THE PREFECT

Also by Alastair Reynolds from Gollancz:

Chasm City
Revelation Space
Redemption Ark
Absolution Gap
Century Rain
Pushing Ice
Diamond Dogs, Turquoise Days
Galactic North

THE PREFECT

Alastair Reynolds

First published in Great Britain in 2007 by
Gollancz
An imprint of the Orion Publishing Group
Orion House, 5 Upper St Martin's Lane, London WC2H 9EA
An Hachette Livre UK Company

This edition published in Great Britain in 2008 by Gollancz

3 5 7 9 10 8 6 4

A CIP catalogue record for this book is available
from the British Library

ISBN 978 0 57508 218 2

Typeset by Input Data Services Ltd, Frome

Printed and bound in Great Britain by
Mackays of Chatham plc, Chatham, Kent

www.orionbooks.co.uk

To my Mum and Dad,
for forty years of love and encouragement.

CHAPTER 1

Thalia Ng felt her weight increasing as the elevator sped down the spoke from the habitat's docking hub. She allowed herself to drift to the floor, trying to judge the point at which the apparent force reached one standard gee. Thalia hoped this was not one of those habitats that insisted on puritanically high gravity, as if it was somehow morally improving to stagger around under two gees. Her belt, with her whiphound and polling-core-analysis tools, already weighed heavily on her hips.

'Thalia,' Dreyfus said quietly as the elevator slowed to a halt, 'try not to look so nervous.'

She tugged down the hem of her tunic. 'I'm sorry, sir.'

'You're going to do fine.'

'I wish there'd been more time, sir. To read up on House Perigal, I mean.'

'You were informed of our destination as soon as we left Panoply.'

'That was only an hour ago, sir.'

He looked at her, his lazy right eye nearly closed. 'What's your speed-reading index?'

'Three, sir. Nothing exceptional.'

Dreyfus took a sip from the bulb of coffee he'd carried with him from the ship. Thalia had conjured it for him: black as tar, the way her boss liked it. 'I suppose it *was* quite a long summary file.'

'More than a thousand paragraphs, sir.'

'Well, there's nothing you need to know that wasn't covered in training.'

'I hope so. All the same, I couldn't help noticing . . .'

'What?' Dreyfus asked mildly.

'Your name's all over the summary file, sir.'

'Caitlin Perigal and I've had our fair share of run-ins.' He smiled tightly. 'As I'm sure she'll be at pains to remind me.'

'Count on it,' said Sparver, the other deputy field on the lock-down party.

Dreyfus laid a thick-fingered hand on Thalia's shoulder. 'Just remember you're here to do one thing – to secure evidence. Sparver and I'll take care of any other distractions.'

When the elevator doors puckered open, a wave of heat and humidity hit like a hard, wet slap. Steam billowed in the air as far as Thalia could see. They were standing at the entrance to an enormous cavern hewn into the rocky torus of the wheel's rim. Much of the visible surface consisted of pools of water arranged on subtly different levels, connected by an artful system of sluices and channels. People were bathing or swimming, or playing games in the water. Most of them were naked. There were baseline humans and people very far from human. There were sleek, purposeful shapes that might not have been people at all.

Dreyfus pulled a pair of bulbous glasses from his tunic pocket and rubbed the condensation from the dark lenses onto his sleeve. Thalia followed his cue and slipped on her own glasses, taking note of the changes she saw. Many of the apparently naked people were now masked or clothed, or at least partly hidden behind shifting blocks of colour or mirage-like plumage. Some of them had changed size and shape. A few had even become invisible, although the shades provided a blinking outline to indicate their true presence. Luminous branching structures – Thalia couldn't tell if they were sculptures or some form of data visualisation related to an ongoing mindgame – loomed over the complex of pools.

'Here comes the welcome,' Dreyfus said.

Something strode towards them, following a dry path that wound between the bathing pools. A pair of shapely, stockinged female legs rose to support a flat tray arrayed with drinks. High heels clicked as the legs approached, placing one foot before the other with neurotic precision. The fluid in the glasses remained rock steady.

Thalia's hand moved to her belt.

'Steady,' Dreyfus breathed.

The servitor halted before them. 'Welcome to House Perigal, Prefects,' it said in a squeaky voice. 'Would you care for a drink?'

'Thanks,' Thalia said, 'but we should—'

Dreyfus put down the coffee bulb and dithered his hand over the tray. 'What do you recommend?'

'The red's acceptable.'

'Red it is, then.' He took a glass and lifted it towards his lips, just close enough to sniff the aroma. Thalia took a glass for herself. Only Sparver abstained: his metabolism couldn't cope with alcohol.

'Follow me, please. I'll take you to the matriarch.'

They followed the legs through the cavern, winding between the pools. If their arrival had gone apparently unnoticed, that luxury had passed. Thalia could feel the back of her neck prickling from the uneasy attention they were now warranting.

They climbed to one of the highest pools, where four ornamental iron fish vomited water from their gaping mouths. Three adults were floating in the water, up to their chests in perfumed froth. Two were men. The third was Caitlin Perigal, her face recognisable from the summary file. Her muscular shoulders and arms tapered to elegant webbed hands with acid-green fingernails. A peacock's feather adorned her hair. Green nymphs and satyrs buzzed around her head.

'Prefects,' she said, with all the warmth of superfluid helium.

'Matriarch Perigal,' Dreyfus said, standing with his feet a few centimetres from the edge of the pool. 'My companions are Deputy Field Prefects Sparver Bancal and Thalia Ng. We've met, of course.'

Perigal turned languidly to her two companions. 'The sleepy-looking fat one is Tom Dreyfus,' she explained.

One of them – an aristocratic man with long, white hair – examined Dreyfus through clinical grey eyes. His plumage rendered him in impressionist brushstrokes. 'Your paths have crossed before, Caitlin?'

Perigal stirred, breaking the water with the muscular fluked tail that had been grafted on in place of her legs. Thalia touched the stud on the side of her shades to verify that the tail was real, not a hallucination.

'Dreyfus's function in life seems to be finding obscure legal channels through which to harass me,' Perigal said.

Dreyfus looked unimpressed. 'I just do my job. It's not my fault that you keep being a part of it.'

'And I do, don't I?'

'So it seems. Nice tail, by the way. What happened to the legs?'

Perigal nodded at the walking tray. 'I keep them around as a conversation piece.'

'Each to their own.'

'Yes, that's the general principle.' Perigal leaned forward in the pool, her voice hardening. 'Well, pleasantries over with. Make your inspection, do whatever you have to do, then get the hell off my habitat.'

'I haven't come to inspect the habitat,' Dreyfus said.

Thalia tensed despite herself. This was the moment she had been both dreading and quietly anticipating.

'What, then?' Perigal asked.

Dreyfus removed a card from his tunic pocket and held it up to his face, squinting slightly. He glanced briefly at Thalia and Sparver before reading, 'Caitlin Perigal, as matriarch of this habitat, you are hereby charged with a category-five infringement of the democratic process. It is alleged that you tampered with the polling apparatus, to the intended benefit of your house.'

Perigal stuttered something, her cheeks flushing with indignation, but Dreyfus held up a silencing hand and continued with his statement.

'While the investigative process is in operation, your habitat is to be placed under lockdown. All physical traffic between House Perigal and the rest of the system, including Chasm City, is now suspended. No incoming or outgoing transmissions will be permitted. Any attempts to break these sanctions will be countered with destructive force. This is final and binding.' Dreyfus paused, then lowered the card. 'The state of lockdown is now in effect.'

There was an uneasy silence, broken only by the gentle lapping of water against the side of the pool.

'This is a joke, isn't it?' the grey-eyed man said eventually, looking encouragingly at Perigal. 'Please tell me it's a joke.'

'So it's come to this,' the matriarch said. 'I always knew you were dirty, Dreyfus, but I never thought you'd stoop quite this low.'

Dreyfus placed the card beside the pool. 'This is a summary of the case against you. Looks watertight to me, but then I'm only a lowly field prefect.' He touched a finger to his chin, as if he'd just remembered an errand. 'Now I need a small favour.'

'You're insane.'

'Kindly issue a priority interrupt to all your citizens and guests. Tell them that a lockdown is in force, and that they're about to lose contact with the external universe. Remind them that this state of affairs could last for anything up to one century. Tell them that if they have thoughts or messages to convey to loved ones beyond House Perigal, they have six hundred seconds in which to do so.'

He turned to Thalia and Sparver and lowered his voice, but not so low that Perigal wouldn't have been able to hear him. 'You know what to do, Deputies. If anyone obstructs you, or refuses to cooperate, you have clearance to euthanise.'

The rim transit moved quickly, its motion counteracting the centrifugal gravity of the slow-turning wheel. Thalia sat next to Sparver, brooding.

'It isn't fair,' she said.

'What isn't?'

'All those people stuck here by accident, the people who just happened to be visiting.'

'Sometimes the only workable solution isn't a fair one.'

'But cut off from the Glitter Band, from Yellowstone, from friends and family, from abstraction, from their medical programmes ... some of them could actually die in here before the lockdown's over.'

'Then they should have thought about that before. If you don't like the idea of being caught in a lockdown, do the homework on your habitat.'

'That's a very callous outlook.'

'They screwed with democracy. I'm not going to lose much sleep when democracy screws them back.'

Thalia felt her weight returning as they neared their destination and the transit slowed. The two prefects disembarked into another cavern, smaller and brighter than the first. This time the floor was an expanse of interlocking black and white tiles, polished to a luxurious gleam. A cylindrical structure rose from a hole in the centre of the floor, wide as a tree trunk, its spired tip almost touching the ceiling. The cylinder's black surface flickered with schematic representations of data flows: rapidly changing red and blue traceries. A railingless spiral staircase wrapped around the pillar, offering access to the stump-like branches of interface ports.

A man in beige uniform – some kind of technician or functionary, Thalia decided – stood by the base of the trunk, his face a study in suspicion.

'Don't come any closer,' he said.

Sparver answered him. 'Didn't Perigal make it clear we were on our way, and that we weren't to be hindered?'

'It's a trick. You're agents of House Cantarini.'

Sparver looked at him sceptically. 'Do I look like an agent of House Cantarini?'

'An agent could look like anyone.'

'I'm a pig. How likely is it that they'd send an ugly specimen like me when there was an alternative?'

'I can't take the risk. You touch this core, I lose my job, my standing, everything.'

'Step aside, sir,' Thalia said.

'I'm sorry. I can't let you any nearer.' The man opened his hand to reveal a matt-silver device cuffed to his palm, inset with a red firing stud. 'There are weapons already trained on you. Please don't make me use them.'

'You kill us, Panoply will just send more prefects,' Sparver said.

Thalia's skin prickled. She could feel the scrutiny of those hidden weapons, ready to wipe her out of existence at the twitch of the man's thumb.

'I won't kill you if you turn and leave.'

'We'll leave when we have the evidence.' Sparver's hand moved to his belt. He unclipped the handle of his whiphound and flicked it to deploy the filament. It cracked as it spun out to its maximum extension, lashing the floor.

'He's right,' Thalia said, fighting to keep the tremor from her voice. 'We're Panoply.'

'Please.' The man's thumb caressed the firing stud. 'I'll do what needs to be done to protect the core.'

Sparver released the whiphound. The handle remained at waist height, supported by the coiled extremity of its stiffened filament. It swayed from side to side with the questing motion of a snake. Then it curled around and aimed itself at the man.

A bright red dot appeared on his Adam's apple.

'I need you to answer a question for me,' Sparver said. 'How attached are you to your fingers?'

The man inhaled and held his breath.

'The whiphound has a mark on you now,' Sparver continued. 'If it detects hostile intent – and it's very, very good at detecting hostile intent – it'll be on you faster than a nerve impulse can travel down your arm. When it reaches you, it'll do something quite nasty with the sharp edge of that filament.'

The man opened his mouth to say something, but all that came out was a dry croak. He spread both his hands, opening his fingers and thumbs as wide as they would go.

'Sensible,' Sparver said. 'Now hold that pose, but step away from the core.' He nodded at Thalia, giving her the go-ahead to start securing the evidence. The whiphound stayed by his side, its blunt head tracking the man as he inched away from the central column.

Thalia walked to the core. It was a standard design, installed within the last twenty years, so she knew exactly where to start.

'This is Deputy Field Prefect Thalia Ng,' she said aloud. 'Confirm recognition.'

'Welcome, Deputy Field Prefect Ng,' it replied, in the neutrally sexless voice common to all cores. 'How may I assist you?'

Thalia brought to mind the one-time code with which she had been briefed after the cutter's departure from Panoply. 'Acknowledge security access override Narcissus Eight Palisander.'

'Override confirmed. You now have six hundred seconds of clearance, Deputy Field Prefect Ng.'

'Disable two-way access to the exterior abstraction.'

'Access is now blocked.'

The red lines vanished. Now the pillar showed only blue traffic. No signals were reaching or leaving the habitat. Almost immediately the blue traffic intensified as the citizenry began to panic, sending emergency queries to the core.

Thalia glanced at the man Sparver's whiphound was still detaining. For the first time in his life, his implants would no longer be in constant communication with the informational matrix beyond House Perigal. It must have felt like the drop of a guillotine.

She returned her attention to the core. 'Prepare me triplicate physical summary packages for all data traffic in and out of this habit in the last thousand days.'

'I am preparing the packages. Please wait a moment.'

Thalia reached up and touched her throat microphone. 'Thalia, sir. We're securing the evidence now. We should be back with you within ten minutes.'

There was no response. She waited a few moments, giving Dreyfus time to activate his own microphone, but still nothing came.

She shot a look at Sparver. 'I'm not getting anything.'

'The boss man could be preoccupied,' Sparver said.

'He should have answered by now. I'm worried. Maybe we ought to get back there, see—'

'We need those summary packages, Thalia. In five minutes you'll be locked out of the core again.'

Sparver was right. The one-time code – good for ten minutes of unrestricted activity – would not buy her access to the core a second time.

'Hurry up,' she said, through clenched teeth.

She tried Dreyfus again, but still there was no reply. After what felt like an eternity, the core ejected the summary packages from a slot near its base. Thalia clipped together the thick diskettes and then secured them to her belt. Absurd as it was, she swore she could feel the weight of the information inside them. It would have taken days to squeeze that amount of data across a beam.

'You done?' Sparver asked.

'This is all we need. We can leave the local abstraction running.'

'And if they try to get around the block you just put in?'

'They'll have a dead core on their hands. They'll be lucky if life support still works after that, let alone abstraction.' Thalia turned back to the core and authorised it to rescind the Panoply access privilege it had just granted her. 'That's it, then,' she said, feeling an unexpected sense of anticlimax.

'There. Wasn't so hard, was it?'

'I'm worried about the boss.'

'It's just the rock this thing's made of, blocking our signals.' Sparver smiled at the technician again. 'We're done. Can I trust you not to do anything silly if I pull the whiphound off you?'

The man swallowed painfully and twitched his head in a nod.

'I'll take that as a "yes",' Sparver said. He reached out his hand and beckoned the whiphound. With a flick of its tail, the weapon sprang its handle into Sparver's grip, the tail whisking back into the housing with a lashing sound.

Sparver patted the handle and reattached it to his belt. 'Let's go check on the boss man.'

But when they rode the rim transit back to Dreyfus, they found him standing alone and still, amidst a scene of almost unspeakable carnage. He held his glasses in one hand and the whiphound in the other.

Thalia snatched off her own glasses so that she could see things as they really were. People were screaming, scrambling and splashing to get away from the prefect and the objects of his attention. Caitlin Perigal's two male guests were both slumped in the pool, in water that was now bloodstained pink. The man with the grey hair had lost his forearm: it was lying on the marble poolside, the hand pointing accusingly at Dreyfus. Behind the wrist, the skin bulged as if a bone-grafted weapon had been trying to push its way through to the surface. The other man, trembling as if in the throes of a seizure, had blood running from both his nostrils. His eyes were wide open, fixated on the ceiling. Three or four nearby guests were nursing wounds of varying severity. With all the blood in the water – draining from pool to pool via the waterfalls and sluices – it was difficult to be certain how many people had been hurt. Medical servitors had already arrived and were attending to the most seriously injured, but even the machines appeared confused.

Perigal was still alive, albeit breathing heavily. A vivid gash cut her across the right cheek, running from the corner of her mouth to her ear. She breathed heavily, her eyes wide and white with fury and fear.

'You're wrong about this,' she breathed. 'You're wrong about this and you're going to pay.'

Dreyfus turned slowly at the approach of Thalia and Sparver. 'Got the packages?'

Thalia's mouth was dry. 'Yes,' she said, forcing the word out, striving to maintain professional composure.

'Then let's go. We're done here.'

CHAPTER 2

Dreyfus had closed half the distance to the middle of the supreme prefect's office when the safe-distance tether jerked him to a halt. For a moment Jane Aumonier appeared unaware of his presence, absorbed in one of her wall displays. He coughed quietly before speaking.

'If you want my resignation, it's yours.'

Aumonier turned her head to face him, without moving the rest of her body. 'On what grounds, Tom?'

'You name it. If I committed an error of procedure, or was guilty of improper judgement, you only have to say the word.'

'If you committed an error, it was in not going far enough to defend yourself and your deputies. What was the final body count?'

'Six,' Dreyfus said.

'We've done worse. Perigal was always going to be a tough nut. A single-figure body count strikes me as entirely acceptable, given all that we could have expected.'

'I was hoping things wouldn't get quite so messy.'

'That was Perigal's call, not yours.'

'I still don't think we're finished with her. What she said to me . . .' Dreyfus paused, certain that Aumonier had enough to worry about without being burdened with his doubts. 'I feel as if a debt has been settled. That isn't a good way for a prefect to feel.'

'It's human.'

'She got away with it in the past because we weren't clever or fast enough to audit her before the evidence turned stale. But even if we'd been able to pin anything on her, her crimes wouldn't have merited a full century of lockdown.'

'And we don't know that it will come to that this time, either.'

'You think she'll slip through again?'

'That'll depend on the evidence. Time to make use of that bright new expert on your team.'

'I have every confidence in Thalia.'

'Then you've nothing to fear. If Perigal's guilty, the state of lockdown will continue. If the evidence doesn't turn anything up, House Perigal will be allowed re-entry into the Glitter Band.'

'Minus six people.'

'Citizens panic when they lose abstraction. That isn't our problem.'

Dreyfus tried to read Aumonier's expression, wondering what he was missing. It wasn't like her to need to ask him how many people had died during an operation: normally she'd have committed the figures to memory before he was back inside Panoply. But Aumonier's emotionless mask was as impossible to read as ever. He could remember how she looked when she smiled, or laughed, or showed anger, how she'd been before her brush with the Clockmaker, but it took an increasing effort of will.

'Pardon me,' he said, 'but if this isn't a reprimand ... what exactly do you want me for?'

'The conversation? The banter? The warmth of human companionship?'

'I don't think so.'

'Something's come up. The news broke while you were outside. It's as delicate as the Perigal affair, if not more so. Urgent, too. We need immediate action.'

Dreyfus had not heard of anything brewing. 'Another lockdown?'

'No. There wouldn't be much point, unfortunately.'

'I'm sorry?'

Aumonier extended a hand to the wall, enlarging one of the display facets. It filled with an image of a spherical habitat, a grey ball blurred with microscopic detail, banded by tropical sun-panels, with an array of vast mirrors stationed at the poles and around the equator. The scale was difficult to judge, though Dreyfus doubted that the habitat was less than a kilometre wide.

'You won't recognise it. This is a recent image of the Ruskin-Sartorious Bubble, a fifth-magnitude shell habitat in the high outer orbits. It's never fallen under Panoply scrutiny before.'

'What have they done wrong now?'

'Here's a more recent image, taken three hours ago.'

The Ruskin-Sartorious Bubble had been cut open, sliced along its midsection like an eyeball gouged by a razor. The cut had almost split the habitat into two hemispheres. On either side of the cut, the habitat's fabric had been scorched to a crisp midnight black. Structures inside were still glowing cherry-red.

'Casualties?' Dreyfus asked, holding his horror at bay.

'Last census put the population at nine hundred and sixty. We think they all died, but we need to get a team in and make an immediate physical inspection. Survivors can't be ruled out. At the very least, there may be beta-level recoverables.'

'Why isn't this all over the Band?'

'Because we're keeping a lid on it. This doesn't look like an accident.'

'Someone will have noticed Ruskin-Sartorious dropping off the networks.'

'They only participated in abstraction at a shallow level, enough that we can continue to simulate the existence of the fully functional habitat for the time being, using our network privileges.'

'And the time being . . . would be how long?'

'Best guess? Less than twenty-six hours. Thirteen might be nearer the mark.'

'And when the story breaks?'

'We'll have a major crisis on our hands. I think I know who did this, but I'll need to be absolutely certain before I move on it. That's why I want you to get out to Ruskin-Sartorious immediately. Take whoever you need. Secure evidence and recoverables and get back to Panoply. Then we'll hold our breath.'

Dreyfus looked again at the image of the wounded habitat. 'There's only one thing that could have done that, isn't there? And it isn't even a weapon.'

'We see things similarly,' Aumonier said.

The walls of the tactical room were finely grained teak, varnished to a forbidding gleam. There were no windows or pictures, no humanising touches. The heavy, dark furniture was all inert matter: grown, cut and constructed by nature and carpentry. The double doors were cased in hammered bronze, studded with huge brass bolts, each door inlaid with a stylised version of the raised gauntlet that was Panoply's symbol. The gauntlet was supposed to signify protection, but it could just as easily be interpreted as a threatening fist, clenched to smash down on its enemies or those who failed it.

'Begin please, Ng,' said the man sitting opposite Thalia, Senior Prefect Michael Crissel.

She placed the recovered diskettes on the table's edge, almost dropping them in her nervousness. 'Thank you, Senior Prefect. These are the triplicate physical summary packages from the Perigal polling core.' She nodded at the clockwork-gear shape of the Perigal habitat, imaged as a tiny representation in the tactical room's Solid Orrery, enlarged and elevated above its real orbital plane. 'The data has now been copied into our archives, all one thousand days' worth of it. I've verified that the three triplicate summaries are consistent, with no indication of tampering.'

'And your findings?'

'I've only had a few hours to look into things, which really isn't enough time to do more than skim—'

Senior Prefect Gaston Clearmountain growled his impatience. 'Cut the blather, Ng. Just tell us what you have.'

'Sir,' Thalia said, almost stammering. 'Preliminary analysis confirms everything in the lockdown report. House Perigal were indeed guilty of tampering with the democratic process. On at least eight occasions they were able to bias voting patterns in marginal polls, either to their advantage, or to the advantage of their allies. There may be more instances. We'll have a clearer picture when we've run a full audit on the packages.'

'I was hoping for a clearer picture now,' Clearmountain said.

Senior Prefect Sheridan Gaffney leaned forward in his huge black chair with a creak of leather. 'Easy on her, Gaston,' he growled. 'She's been under a lot of pressure to pull this together at short notice.'

Gaffney had a reputation for having a short fuse and a marked intolerance for fools. But as head of both Internal Security and whiphound training, the gruff-voiced Gaffney had always treated Thalia with impeccable fairness, even encouragement. She now perceived him as her only unambiguous ally in the room. It would have been different if Dreyfus or Jane Aumonier had been present, but Dreyfus was absent (his Pangolin clearance would have allowed him to sit in on the meeting even though he wasn't a senior) and the position where the supreme prefect normally manifested – beamed into the room as a projection – was conspicuously empty. On her way to the room, Thalia had picked up rumours that some other crisis was brewing, something unrelated to the lockdown they'd recently performed.

The other seniors were neither on her side nor against her. Michael Crissel was a gentle-looking man with scholarly features and a diffident manner. By all accounts he'd been an excellent field prefect once, but he'd spent most of the last twenty years inside Panoply, becoming detached from the hard reality of duty outside. Lillian Baudry's field career had come to an end when she was blown apart by a malfunctioning whiphound. They'd put her back together again, but her nervous system had never been the same. She could have surrendered herself to the medical expertise available elsewhere in the Glitter Band, but the security implications of receiving outside treatment would have meant her leaving Panoply for good. So she'd chosen duty over well-being, even though that meant sitting in meetings like a stiffly posed china doll.

It was a measure of the importance attached to Thalia's report that only four seniors were present. Normally at least six or seven of the ten permanent seniors would have been in attendance, but today there were more than the usual number of empty places around the table. Yes, they wanted this affair tied up as quickly as possible – but that didn't mean they saw it as anything other than a blip in Panoply's schedule of business.

'Let's cut to the chase,' Clearmountain said. 'We've got the packages. They confirm our existing suspicions, which is that Perigal had her hands in the pie. The lockdown can hold. Now all we need to do is seal the leak before someone else exploits it the same way.'

'I agree, sir,' Thalia said.

'Exactly how much damage did these polling violations cause?' asked Baudry.

'In the scheme of things, nothing major,' Thalia answered. 'They were all polls on relatively minor issues. Caitlin Perigal might have wanted to tip the balance in more significant polls, but discovery would have been even more likely if she'd tried. Frankly, with the amount of oversight and scrutiny we already have in place whenever something big comes up, I can't imagine anyone managing to bias the votes to a statistically useful degree.'

'It's your *job* to imagine it,' Michael Crissel said.

'She knows that,' Gaffney said in a whisper.

Thalia acknowledged Crissel. 'I'm sorry, sir. I just mean – given everything we know – it's unlikely. The system can't ever be proven to be inviolable; Gödel's Incompleteness Theorem—'

'I don't need to be lectured on Gödel, Ng,' Crissel said tersely.

'What I mean, sir, is that the system tests itself through being used. House Perigal has actually done us a favour. Now we're aware of a logical flaw we hadn't seen before: one that permits a tiny bias in the polls. We'll fix that and move on. Somewhere down the line, someone else will get creative and find another loophole. We'll fix that as well. That's the process.'

'So you're confident we can plug this hole?' Baudry asked.

'Absolutely, Senior. It's trivial.'

'If it's "trivial", how did we miss it until now?'

'Because we introduced it,' Thalia said, trying not to sound too full of herself. 'We plugged one hole – thinking we were being clever – and inadvertently opened another. The fault was deep in our error-handling routine. It was designed to stop valid votes being lost, but it accidentally allowed additional votes to be registered fraudulently.'

'Probably not the first time in history that's happened,' Crissel said dryly.

Thalia laced her hands together on the table, trying to strike the right note between defensiveness and professional detachment. 'It was regrettable. But to date only a handful of habitats have exploited the loophole.'

'Regrettable?' Clearmountain said. 'I call it reprehensible.'

'Sir, the existing error-handling routine already ran to twenty-two million lines of code, including some subroutines written more than two hundred and twenty years ago, in the First System. Those programmers weren't even speaking modern Canasian. Reading their documentation is like ... well, deciphering Sanskrit or something.'

'Ng's right,' Gaffney said. 'They did the best they could. And the secondary loophole was subtle enough that only five habitats in ten thousand ever attempted to exploit it. I think we can put this one down to experience and move on.'

'Provided, of course, we have a reliable fix,' Baudry said. She nodded stiffly at Thalia. 'You did say it would be a simple matter?'

'For once, yes. The correction isn't anything like as complicated as the alteration that introduced the fault in the first place. Just a few thousand lines that need changing. Having said that, I'd still like to run the first few installations manually, just to iron out any unanticipated issues due to different core architectures. Once I'm satisfied, we can go live across the entire ten thousand.'

Gaffney looked sharply at Thalia. 'It's clear that we need to get this whole mess tidied up as quickly as possible. By the time the

Perigal lockdown becomes binding – as I have no doubt it will – I want us ready to begin implementing the upgrade. The special evidential board has access to the summary packages?'

'Since this morning, sir.'

Gaffney took out a handkerchief and dabbed at the perspiration glistening on his forehead. 'On past form we can expect their decision within ten days. Can you match that?'

'We could go live in two, sir, if you demanded it. I'm confident that the tests won't throw up any anomalies.'

'We were confident last time,' Gaffney reminded her. 'Let's not make the same mistake twice.'

But there's a difference between then and now, Thalia thought to herself. She hadn't been on the team when the last upgrade was made. She couldn't speak for her predecessors, but she would never have allowed that error to slip through.

'We won't,' she said.

Dreyfus took in the scene of the crime from the vantage point of a Panoply cutter. It would have been quick, he reflected, but perhaps not fast enough to be either painless or merciful. The habitat was a corpse now, gutted of pressure. When whatever gouged that wound had touched the atmosphere inside the shell, it would have caused it to expand in a scalding ball of superheated air and steam. There'd have been no time to reach shuttles, escape pods or even armoured security vaults. But there'd have been time to realise what was happening. Most people in the Glitter Band didn't expect to die, let alone in fear and agony.

'This isn't looking good,' Sparver said. 'Still want to go in, before forensics catch up with us?'

'We may still be able to get something from hardened data cores,' Dreyfus answered, with gloomy resignation. He wasn't even confident about the cores.

'What kind of weapon did this?'

'I don't think it was a weapon.'

'That doesn't look like any kind of impact damage to me. There's scorching, suggesting some kind of directed energy source. Could the Conjoiners have dug out something that nasty? Everyone says they have a few big guns tucked away somewhere.'

Dreyfus shook his head. 'If the Spiders wanted to pick a fight with an isolated habitat, they'd have made a cleaner job of it.'

'All the same—'

'Jane has a shrewd idea of what did this. She just isn't happy about the implications.'

Dreyfus and Sparver passed through the cutter's suitwall into vacuum, and then through a chain of old-fashioned but still functional airlocks. The locks fed them into a series of successively larger reception chambers, all of which were now dark and depressurised. The chambers were full of slowly wheeling debris clouds, little of which Dreyfus was able to identify. The internal map on his facepatch was based on the data Ruskin-Sartorious had volunteered during the last census. The polling core – which was likely to be where any beta-levels had been sequestered – was supposedly on the sphere's inside surface near the equator. They would just have to hope that the beam had missed it.

The main interior spaces – the two-kilometre-wide Bubble had been partitioned into chambered habitat zones – were charred black caverns, littered only with heat-warped or pressure-mangled ruins. Near the cut, traceries of structural metal were still glowing where the killing beam had sliced through them. It appeared that the Bubble had been a free-fall culture, with only limited provision for artificial gravity. There were many places like that in the Band, and their citizens grew elegant and willowy and tended not to travel all that much.

Sparver and Dreyfus floated through the heart of the sphere, using their suit jets to steer around the larger chunks of free-fall debris. The suits had already begun to warn of heightened radiation levels, which did nothing to assuage Dreyfus's suspicions that Aumonier was right about who had done this. But they'd need more than just suit readings to make a case.

'I've found something,' Sparver said suddenly, when they had drifted several tens of metres apart.

'What?'

'There's something big floating over here. Could be a piece of ship or something.'

Dreyfus was sceptical. 'Inside the habitat?'

'See for yourself, Boss.'

Dreyfus steered his suit closer to Sparver and cast his lights over the floating object. Sparver had been right in that at first glance the thing resembled a chunk of ship, or some other nondescript piece of large machinery. But on closer inspection it was clear that this was nothing of the sort. The blackened object was a piece of artwork, apparently only half-finished.

Someone had begun with a chunk of metal-rich rock, a potato-shaped boulder about ten or twelve metres across. It had a dark-blue lustre, shading to olive green when the light caught it in a certain fashion. One face of the boulder was still rough and unworked, but the other had been cut back to reveal an intricate sculptural form. Regions of the sculpted side of the boulder were still at a crude stage of development, but other areas gave the impression of having been finished to a very high degree, worked down to a scale of centimetres. The way the rock had flowed and congealed around the worked-in areas suggested that the artist had been sculpting with fusion torches rather than just cutting drills or hammers. The liquid forms of the molten rock had become an integral part of the piece, incorporated into the composition at a level that could not be accidental.

Which didn't mean that Dreyfus had any idea as to what it represented. There was a face emerging from a rock, that of a man, but oriented upside down from Dreyfus's present point of view. He spun the suit around and for a moment, fleetingly, he had the impression that he recognised the face, that it belonged to a celebrity or historical figure rather than someone he knew personally. But the moment passed and the face lost whatever sheen of familiarity it might have possessed. Perhaps it was better that way, too. The man's expression was difficult to read, but it was either one of ecstasy or soul-consuming dread.

'What do you make of it?' Sparver asked.

'I don't know,' Dreyfus said. 'Maybe the beta-levels will tell us something, if any of them turn out to be recoverable.' He pushed his suit closer and fired an adhesive marker onto the floating rock so that forensics would know to haul it in.

They moved on to the entry wound, until they were hovering just clear of the edge of the cut. Before them, airtight cladding had turned black and flaked away, exposing the fused and reshaped rock that had formed the Bubble's skin. The beam had made the rock boil, melt and resolidify in organic formations that were unsettlingly similar to those in the sculpture, gleaming a glassy black under their helmet lights. Stars were visible through the ten-metre-wide opening. Somewhere else out there, Dreyfus reflected, was all that remained of the habitat's interior biome, billowing away into empty space.

He steered his suit into the cleft. He floated down to half the depth of the punctured skin, then settled near a glinting object embedded in the resolidified rock. It was a flake of metal, probably a piece of cladding that had come loose and then been trapped when the rock solidified. Dreyfus unhooked a cutter from his belt and snipped a palm-sized section of the flake away. Nearby he spotted another glint, and then a third. Within a minute he had gathered three different samples, stowing them in the suit's abdominal pouch.

'Got something?' Sparver asked.

'Probably. If it was a drive beam that did it, this metal will have mopped up a lot of subatomic particles. There'll be spallation tracks, heavy isotopes and fragmentation products. Forensics can tell us if the signatures match a Conjoiner drive.'

Now he'd said it, it was out in the open.

'Okay, but no matter what forensics say, why would Ultras do this?' Sparver asked. 'They couldn't hope to get away with it.'

'Maybe that's exactly what they were hoping to do – cut and run. They might not be back in this system for decades, centuries even. Do you think anyone will still care about what happened to Ruskin-Sartorious by then?'

After a thoughtful moment, Sparver said, 'You would.'

'I won't be around. Neither will you.'

'You're in an unusually cheerful frame of mind.'

'Nine hundred and sixty people died here, Sparver. It's not exactly the kind of thing that puts a spring in my step.' Dreyfus looked around, but saw no other easily accessible forensic samples. The analysis squad would arrive shortly, but the really heavy work would have to wait until the story had broken and Panoply were not obliged to work under cover of secrecy.

By then, though, all hell would have broken loose anyway.

'Let's get to the polling core,' he said, moving his suit out of the cut. 'The sooner we leave here the better. I can already feel the ghosts getting impatient.'

CHAPTER 3

Whether by accident or design – Dreyfus had never been sufficiently curious to find out – the four main bays on the trailing face of Panoply conspired to suggest the grinning, ghoulish countenance of a Hallowe'en pumpkin. No attempt had been made to smooth or contour the rock's outer crust, or to lop it into some kind of symmetry. There were a thousand similar asteroids wheeling around Yellowstone: rough-cut stones shepherded into parking orbits where they awaited demolition and reforging into sparkling new habitats. This was the only one that held prefects, though: barely a thousand in total, from the senior prefect herself right down to the greenest field just out of the cadet rankings.

The cutter docked itself in the nose, where it was racked into place alongside a phalanx of similar light-enforcement vehicles. Dreyfus and Sparver handed the evidential packages to a waiting member of the forensics squad and signed off on the paperwork. Conveyor bands pulled them deeper into the asteroid, until they were in one of the rotating sections.

'I'll see you in thirteen hours,' Dreyfus told Sparver at the junction between the field-training section and the cadets' dormitory ring. 'Get some rest – I'm expecting a busy day.'

'And you?'

'Some loose ends to tie up first.'

'Fine,' Sparver said, shaking his head. 'It's your metabolism. You do what you want with it.'

Dreyfus was tired, but with Caitlin Perigal and the implications of the murdered habitat dogging his thoughts, he knew it would be futile trying to sleep. Instead he returned to his quarters for just long enough to step through a washwall and conjure a change of clothing. By the time he emerged to make his way back through the rock, the lights had dimmed for the graveyard shift in Panoply's twenty-six-hour operational cycle. The cadets were all asleep; the refectory, training rooms and classrooms empty.

Thalia, however, was still in her office. The passwall was transparent, so he entered silently. He stood behind her like a father admiring his daughter doing homework. She was still dealing with the implications of the Perigal case, seated before a wall filled with scrolling code. Dreyfus stared numbly at the lines of interlocking symbols, none of which meant anything to him.

'Sorry to interrupt your flow,' he said gently when Thalia didn't look up.

'Sir,' she said, starting. 'I thought you were still outside.'

'Word obviously gets around.'

Thalia froze the scroll. 'I heard there was some kind of crisis brewing.'

'Isn't there always?' Dreyfus plopped a heavy black bag down on her desk. 'I know you're already busy, Thalia, but I'm afraid I'm going to have to add to your burden.'

'That's okay, sir.'

'Inside that bag are twelve beta-level recoverables. We had to pull them out of a damaged core, so in all likelihood they're riddled with errors. I'd like you to fix what you can.'

'Where did they come from?'

'A place called Ruskin-Sartorious. It doesn't exist any more. Of the nine hundred and sixty people who used to live there, the only survivors are the patterns in these beta-levels.'

'Just twelve, out of all those people?'

'That's all we got. Even then, I doubt you'll get twelve stable invocations. But do what you can. Call me as soon as you recover something I can talk to.'

Thalia looked back at the code wall. 'After I'm done with this, right?'

'Actually, I'd like those invocations as quickly as possible. I don't want you to neglect Perigal, but this is looking more serious by the hour.'

'What happened?' she breathed. 'How did those people die?'

'Badly,' Dreyfus said.

The safe-distance tether jerked him to a halt in Jane Aumonier's presence.

'Forensics are on the case,' he said. 'We should have an answer on those samples within the hour.'

'Not that there's much room for doubt,' Aumonier said. 'I have every confidence – if that's the word – that they'll tie the damage to the output beam of a Conjoiner drive.' She directed Dreyfus's attention to a portion of the wall she had enlarged before his arrival. Frozen there was a sleek silver-grey thing like a child's paper dart. 'Gaffney's been talking to Centralised Traffic Control. They were able to backtrack the movements of this ship. Her name is *Accompaniment of Shadows*.'

'They can place her at the Bubble?'

'Close enough for our purposes. No other lighthugger was anywhere near.'

'Where's she now?'

'Hidden in the Parking Swarm.'

Aumonier enlarged another portion of the wall. Dreyfus saw a ball of fireflies, packed too tightly in the middle to separate into individual motes of light. A single ship would have no difficulty losing itself in the tight-packed core.

'Have any left since the attack?' he asked.

'None. We've had the Swarm under tight surveillance.'

'And in the event that one should break cover?'

'I'd rather not think about it.'

'But you have.'

She nodded minutely. 'Theoretically, one of our deep-system cruisers could shadow a lighthugger all the way out to the Oort cloud. But what good would it do us? If they don't want to stop, or let us board ... nothing *we* have is going to persuade them. Frankly, direct confrontation with Ultras is the one situation I've been dreading ever since they gave me this job.'

'Do we have any priors on this ship?'

'Nothing, Tom. Why?'

'I was wondering about a motive.'

'Me, too. Maybe one of the recoverables can shed some light on that.'

'If we're lucky,' Dreyfus said. 'We only got twelve, and most of those are likely to be damaged.'

'What about back-ups? Ruskin-Sartorious wouldn't have kept all their eggs in that one basket.'

'Agreed. But it's unlikely that the squirts happened more frequently than once a day, if that. Once a week is a lot more likely.'

'Stale memories may be better than nothing, if that's all we have.' Her tone shifted, becoming more personal. 'Tom, I have to ask another favour of you. I'm afraid it's going to be even more difficult and delicate than Perigal.'

'You'd like me to talk to the Ultras.'

'I want you to ride out to the Swarm. You don't have to enter it yet, but I want them to know that we have our eye on them. I want them to know that if they attempt to hide that ship – or aid its evasion of justice in any way – we won't take it lightly.'

Dreyfus skimmed mental options, trying to work out what kind of ship would send the most effective signal to the Ultras. Nothing in his previous experience with the starship crews had given him much guidance.

'I'll leave immediately,' he said, preparing to haul himself back to the wall.

'I'd rather you didn't,' Aumonier replied. 'Get some rest first. We're up against the clock on this one, but I still want the Ultras to stew a little, wonder what our response is going to be. We're not totally clawless. We can hit them in the trade networks, where it really hurts. Time to make *them* feel uncomfortable for once.'

Elsewhere, an object fell through the Glitter Band.

It was a two-metre-wide sphere, following a carefully calculated free-fall trajectory that would slip it through the transient gaps in civilian, CTC and Panoply tracking systems with the precision of a dancer weaving between scarves. The nonvelope's path was simply an additional precaution that had cost nothing except a tiny expenditure of computing time and an equally small delay to its departure time. It was already nearly invisible, by the standards of all but the most probing close-range surveillance methods.

Presently it detected the intrusion of light of a very particular frequency, one that it was programmed not to deflect. Machinery deep in the nonvelope processed the temporal structure of the light and extracted an encoded message in an expected format. The same machinery composed a response and spat it out in the opposite direction, back to whatever had transmitted the original pulse.

A confirmatory pulse arrived milliseconds later.

The nonvelope had allowed itself to be detected. This was part of the plan.

Three hours later, a ship positioned itself over the nonvelope, using gravitational sensing to refine its final approach. The nonvelope was soon safely concealed inside the reception bay of the ship. Clamps locked it into position. Detecting its safe arrival, the nonvelope relaxed the structure of its quickmatter envelope in preparation for disgorging its cargo. As lights came on and air flooded into the bay, the nonvelope's surface flicked to the appearance of a large chromed marble. Weight returned as the ship powered away from the rendezvous point.

A figure in an anonymous black spacesuit entered the bay. The figure crouched next to the nonvelope and observed it open. The sphere cracked wide, one half folding back to reveal its occupant. A glassy cocoon of support systems oozed away from his foetal form. The man was breathing, but only just on the edge of consciousness.

The man in the suit removed his helmet. 'Welcome back to the world, Anthony Theobald Ruskin-Sartorious.'

The man in the nonvelope groaned and stirred. His eyes were gummed with protective gel. He pawed them clean, then squinted while they found their focus.

'I've arrived?'

'You're aboard the ship. Just like you planned.'

His relief was palpable. 'I thought it was never going to end. Four hours in that thing ... it felt like a million years.'

'I wouldn't mind betting that's the first physical discomfort you've ever known in your life.' The man in the black spacesuit was standing now, his legs slightly apart, braced in the half-gravity produced by the ship's acceleration.

Anthony Theobald narrowed his eyes at the figure. 'Do I know you?'

'You do now.'

'I was expecting to be met by Raichle.'

'Raichle couldn't make it. I came instead. You're okay with that, I assume?'

'Of course I'm ...' But Anthony Theobald's usual self-control was betraying him. The man in the suit felt waves of fear rippling off him. Waves of fear and suspicion and an arrogant unwillingness to grasp that his escape plans hadn't been as foolproof as they'd looked when he climbed into the nonvelope. 'Did it really happen? Is Ruskin-Sartorious gone?'

'It's gone. The Ultras did a good job. You got out just in time.'

'And the others? The rest of us?'

'I'd be surprised if there's a single intact strand of human DNA left anywhere in the Bubble.'

'Delphine ...' There was a heartbreaking crack in his voice. 'My poor daughter?'

'You knew the deal, Anthony Theobald. You were the only one with a get-out clause.'

'I demand to know who you are. If Raichle didn't send you, how did you know where to find the nonvelope?'

'Because he told me, that's why. During interrogation.'

'Who are you?'

'That isn't the issue, Anthony Theobald. The issue at hand is what you were doing sheltering that evil thing in your nice little family-run habitat.'

'I wasn't sheltering anything. I don't know what you're talking about.'

The man in the suit reached behind the small of his back and unclipped a small, handle-shaped object. He hefted it in his palm as if it might be a cosh or truncheon.

'I think it's about time you met a close, personal friend of mine.'

'You've got it wrong. The thing underground was just—'

The man made an odd flicking motion with the handle and something whipped out, extending all the way to the floor. It was almost invisibly fine, catching the light only intermittently. It appeared to swish against the flooring of its own volition, as if searching for something.

The man let go of the handle. The handle remained where it was, its coiled filament stiffening to support it. The handle tracked around until the black cylinder of its head was aimed directly at Anthony Theobald. He raised a hand against the laser as it scratched a bright, oscillating line across his eyes.

It had a mark on him now, confirmed by a minute nod from the man in black.

'Keep that thing away from me.'

'This is a Model C whiphound,' the man in the suit said. 'It's got a few additional features compared to the last version. One of them's called "interrogation mode". Shall we give it a spin?'

The whiphound began to slink closer to Anthony Theobald.

Dreyfus was alone in his quarters. He had prepared some tea, losing himself in the task. When he was finished, he knelt at a low, black table and allowed the hot ginger-coloured brew to cool before drinking it. The room filled itself with the tinkling sound of distant wind chimes, a ghost-thin melody implicit in the apparent randomness. Normally it suited his mood, but today Dreyfus waved the music quieter, until he had near-silence. He sipped at the tea but it was still too hot.

He faced a blank rice-paper wall. He raised a hand and shaped a basic conjuring gesture, one that he had practised thousands of times. The wall brightened with blocky patches of vivid colour. The colours resolved into a mosaic of faces, several dozen of them, arranged in a compositional scheme with the larger images clustered near the middle. The faces were all the same woman, but taken at different stages in her life, so that they almost looked like images of different people. Sometimes the woman was looking into the camera; sometimes she was looking askance, or had been snapped candidly. She had high cheekbones, a slight overbite and eyes of a startling bronze, flecked with chips of fiery gold. She had black hair that she usually wore in tight curls. She was smiling in many of the images, even the ones where she hadn't been aware that she was being photographed. She'd smiled a lot.

Dreyfus stared at the pictures as if they were a puzzle he had to solve.

Something was missing. In his mind's eye he could see the woman in the pictures turning to him with flowers in her hand, kneeling in newly tilled soil. The image was vivid, but when he tried to focus on any particular part of it the details squirmed from his attention. He knew that memory had to come from somewhere, but he couldn't relate it to any of the images already on the wall.

He'd been trying to place it for nearly eleven years.

The tea was cool enough to drink at last. He sipped it slowly, concentrating on the mosaic of faces. Suddenly the composition struck him as jarringly unbalanced in the top-right corner, even though he'd been satisfied with it for many months. He raised a hand and adjusted the placement of the images, the wall obeying his gestures with flawless obedience. It looked better now, but he knew it would come to displease him in time. Until he found that missing piece, the mosaic would always be disharmonious.

He thought back to what had happened, flinching from the memory even as he embraced it.

Six missing hours.

'You were okay,' he told the woman on the wall. 'You were safe. It didn't get to you before we did.'

He made himself believe it, as if nothing else in the universe mattered quite as much.

Dreyfus made the images disappear, leaving the rice-paper wall as blank as when he'd entered the room. He finished the tea in a gulp, barely tasting it as it sluiced down his throat. On the same portion of the wall he called up an operational summary of the day's business, wondering if the forensics squad had managed to get anything on the sculpture Sparver and he had seen in Ruskin-Sartorious. But when the summary sprang onto the wall, neither the images nor the words were legible. He could make out shapes in the images, individual letters in the words, but somewhere between the wall and his brain there was a scrambling filter in place.

Belatedly, Dreyfus realised that he'd neglected to take his scheduled Pangolin shot. Security dyslexia was kicking in as his last clearance boost faded.

He stood from the table and moved to the part of the wall where the booster was dispensed. As he reached towards the pearly-grey surface, the booster appeared in an alcove. It was a pale-grey tube marked with the Panoply gauntlet and a security barcode matching the one on his uniform. Text on the side of the booster read: *Pangolin clearance. To be self-administered by Field Prefect Tom Dreyfus only. Unauthorised use may result in permanent irreversible death.*

Dreyfus rolled up his sleeve and pressed the tube against the skin of his forearm. He felt a cold tingle as the booster rammed its contents into his body, but there was no discomfort.

He retired to his bedroom. He slept fitfully, but without dreams. When he woke three or four hours later, the summary on the wall was crystal clear.

He studied it for a while, then decided he'd given the Ultras long enough.

CHAPTER 4

An alert chimed on the cutter's console. Dreyfus pushed the coffee bulb back into the wall and studied the read-out. Something was approaching from the Parking Swarm, too small to be a lighthugger. Guardedly, he notched up the cutter's defensive posture. Weapons unpacked and armed, but refrained from revealing themselves through the hull. Dreyfus concluded that the approaching object was moving too slowly to make an effective missile. A few moments later, the cutter's cams locked on and resolved the foreshortened form of a small ship-to-ship shuttle. The vehicle had the shape of an eyeless equine skull. Black armour was offset with a scarlet dragonfly, traced in glowing filaments.

He received an invitation to open audio-only communications.

'Welcome, Prefect,' said an accentless male voice in modern Russish. 'How may I be of assistance?'

With some effort, Dreyfus changed verbal gears. 'You can be of assistance by staying right where you are. I haven't entered the Swarm.'

'But you're very close to the outer perimeter. That would suggest an intention to enter.'

'To whom am I speaking?'

'I might ask the same question, Prefect.'

'I have legal authority in this airspace. That's all you need to know. I presume I'm dealing with an assigned representative of the Swarm?'

After a pause – which had nothing to do with timelag – the voice replied: 'You may call me Harbourmaster Seraphim. I speak for all ships gathered in the Swarm, or docked at the central servicing facility.'

'Would that make you an Ultra?'

'By your very narrow definition of the term, no. I do not owe my allegiance to any single ship or crew. But while they are here, all crews are answerable to me.'

Dreyfus racked his memory, but he did not recall any prior dealings with anyone called Seraphim, Ultra or otherwise.

'That'll make life a lot easier, then.'

'I'm sorry, Prefect?'

'It could be that I need access to one of your crews.'

'That would be somewhat irregular.'

'Not as irregular as turning a drive beam on a habitat containing nine hundred and sixty people, Harbourmaster.'

Again, there was a lengthy pause. Dreyfus felt a prickle of sweat on the back of his hands. He had jumped the gun by mentioning Ruskin-Sartorious, which was in express contravention of Jane Aumonier's instructions. But Aumonier had not counted on Dreyfus being approached by someone willing to speak for the entire Swarm.

'Why are your weapons in a state of readiness, Prefect? I can see them through your hull, despite your baffle-cladding. You're not nervous, are you?'

'Just sensible. If I could see your weapons, I'd expect them to be in a state of readiness as well.'

'Touché,' Harbourmaster Seraphim said, with a chuckle. 'But I'm not nervous. I have a duty to protect my Swarm.'

'One of your ships could do a lot more damage than one of ours. I think that's already been adequately demonstrated.'

'Yes, so you said. That's a serious accusation.'

'I wouldn't make it if I didn't have solid proof.'

'Such as?'

'Shipping movements. Forensic samples from the habitat, consistent with torching from one of your drives. I can even give you the name of a ship, if you—'

'I think we need to speak in person,' Harbourmaster Seraphim said, with an urgency Dreyfus hadn't been expecting. 'Stand your weapons down, please. I am about to approach and initiate hard docking with your ventral airlock.'

'I haven't given you permission.'

'But you're about to,' Harbourmaster Seraphim replied.

As the lock cycled – coping with the different pressure and atmospheric-mix protocols in force on both ships – Dreyfus emptied his mind of all preconceptions. It never paid to make assumptions about the physical manifestations of Ultras. They could look as fully human as any Panoply operative, and yet be crawling with furtive and dangerous machines.

Dreyfus had seen stranger than Harbourmaster Seraphim, though. His limbs and torso were encased in the bright green armour of a powered exoskeleton. His head had a shrunken look to it, his mouth and nose hidden behind a grilled silver breathing device that appeared to be grafted in place. There was a chrome-plated input socket set into the left side of his skull – Ultras favoured direct hook-up when they interfaced with their machines – but other than that there was no suggestion of extensive cyborgisation. He had long, black hair drawn back into a single braided tail. His delicate, pale hands reminded Dreyfus of the imprint of a bird's wings in ancient rock.

'Thank you for letting me aboard,' Seraphim said, the voice emanating from somewhere beneath his throat.

Dreyfus introduced himself, then escorted the Ultra into the cutter's habitation area. 'Is there anything I can offer you by way of hospitality?'

'Can you run to blood dialysis?'

'I'm afraid not.'

'That's a pity. My ship's having trouble purging my fatigue poisons. I think the filters need changing, but I can't ever seem to find the time to return to the central servicing facility.'

'How about coffee instead?'

'I'll pass, Prefect. Now: concerning this disagreeable subject we were about to touch on.'

'Nine hundred and sixty casualties. That's way beyond disagreeable. Those people weren't ever on my radar, Harbourmaster. That means they were just decent human beings trying to get on with their lives without hurting anyone else. None of them made it out alive.'

'I'm sorry about the deaths. Truly, I am. We do have souls, Prefect Dreyfus. We do have consciences. But I assure you this could not have been what it appears to be.'

'I can place the *Accompaniment of Shadows* near enough to rule out the involvement of any other ship.'

Seraphim touched one hand to the side of his breather mask, as if making some microscopic adjustment to his airflow settings. 'Have you considered the possibility that someone else committed the crime, yet wished it to appear the work of an innocent crew who just happened to be in the neighbourhood?'

'There's nothing my boss and I would rather have than an excuse not to stir up trouble with the Ultras. But we know of only one thing that could have sliced open the Ruskin-Sartorious Bubble, and that's a Conjoiner drive.'

'You've ruled out the possibility of something else: a weapon, for instance?'

'There's nothing that could have done that.'

'Maybe nothing known to us now. But no one would deny that things were created in the past – terrible, destructive things – that may have survived into the present era. We've all heard talk of the hell-class weapons—'

'I'm a prefect, Seraphim,' Dreyfus said patiently. 'I deal in known facts, not speculation. And I don't have to look for some fabled weapon from the dark ages. I have proof that a drive was involved. That's all I need.'

'There must still be a mistake. No crew would perpetrate such an atrocity.'

'Even if a deal went sour?'

'Children act out of spite, Prefect Dreyfus. We're not children.'

'All right. What about an accident?'

'A Conjoiner drive doesn't just *switch on* spontaneously.'

'Fine. Then someone had to have their hands on the controls. Glad we cleared that up.'

'We've cleared nothing up. What are you expecting me to do?'

'I want you to prevent the *Accompaniment of Shadows* from leaving the Swarm. That's step one. Step two is you stop any of her crew from jumping ship. Step three is you use your influence to bring the captain to justice.'

'That's a lot of steps you're asking for, Prefect.'

'It's my job.'

'And if I don't do as you say?'

'We'll have to review the existing trading arrangements. There are ten thousand habitats open for business in the Glitter Band, Harbourmaster. But you don't get to talk to any of them without our blessing.'

'We'd find workarounds.'

'I don't doubt it. But I'd like to see how your profit margins hold up. I imagine things might get very unpleasant for a man in your position.'

'Don't ever threaten us, Prefect,' the Harbourmaster said.

'Why not?'

'Because you need us a great deal more than we need you.'

Sparver knocked before entering Thalia's office, even though the passwall was transparent. As a Deputy Field III – the highest ranking before promotion to full field status – Sparver was two full grades above Thalia. He would have been within his official rights had he walked in unannounced, as Dreyfus would most likely have done. But in all his dealings with Thalia, ever since she'd joined the team, Sparver had scrupulously treated her as an exact equal. The daughter of Jason Ng had enough to deal with without petty displays of rank, especially from another deputy.

'Boss man keeping you busy?' he said, as Thalia looked around from her work.

'It can't be helped.' She took a swig from a coffee flask before rubbing her eyelids. 'The Perigal issue was already a high-priority item before Ruskin-Sartorious came in. I'm just glad that Dreyfus trusts me to handle both tasks.'

Sparver stood next to her console, scanning the information scrolling past on multiple panes. Thalia made light of her speed-reading ability, but her Klausner index was still much higher than his own.

'The boss trusts you. Don't worry about that.'

'But he has his doubts.'

'Why d'you say that?'

Thalia stopped the scrolling panes. 'It would have made sense for me to go out to the Ruskin-Sartorious Bubble. I know core architecture better than anyone.'

'But you were already busy.'

'I'm even busier now. That wasn't really an argument for me not coming along.'

'Dreyfus knew I could take care of the core,' Sparver said. 'If we'd run into anything thorny, you could have signed out a cutter and met us at the Bubble within an hour.'

'I suppose so.'

'Thalia, listen to me. The boss thinks very highly of you. He may not show it, but that's just his way. He wouldn't have brought you onto the team in the first place if he thought otherwise. Trust me on this.'

'I'm just worried that he thinks I'm underperforming.'

'Has he said anything to that effect?'

Thalia frowned. 'Not exactly, no.'

'Well, then.'

'I still can't help wondering why he didn't ask me along to the Bubble.'

'Because it was a potentially dangerous operation.'

'More so than a lockdown?'

'Potentially. If someone wanted to destroy the Bubble that badly, they could easily have come back for another go if they saw prefects crawling all over it.'

'But they didn't.'

'Point still stands. Reason Dreyfus didn't ask you to join the team – apart from the fact that he was trying not to exhaust you – was that he didn't want to place one of his best deputies in a high-risk environment. Lockdown's different – you had to be on the squad. But this time? I think the boss made the right call. And it has nothing to do with your abilities not measuring up.'

Thalia looked sheepish. 'I guess all this sounds silly to you.'

'Not at all. When I first started working with him, I spent months wondering what the hell I was doing wrong. Not a word of praise ever escaped his lips. Then slowly it dawned on me: if Dreyfus keeps you on the team, that's the praise.'

'But now ... it's different, right?'

'Not really. Once in a blue moon he throws me a crumb of encouragement, but other than that I get exactly the same treatment as you.'

'It doesn't look that way.'

'That's because you're still the new addition to the team. When I make full field, I'll get promoted to another section and you'll fill my slot. Then Dreyfus'll bring in someone new, someone who'll feel exactly the way you do now.'

Thalia glanced over his shoulder at the waiting passwall. 'Do you like him, Sparver?'

'There's no one in Panoply I'd rather work for.'

'Not what I asked.'

'I know, but that's the answer you're getting.' He spread his hands. 'I'm a pig, Thalia. There are prefects who won't look me in the eye because of that. Dreyfus specifically requested I be assigned to his team. He can be as cold-hearted and uncommunicative as he wants, and I'll still owe him for that.'

'There are prefects who won't look me in the eye either,' Thalia said.

'There you go. We both owe the boss man. Now why don't you pipe some of that workload over to me and I'll see what I can do to take the burden off you?'

'You don't have to do this.'

'And I'm not claiming to know as much about beta-levels as you. But I thought there might be some routine tests I can run while you're getting on with the clever stuff.'

'Actually, now that you mention it . . .' Thalia's hands moved over the console again. 'I've run standard recovery algorithms on all twelve recoverables, using the Tianjun protocols. Five or six of them look hopelessly corrupted, but I need to run a second set of tests to make absolutely sure.'

Sparver nodded. 'Using the Lisichansk protocols, I'm guessing?'

'It probably won't make any difference – if you can't get a clean resurrection with Tianjun, Lisichansk isn't likely to do any better. But for the sake of completeness, it has to be done.'

'I'll get on it.'

'Appreciated, Sparver.'

'Anything else I can do for you?'

Thalia looked down at her hands, still poised above the console. 'There is something. But it isn't that kind of favour.'

'Go ahead.'

'When I joined the team, I asked you what had happened to Dreyfus, why he is the way he is.'

'I vaguely remember.'

'You said you didn't have all the answers, but one day you'd tell me what you knew.'

'I did,' he admitted.

'It's been five years, Sparver. You can give me something now.'

'Have you asked around?'

'I don't do much asking around, in case you hadn't noticed.'

'Fair point. Have you run a query through the Turbines?'

'It didn't seem right, digging around behind his back.'

'Whereas talking about him isn't a problem?'

'It's different,' she said, giving him a warning look. 'I'm asking you as a friend to tell me what happened to him.'

Sparver felt something in him give way. He'd made a promise to her when she joined the team and he couldn't renege on that now, even though he'd hoped she'd forgotten. 'It's not what happened to Dreyfus. It's what happened to someone he cared about. Her name was Valery Chapelon.'

He could tell that the name meant nothing to Thalia.

'Was she his wife?'

Sparver nodded slowly, feeling as if he'd committed a grievous betrayal of confidence.

'What happened?' Thalia asked.

'It was eleven years ago. Now ask yourself how long Jane Aumonier's been the way she is, and that should tell you all you need to know.'

He waited for the reaction to show itself in her face.

Jane Aumonier floated with her arms folded, her chin lifted, her eyes bright with intense focus.

'You're back sooner than I expected,' she said, when the safe-distance tether brought Dreyfus to a stop.

'I made progress.'

'I seem to recall that my recommendation was that you were not to engage.'

'They forced my hand. I didn't enter the Swarm, but I did have a talk with someone claiming to speak for it.'

'I'm guessing you encountered the harbourmaster, in that case.'

'I didn't know you'd met.'

'Once or twice in the past. Never face to face. He's a slippery customer, but all told I'd rather deal with him than most of his predecessors. My impression is that he's open to reasoned debate.'

Dreyfus would have shifted awkwardly were he not floating on the end of the tether. 'I hope so.'

Aumonier's normally inexpressive face became stern. 'You didn't push him, did you?'

'We don't have time to pussyfoot. Once the story breaks that Ultras are torching habitats, Seraphim and his friends are going to have a lot more to worry about than a few gentle hints from me.'

Aumonier's attention flicked back to one of her read-outs. Her eyes glazed: for a moment, she could have been light-seconds away in body and mind. 'Well, you're right that we don't have much time. Our effort to mask the catastrophe is still holding but we're fending off more queries by the hour. Word is beginning to reach the other habitats that *something* may have happened. It's only a matter of time before someone decides to have a look-see, or sends a query we can't answer in a convincing fashion.'

'Then what?'

'Then life gets interesting,' Aumonier said darkly.

'In which case, I'm glad I was forceful. If Seraphim's the reasonable man you say he is, maybe we'll get somewhere.'

'We're playing with fire, Tom.'

'We didn't choose the game,' he reminded her. 'This is what they pay us for.'

Aumonier was silent. Dreyfus began to think she was done with him, that she had returned her attention to the ever-shifting display wall and forgotten his presence. It had happened before, and he took no slight from it. But when she spoke he knew that she had only been summoning the courage to talk about something painful.

'Tom, there's something you need to know. It's about the scarab.'

'Good news?' he asked, despite the fact that everything in her tone said otherwise.

'Not good news, no. Or at least something we don't understand. As far as I'm concerned, that's bad news by definition.'

'Tell me.'

'You know what sometimes worries me the most? It's not that they won't ever be able to get it off me. I have confidence in their abilities, maybe more than they do. Demikhov's team is the best I could ever hope for.'

'So what's worrying you?' asked Dreyfus softly.

'That I won't be able to dream. What happens when you don't dream for eleven years, Tom? Does anyone really know?'

'I'm sure you'll be able to dream.'

'But we don't know for sure. What if the parts of my brain that used to dream have withered away from not being used? What if they've been taken over by some other part? That happens, you know. The brain rewires itself all the time.'

'You'll dream,' he said, as if that should be reassurance enough.

After a silence, Aumonier said, 'They've detected a change inside it. Components have moved. I felt it myself. They don't know what to make of the change.'

'I thought Demikhov said they understood everything inside it.'

'He's never claimed that, just that they know enough to be able to get it off me, one day.'

Dreyfus studied the thing attached to the back of Aumonier's neck. It was a fist-sized machine shaped like a red chromed beetle, clamped into place by its legs, a dozen sterile prongs that dug into her skin.

'Why now?' he asked.

'These last few days have been stressful for all of us. I can't get much out of Demikhov, but I can guess what he's thinking. We already know the scarab has a tap into my spine, so that it can read my blood chemistry. We also suspect that it has a field trawl, so that it can tell if I start falling asleep. I've no doubt about that – occasionally I feel the itch as it runs its fingers through my brain. I think it has enough to go on, Tom. It's responding to my stress levels. Something in me has crossed a threshold, and the scarab has responded accordingly.'

'But apart from the change, the movement of components, it's done nothing?'

'It may be preparing for something, waiting for my stress levels to notch higher. But no one in the Sleep Lab will tell me anything. I think they're concerned about what might happen were I to become even more stressed.'

'I'll talk to Demikhov,' Dreyfus said. 'Get the straight story.'

'I'd appreciate that.'

'It's the least I can do.'

'The thing is, I can't let this distract me from the present crisis. But I thought you deserved to know.' She swallowed hard. 'In case something happens to me.'

CHAPTER 5

The passwall sealed itself into non-existence behind Senior Prefect Gaffney. He had just returned from Hospice Idlewild, and his sinuses were still blocked after exposure to the furnace-dry air aboard the corvette. He picked at a nostril, then smeared the offending nasal matter against the wall, where it melted away into the absorbing matrix of quickmatter.

The room – the heart of Internal Security – was as cold and still and empty as the deepest, clammiest part of a cave system. But as Gaffney moved further into it, the systems responded to his presence and conjured furniture and amenities into being, shaped to his usual ergonomic preferences. Gaffney settled himself before a wraparound console from which rose several membrane-thin display panes. Symbols appeared on the console, outlined in neon blue. Gaffney's fingers skated over them, entering complex chains of richly syntactic security commands, stringing them together like beads on a wire. Text and graphics churned over the display facets, flickering past at high speed. Within Panoply, Gaffney prided himself on having one of the highest speed-reading faculties of any operative.

Far away, in the weightless heart of Panoply, the Search Turbines threshed their way through unthinkable quantities of archived knowledge. It was illusory, but Gaffney swore he could feel the subterranean rumble of those questing machines; could almost feel the fire-hose pressure of the data rocketing through them.

He slowed the flow as he neared the focus of his search.

'Warning,' the system advised him. 'You are entering a high-security data trove. Pangolin clearance is now mandatory. If you do not have Pangolin clearance, desist from further queries.'

Gaffney pressed on. He not only had Pangolin clearance, he got to decide who else had it.

'Category: weapon systems, archival, interdicted,' said the system.

Gaffney refined his query parameters one final time.

'Specific retrieval item,' the system said. 'War robot. Weevil class.'

'Show me,' Gaffney breathed as his hands echoed the verbal command.

Line diagrams and cutaway illustrations crammed the display panes. Gaffney narrowed his eyes and peered closer. In some of the views, the weevils were accompanied by human figures to lend scale. The robots were smaller than he'd been expecting, until he remembered that one of their prime uses had been infiltration. By all accounts they were fast, with a high degree of tactical autonomy.

Not that anyone alive had clear memories of weevils. The date-stamps on the annotations were all at least a century old.

Gaffney's hands moved again. Now the panes filled with scrolling lines of text and symbols in MAL, the human-readable Manufactory Assembler Language. The instructions became a whizzing blur. The blur began to dance and squirm in subtle rhythms, betraying large-scale structure in the sequencing code. Here were the commands that, if fed into a sufficiently equipped manufactory, would result in the production of a fully operational weevil.

Or more than one.

Having verified that the MAL script was complete and error-free, Gaffney encysted the code in a private partition of his own security management area. In the unlikely event of anyone stumbling on it, all they would see would be routine entry/exit schedules for pressure-tight passwalls inside Panoply.

He backed-up the top level of the query stack. His hands dithered over the keys. He switched to voice-only.

'Retrieve priors on search-term Firebrand.'

'Repeat search term, please.'

'Firebrand,' Gaffney said, with exaggerated slowness.

He'd been expecting some hits, but nothing like the multitude of priors that filled the panes. He applied filters and whittled down the stack. Yet when he was finished it was still hopelessly large, and he wasn't seeing anything remotely connected with Panoply, or the thing that so interested Aurora.

Firebrand.

What the hell did it mean? Anthony Theobald had given him the word, and he'd allowed himself to believe it was something useful, enough to stop trawling the man before he became an unwilling recruit for the Persistent Vegetative State. But now that he had let the man go, now that he was alone with the Search Turbines, Gaffney wondered whether he should not have gone deeper.

'You sold me a dud, Tony,' Gaffney said aloud. 'You naughty, naughty boy.'

But even as he spoke, he remembered something else Anthony Theobald had told him. The men who'd let slip that codeword had once told him that their operations were superblack. Untraceable, unaccountable and officially deniable at all levels of Panoply command and control, right up to the Queen of the Scarab herself.

In other words, it was hardly surprising that he hadn't found anything significant in a two-minute search. Firebrand might still mean something. But it was going to take more than sitting at a console to get any closer to the truth.

Gaffney spent the next five minutes covering his tracks, erasing any trace of his rummaging from the query logs of the Search Turbines. Then another five minutes covering traces of *that*. By the time he was done, Gaffney was confident that even he wouldn't have been able to follow his own trail.

He stood from the console and conjured it back into the room, together with the seat he had been using. Then he wiped the sleeve of his tunic across his brow, ran fingers through his wiry red hair and headed for the passwall.

He knew that what he had just done was 'wrong', just as it had been 'wrong' to intercept, trawl and discard the hapless Anthony Theobald. But everything, as Aurora liked to remind him, depended on viewpoint. There was nothing wrong with protecting the citizenry, even if what they most needed protection from was their own worst natures.

And Aurora was always right.

The beta-level regarded Dreyfus with cold indifference. Dreyfus stared at him obligingly, as if waiting for the punch line to a joke. It was an old interview technique that usually obtained a result.

The imaged figure was male, taller than Dreyfus, thin of face, his body hidden under the voluminous folds of a purple robe or gown. His right shoulder and arm were clothed in quilted black leather, his visible hand gloved and ringed. His cropped greying hair, the aquiline curve of his nose, the solemnity of his expression, his general stance, brought to mind a statue of a powerful Roman senator. Only a slight translucence made the figure appear less than totally solid.

After the silence had stretched almost to snapping point, Anthony Theobald said, 'If you didn't want to ask me questions, perhaps you shouldn't have brought me back to life, Prefect.'

'I've got a lot of questions,' Dreyfus said easily. 'I just wanted to give you the chance to have your say first.'

'I suppose you'd be the man your colleague mentioned during my last invocation.'

Thalia had already activated the beta-level to test its readiness for interviewing. Of the twelve beta-levels saved from Ruskin-Sartorious, only three had been deemed sufficiently functional to offer useful testimony, despite the best efforts of Thalia and Sparver to mend the remaining nine.

'I'm Dreyfus,' he said pleasantly. 'Welcome to Panoply, Citizen.'

'Perhaps it's me, but "welcome" doesn't have quite the necessary degree of solemnity.'

'I was just being polite,' Dreyfus replied. 'My personal belief is that beta-levels have no claim on consciousness. As far as I'm concerned, you're just an item of forensic evidence. The fact that I can talk to you – the fact that you might claim to feel alive – is entirely irrelevant.'

'How reassuring to meet someone with such an enlightened viewpoint. What's your opinion on women? Do you consider them capable of full sentience, or do you have lingering reservations about them as well?'

'I don't have a problem with women. I do have a problem with software entities that pretend to be alive and then expect to be accorded the rights and privileges of the living.'

'If I'm not alive, how can I "expect" anything?'

'I'm not saying you can't be persuasive. But the instant I sense evasion or concealment I'll send you back to the deepfreeze. Once you're there, I can't vouch for your safety. Things go astray. Files get deleted by mistake.'

'A policeman of the old school,' Anthony Theobald said, nodding approvingly. 'Skip the appetiser and straight on to the main course of threats and bullying. Actually, I welcome it. It's a refreshingly direct approach.'

'Just so we understand each other.'

'Now are you ready to tell me what happened?'

Dreyfus scratched at the bulge of neck fat lapping against the back of his collar. 'My background files say that you were the head of the family in the Bubble. According to the last census, you were lording it over more than nine hundred subjects.'

'Free family members and citizens. Again: what happened?'

'How much did my deputy tell you?'

'Nothing useful.'

'Good for her. I'll begin by telling you that Ruskin-Sartorious no longer exists. Your habitat was gutted by the drive exhaust from a lighthugger space vehicle, the *Accompaniment of Shadows*. It appears to have been a deliberate act. Do you remember this event?'

Anthony Theobald lost some of his composure, the set of his jaw slackening. 'I have no recollection of it.'

'What's the last thing you do remember? Does the name of the ship ring any bells?'

'It rings more than bells, Prefect. We were in negotiations with the *Accompaniment of Shadows*. The ship was parked near Ruskin-Sartorious.'

'Why wasn't she using the Swarm, like all the other ships?'

'I gather there was a problem with their long-distance shuttle. It was simpler to move the entire ship and rely on one of our own short-range shuttles. We had the facilities to cope, and Dravidian's crew seemed happy enough to be entertained at our expense.'

It was the first mention of the captain's name.

'Trade talks?'

Anthony Theobald looked at Dreyfus as if the question was absurd. 'What other reason is there to deal with Ultras?'

'Just asking. How were the talks running?'

'Agreeably, at first.'

'And then?'

'Less agreeably. We weren't experienced in dealings with Ultras. I'd hoped matters wouldn't come to such a sorry pass, frankly. We had some financial difficulties and I'd been hoping that the affair between Vernon and Delphine would ease matters somewhat ... but that wasn't to be. In the end we had no choice but to deal with Ultras.'

'What were you hoping to sell?'

'Delphine's works, of course.'

Dreyfus nodded as if nothing more needed to be said, but filed the information away for future reference. Thalia had already informed him that the other two stable witnesses were Delphine Ruskin-Sartorious and her lover, Vernon Tregent. 'And when the crew visited you – who were you dealing with, primarily?'

'Dravidian, in the main.'

'How'd you take to him?'

'I found him straightforward enough for a cyborg, or chimeric, or however they wish to be called. He appeared interested in some samples of Delphine's work. He felt he could get a good price for them around one of the other worlds.'

'Where was his next port of call?'

'I confess I don't recall. Fand, Sky's Edge, the First System, some other godforsaken place. What did it matter to me, once the works were sold?'

'Maybe it mattered to Delphine.'

'Then you can take it up with her. My sole concern was the economic benefit to Ruskin-Sartorious.'

'And you got the impression Dravidian was offering a fair price?'

'I'd have preferred more, naturally, but the offer appeared reasonable enough. Judging by the state of his ship and crew, Dravidian had his own financial difficulties.'

'So you were happy with the deal. You sold the goods to the Ultras. Dravidian said goodbye and took his ship away. What happened next?'

'That isn't how things played out. Negotiations were winding to a close when Delphine received an anonymous message. She brought it to my immediate attention. It suggested that Dravidian was not to be trusted: that the price he was offering us was far below a realistic market value, and that we would be much better off dealing with other Ultras.'

'But you had no access to anyone else.'

'Until then. But the message hinted that there might in fact be interested parties.'

'How'd you react?'

'We consulted. I was suspicious, urging that we should conclude our business with Dravidian. We had a deal. But Delphine demurred. She used executive privilege to block the transaction. Vernon supported her, of course. I was furious, but not half as furious as Dravidian. He said the honour of his ship and crew had been impugned. He issued threats, saying that what we'd done would cost Ruskin-Sartorious gravely.'

'And then what?'

'His crew returned to their ship. Our shuttle came back. We saw the *Accompaniment of Shadows* move away.' Anthony Theobald spread his hands. 'And that is all I remember. As you have been so thoughtful as to remind me, I am a beta-level simulation: reliant for my perceptions on the distributed surveillance systems of the habitat. Those perceptions would have been processed and consolidated in the core, but it would not have been an instantaneous process. There would not have been enough time to incorporate those final observations into my personality model before Ruskin-Sartorious was destroyed.'

'At least you remember something.'

'You'll hear the same story from the others.' Anthony Theobald peered intently at Dreyfus. 'There are others, aren't there?'

'I can't say. I haven't completed my interviews.'

'Do you intend to question Dravidian?'

'I'll question anyone I think might have an angle on the attack.'

'You can't let this atrocity go unpunished, Prefect. Something unspeakable happened to Ruskin-Sartorious. Someone must pay for that.'

'I'm pretty sure someone will,' Dreyfus said.

When he had returned the simulation to storage – very much against its wishes – Dreyfus took a minute to note his own thoughts into his compad. Perhaps his clarifying statement concerning his views on beta-levels hadn't helped matters, but he'd sensed an undeniable hostility from the Ruskin-Sartorious patriarch. It would be a mistake to read too much into that, though. No one liked Panoply very much, and the resurrected dead were no exception.

He invoked the second valid recoverable, opting to take a slightly less harsh tack.

'Hello, Vernon,' Dreyfus said, addressing the younger-looking man who'd just appeared. He had a pleasant, trustworthy face and a headful of tight blond curls. 'Welcome to Panoply. I'm very sorry to have to tell you this, but in case my colleague didn't make it clear, your primary is dead.'

'I gathered,' Vernon Tregent said. 'I still want to know about Delphine. Your colleague wouldn't tell me anything. Did she make it out? Did you get anything from her beta?'

'We'll get to that. I just need to clarify something first. I don't mean this to sound hurtful, but there are people who believe in the sanctity of beta-levels, and people who don't, and I'm afraid I'm one of the latter.'

'That's fine,' Vernon said, with an easy shrug. 'I don't believe in the sanctity of beta-levels either.'

Dreyfus blinked a double-take. 'How can you not believe? You *are* one.'

'But my responses are governed by Vernon's beliefs, as demonstrated on countless occasions. Vernon didn't think beta-levels were anything more than clever simulacra. He was very vocal in that opinion. Hence, I share that view.'

'Good ...' Dreyfus said, less sure of himself. 'That'll make life a lot easier.' Then some impulse caused him to volunteer more information than he'd normally have considered wise. 'We've recovered Delphine. I still have to interview her, but my colleague thinks there'll be enough there to serve as a useful witness.'

Vernon closed his eyes. He raised his chin, as if giving thanks to the blank white infinity that served as a ceiling. 'I'm glad. If anyone deserved to get out, it was Delphine. Now tell me what happened.'

'Does the name Dravidian mean anything to you?'

'If you mean the Ultra captain ... then yes, it means a lot. What happened?'

'You don't remember?'

'I wouldn't be asking if I did.'

It was the same story as Anthony Theobald, Dreyfus thought. No memory of the final events because the recording systems hadn't had time to update the beta-level models in the processor cores. 'Your habitat was destroyed,' he said. 'The captain – we'll assume Dravidian gave the order – appears to have decided to slash it open with his engine.'

'Dravidian wouldn't have ...' But Vernon trailed off, as if the very repugnance of the crime was only now hitting home. 'I can't believe he'd have done something so vicious, so out-of-proportion. There's no doubt that this happened?'

'I've crawled over the ruin myself. Forensic evidence is watertight. And one of my other witnesses says that Dravidian didn't like it when the deal went sour.'

Vernon pushed his fingertips against his temples, screwing up his eyes. 'I remember that we were close to settling things. Then the message came through ... Delphine received it, I remember.'

'Saying not to trust Dravidian?'

'Saying we could get a better offer elsewhere. Anthony Theobald was angry, of course: he wanted those funds so badly he was prepared to sell Delphine's art for its scrap value.' Vernon clenched his fist in emphasis. 'But it was her life's work! She'd put her soul into it. I couldn't stand by and see it sold off for less than a fair price.'

'So you and Delphine decided to break off negotiations.'

'We wished Dravidian no hard feelings.'

'But he didn't take it well.'

'He seemed put out, exasperated, as if he genuinely thought he was offering an honest price for Delphine's art. He said he'd have to think twice about ever doing business with us again. He said that to withdraw from negotiations so late in a discussion was most irregular.' Vernon shook his head. 'But to go from that to ... destroying Delphine's home ... nothing he said indicated that he was *that* angry. I mean, there's a difference between angry and murderous. Isn't there?'

'Less than you'd think.'

'Do you think he did it, Prefect? Do you think Dravidian was capable of this?'

'Let's get back to Delphine. Was she an artist of some kind?'

'Some of us thought so.'

'What kind of work?'

'Sculpture, mostly. Her work was brilliant. She was right to want the best price for it.'

Dreyfus thought back to the face he'd seen carved into the rock drifting through the ruins of Ruskin-Sartorious. He couldn't deny the power of the piece, but there'd been nothing useful about it in the forensics summary.

'Was she working on anything at the time of the attack?'

'Well, not literally, but she'd been busy with a big piece for several months. Part of her Lascaille series.' The young man shrugged. 'It was just a phase she was going through.'

The word 'Lascaille' meant something to Dreyfus, just as he was sure he'd recognised the face in the rock, but neither shed any immediate light on the other. It was only a work of art, but anything that offered a window into Delphine's head might be useful in determining her role in events. He made a mental note to look into the matter later.

'How did you come to know her?' he asked. 'Were you married?'

'We were supposed to be married. Ruskin-Sartorious was in financial difficulties and Anthony Theobald thought he could solve the Bubble's problems by marrying his daughter off to the son of another habitat. He already had ties to Macro Hektor Industrial: we'd installed his anti-collision defences and he was in debt to us.

I was the scion of one of the most powerful family lines within Industrial. Negotiations took place behind our backs. Delphine and I didn't like that very much.' He smiled sadly. 'But that didn't stop us from falling in love for real.'

'So Anthony Theobald got what he wanted?'

'Not exactly. My family had expectations that I'd become another partner in the defence-design business. Unfortunately, I had other plans. I decided to leave Industrial, severing ties to both my family and the business, and join Delphine in the Bubble. I'd become inspired by her art, convinced that I might have something of the same genius lying untapped within myself. It took me about three months to realise that I had no undeveloped talent whatsoever.'

'Takes some people a lifetime.'

'But I did realise that I could help Delphine. I decided to become her agent, publicist, broker, whatever you want to call it. That's why I was so reluctant to accept Dravidian's offer.'

'I take it Anthony Theobald wasn't exactly thrilled by either course of events: you severing ties with your rich family, and then souring the Dravidian deal.'

'I sensed some issues there, yes.'

'Do you think he was angry enough to want to kill his own daughter and family?'

'No. Anthony Theobald and I might not have seen eye to eye, but I knew he loved his daughter. He'd have played no part in this.' Vernon Tregent looked intently at Dreyfus. 'Why look for another angle, though, when you already have Dravidian?'

'I'm just making sure I don't miss anything. If you think of something, you'll be sure to tell me, won't you?'

'Certainly.' But then a shadow of suspicion crossed the young man's face. 'I'd have to know I could trust you, of course.'

'Why wouldn't you trust me?'

'How do I know that you're really a prefect, to begin with, or that Ruskin-Sartorious really has been destroyed? For all I know I could have been kidnapped by data-pirates. I don't have any evidence that this is Panoply.'

'Nothing I can show you or tell you will make any difference to that.'

Vernon pondered that for a long while before responding. 'I know. And right now I'm not sure I've seen or heard enough to be able to make a sound judgement.'

'If you know anything that could assist in the investigation, you should tell me now.'

'I want to talk to Delphine.'

'Out of the question. You're both material witnesses. I can't have your individual testimonies invalidated by cross-contamination.'

'We're in love, Prefect.'

'Your human counterparts were in love. There's a difference.'

'You really don't believe in us, do you?'

'Nor do you.'

'But Delphine does. She believes, Prefect. That's all that matters to me.' Vernon's eyes seemed to shine right through him. 'Crush me, by all means. But don't crush Delphine.'

'Hold invocation,' Dreyfus said.

When the room was empty, Dreyfus retrieved the compad from between his knees and began to organise his thoughts about Vernon, using the ancient stylus entry mode that he favoured. Yet something stilled his hand, however: some tingle of disquiet that he could not ignore. He'd interviewed beta-level simulations on many previous occasions, and he considered himself well versed in their ways. He had never sensed a soul behind the clockwork, and he would not have said that he sensed one now. But *something* was different. He had never before felt that he had to earn the trust of a beta-level, nor had he ever considered what the earning of that trust might signify.

One trusted machines. But one never expected machines to return the favour.

'Invoke Delphine Ruskin-Sartorious,' Dreyfus said.

The woman assumed solidity in the interview room. She was taller than Dreyfus, dressed in a simple white smock and trousers, her sleeves rolled up to the elbow, the trousers rolled to just below the knee, flat white slippers on her feet, arms crossed. She was leaning to one side, weight on one leg, as if waiting for something to happen. She had silver bracelets on her wrists, but no other ornamentation. Her heart-shaped face was plain without being ugly. She had simple, minimalist features, unadorned with cosmetics. Her eyes were a very pale sea-green. Her hair was scrunched back from her brow, tied with what looked like a dirty rag. A few coiled strands had escaped to frame the side of her face.

'Delphine?' Dreyfus asked.

'Yes. Where am I?'

'You're in Panoply. I'm afraid I have very bad news. Ruskin-Sartorious has been destroyed.'

Delphine nodded, as if the news was something she'd been quietly dreading. 'I asked your colleague about Vernon. She wouldn't tell me anything, but I read between the lines. I knew it had to be something bad. Did Vernon—'

'Vernon died. So did everyone else. I'm sorry. But we managed to recover Vernon's beta-level.'

She closed her eyes briefly, reopened them. 'I want to speak to him.'

'That isn't possible.' Some impulse made Dreyfus add: 'Not right now, at any rate. Maybe later. But I need to talk to you alone first. What happened to the Bubble doesn't look like an accident. If it was deliberate, it ranks as one of the worst crimes committed since the Eighty. I want to see justice served. But to do that I need the full cooperation of all surviving witnesses.'

'You said no one survived.'

'All we have are three beta-levels. I think I've begun to piece together what happened, but your testimony will count just as much as the others.'

'If I can help, I will.'

'I need to know what went on right at the end. I understand you were hoping to sell some of your artwork to a third party.'

'Dravidian, yes.'

'Tell me everything you know about Dravidian, starting from the beginning. Then tell me about the art.'

'Why would you care about the art?'

'It's connected to the crime. I feel I need to know about it.'

'Then that's it? No interest in the art beyond that?'

'I'm a man of simple tastes.'

'But you know what you like.'

Dreyfus smiled slightly. 'I saw that sculpture you were working on – the big one with the face.'

'And what did you think of it?'

'It unsettled me.'

'It was meant to. Perhaps you're not a man of such simple tastes as you think.'

Dreyfus studied her for several moments before speaking. 'You appear to be taking the matter of your death quite lightly, Delphine.'

'I'm not dead.'

'I'm investigating your murder.'

'As well you should – a version of me has been killed. But the one that counts – the one that matters to me now – is the one talking to you. As difficult as it may be for you to accept, I feel completely alive. Don't get me wrong: I want justice. But I'm not going to mourn myself.'

'I admire the strength of your convictions.'

'It's not about conviction. It's about the way I feel. I was raised by a family that regarded beta-level simulation as a perfectly natural state of existence. My mother died in Chasm City, years before I was born from a cloned copy of her womb. I only knew her from her beta-level, but she's been as real to me as any person I've ever known.'

'I don't doubt it.'

'If someone close to you died, would you refuse to acknowledge the authenticity of their beta-level?'

'The question's never arisen.'

She looked sceptical. 'Then no one close to you – no one with a beta-level back-up – has ever died? In *your* line of work?'

'I didn't say that.'

'Then someone has died?'

'We're not here to talk about abstract matters,' Dreyfus said.

'I'm not sure I can think of anything less abstract than life and death.'

'Let's get back to Dravidian.'

'I touched a nerve, didn't I?'

'Tell me about the Ultras.'

But just as Delphine started speaking – the look on her face said she wasn't going to answer his question directly – the black outline of a door appeared in the passwall behind her. The white surface within the outline flowed open enough to admit the stocky form of Sparver, then resealed behind him.

'Freeze invocation,' Dreyfus said, irritated that he'd been disturbed. 'Sparver, I thought I said that I wasn't to be—'

'Had to reach you, Boss. This is urgent.'

'Then why didn't you summon me on my bracelet?'

'Because you'd turned it off.'

'Oh.' Dreyfus glanced down at his sleeve. 'So I did.'

'Jane told me to pull you out of whatever you were doing, no matter how much you screamed and kicked. There's been a development.'

Dreyfus whispered a command to return Delphine to storage. 'This had better be good,' he told Sparver when the beta-level had vanished. 'I was close to getting a set of watertight testimonies tying the *Accompaniment of Shadows* to the Bubble. That's all the ammunition I need to take back to Seraphim. He'd have no choice but to hand over the ship then.'

'I don't think you need to persuade him to hand over the ship.'

Dreyfus frowned momentarily, still irked. 'What?'

'It's already on its way. It's headed straight for us.'

CHAPTER 6

When Sparver prodded Dreyfus awake, they'd arrived within visual range of the *Accompaniment of Shadows*. Dreyfus untangled himself from the hammock webbing and followed his deputy into the spacious flight deck of the deep-system cruiser. Field prefects were authorised to fly cutters, but a ship as big and powerful as the *Democratic Circus* needed a dedicated team. There were three operatives on the flight deck, all wearing immersion glasses and elbow-length black control gloves. The chief pilot was a man named Pell, a Panoply operative Dreyfus knew and respected. Dreyfus grunted acknowledgement, had Sparver conjure him a bulb of coffee, then asked his deputy to bring him up to date.

'Jane polled on the nukes,' the hyperpig said. 'We're good to go.'

'What about the harbourmaster?'

'No further contact with Seraphim, or any other representative of the Ultras. But we do have a shipload of secondary headaches to worry about.'

'Just when I was starting to get used to the ones we already had.'

'Headquarters says there's a storm brewing over Ruskin-Sartorious – the news is beginning to break. Not the full facts – no one else knows exactly which ship was involved – but there are a hundred million citizens out there capable of joining the dots.'

'Are people starting to work out that Ultras had to be involved?'

'Definite speculation along those lines. A handful of spectators have noticed the drifting ship and are beginning to think it must be tied to the atrocity.'

'Great.'

'In a perfect world, they'd see the ship as evidence that a crime has been committed and that the Ultras have acted with the necessary swiftness, punishing their own.'

Dreyfus scratched at stubble. He needed a shave. 'But if this was a perfect world, you and I'd be out of a job.'

'Jane says we have to consider the very real possibility that some parties may attempt unilateral punitive action if they conclude that Ultras were responsible.'

'In other words, we could be looking at war between the Glitter Band and the Ultras.'

'I'm hoping no one will be *quite* that stupid,' Sparver said. 'Then again, this is baseline humans we're dealing with.'

'I'm a baseline human.'

'You're weird.'

Captain Pell turned away from the console towards them and flipped up his goggles. 'Final approach now, sir. There's a lot of debris and gas boiling off, so I suggest we hold at three thousand metres.'

Pell had turned most of the hull transparent, so that the *Accompaniment of Shadows* was visible alongside. Something was very wrong with it, Dreyfus observed. The engine spars ended in ragged, splayed stumps of tangled metal and hull plating, with no sign of the engines themselves. It was as if they had been ripped off; amputated. The vessel was crabbing, moving sideways instead of nose-first. The hull itself showed evidence of grave assault: great fissures and sucking wounds where armour had been plucked away to reveal hidden innards; machinery that was now glowing red-hot from some unspecified assault. Coils of blue-grey vapour bled into space, forming a widening spiral trail behind the slowly tumbling wreck.

The ship, Dreyfus realised, was burning from inside.

'I guess we're seeing what passes for justice in Ultra circles,' Sparver said.

'They can call it what they like,' Dreyfus snapped back. 'I asked for witnesses, not a shipload of charred corpses.' He turned to Pell. 'How long until it hits the edge of the Glitter Band?'

'Four hours and twenty-eight minutes.'

'I told Jane we'd destroy it three hours before it reaches the outer habitat orbit. That gives us ninety minutes' grace. How are the nukes coming along?'

'Dialled and ready to go. We've identified impact sites, but we'll be happier if we stabilise the tumble before we blow. We're looking at options for tug attachment now.'

'Quick as you can, please.'

The tug specialists were good at their job, and by the time Dreyfus had finished his coffee they had already anchored the three units in position at various stress-tolerant nodes along the wreck's ruined hull.

'We're applying corrective thrust now, sir,' one of the tug specialists informed him. 'Going to take a while, though. There's a million tonnes of ship to stop tumbling, and we don't want her snapping like a twig.'

'Any sign of movement or activity aboard?' Dreyfus asked.

'Fires are out,' Captain Pell said. 'All available air appears to have vented to space by now. Too much residual heat to start looking for thermal hotspots from survivors inside the thing, but we're still sweeping her for electromagnetic signatures. Anyone human still alive in that thing has to be wearing a suit, and we may pick up some EM noise from life-support systems. It's really not likely that we'll find anyone, though.'

'I didn't ask for a likelihood estimate,' Dreyfus said, nerves beginning to get the better of him.

It took another thirty minutes to bring the tumbling ship under control. The specialists rotated the hull so that its long axis was pointed at the Glitter Band, minimising its collision cross section should something go amiss with the nukes. There was no possibility of using the tugs to shove the lighthugger onto a safe trajectory; at best, all that could be done would be to aim her at one of the less densely populated orbits and hope that she slipped through the empty space between habitats. From this far out, the Glitter Band appeared to be a smooth, flat ring of tarnished silver: the individual glints from ten thousand habitats blurring into a solid bow of light.

Dreyfus kept reminding himself that it was still mostly empty space, but his eyes couldn't accept it.

'How long?' he asked.

'You have just under an hour, sir,' Pell informed him.

'Give me an airlock as close to the front kilometre of the ship as you can manage. If anyone's survived, that's where they'll be.'

Pell seemed reticent. 'Sir, I think you need to look at this first, before you go aboard that thing. We just picked up a burst of radio, stronger than anything we've heard since we began our approach.'

'What kind of burst?'

'Voice-only comms. It was faint, but we still managed to localise it pretty well. As it happens, it matched one of the hotspots we're already monitoring.'

'I thought you said you couldn't see any hotspots because of all the thermal noise.'

'I was talking about hotspots inside the ship, sir. This one's coming from outside.'

'Someone's escaped?'

'Not exactly, sir. It's as if they're on the outside of the hull. We should have an image for you once we're a bit closer.'

Pell started bringing the deep-system cruiser closer to the *Accompaniment of Shadows*. It was a fraught operation. Even though the lighthugger had been stabilised and was most likely completely drained of air, it was still giving off vapour at a prodigious rate as the ship's water reserves boiled away into space. With the outgassing vapour came a steady eruption of debris, ranging from thumb-sized twinkling shards to chunks of warped metal the size of houses. The cruiser's hull pinged and clanged with each nerve-jarring impact. Occasionally Dreyfus felt the subsonic burp as one of the *Democratic Circus*'s automatic guns intercepted one of the larger pieces of junk.

Forty-five minutes now remained.

'I've isolated the sound burst, sir,' Pell told Dreyfus. 'Do you want me to replay it?'

'Go ahead,' Dreyfus said, frowning.

But when the fragment burst over the cruiser's intercom, he understood Pell's unwillingness to transmit it without warning. It was just a momentary thing, like a squall of random sound picked up when scanning across radio frequencies. But in that squall was something unspeakable, an implicit horror that pierced Dreyfus to the marrow. It was a voice calling out in pain or terror or both; a voice that encapsulated some primal state of human distress. There was a universe of misery in that fragment of sound; enough to open a door into a part of the mind that was usually kept locked and bolted.

It was not a sound Dreyfus ever wanted to hear again.

'Do you have that image ready for me?'

'Zeroing in now, sir. I'll put it on the wall.'

Part of the transparent hull revealed an enlargement of the prow of the lighthugger. It zoomed in dizzyingly. For a moment Dreyfus was overwhelmed by the intricate, gothic detail of the ship's spire-like hull. Then he made out the one thing that didn't belong.

There was a figure on the hull. The spacesuited form was spread out, limbs splayed as if it had been nailed in place. Dreyfus knew, beyond a shadow of a doubt, that he was looking at Captain Dravidian.

And that Captain Dravidian was still alive.

The Ultras had done a thorough job with their victim. They'd nailed his extremities to the hull, with his head nearest to the prow. Some form of piton had been rammed or shot into his forearms and lower legs, puncturing suit armour and penetrating the hull's fabric. Dreyfus judged that it was the same kind of piton that ships used to guy themselves to asteroids or comets: hyperdiamond-tipped, viciously barbed against accidental retraction. The entry wounds had been sealed over with rapid-setting caulk, preventing pressure loss. Thus immobilised, Dravidian had been welded to the hull along the edges of his limbs and the midpoint of his torso. A thick silvery line of fillet-weld connected him to the plating of the ship, creating a seamless bond between the armour of his suit and the material of the hull. Dreyfus – standing weightless next to Dravidian, anchored to the hull by the soles of his boots – stared at the spectacle and realised that no expertise with cutters would suffice to free his witness in the time remaining.

He was going to ride his ship all the way to its doom, whether that meant a collision in the Glitter Band or an instant of nuclear annihilation. Through Dravidian's faceplate, eyes tracked Dreyfus and Sparver. They were wide and alert, but utterly without hope.

Dravidian knew exactly how good his chances were.

Dreyfus used his left hand to unreel the froptic line from his right wrist. The design of Dravidian's suit was unfamiliar to him: it was probably a jerry-built lash-up of home-made parts and ancient pieces, some of them dating back to the era of chemical rocketry. But almost all suits were engineered for a degree of inter-compatibility. Air- and power-line jacks conformed to a handful of standard interfaces, and had done for centuries. It was the same for comms inputs.

Dreyfus found the corresponding jack in Dravidian's sleeve and slid the froptic in. He felt the minute click as the contacts docked, followed an instant later by a hiss of foreign air-circulator noise in his helmet. He was hearing Dravidian's life-support system.

'Captain Dravidian? I hope you can hear me. I'm Field Prefect Tom Dreyfus, of Panoply.'

There was a pause longer than Dreyfus had been expecting. He was almost ready to give up on the attempt to talk when he heard Dravidian take in a laboured breath.

'I can hear you, Prefect Dreyfus. And yes, I'm Dravidian. It was very astute of you to guess.'

'I wish we could have reached you sooner. I heard your transmission. You sounded in pain.'

There came something like a chuckle. 'I was.'

'And now?'

'That at least has passed. Tell me: what have they done? I felt great pain in my extremities ... but I couldn't see. They were holding me down. Did they cut me into pieces?'

Dreyfus surveyed the welded form, as if he needed to reassure himself that all of Dravidian was there. 'No,' he said. 'They didn't cut you into pieces.'

'That's good. It means I go with some dignity.'

'I'm afraid I don't understand.'

'There is a scale of punishment amongst Ultras, when a crime is said to have been committed. As it is, my guilt has been deemed highly probable. But not certain. If they thought all possibility of innocence had been eliminated, then they would have cut me into pieces.'

'They've nailed you to the ship,' Dreyfus said. 'Nailed you and then welded you.'

'Yes, I saw the light.'

'I can't get you out of that suit, or cut the suit away from the hull. I can't cut away a section of the hull, either. Not in thirty minutes.'

'Thirty minutes?'

'I'm afraid I have orders to destroy this ship. I am sorry that you have been made to suffer, Captain. I can promise you that *my* justice will be swift and clean, when it comes.'

'Nukes?'

'It'll be fast. You have my word on that.'

'That is kind of you, Prefect. And no, I didn't seriously think there was any possibility of rescue. When Ultras do something ...' He left the remark hanging, unfinished.

Dreyfus nodded, for there was no need to complete the sentence.

'But you talk of justice,' Dravidian continued, when he had recovered either breath or clarity of mind. 'I assume that means you have a fixed opinion as to my guilt?'

'A terrible crime took place, Captain. The evidence in my

possession leaves little room for doubt that your ship was involved.'

'I ran,' Dravidian said. 'I ran for the shelter of the Parking Swarm, thinking I would be safe there, that my argument would fall on sympathetic ears. I should never have run. I should have trusted your justice over that of my people.'

'I'd have listened to whatever you had to say,' replied Dreyfus.

'What happened ... was not what it appeared.'

'Your drive did destroy that habitat.'

'Yes, I concede that much.'

'You left it in a state of anger, having been cheated out of a lucrative deal.'

'I was sorry that the family did not choose to close negotiations. But that doesn't mean I planned to kill them all.'

'It wasn't an accident, Dravidian. No one's going to buy that.'

'I never said it was. It was a deliberate act of murder against an innocent habitat. But I had no hand in it.' With sudden intensity, he added: 'Nor did my crew.'

'Either it happened or it didn't.'

'Someone *made* it happen, Prefect. Someone infiltrated the *Accompaniment of Shadows* and used her against the Ruskin-Sartorious Bubble. We were a weapon, not the murderer.'

'You mean someone got aboard the ship and worked out how to turn the engines on and off at just the right moment to kill the Bubble?'

'Yes,' Dravidian said resignedly, as if all his hopes of being believed had just evaporated. 'Exactly that.'

'I wish I could take you at your word.'

'Prefect, ask yourself this: what could I possibly stand to gain from lying now? My crew has been slaughtered, burnt alive aboard their own ship. They let me hear their screams, their pleas for mercy. My vessel has been ripped apart like a rabid animal tossed to the wolves. I have been tortured and welded to the hull. Very shortly I am going to die.'

'I still—' Dreyfus began.

'I don't know why anyone wanted this to happen, Prefect. It's not my job to answer that question, it's yours. But I swear no crime was committed by my crew.'

'We need to start thinking about getting off this thing,' Sparver said quietly.

Dreyfus held up a silencing hand. To Dravidian he said: 'But surely someone in your crew had to have been responsible.'

'No one that I trusted. No one that I really considered crew. But someone else ... maybe.'

'Who?'

'We took on new recruits after we arrived around Yellowstone. Some crew left to join other ships; others came aboard. It's possible that one of those recruits ...'

'Captain?'

Dravidian's tone changed, as if something new had just occurred to him. 'Something odd happened. Our shuttle developed a fault. That was why we had to move the entire ship close to Ruskin-Sartorious, rather than just shuttle over to it from the Swarm. There wasn't time to worry about the cause of the fault, not when we had a deal to close. But now that I look back on it ... now that I don't have any other distractions ... the more I'm convinced that the shuttle's malfunction could only have been sabotage.'

'I don't understand.'

'Someone put the shuttle out of action, Prefect. Someone wanted an excuse to bring the *Accompaniment of Shadows* within kill-range of the Bubble. Until now I've been thinking that whatever happened, whatever was done in our name, was done in anger, because of the way that deal collapsed. That maybe someone on the ship thought Ruskin-Sartorious needed to be punished for that. Now I'm not so sure.' He fell silent, the face behind the glass completely still. Just when Dreyfus was starting to think that the captain had died or lost consciousness, his lips moved again: 'Now I'm wondering if it wasn't premeditated.'

'Not just murder, but murder in cold blood?'

'I can only tell you what happened.'

'These recruits ... can you tell me anything about them?'

'Six or seven of them. The usual mix. Hardcore types who've already crewed on other ships. Green-behind-the-ears newcomers who don't know one end of a hull from the other. I didn't meet any of them in person, just delivered the usual blood-and-thunder speech when they came aboard.'

'No names, nothing?'

'I'm sorry, Prefect. If I had more to give you, you'd be hearing it.'

Dreyfus nodded. There was no earthly reason for Dravidian to withhold evidence now, if he truly believed in his own innocence. 'What I don't understand is why anyone would want to destroy the Bubble, if it wasn't revenge for a deal that went sour?'

'You're the investigator, Prefect. You tell me.'

'You're going to die,' Dreyfus said softly. 'Nothing I say or do can change that now.'

'But you believe I may be telling the truth.'

'I believe that the investigation has yet to run its course. If the facts confirm your innocence, I'll make sure that they're heard.'

'I hope you're good at your job.'

'That's not for me to say.'

'Whoever did this was prepared to kill nearly a thousand people. More now that my crew have paid with their lives. They won't take kindly to a prefect snooping around trying to undermine their good work.'

'They don't pay us to be popular.'

'You strike me as a decent man, Prefect Dreyfus. I can hear it in your voice. We Ultras aren't such bad judges of character. My crew were decent people, too. Even if you can't exonerate me, I beg of you this much: do what you can to lift this shame from their heads. They didn't deserve to die like this. The *Accompaniment* was a good ship, right to the end. She didn't deserve to die like this either.' He hesitated, then added: 'How are those nukes coming along?'

Dreyfus glanced at Sparver. Sparver tapped his sleeve, as if there was a wristwatch there.

'Twenty minutes, Boss.'

Dreyfus looked along the prow, in the direction of the dead ship's flight. He was also looking straight at Yellowstone and the Glitter Band. The planet was still lit up on its dayside. It was not his imagination that the arc of the Band appeared wider than when he had last seen it. He felt as if he could make out the twinkling granularity of individual habitats. With time and patience, and his ingrained knowledge of their orbits, he was sure he could even have begun to pick out the largest structures by eye. There, for instance: wasn't that silvery glint near the planet's westward limb Carousel New Venice, moving in the congested real estate of the central orbits? And a little to the right: wasn't that string of ruby-red sparks the signature of the eight habitats of the Remortal Concatenation? If so, then that blue-tinged glint to the east had to be House Sammartini, or perhaps the Sylveste Institute for Shrouder Studies.

'I think I'm about done here, Captain.'

'Just one thing, Prefect. Maybe it's nothing, or maybe it'll help you. You'll have to decide for yourself.'

'Go on.'

'Our negotiations with Ruskin-Sartorious were conducted with the usual degree of secrecy. It's how we do things. Yet someone from outside the Bubble was still able to contact Delphine and promise her a better offer than the one already on the table. That means someone knew what was going on.'

'Could have been a lucky break. They saw your ship parked near the Bubble; they knew Delphine's art was on the market, put two and two together.'

'And outbid us by a calculatedly effective margin? I don't think so, Prefect. Someone had already gone to great lengths to position the *Accompaniment* as a murder weapon. All they needed then was to make it look as if we struck back in anger. For that they needed a plausible motive.'

'So what you're saying is ... the whole thing about the deal collapsing was just a ruse, to provide a justification for you hitting back?'

'Exactly so.'

In his head Dreyfus felt the ominous sliding of mental chess pieces moving into a new and threatening configuration. 'Then there must have been another reason why someone wanted to destroy the Ruskin-Sartorious Bubble.'

'Now all you have to do is find out why,' Dravidian answered.

Captain Pell let the missiles streak away, sprinting across the gap to the *Accompaniment of Shadows*. At twenty gees they reached the wreck in slightly more than a minute and a half. In the last instant before impact, the missiles fanned out and then vectored in again from different angles, so that their bright fusion exhausts formed the talons of a gripping three-clawed hand, closing around Dravidian's ship with swift predatory eagerness.

The three nuclear explosions blurred together into a single inseparable flash. When the radiation and debris had dissipated, nothing remained of the killing ship, nor of its captain.

Dreyfus turned from the hull window with a cold, hard feeling that he still had work to do.

CHAPTER 7

In the cloistered cool of his private security annexe, Senior Prefect Sheridan Gaffney found himself looking at the face of Aurora. She was coming through on an untraceable channel, their mutual communication disguised as an exchange of routine housekeeping data. He'd been expecting her; he'd composed his thoughts and marshalled a set of likely questions and responses, and yet still she made him feel flustered and ill-prepared, simply by the withering force of her regard. This, he thought, and not for the first time, was how it must feel to be interrogated by a goddess.

'It's been a while, Sheridan,' she said.

'I'm sorry,' he replied, wiping a sleeve across his brow. 'Things have been complicated around here. But everything's under control.'

'Everything, Sheridan? Then you're confident that there'll be no untoward ramifications concerning the Ruskin-Sartorious incident?'

'I don't think so.'

He was looking at a child-woman, a girl of indeterminate age, sitting on a simple wooden throne. She wore a gold-trimmed brocaded gown of dark green over a brocaded dress of fiery red, patterned again in gold. Her fingers curled around the edges of the armrests, toying with them in a manner that suggested mild restlessness more than actual boredom or impatience. Her auburn hair was parted in the middle and fell to her shoulders in perfect symmetry, framing a face of startling, ravishing serenity. Behind her head, suggesting a halo, was a shining gold motif worked into bas-relief panelling. Her eyes were liquid blue, brimming with puzzled intelligence. He knew he would do anything for those eyes, that face.

'You don't *think* so?' she asked.

'Dreyfus is on the case, unfortunately. I could do without him nosing around in the whole business, but there was no way I could get him off the investigation without drawing attention to myself.'

'You're head of security, Sheridan. Couldn't you have been more creative?'

'I've had my hands full preparing the ground for Thalia Ng. That's required more than enough creativity, I assure you.'

'Nonetheless, this man – this Dreyfus – is a rogue element. He must be brought under control.'

'Not that easy,' Gaffney said, feeling as if they'd had this discussion a thousand times already. 'He's Jane Aumonier's pet field prefect. She's even given him Pangolin clearance, despite my protestations. If I interfere too much, I'll have Jane on my back, metaphorically speaking.' He tested Aurora with a smile. 'Right now that would *not* be a good idea.'

'Jane is a problem,' Aurora said, signally failing to acknowledge his smile. 'We can't put off dealing with her for ever, either. Once the Thalia situation is stable, I'd like you to direct some energy into removing Aumonier.'

Gaffney dredged up some outrage. 'I hope you're not asking me to kill her.'

'We're not murderers,' Aurora said, looking suitably shocked at the suggestion.

'We just took out nine hundred and sixty people. If that's not murder, it's a hell of a way to make friends.'

'They were the unavoidable victims of a war that has already begun, Sheridan. I grieve for those people. If I could have spared one of them, I would have. But we must think of the millions we shall save, not the hundreds we must sacrifice.'

'Not that you'd blink an eyelid at killing Jane, if she got in our way.'

'She doesn't *have* to die, Sheridan. She's a brave woman and a good prefect. But she has principles. They're admirable, in their own way, but they'd compel her to obstruct our arrangements. She would commit the error of placing loyalty to Panoply above the greater good of the people.'

Gaffney ruminated over the possibilities. 'Aumonier's been under a lot of pressure lately, that's for sure.'

'Enough to concern Doctor Demikhov?'

'So I gather.'

'Well, things are certainly not going to get any less stressful for the supreme prefect any time soon. Perhaps you could arrange her removal from power on compassionate grounds?'

'The other seniors won't go for it if they think I'm after her job.'

'We don't need you in the hot seat, Sheridan, we just need Jane out of it. The other key players – Crissel, Baudry, Clearmountain ... which one would be her natural successor?'

'Baudry has automatic seniority.'

'How will she perform?'

'Baudry's competent, but she's detail-focused, not someone with Jane's strategic overview. There are going to be a lot of balls in the air when we go live. I think Baudry could end up dropping a few.'

'In other words, she'd suit our requirements very well.' Aurora looked pleased with him, or with herself: he wasn't usually able to tell. 'Start making arrangements, Sheridan.'

'I'm still concerned about Dreyfus. You can bet he'll fight Jane's corner. Baudry and the other seniors have a lot of respect for him, so it'll be difficult to squeeze Jane out while he's around.'

'Then I see only one possibility, Sheridan. You'd better remove Dreyfus from the picture. He's a field prefect, correct?'

'Long in the tooth, but still one of the best.'

'It can be dangerous work, being a field prefect.' For a moment she seemed absent, as if the face had pulled away from the mask. Gaffney drummed his fingers against the pedestal of his chair until she returned, feeling like a little schoolboy left alone in a big office. 'Perhaps I can help,' she continued. 'I'll need to know his movements when he's outside Panoply. I presume you can feed them to me?'

'It'll be risky, but—'

'You'll do your best. See to it, Sheridan,' she urged. 'And *don't worry*. I know that you are a good man and that deception does not come easily to you. Your natural instincts are to duty and loyalty, to the service of the people. I've known that since Hell-Five. You stared into the moral abyss of that horror, saw what freedom can lead to when freedom is unchecked, and you said *no more*. You knew that something must be done, even if it meant good men doing unpleasant things.'

'I know. It's just that occasionally I have doubts.'

'Purge them. Purge them utterly. Have I not vouchsafed unto you the consequences of our inaction, Sheridan? Have I not shown you glimpses of the world to come, if we do not act now?'

She had, too, and he knew that everything boiled down to a choice between two contending futures. One was a Glitter Band under the kindly rule of a benevolent tyrant, where the lives of the hundred million citizens continued essentially as they did now, albeit with some minor restrictions on civil liberty. The other was a Glitter Band in ruins, its population decimated, its fallen glories stalked by ghosts, revenants and monsters, some of which had once been people.

'I have the weevil data,' he said, when the silence had become unendurable.

'I must see it immediately.'

'I'm encapsulating it into the comms feed.'

Aurora closed her eyes. Her lips opened slightly, as if she was in transports of indescribable ecstasy. He imagined the data streaming out of Panoply, into the labyrinthine tangle of the Glitter Band data network, Aurora – whatever she was, human or machine – drinking it in somewhere at the end of a complex chain of routers and hubs.

Her mouth closed again as her eyes opened. 'Well done, Gaffney. All appears to be in order. You've done *very well* indeed.'

'Then you have all that you need? To make the weevils?'

'I won't know for sure until I have access to a functioning manufactory. The proof of the pudding, as they say. But I've no reason to doubt that things will work exactly as intended.'

'I read the tech notes,' Gaffney said. 'Those things are nightmares.'

'And that's why they'll only be used as an absolute last resort. But we must have the means, Sheridan, if we are to prevent the unnecessary loss of life. We would be negligent otherwise.'

'People are going to die when we do this.'

'People will die if we don't. Oh, Sheridan – you've come so far, done so much good work for the cause. Please don't quail now, at the final hurdle.'

'I won't "quail",' he said, resenting her tone.

'You trust me, don't you? Absolutely, unquestioningly?'

'Yes.'

'Then you know that we are doing the right thing, the decent thing, the only *human* thing. When the time of transition is complete, the citizenry will thank us from the bottom of their hearts. And the time will be soon, Sheridan. Now that all but these last few trifling obstacles have been removed ...'

Gaffney had learned that brazen honesty was the only sensible approach when dealing with Aurora. She pierced lies, penetrated evasion like a gamma-ray laser burning through rice paper.

'There is still one larger problem we haven't dealt with,' Gaffney began.

'I confess I don't understand.'

'The Clockmaker is still out there.'

'We destroyed it. How can it possibly be a problem?'

Gaffney shifted on his seat. 'The intelligence was flawed. They'd moved the Clockmaker before we destroyed Ruskin-Sartorious.'

He'd been expecting fury. The mild reaction he got was worse, since it implied fury being bottled away, stored up for later dispensing. 'How can you be sure?'

'Forensics swept the ruin. They'd have flagged anything anomalous, even if they didn't recognise what they were dealing with.'

'We know it was there recently. What happened?'

'Someone must have decided to move it somewhere else.'

'Why would they do that?'

'Probably because they got word that someone was nosing around their secret.'

'And that someone would be ...' Aurora asked.

'You ordered me to ferret out the location of the Clockmaker. I did the best I could, but it meant digging into data outside my control, where I couldn't always hide my enquiries. I made that abundantly clear before you asked me to find it.'

'So why did you wait until now to tell me you thought it had been moved?'

'Because I have another lead, one I'm still following. I thought it best to wait and see where it leads before taking up any of your valuable time.'

If his sarcasm grated on her, she didn't show it. Aurora merely looked unimpressed. 'And this lead?'

'Anthony Theobald survived the destruction of the habitat. The weasel must have suspected something was going down. But he didn't get far. I intercepted him and ran some extraction procedures.'

'He'd hardly have been likely to know where they were taking the Clockmaker.'

'He knew *something*.'

Now she looked vaguely interested again. 'Names, faces?'

'Names and faces wouldn't mean anything – the operatives who visited the Clockmaker wouldn't have been using their official identities. But it appears they *were* occasionally indiscreet. One of them dropped a word into the conversation once, something Anthony Theobald obviously wasn't meant to hear.'

'A word.'

'Firebrand,' Gaffney said.

'That's all? One word, which could mean almost anything?'

'I hoped you might be able to shed some light on it. I've run a database search, but it didn't reveal any significant priors.'

'Then it means nothing.'

'Or it refers to something so dark that it doesn't even show up in maximum-security files. I can't dig any deeper without the risk of stumbling into the same kinds of tripwire that may already have alerted them to our interest in the Clockmaker. But I thought you—'

She cut him off brusquely. 'I am not omniscient, Sheridan. There are places you can go that I can't, and vice versa. If I knew everything, saw everything, why would I need you?'

'That's a very good point.'

'Maybe there *is* something called Firebrand.' It sounded like a conciliatory line, but he could feel the stinger coming. 'Perhaps that is the name of the group or cell who have been studying the Clockmaker. But if so it tells us nothing we didn't already know.'

'It's a handle. It's leverage.'

'Or random noise, plucked out of a dying man's head by the grabbing fingers of a trawl. What do *you* think?'

'I think we're dealing with Panoply,' Gaffney said.

'You believe your own organisation chose to keep it alive, after all it did to them?'

'Look, it makes a kind of sense. When the Clockmaker got loose, it was Panoply that put it back in the bottle. But we still didn't know what it was or where it had come from. Who'd have been better placed to smuggle that bottle away for further study? Who, frankly, would have been negligent *not* to do something like that?'

After a while she said, 'There may be some merit in your reasoning, Sheridan.'

'That's why I think Firebrand might be the codename for a unit inside Panoply. Now I need to find out who's *inside* Firebrand. They'll know where the thing is now. If I can get to one of them, isolate and trawl ...' As he spoke, his hand stroked the black haft of his Model C whiphound.

'Apart from Jane Aumonier, you wouldn't know where to start.'

'I can run a systematic search: look at who was involved eleven years ago, however peripherally, who's still in the organisation.' He risked another smile. 'I've got one thing on my side, Aurora. They're beginning to panic, which means they're likely to screw up.'

He'd hoped his words would console her, but they had exactly the opposite effect. 'We don't want them to err, Sheridan. If these people make mistakes, they may allow the Clockmaker to slip free. Such an outcome wouldn't just be catastrophic for our plans. It would be catastrophic for the Glitter Band, as it very nearly was eleven years ago.'

'I'll exercise due discretion. Believe me, that thing isn't going to escape a second time. And even if it does, we know what we have to do to catch it again.'

'Yes,' Aurora said. 'And while we were doing it we'd hope and pray that the same thing worked twice, wouldn't we? Answer me this, just out of interest: could *you* have given that order?'

'Which order would that be?'

'You know exactly which one I mean. The thing they don't like to talk about. The thing they did before they nuked the Sylveste Institute for Artificial Mentation.'

'I wouldn't have blinked,' he said.

Thalia felt a chill on her neck as the heavy double doors swung open behind her. As they entered, the other prefects were engaged in low, whispered conversations that had obviously been going on for some time. Thalia had been too absorbed in her duties to pay much attention to the crisis that had been unfolding during the last twenty-six hours, but it was clear that this meeting was considered a necessary but disagreeable diversion.

'Let's keep this brief, Thalia,' said Senior Prefect Gaffney. 'We all have work to be getting back to. Can we conclude that you've closed the leak in the polling apparatus?'

'Sir,' Thalia said, almost stammering, 'I've completed work on the update. As I said before, it only amounted to a couple of thousand lines of changes.'

'And you're confident this will plug the security hole Caitlin Perigal was able to abuse?'

'As confident as we can ever be, sir. I've subjected the new code to the formal testing process, and the validation system found no errors after simulating fifty years' worth of polling transactions.

That's a better error rate than we accepted before the last upgrade, sir. I can see no reason not to go live.'

Gaffney looked at her distractedly, as if his mind had already strolled out of the room, into another more urgent meeting. 'Across the entire ten thousand?'

'No, sir,' Thalia said patiently. She'd already explained her plans the last time she'd been sitting in that room, but obviously she'd have to go through it one more time. 'The changes to the code are relatively simple, but the upgrade will involve high-level access to all ten thousand polling cores. It'll go smoothly with most of the newer cores, but there are some issues with older installations that I'd like to resolve in the field. By that I mean physical visits, sir.'

'On-site installation?' asked Michael Crissel.

Thalia nodded keenly. 'But only for the following habitats.' She raised a hand to the Solid Orrery, a gesture she had primed it to wait for. On command, the invisibly fine ceiling threads retracted five orbiting bodies from the frozen swirl of the Glitter Band. Quickmatter oozed down the threads and swelled the representations a hundredfold. One of the five bodies was Panoply itself, instantly recognisable to all present in the room. Thalia pointed instead to the other four, naming each in turn. 'Carousel New Seattle-Tacoma. The Chevelure-Sambuke Hourglass. Szlumper Oneill. House Aubusson.' Scattered red laser-light flicked between the four habitats and Panoply, revealing Thalia's intended route. 'In all cases, I think we can be in and out well inside thirteen hours per habitat. Abstraction downtime will be in the order of milliseconds: not long enough for anyone to actually notice.'

'We can't spare four ships in the current emergency,' Gaffney said.

'I'm not expecting you to, sir. I'd like to be on-site for all the installations myself, which means doing them sequentially. But even allowing for sleep and travel time between the four habs, I can have all four upgrades complete inside sixty hours.'

'And then you'll go live across the whole Band?'

'Provided no issues come to light during the four test installations, I don't see any reason to delay.'

'I think we should hold off until the Ruskin-Sartorious mess has blown over,' said Senior Prefect Baudry, holding her usual electrified posture. 'Any nonessential activity at this time is a stretch on our resources we can do without. I don't doubt that Thalia's counting on a full support team. Frankly, we can't afford to reallocate key personnel at such a sensitive time, with the citizenry straining at the leash to punish the Ultras.'

'Maybe you're right,' Gaffney said. 'I know Jane wants closure on the polling anomaly as quickly as possible, but she'll also understand that we have to contain the aggressors until something else comes along to occupy their time.'

'Begging your pardon, sir,' Thalia said, 'but I'm not counting on anything other than myself and a cutter to get me between habitats. I can handle the upgrades single-handedly.'

Gaffney looked unconvinced. 'Quite a responsibility, Ng.'

'It makes sense, sir. I'm intimately familiarly with the software changes and the procedure for installing them. It's been my speciality since I joined the organisation. It's what I live and breathe. I don't think there's anyone else in Panoply who understands the polling mechanism as thoroughly as I do.'

'All the same, it's still a heavy burden for one person.'

'I can do it, sir. In sixty hours, less if things go smoothly, this whole business could be behind us.'

Crissel and Gaffney exchanged glances. 'It would be good to get it off the table,' Crissel said quietly. 'And if Ng thinks she can handle this on her own ... it won't impact on our existing activities.'

'I still say she should wait,' Baudry put in.

'We have no idea how long the crisis with the Ultras is going to last,' Crissel said. 'We could still be putting out fires a month from now. We can't leave the security hole unplugged until then – there are critical polls coming up and we need the apparatus in a fit state to handle them.'

'If she runs into trouble,' Baudry said, 'we won't be able to spare a Heavy Technical Squad to help her out.'

'I won't run into trouble,' Thalia replied.

Baudry looked unimpressed. 'You sound spectacularly sure of yourself. No update to a polling core is *routine*, Ng. You take the local abstraction down and then can't get it back up, you'll have a rioting mob on your hands. One whiphound isn't going to make much difference in that situation.'

'I promise there'll be no technical difficulties. Aside from a few habitat seniors, no one else need even know that I'm on the premises.'

'She talks a good talk,' Gaffney said, with the tone of a man who had no great stomach for argument. 'Part of me says hold off this until we can give it our full attention. Another part says, hell, if she thinks she can do it unassisted—'

'I can, sir,' Thalia said.

'Maybe we should bounce this one off Jane,' Crissel said.

'The supreme prefect expressly requested not to be troubled with matters of minor procedure,' said Baudry. 'As she's made abundantly clear, she can only be expected to concentrate on so many matters at once.'

Gaffney pulled a face, racked by indecision. 'Sixty hours, you say?'

'Starting from now, sir. I can leave immediately for New Seattle-Tacoma.' Thalia nodded towards the red laser-line trajectory. 'The conjunction's favourable. Assign me a cutter and I can be on-site inside Sea-Tac within two hours.'

'All right,' Gaffney said. 'We'll spare you a cutter. No weps or heavy armour, though.'

'I won't let you down,' Thalia said.

'You'll need one-time pads for core access, I take it?'

'Just the four, sir. Most of the work shouldn't require deep-level changes, so I ought to be able to manage with six-hundred-second access windows.'

'I'll have Vantrollier issue them.' Gaffney looked at her warningly. 'You're good, Ng. None of us needs convincing about that. But that doesn't mean we'll cut you an easy ride if things go wrong. This is in your hands now. Don't fuck it up.'

'I won't, sir.'

'Good. Then get out there and update those cores.'

CHAPTER 8

The gallery of clocks covered two long walls, with each timepiece resting in a glass-sealed alcove next to a small black plaque denoting the date and precise location of the object's construction, together with any other salient observations. As usual, Dreyfus had no intention of stopping on his way to the inner sanctum of Dr Demikhov's Sleep Lab. But something always caused him to halt, select one of the clocks and use his Pangolin privilege to open the alcove, remove the evil thing and hold it in his hands. This time he chose a clock he did not believe he had examined before, one that was dark and unornamented enough to have escaped his curiosity on previous occasions.

He could hear it ticking behind the glass. It would have been wound by one of Demikhov's technicians.

He read the plaque:

Clock #115
Found: LCS, SIAM, 13:54, 17:03:15 YST.
Finder: Valery Chapelon.
Duration of construction: unknown.
Primary base materials: common ferrous alloys.
Origin of base materials: unknown.
Movement: double-roller anchor escapement.
Remarks: electron microscopy reveals atomic-scale fractal patterning in top-right spandrel. Nature of fractal patterning obscure, but may echo visible detail on pendulum hinge of clock #341.
Status: functional.
Known booby traps: none.
Associated fatalities: none.
Estimated hazard level: low.

Dreyfus opened the glass panel. The clock's ticking became louder. He reached in and placed his hands on either side of the black metal case and lifted the clock from its base, holding it at eye level. Like all the clocks it was surprisingly heavy, dense with mechanisms, but in this case there was no delicate tracery of gold-leaf ornamentation or razor-sharp edges to watch for. The clock had a crudely fashioned look, at odds with the complexity and accuracy of the mechanism inside it. No glass protected the dial. The hands were withered wisps of beaten metal, the hour marks irregularly soldered stubs.

Dreyfus hated to hold any of the clocks. But whenever he made the pilgrimage to the Sleep Lab, he found himself unable to resist. The models of the scarab in Demikhov's lab were accurate, but only Jane Aumonier could touch the scarab on her neck. The clocks – all four hundred and nineteen of them – were the only tangible link back to the entity itself.

Dreyfus had long wondered whether there was a message in the clocks. During the long period of its incarceration in SIAM, the clocks it made had grown in sophistication and ingenuity. It had been presumed by those studying it that the entity was learning with each clock, inventing and innovating as it progressed.

This view was now considered incorrect. Analysis of microscopic details engraved onto the main gear of clock thirty-five turned out to anticipate refinements – an elegant grasshopper escapement and gridiron pendulum – incorporated as far along the series as clock three hundred and eighty-eight. Since the entity had been denied access to its artefacts as soon as they were discovered, only one conclusion was possible: the Clockmaker had always known what it was doing.

Which meant that it could easily have been planning its killing spree while the researchers thought they were dealing with something as innocent and guileless as a child, which desired nothing more than to be allowed to make clocks.

Which meant in turn that, in any given clock, there might be a message that had yet to be deciphered: one that spoke of the Clockmaker's intentions for the woman who had spent the most time with it, the one who thought she knew it best of all. Had it hated her more than any of the others?

Dreyfus didn't know, but he hoped that one day a clock might reveal something to him.

Not today, though.

He replaced clock one hundred and fifteen carefully, then sealed the window. Around him the ticking of the other instruments grew more insistent, the ticks moving in and out of phase with subtle rhythms until the hectoring noise forced him further into the Sleep Lab.

For eleven years, Demikhov's department had had no other business than the matter of removing the scarab. Every square centimetre of the Sleep Lab beyond the gallery of clocks (which itself offered an insight into the mentality of the Clockmaker) was testament to that effort: walls and partitions aglow with sectional schematics of both the scarab and its host, scribbled over with eleven years' worth of handwritten notes and commentary. Jane Aumonier's skull and neck had been imaged from every conceivable angle, using scanning devices powerful enough to function from more than seven metres away and yet still resolve nerve and circulatory structure. The metallic probes that the scarab had pushed into her spinal cord were visible in multiple cross sections, at different degrees of structural penetration. The scarab's main body, clamped to her neck, had been subjected to the same variety of analysis modes. Interior details showed in ghostly pastel overlays.

Dreyfus touched certain panels, causing animations to spring into life. These were simulations of planned rescue attempts, all of which had been deemed unsatisfactory. Dreyfus had heard reliable estimates that the scarab's mechanism would require just under six-tenths of a second to kill Aumonier, meaning that if they could get a machine in there and disarm the scarab in less than half a second they might have a hope of saving her. But he did not envy the person who would have to make the decision as to when to go in. It wouldn't be Aumonier: that was one responsibility she had abdicated long ago.

Dreyfus paused by one of the benches and picked up a model of the scarab moulded in smoky translucent plastic. There were dozens like it, littering the benches in various dismantled states. They differed in their internal details, depending on the way the scans had been interpreted. Entire rescue strategies hinged on infinitely subtle nuances of analysis. At any one time, Demikhov's squad consisted of several different teams pursuing radically opposed plans. More than once, they'd almost come to blows over the right course of action. Dreyfus thought of monks, arguing over different interpretations of scripture. Only Demikhov's quiet presence kept the whole operation from collapsing into acrimony. He'd been doing that for eleven years, with no visible reward.

He was at work, leaning over a bench in low, whispered debate with three of his team members. Tools and scarab parts covered the work surface. An anatomical model of a skull – made up of detachable glass parts – sat with the structure of its neck and spine exposed. Luminous markers highlighted vulnerable areas.

Demikhov must have heard Dreyfus approaching. He pulled goggles from his eyes and used his fingers to comb lank strands of hair away from his brow. The subdued red lighting of the Sleep Lab did nothing to ameliorate Demikhov's sagging lantern-jawed features. Dreyfus had seldom met anyone who looked quite as old.

'Tom,' he said, with a weary smile. 'Nice of you to drop by.'

Dreyfus smiled back. 'Anything new for me?'

'No new strategies, although we've shaved another two-hundredths of a second off Plan Tango.'

'Good work.'

'But not good enough for us to go in.'

'You're getting closer.'

'Slowly. Ever so slowly.'

'Jane's patient. She knows how much effort you put in down here.'

Demikhov stared deep into Dreyfus's eyes, as if looking for a clue. 'You've spoken to her recently. How is she? How's she holding up?'

'As well as can be expected.'

'Did she . . .'

'Yes,' Dreyfus said. 'She told me the news.'

Demikhov picked up a scarab model and unclipped its waxy grey casing. The internal parts glowed blue and violet, highlighting control circuits, power lines and processors. He poked a white stylus into the innards, tapping it against a complicated nexus of violet lines. 'This changed. A week ago, there were only three lines running into this node. Now there are five.' He moved the stylus to the right. 'And this mechanical assembly has shifted by two centimetres. The movement was quite sudden. We don't know what to make of either change.'

Dreyfus glanced at the other lab technicians. He presumed they were fully aware of the situation, or Demikhov wouldn't be talking so openly. 'It's getting ready for something,' he said.

'That's my fear.'

'After eleven years: why now?'

'It's probably reading stress levels.'

'That's what she told me,' Dreyfus said, 'but this isn't the first crisis we've had in the last eleven years.'

'Maybe it's the first time things have been this bad. It's self-reinforcing, unfortunately. We can only hope that her elevated hormone level won't trigger another change.'

'And if it does?'

'We may have to rethink that safety margin of which we've always been so protective.'

'You'd make that call?'

'If I felt that thing was about to kill her.'

'And in the meantime?'

'The usual. We've altered her therapeutic regime. More drugs. She doesn't like it, says it dulls her consciousness. She still self-administers. We're treading a very fine line: we have to take the edge off her nerves, but we mustn't put her to sleep.'

'I don't envy you.'

'No one envies us, Tom. We've grown used to that by now.'

'There's something you need to know. Things aren't going to get any easier for Jane right now. I'm working a case that might stir up some trouble. Jane's given me the green light to follow my investigation wherever it leads.'

'You've a duty to do so.'

'I'm still worried how Jane'll take things if the crisis worsens.'

'She won't step down, if that's what you're wondering,' Demikhov said. 'We've been over that a million times.'

'I wouldn't expect her to resign. Right now the only thing keeping her sane is her job.'

Dreyfus sat before his low black table, sipping reheated tea. The wall opposite him, where he normally displayed his mosaic of faces, now showed only a single image. It was a picture of the rock sculpture, the one that Sparver and he had found in the incinerated ruin of Ruskin-Sartorious. Forensics had dragged it back to Panoply and scanned it at micron-level resolution. A neon-red contour mesh emphasized the three-dimensional structure that would otherwise have been difficult to make out.

'I'm missing something here,' Sparver said, sitting next to him at the table. 'We've got the killers, no matter what Dravidian might have wanted us to think. We've got the motive and the means. Why are we fixating on the art?'

'Something about it's been bothering me ever since we first saw it,' Dreyfus said. 'Don't you feel the same way?'

'I wouldn't hang it on my wall. Beyond that, it's just a face.'

'It's the face of someone in torment. It's the face of someone looking into hell and knowing that's where they're going. More than that, it's a face I feel I know.'

'I'm still just seeing a face. Granted, it's not the happiest face I've ever seen, but—'

'What bothers me,' Dreyfus said, as if Sparver hadn't spoken, 'is that we're clearly looking at the work of a powerful artist, someone in complete control of their craft. But why haven't I ever heard of Delphine Ruskin-Sartorious before?'

'Maybe you just haven't been paying attention.'

'That's what I wondered. But when I searched for priors on Delphine, I only got sparse returns. She's been contributing pieces to exhibitions for more than twenty years, but with no measurable success for most of that time.'

'And lately?'

'Things have begun to take off for her.'

'Because people caught on to what she was doing, or because she got better at it?'

'Good question,' Dreyfus said. 'I've looked at some of her older stuff. There are similarities with the unfinished sculpture, but there's also something missing. She's always been accomplished from a technical standpoint, but I didn't get an emotional connection with the older works. I'd have marked her down as another rich postmortal with too much time on her hands, convinced that the world owes her fame in addition to everything else it's already given her.'

'You said you thought you knew the face.'

'I did. But forensics didn't make any connection, and when I ran the sculpture through the Search Turbines, nothing came up. Hardly surprising, I suppose, given the stylised manner in which she's rendered the face.'

'So you've drawn a blank.'

Dreyfus smiled. 'Not quite. There's something Vernon told me.'

'Vernon?' Sparver said.

'Delphine's suitor, Vernon Tregent, one of the three stable recoverables. He told me the work had been part of her "Lascaille" series.

The name meant something to me, but I couldn't quite place it.'

'So run it through the Turbines.'

'I don't need to. Just sitting here talking to you, I know where I've heard that name before.'

And it was true. Whenever he voiced the word in his mind, he saw a darkness beyond comprehension, a wall of starless black more profound than space itself. He saw darkness, and something falling into that darkness, like a white petal floating down into an ocean of pure black ink.

'Are you going to put me out of my misery?' Sparver asked.

'Lascaille's Shroud,' Dreyfus answered, as if that was all that needed to be said.

Thalia was reviewing the summary file on Carousel New Seattle-Tacoma when the call came in. She lifted her eyes from her compad and conjured her master's face into existence before her. Slow-moving habitats, vast and imperious as icebergs, were visible through the slight opacity of the display pane.

'I'm not interrupting anything, am I?' Dreyfus asked.

Thalia tried not to sound flustered. 'Not at all, sir.'

'No one told me you were outside.'

'It all came together quite quickly, sir. I have the patch for the polling bug, the one that allowed Caitlin Perigal to bias the results. I'm going to dry-run it before going live across the whole ten thousand.'

'Good. It'll be one less headache to deal with. Who's with you?'

'No one, sir. I'm handling the initial upgrades on my own.'

Something twitched in the corner of his right eye, the lazy one. 'How many are you doing?'

'Four, sir, ending with House Aubusson. I told the seniors that I can have the upgrades complete inside sixty hours, but I was being deliberately cautious. If all goes well I should be done a lot quicker than that.'

'I don't like the idea of you handling this alone, Thalia.'

'I'm quite capable of doing this, sir. Another pair of hands would only slow me down.'

'That isn't the issue. The issue is one of my deputies going out there without back-up.'

'I'm not going out there to initiate a lockdown, sir. No one's going to put up a fight.'

'We don't start being popular just because we aren't enforcing lockdowns. The citizenry moves from hating and fearing us to guarded tolerance. That's as good as it gets.'

'I've been doing this for five years, sir.'

'But never alone.'

'I was alone in Bezile Solipsist for eight months.'

'But no one noticed you. That's why they call it Bezile Solipsist.'

'I need to prove that I can handle a difficult assignment on my own, sir. This is my chance. But if you really think I ought to come back to Panoply—'

'Of course I don't, now that you're out there. But I'm still cross. You should have cleared this with me first.'

Thalia cocked her head. 'Would you have let me go alone?'

'Probably not. I don't throw assets into risky environments without making damned sure they're protected.'

'Then now you know why I went out without calling you.'

She saw something in his expression give way, as if he recognised this was a fight he could not hope to win. He had chosen Thalia for her cleverness, her independence of mind. He could hardly be surprised that she was beginning to chafe at the leash.

'Promise me this,' he said. 'The instant something happens that you're not happy about ... you call in, understood?'

'Baudry said they won't be able to spare a taskforce, sir, if I run into trouble.'

'Never mind Baudry. I'd find a way to move Panoply itself if I knew one of my squad was in trouble.'

'I'll call in, sir.'

After a moment, Dreyfus said, 'In case you were wondering, I didn't call you to tick you off. I need some technical input.'

'I'm listening, sir.'

'Where House Perigal was concerned, you were able to recover all the communications handled by the core in the last thousand days, correct?'

'Yes,' Thalia said.

'Suppose we needed something similar for the Ruskin-Sartorious Bubble?'

'If the beta-levels didn't come through intact, I don't hold out much hope for transmission logs.'

'That's what I thought. But a message still has to originate from somewhere. That means someone else must have the relevant outgoing transmission somewhere in their logs. And if it travelled more than a few hundred kilometres through the Band, it probably passed through a router or hub, maybe several. Routers and hubs keep records of all data traffic passing through them.'

'Not deep content, though.'

'I'll settle for a point of origin. Can you help?'

Thalia thought about it. 'It's doable, sir, but I'll need access to a full version of the Solid Orrery.'

'Can your ship run a copy?'

'Not a light-enforcement vehicle. I'm afraid it'll have to wait until I return.'

'I'd rather it didn't.'

Thalia thought even harder. 'Then ... you'll need to turn the Orrery back to around the time of this transmission, if you know it.'

'I think I can narrow it down,' Dreyfus said.

'You'll need to pinpoint it to within a few minutes. That's the kind of timescale on which the router network optimises itself. If you can do that, then you can send me a snapshot of the Orrery. Pull out Ruskin-Sartorious and all routers or hubs within ten thousand kilometres. I'll see what I can do.'

Dreyfus looked uncharacteristically pleased. 'Thank you, Thalia.'

'No promises, sir. This might not work.'

'It's a lead. Since I've nothing else to go on, I'll take what I'm given.'

Sparver collected his food from the counter and moved to an empty table near the corner of the refectory. The lights were bright and the low-ceilinged, gently curving space was as busy as it ever got. A group of fields had just returned from duty aboard one of the deep-system vehicles. A hundred or so grey-uniformed cadets were squeezing around three tables near the middle, most of them carrying the dummy whiphounds they'd just been introduced to in basic training. The cadets' eager, over-earnest faces meant nothing to him. Dreyfus occasionally taught classes, and Sparver sometimes filled in for him, but that happened so infrequently that he never had a chance to commit any of the cadets to memory.

The one thing he didn't doubt was that they all knew his name. He could feel their sidelong glances when he looked around the room, taking in the other diners. As the only hyperpig to have made it past Deputy II in twenty years, Sparver was known throughout Panoply. There'd been another promising candidate in the organisation a few years earlier, but he'd died during a bad lockdown.

Sparver couldn't see any hyperpigs amongst the cadets, and it didn't surprise him. Dreyfus had accepted him unquestioningly, had even pulled strings to get Sparver assigned to his team rather than someone else's, but for the most part there was still distrust and suspicion against his kind. Baseline humans had made hyperpigs, created them for sinister purposes, and now they had to live with the legacy of that crime. They were resentful of his very existence because it spoke of the dark appetites of their ancestors.

He began to eat his meal, using the specially shaped cutlery that best fit his hands.

He felt eyes on the back of his neck.

He laid his compad before him and called up the results on the search term he had fed into the Turbines just before entering the refectory. Lascaille's Shroud, Dreyfus had said. But what did Sparver – or Dreyfus, for that matter – know of the Shrouds? No more or less than the average citizen of the Glitter Band.

The compad jogged his memory.

The Shrouds were *things* out in interstellar space, light-years from Yellowstone. They'd been found in all directions: lightless black spheres of unknown composition, wider than stars. Alien constructs, most likely: that was why their hypothetical builders were called the Shrouders. But no one had ever made contact with a Shrouder, or had the least idea what the aliens might be like, if they were not already extinct.

The difficulty with the Shrouds was that nothing sent towards them ever came back intact. Probes and ships returned to the study stations mangled beyond recognition, if they came back at all. No useful data was ever obtained. The only indisputable fact was that the crewed vehicles returned less mangled, and with more frequency, than the robots. Something about the Shrouds was, if not exactly tolerant of living things, at least slightly less inclined to destroy them utterly. Even so, most of the time the people came back dead, their minds too pulverised even for a post-mortem trawl.

But occasionally there was an exception.

Lascaille's Shroud, the compad informed Sparver, was named for the first man to return alive from its boundary. Philip Lascaille had gone in solo, without the permission of the study station where he'd been based. Against all the odds, he'd returned from the Shroud with his body and mind superficially intact. But that wasn't to say that Lascaille had not still paid a terrible price. He'd come back mute, either unwilling or incapable of talking about his experiences. His emotional connection with other human beings had become autistically impoverished. A kind of holy fool, he spent his time making intricate chalk drawings on concrete slabs. Shipped back to the Sylveste Institute for Shrouder Studies, Lascaille became a curiosity of gradually dwindling interest.

That was one mystery solved, but it begged more questions than it answered. Why had Delphine alighted on this subject matter, so many decades after Lascaille's return? And why had her decision to portray Lascaille resulted in a work of such striking emotional resonance, when her creations had been so affectless before?

On this, the compad had nothing to say.

Sparver continued with his meal, wondering how far ahead of him Dreyfus's enquiries had reached.

He could still feel the eyes on his neck.

'Back from whatever busy errand called you away last time, Prefect Dreyfus?' asked the beta-level invocation of Delphine Ruskin-Sartorious.

'I'm sorry about that,' Dreyfus said. 'Something came up.'

'Connected with the Bubble?'

'I suppose so.' His instincts told him that Delphine didn't need to know all the details concerning Captain Dravidian. 'But the case isn't closed just yet. I'd like to talk to you in some detail concerning the way the deal collapsed.'

Delphine reached up and pushed a stray strand of hair back under the rag-like band she wore around her head. She was dressed in the same clothes she'd been wearing during the last invocation: white smock and trousers, sleeves rolled to the elbow, trousers tucked up to the knee. Once again Dreyfus was struck by the paleness of her eyes and the doll-like simplicity of her features.

'How much did Vernon tell you?' she asked.

'Enough to know that someone called through and that was enough to remove Dravidian's offer from consideration. I'd really like to know who that mystery caller was.'

'A representative of some other group of Ultras, intent on undermining Dravidian. Does it really matter now?'

'Play along with me,' Dreyfus said. 'Assume for a minute that Dravidian was set up to make it look as if he intentionally fired on you. What reason might there have been for someone to want to hurt your family?'

Her face became suspicious. 'But it *was* revenge, Prefect. What else could it have been?'

'I'm simply keeping an open mind. Did you or your family have enemies?'

'You'd have to ask someone else.'

'I'm asking you. What about Anthony Theobald? Had he crossed swords with anyone?'

'Anthony Theobald had friends and rivals, like anyone. But actual enemies? I wasn't aware of any.'

'Did he leave the habitat often?'

'Now and then, to visit another state or go down to Chasm City. But there was never anything sinister about his movements.'

'What about visitors – get many of those?'

'We kept ourselves to ourselves, by and large.'

'So no visitors.'

'I didn't say that. Yes, of course people came by. We weren't hermits. Anthony Theobald had his usual guests; I had the occasional fellow artist or critic.'

'None of whom would have had any pressing reason to see you dead?'

'Speaking for myself, no.'

'And Anthony Theobald – what were his guests like?'

He caught it then: the tiniest flicker of hesitation in her answer. 'Nothing out of the ordinary, Prefect.'

Dreyfus nodded, allowing her to think he was content to let the matter stand. He knew he'd touched on something, however peripheral it might prove, but his years of experience had taught him that it would be counterproductive to dig away at it now. Delphine would be conflicted between her blood loyalty to Anthony Theobald and her desire to see justice served, and too much probing from him now might cause her to clam up irrevocably.

He would have to earn her trust.

'The point is,' she went on, 'I really wasn't interested in family or Glitter Band politics. I had – have – my art. That was all that interested me.'

'Let's talk about your art, then. Could someone have been jealous of your success?'

She looked stunned. 'Enough to kill nine hundred and sixty people?'

'Crimes aren't always proportionate to motive.'

'I can't think of anyone. If I'd been the talk of Stoner society, we wouldn't have been dealing with a second-rate trader like Dravidian.'

Dreyfus bit his tongue, keeping his policeman's poker face fixed firmly in place. 'All the same, someone wanted you all dead, and I'll sleep easier when I know the reason.'

'I wish I could help.'

'You still can. I want you to tell me when that call came through.'

'While Dravidian was visiting us.'

'If you could narrow it down, that would help.'

The beta-level closed her eyes momentarily. 'The call came in at fourteen hours, twenty-three minutes, fifty-one seconds, Yellowstone Standard Time.'

'Thank you,' Dreyfus said. 'Freeze—' he began.

'Are we done?' Delphine asked, cutting him off before he had finished issuing the command.

'For now. If there's anything else I need from you, you'll be the first to hear about it.'

'And now you're going to put me back in the box?'

'That's the idea.'

'I thought you wanted to talk about art.'

'We did.'

'No, we discussed the possibility of my art being a motivating factor in the crime. We didn't discuss the art itself.'

Dreyfus shrugged easily. 'We can, if you think it's relevant.'

'You don't?'

'The art appears to be a peripheral detail, unless you think otherwise. You yourself expressed doubt that jealousy could have been a motivating factor.' Dreyfus paused and reconsidered. 'That said, your reputation was building, wasn't it?'

Delphine looked at him sourly. 'You make it sound as if my life story's already written, down to the last footnote.'

'From where I'm standing ...' But then Dreyfus remembered what Vernon had told him concerning Delphine's belief in the validity of beta-level simulation.

'What?' Delphine said.

'Things will be different. Won't they?'

'Different. Not necessarily worse. You still don't believe in me, do you?'

'I'm trying my best,' Dreyfus replied.

'The last time we spoke, I asked you a question.'

'Did you?'

'I asked you if you'd ever lost a loved one.'

'I answered you.'

'Evasively.' She fixed him with a long, searching stare. 'You have lost someone, haven't you? Not just a colleague or friend. Someone closer than that.'

'We've all lost people.'

'Who was it, Prefect Dreyfus? Who did you lose?'

'Tell me why you chose to work on the Lascaille series. Why did you care about what happened to a man you never knew?'

'Those are personal questions for an artist.'

'I'm wondering if you made any enemies when you picked that theme.'

'And I'm wondering why you find it so difficult to acknowledge my conscious existence. This person who died – did something happen that made you turn against beta-levels?' Her eyes flashed an insistent sea-green, daring him to look away. 'Who was it, Prefect? Quid pro quo. Answer my question and I'll answer yours.'

'I've got a job to do, Delphine. Empathising with software isn't part of it.'

'I'm sorry you feel that way.'

'No,' Dreyfus said, something inside him snapping, 'you aren't "sorry". 'Sorry" would imply the presence of a thinking mind, a sentient will capable of experiencing the emotion called "regret". You're saying that you are sorry because that's what the living Delphine would have said under similar circumstances. But it doesn't mean you feel it.'

'You really don't think I'm alive, in any sense of the word?'

'I'm afraid not.'

Delphine nodded coolly. 'In which case: why are you arguing with me?'

Dreyfus reached for an automatic answer, but nothing came. The moment dragged, Delphine regarding him with something between amusement and pity. He froze the invocation and stood staring at the empty space where she had been standing.

Not a she, he told himself. An it.

'Hello?' Thalia called into an echoing, dank darkness. 'This is Deputy Field Prefect Ng. Is anyone there?'

There was no answer. Thalia stopped and put down the heavy cylinder she'd been carrying in her left hand. She touched her right hand to the haft of her whiphound, and then chided herself for her unease. Letting go of the weapon, she extracted her glasses, slipped them on and keyed image-amplification. The darkness of the chamber abated, revealing a doorway in one wall. Thalia touched the glasses again, but the entoptic overlay changed nothing. If a habitat citizen had been standing in Thalia's place with a skullful of sense-modifying implants, they'd still have seen only the same drab walls.

'Moving deeper into the hab,' Thalia said, reporting back to her cutter. 'So far I'm not exactly overwhelmed by the welcoming committee.'

She picked up the equipment cylinder in her left hand. Caution prevailed, and this time she chose to release the whiphound. 'Proceed ahead of me at defence posture one,' she instructed, before letting go. Red eye bright, the whiphound nodded its haft once to indicate that it had understood her order and was now in compliance. Then it turned the haft away from her and slunk forward, gliding across the ground on the coiled tip of its filament, like a sketch of a cobra.

The doorway led to a damp tunnel with cracked flooring. Ahead, the tunnel began to curve around. The whiphound slinked forward, the red light of its scanning eye reflecting back from moist surfaces. Thalia followed it into the tunnel, around a gentle curve, until the tunnel widened out into a gloomily lit plaza. The curvature of the habitat was evident in the continuous gentle up-sweep of the floor, rising ahead of her until it was hidden by the similarly curving ceiling. The only illumination came from sunlight creeping through immense slatted windows on either side, their glass panes tinting the light sepia-brown through a thick caking of dust and mould. Rising high above Thalia, interrupted only by the windows, were multi-levelled tiers of what had once been shops, boutiques and restaurants. Bridges and ramps spanned the space between the two walls, some of them sagging or broken. Glass frontages lay shattered, or were covered with various forms of mould or foliage-like infestation. In some of the shops there was even evidence of unsold merchandise, cobwebbed into obscurity.

Thalia didn't like the place at all. She was glad when she found another tunnel leading out of the plaza. The whiphound slinked ahead of her, its coil making a rhythmic hissing sound against the flooring.

Without warning, it vanished.

An instant later Thalia heard a sound like two pieces of scrap metal being smashed against each other. Cautiously she rounded the curve and saw the whiphound wrapped around the immobilised form of a robot, which had toppled over onto its side, its rubber-tyred wheels spinning uselessly. Thalia stepped closer, putting down the cylinder. She appraised the fallen machine for weapons, but there was no sign that it was anything other than a general-purpose servitor of antique design.

'Release it,' she said.

The whiphound uncoiled itself and pulled back from the robot, while still keeping its eye locked on the machine. Laboriously, the robot extended telescopic limbs to right itself. A slender pillar rose from the wheeled base, with limbs and sensors sprouting at odd, asymmetric angles from the pillar.

'I am Deputy Field Prefect Thalia Ng, of Panoply,' she said. 'Identify your origin.'

The robot's voice was disconcertingly deep and emphatic. 'Welcome to Carousel New Seattle-Tacoma, Deputy Field Prefect Ng. I trust your journey was pleasant. I apologise for my lateness. I have been tasked to escort you to the participatory core.'

'I was hoping to talk to Citizen Orson Newkirk.'

'Orson Newkirk is in the participatory core. Shall I assist you with your luggage?'

'I can manage,' Thalia said, shaking her head.

'Very well, Deputy Field Prefect Ng. Please follow me.'

'Where is everyone? I was expecting a population of one point three million people.'

'The current population is one million, two hundred and seventy-four thousand, six hundred and eighteen people. All are accounted for in the participatory core.'

'You keep saying that – what's a "participatory core"?'

'Please follow me.'

The robot spun around, tyres hissing against the wet flooring, and began to amble down the corridor, trailing an electrical burning smell in its wake.

From seven and a half metres away Jane Aumonier smiled tightly. 'You're like a dog with a bone, Tom. Not everything in life is a conspiracy. People do sometimes get mad and do stupid and irrational things.'

'Dravidian sounded neither mad nor irrational to me.'

'One of his crew, then.'

'Acting according to plan. Following a script to make the whole attack look like a heat-of-the-moment thing, when in fact it was set up long before Dravidian ever met Delphine.'

'You really think so?'

Dreyfus had just run the Solid Orrery in his room. He'd back-tracked the configuration of the Glitter Band to the time when Delphine Ruskin-Sartorious said the call had come in. The data was now sitting in Thalia's cutter, waiting for her to get to it when she completed her current upgrade.

'You've always trusted my instincts in the past,' Dreyfus said. 'Now they're telling me that there's something going on here that we're supposed to overlook.'

'You've spoken to the betas?'

'They can't think of anyone who'd do this to the family.'

'So you've no hint as to what the motive might have been?'

'No, not yet. But I'll tell you this. If you just wanted to hurt a family, there are any number of assassination weapons capable of doing the job without leaving a forensic trail.'

'Agreed . . .' Aumonier said, her tone non-committal, letting him know that she was going along with him for the sake of argument alone.

'But whoever did this wanted to take out more than just the family. They killed all the people in that habitat and then they killed the habitat itself.'

'Maybe they didn't have access to assassination weapons.'

Dreyfus pulled a sceptical expression. 'Yet they did have the means to infiltrate an Ultra ship and manipulate its Conjoiner drive?'

'I'm not sure where you're going with this, Tom.'

'I'm saying that it would have been harder for them to use Dravidian than to get their hands on any number of assassination tools. Which means they really needed that ship. They used it for a reason. Killing the family wasn't enough. They had to incinerate them, wipe every trace of them out of existence. Short of a foam-phase bomb or a nuke, how else do you do that, except with a Conjoiner drive?'

'It still doesn't add up to much,' Aumonier said.

'At least the ship gave them a chance to pin it on the Ultras, rather than making it look like the work of another habitat. But I think Dravidian and his crew were innocent.'

Aumonier looked wearily at the wall of displays jostling for her attention. Even at a glance, Dreyfus could see that almost all of them referred to her efforts to contain the escalating crisis between the Glitter Band and the Ultras. The screens wrapped the room from pole to pole, the combined pressure of them pushing in from all directions like the impaling spikes of an iron maiden.

'If I did have proof,' she said, 'if I could demonstrate that the Ultras were innocent, that would certainly ease matters.'

'I've got Thalia Ng helping me to trace the caller who set up Dravidian.'

She looked at Dreyfus questioningly. 'I thought Ng was outside on field duty. The update to the polling cores, wasn't it? Vantrollier asked me to sign off on the pad release.'

'Thalia's outside,' Dreyfus confirmed. 'And she's helping me as well, between upgrades.'

Aumonier nodded approvingly. 'A good deputy.'

'I don't employ any other kind.'

'And I don't employ any other kind of field prefect. I want you to understand that you are appreciated, no matter how ... frustrating you must occasionally find your position.'

'I'm perfectly happy with my role in the organisation.'

'I'm glad you feel that way.'

There was a lull.

'Tell me something, Jane. Now that we're having this conversation.'

'Go ahead, Tom.'

'I want you to answer truthfully. I'm going to be poking around under some stones. There may be things under them that bite back. I need to be certain that I have your complete confidence when I go out there to do my job.'

'You have it. Unconditionally.'

'Then there's no reason for me to think that I might have disappointed you, or underperformed, in my line of work?'

'Why would you feel that way?'

'I sense that I have your confidence. You've given me Pangolin clearance, which I appreciate. I'm entitled to sit in with the senior prefects. But I'm still a field, after all these years.'

'There's no shame in that.'

'I know.'

'If it wasn't for this ... thing on my neck, maybe I'd still be out there as well.'

'Not very likely, Jane. You'd have been promoted out of fieldwork whether you liked it or not. They'd have kept you inside Panoply anyway, where you can be of most benefit to the organisation.'

'And if I'd said no?'

'They'd have thanked you for your opinion and ignored you anyway. People get promoted out of field while they're still at the top of their game. That's the way it works.'

'And if I told you I thought the best way for you to serve Panoply was to remain a field prefect?'

'I'm getting old and tired, Jane. I've started making mistakes.'

'None that have reached my attention.' She addressed him with sudden urgency, as if she'd been indulging him until then but now it was time to lay down the law. 'Tom, listen to me. I don't want to hear any more of this. You're the best we have. I wouldn't say that if I didn't mean it.'

'Then I have your confidence?'

'I've said it once already. Go and look under as many stones as you want. I'll be right behind you.'

CHAPTER 9

Ahead, the whiphound was a nervous black squiggle against a brightening red glow. The escort servitor had broken down, but it had given Thalia clear instructions about where she should go. Now she quickened her pace, the cylinder weighing heavily on her wrist, until she emerged into a huge arena-like space. She appeared to be standing on a railed balcony, the opposite wall an easy hundred metres away. The wall was divided into endless boxlike partitions, stacked on many levels, but the blood-red light was too dim for Thalia to see more than that. Above was only inky darkness, with no suggestion of how high the ceiling was.

Next to her, the whiphound snapped around agitatedly, sizing up the new space in which it found itself.

'Easy,' she whispered. 'Maintain defence posture one.'

That was when a new voice boomed out of nowhere. 'Welcome, Thalia. This is Orson Newkirk speaking. I'm sorry about your tribulations with the servitor.'

She raised her own voice in return. 'I can't see you, Citizen Newkirk.'

'My apologies. It's spectacularly bad form not to be there to greet your guests, but I haven't been unplugged in a while and there was a problem with one of my disconnect valves. All fixed now, though. I'm on my way down as I speak. Be with you in a jiffy.'

'On your way down?' she asked, looking up.

'How much do you know about us, Thalia?' he asked, his voice cheerfully playful.

'I know that you stay out of trouble with Panoply,' she said, giving a non-answer that she hoped would mask her ignorance.

'Well, that's good. At least you haven't heard anything bad.'

Thalia was getting a crick in her neck. 'Should I have?'

'We have our critics. People who think the level of abstraction we practise here is somehow wrong, or immoral.'

'I'm not here to judge. I'm here to install a software patch.'

She could see something now: a mote of light in the darkness above, descending towards her. As Orson Newkirk came fully into view, Thalia saw that he was contained inside a rectangular glass box, which was being lowered down on a barely visible line. The box wasn't much larger than a suitcase.

He was a bust, Thalia thought: a human head, half of the upper torso, and *nothing else*. Nothing below the ribs. No arms, no shoulders. Just a head and a chest, the base of his torso vanishing into a ring-shaped life-support device. A padded framework rose up behind him, supporting the torso, neck and head.

'They say we're just heads,' Newkirk said chattily. 'They couldn't be more wrong! Anyone can keep a head alive, but without the hormonal environment of the rest of the body, you don't get anything remotely resembling the rich texture of human consciousness. We're creatures of chemistry, not wiring. That's why we keep as much as possible, while throwing out everything we don't need. I still have glands, you know. Glands make all the difference. Glands maketh the man.'

'*All* your glands?' Thalia asked, glancing at the truncated torso.

'Things can be moved around and rerouted, Thalia. Open me up and you'd find a very efficient utilisation of space.'

The box came to a halt with Newkirk's head level with Thalia's.

'I don't understand,' she said, thinking about the echoing, musty spaces she had already walked through. 'Why have you done this to yourself? It can't be that you need the room.'

'It's not about room. It's about resources.' Newkirk smiled at her. He had a young man's face, not unattractive when one ignored everything else about him. His eyes were white orbs, blank save for a tiny dot of a pupil. They trembled constantly, with the coordinated motion of someone in deep REM sleep.

'Resources?' she asked.

'Funds have to be used in the most efficient manner possible. There are more than a million people living in Sea-Tac. If every single one of them had the mass-energy demands of an adult human, we'd be spending so much money keeping them all fed and watered that we wouldn't have a penny left over for bandwidth.'

'Bandwidth?' Thalia asked, blearily conscious of where this was heading.

'For abstraction, of course,' Newkirk said, sounding surprised that this wasn't obvious.

'But there isn't any. My glasses were dead.'

'That's because you were outside the participatory core. It's heavily shielded. We don't waste a watt broadcasting abstraction where it isn't needed.'

She cut him off. 'Where is everyone, Citizen?'

'We're all right here.'

Lights blazed on, descending in a wave from a vanishing point that appeared to be almost infinitely far above. Thalia saw tier upon tier of compartments, each of which held an identical glass box to the one in which Newkirk resided. There wasn't room for this inside the habitat, she started to think, before realising that she must be looking along one of the connecting spokes, all the way to the weightless hub.

'Why have you done this to yourselves?'

'That's not the right question. What you should be asking is, who do I have to kill to join?'

She grinned nervously. 'No thanks.'

'You don't know what you're missing.'

'Maybe not. I do know that I quite like having a body, being able to walk around and breathe.'

'But you know nothing of abstraction. If you had any experience of it before you became a prefect, it must be just a fading memory by now. Like a glimpse of the gates of heaven between a crack in the clouds. Before the clouds closed again.'

'I've sampled abstraction – I had implants before I joined Panoply.'

'You've sampled it, yes. But only in Sea-Tac would you know the euphoric bliss of total immersion.'

Thalia looked across the open space, at the boxes ranked on the far wall, the endless parade of human busts. 'They're all somewhere else, aren't they? Mentally, I mean. Their minds aren't in Sea-Tac at all.'

'What would be the point? My people are the only real citizens of the Glitter Band, the only ones who truly inhabit it. Their minds are out there now, Thalia: spread across the entire volume of near-Yellowstone space, a choir invisible, singing the body electric, angels in the architecture.'

'They've paid a price for it.'

'One they'd all gladly pay ten times over.'

'I really should be getting on with the upgrade,' Thalia said.

'The polling core's at the bottom of the shaft. Follow the walkway and it'll bring you to the base in two rotations.'

Thalia did as Citizen Newkirk instructed. When she reached the bottom of the shaft – Newkirk lowering down to match her descent until he was hovering only a metre above the floor – she reached out her right hand and summoned the whiphound back. It sprang into her grip, retracting its filament with a supersonic crack. She locked the whiphound back onto her belt.

'I'll run through what I need to do. I'm going to open a ten-minute access window into the polling core's internal operating architecture.' Thalia patted the cylinder she had brought with her. 'Then I'm going to implement a minor software upgrade. I won't need to take abstraction down for more than a few milliseconds.' She cast a glance at the wall of busts. 'They won't notice it, will they?'

'A few milliseconds? Not very likely. Buffering software in their implants will smooth over any glitches, in any case.'

'Then there's no reason for me not to begin.'

Thalia's cylinder opened like a puzzle box, revealing racks of specialised tools and colour-coded data diskettes. She pulled out the first of the four one-time pads and held the rectangle up to eye level. She applied finger pressure and watched text spill across the rectangle's surface.

'This is Deputy Field Prefect Thalia Ng. Acknowledge security access override Probity Three Saxifrage.'

'Override confirmed,' the apparatus replied. 'You now have six hundred seconds of clearance, Deputy Field Prefect Ng.'

'Present entry port sixteen.'

The polling core sank into the floor like a descending periscope, rotating on its axis as it did so. An illuminated slot came into view. Thalia reached into her cylinder and extracted the diskette containing the relevant software upgrade. She slid the diskette into the slot, feeling the reassuring tug as the pillar accepted it. The diskette vanished into the polling core, accompanied by a series of faint rumbles and thuds.

'The diskette contains a data fragment. What do you wish me to do with this data fragment, Deputy Field Prefect Ng?'

'Use the fragment to overwrite the contents of executable data segment alpha alpha five one six.' She turned to Newkirk and whispered, 'This will only take an instant. It's a run-time fragment, so there won't be any need to recompile the main operating stack.'

'I cannot overwrite the contents of executable data segment alpha alpha five one six,' the core said.

Thalia felt a tingle of sweat on her brow. 'Clarify.'

'The requested operation would introduce a tertiary-stage conflict in the virtual memory array addressing the executable image in segment kappa epsilon nine nine four.'

'A problem, Prefect?' Newkirk asked mildly.

Thalia wiped her brow dry. 'Nothing we can't work around. The architecture's just a bit knottier than I expected. I might have to take abstraction down for slightly longer than a few milliseconds.'

'What counts as "slightly longer"?'

'Maybe a tenth of a second.'

'*That* won't go unnoticed.'

'You now have four hundred and eighty seconds of access, Deputy Field Prefect Ng.'

'Thank you,' she said, struggling not to sound flustered. 'Please evaluate the following. Suspend run-time execution of all images between segments alpha alpha to kappa epsilon inclusive, then perform the data segment overwrite I already requested. Confirm that this would not involve a suspension of abstraction access exceeding one hundred milliseconds—'

'The aforementioned tertiary-stage conflict would now be resolved, but a quaternary-stage conflict would then arise.'

Thalia swore under her breath. Why had she not probed the architecture before initiating the one-time access window? She could have learned everything she needed to without invoking Panoply privileges.

'Turn it around,' she said, suddenly seeing a way. 'Tell me what would be required to perform a clean installation of the new data segment.'

'The new data segment can be installed, but it will entail a complete rebuild of all run-time images in all segments between alpha alpha and kappa epsilon inclusive.'

'Status of abstraction during downtime?'

'Abstraction will be fully suspended during the rebuild.'

'Estimated build-time?' Thalia asked, her throat dry.

'Three hundred and forty seconds, plus or minus ten seconds, for a confidence interval of ninety-five per cent.'

'State remaining time on access window.'

'You now have four hundred and six seconds of access, Deputy Field Prefect Ng.'

She looked at Newkirk, who was studying her with a distinctly unamused expression, in so far as his wax-like mask was capable of expression.

'You heard what the machine said,' Thalia told him. 'You're going to lose abstraction for more than five minutes. I have to begin the build in the next minute to stand a chance of it finishing before my window closes.'

'If it doesn't build in time?'

'The core will default to safe mode. It'll need more than a six-hundred-second pad to unlock it then. You could be down for days, with the way Panoply's tied up at the moment.'

'Losing abstraction for five minutes will cost us dearly.'

'I wish there was some other way. But I really need to start that build.'

'Then do whatever you must.'

'Do you wish to warn the citizens?' Thalia asked.

'It wouldn't help them. Or me, for that matter.' His voice turned stern. 'Begin, Prefect. Get this over with.'

Thalia nodded and told the polling core to commence the build. 'Abstraction will be interrupted in ten seconds,' the pillar informed her. 'Predicted resumption in three hundred and forty seconds.'

'Time on window.'

'Access window will close in three hundred and forty-four seconds.'

'You like to cut it fine,' Newkirk said.

Thalia made to respond, but even as she was opening her mouth she saw that there would be no point. The man's face had frozen into mask-like stiffness, his eyes no longer quivering in their sockets. He looked dead; or rather he had become the dead stone bust he had always resembled.

They would all be like that, Thalia realised. All one million, two hundred and seventy four thousand, six hundred and eighteen people inside Carousel New Seattle-Tacoma would now be in a state of limbo, severed from the realm of abstract reality that for them was the entire meaningful world. Just from looking at Newkirk, she knew that there was no consciousness going on inside his skull. If his mind could be said to exist at all, it was somewhere else, locked out, knocking on a door that would remain resolutely shut for another five minutes.

Thalia was utterly alone in a room containing more than a million other people.

'Give me an update,' she queried.

'Rebuild is proceeding on schedule. Estimated time to resumption of abstraction is now two hundred and ninety seconds.'

Thalia clenched her fists. It was going to be the longest three minutes of her life.

'Sorry to bother you again,' Dreyfus said as the beta-level copy of Delphine Ruskin-Sartorious resumed existence in the interview suite, 'but I wondered if you wouldn't mind answering a few more questions.'

'I'm at your disposal, as you've already made abundantly clear.'

Dreyfus smiled briefly. 'Let's not make this any harder than it has to be, Delphine. We may not agree on the sanctity of beta-level simulation, but we both agree a crime's been committed. I need your help to get to the bottom of it.'

She had her arms crossed before her, silver bracelets hanging from her wrists. 'Which will inevitably lead us back to the vexed question of my art, I suppose.'

'Something made someone angry enough to destroy your habitat,' Dreyfus went on. 'Your art may have been a factor in that.'

'We're back to the jealousy thing.'

'I'm wondering if it was more than that. You may have strayed into a politically sensitive area when you picked Philip Lascaille as your subject matter.'

'I'm not sure I follow you.'

'Don't take this the wrong way, but I looked at your history as an artist and until recently you were keeping something of a low profile. Then suddenly – well, I won't say you became an overnight celebrity, but all of a sudden your work was being talked about, and your pieces were starting to sell for more than just small change.'

'These things happen. It's why we keep struggling.'

'All the same, it appears that your work started attracting attention from about the time you began work on the Lascaille series.'

Delphine shrugged, giving nothing away. 'I've worked on many thematic sequences. This is just the most recent one.'

'But it's the one that got people looking at your work, Delphine. For one reason or another, *something* happened. Why did you settle on Lascaille for your subject matter?'

'I'm not sure where you're going with this, Prefect. Lascaille and everything that happened to him is part of our shared history.

There are already a million works of art inspired by his visit to the Shroud. Is it any great surprise that I have incorporated a tragic and familiar figurehead into my own?'

Dreyfus made an equivocal face. 'But it *was* a long time ago, Delphine. We're going back to the time of the Eighty. Those wounds healed years ago.'

'Doesn't mean there isn't still resonance in the theme,' she countered.

'I don't deny it. But has it occurred to you that you might have raked over some ground that was better left undisturbed?'

'With Lascaille?'

'Why not? The man came back a lunatic. He was barely capable of feeding himself. Word is he drowned himself in the Sylveste Institute for Shrouder Studies. That made some of the other organisations with an interest in the Shrouders very unhappy. They'd long wanted to get their own hands on Lascaille, so that they could look into his skull and see what the hell had happened to him. Then word got out that he'd drowned himself in an ornamental fish pond.'

'He was more than likely suicidal. You're not suggesting someone murdered him?'

'Only that his dying didn't look good for House Sylveste.'

'So what you're saying is – let me get this right – someone killed me and my family, not to mention my entire habitat, because I had the temerity to refer to Philip Lascaille in my art?'

'It's a theory. If someone connected to the Sylveste family perceived your art as a veiled critique of their actions, they might well have considered retaliation.'

'But why not just kill me, if I made them so angry?'

'I don't know,' Dreyfus admitted. 'But it would help if I knew that you really hadn't intended that work to embarrass the Sylvestes.'

'Would that have been a crime, if I had?'

'No, but if you'd intended the art to provoke a response, it wouldn't be too surprising that you got one.'

'I can't speculate on the motives of the Sylveste family.'

'But you can tell me why you picked Lascaille.'

She looked at him witheringly, as if she'd only just appreciated his true worth. 'You think it's that easy? You think I can articulate my reasons for choosing that subject matter as if it was no more complicated or involved than picking the colour of a chair?'

'I'm not saying—'

'You've precious little insight into the artistic process, Prefect. It's a shame; I pity you. You must see the world in such drab, mechanistic terms. What a crushing, regimented, soullessly predictable universe you must inhabit. Art – anything that can't be described in strictly procedural terms – is utterly alien to you, isn't it?'

'I knew my wife,' Dreyfus said quietly.

'I'm sorry?'

'She was an artist.'

Delphine looked at him for long moments, her expression softening. 'What happened to her?' she asked.

'She died.'

'I'm sorry,' Delphine said, Dreyfus hearing genuine remorse in her voice. 'What I just said to you – that was cruel and unnecessary.'

'You were right, though. I've no artistic side. But I spent enough time with my wife to understand something of the creative process.'

'Do you want to tell me what happened to her?'

Dreyfus shot her a steely smile. 'Quid pro quo is the phrase, I believe.'

'I don't need to know about your wife. But you do need to know about my art.'

'You're curious, though. I can tell.'

She breathed out through her nose, looking down it at him. 'Tell me what kind of an artist she was.'

'Valery wasn't exceptionally talented,' Dreyfus said. 'She discovered that early enough in her career for it not to cause her too much grief and disappointment when she brushed against real genius. But she still wanted to find a way to make art her vocation.'

'And?'

'She succeeded. Valery became interested in art created by machine intelligences. Her mission was to prove that it was as valid as purely human art; that there wasn't some essential creative spark that required the input of a flesh-and-blood mind.'

'That's reassuring, given that I'm no longer a flesh-and-blood intelligence myself.'

'Valery would have insisted that your art be taken just as seriously now as when you were alive. But she wasn't so much interested in what beta-level simulations could produce as she was in art created by intelligences that had no human antecedents. That was what took her to SIAM.'

'That rings a bell.'

'The Sylveste Institute for Artificial Mentation.'

'That family again.'

'Yes, they do tend to crop up.'

'What did they want with your wife, Prefect Dreyfus?'

'In SIAM they were building experimental machine intelligences based on a raft of different neural architectures. Valery was assigned to the Laboratory for Cognitive Studies, a department within SIAM. Her function was to evaluate the creative potential of these new minds, with the goal of creating a generation of gamma-level intelligences with the ability to solve problems by intuitive breakthrough, rather than step-by-step analysis. In essence, they wanted to create gamma-levels that were not only capable of passing the standard Turing tests, but which had the potential for intuitive thinking.' Dreyfus touched a finger to his upper lip. 'Valery tried to coax these machines into making art. To one degree or another, she usually got something out of them. But it was more like children daubing paint with their fingers than true creative expression. Valery began to despair of finding anything with an artistic impulse. Then she was introduced to a new machine.'

'Wait a minute,' Delphine said, uncrossing her arms. 'I knew I'd heard of SIAM before. Wasn't that where the Clockmaker happened?'

Dreyfus nodded. 'That was the machine. Its origin was obscure: there was secrecy and interdepartmental rivalry within SIAM, as in any organisation of that nature. What was clear was this: someone had created an artificial mind unlike anything that had gone before. Not just a brain in a bottle, but an autonomous robotic entity with the ability to move and interact with its surroundings. By the time my wife got to see it, it was already making things. Toys. Puzzles. Little ornaments and objets d'art. Clocks and musical boxes. Soon it started making more clocks than anything else.'

'Did you know about it at the time?'

'Only through what my wife told me. I expressed concern. The Clockmaker's ability to manipulate its surroundings and alter its own structure suggested a robot embodying advanced replicating technology, the kind of thing Panoply was supposed to police.'

'What did Valery say?'

'She told me not to worry. As far as she was concerned, the Clockmaker was no more dangerous than a child eager to please. I told her I hoped it wouldn't throw a temper tantrum.'

'You sensed the possibilities.'

'No one knew where the thing had come from, or who was responsible for creating it.'

'You were right to be worried.'

'One day it made something evil. Clock number two hundred and fourteen looked no different from a dozen that had preceded it. Valery wasn't the one who found it. It was another SIAM researcher, a woman named Krafft. At twelve fifty-eight in the morning she picked up the clock, preparing to carry it back to the analysis area. She was still on her way when the clock struck thirteen. A spring-loaded barb rammed out of the dial, pushing its way into Krafft's chest. It penetrated her ribs and stabbed her in the heart. She died instantly.'

Delphine shuddered. 'That was when it began.'

'We lost contact with SIAM at thirteen twenty-six, less than half an hour after the discovery of clock number two hundred and fourteen. The last clear message was that something was loose, killing or maiming people wherever it encountered them. Yet all the while it found time to stop and make clocks. It would absorb materials into itself, into the flickering wall of its body, and spew out ticking clocks a few seconds later.'

'I have to ask – what happened to your wife? Did the Clockmaker kill her?'

'No,' Dreyfus said. 'That wasn't how she died. I know because a team of prefects entered SIAM within an hour of the start of the crisis. They established contact with a group of researchers holed up in a different section of the facility. They'd managed to contain the Clockmaker behind emergency decompression barriers, sealing it into one half of the habitat. My wife was one of the survivors, but the prefects couldn't reach them, or arrange for their evacuation. Instead they concentrated on neutralising the Clockmaker and gathering its artefacts for further study. Jane Aumonier was the only one of those prefects to make it out alive. She was also the only one to survive a direct encounter with the entity.'

'Jane Aumonier?'

'My boss: the supreme prefect. She was still alive when we got to her, but the Clockmaker had attached something to her neck. It had told her that the device would kill her if anyone attempted to remove it. That wasn't all, though. The prefects had sixty minutes to get Jane back to Panoply and into a weightless sphere. When that sixty minutes was up, the device would execute her if anyone – and almost anything – came within seven and a half metres of her.'

'That's horrific.'

'That wasn't the end of it. The scarab – that's what we came to call the device – won't allow her to sleep. It's not that it's keeping her awake artificially. Her body's screaming for sleep. But if the scarab detects unconsciousness, it'll kill her. Drugs have kept Jane in a state of permanent consciousness for eleven years.'

'There must be something you can do for her. All the resources of this place, of the entire Glitter Band—'

'Count for nothing against the ingenuity of the Clockmaker. Which isn't to say that there aren't good men and women spending every waking minute of their lives trying to find a way to relieve Jane of her torment.' Dreyfus offered a pragmatic shrug. 'We'll get it off her one way or another. But we'll have to be certain of success before we attempt it. The scarab won't give us a second chance.'

'I'm sorry about your boss. But you still haven't told me what happened to your wife. If she was isolated from the Clockmaker—'

'After we got Jane out, we knew there was no point sending in more prefects. They'd have been butchered or worse. And the Clockmaker was beginning to break down the barricades. It was only a matter of time before it had free run of SIAM. From there, given its speed and cleverness, it might have been able to hop to another habitat, somewhere with millions of citizens.'

'You couldn't take that chance.'

'Albert Dusollier – supreme prefect at the time – took the decision to nuke SIAM. It was the only way to ensure that the Clockmaker didn't get loose.'

Delphine nodded slowly. 'I remember they destroyed it. I didn't realise there were still people inside.'

'There was never any cover-up. It's just that most of the reports dwelled on what had been prevented, not on the costs of the action.'

'Were you there when it happened?'

He shook his head automatically. 'No. I was on the other side of the Glitter Band when the crisis broke. I started making my way there as quickly as possible, hoping that there'd be a way to get a message through to Valery. I didn't make it in time, though. I saw the flash when they destroyed SIAM.'

'That must have been very difficult for you.'

'At least the Clockmaker didn't have time to get to Valery.'

'I'm sorry about your wife, Prefect. I'd like to have met her. It sounds as if we'd have found a great deal to talk about.'

'I'm sure you would have.'

After a moment, Delphine said, 'I remember the name Dusollier now. Didn't something happen to him after the crisis?'

'Three days later he was found dead in his quarters. He'd used a whiphound on himself, set to sword mode.'

'He couldn't live with what he'd done?'

'So it would appear.'

'But surely he'd had no choice. He would have needed to poll the citizenry to be able to use those nukes in the first place. He'd have had the will of the people behind him.'

'It obviously wasn't enough for him.'

'There was no explanation, no suicide note?'

Dreyfus hesitated. There had been a note. He'd even read it himself, using Pangolin privilege.

We made a mistake. We shouldn't have done it. I'm sorry for what we did to those people. God help them all.

'There was no note,' he told Delphine. There was no note, just as there was no anomalous six-hour timelag between the rescue of Jane Aumonier and the destruction of SIAM. There was no timelag, just as there was no inexplicable connection with the mothballed spacecraft *Atalanta*, moved from its prior orbit to a position very near SIAM at exactly the time of the crisis.

There were no mysteries. Everything was accounted for.

'I still don't understand why the man killed himself,' Delphine said.

Dreyfus shrugged. 'He couldn't forgive himself for what he'd done.'

'Even though it was absolutely the only right thing to do?'

'Even though.'

Delphine appeared to reflect on his words before speaking again. 'Was there a beta-level copy of your wife?'

'No,' Dreyfus said.

'Why not?'

'Valery didn't believe in them. She refused to accept that a beta-level simulation could be anything other than a walking, talking shell. It might look and sound like her, it might mimic her responses to a high degree of accuracy, but it wouldn't be her on the inside. It wouldn't have an interior life.'

'And you believe the same thing, because it's what your wife believed.'

Dreyfus offered his palms in surrender. 'I'm sorry. That's just the way it is.'

'Did your wife ever consider alpha-level simulation?'

'She'd have had no philosophical objection to it. But my wife and I grew up in the shadow of the Eighty. I know the methods have improved since then, but there are still risks and uncertainties.'

'I understand now why you have a problem with the likes of me.' Delphine blunted the harshness of the remark with a sympathetic smile. 'And I'm not angry. You lost someone dear to you. To admit that I have some claim on consciousness would be to repudiate Valery's beliefs.'

Dreyfus made a self-deprecatory gesture. 'Trust me, I'm not that complicated.'

'But you're human. It's not a crime, Prefect. I'm sorry I prejudged you.'

'You weren't to know.'

Delphine took a deep breath, as if she was preparing to submerge herself underwater. 'I made a promise. You've told me something personal, and now you want to know about my reasons for working on the Lascaille series. I'll do my best to explain, but I think you're going to be disappointed. There was no blinding flash when I woke up one day and realised I had to devote myself to his story.'

'But *something* happened.'

'I just felt this thing building up inside me, like a kind of pressure trying to force its way out. It was like an itch I couldn't scratch, until I'd told Philip's side of events.'

'How familiar were you with the story?'

Delphine looked equivocal, as if this was a question she'd never really asked herself. 'As familiar as anyone, I suppose. I'd heard of him, I knew something of what had happened—'

'But was there a defining moment when you realised you had to tackle him? Did you see a reference to him, hear something about the Sylveste family or the Shrouds?'

'No, nothing like that.' She paused and something flashed in her eyes. 'But there was *that* day. I was working in the habitat, cutting rock in my vacuum atelier. I was suited, of course – the heat from the plasma torches would have killed me even if there'd been air to breathe. I was directing the cutting servitors, working on a completely unrelated composition. Imagine a conductor standing before an orchestra. Then think of the musicians shaping solid rock with plasma-fire and atomic-scale cutting tools instead of making music with traditional instruments. That was what it felt like: I only had to imagine a shape or texture and my implants would steer the machines to do my bidding. It became a near unconscious process, dreaming rock into art.'

'And then?'

'I pulled back from the piece I was working on and realised that I'd been taking it in a direction I hadn't intended. The face wasn't supposed to be anyone in particular, but now it reminded me of someone. Once I'd made that connection, I knew my subconscious was pushing me towards Philip Lascaille as subject matter.'

'Beyond that, though, you can't explain why you focused on him?'

Delphine looked apologetic. 'I wish I could rationalise it. But as I'm sure your wife would have agreed, art doesn't work that way. Some days we just tap into something inexplicable.'

'I appreciate your honesty.'

'Does this invalidate your theory that someone took offence at my art?'

'Not necessarily. You might have provoked something without meaning to. But I admit it's difficult to see how merely referencing Philip Lascaille would have been enough to push someone to mass murder.' Dreyfus straightened – he'd been getting stiff in the back. 'All the same, the crime happened. I think I have enough to be going on with for now, Delphine. Thank you for your time.'

'What's your next move?'

'One of my deputies – you met her – is working on backtracking the incoming call to your habitat. When I have a result from her, I'll see where it leads.'

'I'm curious to know the outcome.'

'I'll make sure you hear about it.'

'Prefect, before you turn me off again – would you reconsider my earlier request? I'd like to be able to talk to Vernon.'

'I can't risk cross-contamination.'

'Neither of us has anything to hide from you. I've told you everything I know.'

'I'm sorry, but I just can't take the risk.'

'Prefect, there's something you need to understand about us. When you turn me off, I don't have any existence.'

'That's because your simulation undergoes no state changes between episodes of invocation.'

'I know – when you switch me back on again, I remember nothing except our last meeting. But I can tell you this: I still feel as if I've been somewhere else.' She looked him hard in the eyes, daring him to look away. 'And wherever it is, it's a cold and lonely place.'

A message from Thalia awaited him when he turned his bracelet on again. He called her back.

'I see you're en route. How are things going?'

Her response returned with no detectable timelag. 'Well enough, sir. I've finished the first installation.'

'All went smoothly?'

'Couple of hiccups, but they're up and running now.'

'In other words, one hole closed, three to go. You're ahead of schedule, I see.'

'In all honesty, sir, I don't expect any of these upgrades to need all the time I allocated. But I thought it was better to be safe than sorry.'

'Very wise of you.'

After a pause, Thalia said, 'I guess you're wondering about the network analysis, sir?'

'I don't suppose you've made any progress?' he asked, his tone hopeful.

'The snapshots you sent through were all I needed. I might even have a lead for you. Assuming that the stated time for the incoming transmission to the Ruskin-Sartorious Bubble was correct to within twenty minutes, I see only one likely candidate for the network router that would have handled that data traffic.'

'Which would be?'

'It's nowhere you're likely to have heard of, sir. Just a free-floating network router named Vanguard Six. Basically it's nothing more than a boulder floating in the Glitter Band, with an automated signal-forwarding station built into it.'

He made a mental note of the name. 'And you think this router will have kept a record of traffic it handled?'

'Enough to tell you where the message originated, sir. Even if that point of origin turns out to be another router, you should still be able to keep backtracking it until you reach the original sender.

It would be unusual for a message to pass through more than two or three relay stages.'

'Sparver should be able to handle the technical issues. It can't be done remotely, can it?'

'No, sir. Someone needs to be physically present. But you're right – Sparver will know exactly what to do.'

'I'm sure he will,' Dreyfus said.

Without another word he closed the connection and prepared to rouse his other deputy.

CHAPTER 10

They did not look like people at all, but rather luminous pink branching coral formations, vast, dendritic and mysteriously chambered. For many seconds, Gaffney stared in mesmerised fascination at the three-dimensional patterns, awed at what he was seeing. If human souls could be frozen and captured in light, they would look something like this. Now that the flesh-and-blood individuals were deceased, and since none of the three had subjected themselves to alpha-level scanning, these beta-levels represented the last link with the living as far as Vernon Tregent, Anthony Theobald and Delphine Ruskin-Sartorious were concerned.

Panoply might not regard beta-levels as anything other than forensic information, akin to photographs or bloodstains, but Gaffney was more open-minded. He didn't hold with the orthodox view that only alpha-level simulations were to be accorded full human rights. The exterior effect was the only thing that mattered, not what was going on behind the mask. That was why it did not unduly concern him that he did not know exactly what Aurora was. So she might be a machine, rather than a living person. So what? What mattered was her compassion, her evident concern for the well-being of the hundred million souls orbiting Yellowstone.

He'd had his doubts at first, of course.

She had come to him five years earlier, four years after he'd been promoted to head of Panoply's Internal Security division. He'd been a senior for years before that, and an outstanding field for as long again. He'd given his life to Panoply, and asked for nothing in return except the assurance that his colleagues cared about their duties as much as he did. He had invested his own identity in the idea of service, eschewing marriage and social relationships in preference to a life of disciplinary self-control. He lived and breathed the ideals of Panoply, the martial life of a career prefect.

He didn't just accept the sacrifices of his profession, he welcomed them.

But then something had happened that caused Gaffney to question the worth of Panoply, and by inference his own fitness as a human being. He had been sent to investigate possible voting anomalies in a habitat known as Hell-Five. It was a strange world, built around a perfect hemisphere of rock, as if a round asteroid had been sliced in two. Airtight structures rose up from both the flat face and the underlying pole, densely packed skyscrapers wrapped in coiling pressurised passageways. Once, Hell-Five had been a gambler's paradise, before the fashion for such things waned. It had moved through several social models after that, each less remunerative than the last, before settling on the one Gaffney had witnessed during his visit. Within months of assuming its new identity, Hell-Five had become a dazzling success, with other habitats paying handsomely to access its lucrative new export.

That export was human misery.

Once a month, one of the habitat's extremely wealthy citizens was selected at random. That unfortunate individual would be tortured, their excruciation prolonged via medical intervention until they eventually succumbed to death. Money flowed into Hell-Five's coffers via the sale of viewing rights and the fact that the citizens of other habitats could sponsor a particular mode of torture, often after a series of escalating auctions.

The system sickened Gaffney to the marrow. He'd observed many extremes of human society in his tours of the Glitter Band, but nothing to compare with the depravities of Hell-Five. One glimpse of one of the victims-in-progress had sent him reeling. He had experienced a deep-seated conviction that Hell-Five was simply *wrong*; a social abomination that needed to be corrected, if not wiped out of existence.

But Panoply – and therefore Gaffney himself – could do nothing to curtail it. Panoply was concerned only with matters of security and voting rights as they pertained to the Glitter Band as a whole. What went on inside a given habitat – provided those activities did not contravene technological or weapons moratoriums, or deny citizens free voting rights – was entirely outside Panoply's jurisdiction; a matter for local constabulary alone.

By these criteria, Hell-Five had done nothing wrong.

Gaffney found himself unable to accept this state of affairs. The phenomenon of the torture states, and the citizens' collective refusal to see them ended, showed that the people could not be trusted with absolute freedom. Nor could Panoply be trusted to step in when a moral cancer began to spread through the Glitter Band.

Gaffney saw then that something had to be done. Too much power had been devolved to the habitats. For their own safety, central government needed to be reasserted. The citizens would never vote for that, of course; even the moderate states were wary of ceding too much authority to an organisation like Panoply. But needs must, no matter how unwilling the populace. Children were playing with some very sharp knives: it was a wonder more blood hadn't already been spilled.

Gaffney had begun to express his thoughts in his personal journal. It was a way of clarifying and organising his precepts. He saw that Panoply had to change – perhaps even cease to exist – if the people were not to be abandoned to their own worst natures. He was aware that his ideas were heretical; that they cut against everything Sandra Voi's name had stood for these past two hundred years. But history was not made by reasonable or cautious individuals. Sandra Voi had hardy been cautious or reasonable herself.

Aurora had revealed herself to him soon after.

'You're a good man, Sheridan. Yet you feel beleaguered, as if all those around you have forgotten their true responsibilities.'

Gaffney had blinked at the sudden appearance of the face on his private security pane. 'Who are you?'

'A fellow sympathiser. A friend, if you wish.'

He was inside Panoply. If she was reaching him, then she had to be inside as well. But he knew even then that she was not, and that Aurora had powers of infiltration and stealth that made a mockery of walls and doors, whether real or virtual. If she was a beta- or gamma-level, she was cleverer and more agile than most.

'Are you human?'

The question had clearly amused her. 'Does it really matter what I am, provided we share the same ideals?'

'My ideals are my own business.'

'Not now they aren't. I've seen your words, shared your theories.' She nodded in answer to the question he'd barely begun to frame. 'Yes, I've looked into your private journals. Don't be shocked, Sheridan. There is nothing shaming about them. Quite the contrary. I found them courageous. You are that rarest of creatures: a man with the wisdom to see beyond his own time.'

'I'm a prefect. It's my job to think about the future.'

'But some people are better at it than others. You are a seer, Sheridan: much like myself. We just use different methods. Your policeman's instincts tell you that Hell-Five is a symptom, a diagnostic of a looming pathology that may tax even Panoply's resources. I see the future through a different lens, but I perceive the same ominous patterns, the same subtle indications of times of great crisis to come.'

'What do you see?'

'The end of everything, Sheridan. Unless brave men take the right action now to avert that catastrophe.' She had looked at him testingly, like a teacher judging a bright but wayward pupil. 'The words in your journal show that you care. But caring is not enough. Words must become deeds.'

'I'm doing what I can. When my ideas are finalised, I can approach the other seniors—'

'And have them drum you out of the organisation?'

'If I could only express myself properly—'

'It'll make no difference. You're advocating authoritarian control. You know it is the right thing to do, but to most people the very idea is poison.'

'It doesn't have to be like that.'

'Of course it doesn't. You see that, just as you feel it in your heart. Authoritarian control can also be a form of *kindness*, like a mother hugging an infant to her breast to stop it thrashing and wailing. But no amount of rational persuasion will convince the populace. They must simply be shown.'

'Then it'll never happen. Even if Panoply had the will, it'd never have the power to seize the Glitter Band. The citizenry won't even let us carry guns!'

'There are other ways of asserting control, Sheridan. It doesn't have to involve prefects storming every habitat in the ten thousand and declaring a new regime.'

'How, then?'

'It can happen between one moment and the next, if the right preparations are made.'

'I don't follow.'

'For a long time I've been thinking along similar lines to yourself. After much deliberation, I've concluded that the transition to central authority must happen instantly, before there is a possibility of panic and counter-reaction.'

'The means don't exist,' he told her.

'But what if we arranged things such that they do?'

'They'd notice our preparations.'

'Not if we are better than them. That's no problem. Between the two of us, Sheridan, I think we can be very good indeed.'

Years after that first conversation with Aurora, Gaffney found himself thinking of all the preparations they had made, all the perils and impediments they had overcome. The thing that struck him, given all that he now knew, was how Aurora had never once uttered an actual untruth. She had not needed to tell him about her own visions of the future, but she had done so nonetheless. And as their relationship deepened, as the bonds of conspiracy grew thicker and more tangled, so she had allowed him to learn the true nature of that lens of which she had first spoken: the machine called Exordium, and the unwilling sleepers who on her behalf peered into its misty depths and reported what they saw. He had even walked amongst them, privy to a secret that would have ripped the system wide open had it become known. He felt sorry for those dreaming prisoners. But what they were doing was a beautiful, necessary thing.

History would thank them.

Hell-Five had shown Gaffney that the very nature of the Glitter Band embodied the seed of its own destruction. But Aurora had sucked information out of the future and seen *the end* itself: not as some vague, ill-determined catastrophe, but a specific event that could almost be tied down to a specific date.

A time of plague. A time of corruption and foulness.

It was coming and there was nowhere to hide.

But between them they had done something: perhaps not enough to avert the crisis, but at least to deflect some of its impact when it arrived. In a very short while, the Glitter Band would be relieved of the burden of self-determination.

This, Gaffney knew, was the time of the most acute risk. He had taken care of almost everything. But the one thing that might create difficulties for Aurora had still not been neutralised. Now he was also confronted with the thorny issues of the beta-levels. Gaffney had hoped that none would survive the attack, and that any backed-up copies retrieved from other habitats would be too out-of-sync to point Dreyfus towards the truth.

But Dreyfus was on to something.

Gaffney had accessed the logs concerning the other prefect's usage of the Search Turbines. The man was showing an unhealthy interest in the details of Delphine's art, as if he instinctively knew that there was more to the habitat's demise than met the eye. Dreyfus might not be aware of the Clockmaker connection, but given the man's demonstrated resourcefulness, it might only be a matter of time before he found a link.

So he had to be impeded.

Gaffney's hands moved to initiate the command he had already composed. From elsewhere in the data troves laid open for his inspection, he retrieved a slow-acting, high-stealth cybervirus. The software weapon was ancient and wouldn't stand a chance against a properly shielded installation. But the beta-levels were a different matter.

He threaded copies of the virus into their architectures at a level that would withstand superficial scrutiny. For now it did nothing. It was dormant, waiting until it was called into action.

Waiting until the witnesses were resurrected from the dead again.

Sparver was blowing his upturned, flat-ended nose into his sleeve while Dreyfus poured tea. His hyperpig respiratory system liked the air on cutters even less than Dreyfus's did.

'You were quicker than I was expecting,' Dreyfus observed. 'Any hitches?'

Sparver stared at his sleeve until it cleaned itself. 'Not at all. I got in and out without a snag.'

'What did you find?'

'Nothing to write home about. A piece of free-floating junk about the same size as the cutter. I grappled in and spacewalked. Took me about two minutes to find the right module and patch in a froptic. After that it was plain sailing.' His gently slanted eyes were pink-rimmed, as if he'd been up all night drinking vodka. 'Heard from Thalia since I left, Boss?'

Dreyfus shook his head. 'I reckoned she'd work faster without me breathing down her neck every five minutes.'

'She'll get the job done, don't worry about that.'

'I sincerely hope so.'

'You have doubts?'

'I can't help worrying. She's a good deputy, but she's barely out of school. I know she wants to prove to us all how good she is, but sometimes I think she's overcompensating for what happened to her father.'

'What was your take on that?'

'I didn't know Jason Ng all that well. But from what I did know, I never had cause to doubt his abilities or his dedication to Panoply.'

'So you were surprised?'

'We all were.'

'You ever talk to Thalia about it?'

'The subject's never come up.'

Sparver smiled. 'She'd hardly be the one to raise it, would she?'

'Whatever I might think of her father, it has no bearing on my opinion of Thalia. I wouldn't have selected her for my squad if I'd had doubts.' Dreyfus took his cup and sipped at it gently, blowing on the tea to cool it. 'Isn't that all the reassurance she needs?'

'There are still prefects who won't look her in the eye when she goes to the refectory,' Sparver said. 'I know how that feels.'

'They also resent her because she was promoted to Deputy Field One ahead of most of her classmates.'

'I just sometimes wonder if we truly understand what it's like for her, working for the same organisation that tarred and feathered her father.'

Dreyfus shrugged. He had no real opinion on the matter. Jason Ng had been outwardly competent and trustworthy, but it was a matter of record that he had obstructed an investigation into a mid-rank habitat suspected of voting fraud. He had been found dead, having committed suicide in a cargo airlock. Post-mortem audits revealed how Ng had been receiving bribes from parties connected to the habitat. He had killed himself because his culpability was about to be made public, and he wished to spare Thalia the shame of watching her father go through a humiliating tribunal.

Dreyfus didn't care. He did not believe in an inherited disposition for accepting bribes or perverting investigations. If anything, he believed that Thalia would make a better prefect than many of her peers. She wanted both to redeem her father's sins and show that she was not a slave to her genes.

'She's a good deputy,' he said again. 'That's all that matters to me. And I have every confidence that she'll pull this off without our assistance.'

'You didn't sound confident just now.'

'I'm entitled to entertain reasonable qualms. But that's all they are. And face it, Sparv: Thalia chose to bite this one off on her own. She'd hardly welcome the arrival of a back-up squad, even if we could spare the personnel.'

'You're right, as usual. I just have this horrible feeling that we're dancing to someone else's tune, spreading ourselves too thinly. We've got Thalia trying to seal the Perigal security hole; we've got you and me trying to nail whoever murdered Ruskin-Sartorious; we've got the rest of Panoply trying to keep the habitats and the Ultras from cutting each other's throats. Is it me or is this starting to feel like an unusually busy week?'

'Look on the bright side,' Dreyfus said. 'Thalia's going to be done soon: that'll be one case closed. And we're making solid progress on the Ruskin-Sartorious investigation.' He studied Sparver with sudden intensity. 'We *are*, aren't we? Or did you just drop in for tea and sympathy?'

'Tea. For sympathy I go elsewhere. Mind if I use your wall? I want to show you what I got from the router.'

Dreyfus extended a hand. 'Go ahead. It's group-conjurable.'

With the slightly exaggerated patience Dreyfus had sometimes come to recognise in his underlings, Sparver walked him through the data. There were five columns of information: the time of arrival of an incoming transmission, its point of origin (the next node up the line), its intended destination (the next node down the line), the time when it had been forwarded – typically only a few nanoseconds after it had come in – and a final column giving some sketchy information concerning the contents of the transmission.

'There's a lot of CTC traffic coming through,' Sparver said, indicating a proportion of columns with a particular flag in the fifth column. 'That we can dispense with. It's just navigational housekeeping data, keeping tabs on all the ships and drones moving through the Band.' Sparver removed the CTC data, leaving many blank lines in the wall display. Dreyfus felt cheered: they were getting somewhere. But his glad frame of mind didn't last long. The remaining data shuffled up to fill the gaps, leaving the wall looking much as it had before. He reminded himself that he was only seeing a small, illustrative portion of the entire router log, and that there were millions of lines above and below the visible segment.

'Now we do a similar filtering on polling traffic,' Sparver said. 'That takes care of another major chunk of the data. Run the same trick on traffic on the major trade nets and we delete another big chunk. It may not look like an improvement, but we've already shrunk the log by about half. But we can do better still. Clear out all router housekeeping and we drop another ten per cent. Clear out standard abstraction packets and we're down to about twenty per cent of our original file.'

It must still have been tens of thousands of lines. 'We'll need to do better than that, even,' Dreyfus said.

'And we can. Now we filter on the target address of Ruskin-Sartorious.' Sparver scrolled up and down to show that he had now reduced the log to a mere thousand lines or so.

Dreyfus scratched at his left eyebrow. 'Why didn't we just jump to this point in the first place?'

'Doesn't work like that,' Sparver said. 'Like almost every habitat in the Glitter Band, Ruskin-Sartorious would have handled onward forwarding of third-party data, including CTC services, trade talk, abstraction packets, the works. We'd still have had to strip all that from the list even if we narrowed it down to messages only going to Ruskin-Sartorious.'

'Would have been faster, though.'

'But logically equivalent. The system doesn't care in which order you do the filtering.'

'I'll take your word for it. But we're still looking at a mass of data.'

'We're not done. Now we start getting clever.'

'I thought we were already being clever.'

'Not enough.' Sparver smiled – he was clearly enjoying himself. 'See that number in the fourth column?'

'Yes,' Dreyfus said guardedly. 'Timetag for outgoing transmission.'

'That's our clue. The message that came through to Ruskin-Sartorious was voice-only, right?'

'According to Vernon and Delphine. What difference does the message format make?'

Sparver drank from his cup. 'It makes a world of difference. When a transmission goes through the router, it's subjected to a certain amount of routine processing. Cyclic redundancy error-checking, that kind of thing. If there's a fault, the router sends a message back to the previous sender, asking for a repeat transmission.'

Dreyfus nodded provisionally. 'Makes sense.'

'The point is, all that error-checking takes a finite amount of time. And the heavier the data burden – the more *content* there is in the message – the more number-crunching needs to be done.'

'Ah. I think I see where you're going.'

'The key's in the outgoing timetag, Boss. Compared to most of the traffic the router would have forwarded to Ruskin-Sartorious, voice-only comms are hardly worth mentioning. The processing delay would have been almost zero.'

'So when the time difference between the incoming and outgoing tags is smallest—'

'We'll probably have isolated our message. Or at least some possible candidates.'

'Do it,' Dreyfus said excitedly.

Sparver was ahead of him. Now the wall showed only a dozen transmissions, all falling within the likely interval when Delphine had been warned to break off negotiations with the Ultras.

'We're still not down to one—' Dreyfus began.

'But we're getting damned warm. Now we can apply some good old intuitive police work. We look at the originating nodes. Check out the second column, Boss – I've resolved the addresses into recognisable names. Now, I'm willing to bet that most of them will correspond to habitats that have either been in contact with Ruskin-Sartorious over a long period of time, or which are places we'd expect to broadcast to the entire Glitter Band on a fairly regular basis.'

'Can you check that?'

'Already did. You ready for this?' Sparver sent a command to the wall. Now there was only one transmission entry left. 'You'll need to look over the eleven I rejected, but I'm pretty confident we can rule them out. This one, on the other hand, sticks out like the proverbial.'

'In what way?'

'The point of origin isn't anywhere I recognise, which immediately sets off my alarm bells. It's just a rock, a free-floating chunk of unprocessed asteroid drifting in one of the middle orbits.'

'Someone's got to own it.'

'The claim on the rock goes back to a family or combine called Nerval-Lermontov. Whether that means anything or not, I don't know.'

'Nerval-Lermontov,' Dreyfus said, repeating the name slowly. 'I know that family name from somewhere.'

'But then you know a lot of families.'

'They could be innocent. Is there any reason to think this rock isn't just another router?'

'Maybe it is. But here's the odd thing. Whoever made the call, whoever sent that signal from the Nerval-Lermontov rock – whether it originated there, or was just routed through it – that was the only time they ever contacted Ruskin-Sartorious through that particular node.'

'You're right,' Dreyfus said approvingly. 'Alarm bells. Lots of them.'

Sparver put down his tea, the china clinking delicately against Dreyfus's table. 'Never say we pigs don't have our uses.'

A flying horse had been waiting for Thalia when she arrived in the Chevelure-Sambuke Hourglass. The animal's wings beat the air with dreamlike slowness, slender legs treading air as if galloping on the spot. Its skin was transparent, affording an anatomically precise view of its tightly packed internal organs, its highly modified skeleton and musculature. The insectile wings were blade-slender, intricately veined, with no visible skeletal underpinnings.

Thalia's pegasus wasn't the only flying thing in the air. There were other flying horses, visible as slowly flapping translucent forms in the far distance. Some of them had riders; others must have been on their way to pick up passengers or were engaged in some errand of their own. There were also much more colourful things, suggestive of giant patterned moths, striped fish or elaborately tailed Chinese dragon kites. The pegasuses appeared to be confined to the habitat's low-gravity regions (with those prismatic wings it wasn't surprising) but the other flying forms had free roam of the entire interior. Amongst them, almost too small to make out, were the star-shaped forms of flying people, with wings or aerodynamic surfaces of their own. Thalia tried her glasses, but the overlay revealed no significant points of difference compared to naked reality. This confirmed everything that she had read about the Hourglass during her flight: the people here preferred to shape matter, not information.

Gradually, she became aware of gravity pushing her deeper into the saddle. The horse was aiming itself at a tongue-like landing deck, buttressed out from a spired white mansion near the top of a city constructed on the slopes of the Hourglass's midpoint constriction. As she neared the touchdown point, Thalia observed a civic welcoming party gathered around the perimeter of the deck.

A pair of functionaries rushed to the side of the pegasus to help Thalia disembark as soon as the horse's hooves clinked against glass flooring. The pull of gravity could still not have been more than a tenth of a gee, but the horse's wings were beating constantly, fanning the air with an audible whoosh on each twisting downbeat. The functionaries – who were more or less baseline human in appearance – moved out of the way once Thalia was on her feet.

A giant panda-like man, all black and white fur, ambled across to meet her. He moved with remarkable grace despite his obvious mass. His huge head was as wide as a vacuum helmet, his true eyes barely visible in the black ovals of his eyepatches. He stopped munching on a thin greenish stick and passed it to a functionary.

'Welcome, Deputy Field Prefect Ng,' he said in an unctuous tone. 'I am Mayor Graskop. It is a pleasure to welcome you to our modest little world. We trust your stay will be both pleasant and productive.'

He offered her his paw in greeting. Thalia's own small hand disappeared into a padding of warm, damp fur. She noticed that Mayor Graskop had five fingers and a thumb, all digits tipped with a shiny black nail.

'Thank you for sending the horse.'

'Did you like it? We'd have cultured something unique if we'd had more notice of your visit.'

'It was a very nice horse, thank you. You didn't need to go to any more trouble.'

The mayor released his grip. 'Our understanding is that you wish to access our polling core.'

'That's correct. What I have to do won't take too long. It's quite straightforward.'

'And afterwards? You'll stay to enjoy some of our hospitality, won't you? It's not often we get a visitor from Panoply.'

'I'd love to, Mayor, but now isn't a good time.'

He tilted his huge monochrome head. 'Trouble outside, is there? We'd heard reports, although I confess we don't pay as much attention to such matters as we ought.'

'No,' Thalia said diplomatically. 'No trouble. Just a schedule I have to stick to.'

'But you will stay, just for a short while.' When the mayor spoke, she glimpsed fierce ranks of sharp white teeth and caught the sugary whiff of animal digestive products.

'I can't. Not really.'

'But you simply *must*, Prefect.' He looked at the other members of the welcoming party, daring Thalia to disappoint them. Their faces, for the most part, were still recognisably human, albeit furred, scaled or otherwise distorted according to some zoological model. Their eyes were disturbingly beautiful, liquid and intense and childlike. 'We won't detain you without good reason,' the mayor insisted. 'We receive so very few outsiders, let alone figures of authority. On such rare occasions that we do, it's our custom to host an impromptu contest, or tournament, and to invite our honoured guest to participate in the judging. We were hoping you'd help with the adjudication in an air-joust—'

'I'd love to, but—'

He grinned triumphantly. 'Then it's settled. You *will* stay.' He clasped his paws together in anticipation. 'Oh, how wonderful. A prefect as judge!'

'I'm not—'

'Let's deal with the trifling business of the polling core, shall we? Then we can move on to the main event. It will be a wonderful air-joust! Are you happy to follow me? If you don't like our low gravity, we can arrange a palanquin.'

'I'm doing just fine,' Thalia said tersely.

CHAPTER 11

Dreyfus was settled before his console, composing a query for the Search Turbines. He sought priors on the Nerval-Lermontov family, certain that the name meant something but incapable of dredging the relevant information from the event-congested registers of his own ageing memory. Yet he had no sooner launched the request, and was dwelling on the idle possibility of trawling his own mind, when he felt a sudden brief shudder run through the room. It was as if Panoply had suffered an earthquake.

He lifted his cuff, ready to call his deputy, fearing the worst. But he had not even uttered Sparver's name before his console informed him that there had been a major incident in the Turbine hall.

Dreyfus stepped through his clotheswall and made his way from his room through the warrens of the rock to the non-centrifuge section where the Search Turbines were located. Even before he arrived, he realised that the incident had been grave. Prefects, technicians and machines were rushing past him. By the time he reached the entrance to the free-fall hall, medical crews were bringing out the wounded. Their injuries were shocking.

A conveyor band drew him into the vastness of the hall. He stared in stupefied amazement at the spectacle. There were no longer four Search Turbines, but three. The endmost cylinder was gone, save for the sleeve-like anchor points where it emerged from the chamber's inner surface. The transparent shrouding had shattered into countless dagger-like shards, many of which were now embedded in the walling. Dreyfus couldn't imagine the outward force that would have been necessary to rupture the armoured sheathing, which was the same kind of glass-like substance they used to form spacecraft hulls. As for the machinery that would have been whirling inside the glass just before it broke loose, nothing remained except a dusty residue, lathered several centimetres thick over every surface and hanging in the air in a choking blue-grey smog. The Turbine – its layered data stacks and whisking retrieval blades – had pulverised itself efficiently, leaving no components larger than a speck of grit. It was designed to do that, Dreyfus reminded himself, so that no information could be recovered by hostile parties in the event of a takeover of Panoply. But it was not meant to self-destruct during the course of normal operations.

He studied the other Turbines. The sheathing on the nearest of the three, the one that had been closest to the destroyed unit, was riven by several prominent cracks. The apparatus inside was spinning down, decelerating visibly. The other two units were undergoing the same failsafe shutdown, even though their casings appeared intact.

Keeping out of the way of the medical staff attending to hall technicians who'd been lacerated by glass and high-speed Turbine shrapnel – they'd already pulled out the most seriously wounded – Dreyfus found his way to a woman named Trajanova. She was the prefect in charge of archives, and considered supremely competent by all concerned. Dreyfus did not dissent from that view, but he did not like Trajanova and he knew that the feeling was mutual. He'd employed her once as a deputy, then dismissed her because she did not have the necessary instincts for fieldwork. She had never forgiven him for that and their rare meetings were tense, terse affairs. Dreyfus was nevertheless relieved to see that she had suffered no conspicuous injuries save for a gashed cheek. She was pressing her sleeve to it, her uniform dispensing disinfectant and coagulant agents. She had headphones lowered around her neck, glasses pushed up over her brow and a fine dusting of blue-grey debris on her clothes and skin.

Trajanova must have seen the look on his face. 'Before you ask, I have no idea what just happened.'

'I was about to ask if you were all right. Were you in here when it happened?'

'Behind the fourth stack, the furthest one from the unit that blew. Running search-speed diagnostics.'

'And?'

'It just went. One second it was spinning, next second it didn't exist any more. I'd have been deafened if I hadn't had the phones on.'

'You were lucky.'

She scowled, pulling her sleeve away to reveal the dried blood on her cuff. 'Funny. I'd say it was fairly unlucky of me to have been in here in the first place.'

'Was anyone killed?'

'I don't think so. Not permanently.' She rubbed at dust-irritated eyes. 'It was a mess, though. The glass did the worst harm. That's hyperdiamond, Dreyfus. It takes a lot to make it shatter. It was like a bomb going off in here.'

'Was it a bomb? I mean, seriously: could a bomb have caused this?'

She shook her head. 'I don't think so. The unit just spun loose, all of a sudden. There was no bang, no flash, before it happened.'

'Those things run near critical break-up speed, don't they?'

'That's the idea. We spin them as fast as they can go. Any slower and you'd be the first to moan about retrieval lag.'

'Could the unit have overspun?'

She answered his question with look of flat denial. 'They don't do that.'

'Could the assembly have been fatigued?'

'All the units are subjected to routine de-spin and maintenance, one at a time. You don't usually notice because we take the burden on the other three Turbs. The unit that failed got a clean bill of health during the last spin-down.'

'You're sure of that?'

Her face said: *Don't question my competence, and I won't question yours*. 'If it hadn't, it wouldn't be spinning, Prefect.'

'I had to ask. Something went terribly wrong here. Could a badly formed query have caused the break-up?'

'That's a bizarre question.'

'It's just that I sent something through about a second before the accident.'

'The units would have handled millions of queries in that interval,' she said.

'Millions? There aren't millions of prefects.'

'Most of the queries coming through are machine-generated. Panoply talking to itself, consolidating its own knowledge base. The Turbs don't care whether it's a human or a machine sending the query. All are treated with equal priority.'

'It still felt related to me.'

'It can't have been your query that did this. That would be absurd.'

'Maybe so. But I'm conducting a sensitive investigation and just at the point when I think I'm getting somewhere, when I might be about to connect my case to one of our glorious families, when I might be about to *hurt* someone, one of my primary investigative tools is sabotaged.'

'Whatever this was, it can't have been sabotage,' Trajanova said.

'You sound very certain.'

'Maybe it's escaped your attention, but this is an ultra-secure facility inside what is already an ultra-secure organisation. No one gets inside this room without at least Pangolin clearance, and no one – not even the supreme prefect herself – gets to access the Search Turbines from outside the rock. Frankly, I can't think of a facility it would be harder to sabotage.'

'But a prefect could do it,' he said. 'Especially if they had Pangolin clearance.'

'I was keeping our discussion within the realms of possibility,' Trajanova said. 'I can think of a million reasons why our enemies might want to smash the Search Turbines. But a prefect, someone already inside the organisation? You mean a *traitor*?'

'I'm just running through the possibilities. It's not so very difficult to believe, is it?'

'I suppose not,' Trajanova said slowly, staring him hard in the eye. 'After all, there's a traitor's daughter in the organisation even as we speak. Have you talked to her recently?'

'With Thalia Ng? No, she's too busy acquitting herself excellently on field duties.' He smiled coldly. 'I think we're done here, aren't we?'

'Unless you want to help me clean up this mess.'

'I'll leave that to the specialists. How long before we'll have the other Turbs back up to speed?'

She glanced over her shoulder at the intact tubes. 'They'll have to be thoroughly checked for stress flaws. Thirteen hours, at the very minimum, before I'll risk spin-up. Even then we'll be running at a low retrieval rate. Sorry if that inconveniences you, Prefect.'

'It's not that it inconveniences me. What I'm worried about is that it's conveniencing someone else.' Dreyfus scratched dust from the corners of his eyes, where it had begun to gather in gooey grey clumps. 'Keep looking into the sabotage angle, Trajanova. If you find anything, I want to hear about it immediately.'

'Maybe it would help if you told me about this magic query of yours,' she said.

'Nerval-Lermontov.'

'What about Nerval-Lermontov?'

'I wanted to know where the hell I'd heard that name before.'

She looked at him with icy contempt. 'You didn't need the Search Turbines for that, Dreyfus. I could have told you myself. So could any prefect with a basic grasp of Yellowstone history.'

He ignored the insult. 'And?'

'The Eighty.'

It was all he needed to be told.

The corvette was a medium-enforcement vehicle, twice as large as a cutter, and with something in the region of eight times as much armament. Panoply's rules dictated that it was the largest craft that could be operated by a prefect, as opposed to a dedicated pilot. Dreyfus had the necessary training, but as always in such matters he preferred his deputy to handle the actual flying, when the ship wasn't taking care of itself.

'Not much to look at,' Sparver said as a magnified image leapt onto one of the panes. 'Basically just a big chunk of unprocessed rock, with a beacon saying "keep away – I'm owned by somebody".'

'Specifically, the Nerval-Lermontov family.'

'Is that name still ringing a bell with you?'

'Someone jogged my memory,' Dreyfus said, thinking back to his less-than-cordial conversation with Trajanova. 'Turns out that Nerval-Lermontov was one of the families tied up with the Eighty.'

'Really?'

'I remember now. I was a boy at the time, but it was all over the system. The Nerval-Lermontovs were one of the families kicking up the biggest stink.'

'They lost someone?'

'A daughter, I think. She became a kind of emblem for all the others. I can see her face, but not her name. It's on the tip of my tongue . . .'

Sparver dug between his knees and handed Dreyfus a compad. 'I already did *my* share of homework, Boss.'

'Before the Turbines went down?'

'I didn't need them. Remember that case we worked a couple of years ago, involving the disputed ownership of a carousel built by one of the families? I copied reams of Eighty-related stuff onto my compad back then, and it's all still there, with summaries for all the players.'

'Including the Nerval-Lermontovs?'

'Take a look for yourself.'

Dreyfus did as Sparver suggested, plunging deep into Chasm City history. The article was several thousand lines long, a summary that could easily have been expanded by a factor of ten or a hundred had Sparver selected different text filters. The system's major families were nothing if not well documented.

Dreyfus hit the Eighty. One name leapt out at him across fifty-five years of history.

'Aurora,' he said, with a kind of reverence. 'Aurora Nerval-Lermontov. She was just a girl – twenty-two years old when she went under Cal's machines.'

'Poor kid. No wonder they were pissed off.'

They had been, too, Dreyfus remembered. And who wouldn't be? Calvin Sylveste had promised true immortality to his seventy-nine volunteers. Their minds would be scanned at sub-neuronal resolution, with the resultant structures uploaded into invulnerable machines. Rather than just being static snapshots, Calvin's Transmigrants would continue to think, to feel, once they'd been mapped into computer space. They would be true alpha-level simulations, their mental processes indistinguishable from those of a flesh-and-blood human being. The only catch was that the scanning process had to be performed with such rapidity, such fidelity, that it was destructive. The scanned mind was ripped apart layer by layer, until nothing lucid remained.

It wouldn't have mattered if the procedure had worked. All had been well for a while, but shortly after the last volunteer had gone under – Calvin Sylveste had been the eightieth subject in his own experiment – problems began to emerge with the earliest subjects. Their simulations froze, or became locked in pathological loops, or regressed to levels of autistic disengagement from the outside universe. Some vital detail, some animating impulse, was missing from the design.

'Do you believe in coincidence, Sparver?'

Sparver tapped one of the thruster controls. The rock had doubled in size, its wrinkled ash-grey surface details becoming more distinct. The potato-shaped asteroid was more than two kilometres wide at its fattest point.

'Why d'you ask?'

'Because I was already wondering why the Sylveste family kept coming up in this investigation. Now we've got another hit.'

'They're a big octopus. Sooner or later you're bound to trip over another tentacle.'

'So you don't think there's anything odd about this?'

'The Sylvestes weren't a charity. Only families with influence and money were able to buy themselves a slot in Cal's experiment. And only families with influence and money can afford to hold on to rocks like this. The key here is the Nerval-Lermontovs, not the Sylvestes.'

'They tried to take down the Sylvestes, didn't they?'

'Everyone tried. Everyone failed. This is their system. We just live in it.'

'And the Nerval-Lermontovs? They've been quiet since the Eighty, haven't they? They're hardly big players any more. If they were, I'd have recognised the name sooner. So what the hell are they doing implicating themselves in the Ruskin-Sartorious affair?'

'Maybe they were used. Maybe when we dig into this place, we'll find it was just used to bounce signals from somewhere else.'

Dreyfus felt some of his earlier elation abate. Perhaps his cherished instincts had failed him this time. If necessary, they could go outside and read the message stack, just as they'd done with the Vanguard Six router. Sparver had sounded confident that the process was repeatable, but what if it wasn't quite so easy to backtrack the signal a second time?

Dreyfus was musing on that theme when the rock launched its attack.

It came fast and without warning; it was only when the assault was over that he was able to piece together the approximate sequence of events. Across the face of the rock, small regions of the crust erupted outwards as if a dozen low-yield mines had just detonated, showering rubble and debris into space. The shattered material rained into the corvette, the noise like a thousand hammer blows against the hull.

Alarms began to shriek, damage reports cascading across the display surfaces. Dreyfus heard the whine as the corvette's own weapons began to upgrade their readiness posture. Sparver grunted something unintelligible and began to coordinate the response with manual control inputs. But the attack had not really begun in earnest. The eruptions on the rock were merely caused by the emergence of concealed weapons, tucked under ten or twenty metres of camouflaging material. Dark-muzzled kinetic slug-launchers rolled out and spat their cargoes at the corvette. Dreyfus flinched as the walls of the corvette's cabin appeared to ram inwards, before a cooler part of his mind reminded him that this was the corvette doing its best to protect the living organisms inside it. The wall flowed around his body, head to toe, forming an instant contoured cocoon. Then he felt the corvette swerve with what would have been bone-snapping acceleration under any other circumstances. With the little consciousness available to him, he hoped that the corvette had taken similar care of Sparver.

The swerve saved them. Otherwise, the first kinetic slug would have taken them nose-on, where the corvette's armour was thinnest. As it was the slug still impacted, gouging a trench along the entire lateral line of the ship, taking out weapons and sensory modules in a roar of agonised matter that was still nerve-shreddingly loud even through the cushioning of the cocoon. The ship swerved again, and then once more, harder this time. Two more slugs rammed into it. Then the corvette began to give back something of what it had taken.

Many of its weapons had been damaged by the slug impacts, or could not be brought to bear without presenting too much tempting cross section to the still-active slug launchers. But it was still able to respond with an awesome concentration of destructive force. Dreyfus felt rather than heard the subsonic drone of the Gatling guns. Another salvo of debris rained against the hull: that was the Gatling guns churning up the rock's surface even more, kicking more material into space. Four sequenced shoves as the corvette deployed and then traded momentum with its missiles, spitting them out like hard pips. The foam-phase-tipped warheads selected their own targets, punching hundred-metre-wide craters in the crust.

The Gatling guns resumed firing.

Then, with disarming suddenness, all was silent save for the occasional clang as some small piece of debris knocked into the ship.

'I am holding at maximum readiness condition,' the corvette said, its voice dismayingly calm and unhurried, as if it was delivering a weather report. 'Situational analysis indicates that the offensive object has been downgraded to threat status gamma. This analysis may be flawed. If you nonetheless wish me to stand down to moderate readiness, please issue an order.'

'You can stand down,' Dreyfus said.

The cocoon released him. He felt like a single man-sized bruise, with a headache to match. Nothing appeared broken, though, and he was at least alive.

'I think this just stopped being a peripheral investigation,' Sparver said.

Dreyfus spat blood. At some point during the attack he must have bitten his tongue. 'How's the ship doing?' he enquired.

Sparver glanced at one of the status panes. 'Good news is we've still got power, air and attitude control.'

'And the bad news?'

'Sensors are shot to hell and long-range comms don't appear to be working either. I don't think we're going to be able to call home for help.'

The absurdity of their predicament rankled Dreyfus. They were still inside the Glitter Band, in the teeming thick of human civilisation, no more than a thousand kilometres from the nearest inhabited structure. And yet they might as well have been far beyond the system, drifting in interstellar space, for all the difference it made.

'Can we reach anyone else?' he asked. 'We still have signalling lasers. If we can get a visual signal to a passing ship, we might be able to divert them.'

Sparver had already called up a navigation display showing all nearby traffic within a radius of five thousand kilometres. Dreyfus stared at it intently, but the spherical imaging surface kept malfunctioning, crowding with ghost signals caused by the damage the corvette had taken.

'Not much out there,' Sparver observed. 'Certainly not within manual signalling range.'

Dreyfus jabbed a finger at a persistent echo in the display, an object on a slow course through the scanning volume. 'That one's real, and it looks close, too. What is it?'

'Just a robot freighter, according to the transponder flag. Probably inbound from the high-energy manufactories on Marco's Eye.'

'It'll pass within three thousand klicks of us. That's almost nothing out here.'

'But it won't respond to us even if we score a direct hit with the laser. I don't think we've got any option but to limp home, and hope no one runs into us.'

Dreyfus nodded ruefully. In the congested traffic flows of the Glitter Band, a ship with impaired sensor capability was a dangerous thing indeed. That went double for a ship that was stealthed to the point of near-invisibility.

'How long will that take?'

Sparver closed his eyes as he ran the numbers. 'Ninety minutes, maybe a little less.'

'And then another hour before we can reasonably expect to get another ship out here; longer if it has to be reassigned from some other duty.' Dreyfus shook his head. 'Too long. Every instinct in my body says we don't walk away.'

'So we drop a surveillance drone. We're carrying one.'

'A drone won't help us if someone decides to run as soon as we're out of range.'

'I don't think there's anyone down there.'

'We don't know that.' Dreyfus unwebbed himself enough that he could soothe his back, sore after the corvette's spine-jarring evasive swerves. 'Which is why we need to take a look. Maybe we'll find a transmitter when we're down there. Then we can call in the big guns.'

Thalia ran a finger around her collar, stiffening it back into shape. She gathered her equipment and composed herself as the airlock cycled. Spine straight, chin up, eyes sharp. She might feel tired, she might feel embittered by what she had witnessed only a couple of hours earlier, but she was still on duty. The locals would neither know nor care that they were merely the last stop on a demanding itinerary, the last obstacle before sleep and rest and some grudging expression of gratitude from the seniors. She reminded herself that she was still well ahead of her anticipated schedule, and that if all went according to plan from now on she would be back inside Panoply barely a day and a half after she had departed.

The Chevelure-Sambuke Hourglass upgrade had gone flawlessly, but then she'd been detained while the locals had her sit in as a guest adjudicator in their impromptu tournament. It had turned out to be both unpleasant and draining, a combination of beauty pageant and gladiatorial combat, with the entrants all radically biomodified, none of them lacking in teeth and claws. She'd been assured that the most bloodied, humiliated or deceased participants would all be stitched back together again, but the entire experience had left her feeling soiled and manipulated.

Szlumper Oneill had been even worse, but for different reasons.

Szlumper Oneill was a Voluntary Tyranny that had turned nasty, and nothing could be done about it.

Citizens in the Voluntary Tyrannies had no rights at all: no freedoms, no means of expression beyond what they could achieve through the usual voting channels. Their entire lives were under the authoritarian control of whatever regime held sway in their particular habitat. Typically, they'd be guaranteed the basic needs: food, water, heating, minimal medical care, somewhere to sleep, even access to sex and rudimentary forms of entertainment. In return they might have to perform some daily activity, however drudge-like and purposeless the work itself might be. They'd be stripped of identity, forced to dress alike, even – in the most extreme cases – compelled to undergo surgery to eradicate distinguishing features.

For some people – a small but not entirely insignificant fraction of the Glitter Band citizenry – life in a Voluntary Tyranny was perversely liberating because it allowed them to shut off an entire part of their minds that dealt with the usual anxieties of hierarchy and influence. They were looked after and told what to do. It was like becoming a child again, a regression to a state of dependence on the adult machinery of the state.

But sometimes the VTs went wrong.

No one was exactly sure what triggered the shift from benevolent-yet-rigid state to dystopian nightmare, but it had happened enough times that it had begun to look as inevitable as the radioactive decay of an unstable isotope. Something unspeakable would ooze from the social woodwork, a form of corrupting sap. Citizens who tried to resist or leave were rounded up and punished. Panoply could do nothing, since it had no remit to interfere in the government of a state unless the state's citizens were being denied abstraction access and voting rights, or unless there was a majority mandate from the wider citizenry of the ten thousand.

Szlumper Oneill was an object lesson in how bad things could get. Representatives of the Interior Administration had escorted Thalia to the polling core, and they'd done their best to shield her from the populace. But she'd still seen enough to get the picture. While Thalia had been setting up her equipment at the core, an old man had broken through a cordon and rushed to plead with her. He'd fallen to his knees, clutching her trouser hems with knotted, arthritic fingers.

'Prefect,' he said, through toothless gums. 'You can do something for us. Please *do* something, before it's too late.'

'I'm sorry,' she said, barely able to speak. 'I wish I could, but—'

'Help us. Please.'

The police had arrived. They'd fired electrified barbs into the man and dragged him away, his body still palsied by the stun currents. He couldn't speak, but he'd managed to keep his face directed at Thalia as he receded, his lips still forming a plea. As the cordon closed around him again, Thalia made out a blur of fists and sticks raining down on frail bones.

She'd completed the upgrade. She did not want to think about what had happened to the old man. She prayed that this next and final upgrade would go smoother, so that she could return to Panoply and wipe the mild taste of complicity from her mouth. She was glad now that she had left House Aubusson till last. It promised to be the simplest of the upgrades; the one that would place the least demands on her concentration.

The habitat had the form of a hollow cylinder with rounded ends, rotating slowly around its long axis to provide gravity. From a distance, just before she dozed off during transit, Thalia had seen a pale-green sausage banded by many sets of windows, their facets spangling as the habitat's dreamily slow spin caused sunlight to flare off them. At the nearer end ticked the intricate clockwork of de-spun docking assemblies, where huge ships were reduced to microscopic details against the mind-numbing scale of the structure. The sausage was an entire world, sixty kilometres from end to end, more than eight kilometres across.

Weightlessness prevailed even after Thalia had disembarked from the cutter and passed through a series of rotating transfer locks. Instead of the teeming concourse she had been expecting, she found herself in a diplomatic receiving area. It was a zero-gravity sphere walled in pale-pink marble, inlaid with monochrome friezes depicting the early history of space colonisation: men in bulbous spacesuits covered in what looked like canvas; surface-to-orbit transports that resembled white fireworks lashed together; space stations so ramshackle in appearance that they looked as if they'd fall apart at the first breath of solar wind. Laughable, yes, Thalia thought: undoubtedly so. But without those canvas suits and firework rockets, without those treehouse space stations, Deputy Field Prefect Thalia Ng would not be floating in the marbled reception bay of a sixty-kilometre-long habitat, one of ten thousand other structures that carried a human freight of one hundred million souls, orbiting an inhabited world that happened to host the most dazzling, bejewelled city in human experience, a world that circled the sun of another solar system entirely, a system that formed the mercantile and cultural nexus of a human civilisation encompassing many such worlds, many stars, bound together by wonderful sleek ships that crossed the interstellar night in mere *years* of starflight.

This was the future, she thought. This was what it felt like to be alive in a time of miracles and wonders.

And she had the nerve to feel *tired*?

A servitor, resembling a mechanical owl assembled from sheets of hammered bronze, floated in the middle of the space. It spread its wing primaries and clacked open its hinged beak. It had the piping voice of a steam-age automaton.

'Greetings, Deputy Field Prefect Ng. I am Miracle Bird. It is a pleasure to welcome you inside House Aubusson. A reception is waiting on the half-gravity landing stage. Please be so kind as to follow me.'

'A reception,' Thalia said, gritting her teeth. 'That'll be nice.'

The bronze bird led Thalia into an elevator carriage. The carriage's windowless interior was covered in polished teak and dimpled maroon plush, offset with ivory Japan-work. The bird inverted itself and tucked its talons into hooks on what was evidently to become the ceiling. With a whirr of geared mechanics, its head spun around. 'We will descend now. Please be so kind as to fold down the seat and secure yourself. Gravity will increase.'

Thalia took the cue and parked herself on the fold-out seat, tucking her equipment cylinder between her knees. She felt a rush of acceleration, blood pooling in the top of her head.

'We are descending now,' the bird informed her. 'We have some distance to travel. Would you care to see the view on the way?'

'If it isn't too much trouble.'

The panel opposite Thalia morphed into transparency. She found herself looking down the length of House Aubusson, all sixty kilometres of it. She had boarded the elevator on the inner surface of one of the endcaps of the sausage-shaped habitat, and was now travelling from the pole of the endcap hemisphere towards the point where it joined the main cylinder of the structure. The elevator's trajectory curved gradually from vertical to horizontal, even though the cabin remained at the same angle. They had been moving for some while already, yet the ground was still the better part of four kilometres below, enough to make even the nearest surface features appear small and toy-like. For now the sloping terrain whizzing past Thalia consisted of featureless white cladding and fused regolith mined from Marco's Eye, interrupted here and there by some huge Art Deco chunk of environmental-regulation machinery.

Apart from the endcaps, the entire interior surface of the habitat was landscaped. Sixty kilometres away, atmospheric haze diluted detail and colour into a twinkling wash of pale blue, indistinguishable from ocean or sky. Nearer – until about halfway along the cylinder – it was still possible to make out the signatures of communities, grids or whorls embossed like thumbprints into clay. There were no huge cities, but there were dozens, even hundreds, of towns, villages and hamlets nestled amidst dense-packed greenery, curving around the shores of artificial seas and lakes and along the banks of man-made rivers and streams. There were hills, valleys, rock faces and waterfalls. There were sprays of mist shot through with rainbows. There were low-lying clouds, seemingly pasted onto the curving landscape. Nearer still, Thalia made out not merely communities, but individual buildings, marinas, plazas, parks, gardens and recreation grounds. Few of the buildings were more than a few hundred metres tall, as if they dared not violate the wide blue emptiness that made up most of the habitat's volume. There was no interior illumination source, but from her descending vantage point Thalia easily made out the bands of windows she had seen before, from outside. Now that she was looking down the length of the interior of the habitat, they became a series of dark concentric rings, Thalia counting a dozen or more of them before perspective and haze made it difficult to separate one from the next. House Aubusson might pass into the shadow of Yellowstone during each ninety-minute orbit around the planet, but it was most unlikely that its citizens would live or work on anything other than the standard twenty-six-hour cycle of Chasm City time. Far above and below the ecliptic plane of the Glitter Band, client mirrors would steer illumination onto those windows even when the habitat was out of direct line of sight of Epsilon Eridani.

Thalia felt the elevator slowing.

'We are arriving now,' the metal owl said, just as the view outside switched from distant vistas to the interior of a windowed landing stage. The door opened; Thalia disembarked. Her legs felt like springy concertinas in the half-standard gravity. Across the platform, with their backs to the window, stood a motley-looking welcoming committee. There were about a dozen of them, men and women of all ages and appearances, dressed in what appeared to be civilian clothes. Thalia looked around helplessly, wondering who she should be talking at.

'Hello, Prefect,' said a plump woman with apple-red cheeks, stepping forward from the group. There was a nervous catch in her voice, as if she was not accustomed to public speaking. 'Welcome to the halfway house. We'd have met you at the hub, but it's been a long time since any of us were in zero-gravity.'

Thalia put down the cylinder. 'It's all right. I'm used to making my own way.'

A lanky, stooping man raised his hand. 'Did Miracle Bird tell you everything you needed to know?'

'Does the owl belong to you?'

'Indeed,' the man said, beaming. He raised an arm, bent at the elbow, and the owl flapped out of the elevator, crossed the space between Thalia and the party and made a precision touchdown on the man's sleeve.

'I'm an excellent bird,' the owl said.

'It's my hobby,' he said, stroking the creature under its segmented neck. 'Making mechanical animals, using only techniques available to the PreCalvinists. Keeps me off the streets, my wife says.'

'That's nice for you,' Thalia commented.

'They were going to go with one of Bascombe's automata until they remembered what happened the last time one of them malfunctioned. That's when Miracle Bird got bumped to the top of the list.'

'What list?' Thalia looked at the peculiar gathering. There was nothing ragged or untidy about any of the individual members of the group – everyone was well dressed, colourful without being gaudy, well groomed, respectable in demeanour – but the cumulative effect was far from harmonious. Like a circus troupe, she thought, not a civic delegation. 'Who *are* you people?'

'We're your reception committee,' the plump woman said.

'That's what the owl told me.'

Another individual stepped forward to speak. He was a severe-looking gentleman in an ash-grey skin-tight suit with deep lines on either side of his mouth and a shock of stiff grey-white hair shaved close at the temples, his long-boned hands knitted together.

'Perhaps one of us should explain. You are inside one of the most egalitarian states in the Glitter Band.' He had a very low, very reassuring voice, one that made Thalia think of dark knotted wood, polished smooth by generations of hands. 'Comparatively few states practise true Demarchist principles behind their own doors, in the sense of abolishing all governmental structures, all formalised institutions of social control. Yet that is absolutely the case in House Aubusson. Possibly you were expecting a formal reception, attended by dignitaries of varying rank and pomposity?'

'I might have been,' Thalia allowed.

'In Aubusson, there are no dignitaries. There is no authority except the transparent government of the collective will. All citizens wield a similar amount of political power, leveraged through the machinery of democratic anarchy. You ask who we are. I'll tell you, beginning with myself. I am Jules Caillebot, a landscape gardener. Most recently I worked on the redevelopment of the botanic gardens in the quarter adjoining the open-air theatre in Valloton, a community between the fifth and sixth windows.' He gestured towards the plump woman who had been the first to speak.

'I'm an utter nobody,' she said, with a kind of cheery defiance, her earlier nervousness no longer apparent. 'At least *some* people in Aubusson have heard of Jules, but no one knows me from Adam. I'm Paula Thory. I keep butterflies, and not even very rare or beautiful ones.'

'Hello,' Thalia said.

Paula Thory nudged the man who'd made the owl. 'Go on, then,' she said. 'I know you're itching to tell her.'

'I'm Broderick Cuthbertson. I make mechanical animals. It's my—'

'Hobby, yes. You said.' Thalia smiled nicely.

'There's an active subculture of automaton builders in Aubusson. I mean *real* automaton builders, obviously. Strictly PreCalvinist. Otherwise it's just cheating.'

'I can imagine.'

'Meriel Redon,' said a young, willowy-looking woman, raising a tentative hand. 'I make furniture out of wood.'

'Cyrus Parnasse,' another man said, a beefy, red-faced farmer type with a burr to his voice who could have stepped out of the Middle Ages about five minutes ago. 'I'm a curator in the Museum of Cybernetics.'

'I thought the Museum of Cybernetics was in House Sylveste.'

'Ours isn't as big,' Parnasse said. 'Or as flashy or dumbed-down. But we like it.'

One by one the others introduced themselves, until the last of the twelve had spoken. As if obeying some process of collective decision-making that took place too subtly for Thalia to detect, they all turned to look at Jules Caillebot again.

'We were selected randomly,' he explained. 'When it was known that an agent of Panoply was to visit, the polling core shuffled the names of all eight hundred thousand citizens and selected the twelve you see standing before you. Actually, there was a bit more to it than that. Our names were presented to the electorate, so that our fitness for the task could be certified by a majority. Most people voted "no objection", but one of the original twelve was roundly rejected by a percentage of citizens too large for the core to ignore. Something of a philanderer, it seems. He'd made enough enemies that when his one shot at fame arose, he blew it.'

'If you call this fame,' Parnasse, the museum curator, said. 'In a couple of hours you'll be out of Aubusson, girl, and we'll all have returned to deserved obscurity. It *is* that kind of visit, isn't it? If this is a lockdown, no one warned us.'

'No one ever warns you,' Thalia said dryly, not taking to the grumpy undercurrent she had heard in the man's voice. 'But no, this isn't a lockdown, just a routine polling core upgrade. And whether or not you think being part of this reception party is something to be proud of, I *am* grateful for the welcome.' She picked up the cylinder, relishing its lightness before she returned to full gravity. 'All I really need is someone to show me to the polling core, although I can locate it myself if you prefer. You can all stick around if you want, but it isn't necessary.'

'Do you want to go straight to the core?' asked Jules Caillebot. 'You can if you like. Or we can first take some tea, some refreshments, and then perhaps a leisurely stroll in one of the gardens.'

'No prizes for guessing whose gardens,' someone said, with a snigger.

Thalia raised a calming hand. 'It's kind of you to offer, but my bosses won't be too happy if I'm late back at Panoply.'

'We can be at the core in twenty minutes,' Jules Caillebot said. 'It's just beyond the second window band. You can see it from here, in fact.'

Thalia had been expecting the core to be buried in the skin of the world, like a subcutaneous implant. 'We can?'

'Let me show you. The new housing's rather elegant, even if I say so myself.'

'That's one opinion,' Parnasse rumbled, just loud enough for Thalia to hear.

They led her to the window. The remaining two kilometres of the endcap curved away below her to merge with the level terrain of the main cylinder. Caillebot, the landscape gardener, stood next to her and pointed into the middle distance. 'There,' he said, whispering. 'You see the first and second window bands? Now focus on the white bridge crossing the second band, close to that kidney-shaped lake. Follow the line of the bridge for a couple of kilometres, until you come to a ring of structures grouped around a single tall talk.'

'I've got it,' Thalia said. Since it lay directly ahead, the stalk was aligned with her local vertical too closely to be coincidence given the three-hundred-and-sixty-degree curvature of the habitat. She had presumably been directed down the appropriate elevator line for a visit to the polling core.

'Remind you of anything?' Caillebot asked.

'I don't know. Maybe. Milk splashing into milk, perhaps. That ring of stalks, with the little spheres on top of each one, and then the tall one in the middle—'

'That's exactly what it is,' Parnasse said. 'A perfect representation of a physical instant. That's the original Museum of Cybernetics. Then the Civic Planning Committee got it into their heads that what it really needed was a gigantic single stalk rising from the middle, to house the polling core in the sphere on top. Completely ruined the purity of the original concept, needless to say. You can't get a central stalk *and* a ring of stalks from a single splash, no matter how hard you try.'

'Why did the core need a new housing?'

'It didn't,' Parnasse said, before anyone else had a chance to contribute. 'It worked fine the way it used to be, out of sight and out of mind. Then the Civic Planning Committee decided we needed to *celebrate* our embracing of true Demarchist principles by making the core a visible symbol that could be seen from anywhere in the habitat.'

'Most people like the new arrangement,' Caillebot said, with a strained smile.

Parnasse wasn't having it. 'You're only saying that because they had to rip out the old gardens to accommodate the new stalk. The ones put in by your rival. You'd feel differently if you actually had to work there.'

Thalia coughed, deciding it was best not to take sides at this point. Moving a core was hardly routine, but Panoply would have been consulted, and if there had been any technical objection it would not have been permitted. 'I need to see it close up, no matter what the controversies,' she said.

'We'll be there in no time at all,' Caillebot said, extending a hand back towards the wall where a row of elevator doors stood open. 'Would you like some help with that equipment? It'll be heavier on the surface.'

'I'll cope,' Thalia said.

Miracle Bird opened its metal beak and emitted a raucous mechanical chime as it took flight and led the way towards the elevators.

CHAPTER 12

Dreyfus held his breath, still anticipating an attack despite the evidence from the scans. The corvette's sensors had probed the rock's embattled surface and revealed no further evidence of active weaponry, although he considered it likely that there were still guns buried in the other hemisphere. The same scans had pinpointed a likely entry point, what appeared to be an airlock leading to some kind of subsurface excavation. The scans could only hint at the depth and extent of the tunnel system. The corvette now lay with its dorsal lock positioned over the surface entry point, separated by only a couple of metres of clear space.

'I can do this alone,' Dreyfus said, ready to push himself through the suitwall. 'We don't both need to go inside.'

'And I'm not babysitting the corvette while you have all the fun,' Sparver replied.

'All right,' Dreyfus said. 'But understand this: if something happens to one of us down there – whether it's you or me – the other one gets out of there as fast as he can and concentrates on warning Panoply. Whatever we're dealing with here, it's bigger than the life of a single prefect.'

'Message received,' Sparver said. 'See you on the other side.'

Dreyfus pushed himself through the grey surface of the suitwall. As always, he felt ticklish resistance as the suit formed around him, conjured into being from the very fabric of the suitwall. He turned around in time to observe Sparver's emergence: seeing the edges of the suit blend into the exterior surface of the suitwall and then pucker free. For a moment, the details of Sparver's suit were blurred and ill-defined, then snapped into sharpness.

The two prefects completed their checks, verifying that their suits were able to talk to each other, and then turned to face the waiting airlock that would allow entry into the rock. Nothing about it surprised Dreyfus, save the fact that it existed in the first place. It was a standard lock, built according to a rugged, inert-matter design. The lock had been hidden before the engagement, tucked away near the base of one of the slug cannons. A concealed shaft must have led down from the surface before the cannons deployed.

There was no need to invoke the manual operating procedure since the lock was still powered and functional. The outer door opened without hesitation, admitting Dreyfus and Sparver to the lock's air-exchange chamber.

'There's pressure on the other side,' Sparver said, indicating the standard-format read-out set into the opposite door. 'There's probably no one inside this thing, but there *might* be, so we can't just blow it wide open.'

It was a complication Dreyfus could have done without, but he concurred with his deputy. They would need to seal the door behind them before they advanced further.

'Close the outer door,' Dreyfus said.

The lock finished pressurising. Dreyfus's suit tasted the air and reported that it was cold but breathable, should the need arise.

He hoped it wouldn't.

'Stay sharp,' he told Sparver. 'We're going deeper.'

Dreyfus waited for the inner door to seal itself before moving off. Common lock protocol dictated both inner and outer doors be closed against vacuum unless someone was transitioning through.

'I can't see a damn thing,' he said, knowing that Sparver's vision was at least as poor as his own. 'I'm switching on my helmet lamp. We'll see if *that*'s a good idea in about two seconds.'

'I'm holding my breath.'

The helmet revealed that they had arrived in a storage area, a repository for tools and replacement machine parts. Dreyfus made out tunnelling gear, some spare airlock components, a couple of racked spacesuits of PreCalvinist design.

'Want to take a guess at how long this junk's been here?' Sparver said, activating his own lamp.

'Could be ten years, could be two hundred,' Dreyfus said. 'Hard to call.'

'You don't pressurise a place if you're planning to mothball it. Waste of air and power.'

'I agree. See anything here that looks like a transmitter, or that might send a signal?'

'No joy.' Sparver nodded his helmet lamp towards the far wall.

'But if I'm not mistaken, that's a doorway. Think we should take a look-see?'

'We're not exactly overwhelmed with choices, are we?'

Dreyfus kicked off from the wall and aimed himself at the far doorway, Sparver following just behind. Doubtless the rock's gravity would eventually have tugged him there, but Dreyfus didn't have time to wait for that. He reached the doorway and sailed on through into a narrow shaft furnished only with rails and flexible hand-grabs. When the air began to impede his forward drift, he grabbed the nearest handhold and started yanking himself forward. The shaft stretched on far ahead of him, pushing deeper into the heart of the rock. Maybe the shaft had been there for ever, he thought: sunk deep into the rock by prospecting Skyjacks, and someone had just come along and used it serendipitously. But the tunnelling equipment he'd already seen didn't have the ramshackle, improvised look of Skyjack tools.

He was just pondering that when he caught sight of the end of the shaft.

'I'm slowing down. Watch out behind me.'

Dreyfus reached the bottom and spun through one hundred and eighty degrees to bring his soles into contact with the surface at the base of the shaft. Up and down still had little meaning in the rock's minimal gravity, but his instincts forced him to orient himself as if his feet were being tugged toward the middle.

He assessed his surroundings as Sparver arrived next to him. They'd come to an intersection with a second shaft that appeared to run horizontally in either direction, curving gently away until it was hidden beyond the limit of the illumination provided by their helmet lamps. The rust-brown tunnel wall was clad with segmented panels, thick braids of pipework and plumbing stapled to the sides. Every now and then the cladding was interrupted by a piece of machinery as rust-brown and ancient-looking as the rest of the tunnel.

'We didn't see deep enough to map this,' Dreyfus said. 'What do you make of it?'

'Not much, to be frank.'

'Judging by the curvature, we could be looking at a ring that goes right around the middle of the rock. We need to find out why it's here.'

'And if we get lost?'

Dreyfus used his suit to daub a luminous cross onto the wall next to their exit point. 'We won't. If the shaft's circular, we'll know when we come back to this point, even if something messes around with our inertial compasses.'

'That's me fully reassured, then.'

'Good. Keep an eye out for anything we can use to squeeze a signal back to Panoply.'

Dreyfus started moving, the brown walls of the shaft drifting past him. His own shadow stalked courageously ahead of him, projected by the light from Sparver's lamp. He glanced down at the suit's inertial map, displayed just below his main facepatch overlay.

'So do you have a theory as to what the Nerval-Lermontov family needs with this place?' Sparver asked. 'Because this is beginning to look like a lot more than a simple case of inter-habitat rivalry, at least from where I'm standing.'

'It's bigger, definitely. And now I'm wondering if the Sylveste family might have a part in this after all.'

'We could always pay them a visit when we're done here.'

'We wouldn't get very far. The family's being run by beta-level caretakers. Calvin Sylveste's dead, and his son's out of the system. The last I heard, he's not due back for at least another ten or fifteen years.'

'But you still think there's a Sylveste angle.'

'I'm all for coincidence, Sparv, and I agree that the family has a lot of tentacles. But as soon as the Eighty popped up in our investigation, I got the feeling there was more to it than chance.'

After a pause, Sparver said, 'Do you think the Nerval-Lermontovs are still around?'

'Someone's been here recently. A place feels different when it's deserted, when no one's visited it for a very long time. I'm not getting that feeling here.'

'I was hoping it was just me,' Sparver said.

Dreyfus set his jaw determinedly. 'All the more reason to investigate, then.'

But in truth he felt no compulsion to continue further along the corridor. He also felt Sparver's unease. There was nothing he would rather have done than return to the corvette and await back-up, however long it took to arrive.

They hadn't gone more than a couple of hundred metres along the gently curving shaft when Sparver brought them to a halt next to a piece of equipment jutting from the wall. To Dreyfus it looked almost indistinguishable from the countless rust-coloured items of machinery they had already passed, but Sparver was paying it particular attention.

'Something we can use?' Dreyfus asked.

Sparver flipped aside a panel, revealing a matrix of tactile input controls and sockets. 'It's a tap-in point,' he said. 'No promises, but if this is hooked up to any kind of local network, I should be able to find my way to the transmitter and maybe open a two-way channel to Panoply.'

'How long will it take?'

Sparver's suit had been conjured with a standard toolkit. He dug into it and retrieved a strand of luminous cabling with a writhing, slug-shaped quickmatter universal adaptor at the end. 'I should know within a few minutes,' he said. 'If it doesn't work, we'll move on.'

'See what you can get out of it. I'll be back here in five or ten minutes.'

Sparver's eyes were wide behind his facepatch. 'We should stay together.'

'I'm just taking a look a little further along this shaft. We'll remain in contact the whole time.'

Dreyfus left his deputy attending to the equipment, fiddling with adaptors and spools of differently coloured froptic and electrical cabling. He had no doubt that if there was a way to get a message to Panoply, Sparver would find it. But he could not afford to wait around for that to happen. Elsewhere in the rock, someone might be erasing evidence or preparing to make their escape via a hidden ship or lifepod.

Eventually Dreyfus looked back and saw that Sparver had vanished around the curve of the shaft.

'How are you doing?' he asked via the suit-to-suit comms channel.

'Making slow progress, but I think it's doable. The protocols are pretty archaic, but nothing I haven't seen before.'

'Good. Keep in touch. I'm pressing on.'

Dreyfus passed through a constriction in the cladding of the tunnel, tucking his elbows in to avoid banging them against the narrow flange where the walls pinched tighter. Looking back now, he could not even see the faint glow caused by the light spilling from Sparver's helmet lamp. Psychologically, it felt as if they were kilometres apart rather than the hundreds of metres that was really the case.

Suddenly there came a bell-like clang, hard and metallic. Dreyfus's gut tightened. He knew exactly what had happened, even before his conscious mind had processed the information. Where the constriction had been was now a solid wall of metal. A bulkhead door – part of an interior airlock system – had just slammed down between him and Sparver.

He returned to the door and checked the rim for manual controls, but found nothing. An automatic system had sealed the door, and the same automatic system would have to open it again.

'Sparver?'

His deputy's voice came through chopped and metallic. 'Still reading you, but faintly. What just happened?'

'I tripped a door,' Dreyfus said, feeling sheepish. 'It doesn't want to open again.'

'Stay where you are. I'll see if I can work it from my side.'

'Leave it for now. We made a plan and we'll stick to it, even if I have to stay here until help arrives. If necessary I should be able to cut through with my whiphound, provided the door doesn't incorporate any active quickmatter. In the meantime I'll try circumnavigating and see if I can meet you from the other side.'

'Try not to trip any more doors on the way.'

'I will.'

'You should think about conserving air,' Sparver said, in a gently reminding tone. 'These m-suits don't recirculate, Boss. You're only good for twenty-six hours.'

'That's about twenty-four hours longer than I expect to be here.'

'Just saying we need to allow for all eventualities. I can make it back to the corvette; you may not be able to.'

'Point taken,' Dreyfus said.

The suit was indeed still assuring him that the air surrounding him was breathable. He clearly had little to lose by trusting it. He reached up and unlatched the helmet; the suit had been conjured in one piece, but it obliged by splitting into familiar components.

He sucked in his first lungful of cold, new air. After the initial shock of it hitting his system, he judged that it was tolerable, with little of the mustiness he'd been anticipating.

'I'm breathing ambient air, Sparv. No ill effects so far.'

'Good. All I've got to do now is kid this system that I'm a valid user, and then we should get ourselves a hotline to Panoply. I'll be out of touch when I'm calling home – I'll have to reassign the suit-to-suit channel to make this work.'

'Whatever you have to do.'

Dreyfus pressed the helmet against his belt until it formed a cusp-like bond. He'd made perhaps another hundred metres of progress when he encountered a junction in the shaft. The main tunnel, the one he'd been following, continued unobstructed ahead, but now it was joined by another route, set at right angles and leading towards the centre of the rock.

'Sparver,' he said, 'slight change of plan. While I'm not using suit air, I'm going to explore a sub-shaft I've just run into. It appears to head deeper. My guess is it leads to whatever this place is concealing.'

'You be careful.'

'As ever.'

The new shaft turned out to be much shorter than the one they'd descended from the surface, and within thirty metres he detected a widening at the far end. Dreyfus continued his approach, caution vying with curiosity, and emerged into a hemispherical chamber set with heavy glass facets. His helmet lamp played across the bolted and welded partitions between the window elements. Beyond the glass loomed a profound darkness, more absolute than space itself, as if the very heart of the rock had been cored out.

'It's hollow, an empty shell,' he said to himself, as much in wonder as perplexity.

The hemispherical chamber was not just some kind of viewing gallery. One of the facets was covered with a sheet of burnished silver rather than glass, and next to that was a simple control panel set with tactile controls of old-fashioned design. Dreyfus propelled himself to the panel and appraised its contents. The chunky controls were designed to be used by someone wearing a spacesuit with thick gloves, and most of them were labelled in antiquated Canasian script. Most of the abbreviations meant nothing to Dreyfus, but he saw that one of the controls was marked with a stylised representation of a sunburst.

His hand moved to the control. At first it was so stiff that he feared it had seized into place. Then it budged with a resounding clunk, and vast banks of lights began to blaze on beyond the armoured glass.

He'd been wrong, he realised. The hollowed-out interior of the Nerval-Lermontov rock was not empty.

It contained a ship.

'I've found something interesting,' he told Sparver.

'What I don't understand,' Thalia said as the train whisked the entourage across the first window band of House Aubusson, 'is how this place pays for itself. No offence, but I've spoken to most of you by now and I'm puzzled. I assume you're a representative slice of the citizenry, or you wouldn't have been selected for the welcoming party. Yet none of you seem to be doing any work that's marketable outside Aubusson. One of you breeds butterflies. Another designs gardens. Another one of you makes mechanical animals, for fun.'

'There's no law against hobbies,' said Paula Thory, the plump butterfly-keeper.

'I totally agree. But hobbies won't pay for the upkeep of a sixty-kilometre-long habitat.'

'We have a full-scale manufactory complex in the trailing endcap,' Caillebot said. 'We used to make ships. Lovely things, too: single-molecule hulls in ruby and emerald. It hasn't run at anything like full capacity for decades, but smaller habitats occasionally contract us to build components and machines. The big enterprises on Marco's Eye will always out-compete us when it comes to efficiency and economies of scale, but we don't have to lift anything out of a gravity well, or pay Glitter Band import duties. That takes care of some of our finances.'

'Not all of it, though,' Thalia said. 'Right?'

'We vote,' Thory said.

'So does everyone,' Thalia replied. 'Except for Panoply.'

'Not everyone votes the way we do. That's the big difference. There are eight hundred thousand people in this habitat, and each and every one of us takes our voting rights very seriously indeed.'

'Still won't put food on your plates.'

'It will if you vote often enough, and intelligently enough.' Thory was looking at Thalia quite intently now, as the train whisked through a campus of low-lying buildings, all of which had the softened outlines and pastel coloration of candied marshmallows. 'You're Panoply. I presume you're adequately familiar with the concept of vote weighting?'

'I recall that the mechanism allows it, under certain circumstances.'

Thory looked surprised. 'You "recall". Aren't you supposed to be the expert here, Prefect?'

'Ask me about security, or about polling core software, and I'll keep you enthralled for hours. Vote processing is a different area. That's not my remit.' Thalia had her hands laced in her lap, with the cylinder between her knees. 'So tell me how it works for Aubusson.'

'It's common knowledge that the apparatus logs every vote ever entered, across the entire Glitter Band,' Thory said. 'That's at least a million transactions every second, going back two hundred years. What people don't generally realise is that the system occasionally peers back into its own records and looks at voting patterns that shaped a particular outcome. Suppose, for instance, that a critical vote was put to the population of the entire Band, all hundred million of us. A hypothetical threat had been identified, one that could be met with a variety of responses ranging from a pre-emptive attack to the simple decision to do nothing at all. Suppose furthermore that the majority voted for one particular response out of the options available. Suppose also that action was taken based on that vote, and that with hindsight that action turned out to have been the wrong thing to do. The apparatus is intelligent enough to recognise democratic mistakes like that. It's also intelligent enough to look back into the records and see who voted otherwise. Who, in other words, could be said to have been right, while the majority were wrong.'

Thalia nodded, recalling details she had once learned and then buried under more immediately relevant knowledge. 'And then, having identified those voters as being of shrewd judgement, it attaches a weighting bias to any future votes they might cast.'

'In essence, that's how it works. In practice, it's infinitely more subtle. The system keeps monitoring those individuals, constantly tuning the appropriate weighting factor. If they keep on voting shrewdly, then their weighting remains, or even increases. If they show a sustained streak of bad judgement, the system weights them back down to the default value.'

'Why not just remove their voting rights entirely, if they're that bad?'

'Because then we wouldn't be a democracy,' Thory replied. 'Everyone deserves a chance to mend their ways.'

'And how does this work for Aubusson?'

'It's how we make our living. The citizenry here possesses a very high number of weighted votes, well above the Glitter Band mean. We've all worked hard for that, of course: it isn't just a statistical fluctuation. I have a weighting index of one point nine, which means that every vote I cast has nearly double its normal efficacy. I'm almost equivalent to two people voting in lockstep on any issue. One point nine is high, but there are fifty-four people out there who have indices nudging three. These are people whom the system has identified as possessing an almost superhuman acumen. Most of us see the landscape of future events as a bewilderingly jumbled terrain, cloaked in a mist of ever-shifting possibilities. The Triples see a shining road, its junctions marked in blazing neon.' Thory's voice became reverential. 'Somewhere out there, Prefect, is a being we call the Quadruple. We know he walks amongst us because the system says he is a citizen of House Aubusson. But the Quad has never revealed himself to any other citizen. Perhaps he fears a public stoning. His own wisdom must be a wonderful and terrifying gift, like the curse of Cassandra. Yet he still only carries four votes, in a population of a hundred million. Pebbles on an infinite beach.'

'Tell me how you stay ahead of the curve,' Thalia said.

'With blood, sweat and toil. All of us take our issues seriously. That's what citizenship in Aubusson entails. You don't get to live here unless you can hold a weighted voting average above one point two five. That means we're all required to think very seriously about the issues we vote on. Not just from a personal perspective, not just from the perspective of House Aubusson, but from the standpoint of the greater good of the entire Glitter Band. And it pays off for us, of course. It's how we make our living – by trading on our prior shrewdness. Because our votes are disproportionately effective, we are *very* attractive to lobbyists from other communities. On marginal issues, they pay us to listen to what they have to say, knowing that a block vote from Aubusson may swing the result by a critical factor. That's where the money comes from.'

'Political bribes?'

'Hardly. They buy our attention, our willingness to listen. That doesn't guarantee that we will vote according to their wishes. If all we did was follow the money, our collective indices would ramp down to one before you could blink. Then we'd be no use to anyone.'

'It's a balancing act,' put in Caillebot. 'To remain useful to the lobbyists, we must maintain a degree of independence from them.

This is the central paradox of our existence. But it is the paradox that allows me to spend my time designing gardens, and Paula to breed her butterflies.'

Thory leaned forward. 'Since we've been on this train, I've already participated in two polling transactions. There's a third coming up in two minutes. Minor issues, in the scheme of things – the kinds of things most citizens let their predictive routines take care of.'

'I didn't notice.'

'You wouldn't have. Most of us are so used to the process now that it's almost autonomic, like blinking. But we take each and every vote as seriously as the last.' Thory must have seen something amiss in Thalia's expression, for she leaned forward concernedly. 'Everything I've just described is completely legal, Prefect. Panoply wouldn't allow it to happen otherwise.'

'I know it's legal. I just didn't think it had become systematized, made the basis for a whole community.'

'Does that distress you?'

'No,' Thalia answered truthfully. 'If the system allows it, it's fine by me. But it just reminds me how many surprises the Glitter Band still has in store.'

'This is the most complex, variegated society in human history,' Thory said. 'It's a machine for surprising people.'

Dreyfus studied the spectacle of the ship floating before him, pinned in the vivid blue lights at the core of the Nerval-Lermontov rock. It was a midnight-black form in a pitch-black cavern. He did not so much see the ship as detect the subtle gradation in darkness between its hull and the background surface of the rock's hollowed-out heart. It was like an exercise in optical trickery, a perceptual mirage that kept slipping out of his cognitive grasp.

But he knew exactly what he was looking at. Though it was smaller than most, the vehicle was clearly a starship. It had the sleek, tapering hull of a lighthugger, and the two swept-back spars that held the complicated nacelles of its twin drives. He remembered the burning wreck of the *Accompaniment of Shadows*, its own engines snipped off to become prizes for other Ultras. But as soon as its shape stabilised in his imagination, he knew that this was no Ultra starship.

Dreyfus smiled to himself. He'd felt the scope of the investigation widening the moment a connection to the Eighty entered the frame. But nothing had prepared him for this shift in perspective.

'Keep talking to me, Boss. I'm still on the line.'

'There's a Conjoiner ship here. It's just sitting in the middle of the rock.'

Sparver paused before answering. Dreyfus could imagine him working through the ramifications of the discovery.

'Remind me: what have Conjoiners got to do with our case?'

'That's what I'm very eager to find out.'

'How did the ship get where it is?'

'No idea. Can't see any sign of a door in the chamber, and there definitely wasn't one on the outside. Almost looks as if it's been walled-up in here, encased in rock.'

'You think the Conjoiners hid it here for a reason?'

Dreyfus brushed his hand over the control panel again. 'I don't think so. Apart from the ship itself, nothing in the rock looks Conjoiner. It's more as if the ship's being held here by someone else.'

'Someone managed to capture and contain a Conjoiner ship? That's a pretty good trick in anyone's book.'

'I agree,' Dreyfus said.

'Next question: why would anyone do that? What would they hope to gain?'

Dreyfus looked at the one facet in the chamber that was burnished silver and realised that it was a sealed door rather than an opaque panel in the bank of windows. The chamber's illumination traced the ribbed tube of a docking connector, stretching across space from the door panel to meet the light-sucking hull of the ship.

'That's what I'm going to have to go aboard to find out.'

'I don't think that's a good idea, Boss.'

Dreyfus turned to the panel again. Every cell in his body was screaming at him to leave. But the policeman in him had to know what was inside that ship; what secret was worth murdering to protect.

His hand alighted on another toggle control, this one marked {X} – the universal symbol for an airlock actuator. The silver panel whisked aside silently and smoothly. Sensing his intentions, lights came on in sequence along the connector. The golden band arced down until it vanished into a docking port on the side of the lighthugger.

Nothing now prevented him from boarding.

'I'm going inside. Call me back as soon as you get through to Panoply.'

While Thalia had been talking with her House Aubusson companions, they had crossed another window band spanning a brief ocean of space and stars (most of which were in fact other habitats), and now the train was slowing as it neared its destination. They crossed a series of manicured lawns, skimming high above them on a filigreed wisp of a bridge, then descended back down to ground level. On either side, Thalia saw the tapering stalks of the Museum of Cybernetics, each structure rising at least a hundred metres into the air, each surmounted by a smooth blue-grey sphere, each sphere marked with a symbol from the hallowed history of information processing. There was the ampersand, which had once symbolised a primitive form of abstraction. There was an ever-tumbling hourglass, still the universal symbol for an active computational process. There was the apple with a chunk missing, which (so Thalia had been led to believe) commemorated the suicidal poisoning of the info-theorist Turing himself.

The train plunged into a tunnel, then slowed to a smooth halt in a plaza under the central stalk of the polling core. People came and went from trains parked at adjoining platforms, but Thalia's party had an entire section of the station to themselves, screened off by servitors and glass barriers. They rode escalators into hazy daylight, surrounded by the ornamental gardens and rock pools clustering around the base of the main stalk. Nearby, a bright blue servitor was diligently trimming a hedge into the shape of a peacock, its cutting arms moving with lightning speed as it executed the three-dimensional template in its memory.

Thalia craned her head back to take in the entirety of the stalk. It rose from a gradually steepening skirt, climbing five or six hundred metres above the ground before tapering to a neck that appeared only just capable of supporting the main sphere. The sphere was much larger than those balanced on the smaller stalks, banded with tiny round windows where they were blank. Geometric shapes were in constant play on its surface, indicating – so Thalia guessed – the changing parameters of abstraction flow and voting patterns.

Thalia's party walked into the shaded lobby of the stalk. The structure appeared to be hollow, its inward-leaning interior walls given over to towering murals, each of which depicted a great visionary of the PreCalvinist cybernetic era. A thick column rose up through the middle of the dizzying space, buttressed to the walls by filigreed arches. That had to be the main data conduit, Thalia judged, carrying abstraction services and voting packets to the polling core high above her head. The citizens here might not be as thoroughly integrated into abstraction as those in New Seattle-Tacoma, but their enthusiasm for the voting process would nonetheless ensure hefty data traffic. Thalia imagined the flow of information in the pipe, like high-pressure water searching for a loose rivet or leaky valve. Rising next to the column, but separated from it by a few metres of clear space, was the thinner tube of an elevator shaft, with a spiral walkway wrapped around it in ever-receding vertigo-inducing loops. The data conduit, elevator shaft and spiral staircase plunged through the ceiling at the top of the stalk, into the sphere that sat above it.

Thalia knew she was rubbernecking, that even this tower would have been considered unimpressive by Chasm City standards, but the locals looked happy that she was impressed.

'It's an ugly big bastard all right,' Parnasse said, which was presumably his way of showing a fragment of civic pride.

'We go up?' Thalia asked.

Paula Thory nodded. 'We go up. The elevator should already be waiting for us.'

'Good,' Thalia said. 'Then let's get this done so we can all go home.'

Not for the first time in his life, Sparver found himself cursing the inadequacy of his hands. It was not because there was anything wrong with them from a hyperpig's point of view, but because he had to live in a world made for dextrous baseline humans, with long fingers and thumbs and an absurd volume of sensorimotor cortex dedicated to using them. The stubby, gauntleted fingers of his trotter-like hands kept pushing two keys at once, forcing him to backtrack and initiate the command sequence all over again. At last he succeeded, and heard a chirp in his helmet signifying that he was in contact with Panoply, albeit on a channel not normally used for field communications.

'Internal Prefect Muang,' a voice announced. 'You have reached Panoply. How may I be of assistance?'

Sparver knew and liked Muang. A small, stocky man himself, with looks that were at best unconventional, he had no conspicuous problem with hyperpigs.

'This is Sparver. Can you hear me?'

'Loud and clear. Is something wrong?'

'You could say that. Prefect Dreyfus and I were investigating a free-floating rock owned by Nerval-Lermontov, as part of a case we're working. As we were making our final approach the rock opened fire on our corvette and took out our long-range communications.'

'The rock attacked you?'

'There were heavy anti-ship weapons concealed under its surface. They popped out and started shooting at us.'

'My God.'

'I know. Don't you just hate it when that happens? Thing is, we could use some assistance out here.'

'Where are you now?'

'I'm patching in via a transmitter inside the rock itself, but I don't know how long this link is going to hold up.'

'Copy, Sparver. With luck we can rustle up a deep-system vehicle. Do you need a medical team? Are either of you injured?'

'We're separated from each other, but otherwise both okay. If I could put Dreyfus through, I would, but it's all I can do to rig this connection from my own suit.'

'Is your ship flightworthy?'

'We could limp home if we had to, but it would be better if Panoply sent out a couple of heavy ships to pick over this place.'

'Do you have orbital data for this rock?'

'Aboard the ship. But all you have to do is check the assets of the Nerval-Lermontov family. We're sitting on a two-kilometre-wide lump of unprocessed rock in the middle orbits. You should be able to image our corvette, even if you can't pick out the debris cloud from the attack.'

'Should narrow it down. Sit tight and I'll get the wheels moving.'

'Tell those ships to come in cautiously. And make sure they know Dreyfus and I are sitting inside this thing, in case anyone gets trigger-happy.'

'I'll get the message through immediately. You shouldn't have to wait more than an hour.'

'I'm not going anywhere,' Sparver said.

He closed the link and re-established contact with Dreyfus, glad when he heard his laboured breathing coming through nice and regularly, as if Dreyfus was pulling himself along a docking connector.

'I got through, Boss. Cavalry's coming.'

'Good.'

'So now might be the time to rethink that plan of yours to board the ship.'

'I'm nearly there. Might as well go all the way, after coming this far.' Dreyfus took deep breaths between sentences. 'There's no telling what mechanisms might kick in to destroy evidence if the rock senses our intrusion.'

'Or which might kick in to destroy us. That's also a possibility.'

'I'm still going in. I suggest you return to the corvette and await the back-up.'

That sounded like an excellent idea to Sparver as well, but he had no intention of abandoning Dreyfus inside the rock. Besides, what his boss had just said was equally applicable to the data stored in the rock's router log.

It did not take very long, now that he knew his way around the architecture. But when the list of outgoing message addresses spilled across his facepatch, he assumed there must be some mistake. He'd been expecting hundreds, even thousands, of entries in the last hundred days. But there were only a few dozen. Whoever was controlling the Nerval-Lermontov rock had been very sparing with their usage.

Looking down the list, he recognised the address of the Ruskin-Sartorious sphere, with a timetag corresponding to just before the attack by the *Accompaniment of Shadows*. That was the message that had prompted Delphine to break off negotiations with Dravidian. Yet as pleasing as it was to see that in the log – confirmation that they'd been following the right leads – it was dismaying to see some of the other entries.

There were about a dozen different addresses Sparver didn't recognise off the top of his head. But there were another dozen entries that were shockingly familiar.

They consisted of two different addresses, interspersed randomly. Apart from the last three digits, one was identical to the format he'd just used to contact Muang.

Someone had been using the Nerval-Lermontov rock to call Panoply.

But if anything it was the second of the two addresses that unnerved Sparver the most. He recognised it instantly, for it was still fresh in his mind from his most recent investigation. But it had no business being any part of this one.

It was the address of House Perigal.

'This doesn't make sense,' he said, mouthing the words in something more than a whisper. 'There's no connection. The cases don't belong together.'

But there was no mistake. The numbers weren't going away.

'You still there, Boss?'

'I'm nearly at the airlock. What's up?'

'I don't know. I've just discovered something that doesn't make any sense.'

'Tell me.'

'Someone used this rock to contact House Perigal.'

'You mean Ruskin-Sartorious,' Dreyfus said testily.

'No, I mean exactly what I just said. There've only been a handful of outgoing messages, but they include transmissions to both Panoply and House Perigal, in addition to Ruskin-Sartorious. That means there's a connection between the two cases, *and* a Panoply connection.'

'There can't be,' Dreyfus said.

'The evidence is staring right back at me. There's a link.'

'But Perigal was an open-and-shut case of polling fraud. It has no bearing on the murder of Ruskin-Sartorious.'

'Boss, we may not be able to understand the link, but I'm telling you it exists. We already know this case is bigger than a simple incident of revenge or assassination – we'd figured that much out before you went and found a Conjoiner ship buried inside this rock.' Sparver paused: he could feel something behind his eyes trying to come into clarity, but not quite succeeding. 'We went after Perigal because of voting fraud,' he said. 'We nailed her, too, and all along it felt too easy.'

'Too much like a debt being settled,' Dreyfus said, echoing Sparver's tone.

'Maybe what we should be focusing on is the consequence of that case. Not the fact that Perigal's under lockdown, but the security hole it drew our attention to.'

He heard a silence on the end of the line. Then: 'We're closing that hole, Sparv. That's what Thalia's doing.'

'That's what we *think* she's doing. But what if we've been led up the garden path?'

'We can trust Thalia,' Dreyfus said.

'Boss, we don't have time to think through all the implications.

All we know is that something's wrong, and that, knowingly or otherwise, Thalia may be a part of it.'

'You're right,' Dreyfus said eventually. 'I don't like it, but ... something doesn't fit.'

'Thalia's still out there, isn't she?'

'As far as I know.'

'We have to get a message to her. She has to stop those upgrades until we figure out what's going on.'

'Can you contact Panoply again?'

'No reason why not,' Sparver said. 'But it'll mean me dropping out of contact with you again until I'm done.'

'Do it immediately. Call me back when you've got word to Thalia. Do it now, Sparv.'

He closed the connection with Dreyfus and re-established the jury-rigged link with Panoply.

'I wasn't expecting to hear from you again so soon,' Muang said, before Sparver could get a word in. 'Good news is Jane expedited immediate retasking of a deep-system vehicle. It's on high-burn as we speak. Should be on your position inside forty-five minutes.'

'Good,' Sparver said, barely hearing what Muang had to say. 'Now listen to me. Has Deputy Field Ng returned from her mission?'

There was no need to elaborate. Everyone in Panoply knew of Jason Ng's daughter.

'I don't know. I can check with Thyssen, but—'

'Never mind, there isn't time. Can you patch me through to Thalia? I need to talk to her urgently.'

'Wait a moment. I'll see what I can do.'

Sparver did not breathe. It could only have been tens of seconds before Muang spoke again, but it felt like hours. 'She isn't aboard her cutter, which is currently docked at House Aubusson. I'm trying to contact her through her bracelet, but if she's out of range of the cutter, the transmission will have to be routed through the habitat's own abstraction services. This may take a moment—'

'No one's going anywhere,' Sparver said.

After another eternity, Muang said, 'I'm picking up her bracelet, Deputy. It's ringing. If she's wearing it, she'll hear you.'

Dreyfus slowed his passage along the tube, gripped by an almost overwhelming urge to turn back. But he focused his resolve and continued until he reached the black wall of the entry lock. There was no suggestion of a door. He touched the armour of the

Conjoiner ship and felt it ease inwards under the pressure of his fingers. It was neither metal nor ordinary quickmatter.

The only visible controls consisted of a smaller version of the panel he had already used. It had been glued to the side of the hull, fixed into place by crusty dabs of bright green adhesive. There were only two toggles. Dreyfus reached for the one marked with the airlock symbol and gave it a hefty twist. After a moment, a luminous blue outline appeared in the black, defining the rectangular shape of a door. The outline thickened, and then the entire rectangular part pushed outwards and sideways, unassisted by any visible mechanisms or hinges.

Dreyfus pushed himself into the interior of the Conjoiner vehicle. He looked back, holding his breath until he was satisfied that the rectangular door was not going to seal him in. He followed a winding, throat-like corridor until he reached a junction. Five corridors converged on this point, arriving from different angles. Light – of a peculiar blue-green sickliness – was leaking down one of the routes. The others were singularly dark and uninviting, and appeared to feed back towards the rear of the ship.

He followed the light. When he estimated that he had moved twenty or thirty metres towards the bow, he found himself emerging into a very large room. The light, which had appeared bright from a distance, now revealed itself to be meagre, obscuring detail and scale. Dreyfus unfixed his helmet from its bonded connection with his belt and used the crown lamp to investigate his surroundings. His illumination glanced off steely surfaces, glass partitions and intricate tangles of plumbing.

That was when he felt something cold and sharp press against his naked throat.

'There are lights, for emergency use,' a woman's voice said, speaking very calmly into his ear. 'I shall bring them on now.'

Dreyfus kept very still. In his lower peripheral vision he could see the gauntleted knuckle of a hand. The hand was holding a blade. The blade was tight against his Adam's apple.

The lights came on at full strength, yellow shading to pale green, and after a few moments of blinking in the sudden brightness Dreyfus saw a room full of sleepers, wired into complicated apparatus. There were dozens of them, eighty or ninety easily, maybe more. They'd been arranged in four long rows spaced equidistantly around an openwork catwalk. The sleepers did not lie in closed caskets, but rather on couches, to which they were bound by black restraining straps and webs of silver meshwork. Transparent lines ran in and out of their bodies, pulsing not just with what Dreyfus presumed to be blood and saline but with vividly coloured chemicals of obscure function. The sleepers were all naked and they were all breathing, yet so slowly that Dreyfus had to study the rise and fall of a single chest intently before he convinced himself that he was looking at anything other than a corpse. It was sleep dialled down almost all the way to death. He could make out nothing of their heads, for each sleeper wore a perfectly spherical black helmet sealed tight around the neck, which in turn sprouted a thick ribbed black cable from its crown, connected into a socket recessed into the adjoining wall. The impression of a room full of faceless human components, smaller parts plugged into a larger machine, was total.

The knife was still pressing against his throat.

'Who are you?' he asked, speaking quietly, fearful of moving his throat.

'Who are you?' the woman asked back.

There was no reason for subterfuge. 'Field Prefect Tom Dreyfus, of Panoply.'

'Don't try anything rash, Prefect. This knife cuts very well. If you doubt me, take a look around you.'

'At what?'

'The sleepers. See what I've done to them.'

He followed her instruction. He saw what she meant.

Not all of the sleepers were whole.

The confusion of restraints, surgical lines and helmets had hidden the truth at first. But once Dreyfus had become accustomed to the fact of the sleepers, and the mechanisms that sustained them, he realised that many of them were incomplete. Some were missing hands and arms, others lower legs or the whole limb. Perhaps a third of the sleepers had suffered a loss of some kind. Dreyfus started thinking back to the wars the Conjoiners had been involved in – perhaps this ship had been carrying the injured from one of those engagements, waylaid on their passage to the Conjoiner equivalent of a hospital.

But that couldn't be the answer. This ship had probably been here for decades, and yet the injuries looked fresh. Some form of turquoise salve had been spread over the wounds, but beneath the salve the stumps were still raw. The sleepers hadn't even received basic field care, let alone the emergency regenerative medicine that the Conjoiners should have been able to utilize.

'I don't understand—' he began.

'I did it,' the woman said. 'I cut them. I cut them all.'

'Why?' Dreyfus asked.

'To eat them,' she said, sounding amazed at his question. 'What other reason would there have been?'

CHAPTER 13

Thalia found herself once again confronting a waiting polling core. She was somewhere in the sphere: most likely on a floor about halfway up its hundred-metre diameter, judging by the spacious dimensions of the room housing the machinery. Large porthole-shaped windows ringed the enormous space. The beige walls were covered in mazelike white patterns derived from the designs of early integrated circuits. A number of chairs and tables had been provided for the comfort of the visitors. The furniture was all safely inert; no quickmatter was permitted near a polling core, save that essential for the functioning of the core itself. The core was a pearl-coloured cylinder rising from the middle of the floor and piercing the ceiling, surrounded by a low metal railing. Resting on a heavy-looking plinth just outside the railinged area was a glass-cased architectural model of the Museum of Cybernetics, rendered with sterile precision.

Thalia had already explained what she would have to do; that if everything went to plan she would be on her way within less than twenty minutes; that at most her guests could expect a subliminal interruption in their access to abstraction. She had already examined the core and satisfied herself that there would be no surprises once she had opened the access window. 'Really,' she said, in her best self-deprecating tone, 'it's not all that interesting. If it was serious, they wouldn't entrust it to just one field prefect.'

'I'm sure you're understating your abilities,' said Caillebot, lounging in a blocky blue chair, one leg hooked over the other.

'All I'm saying is, if you don't want to hang around and see me mutter a few boring incantations, I won't be offended. I know my way down now. If you want to wait by those goldfish ponds, I can find you when I'm done.'

'If it doesn't inconvenience you, I think we'd all like to stay,' Paula Thory said, looking to the others for support. 'It's not often we see the beating heart of the voting apparatus laid open for examination.'

Thalia scratched at her damp collar. 'If you want to stick around, I have no problem with that. I'm about ready to begin.'

'Do what you must, Prefect,' Thory said.

She opened the cylinder, conscious of the eyes on her, and retrieved the last of the four one-time pads. 'I'm going to read out three magic words here. They'll give me access to the core for six hundred seconds. There's no going back once I've initiated that window, so it'd be best if I'm not interrupted unless absolutely necessary. Of course, I'll keep you informed about what's happening.'

'We appreciate the gesture. Please, continue your work and don't pay any heed to us,' Caillebot said.

Thalia stepped through a gap in the surrounding railing, placed her cylinder on the ground and faced the flickering pillar of the core. She cleared her throat. 'This is Deputy Field Prefect Thalia Ng. Acknowledge security access override Hickory Crepuscule Ivory.'

'Override confirmed,' answered the core. 'You now have six hundred seconds of clearance, Deputy Field Prefect Ng.'

Thalia removed the final upgrade diskette from her cylinder. 'I'm going to insert this into the core,' she said. 'It contains new software instructions to cover a minor security loophole identified by Panoply.'

She had the core present a data-entry slot for her use. She pushed the thick diskette into the pillar, then stood back while the machine digested its contents. Thalia was anxious, but not nervous. She had run into difficulties in Carousel New Seattle-Tacoma, but all her instincts assured her that nothing like that would happen here.

'The diskette contains a data fragment,' the core said. 'What do you wish me to do with this data fragment?'

Thalia started to answer, but at that moment her bracelet began chiming. She lifted her cuff and glared at it in irritation. What was Prefect Muang trying to reach her about, now of all times? Muang was not one of the bastards who gave her grief about her father, but he wasn't Dreyfus or Sparver, or one of the senior prefects she was doing her best to impress. Whatever he was calling about, it could not possibly be that urgent. Certainly not urgent enough to interrupt a sensitive field upgrade, especially now that she'd actually opened the six-hundred-second access window.

She would call him back when she was done. The world wasn't

going to end because she kept Muang waiting for a few minutes.

'I'm sorry,' Thalia said, squeezing the suppress button.

The core repeated its enquiry. 'The diskette contains a data fragment. What do you wish me to do with this data fragment?'

Thalia pulled down her cuff. 'Use it to overwrite the contents of executable data segment alpha alpha five one six, please.'

'Just a moment.' Lights flashed while the pillar cogitated. 'I am ready to execute the overwrite order. I anticipate that the operation will entail a brief loss of abstraction, not exceeding three microseconds. Please confirm that the overwrite order is to be executed.'

'Confirm,' Thalia said.

'The executable data segment has now been overwritten. Abstraction was down for two point six eight microseconds. All affected transactions were buffered and have now been successfully reinstated. A level-one audit indicates no software conflicts have arisen as a result of this installation. Do you have further instructions for me?'

'No,' Thalia said. 'That will be all.'

'There are four hundred and eleven seconds remaining on your access window. Do you wish the window to remain open until its scheduled termination, or shall I invoke immediate closure?'

'You can close. We're done here.'

'Access is now terminated. Thank you for your visit, Deputy Field Prefect Thalia Ng.'

'It's been a pleasure.' After retrieving the upgrade diskette from the pillar, Thalia snapped it back into the cylinder and then sealed the cylinder itself. She tried to keep her composure, but now that she was done, she could not help but feel a giddy elation. It was a little like being drunk on an empty stomach. *I did it!* she thought. She had completed all four installations. All on her own, without Dreyfus looking over her shoulder, without even the benefit of another field agent to help her with the technical workload. If anyone had ever doubted her abilities, or wondered how well she would function outside a team context, this would silence them. *I, Thalia Ng, not only designed the security plug, I field-installed it myself, by hand, with just a cutter for company.*

Four habitats completed. The plan had been executed. And now that she had satisfied herself that the upgrade was robust by installing it in four worst-case examples, there was nothing to stop her going live across the entire Glitter Band, all ten thousand habitats.

Bring them on, Thalia thought, and then worked very hard to wipe the look of self-satisfaction from her face as she turned to her audience again, because it would be neither seemly nor dignified in a prefect.

'Is there a problem?' Jules Caillebot asked, still sitting in the blue armchair but no longer in the relaxed pose of a few minutes earlier.

'Not from my end,' Thalia said. 'It all went like a dream. Thanks for your cooperation.' Maybe Muang had been calling her to inform her of a temporary comms blackout, she thought. It happened sometimes. Nothing to worry about. 'You know what? Now that we're done, maybe I will take a walk in some of the gardens after all.'

'Abstraction is down,' Caillebot said quietly.

Thalia felt the first itch of wrongness. 'I'm sorry?'

'We have no abstraction. You said it would be off-line for a few microseconds, too short to notice. But it's still down.' His voice became firmer and louder. 'Abstraction is down, Prefect. *Abstraction is down.*'

Thalia shook her head. 'You're mistaken. It can't be down.'

'There is no abstraction,' Paula Thory said, standing up from her own chair. 'We're out of contact, Prefect. Something appears to have gone wrong.'

'The system ran an audit on itself. It confirmed that abstraction had only been interrupted for an instant. The system doesn't make mistakes.'

'Then why were you here in the first place, if it wasn't to correct a failing in the apparatus?' asked Caillebot.

'Maybe it's just us,' said Broderick Cuthbertson. His mechanical owl twitched its head in all directions, as if following the flight of an invisible wasp.

'Your bird's confused,' Cyrus Parnasse said. 'I'm guessing it depends on abstraction to orient itself.'

Cuthbertson comforted his creation with a finger-stroke. 'Easy, boy.'

'Then it's at least everyone – *everything* – in this building,' Thory said, colour draining from her cheeks. 'What if it's not just the building? What if we're looking at a major outage across the whole campus?'

'Let's look out of the windows,' said Meriel Redon. 'We can see half of Aubusson from here.'

They were paying no attention to Thalia. She was just a detail in the room. For now. She walked behind them as they stood from their chairs and sofas and stools – those who weren't already standing – and dashed to the row of portholes, two or three of them crowding behind each circular pane.

'I can see people down in the park,' said a clean-shaven young man whose name Thalia didn't remember. He wore an electric-blue suit with frilled black cuffs. 'They're behaving oddly. Clumping together all of a sudden, as if they want to talk. Some of them are starting to run for the exits. They're looking up, at us.'

'They know there's a problem,' Thory said. 'It's no wonder they're looking up at the polling core. They're wondering what the hell's happening.'

'There's a train stopped on the line,' said a woman in a flame-red dress, standing at another porthole. 'It's the other side of the nearest window band. Whatever this is, it isn't local. It isn't just happening to us, or to the museum.'

'There's a volantor,' someone else said. 'It's making an emergency landing on the roof of the Bailter Ziggurat. That's two whole bands towards the leading cap. Nearly ten kilometres!'

'It's the whole habitat,' Thory said, as if she'd just seen a fearful omen. 'The whole of House Aubusson, all sixty kilometres of it. Eight hundred thousand people have just lost abstraction for the first time in their lives.'

'This can't be happening,' Thalia whispered.

The knife was still hard against Dreyfus's throat. He cursed himself for not donning the helmet when he'd had the chance. He tried to reason that the woman would have killed him by now if that was her intention, but he could think of a multitude of reasons why she might want to keep him talking now and kill him later.

'What year is it?' she asked, as if the question had just popped into her head.

'What *year*?'

The pressure of the knife increased. 'Is there a problem with my diction?'

'No,' Dreyfus said hastily. 'Not at all. The year is two thousand, four hundred and twenty-seven. Why do you ask?'

'Because I've been inside this place a very long time.'

'Long enough to lose track of the year?'

'Long enough to lose track of everything. I had my suspicions, though.' He caught a note of proud defiance in her voice. 'I wasn't so very far off the mark.'

He'd still not seen her face, or any part of her save the gauntleted hand holding the knife. 'Are you a member of the Nerval-Lermontov family?' he asked.

'Is that who you are looking for?'

'I'm not looking for anyone in particular. I'm a policeman. I'm investigating a crime. My inquiries brought me to this asteroid.'

'Alone?'

'I came in a ship, with my deputy. We were attacked during our approach and the ship was damaged. We could have limped back to Panoply, but we decided to see if we could use the rock to get a message to them quicker. That's what my deputy's doing now. I also wanted to see what was worth attacking us to protect.'

The knife scratched against his skin. It felt cold. He wondered if it had drawn blood yet.

'You've seen it now,' the woman said, obviously meaning the ship in which they were floating. 'Tell me what you make of it.'

'It's a Conjoiner spacecraft. That's as much as I was able to tell from outside. I came aboard and I've seen *this*.' He meant the room full of dismembered sleepers, the ones that the woman said she had been eating. 'That's all. Now are you going to tell me what this means?'

'Try moving,' she said. 'Move an arm or a leg. I won't stop you.'

Dreyfus tried, but although he could move his limbs, they encountered stiff resistance against the interior of his suit. He was effectively paralysed.

'I can't.'

'I've reached into your suit and disabled its motor and communication functions. I can turn them on and off as easily as I can blink. With the suit immobilised like that, you won't be able to move or remove it. You'll starve here and die. It would take a long time and it would not be pleasant.'

'Why are you telling me this?'

'So that you understand, Prefect. So that you grasp that I have complete control over you.' The pressure from the knife eased. 'So that you understand that I don't need *this* to kill you.'

Her hand pulled away.

'You must be a Conjoiner,' he said. 'No one else could perform a trick like that.' When she offered neither confirmation nor denial, he said, 'You must be from this ship. Am I right?'

'So you are not completely incapable of deductive reasoning. For one of the retarded, you must be quite bright.'

'I'm just a prefect trying to do my job. Are you being held captive here?'

'What do you think?' she asked, with acid sarcasm.

'Let's establish some ground rules. I'm not your enemy. If someone is keeping you here against your will, I want to find out who they are and why they're doing it. We're on the same side. We should be able to trust each other.'

'Shall I tell you why I have difficulty trusting you, Prefect? A man like you came here already. He saw what was being done to us and did nothing.'

'What do you mean, a man like me?'

'He wore the same kind of suit.'

'That doesn't mean anything.'

'I mean *exactly* the same kind. If a prefect is what you are, then this man was a prefect as well.'

'That's not possible,' Dreyfus said. But even as he spoke he recalled the link that Sparver had found connecting this rock to Panoply. Could someone else have come here, making independent inquiries? Perhaps. But if so, how could Jane Aumonier not have known about it?

'I saw him myself. There was no mistake. I could not see into his head, and I can't see into yours. Your kind never carry neural implants, do they?'

His own voice sounded distant and strangulated. 'This man ... does he come on his own, or are there others?'

'Only the man comes in person. But there are other visitors.'

'You're confusing me.'

'That is because they confuse me. I know when the man comes because I sense the electromagnetic noise from the opening and closing of airlocks. I sense his suit, although I can never get close enough to paralyse him. But the others don't arrive like that. Suddenly they are simply *here*, like a change in the wind. One in particular makes her presence very clear to me. She likes to walk in our heads, as if she is taking a stroll through an ornamental garden. She toys with us. She takes pleasure in our confinement, in our distress.'

'You're talking about an artificial intelligence, then. A beta-level simulation, something like that. A simulacrum that looks and acts like a real person, but has no interior life.'

'No,' the Conjoiner said carefully. 'I am talking about something vastly more than that. A mind like a thundercloud, brimming with terrible lightning, terrible darkness. It was never a beta-level simulation. It has the structure of human consciousness, but warped, magnified, perverted. Like a mansion gone wrong, a great house turned evil.'

'Does she have a name?'

'One,' the Conjoiner affirmed. 'She professes to hide her true identity from us, but I have seen through her concealments. She is too vain to hide herself perfectly. She desires to be known, I think.'

Dreyfus hardly dared ask. 'Tell me the name.'

'She calls herself Aurora.'

'I made no mistake,' Thalia said. 'I swear I did everything by the book.'

Thory's eyes had shrunk to nasty little dots. 'Then maybe the book is wrong. Every second that we don't have abstraction will cost our standing with the lobbyists. You have no idea of the financial hurt I'm talking about. Each and every one of us is a stakeholder in Aubusson society. Damage the habitat's finances and you damage us. That means *me*, personally.'

Thalia's voice had become absurdly timid and small. She felt like a schoolgirl being required to explain late homework. 'I don't know what the problem is.'

'Then perhaps you should start investigating!' Thory glared at her with venomous intent. 'You broke this, Prefect. It's your responsibility to fix it. Why don't you start, instead of just standing there like a petrified tree?'

'I ... don't have access,' Thalia said. Under her tunic she could feel a cold line of sweat trickling down her back. 'They gave me a six-hundred-second window. I used it. There's no way back in again.'

'Then you'd better think of something else,' Caillebot said. 'And be fast about it.'

'There's nothing else to do. I can run some superficial tests on the pillar ... but without core access, I can't see into its guts. And this has to be a fundamental problem, something really deep-rooted.'

It was Parnasse's turn to speak. His voice was a low rumble, yet everyone listened to him. 'They only gave you a single one-time pad, did they, girl?'

'Just the one,' Thalia said.

'Then she's right,' he said, turning to the others. 'I may not be a prefect, but I know a thing or two about the way these things work. She won't get in again without a new pad.'

'Then call home and get one,' Thory said, hissing out the words.

'Nice trick, without abstraction access,' Parnasse replied. He looked at Thalia. 'True, isn't it? Your own comms piggyback abstraction services. You'd need it to be up and running before you can call Panoply.'

Thalia swallowed hard as the truth sank home. 'That's right. We depend on abstraction protocols as well. I'm out of contact with home.'

'Try it, just to be sure,' said Parnasse.

Thalia tried it. She attempted to return the call from Muang, the one she had ignored during the upgrade.

'I'm sorry,' she said, when the bracelet failed to connect. 'I can't see Panoply. I can't even see my ship.'

'Oh, that's clever!' Thory said. 'You gut us open and then you can't even call for help! Whose clever bloody idea was that?'

'It's never caused us a problem before. If we take abstraction down, it's on our terms.'

'Until today,' Thory said.

The mood of the gathering was swerving somewhere unpleasant. They'd been all smiles until she took their sweets away.

'Look,' Thalia said, trying to strike the right conciliatory note, 'this is unacceptable, and you have my sincere apology for any inconvenience I may have caused. But I promise you it won't last long. If the abstraction blackout is as wide as it looks, then that means an entire habitat has just dropped off the network. Not just any old hermit colony, either, but House Aubusson. You've already told me that the lobbyists are in almost constant contact with you. How long do you think it will take before they notice your absence? Probably not more than a few minutes. Maybe a few minutes more before they act on that absence and start calling Panoply, to find out what's gone wrong.' She took a deep breath. 'My bosses will take this very, very seriously, even given the current crisis. At high-burn, a Heavy Technical Squad could be knocking on the door inside forty-five minutes. They'll have new pads, maybe even an emergency field core, everything necessary to get abstraction back up and running. Honestly, you could be back on-line inside an hour, ninety minutes at the max.'

'You talk as if ninety minutes is nothing,' Thory said. 'Maybe it isn't for you. I know how it is for prefects. You've never experienced true abstraction. You have no idea what losing it means to us. Perhaps if your bosses had sent someone more experienced, someone who at least looked as if they knew what they were doing—'

Thalia felt something inside her snap, like a wishbone tearing in two. 'Maybe I don't know what losing abstraction means to you. But I'll tell you this. A few days ago I was part of a lockdown party. It turned nasty. We had to euthanise. So *don't you dare* talk to me as if I'm some wet-behind-the-ears apprentice who's never got her hands dirty.'

'If you think—' Paula Thory began.

'Wait,' Thalia said. 'I'm not done. I'm not *remotely* done. Since we got back from that lockdown – which was regarded as a successful operation, incidentally, despite the casualties – my boss has had to deal with the murder of more than nine hundred innocent people, not including the crew of a ship who were butchered and burnt for their perceived part in that crime, but who were in all likelihood innocent. My boss is still on that case. *His* boss is doing her best just to keep her head in one piece. The rest of Panoply's trying to stop the whole Glitter Band sliding into war against the Ultras, while bracing itself for the civil war that's probably going to follow when we find out who really torched Ruskin-Sartorious.' Thalia stiffened the set of her jaw, making sure she looked at each member of the party in turn. 'Maybe that isn't a typical week in the life of Panoply, people, but it happens to be the week we're dealing with right now. Perhaps you think the loss of ninety minutes of abstraction measures up to what's already on our table. Fine if you do, that's your call. But I'm here to tell you that, as far as I'm concerned, you are a bunch of self-pitying sonsofbitches who at this point in time are doing pretty fucking well just to be breathing.'

No one said anything. They were just looking at her, mouths open, as if she had frozen them all into silence.

Thalia smiled tightly. 'Nothing personal, though. I guess I'd be pretty upset if someone had taken my toys from the pram as well. I'm just saying that right now we could all use a degree of perspective. Because this is not the end of the world.'

She relaxed her stance just enough to let them know that the dressing down was over, for the moment.

'You,' she said, pointing at the woman in the flame-red dress. 'That train you saw earlier. Is it still stopped?'

'Yes,' the woman said, stammering out her answer. 'I can still see it. It's not going anywhere.'

'I was hoping we could take the train back to the endcap. As I said, help'll be on its way soon enough regardless, but if it would make any of you happier, I could use the transmitter on my ship to call Panoply.'

'Would that work?' asked a chastened Caillebot.

'Absolutely. Since it's outside Aubusson, it won't have been affected by the abstraction outage. Looks like we're stuck here for the duration, though, unless any of you knows another way to get to the docking hub.'

'I'm not seeing any aerial traffic,' said a man with a strangely comedic face. 'All flights must have been grounded along with that volantor.'

'We could walk,' Parnasse said. 'It's less than ten kilometres to the endcap.'

'Are you serious?' Paula Thory asked.

'No one's saying you'd have to come with us.' He nodded in Thalia's direction. 'I think the girl's right: once word gets out, they'll send help. But like she said, this is a sticky time for Panoply. We might be looking at a fair bit longer than an hour, or ninety minutes. Could be two hours, could be three, even longer.'

'So what does walking accomplish?' Thory asked.

Parnasse shrugged his broad farmer's shoulders. He'd rolled up his sleeves, revealing hairy red arms knotted with muscle. 'Not much, except it means we'd stand a chance of meeting the specialists when they come through the door. At least Thalia could fill them in on exactly what she was doing before the system went tits-up.' He glanced at her. 'Right, girl?'

'It might save some time,' she said. 'If we can get to the hub, I can also talk to Panoply and give them some technical background before the squad arrives.' The hypothetical squad, she reminded herself. The one she could not say for sure would actually be on its way. 'Either way, it's no worse than staying here. I can't do a thing for the core now.'

'People out there,' Parnasse said, 'are going to be just a tad upset if they see a Panoply uniform. You could be looking at an eight-hundred-thousand-strong lynch mob.'

'They can fume and rage all they want,' Thalia said, touching her whiphound for reassurance. 'I'm the prefect here, not them. And if they want to find out what happens when one of them even thinks of laying a finger on me, they're more than welcome.'

'Fighting talk,' Parnasse said, in little more than a mutter. 'I like the sound of that.'

The gruff curator, Thalia realised, was the only one of them who was unequivocally on her side. Perhaps he had a grudging respect for her ability with cybernetic systems, in spite of all that had just befallen them, or maybe he was just prickly enough to defend her because everyone else wanted her hide.

'We can cover ten kilometres in less than two hours,' she said. 'Provided we don't have to detour to cross those window bands, of course.'

'We won't,' Parnasse said. 'Not much, anyway. We can use the pedestrian bridges under the rail line, and even if those are blocked for one reason or another, there are always the parkland connections. There's a lot of greenery, a lot of cover.'

Thalia nodded: she'd seen where the window bands were bridged by tongues of parkland or tree-lined aqueducts and rail-line viaducts.

'Of course,' she said, 'we'll still have four kilometres to climb to the hub.'

'Shouldn't be a problem,' said Cuthbertson, raising a tentative hand as he spoke. 'Volantors depend on abstraction for nav services, same as Miracle Bird does. But elevators don't. There isn't a reason in the world why they shouldn't work.'

'And the trains?' asked Thory. 'Got an explanation for why *they* aren't running?'

'Someone panicked, that's all. Activated the emergency stop.'

'All over Aubusson?' asked the woman in the red dress. 'I've been looking out of this window for a long time now and can see far enough to make out six or seven lines. I'm damned if I've seen one moving train in all that time.'

Cuthbertson's certainty had slipped a notch. 'So a lot of people panicked. Or maybe Utility pulled the plug because *they* panicked.'

'Could affect the elevators, in that case,' the woman said.

'I don't know. I think the elevators run on a different supply, independent of Utility. Point is, we won't lose anything by finding out.' Cuthbertson turned to face Cyrus Parnasse. 'I'm coming with you, Curator. Miracle Bird can act as look-out, in case we run into any mobs.'

'That bird of yours can still fly, even when it's twitching like that?' asked Thalia.

'It'll manage. It's adapting already.' The mechanical owl turned its dish-like face to look at Cuthbertson. 'Aren't you, boy?'

'I'm an excellent bird.'

'So that's three of us,' Thalia said. 'Not counting the owl. That's a good number. If we encounter trouble, we shouldn't be too conspicuous.'

'I'm coming, too,' said Caillebot. 'If there's anyone who knows the layout of the parks and gardens in this cylinder, it's me.'

'You can count me in as well,' said Meriel Redon.

'You sure?' Thalia asked. 'You'll be safe and sound up here until the back-up squad arrives.'

'I've made my mind up. I've never been one for sitting around when I could be walking. Makes me nervous.'

Thalia nodded heavily. 'I think five is the limit, folks. Any more and we'll be slower than we need to be. The rest of you can sit tight and wait until abstraction comes back up.'

'Are you issuing orders now?' Paula Thory asked.

Thalia thought about it for an instant. 'Yes,' she said. 'Looks like I am. So start dealing with it, lady.'

Dreyfus absorbed the truth of the Conjoiner's revelations, convinced in his heart that she had no reason to lie. 'I think I know who Aurora is,' he said slowly. 'But she shouldn't be here. She shouldn't be anywhere. She should have died – she should have *ended* – fifty-five years ago.'

'Who is she?'

'Unless someone else is using the same name, we're dealing with a dead girl. One of the Eighty, the group of human volunteers who took part in Calvin Sylveste's immortality experiments. Do you know what I'm talking about?'

'Of course. We learned of those experiments with horror and dismay. His methods were conceptually flawed. Failure was inevitable.'

'Except maybe it wasn't,' Dreyfus said, 'because Aurora Nerval-Lermontov appears to be very much with us. At least one of the Transmigrants must have persisted, despite what the records say.'

'You have no evidence of this.'

'I know that her family owned this rock.' By way of an afterthought, he added, 'Do you think you're ready to trust me yet?'

'Turn around,' she said after due consideration. 'I have released my hold on your suit. Your communication functions are still disabled.'

He turned to look at her. She was wearing a suit herself, but of Conjoiner design. It had the glossy sheen of something moulded from luxury chocolate. For a moment he was looking at a featureless black oval instead of a head. Then her helmet melted back into the ruff-like collar of the neck ring.

He saw her face.

He'd seen stranger things in the Glitter Band. There was very little about her that wasn't baseline human, at first glance. She was a woman of uncertain age – he'd have said forty or so, except that he knew she was probably much older than that, because Conjoiners were as long-lived as any human splinter faction. Piercingly intelligent eyes, coloured a very pale green; wide, freckled cheekbones; a jaw that some might have considered too strong, but which was actually exactly in proportion with the rest of her face. She was bald, the top of her skull rising to a sharp mottled ridge that began halfway up her brow, betraying the enlarged cranial cavity she must have needed for her supercharged, machine-clotted brain.

That was where her true strangeness lay: beneath the skin, beneath the bone. The people in the wilder habitats might employ Mixmasters to sculpt themselves into exotic forms, but they seldom did anything to the functional architecture of their minds. Even the people who were wired into extreme levels of abstraction were still human in the way they processed the data entering their brains. That couldn't be said for the Conjoiner woman. She might be able to emulate human consciousness when it suited her, but her natural state of mind was something Dreyfus would never be able to grasp, any more than a horse could grasp algebra.

'Do you want to tell me your name?' Dreyfus asked.

'For your purposes I will call myself Clepsydra. If this is problematic for you, you may call me Waterclock, or simply Clock.'

'You sound as if that isn't your real name.'

'My real name would split your mind open like wood under an axe.'

'Clepsydra it is, then. What exactly are you doing here, assuming you're ready to tell me?'

'Surviving. That has been enough, lately.'

'Tell me about this ship. What's it doing here? What use is it to Aurora?'

'Our ship returned to this system nearly fifty years ago. We were experiencing difficulties. We'd encountered something in deep interstellar space: a machinelike entity of hostile nature. The ship had survived by sloughing part of itself, in the manner of a lizard shedding its tail. On the long return journey it had reorganised itself as best as it could, but it was still damaged. We were attempting to make contact with the Mother Nest, but our communications systems were not functioning properly.' Clepsydra swallowed, a gesture that all of a sudden made her look helplessly human. 'Aurora found us first. She lured us in with promises of help and then swallowed us inside this place. We have been inside it ever since: unable to escape, unable to contact the Nest.'

'That still doesn't tell me what Aurora wanted of you.'

'That is more difficult to explain.'

'Try me.'

'Aurora wanted us to dream, Prefect. That is why she – why it – kept us here. Aurora made us dream the future. She desired our intelligence concerning future events. We prognosticated. And when we saw something in our prognostications that she didn't like, Aurora punished us.'

'No one can dream the future.'

'We can,' Clepsydra said blithely. 'We have a machine that lets us. We call it Exordium.'

CHAPTER 14

Thalia's walking party made their way to the elevator shaft that pierced the middle of the sphere from pole to pole. The high-capacity car was still waiting for them, exactly as they had left it, down to the pale-yellow watercolour panels of scenes from Yellowstone.

'It's powered up,' Parnasse said. 'That's good. Shouldn't be any problem getting down now.'

Thalia, the last of the five to enter, cleared the trelliswork doors. They scissored shut behind her.

'It's not moving. I'm asking it and it isn't moving,' Caillebot said.

'That's because it isn't hearing you. Abstraction's two-way,' Parnasse said, with the weary air of a man who shouldn't have to explain such things.

'Then how do we get it to move? Are there manual controls?'

'We don't need them just yet. Do we, Thalia?'

'He's right,' she said. 'Panoply operatives need to be free to move wherever and whenever we want, even without abstraction. We distribute the voiceprint patterns of authorised personnel to all habitats as a matter of routine.' She spoke up. 'This is Deputy Field Prefect Thalia Ng. Recognise my voiceprint.'

'Voiceprint recognised, Deputy Field Prefect Ng.'

Thalia breathed a little easier. 'Please descend to ground level.'

There was an uncomfortable moment when nothing happened, and then the elevator began to descend.

'Glad that worked,' Thalia said under her breath. Parnasse glanced at her with a sly smile as if he'd overheard.

'That's good,' Caillebot said. 'I was beginning to wonder what would happen if we'd been stuck up there.'

'We'd have taken the stairs,' Parnasse said witheringly. 'You're familiar with the concept of stairs, right?'

Caillebot shot him a warning look but didn't reply.

The elevator continued its smooth descent, passing through the neck connecting the sphere to the stalk. They were in the hollow atrium now. Far below, visible through the trellised glass windows on the outside of the car, the lobby lay completely deserted. Thalia had half-expected that at least some citizens would be converging on the polling core, demanding to know what was wrong and exactly when it would be fixed, but there was no sign of them. She couldn't exactly say why, but something made her touch the whiphound again.

The car completed its descent, coming to a smooth halt at the lobby level, and the trelliswork doors clattered open. Again, Thalia was struck by the emptiness of the lobby. It felt even more still than when they had first passed through it, their footsteps echoing loudly.

'Okay, people,' she said, 'let's stick together. Like the man said, there could be some angry citizens out there, and we may be the ones they decide to take it out on.'

They walked into blue-hazed sunlight, shining down from the arc of the window band eight kilometres above. Around them stood ornamental ponds and lawns, crisscrossed by neatly tended gravel and marble pathways. Fountains were still burbling somewhere nearby. Everything looked utterly normal, exactly as Thalia had expected save for the absence of a rampaging mob. Perhaps she was doing the citizens of Aubusson a disservice. But then she recalled how quickly the reception committee had turned against her. If they were truly representative of the citizenry, then there was every reason to expect a similarly unpleasant reaction from the other eight hundred thousand of them.

'I hear voices,' Caillebot said suddenly. 'I think they're coming from the other side of the stalk.'

'I hear them, too,' Parnasse said, 'but we're not going that way. Straightest path is right ahead, though those trees, directly towards the endcap.'

'Maybe I should speak to them,' Thalia said. 'Tell them what's happened, how it won't be long before things are sorted out.'

'We had a plan, girl,' Parnasse said. 'The idea was to walk and stay out of trouble. Those voices don't sound too happy, the way I'm hearing 'em.'

'I agree,' said Meriel Redon.

Thalia bit her lip. She could hear the voices as well, just above the burble of fountains. A lot of people, sounding agitated and angry. Shouts that were threatening to become screams.

Her hand tightened on the whiphound again. Something was wrong, she knew. That wasn't the sound of a crowd high on its own fury and indignation, wanting the blood of whoever had taken down their precious abstraction.

That was the sound of frightened people.

'Listen to me,' Thalia said, fighting to keep the fear out of her own voice. 'I need to see what's happening. That's my duty as a prefect. You four keep going, heading towards the endcap. I'll catch you up.'

'That's not a pretty sound,' Parnasse said.

'I know. That's why I need to check it out.'

'It isn't your problem,' Caillebot said. 'Our constables will take care of any civil unrest. That's what they're for.'

'You have a standing police force?'

The gardener shook his head. 'No, but the system will have called up a constabulary from the citizenry, the same way we were called up to form the reception party.'

'There is no system,' Parnasse said.

'Then the people who were called up last time will resume their duties.'

'When exactly *was* last time?' Thalia asked. The agitated noise was growing louder. It sounded more like the whooping of excited wildfowl than any sound produced by people.

'I don't remember. A couple of years ago.'

'It was more like ten,' Meriel Redon said. 'And even if the constables self-activate, how are they all going to get where they're needed if the trains are down?'

'We don't have time to talk this over.' Thalia unclipped her whiphound, tightening her hand around the heavy shaft of the handle. 'I'm going to take a look.'

'On your own?' Redon asked.

'I won't have to get too close. The whiphound can give me an advance pair of eyes. In the meantime you keep walking along this path, towards that row of trees. I'll find you.'

'Wait,' Cuthbertson said urgently. 'We have Miracle Bird. Let's use him.'

'How?' Thalia asked.

'He can overfly the crowd and tell us what he sees when he returns. He doesn't need abstraction for that. Do you, boy?'

Miracle Bird's beak clacked in return. 'I can fly,' said the mechanical owl. 'I'm an excellent bird.'

'He doesn't sound as bright as when he met me at the hub,' Thalia said.

Cuthbertson raised his hand, Miracle Bird responding by unfolding and flexing his glittering alloy wings. 'He knows what to do. Shall I release him?'

Thalia glanced at the whiphound. She might need its close-up surveillance mode later, but for now an aerial snapshot would be at least as useful.

'Do it,' she said.

Cuthbertson pushed his arm higher. Miracle Bird released its talons, its wings hauling it aloft with a whoosh of downthrust. Thalia watched it climb higher and recede, sun flaring off its foil-thin feathers with every wingbeat, until it vanished around the side of the stalk.

'It'll know to come back to us?' Thalia asked.

'Trust the bird,' Cuthbertson said.

It was an uncomfortably long time before the owl reappeared, emerging around the other side of the stalk. It loitered above them, then spiralled down for an awkwardly executed landing on Cuthbertson's sleeve. He whispered something to the bird; the bird whispered something back.

'Did he get anything?' Caillebot asked.

'He recorded what he saw. He says he saw people and machines below.'

Caillebot narrowed his eyes. 'Machines?'

'Servitors, probably. But that's all he can tell us himself. He's a smart bird, but he's still PreCalvinist.'

Caillebot looked disgusted. 'Then we haven't achieved anything, other than wasted time.'

'Let's find some shade. Then we'll see what we achieved.'

'What in Voi's name do we need shade for?' Caillebot snapped.

'Find me some and I'll show you.' The automaton-maker tapped a finger against the owl's delicate jewelled eyes. Thalia understood – the eyes looked very much like laser projectors – and started looking around, hoping they would not have to go back into the lobby.

'Will that do?' Meriel Redon asked, pointing to the shadow cast by an ornamental arch at the foot of one of the pond-spanning bridges.

'Good work,' Thalia said. They trooped over to the arch and

made room for Cuthbertson to kneel down, bringing Miracle Bird's head to within thirty centimetres of the dark marbled floor.

'Start playback, boy,' Cuthbertson said. 'Everything you shot, from the moment I let you go.'

The owl looked down. A square of bright colour appeared on the dark-grey marble. Thalia saw faces and clothes, a huddle of people diminishing as the bird took flight. Its point of view shifted as it looked away from them. Blue haze, textured by the faint roads, parks and communities of the farside wall. Then the ivory-white spire of the polling core's stalk filled the owl's field of view. The stalk widened, then veered to the right as the owl swept past it. Now Miracle Bird's point of view shifted smoothly downwards, tracking towards the ground beneath him. Geometric divisions of grass and water slid across the image square. One of the escalator ramps down to the train station. Then a larger green space dotted with the pale, foreshortened blobs of people, many dozens of them.

'Hold it there,' Cuthbertson said. 'Freezeframe and zoom in picture centre, boy.'

The image enlarged. The blobs resolved into individuals. There were at least fifty or sixty people, Thalia judged; maybe more out of sight. They were not just standing around any more, nor had they assembled into the agitated clumps of a restless, bad-tempered crowd.

No. They had formed a single, tight-packed group, jammed closer together than normal social etiquette would have allowed. A thought started to form in Thalia's mind, but Meriel Redon said it aloud.

'They're being herded,' she said, very softly. 'They're being herded by machines.'

The furniture-maker was right, Thalia saw. The people had been shunted together by servitors, at least a dozen of them. Their squat forms were quite unmistakable, even from above. Some of them moved on wheels or tracks, some on slug-like pads, some on legs. She thought she recognised at least one of the bright blue gardening servitors that they had passed on the way to the polling core. She recalled the wicked gleam of its trimmer arms as it carved a peacock out of the hedge.

'This isn't good,' Thalia said.

'The constables must have tasked the servitors to assist them,' Caillebot replied.

Parnasse pointed a stubby finger at the image, indicating the shoulder of a man wearing a bright orange armband. 'Sorry to dampen your enthusiasm, but I think that *is* a constable. The machines seem to be treating him the same way they're treating everyone else.'

'Then he must be an impostor wearing a constable's armband. The machines would only be acting under the supervision of the officially designated constables.'

'Then where are they?' Parnasse asked.

Caillebot looked irritated. 'I don't know. Sending instructions from somewhere else.'

Parnasse looked suitably unimpressed. 'With no abstraction? What are they using, messenger pigeons?'

'Maybe the machines are programmed to act this way when they sense a civil emergency,' Redon said doubtfully. 'They're only doing what the constables would do if they were here.'

'Has anything like this happened before?' Thalia asked.

'Not in my memory,' Redon said.

'There have been disturbances,' Parnasse said. 'Storms in a teacup. But the machines have never started acting like constables.'

'Then I don't think that's what we're looking at,' Thalia said.

'What, then?' Parnasse asked.

He was starting to rankle her, but she kept her composure. 'I'm starting to worry that this is something more sinister. I'm beginning to think that what we're seeing here is some kind of takeover.'

'By whom?' asked Caillebot. 'Another habitat?'

'I don't know. That's why I need to see things with my own eyes. I want you four to stay here and keep quiet until I'm back. If you don't hear from me inside five minutes, start making your way to the endcap.'

'Are you insane?' Redon asked.

'No,' Thalia said. 'Just on duty. There are people in distress here. Since the local law enforcement appears to be failing them, they've become a matter for Panoply.'

'But there's just one of you.'

'Then I'd better make myself count, hadn't I?' Sounding braver than she felt, Thalia tapped her sleeve. 'Five minutes, people. I'm serious.'

She left the shade of the arch, crouching as she made her way from point to point, the whiphound gripped in her right hand like a truncheon. Away from the group, away from their demands and bickering, she found herself starting to think things through.

Servitors were programmed with a degree of autonomy, but – unless they'd been uploaded with some very specialised new crowd-control routines – the kind of coordinated action they had seen via the owl implied that someone was pulling their strings from afar. That in turn meant that abstraction could not be down completely.

She remembered her glasses. Furious with herself for not using them sooner, she delved into her tunic pocket with her left hand and slipped them on. The view hardly changed, confirming that abstraction was absent or at least running at a very low level. But symbols were dancing in her lower-right field of view, indicating that the glasses were detecting signals that very much resembled servitor protocols. *Someone* was puppeting the machines after all. Abstraction wasn't down; it was just that the people had been locked out.

It was all looking too damned coincidental for comfort. She'd been sent in to make a systems upgrade, and at the very moment when the upgrade had gone through, something had thrown a wrench into the system.

Thalia felt dizzy. She'd had a moment of clarity and it had felt like the thin skin of the world opening up beneath her feet.

She reined her thoughts in before they pulled her somewhere treacherous. Still crouched, moving from cover to cover as if evading a sniper, Thalia finally came in sight of the area of lawn where the machines were herding the citizens. She had the protection of a low hedge, just tall enough to shield her when she was crouching. It had been trained into a lattice pattern, offering diamond-shaped peepholes through to the other side. Thalia was grateful for her black uniform. A military-grade servitor would have spotted her already, using thermal imaging or any one of a dozen other sensors designed to sniff out concealed human prey. But these were servitors manufactured to tend formal gardens, not engage in search-and-destroy missions.

From this low angle, it was not easy to tell exactly what was going on. She could see the cordon of robots, with the humans crammed into a mass behind them. The machines had hemmed the people into a corner of the lawn, backed against the angle formed by two tall hedges. About a dozen servitors appeared to be involved in the herding operation. If someone tried to break free of the mass, they would only manage a few steps before one of the fast machines sped around to block their exit.

Most people were making no effort to escape, Thalia noticed. The crowd was more subdued than before. They were quieter, talking more than shouting, and a handful of people even looked quite relaxed. The physical size and mass of the machines was apparently enough of a deterrent against escape – some of the servitors were much taller than a person – but they also had makeshift weapons. Thalia had already seen the blades of the hedge-cutter, but that wasn't all. Amongst their arsenal the servitors also had high-pressure water sprays, to keep the marble tiles clean. They had flails to trim the edges of lawns. They had manipulator arms to handle tools and materials.

Now that the crowd was quieter, she could hear a single voice dominating all others. It was measured, reassuring. It had an amplified edge that suggested it was coming from one of the servitors.

She whispered a command to the whiphound. 'Forward surveillance mode. Advance twenty metres and hold for one hundred seconds before returning. Extreme stealth posture.'

She let go of the handle. With uncanny speed, the whiphound deployed its filament and slithered through one of the diamond-shaped gaps in the hedge. Thalia heard the merest hiss of disturbed foliage, then nothing. She touched a finger to the side of her glasses, opening a window that showed the whiphound's point of view. The image remained level as the machine slinked to its surveillance point, directly ahead of the Thalia. Through the gaps in the hedge she could just see the thin cord of its filament, coiling along the ground with the handle only a few handwidths above the grass.

The machine reached its surveillance point. Nothing but grass stood between the whiphound and the outer cordon of servitors. It halted and slowly elevated its handle until the crowd came into view again. The image zoomed in, clicking through magnification factors. The whiphound had enough smarts to identify people and concentrate its attention on them. Thalia studied the faces, seeing fear and bewilderment on several, anger on others, but also a kind of trusting acceptance on many.

The whiphound's audio pickup pushed an amplified voice into her earpiece. '... state of emergency is now in force,' the voice said. 'Although full information is not yet available, there is credible evidence that House Aubusson has suffered an attack by hostile parties. This incident is still in progress. In addition to the sabotaging of abstraction services, it is believed that an airborne neurotoxic agent has been introduced into the biosphere. Until the focus and extent of this agent have been determined, it is regrettably necessary to suspend normal freedom of movement and communication. In areas where constables cannot be activated or deployed, servitors have been tasked to provide the same function. This temporary measure has been instigated for your safety. Constables are now actively assessing the scale and threat of the attack. Panoply operatives have also been notified of the situation, and are now formulating an appropriate tactical response. In the meantime, please assist the constabulary by cooperating fully with locally designated operatives, be they human or servitor, so that habitat-wide resources can be targeted efficiently on the elimination of the threat. I thank you for your assistance at this difficult time.' The voice fell silent, but only momentarily before what was clearly a recorded loop began again. 'This is Constable Lucas Thesiger, speaking for the constabulary of House Aubusson, under the terms of the Civil Emergency Act. I regret to inform you that a state of emergency is now in force. Although full information is not yet available . . .'

The whiphound broke off its surveillance and commenced its return to Thalia. She snapped off the glasses, folded them and slid them back into her tunic pocket. With a rustle the whiphound emerged through the hedge. She spread the fingers of her right hand and allowed the handle to leap into her grasp, the filament retracting in the same instant.

She looked back the way she had come, plotting her route, and saw the moving form of a large six-wheeled servitor. Only the top half of the machine was visible, the rest of it obscured by the line of a hedge. It was an orange robot with a high-gloss shell, the claws and scoop of heavy-duty waste-collection apparatus just visible at the front. The machine was trundling along a gravel-lined path, crunching stones beneath its tyres. Thalia replayed the route she had followed and reckoned that the robot would be on her in fifteen or twenty seconds; sooner if she returned the way she had come.

It might do nothing. It might just rumble past her, on some preprogrammed errand.

She wasn't going to take that chance.

She crouch-walked as fast as she dared, holding the whiphound tight. She reached a dead end where three sets of hedges converged, blocking her in. The servitor rumbled closer. She risked a glance back and saw blue-hazed sunlight flare off its shell. With the outspread axles of its six wheels, its claw-like waste-collection system and the dim-looking cluster of cameras tucked under the shell's forward lip, there was something fierce and crablike about the advancing machine. An hour ago she would have walked past it without giving it a glance. Now it made her feel mortally frightened.

Thalia thumbed one of the heavy-duty controls set into the whiphound's handle. *Sword mode.* The filament whisked out to a length of one metre, but stiffened to the rigidity of a laser beam. Gripping the thing in both hands, Thalia pushed the blade into the hedge. She sliced sideways, the whiphound automatically twisting the blade to bring the microscopic ablative mechanisms of the cutting edge into play. There was no detectable resistance. A downward swoop, a sweep across, a sweep up. She retracted the blade, then pushed against the cube of hedge she had cut free. It eased inwards, then flopped back onto the turf on the other side. With hindsight, she should have cut a wider hole.

She didn't have time for hindsight.

She wriggled through. Her heels must have been clearing the gap when the robot rounded the final corner. Thalia crouched low and still. She had emerged onto an area of lawn bounding one of the ponds, out of sight of the other servitors. The pond was circular, with an ornamental fountain at its centre.

The machine approached, its progress silent save for the steady crunch of gravel under its wheels. Thalia tensed, convinced that the machine was going to slow or stop. It would see the hole, she thought; it would find her, then it would summon others. But the machine did not stop, even when it reached the cut in the hedge. Thalia remained as still as possible until the crunching noise had receded into the background sounds – the burble of the fountain, the distant voices of the herded crowd and the endlessly cycling message of reassurance from Constable Lucas Thesiger.

When at last she was certain that the machine was not about to return, she poked her head above the level of the hedge. No other servitors were nearby, or at least none large enough to see. The orange machine was turning, changing its course to proceed at ninety degrees to the hedge Thalia had cut, but not in a direction that would take it further away. She looked along the line of the hedge that the machine was traversing and spotted an opening at its far end, one she had missed on her first inspection. If the machine reached that spot and then turned in towards her, she would be exposed and obvious. Thalia stowed the whiphound. She returned through the hole she had cut, the gravel chips digging into the skin of her palms as she pushed herself up to a crouching position. Holding still again, she watched the orange servitor make its way to the end of the hedge and then turn into the enclosure around the pond. She had been right to dodge back through the hedge. Even if the machine carried only a rudimentary vision system, she would have been obvious.

Instinct told her to move while the machine was engaged in its business, but she forced herself to remain still. She had seen something slumped in the servitor's waste scoop, something that had no business being there.

The machine trundled to the edge of the pond. It raised the scoop, shining pistons elongating. The angle of the scoop tilted down. The slumped thing Thalia had glimpsed slid free into the water. It was a body, a dead man clothed in the brown overalls of a park attendant. As the body entered the pond, limp enough to suggest that death had been recent, Thalia made out a vivid red gash across the man's chest, where he had been cut through his clothes. Then he was gone. For a moment an elbow jutted out of the water, before disappearing under. The fountain laid a white froth over the surface of the pond, obscuring the body completely.

Thalia was shaking. She unclipped the whiphound again. She had not believed the recorded message from Lucas Thesiger, if there was such a person. But until that moment she had at least been prepared to believe that the servitors were acting under some dire-emergency protocol. Perhaps the truth was simply too unsettling to reveal to the citizenry, for fear of inciting panic.

But even in a state of emergency, you didn't bury bodies in civic ponds.

'There were a hundred of us once,' Clepsydra said. 'This room is where we slept, or at least rested our bodies, during interstellar flight. Most of us are still alive, connected via neural connections to the Exordium device.'

'Where is it?' Dreyfus asked.

'Somewhere else in the ship.'

'Can you show it to me?'

'I could, but then I'd have to kill you.'

He couldn't tell if that was an attempt at humour, or whether she was deadly serious.

In total, she'd told him as little about the technology as she could get away with. All Dreyfus was clear about was that Exordium was a kind of quantum periscope, peering into a murky, fog-shrouded sea of overlapping future states. What Clepsydra called the 'retrocausal probability function' was generated by future versions of the same dreamers, plugged into the Exordium machine further down the timeline. It took the minds of those selfsame dreamers to shape the nebulous Exordium data into coherent predictions about things yet to happen.

He looked at the wounded sleepers. 'Please don't tell me they're conscious.'

'It is a state of consciousness akin to lucid dreaming. Their minds have been enslaved for Aurora's purposes, nothing more. With their minds given over to processing Exordium imagery, the sleepers have scarcely any spare capacity for what you might call normal thought. Aurora has made that impossible.'

'And yet you escaped,' Dreyfus said.

'It was planned, with the full cooperation of the remaining sleepers. In the gaps between monitored thoughts we hatched a scheme. It took us years. We knew only one of us could escape. I was chosen at random, but any one of us would have sufficed.'

'Why just one of you? Once you'd escaped, couldn't you ... free the others, or something?'

'We had hopes that I might make it back to civilisation. That proved impossible.'

'How long have you been free?'

'A hundred days. A thousand. I'm not sure. Now at least you understand how I kept myself alive. I have a hiding place elsewhere in the rock, away from Aurora's scrutiny. But I can't stay there all the time. Periodically I must return here, to the ship, and harvest rations. I do it surgically, a little at a time. Just enough to keep me alive for a couple of days, but not enough to cause any additional complications in the donor. I take the harvested food back with me to my hideaway. I cook it as best I can, using a cauterizing tool.' She looked at Dreyfus, her expression challenging him to judge her. 'Then I eat it, slowly and gratefully. Then I return.'

'It's monstrous.'

'It's what we agreed.'

'We?'

'The other sleepers and I. Listen carefully, Dreyfus. This was always the plan. One of us would wake. One and only one. Aurora demanded a single thing of us: a steady stream of Exordium data. If we fell short, if we were perceived not to be performing to expectations, we would be punished. Our neural blockades are effective at neutralising physical pain, but they can do nothing against pain that is administered directly to the brain via cortical stimulation. That was how Aurora made us do what we were told.'

'The helmets?'

'A modification of our own equipment. They connect us to Exordium, but they also administer punishment.'

'Did she hurt you?'

'Aurora hurt all of us. But not by administering pain to the entire group of sleepers. Had Aurora done that, it might have engendered a sense of unity through suffering: a rebellious solidarity that might have given us the strength to refuse to dream. Aurora was cleverer than that.'

'What did she do?'

'Aurora's way was to select one of us and make that sleeper suffer for our collective failure. Aurora picked on certain sleepers again and again. Because we are Conjoiners, we always felt something of the other sleeper's pain: not its totality, but a reflection of it, enough to judge the degree of suffering.'

'And that worked?'

'We learned not to fail her. But by the same token we also strove to find a way to cheat. Aurora monitors our thoughts, but not infallibly. We sensed gaps in the flow of our group consciousness when her attention was elsewhere. In these gaps we devised our scheme.'

'Surely Aurora would have noticed at some point?'

'Aurora cares only about dreams and punishment. The mechanics of how the Exordium prognostications arrive are of little concern. Had I gone on to cause trouble ... then perhaps things would have been different.'

'How were you selected?'

'The honour was bestowed randomly. There were some who thought the escapee should be one of the sleepers Aurora was prone to punish, but that would have risked drawing too much attention to our plan, when the time for the next punishment came around.'

'I understand.'

'The matter of escape was not simple. It required enormous preparation, artful distraction. I learned how to fool the helmet into thinking I was still in the dreaming consciousness state, while in fact being fully lucid, fully awake. I learned how to interfere with its mechanism, to release it, yet not trigger any alarms. All this required more than a year of preparation.'

Dreyfus reeled at the enormity of what he was hearing. 'But once you escaped ... wouldn't there still have been an empty position?'

'That was easily dealt with. I mentioned the accident that had already befallen our ship. There were corpses elsewhere on the vessel, due to be returned to the Mother Nest for component recycling. Before my absence was noted, I retrieved one of these corpses and plugged it into the dreaming apparatus. The life-support system kept the corpse animate. It was incapable of thought, but the other dreamers were able to conceal that from Aurora.'

Dreyfus shook his head, dumfounded, appalled and awed at what he had heard. Speech itself felt like a form of blasphemy, set against so much suffering. 'But if you haven't been able to escape ... hasn't all of this been for nothing?'

'I was beginning to think so. So were the other sleepers. The idea was that I would use my talents to send a message to the Mother Nest, if it still existed. But the machinery in this place would not allow it. I can sense doors opening and closing, the arrival of ships and individuals. But the data architecture depends on optical circuitry, which my implants cannot manipulate.'

Dreyfus nodded grimly. 'Aurora knew exactly which bars would hold you prisoner.'

'Yes, she did. Perhaps your deputy will have more success, if he has the right equipment. But I was mute.'

'But you didn't give up.'

'I shifted my efforts to constructing a transmitter of my own. The ship could grow me such a thing in hours if I sent the right commands to it. But if I did that, Aurora would sense the changes in the ship. She almost certainly knows that you are here, Prefect. I could not risk her killing the sleepers. I was forced to scavenge what I could from the surrounding structure. I have been piecing together parts and tools in my hiding place.'

'How close are you to success?'

'A hundred days, a thousand days.' Then quietly she added, 'Perhaps longer. Nothing is certain.'

'How long could you last?'

'In a few years, I would reach the limit of what could be harvested without causing death. Then difficult decisions would need to be made. I would have made them, without flinching. That is our way. But then something changed.'

'Which was?'

'You arrived, Prefect. And now things can start happening.'

Meriel Redon was waiting for Thalia as soon as she returned to the other four members of the escape party. 'What did you see?' she asked.

Thalia raised a hand until she caught her breath. Her back was aching from all the crouching she'd had to do.

'It's pretty much what I expected, based on what we saw from the bird.' She kept her voice low, breaking off to take deep breaths. 'But it's not as bad as it looked at first. The servitors have been activated under an emergency protocol. I heard the voice of a constable explaining why everyone needs to stay calm.'

'I thought there were no constables,' said Caillebot. 'Except for the one we saw in the crowd, being treated like all the other people.'

'I don't think he had the right to wear a constable's armband,' Thalia said, her mind racing ahead as she tried to anticipate the questions her party might ask. 'The voice was coming from a servitor, anyway. It was broadcasting a looped statement from someone called Lucas Thesiger. Does the name mean anything to any of you?'

'Thesiger was assigned to the constabulary during the Blow-Out Crisis,' said Redon. 'I remember seeing his face on the reports. He was commended for bravery after he saved some people who were stranded outside near the breach. A lot of us said he should be made a permanent constable, to be activated again the next time there was a crisis.'

'Well, it looks like you got your wish. Thesiger's calling the shots now, from somewhere else.'

Cuthbertson looked sceptical. 'Why are the machines doing the work of the constables if the constables are still in charge?'

'Constables can't get everywhere at once,' Thalia told the bird man. 'And there are problems with communication. That's why the machines have been tasked in some areas, like this one. The people are being told to sit tight and wait for the crisis to blow over.'

'What crisis?' Parnasse asked, so quietly that Thalia almost didn't hear him.

'It's not clear. Thesiger says there are indications the habitat was attacked. The attack may even be ongoing. Something nasty might have been released into the air.'

The curator studied her with a look on his face that said Thalia might fool the others, but she wasn't fooling him. 'Then it was just coincidence that abstraction went down the moment you completed that upgrade?'

'Difficult as it may be to believe, that's what it looks like.'

'That's quite some coincidence.'

Thalia nodded earnestly. 'I agree, but right now we don't have time to dwell on that. What we have to focus on is surviving. Thesiger – whoever he is – is right to enforce martial rule to keep the citizenry from panicking too much. In his shoes, it's exactly what I'd do – even if that meant tasking servitors to fill in for constables.'

'But those machines weren't just directing the people to safety,' Cuthbertson said, a strained edge in his voice. 'They were herding them. There was something wrong there.'

'It's okay. The servitors must have been tasked before Thesiger was able to get his recorded message out. Given what had already happened – abstraction going down, the loss of utilities – I can imagine that the people were pretty spooked when the robots started pushing them around. But the machines were just doing what they were instructed to do. Constables would have done it with a smile and a wave of encouragement, but it's no different in the end. The crowd was a lot calmer once Thesiger explained what was happening.'

'I think she's right,' Redon said. 'I can't hear the voices as much now.'

'So what are you proposing?' Caillebot asked. 'That we go and join those people?'

Thalia took her biggest gamble. 'You can if you want. I won't stop you. But unlike those people, you happen to be under Panoply care already. That overrides any local security arrangements, including a habitat-wide curfew.'

'But you mentioned something in the air,' Redon said.

Thalia nodded. 'Thesiger talked about a toxic agent. I'm guessing he has intelligence that says something like that was at least planned. But I think he may be overstating the danger, just to be on the safe side.'

'You can't know that,' the furniture-maker said, her eyes widening with concern.

'No,' Thalia admitted. 'I can't. But I can tell you this. Thesiger wants to round people up to prevent panic, and for now that means holding them in the open air.'

'The larger buildings are all airtight,' Caillebot said, as if just realising it himself. 'They're designed to tolerate another blow-out. Why doesn't he move them to the larger buildings?'

'He's probably going to as soon as he has large enough groups under sufficient control. Once one group of people seal themselves into a building, they're not going to open the door to anyone else. And that will be bad news if the agent is real, and not everyone gets inside in time.'

'But staying with you doesn't help us,' Redon said.

'It does,' Thalia said. 'Our best strategy is to move, and keep moving. The whiphound has a chemosensor. It'll detect harmful elements in the air long before they reach sufficient concentration to do harm.'

'And then what?' the woman asked.

'We'll seek shelter if we have to. But our main objective is to reach my ship. You'll be safe there.'

'What about the others, the people we left behind in the polling core?'

Thalia glanced up at the spherical structure high above them. 'I can't help them now. The sphere's airtight, so they'll be safe from any toxins. They'll just have to sit it out up there until help arrives.'

Parnasse inhaled through his nose and nodded. 'Then we keep walking, the way we were going before.'

'At least we won't have any mobs to worry about,' Cuthbertson said, 'if the machines are putting everyone else under protection—'

'No, we won't have to worry about mobs,' Thalia told him. 'But I don't want to run into any tasked servitors either.'

'Won't they let us through when you explain that you're Panoply?' Caillebot asked.

'One would hope so, but I don't want to have to put that to the test. Those machines aren't reporting back to Thesiger every time they need to make a decision. They're running a one-size-fits-all enforcement program designed to safeguard the mass populace.'

'Then we'll need to avoid machines,' the gardener said. 'That isn't going to be easy, Prefect. Have you any idea how many servitors there are in this place?'

'In the order of millions, I'd guess,' Thalia said. 'But we'll just have to make do as best we can. The whiphound can move ahead of us, securing an area before we enter it.' She unclipped the handle and allowed the whiphound to deploy its filament. 'Beginning now. Forward scout mode. Twenty-metre secure zone. Proceed.'

The whiphound raced ahead, a squiggle moving almost too fast to be tracked by the eye.

'We're moving?' Caillebot asked.

Thalia waited until the whiphound had turned back to her and nodded its laser-eye handle, indicating that it was safe to proceed. 'We're moving,' she said. 'Keep low and keep quiet. Do that, and we'll be fine. One way or the other, we're getting out of here.'

They proceeded along gravel- and marble-lined paths, all stooping to stay below the level of the hedges. Now and then the hedges widened out to enclose a small courtyard or ornamental pond. It was less than ten kilometres to the endcap, but ten kilometres like this was going to feel more like fifty. She just hoped they would be able to move more freely once they had cleared the manicured gardens around the museum campus and entered the denser foliage of wooded parklands. Ahead lay the line of trees they had been making for since leaving the stalk.

Parnasse sidled next to her. Short and stocky, he had the easiest time of all of them when it came to stooping down. 'Very good work, girl,' he said quietly.

'Thank you,' she replied through gritted teeth.

'But what aren't you telling us?'

'Nothing.'

'You came back from the other side of the stalk with a look on your face I haven't seen in a long time. You saw something bad there, didn't you? Something you're frightened to tell us in case we lose it.'

'Just keep moving, Cyrus.'

'Was it true, about that speech from Thesiger?'

'I told you what I heard.'

'But you don't believe a word of it.'

'This is not the time for discussion. The priority now is to keep moving and keep quiet.' She looked at him sharply. 'Or did you miss that part?'

'What's happening to those people?' Parnasse persisted. 'Are the machines doing something bad to them?'

Ahead, the whiphound shook its handle from side to side. An instant later it flattened itself on the ground, looking just like a coil of discarded cable with a thickening at one end. Thalia raised a warning hand to her party.

'Hold it,' she breathed. 'The whiphound can't secure the area ahead of us. Something's there.'

The four froze behind her. The whiphound remained deathly still on the ground. It had been securing the area around a circular pond crossed by a red-painted wooden Chinese bridge. Two other hedge-lined paths converged on the same pond.

'I think we should retreat,' Thalia whispered.

'You *think*?' Caillebot asked.

The whiphound offered no guidance. It was adopting a maximum stealth posture, which could only mean it sensed purposeful movement. Thalia breathed in deeply, forcing herself to make the right decision. If the area could not be secured, it could not be entered. They would be right to retreat, to return to the last junction, where they could explore an alternative route. 'We go back,' she said.

Two servitors emerged into the area around the pond, one from either side. To the left, a gold-carapaced machine moved on three pairs of articulated legs, with a mass of segmented tentacles emerging from its cowled front end. Some kind of general-utility servitor, Thalia decided. To the right, bouncing along on mechanized ostrich-legs, was a multi-limbed household model, its black and white cladding suggestive of a butler's uniform.

Thalia held out her hand and barked a command. 'Abandon stealth posture. Immediate return.'

The whiphound lashed into action, scattering gravel as it uncoiled and propelled itself, almost flying into the air. Thalia splayed her fingers. The whiphound raced across the twenty metres separating the party from the servitors. The handle flew into Thalia's grasp, the filament retracting at the last instant. Her palm stung from the impact.

She knelt down, aiming the projected red laser spot at the two machines in turn, thumbing a stud each time. 'Mark as hostile,' she said twice. 'Intercept and detain. Maximum necessary force.'

She flung the handle into the air as if throwing a grenade. The filament lashed out, coiling behind the handle as the whiphound oriented itself. The filament contacted the ground, formed a tractive coil and sped the handle in the direction of the bipedal robot, which the whiphound must have identified as the softer target. Gravel hissed and spat.

'Now we run,' Thalia told her four companions.

She looked back over her shoulder as, still crouching, they worked back the way they had come. Both servitors were now circumnavigating the pond, converging at the foot of the bridge nearest Thalia. The whiphound flung itself into the air at the last moment, then wrapped its filament around the legs of the bipedal robot. Momentum on its own was not enough to topple the machine, but the whiphound constricted its filament, drawing tight the coils it had placed around the robot's legs.

The servitor took a juddering step, then lost its balance. It crashed to the dirt and immediately started trying to right itself. The whiphound resettled itself, then flexed its filament through one hundred and eighty degrees to bring the cutting edge into contact with the servitor's legs. As it cut into the machine, blue fluid sprayed out at arterial pressure. The servitor's upper limbs thrashed the ground, but the whiphound had the better of it. Sensing that the target was immobilised, it slithered free and focused its attention on the larger machine, the six-legged utility robot that was now increasing speed towards Thalia's party. The segmented tentacles at the front were flailing the air, giving a convincing impression of a machine driven into a berserker-like rage. The whiphound flung itself into combat again, wrapping metres of sharp-edged filament around the roots of the flailing arms. Thalia kept up her running crouch, glancing back all the while. 'Stay this side of the hedge,' she shouted ahead.

The battle between whiphound and servitor had become a blur of furious metal. Thumb-sized pieces of severed machine parts sprayed in all directions. The whiphound must have impaired the servitor's guidance system, for it was moving erratically now, swerving from side to side. A larger length of severed tentacle came spinning out of the maelstrom. The sound of the battle was like a hundred lashes being administered in unison against rusted steel. The servitor slowed, one of its legs severed. Blue-grey smoke belched from under the gold carapace.

Perhaps it was going to work, Thalia dared to think.

Then something dark came winging out of the chaos, flung aside by the tentacles. It was the handle of the whiphound, trailing a line of limp filament. It thudded at Thalia's heels, a buzzing sound coming from the handle, the tail twitching spasmodically.

The servitor was still approaching.

Thalia slowed as a cold, clear thought shaped itself. The whiphound was damaged, useless as a weapon now except in one very terminal sense. Thalia stopped, spun on her heels and grabbed at the handle. There was a gash in the casing, exposing obscene layers of internal componentry, things she had never been meant to see. The handle was warm, and every time it buzzed she felt it tremor in her hands. The tail drooped in a plumb line.

Thalia twisted the knurled dials at the end of the handle, bringing two tiny red dots into alignment. The dots lit up and started pulsing.

Grenade mode. Minimum yield. Five-second fuse on release.

The tail sped back into the housing. The black handle was still buzzing in her hand, but the training slammed home with the icy clarity of something that had been burnt into muscle memory by agonising repetition.

She flung the whiphound. It left her hand, following a smooth arc towards the still-approaching servitor. She had aimed it to land just ahead of the machine, directly in its path. Too close and the manipulators would have time to pick it up and fling it aside. Too early, and it wouldn't do enough damage. She'd have liked the luxury of requesting maximum yield, but while that would have taken care of the advancing machine, it wouldn't have done wonders for Thalia or her party.

One second.

'Get down!' she shouted, preparing to fling herself against the ground.

Two seconds.

Suddenly the servitor wasn't moving. The smoke was billowing out in greater intensity. It was fatally damaged, Thalia thought. The whiphound had done its job, and now she was going to waste it by having it blow up unnecessarily, when the servitor was already immobilised.

Three seconds.

'Rescind!' Thalia shouted. 'Rescind!'

Four seconds. Then five. The whiphound lay still on the ground. Six seconds oozed into seven. The grenade order had been cancelled, but she could still not shake the sense that she had created a bomb, one that was now compelled to detonate, much as a sword must draw blood before it could be returned to its scabbard.

She crept back towards the whiphound, knees wobbling underneath her. The damaged servitor was still twitching its manipulator tentacles, brushing the gravel only a few centimetres from where the handle had fallen. The citizens were looking back, no doubt wondering what she was doing. Thalia knelt and reached out, fingers advancing gingerly towards the damaged whiphound. The servitor's tentacles stirred and made one last-ditch effort to trap her, but Thalia was faster. Her hand closed around the warm handle of the whiphound and snatched it back. She almost fell on her haunches, before pushing herself to her feet. She quickly turned the arming dials back to their neutral settings.

'What now?' Caillebot asked, his hands on his hips. The party had stopped; they were all looking at her, not so much expecting guidance as demanding it.

Thalia clipped the damaged handle to her belt. It continued to buzz and tremble. 'We can't go on. It'll be too risky with the whiphound the way it is.'

'I say we just surrender ourselves to Thesiger's constables,' Caillebot said. 'What do we care if they're machines or people? They'll look after us.'

'Tell them,' Parnasse said, nodding in Thalia's direction.

Her mouth was dry. She wanted to be anywhere other than here, in this situation, with nothing to protect her or her party but one damaged whiphound.

'Tell us what?' Meriel Redon asked, fear staining her voice.

Thalia wiped gravel dust from her hands onto the hem of her tunic. It left grey finger smears. 'We're in trouble,' she said. 'Worse trouble than I wanted you to know. But Citizen Parnasse is right – I can't keep it from you any longer.'

'Keep what?' Redon asked.

'I don't think Thesiger is in control. I think that's just a ruse to get the citizens to accept the machines. My guess is Thesiger is either dead, already rounded up or fighting for his life. I don't think there are any human constables active inside Aubusson.'

'Meaning what?' the woman persisted.

'The machines are running things now. The servitors are the new authority. And they've started killing.'

'You can't know that.'

'I can,' Thalia said. She pushed sweat-damp hair back from her forehead. 'I've seen where they bury the bodies. I saw a man . . . he was dead. He'd been killed by one of those things. Butchered by a machine. And he was being hidden somewhere we wouldn't see him.'

Cuthbertson took a deep breath. 'Then what we were doing . . . trying to get out of here . . . that *was* the right thing to try. Wasn't it?

'It was,' Thalia said. 'But now I see I was wrong. We'd never have made it with just one whiphound to protect us. It was a mistake. *My* mistake, and I'm sorry. We shouldn't have left the stalk.'

They all looked back at the slender tower, with the windowed sphere of the polling core still gleaming against the blue-hazed pseudo-sky of the habitat's opposite wall.

'So what do we do now?' Caillebot asked.

'We get back up there,' Thalia said, 'as fast as we can, before more machines arrive. Then we secure it.'

If luck had been against them in their attempt to leave the museum campus, it held until they were back inside the cool, shadowed silence of the stalk's lobby. No machines had arrived to block their way, or shepherd them to be detained with the prisoners on the lawn. On one level, it felt as if many hours had passed since the loss of abstraction and the first hints that this was more than just a technical failure. But when Thalia checked the time she was dismayed to see that less than forty minutes had passed since she had completed her upgrade. As far as Panoply was concerned, she wouldn't even be overdue yet, let alone a matter for concern. Help might arrive eventually, but for now – and quite possibly for hours to come – Thalia was on her own.

As if to emphasize how little time had passed, the elevator car was still waiting in the lobby. Thalia beckoned the others inside, the doors snicking closed behind them. Her voice sounded ragged, on the slurred edge of exhaustion and burn-out.

'This is Deputy Field Prefect Thalia Ng. Recognise my voiceprint.'

After an agonising wait – which could only have been a fraction of a second – the door answered her.

'Voiceprint recognised, Deputy Field Prefect Ng.'

'Take us up.'

Nothing happened. Thalia held her breath and waited for movement, that welcome surge as the floor pushed against her feet. Still nothing happened.

'Is there a problem?' Caillebot asked.

Thalia whirled on him with vicious speed, all her tiredness wiped away in an instant. 'What does it look like? We're not moving.'

'Try again,' Parnasse said calmly. 'Could be it didn't understand you the first time.'

'This is Thalia Ng. Please ascend.' But still the elevator refused to move. 'This is Deputy Field Prefect Thalia Ng,' she said again. 'Recognise my voiceprint!'

This time the elevator stayed mute.

'Something's broken,' Parnasse said, still keeping his voice low and disengaged, as if he was commenting on the action rather than participating in it. 'I suggest we consider using the stairs instead.'

'Good idea,' Meriel Redon said. 'I'm starting to feel locked in here—'

'Try the doors,' Parnasse said.

Thalia pressed her hand against the manual-control panel. Her palm was cut and bruised from her battle with the servitors, tiny chips of stone still embedded in her skin.

'No dice. They aren't opening.'

'Try again.'

Thalia already had. 'Nothing doing. I don't suppose asking nicely's going to help either.'

'You could try.'

With a sense of futility, she said, 'This is Thalia Ng. Open the doors.' She hammered the panel again. 'Open the doors. *Open the fucking doors!*'

'Machines,' Cuthbertson said.

They all followed his gaze, through the trelliswork doors, across the shadowed emptiness of the lobby to the daylight beyond, where a squad of servitors glinted and shone as they made a slow but deliberate approach towards the stalk. There were eight or nine of them, all of different designs, wheeling, perambulating or sliding, with manipulators and cutting tools raised high.

'They've trapped us,' Caillebot said, marvelling. 'They let us get back here because they knew we'd take the elevator. That was another of your ideas, Prefect.'

'Do you want to shut up now, or after I've rammed this down your throat?' Thalia asked, unclipping the buzzing warm handle of her whiphound.

The leading machines had reached the shadow of the overhang sheltering the wide doorway leading into the lobby. Three marbled steps led up to the level of the main floor, where the lift was situated. The walking machines began ascending the steps with slow but deliberate intent.

Thalia felt the whiphound tremble in her grip, as if its heart was racing.

'You already said it was damaged,' Caillebot said. 'How much use is it going to be against all those if it could barely hold back two?'

Thalia thumbed the heavy control that invoked sword mode and hoped that there was still enough functionality left in the whiphound to spool out and stiffen its filament. The handle buzzed like a trapped wasp; nothing happened. She thumbed the control again, willing the whiphound to respond.

The filament inched out, the buzzing intensifying. Ten centimetres, then fifteen. Twenty before it reached its limit. But it appeared to be rigid and straight.

Thalia sliced into the black metal trelliswork of the elevator doors. She felt more resistance than when she had cut through the hedge, but that was only to be expected. Keeping her cool, knowing that nothing would be gained from panicking, she worked her way methodically across and then down. She directed the whiphound blade back up to the point where she had started, the last few cuts taking almost as long as the dozen or so that had preceded them. Then the rectangle of trelliswork clattered outwards onto the marble floor. The servitors had already reached the top of the stairs and were beginning to cross the expanse of the lobby. Two of the ambulatory machines were even assisting one of the wheeled variants over the obstacle of the steps.

'The stairs,' Thalia said. 'Run like hell, and don't stop running until you get to the top.'

Thalia moved with the party, but kept herself between them and the machines. She walked backwards, facing the servitors, holding the damaged whiphound in front of her. She had turned the arming dials into alignment again, ready to throw the broken weapon as a grenade. But as her heels touched the stairs, something made her change her mind. Nothing would be gained from attacking these machines now; more would always follow.

Thalia clipped the whiphound back onto her belt and started climbing the stairs behind the others.

CHAPTER 15

Gaffney experienced a moment's hesitation as he clipped the safe-distance line to his belt. How easy it would be to fail to secure the latch, so that the line snapped off just when he reached its maximum extension. Then he would sail on through the boundary of the exclusion volume, into the sphere of space around Jane Aumonier into which the scarab forbade the intrusion of all but the smallest of objects. Aumonier would have a second or two to register both the failure of the line and the Euclidean inevitability of Gaffney's onward progress. No force in the universe could stop him from colliding with her.

How fast would it be? he wondered. How clean, how merciful? He'd pondered the literature concerning sudden, non-medical decapitation. It was confusing and contradictory. Very few subjects had survived to testify to their experiences. There'd be blood, certainly. Litres of it, at arterial pressure.

Blood did interesting, artistic things in weightlessness.

'Prefects,' Aumonier said as she became aware of the delegation's presence. 'I wasn't expecting a visit. Is something the matter?'

'You know what this is about, Jane,' Gaffney said, beginning his drift into the chamber. Next to him, Crissel and Baudry fastened their own safe-distance tethers and kicked off from the wall. 'Please don't make it any more difficult than it already is.'

'I'm not sure I understand.'

'We've come to announce our decision,' Crissel said, in a regretful tone of voice. 'You must stand down for the duration, Jane. Until the present crisis is averted, and the nature of the change in the scarab has become clear to us.'

'I can still do my job.'

Baudry spoke next. 'No one's doubting that,' she said. 'Whatever else this is about, it has absolutely nothing to do with your professional competence, now or at any time in the past.'

'Then what the hell is it about?' Aumonier snapped back.

'Your continued well-being,' Gaffney said. 'I'm sorry, Jane, but you're simply too valuable an asset to risk in this way. That may sound mercenary, but that's just the way it is. Panoply wants to have you around next week, not just today.'

'I'm managing fine, aren't I?'

'Demikhov and the other specialists feel that the scarab's recent state-changes may have been triggered by alterations in your body's biochemical equilibrium,' Crissel said. 'You could cope when all we had to deal with was the occasional lockdown, but with the possibility of all-out war between the Ultras and the Glitter Band—'

'I'm coping, damn you.' She looked Crissel hard in the eyes, doubtless trying to connect with the sympathetic ally she had always been able to count on in the past. 'Michael, listen to me. The crisis is past its point of maximum severity.'

'You can't know that for sure.'

Aumonier nodded firmly. 'I can. Dreyfus has a firm lead. He's zeroing in on whoever murdered Ruskin-Sartorious and I expect to hear a name from him any time now. Once we have hard evidence, we'll broadcast a statement to the entire Band, ordering calm. The Ultras will be exonerated.'

'*If* he gives you a name,' Crissel said.

'I think Tom can be relied upon, don't you?' Then a subtle shift in mood revealed itself on her face. 'Wait a minute. The fact that Tom isn't here – the fact that he's outside on field duty – isn't in any way accidental, is it? You've timed this exquisitely.'

'Dreyfus's presence or absence is irrelevant,' Gaffney said. 'And so, it must be said, is your compliance. We have a majority vote, Jane. That means you must stand down, irrespective of your wishes. Must and will. You have no further say in the matter.'

'Take a look around you,' Jane Aumonier said. 'A good, long look. This is my world. It's all I've known for eleven years of uninterrupted consciousness. None of you can even begin to imagine what that means.'

'It means you could use a good rest,' Gaffney said. Then he raised his arm and spoke into his cuff. 'Commence shutdown, please.'

One by one, habitat by habitat, the displays blanked out, leaving only the black interior surface of Aumonier's office sphere. The blackness was soon absolute, with the entry door the only source of illumination in the space.

Jane Aumonier made a small clicking noise, as if she'd touched her tongue against the roof of her mouth. 'This is an outrage,' she said, her voice hardly raised above a whisper.

'It's necessary and you'll thank us for it later,' Gaffney replied. 'As of now, your authority is suspended on medical grounds. As we've stressed, this action isn't being taken on disciplinary grounds. You may not like us right now, but you still have our utmost respect and loyalty.'

'Like hell I do.'

'Get it out of your system now, Jane. We understand your rage. We'd be surprised if you weren't angry with us.'

'You didn't have to take the habitats away from me.' She was speaking slowly, with a kind of iron calm. 'If you wanted to take me out of the command loop, all you had to do was remove my ability to give orders or offer guidance. *You didn't have to take the habitats away from me.*'

'But we did,' Gaffney said. 'You're too much of a professional, Jane. Do you honestly think you'd stop worrying about the crisis just because we took away your authority? Do you honestly think you'd stop fretting, stop obsessing, every time a new piece of data comes in? Do you honestly think your stress levels wouldn't actually get worse if we let you see but not act? I'm sorry, I know this is hard, but this is the way it has to be.'

'We've discussed the matter with Demikhov,' Baudry said. 'He agrees that the present crisis poses an unacceptable risk to your mental well-being. He consented to this action.'

'You'd have found a way to twist his advice to suit your purpose no matter what he said.'

'That isn't fair,' Crissel said indignantly. 'And we're not going to leave you in the dark, so to speak. We can assign other inputs to the sphere. Historical feeds. Fictions. Puzzles. Enough to keep you occupied.'

'Don't even think of lecturing me about keeping occupied,' Aumonier said to him, with genuine menace.

'We're just trying to help,' Baudry said. 'That's all we've ever wanted to do.'

'I wish you'd acknowledge the reasonableness of our actions,' Gaffney said, 'but your refusal to do so in no way alters what must be done. We'll leave you now. Your usual medical care regime will of course continue unaffected. You may request any data feed, within reason. Access to the usual habitat-monitoring channels will of course be embargoed ... and for the time being, I don't think it's a good idea for you to be able to tap into any of the news networks. Contact with Panoply personnel will also have to restricted—'

'When Tom gets back—' she began.

'He'll bow to our authority,' Gaffney said.

Dreyfus and the Conjoiner woman exited the sleeping chamber and made their way out of the sinuous labyrinth of her ship. Dreyfus kept looking over his shoulder, wary that some restless and vengeful spirit might be following them from that house of abominations.

'My trust in you is provisional,' Clepsydra said, before reminding him that she still had control over the musculature of his suit. 'If you can help me reach other Conjoiners, and bring help to save the rest, you shall have my gratitude. If I suspect that you are like the other man, the one who wears the same kind of suit, you shall discover the consequences of betraying me.'

Dreyfus decided not to dwell on her threat. He was simply glad to be out of the butcher's theatre of the dismembered dreamers. 'Can I call my deputy?'

'You may, but I am detecting no incoming carrier signal.'

Dreyfus tried. Clepsydra was right. 'He must still be attempting to contact Panoply for help.'

'You'd better hope it comes quickly, in that case. Aurora almost certainly knows you're here.'

'Will she harm the sleepers?'

'She may, if only to stop anyone else obtaining access to Exordium.' Clepsydra moved with panther-like speed and grace as they ascended the long thread of the docking connector. 'But that would be the only reason. Lately she has bored of us. We're a toy that won't do what she wants.'

Dreyfus recalled something Clepsydra had told him earlier. 'You said she punished you if you dreamed something she didn't like. What did you mean by that?'

'Aurora expected to glean certain truths from the future. When our prognostications conflicted with her expectations, she grew resentful, as if we were lying to her out of spite.'

'Were you?'

'No. What we told her was what we saw. She just didn't like the message she was being given.'

'Which was?'

'That something bad is going to happen. Not today, not tomorrow. Not for years to come. But not so far in the future that it isn't of concern to her. If I have learned one thing from the glimpses of her mind, it is that she is a cold and cunning strategist, profoundly concerned with her own long-term survival.'

'And your message gave her something to be scared about?'

'So it would appear,' Clepsydra said.

'Care to elaborate?'

'Only to say that everything you cherish, everything you work for, everything you hold precious will have its end. You are very proud of this intricate little community of yours, with its ten thousand habitats, its ticking clockwork mechanisms of absolute democracy. And perhaps in your own small way you are entitled to some of that pride. But it won't last for ever. One day, Prefect, there will be no Glitter Band. There will be no Panoply. There will be no prefects.'

They reached the viewing station where Dreyfus had first glimpsed the imprisoned ship. When they had both cleared the docking connector, he used the control panel to dim the lights and seal the silver door.

'What disaster did you foresee?'

'A time of plague,' Clepsydra said.

Dreyfus shivered, as if someone had just walked over his grave. 'What does Aurora think about that?'

'It concerns her. In the thoughts that she lets slip, I've sensed a great plan being pushed towards reality. She fears the future we have shown her. She will fear it less if she controls it.'

'In what way?'

'For now she hides, flitting furtively from shadow to shadow, surviving by her wits. She lives in your world, but her influence over it is limited. I believe she means to change that. She means to become more powerful. She will rip control of human affairs from your fumbling hands.'

'You're talking about a takeover,' Dreyfus said.

'Call it what you will. You must be ready for her when she shows herself. She will move quickly, and you will not have much time to react.'

It did not take long to return to the sealed door, the one that had cut him off from Sparver and the corvette. It stood as intact and impervious as when he had left it.

'This shaft goes all the way around the rock, doesn't it?'

Clepsydra's expression was blank. 'Yes. Why?'

'Because we'll have to work our way around if we're going to reach the shaft that leads to my ship. Assuming we don't encounter any more obstructions on the way ...'

Clepsydra closed her eyes, jamming them tight as if she was trying to remember the name of an old acquaintance. She raised her palm to the door, tensing the fingers slightly as if holding some fierce, slavering creature at bay.

Something clicked in the mechanism and the door hummed open.

'I didn't realise—' Dreyfus began.

'I said I could not tap into the optical architecture. I mentioned nothing of doors.'

'I'm impressed. Can you all do stuff like that?'

'Not all of us, no. Very small children need tuition before they have the necessary finesse.'

'Very small children.'

'It's nothing for a Conjoiner. We feel the same way about talking to machines as fish do about swimming in water. We hardly notice we're doing it.' Then she cocked her head slightly. 'There is a carrier signal now.'

'Sparver?' Dreyfus asked. 'Are you reading me?'

'Loud and clear. You must be closer than before.'

'I'm on my way back up to the surface lock. I have a witness with me, so don't be too surprised.'

'I'm in the storage area just under the lock. I was coming back down to you with a plasma torch.'

'No need now. You can meet us aboard the ship. Did you manage to get that message through to Thalia?'

'I got a message through to Muang, but Thalia wasn't answering.'

Dreyfus felt his spirits dip. 'Did you tell him to keep trying?'

'It's worse than that.' Sparver sounded genuinely sorry that he had to be the bearer of bad news. 'Muang's lost contact with her completely. He isn't even receiving a signal from her bracelet.'

'Did he have time to get any kind of message through to her?'

'Nothing, Boss. But at least help's on its way to us.'

'Can you cope with a vacuum crossing?' Dreyfus asked Clepsydra, preparing to fix his own helmet back into place. 'Our ship isn't mated with the exterior airlock. You'll have to pass through a suitwall as well.'

'I'd survive vacuum even if I didn't have a suit. Worry about yourself before you worry about me.'

'Just asking,' Dreyfus said.

They were back aboard the corvette in less than five minutes. Sparver was waiting for them on the other side of the suitwall, his arms crossed in anticipation. Clepsydra's suit stayed intact during its passage through the wall, but once she was inside the corvette she made a point of removing her helmet rather than simply folding it back into her suit, and pressed it against an adhesive area on the wall with a natural fluency that suggested she'd been on similar ships a thousand times before. Dreyfus could not help but interpret the gesture as indicative of Clepsydra's provisional trust in her new hosts.

'This is my partner, Deputy Field Prefect Bancal,' Dreyfus told Clepsydra, introducing Sparver. 'I don't know what you've heard about hyperpigs, but there's nothing you need fear from him.'

'Nor does he have anything to fear from me,' Clepsydra answered, her voice low and level.

'Is she a guest or a prisoner?' Sparver asked.

'She's a protected witness. She's been through hell and now we have to safeguard both Clepsydra and her colleagues.'

'How many more of them are there down there?'

'A lot. But we can't do anything for them right now, not until help arrives. I hope you impressed the seriousness of our situation on Muang.'

'He got the message.'

'There are nearly a hundred Conjoiners aboard that ship. When help arrives I'll call Jane and get her to task some more assets. We're going to need a Heavy Medical Squad as well. ETA, roughly?'

Sparver glanced through the flight deck passwall just as the console chimed. 'Proximity alert,' he said. 'Guess that's the help arriving. That was quick.'

'Too bloody quick,' Dreyfus said, a bad feeling brewing low in his gut.

Without seeking permission from either of her hosts, Clepsydra hauled herself across the cabin and through into the vacant flight deck. 'This is the other vehicle from Panoply?' she asked.

'Hopefully,' Sparver said.

'Then why is it coming in on such a fast approach?'

'Guess they're in a bit of a hurry to get to us,' Sparver said.

'They're in more than a hurry. Not even a Conjoiner vehicle

could slow down from that kind of speed without pulping everyone aboard.'

'Then maybe they're planning to overshoot the rock and come back around on a second pass,' Sparver answered.

'They're not overshooting,' Clepsydra said. 'If your tracking system is correct, the incoming ship is on a collision vector.'

Quickly Dreyfus pulled himself into the flight deck and checked the proximity display. He saw the icon of the approaching vehicle and recognised its identifier tag.

'It's not the deep-system vehicle we were hoping for,' he said. 'It's the freighter from Marco's Eye that we saw earlier.'

'Aurora must have tapped into its navigation system, deviating it from its usual flight-path,' Clepsydra said. 'She is going to use it to ram you out of existence, and destroy the evidence of this rock.'

'She's that powerful?' Dreyfus asked.

'It would not take great power, merely great cunning and stealth.'

Sparver joined them. 'How long have we got?'

'Eighty-five seconds,' Clepsydra said.

'Then we're in trouble,' Sparver replied. 'We can't get this thing moving inside of a minute, and even then we wouldn't get far enough away from the surface to make a difference.'

'Seventy-five seconds.'

'We can suit up, return to the rock. If we can get far enough underground—'

'The rock will be destroyed,' Clepsydra said, with stony detachment.

'There isn't time in any case,' Dreyfus said. 'It'd take too long to cycle through the airlock.'

'We have less than a minute,' said Clepsydra.

'The countdown isn't helping,' Sparver replied. 'Maybe we should start thinking about the pods. We've got enough for all three of us. We don't have much time, but—'

'Will they eject us away from the rock, or towards it?' Clepsydra asked.

'They're dorsal pods. We're belly-down now, so—'

'They'll eject us into space,' Dreyfus finished.

'We have thirty-eight seconds,' Clepsydra said. 'I suggest we adjourn to the pods.'

They were designed to be used in dire emergency, when every second counted, so there was little in the way of preliminaries to attend to. Even so, Dreyfus sensed that they were down to the last ten seconds before all three of them were safely ensconced in their own single-person pods.

'The pods have transponders,' he told Clepsydra, just before they sealed the door on her. 'The deep-system vehicle will pick all of them up, but it may take some time.'

Five seconds later he was webbed into his own unit. He reached up over his forehead and tugged down the heavy red handle that triggered the pod's escape system. Quickmatter erupted into the empty spaces to cocoon him against the coming acceleration. When it arrived, it still felt as if the bones of his spine were being compressed to the thickness of parchment.

Then he lost consciousness.

Thalia snapped on her glasses and peered into the gloom of the windowless chamber, while Cyrus Parnasse stood back with his veined, muscular hands planted on his hips, for all the world like a farmer surveying his crops. They were alone in a section of the polling core sphere located well below the viewing gallery where the other citizens were holed up. Boxy grey structures loomed out of the darkness, stretching away into the distance.

She tapped a finger against the side of the glasses, keying in additional amplification. 'What am I looking at here, Citizen Parnasse? It just looks like a load of boxes and junk.'

'Exactly what it is, girl. This is a storage room for the Museum of Cybernetics, full of stuff they haven't got room for in the main exhibit areas. There're hundreds of rooms like this, right across the campus. But this is the only one we can reach without going back down to the lobby.'

'Oh.'

'I reckoned we could use some of this stuff to barricade those stairs. What d'ya think?'

'I didn't think any of those machines would be able to get up the stairs.'

'They won't: too big, most of 'em, or with the wrong kind of design. But there are plenty of machines out there that'll fit the bill. Now that they know we're up here, how long do you think it'll be before they arrive and start climbing?'

'Not long,' she said. 'You're right. I should have thought of that sooner.'

'Don't be too hard on yerself. Had a lot to think out in the last few hours, I dare say.'

True, Thalia thought. *True but still entirely inexcusable.* 'You don't think we're too late, do you?'

'Not if we get a shift on. There's enough junk here to block the stairs, provided we get a chain movin' it. We'll need to take care of the elevator shaft as well.'

'I hadn't forgotten that, just didn't think there was much we could do about it.'

The elevator was still at the bottom of the shaft, waiting in the lobby where they had abandoned it.

'If that whip-thing of yours still works, we can cut a hole into the shaft and drop as much of this stuff down it as we can manage. That's five hundred metres straight down. It won't stop the machines for ever, if they're really determined to get the elevator moving, but it'll definitely put a dent in their plans.'

'From where I'm standing, that sounds a lot better than nothing.' But when she touched her whiphound, it responded by buzzing against her belt, giving off an acrid smell. They'd had to use it to cut through the locked door into the storage room and now it was protesting again. Thalia wondered how long it would last before giving out on her completely; it was already of limited utility as a weapon, unless employed as a one-off grenade.

'We shouldn't hang around,' Parnasse said. 'I'll start moving boxes if you go and round up some help.'

'I hope they're in a mood to take orders.'

'They will be if they think you know exactly what you're doing.'

'I don't, Citizen Parnasse. That's the problem.' Thalia pulled off her glasses and slipped them into her pocket. 'I've been putting a brave face on it, but I'm seriously out of my depth here. You saw what we had to deal with outside.'

'I saw you coping, girl. You might not feel like it, but you look as if you're doing a decent enough job.' Thalia's expression must have been sceptical, because he added: 'You got us all back here alive, didn't you?'

'Right back where we started, Citizen Parnasse. My escape attempt didn't actually achieve much, did it?'

'It was the right thing to try. And we didn't know about the servitors when we started off, did we?'

'I suppose not.'

'Think of it as a scouting expedition. We went out and gathered intelligence on our situation. We learned things we wouldn't have learned if we'd just stayed up here, waitin' for help to come.'

'Put it like that, it almost sounds as if I knew what I was doing.'

'You did know. You've convinced me already, girl. Now all you have to do is convince the others. And you know where that starts, don't you?'

There was a heavy feeling in her stomach, but she forced herself to smile. 'With me. I've got to start acting as if I know exactly what to do, or else the others aren't going to listen.'

'That's the spirit.'

She looked into the darkness of the storage room. 'Maybe we can block the stairs and the shaft. But what do we do afterwards? Sooner or later those machines are going to find a way to get to us, just like they've got to the other citizens outside. Everything we've seen says they're being directed by an external intelligence, something with problem-solving capability.' She thought of the way the citizens had been rounded up and pacified, cowed into submission by warnings of an attack against the habitat. 'Something smart enough to lie.'

'One step at a time,' Parnasse said. 'We deal with the barricades first. Then we worry about a dazzling encore.'

He made it sound so effortless, as if all they were talking about was the right way to cook an egg.

'All right.'

'You're a prefect, girl. A lot might've changed since you dropped by today, but you're still wearing the uniform. Make it count. The citizens are depending on you.'

CHAPTER 16

Dreyfus was still drowsing as the deep-system cruiser completed its docking, nudging home into its skeletal berthing rack. He'd slept all the way back to Panoply, from almost the moment when his escape pod was brought aboard the ship and he was reunited with Sparver and Clepsydra. He dreamed of reeking halls of raw human meat hanging from bloodstained hooks, and a woman gorging herself on muscle and sinew, her mouth a red-stained obscenity. When he woke and sifted through his memories of recent events, his experiences in the Nerval-Lermontov rock felt like something that had happened yesterday, rather than a handful of hours earlier. The rock itself no longer existed. The impact of the fully laden and fuelled freighter had pulverised it, so that nothing now remained of its secrets except a cloud of expanding rubble; a gritty sleet that would rain against the sticky collision shields of the Glitter Band habitats for many orbits. Even if Panoply had the resources, there'd have been little point in combing that debris cloud for forensic clues. Clepsydra was now Dreyfus's only witness to the unspeakable crime that had been visited upon her crewmates.

But it wasn't Clepsydra who was foremost in his thoughts.

As soon as he pushed through the cruiser's suitwall, Dreyfus badgered Thyssen, the tired-looking dock attendant. 'Thalia Ng, my deputy. When did she get in?'

The man glanced at his compad. He had red rings around his eyes, vivid as brands. 'She's still out there, Tom.'

'On her way back?'

'Not according to this.' The man tapped his stylus against a line of text. 'CTC haven't logged her undocking from House Aubusson. Looks as if she's still inside.'

'How long since she docked there?'

'According to this . . . eight hours.'

Dreyfus knew that Thalia had only had a six-hundred-second access window. No matter what obstacles she'd encountered, she should have been out of there by now.

'Has anyone managed to get through to her since Deputy Sparver's attempt?'

The man looked helpless. 'I don't have a record of that.'

'She has one of your ships,' Dreyfus snapped. 'I'd say it was your duty to keep adequate tabs on her, wouldn't you?'

'I'm sorry, Prefect.'

'Don't apologise,' Dreyfus growled. 'Just do your job.' He grabbed a handhold and pulled himself towards the exit.

'If you think you're having a shitty day,' Sparver told Thyssen, 'you should try ours on for size.'

The two prefects and their Conjoiner guest cleared the dock and transitioned through to one of the standard-gravity wheels. They detoured to the medical section and left Clepsydra in the care of one of the doctors, an impish man named Mercier whom Dreyfus trusted not to ask awkward questions. Mercier affected the appearance and manners of a bookish scholar of the natural sciences from some remote candlelit century. He dressed impeccably, with a white shirt and cravat, his eyes forever hidden behind green-tinted half-moon spectacles, and chose to surround himself with facsimiles of varnished wooden furniture, conjured museum-piece medical tools and gruesome illustrative devices. He had a perplexing attachment to paperwork, to the extent that he made many of his reports in inked handwriting, using a curious black stylus that he referred to as a 'fountain pen'. Yet for all his eccentricities, he was no less competent than Dr Demikhov, his counterpart in the adjoining Sleep Lab.

'This is my witness,' Dreyfus explained. 'She's to be examined humanely, treated for malnutrition and dehydration and then left well alone. I'll return in a few hours.'

Clepsydra cocked her crested bald egg of a head and narrowed her eyes. 'Am I now to consider myself a prisoner again?'

'No. Just a guest, under my protection. When the crisis is over, I'll do all in my power to get you back to your people.'

'I could call my people myself if you give me access to a medium-strength transmitter.'

'Part of me would like nothing better. But someone was prepared to kill to keep you a secret. They succeeded in killing your compatriots. That means they'll be more than prepared to kill again if they know you're here.'

'Then I should leave. Immediately.'

'You'll be safe here.'

'I think I can trust you,' Clepsydra said, her attention on Dreyfus, as if no one else was in the room. 'But understand one thing: it is a significant thing for a Conjoiner to trust a baseline human being. People like you did terrible things to people like me, once. Many of them would do the same things again if the chance arose. Please do not give me cause to regret this.'

'I won't,' Dreyfus said.

Dusk was falling in the long shaft of House Aubusson. The mirror-directed sunlight pouring through the window bands was being slowly dimmed as the bands lost their transparency. Soon the habitat would be dark even when its orbit brought it around to Yellowstone's dayside.

From the curved viewing gallery of the polling core, more than five hundred metres above the ground, Thalia watched the shadows encroach like an army of stalking cats. She could still make out the pale-grey trajectory of the pathway they had tried to follow out of the formal gardens, towards the objective of the endcap wall. But the grey was darkening, losing definition as darkness won. Soon even the concentric black hoops of the window bands would be indistinguishable from the surrounding terrain. She would be able to make out neither the path nor the endcap. The attempted crossing, which had seemed achievable only hours earlier, now struck her as hopelessly misguided. It would have been ill-conceived if all they had to contend with was enraged and panicked citizenry looking for someone to mob. But now Thalia knew that the darkening landscape was in all likelihood crawling with dangerous machines, serving an agenda that definitely did not involve the preservation of human life.

But, she thought, seeking composure before she turned around, the citizens in her care must not see how frightened she was. She had come into their world bearing the authority of Panoply and that was the role she was obliged to continue playing. She had failed them once; twice if she included the mistake with the polling core that had created this mess in the first place. She could not let them down again.

'So what's the next step in your plan?' Caillebot asked, with a sarcastic lilt that Thalia couldn't help but detect.

'The next step is we stay put,' she said.

'Up here?'

'We're safe here,' she said, mentally deleting the 'for now' that she had been about to add. 'This is as good a place to wait as anywhere we could have picked in the habitat.'

'Wait for what, exactly?' Caillebot asked.

She'd been expecting the gardener to start needling her as soon as they were inside the core. 'For Panoply, Citizen. They're on their way. There'll be a deep-system cruiser docked with us before you can blink.'

'It'll take more than a few prefects to deal with those machines.'

Thalia touched the buzzing remains of her whiphound. It was uncomfortably hot against her thigh, like a metal bar cooling down from a furnace. 'They'll have the tools for the job, don't you worry about that. All we have to do is hold out until they get here. That's our part of the equation.'

'"Hold out",' repeated Paula Thory mockingly. The plump woman was sitting on one of the inert-matter benches encircling the pearl-grey pillar of the polling core. 'You make it sound so easy, like waiting for a train.'

Thalia walked over to the woman and knelt down to bring them face to face. 'I'm not asking you to run a mile. We're perfectly safe up here.'

'Those barricades won't hold for ever.'

'They don't have to.'

'Well, isn't *that* reassuring.'

Thalia fought to keep herself from snapping at the woman, or worse. Paula Thory had only joined the chain gang grudgingly, when she realised that she would be the only one refusing to assist in the work effort. It had been difficult and exhausting, but between them they must have shoved at least three tonnes of junk down the elevator shaft, and at least as much again down the winding spiral of the staircase. They'd created a barricade out of ancient dead servitors and decrepit computers and interface devices, many of which must have come to the Yellowstone system from Earth and were probably several hundred years old at the very least. There'd even been something huge and metal, a kind of open iron chassis crammed with cogs and ratchets. It had made a most impressive racket as it tumbled down the stairs.

Thalia had called for a rest period, but three citizens – Parnasse, Redon and Cuthbertson – were still shovelling junk down the lift shaft and stairs. Every now and then Thalia would hear a muffled *crump* as the material hit the bottom of the shaft, or a more drawn-out avalanche of sound as something tumbled down the stairs.

'It doesn't have to hold for ever because we're not staying up here for ever,' she said. 'Help will arrive before the machines get through the barricades. And even if it doesn't, we're working on a contingency plan.'

Thory looked falsely interested. 'Which would be?'

'You'll hear about it when all the pieces are in place. Until then all you have to do is sit tight and help with the barricades when you feel willing and able.'

If Paula Thory took that as a barb, she showed no evidence of it. 'I think you're keeping something from us, Prefect – the fact that you haven't got a clue how we're going to get out of this mess.'

'You're perfectly welcome to leave, in that case,' Thalia said, with exaggerated niceness.

'Look!' Jules Caillebot called suddenly from his vantage point by the window.

Thalia stood up, grateful for any excuse not to have to deal with Thory.

'What is it, Citizen?' she said as she strolled over.

'Big machines are moving in.'

Thalia looked out over the darkening panorama. Though it was becoming increasingly difficult to make out distinct objects anywhere in the habitat – nightfall had come with dismaying speed – the machines Caillebot spoke of were at least partially illuminated. As large as houses, they were moving in several slow processions through the civic grounds around the Museum of Cybernetics. They advanced on crawler tracks and huge lumbering wheels, crushing their way across walkways and through tree lines.

'What are they?' Thalia asked.

'Heavy construction servitors, I think,' Caillebot said. 'There's been a lot of building work going on lately, especially around the new marina at Radiant Point.'

Thalia wondered what kind of damage those machines could do to the stalk supporting the polling core. Although she had not voiced her thoughts to the others, she had convinced herself that the machines would not do anything that might damage the core itself. Abstraction might be down for the citizens, but as far as she could tell, the machines were still being coordinated via low-level data transmissions that were dependent on the core. But that was just her theory, not something she was in any mood to see put to the test.

'They're carrying stuff,' Caillebot reported. 'Look at the hopper on the back of that one.'

Thalia struggled to make out detail. She remembered her glasses and slipped them on, keying in both magnification and intensity-amplification. The view wobbled, then stabilised. She tracked along the procession until she identified the machine Caillebot had indicated. It was a huge wheeled servitor, thirty or forty metres long, with scoops at either end feeding the trapezium-shaped hopper it carried on its back. The hopper was piled high with debris: rubble, dirt, torn sheets of composite mesh, chunks of machined metal of unfathomable origin. Thalia moved her view-point along the procession and saw that there was at least one other servitor hauling a similar load.

'You say those machines were working at the marina?'

'I think so.'

'If they're being tasked to work elsewhere, why would they be carrying all that junk?'

'I don't know.'

'Me neither. Maybe it's just debris left over from the work on the marina, and they just haven't been sent a specific command to unload it before moving elsewhere.'

'Possible,' said Caillebot doubtfully, 'but the marina wasn't built on the remains of an older community. They'd have needed to landscape soil, but I can't imagine there'd have been much in the way of actual debris to clear.'

Thalia snapped her focus to the head of the column. 'The procession's stopping,' she said. The machines had reached the base of one of the stalks that formed the ring surrounding the Museum of Cybernetics, close to the point where Thalia's party had emerged from the underground train station. 'I don't like this, Citizen Caillebot,' she said, temporarily forgetting her promise to Cyrus Parnasse that she would look and act at all times as if she was confident both in her abilities and of shepherding the citizens to safety.

She'd lied when she said an escape plan was being hatched. In truth, they had progressed no further than working out their options for barricading the machines. Parnasse had tried to put an optimistic face on it, but they both knew those barricades wouldn't hold for ever against determined brute force.

'I don't like it either,' the landscape gardener said.

The procession broke up, with various machines moving slowly into position around the base of the stalk. Thalia had the eerie impression that she was watching some kind of abstract ballet. It all happened silently, for the windows of the polling sphere were both airtight and thoroughly soundproofed. The debris-carriers were standing back from the stalk, while what were clearly specialised demolition and earthmoving servitors brought their brutal-looking tools into play. The machines commenced their labours almost immediately. Shovels and claws began to dig into the flared base of the stalk, chipping away boulder-sized scabs of pale cladding. At the same time, a little further around the curve of the stalk, Thalia saw the sun-bright strobe of a high-energy cutting tool.

'It doesn't make any sense,' she said, as much for her own benefit as Caillebot's. 'They're attacking the wrong stalk. They know we're not at the top of that one.'

'Maybe attacking it isn't the idea.'

She nodded. Caillebot had been on her case after the upgrade had failed, but now his tone of voice and body language suggested he was prepared to bury the hatchet, at least for now. 'I think you're right,' she said. Then she tracked her glasses onto one of the other processions, at least a kilometre away, tilted gently towards her on the footslopes of the habitat's curving wall. 'Those machines are dismantling something as well. Can't tell what it is.'

'Mind if I take a look?' Caillebot asked.

She passed him the glasses. He pressed them cautiously to his eyes. Prefects weren't meant to share equipment like that, but she supposed if there was ever a time when the rules were meant to be bent, this was it.

'That's the open-air amphitheatre at Praxis Junction,' the gardener said. 'They're tearing into that as well.'

'Then it isn't just us. Something's going on here, Citizen Caillebot.'

He returned her glasses. 'You notice anything about those lines of machines?'

'Like what?'

'They're all moving in more or less the same direction. Maybe they didn't come from the marina after all, but they've still come from the direction of the docking endcap, where you came in. It looks to me as if they've been working their way along the habitat, stopping to demolish anything that takes their fancy.'

'How would machines cross the window panels?'

'There're roads and bridges for that kind of thing. Even if there weren't, the glass could easily take the weight of one of those machines, even fully loaded. The panels wouldn't have been an obstacle to them.'

'Okay, then. If they're headed away from the docking endcap, where are they likely to end up?'

'After they've swept through the whole habitat? Only one place to go – the trailing endcap. No major docking facilities there, so it's a dead end.'

'But they can't be carrying all that stuff for nothing. They must be gathering it for a reason.'

'Well, there's the manufactory complex, of course,' he said off-handedly. 'But that doesn't make any sense either.'

Thalia experienced a premonitory chill. 'Tell me about the manufactory complex, Citizen Caillebot.'

'It's practically dead, like I already told you. Hasn't run at normal capacity for years. Decades. Longer than I can remember.'

Thalia nodded patiently. 'But it's still there. It hasn't been removed, gutted, replaced or whatever?'

'You think they're going to crank it up again. Start making stuff on a big scale, feeding it with the junk the machines are collecting.'

'It's just an idea, Citizen Caillebot.'

'Ships?' he asked.

'Not necessarily. If you can make single-molecule hulls, there's nothing you can't make.' As an afterthought, she added: 'Provided you have the construction blueprint, of course. The manufactory won't be able to make anything unless it's given the right instructions.'

'You sound relieved.'

'I probably shouldn't be. It's just that I was thinking of all the unpleasant things you *could* make with a manufactory if you had the right blueprints. But the point is the only blueprints in the public domain are for things you can't hurt anyone with.'

'You sound pretty sure of that.'

'Try locating the construction blueprint for a space-to-space weapon, Citizen Caillebot, or an attack ship, or a military servitor. See how far you get before a prefect comes knocking.'

'Panoply keeps tabs on that kind of thing?'

'We don't just keep tabs. We make sure that data isn't out there. On the rare occasions when someone needs to make something nasty, they come to us for permission. We retrieve and unlock the files from our archives. We issue them and make damned sure they're deleted afterwards.'

'Then you're certain nothing nasty can come out of that manufactory?'

'Not without Panoply's help,' Thalia said bluntly.

Caillebot responded with a knowing nod. 'A day ago, Prefect, I'd have found that statement almost entirely reassuring.'

Thalia turned back to the window, ruminating on what the gardener had just said. The machines were working with the manic industry of insects. They had chewed deep into the lowest part of the stalk, exposing the geodesic struts that formed the structure's scaffolding. Judging by the rubble and remains being shovelled into a waiting hopper, the cutting tools were making short work of that as well.

'It's not going to last long,' Thalia said. Then she turned around and looked at the polling core, hoping that she was right about the machines needing to keep it intact, and therefore being unable to launch an all-out attack on the stalk supporting the sphere in which they were sheltering.

She'd been wrong about several things already today.

She hoped this wasn't another.

Dreyfus knew something was amiss as soon as he approached the passwall into Jane Aumonier's sphere and saw the two internal prefects waiting on either side of it, whiphounds drawn, tethered by quick-release lines that ran from their belts to eyelets in the doorframe. The passwall itself was set to obstruct.

'Is there a problem?' Dreyfus asked mildly. He'd occasionally been barred from talking to Aumonier when she was engaged in some activity that exceeded his Pangolin clearance. But it had never required the presence of security guards, and Aumonier had generally given him fair warning.

'Sorry, sir,' said the younger of the two guards, 'but no one's allowed to speak to Prefect Aumonier at the moment.'

'Why don't you let me be the judge of that?'

'Not without authorisation from the supreme prefect, sir.'

Dreyfus looked at the kid as if he was being asked to answer a deceptively simple riddle. 'She *is* the supreme prefect.'

The young guard looked embarrassed. 'Not presently, sir. Prefect Baudry is now acting supreme.'

'On what grounds was Prefect Aumonier removed from her position?' Dreyfus asked disbelievingly.

'I'm authorised to tell you that the decision was taken on the basis of medical fitness, sir. I thought you'd been informed, but—'

'I hadn't.' He was trying to keep his fury in check, not wanting to take out his anger on this kid the way he had abused Thyssen earlier. 'But I still want to talk to Prefect Aumonier.'

'Prefect Aumonier is in no fit state to talk to anyone,' said a gruff male voice behind Dreyfus. He pushed himself around to see Gaffney floating towards him along the same corridor he'd just traversed. 'I'm sorry, Field, but that's just the way it is.'

'Let me talk to Jane.'

Gaffney shook his head, looking genuinely regretful. 'I hardly need impress on you how precarious her situation is. The last thing she needs right now is someone upsetting her unnecessarily.'

'Jane isn't going to be the one who's upset if I don't get to see her.'

'Easy, Field. I know you've had a tough time today. But don't use it as an excuse to lash out at your superiors.'

'Did you have any part in removing Jane?'

'She wasn't "removed". She was relieved of the burden of command at a time when it would have been an intolerable imposition for her to have continued.'

In his peripheral vision, Dreyfus saw that the two guards were looking straight ahead with resolutely neutral expressions, pretending that they were not party to this high-level scuffle. Neither man had summoned the senior prefect. Gaffney must have been lurking nearby, Dreyfus thought: waiting until he tried to visit Aumonier.

'What's your angle here?' Dreyfus asked. 'Lillian Baudry's a good prefect when it comes to the details, but she doesn't have Jane's grasp of the big picture. You're counting on her making a mistake, aren't you?'

'Why on Earth would I want Lillian to fail?'

'Because with Jane out of the picture, you're one step closer to becoming supreme prefect.'

'I think you've said more than enough. If you had the slightest idea how ludicrous you sound, you'd stop now.'

'Where's Baudry?'

'In the tactical room, no doubt. In case it's escaped your attention, a crisis has been brewing while you've been pursuing your own interests.'

Dreyfus spoke into his bracelet. 'Get me Baudry.'

She answered immediately. 'Prefect Dreyfus. I was hoping to hear from you before too long.'

'Let me talk to Jane.'

'I'm afraid that wouldn't be wise. But would you mind coming up to tactical immediately? There's something we need to discuss.'

Gaffney looked on with a faint smile. 'I was on my way there before I ran into you. Why don't we go there together?'

Baudry, Crissel and Clearmountain were in attendance when Dreyfus and Gaffney arrived in the tactical room. The seniors were peering at the Solid Orrery from different angles. Dreyfus noticed that four habitats had been pulled out of the swirl of the ten thousand and enlarged until their structures were visible.

Crissel indicated a vacant position. 'Take a seat, Field Prefect Dreyfus. We were hoping you could explain something to us.'

Dreyfus remained standing. 'I understand you were part of the lynch mob that removed Jane from power while I was outside.'

'If you insist on characterising events in those terms, then yes, I was party to that decision. Do you have a problem with it?'

'Have a guess.'

Crissel stared at him equably, refusing to take the bait. 'Perhaps you haven't been paying attention, but there have been worrying changes in the state of the scarab, likely harbingers of something medically catastrophic.'

'I've been paying plenty of attention.'

'Then you'll know that Demikhov is deeply concerned about Jane's future prognosis. All that thing on her neck is waiting for is a trigger. When her stress hormones float above some arbitrary level, it's going to snip her spine in two, or blow her to pieces.'

'Right,' Dreyfus said, as if he was seeing something clearly for the first time. 'And you think removing her from office is the key to lowering her stress levels?'

'She's in the safest therapeutic regime we can devise. And when this is over, when the crisis is averted, we'll look into a strategy for returning Jane to at least some level of functional responsibility.'

'Is that what you told her? Or did you lie and say she could have her old job back when things have blown over?'

'We don't have time for this,' Gaffney purred, the first time he had spoken since their mutual arrival. He'd taken a seat next to Lillian Baudry. His hands rested on the table, the fingers of one caressing the clenched fist of the other. 'Take a look at the Solid Orrery, Field.'

'I've seen it, thanks. It's very pretty.'

'Take a better look. Those four habitats – ring any bells?'

'I don't know.' Dreyfus smiled sarcastically. 'What about you, Senior Prefect Gaffney?'

'Let me spell it out for you. You're looking at New Seattle-Tacoma, Chevelure-Sambuke, Szlumper Oneill and House Aubusson. The four habitats Thalia Ng was scheduled to visit and upgrade.'

Dreyfus felt some of his certainty evaporate. 'Go on.'

'As of just over six hours ago, all four habitats have been unreachable. They've dropped off abstraction.' Gaffney scrutinised Dreyfus's reaction and nodded, as if to emphasize that matters were exactly as grave as they sounded. 'All four habitats dropped off the net within sixty milliseconds of each other. That's comfortably inside the light-crossing time for the Glitter Band, implying a pre-planned, coordinated event.'

'You've always vouched for Thalia Ng,' Crissel said. 'Her promotion to field was fast-tracked on your recommendation. Beginning to look like a mistake now, isn't it?'

'I still have total faith in her.'

'Touching, undoubtedly, but the fact is she's visited four habitats and now they've all fallen silent. All she had to do was make a series of minor polling core upgrades. At the very least, doesn't that suggest procedural incompetence?'

'Not from where I'm standing.'

'What, then?' Crissel asked, fascinated.

'I think it's possible ...' But Dreyfus tailed off, feeling a sudden reluctance to state his theory openly. The seniors regarded him with stony-faced indifference. 'The deep-system cruiser that rescued us – is it still flight-ready?' he asked.

Baudry spoke now. 'Why do you ask?'

'Because the one way to settle this is to pay a visit to Aubusson. That's where Thalia was due last. If one of my deputies is in trouble, I'd like to know about it.'

'You've done enough gallivanting around for now,' Gaffney said.

'We're in a state of emergency, in case you hadn't noticed.'

Baudry coughed gently. 'Let's deal with the other matter, shall we? And please – sit down.'

'What matter would that be?' asked Dreyfus with exaggerated civility. But he took his seat as Baudry had requested.

'You brought a Conjoiner into Panoply, in express contravention of protocol.'

Dreyfus shrugged. 'Protocol can take a hike.'

'She can read our goddamn machines, Tom.' Baudry looked to the others for support. 'She's a walking surveillance system. Every operational secret in our core is hers for the taking, and you let her stroll into Panoply without even putting a Faraday cage around her skull.'

Dreyfus leaned closer. 'Isn't it written down somewhere that we look after victims and go after criminals?'

Crissel looked exasperated. 'We're not the law-enforcement agency you seem to think we are, Tom. We're here to ensure that the democratic apparatus functions smoothly. We're here to punish fraudulent voting. That's it.'

'My personal remit extends further than that, but you're welcome to yours.'

'Let's focus on the matter at hand – the Conjoiner woman,' Baudry said insistently. 'She may already have done incalculable harm in the short time she's been inside Panoply. That can't be helped now. What we can do is make sure that she doesn't do any more damage.'

'Do you want me to throw her into space, or will you do it?'

'Let's be adult about this, shall we?' Crissel said. 'If the Spi– if the *Conjoiner* woman is a witness, then naturally she must be protected. But not at the expense of our operational secrets. She must be moved to a maximum-security holding facility.'

'You mean an interrogation bubble.'

Crissel looked pained. 'Call it what you like. She'll be safer there. More importantly, so will we.'

'She'll be moved when Mercier says she's well enough,' Dreyfus said.

'Is she breathing?' When Dreyfus said nothing, Crissel looked satisfied. 'Then she's well enough to be moved. She isn't going to *die* on us, Tom. She's a survival machine. The human equivalent of a scorpion.'

'Or a spider,' Dreyfus said.

There was a gentle tap on the main doors. Crissel's eyes flashed angrily to the widening gap. A low-ranking operative – a girl barely out of her teens, with a pageboy haircut – entered the room timidly. 'Pardon, Seniors, but I was asked to bring this to your attention.'

'It'd better be good,' Crissel said.

'CTC contacted us, sirs. They say they're picking up reports about House Aubusson and the Chevelure-Sambuke Hourglass.'

'They're off the network. Yes. We know.'

'It's more than that, sir.' The girl placed the compad on the table, next to Gaffney. He picked it up by one corner, inhaling slowly as he digested its message. Without a word he slid it to Crissel. He glanced at it, glanced again, then passed the compad to Baudry. She read it, her lips moving slowly as she did so, as if she needed the sound of her own voice to lend the report a degree of reality.

Then she slid the compad over to Dreyfus.

'He doesn't have authority,' Crissel said.

'His deputy's inside Aubusson. He needs to see this.'

Dreyfus took the compad and read it for himself. His Pangolin boost was fading and it took more than the usual effort to read the words. At first he was convinced that he had made a mistake, despite the fears he was already nursing.

But there had been no error.

Two separate but similar incidents had occurred, within a few minutes of each other. One ship had been on final approach for docking at the Chevelure-Sambuke Hourglass when it was fired on by the habitat with what appeared to be normal anti-collision defences. The ship had sustained a near-fatal hull breach, too large to be patched by the intervention of quickmatter repair systems. The ship had abandoned its docking approach and put out an emergency distress signal, to which CTC had responded by redirecting two nearby vessels. The crew of the damaged ship had all survived, albeit with decompression injuries.

The second ship, on an approach to House Aubusson, had been less fortunate. The anti-collision defences had gored it open in an instant, spilling air and life into space. Its crew had died with merciful speed, but the ship itself had retained enough sentience to put out its own distress signal. CTC had again directed passing traffic to offer assistance, but this time there was nothing that could be done to save the victims.

All this had happened within the last eighteen minutes.

'I think we can safely rule out coincidence,' Dreyfus said, placing the compad back on the table.

'What are we dealing with?' Baudry asked with rigid composure. 'A systemic defence-system malfunction triggered by the loss of abstraction? Could that be the answer?'

'Everything I know about defence systems says that they can't malfunction in this way,' Crissel said.

'Yet it rather looks as if someone doesn't want anyone coming or going from those habitats,' Gaffney observed, reading the CTC report again.

'And the other two?' Baudry asked. 'What about those?'

'They're isolationist,' Dreyfus said. 'New Seattle-Tacoma is a haven for people who want their brains plugged into abstraction and don't care what happens to their physical bodies. Szlumper Oneill is a Voluntary Tyranny gone sour. Either way, neither's going to see much in- or outgoing traffic on a given day.'

'He's right,' Crissel said, favouring Dreyfus with a conciliatory nod. He turned to the still-waiting operative. 'You're still in contact with CTC?' Without waiting for an answer or conferring with the other seniors, he continued, 'Have them identify four unmanned cargo drones currently passing near the four habitats. Then put them on normal docking trajectories, just as if they were on scheduled approaches. If these were malfunctions, then someone inside may have had time to disable the anti-collision systems by now. If they weren't, we'll have confirmation that we're not dealing with one-off incidents.'

'There'll be hell to pay,' Gaffney said, shaking his head. 'Whatever those cargo drones are hauling, someone owns it.'

'Then I hope they have good insurance,' Crissel replied tersely. 'CTC has the right to requisition any civilian traffic moving inside the Glitter Band, manned or otherwise. Just because that clause hasn't been invoked in a century or so doesn't mean it isn't still valid.'

'I agree,' Dreyfus said. 'This is the logical course of action. If you were still allowing Jane her rightful authority, she'd agree to it as well.'

The operative coughed awkwardly. 'I'll get on to CTC immediately, sir.'

Crissel nodded. 'Tell them not to hang around. I don't want to have to wait hours before finding out what we're looking at here.'

An icy silence endured for many seconds after the girl had left the room. It fell to Dreyfus to break it. 'Let's not kid ourselves,' he said. 'We know exactly what's going to happen to those drones.'

'We still need confirmation,' Crissel said.

'Agreed. But we also need to start thinking about what we do once the news comes in.'

'Hypothesise for a moment,' Baudry said, a quaver in her voice that she could not quite conceal. 'Could we be dealing with a breakaway movement? Four states that wish to secede from the umbrella of Panoply and the Glitter Band?'

'If they wanted to, they'd be free to do so,' Dreyfus said. 'The mechanism already exists, and it doesn't require shooting down approaching ships.'

'Maybe they don't want to secede on our terms,' Baudry said, in the manner of one advancing the suggestion for debating's sake rather than out of any deep personal conviction that it was likely.

Crissel nodded patiently. 'Maybe they don't. But once you've decided to opt out of Panoply's protection, out of the democratic apparatus, what do you gain from staying inside the Glitter Band anyway?'

'Not much,' Dreyfus said. 'Which is why this can't be an attempt at secession.'

'A hostage situation?' Baudry speculated. 'Fits the facts so far, doesn't it?'

'For now,' Dreyfus allowed.

'But you don't think that's what we're looking at.'

'You don't take hostages unless there's something you want that you don't already have.'

Crissel looked pleased with himself. 'Everyone wants to be richer.'

'Maybe they do,' Dreyfus answered, 'but there's no way hostage-taking is going to achieve that for you.'

'So they're not trying to become richer,' Baudry said. 'That still leaves a universe of possibilities. Suppose someone doesn't just want to opt out of our system of government, but dismantle it completely?'

Dreyfus shook his head. 'Why would they want to? If someone wants to experiment with a different social model, they're welcome to do so. All they have to do is recruit enough willing collaborators to set up a new state. Provided they let their citizens have the vote, they can even stay within the apparatus. That's why we have freak shows like the Voluntary Tyrannies. Someone somewhere decided they wanted to live in that kind of place.'

'But like you said, they have to abide by certain core principles. Maybe they find even those basic strictures too stifling. Perhaps they want to force a single political model on the entire Glitter Band. Ideological zealots, for instance: political or religious extremists who won't rest until they force everyone else to see things their way.'

'You might have something if we weren't looking at four completely disparate communities. Thalia's habitats have almost nothing in common with each other.'

'All right,' Baudry said, clearly wearying of debate. 'If it isn't about forcing through a political end, what is it about?'

Once again Dreyfus thought back to the things he had learned inside the Nerval-Lermontov rock, including the possibility that not everyone in the room could necessarily be trusted. He had wanted more time to evaluate his position, more time in which to bring at least one of the other seniors around to his side and use them as leverage to put Aumonier back into the saddle. But the news concerning the latest attacks had forced his hand sooner than he would have wished. He had to say something or he would be guilty of withholding vital data from his own organisation.

'The prisoner told me something,' he said, choosing his words with exquisite care, like a man picking his way through a minefield. 'Obviously, I can't be certain that she was telling the truth, or that her isolation hadn't turned her insane. But all my instincts – all my old policeman's instincts, you might say – told me she was on the level.'

'Then perhaps you'd better tell us,' Gaffney said.

'Clepsydra believes that some group or organisation within the Glitter Band has obtained intelligence concerning a coming crisis. Something worse than what we're facing now, even given the latest news.'

'What kind of crisis?' Baudry asked.

'Something catastrophic. Something in the order of a collapse of the entire social matrix, if not the end of the Glitter Band itself.'

'Preposterous,' Crissel said.

Gaffney raised a restraining hand. 'No. Let's hear him out.'

'Clepsydra believes that this group or organisation has devised a plan for averting whatever disaster they've seen coming, even if that means denying us our usual liberties.'

Baudry nodded in the general direction of the Solid Orrery. 'And the blackout, the hostile actions we've just heard about?'

'I think we could be seeing the start of a takeover bid.'

'Voi,' Baudry answered sharply. 'You're not serious. Surely you're not serious.'

'Makes perfect sense to me,' Dreyfus said. 'If we couldn't be trusted to guarantee the future security of the Glitter Band, what would you do?'

'But only four habitats ... there are ten thousand more out there that are still ours!'

'I think Thalia was the key,' Dreyfus said. 'Unwittingly, of course. Her code was contaminated. It must have been tampered with to open a security loophole that didn't exist before. Thalia was *supposed* to make that upgrade Bandwide, across the entire ten thousand, in one fell swoop.'

'But she didn't want to do that, I recall,' said Baudry.

'No,' said Dreyfus. 'She insisted on identifying four of the likely worst cases and running manual installations. That way she could correct errors in real-time, on the spot, and make sure no one was without their precious abstraction for more than a few minutes. Once she'd supervised those four installations, she could tweak the code to make sure the remaining ten thousand went without a hitch.'

'But those habitats have been without abstraction for hours,' Crissel said.

'That isn't Thalia's fault. Her diligence didn't cause this, Michael. It prevented an even worse crisis. If Thalia had done the easy, obvious thing, we wouldn't be looking at four habitats off abstraction, we'd be looking at ten thousand. The takeover would be complete. We'd have lost the Glitter Band.'

'Now let's not get carried away,' Gaffney said, smiling at the others. 'We have enough of a mess to deal with without indulging in apocalyptic fantasies.'

'It isn't a fantasy,' Dreyfus said. 'Someone wanted this to happen.'

'Why, though?' Crissel asked. 'What group of people could possibly organise themselves to seize control of the entire Band? It's one thing to take habitats off abstraction. But the citizens inside won't just roll over and accept that. You'd need an armed militia to actually subjugate them. Thousands of people for each habitat, at the very least. We'd be looking at an invisible army ten million strong just to have a chance of making this work. If there was a movement that powerful, that coordinated, we'd have seen it coming years ago.'

'Maybe it's a different kind of takeover,' Dreyfus said.

'What did the Conjoiner say about the people behind this?' asked Baudry.

'Not much.' Dreyfus hesitated, conscious that every divulgence carried a measurable risk. 'I got a name. A figure called Aurora. She may have some connection to the Nerval-Lermontov family.'

Baudry peered at him. 'They lost a daughter in the Eighty. Her name was Aurora, I believe. You're not seriously suggesting—'

'I'm not making any inferences. Maybe I can get more out of Clepsydra when she's feeling stronger, and she's certain she can trust us.'

'You're worried about *her* trusting *us*?' Baudry said.

A knock at the door signalled the return of the operator. She entered the room with a trace less diffidence than before.

'And?' Gaffney asked.

'The drones have been requisitioned, sirs. First is scheduled to dock at Szlumper Oneill in eleven minutes. Within twenty-two minutes, the remaining three will have completed approaches to their respective habitats.'

'Very good,' Gaffney allowed.

'I've secured high-res visual feeds of all four habitats, sirs. I can pipe the observations through to the Solid Orrery, with your permission.'

Gaffney nodded. 'Do it.'

The Solid Orrery reconfigured itself, allocating much of its quick-matter resources to providing scaled-up representations of the four silent communities. They swelled to the size of fruit, while the rest of the Glitter Band shrank down to a third of its former size. Tiny moving jewels signified the requisitioned drones, steered onto docking approaches. The prefects watched the spectacle wordlessly as the minutes oozed by.

Make me wrong, Dreyfus thought. *Make all this turn out to be the deluded fabulation of a worn-out field prefect, resentful at the shabby treatment accorded his boss. Make Clepsydra's testimony turn out to be the burblings of a mad woman, driven insane by years of isolation. Show us that Thalia Ng really did make mistakes, despite everything I know to the contrary. Show us that the first two attacks were accidents caused by hair-trigger defence systems twitching like headless snakes when abstraction went down.*

But it wasn't to be. Eleven minutes after the girl had spoken, the anti-collision systems of Szlumper Oneill opened fire on the approaching drone, destroying it utterly. If anything the fire was more concentrated, more purposeful, than on the previous two occasions. The jewel-like representation of the drone swelled to a thumb-sized smear of twinkling light, then reformed into the pulsing tetrahedral icon that symbolised an object of unknown status.

Three minutes later a second drone attempted to dock at House Aubusson, and met with precisely the same fate. Five minutes after that, a third drone was annihilated as it braked to engage with Carousel New Seattle-Tacoma. Three minutes after that, twenty-two minutes since the girl had spoken, the guns of the Chevelure-Sambuke Hourglass directed savage fire on the final drone.

The Solid Orrery reformed itself into its usual configuration. A brittle silence ensued.

'So maybe it's war after all,' Baudry said eventually.

CHAPTER 17

The isolation chamber was clad in a honeycomb of identical interlocking grey panels, one of which functioned as a passwall. A handful of the panels were illuminated at any one time, but the pattern changed slowly and randomly, robbing the weightless prisoner of any fixed frame of reference. Clepsydra was floating, knees raised to her chest, arms linked around her shins. The patterns of lights erased all shadow, lending her the two-dimensional appearance of a cut-out. She appeared to be unconscious, but it was common knowledge that Conjoiners did not partake of anything resembling normal mammalian sleep.

Since his emergence through the passwall didn't appear to have alerted her to his presence, Dreyfus cleared his throat gently. 'Clepsydra,' he announced, 'it's me.'

She turned her crested skull in his direction, her eyes gleaming dully in the subdued light of the bubble. 'How long has it been?'

The question took Dreyfus aback. 'Since you were transferred from Mercier's clinic? Only a few hours.'

'I'm losing track of time again. If you had said "months" I might have believed you.' She pulled a face. 'I don't like this room. It feels haunted.'

'You must feel very cut off in here.'

'I just don't like this room. It's so dead that I'm starting to imagine phantom presences. I keep seeing something out of the corner of my eye, then when I look it isn't there. Even the inside of the rock wasn't like this.'

'I apologise,' Dreyfus said. 'I committed a procedural mistake in allowing you into Panoply without considering our operational secrets.'

Clepsydra unfolded herself with catlike slowness. In the sound-absorbing space, the acoustics of her voice had acquired a metallic timbre. 'Will you get into trouble for that?'

He smiled at her concern. 'Not likely. I've weathered worse storms than a procedural slip-up. Especially as no damage was done.' He cocked his head. 'No damage *was* done, I take it?'

'I saw many things.'

'I don't doubt it.'

'Many things that were of no interest to me,' she added. 'It may reassure you to know that I've buried those secrets far below conscious recall. I can't simply forget them: forgetting isn't a capacity we possess. But you may consider them as good as forgotten.'

'Thank you, Clepsydra.'

'But that won't be the end of it, will it? You might believe me. The others won't.'

'I'll see to it that they do. You're a protected witness, not a prisoner.'

'Except I'm not free to leave.'

'We're worried someone wants to kill you.'

'That would be my problem, wouldn't it?'

'Not when we still think you can tell us something useful.' Dreyfus had come to a halt a couple of metres from Clepsydra's floating form, oriented the same way up. Before entering the bubble, he'd divested himself of all weapons and communications devices, including his whiphound. It occurred to him, in a way it had not before, that he was alone in a surveillance blind spot with an agile humanoid-machine hybrid that could easily kill him. Autopsies of dead Conjoiners had revealed muscle fibres derived from chimpanzee physiology, giving them five or six times normal human strength. Clepsydra might have been weakened, but he doubted that she'd have much trouble overpowering him, if she wished.

Some flicker of that unease must have showed on his face.

'I still frighten you,' she said, very quietly. 'But you came unarmed, with not even a knife for protection.'

'I've still got my acid wit.'

'Now tell me exactly what it is *I* have to fear. Something's happened, hasn't it? Something very, very bad.'

'It's begun,' Dreyfus said. 'Aurora's takeover. We've lost control of four habitats. Attempts to land ships on them have been met by hostile action.'

'I didn't think it would be so soon.'

'When Sparver and I found you, she must have realised Panoply were closing in fast. She decided to go with just the four habitats that were already compromised rather than wait for the upgrade software to be installed across the entire ten thousand.'

Clepsydra looked puzzled. 'What good will that do her? Even if you have lost control of those habitats now, you still have access to the resources of the rest of the Glitter Band, not to mention Panoply's own capabilities. Aurora will not be able to hold out indefinitely.'

'I'm guessing she assumes she can.'

'All the times I sensed Aurora's mind, I detected an intense strategic cunning; a constantly probing machinelike evaluation of shifting probabilities. This is not a mind capable of pointless gestures, or elementary lapses of judgement.' Clepsydra paused. 'Have you had any formal contact with her?'

'Not a squeak. Other than our theory about the Nerval-Lermontovs, we still don't really know who she is.'

'You believe she was one of the Eighty?'

Dreyfus nodded. 'But everything we know says that all of the Eighty failed. Aurora was one of the most famous cases. How can we have been wrong about that?'

'What if there was something different about her simulation? Some essential detail that varied from the others? I told you that we were aware of Calvin Sylveste's procedures. We know that he fine-tuned some of the neural-mapping and simulation parameters from one volunteer to the next. Superficially, it appeared to make no difference to the outcome. But what if it did?'

'I don't follow. She either died or she didn't.'

'Consider this, Prefect. After her Transmigration, Aurora was truly conscious in her alpha-level embodiment. She was aware of the other seventy-nine volunteers, in close contact with many of them. They'd hoped to form a community of minds, an immortal elite above the rest of corporeal humanity. But then Aurora saw the others failing: their simulations stalling, or locking into endless recursive loops. And she began to fear for herself, even as she suspected that she might be different, immune to whatever deficiency was stalking her comrades. But she was truly fearful for another reason.'

'Which was?' Dreyfus asked.

'By the time the last of the Eighty was scanned, the true nature of what Calvin was attempting had begun to percolate through to the mass consciousness. What he had in mind was not simply a new form of immortality, to improve upon what was already available via drugs and surgery and medichines. Calvin sought the creation of an entirely new and superior stratum of existence. The Eighty wouldn't just be invulnerable and ageless. They'd be faster, cleverer, almost limitless in their potentiality. They would make the Conjoiners seem almost Neanderthal. Can you guess what happened next, Prefect?'

'A backlash, perhaps?'

'Groups began to emerge, petitioning for tighter controls over the Eighty. They wanted Calvin's subjects to be confined to firewall-shielded computational architectures – minds in cages, if you will. More hardline elements wanted the Eighty to be frozen, so that the implications of what they were could be studied exhaustively before they were allowed to resume simulated consciousness. Even more extreme factions wanted the Eighty to be deleted, as if their very patterns were a threat to civilised society.'

'But they didn't get their way.'

'No, but the tide was growing. Had the Eighty not begun to fail of their own accord, there's no telling how strong the anti-Transmigration movement might have become. Those of the Eighty who were still functioning must have seen the walls closing in.'

'Aurora amongst them.'

'It's just a theory. But if she suspected that her kind were going to be hounded and persecuted, that her own existence was in danger even if she didn't succumb to stasis or recursion, might she not have devised a scheme to ensure her own survival?'

'Fake her own stasis, in other words. Leave a data corpse. But in the meantime the real Aurora was somewhere else. She must have escaped into the wider architecture of the entire Glitter Band, like a rat under the floorboards.'

'I think there is a very real possibility that this is what happened.'

'Were there other survivors?'

'I don't know. Possibly. But the only mind I ever sensed clearly was Aurora's. Even if there are more, I think she is the strongest of them. The figurehead. The one with the dreams and plans.'

'So here comes the big question,' Dreyfus said. 'If Aurora's really behind the loss of those four habitats – and it's starting to look as if she is – what does she want?'

'The only thing that has ever mattered to her: her own long-term survival.' Clepsydra smiled gravely. 'Where you figure in that is another matter entirely.'

'Me personally?'

'I mean baseline humanity, Prefect.'

After a moment Dreyfus asked, 'Would the Conjoiners help us if we were in trouble?'

'As you helped us on Mars two hundred and twenty years ago?'

'I thought we were over all that.'

'Some of us have long memories. Perhaps we would help you, as you might help an animal caught in a trap. Lately, though, we have our own concerns.'

'Even after everything Aurora did to you?'

'Aurora poses no threat to the greater community of the Conjoined. You might as well take revenge on the sea for drowning someone.'

'Then you'll do nothing.'

He thought that was the end of it, but after a long silence she said, 'I admit I would find ... *consolation* in seeing her hurt.'

Dreyfus nodded approvingly. 'Then you do feel something. You've notched down those old baseline human emotions, but you haven't expunged them completely. She did something horrific to you and your crew, and part of you needs to hit back.'

'Except there is nothing to hit.'

'But if we could identify her vulnerabilities, find a way to make life difficult for her ... would you help us?'

'I wouldn't hinder you.'

'I know you looked deep into our data architecture before I brought you into this room. You told me you'd seen nothing of interest. But now that the damage is done, I want you to sift through that information again. It's all in your head. Look at it from different angles. If you can find something, anything, no matter how apparently inconsequential, that sheds any light on Aurora's location or nature, or how we might strike back, I need to know about it.'

'There may be nothing.'

'But there's no harm in looking.'

A tightness appeared in her face. 'It will take a while. Do not expect me to give you an answer immediately.'

'That's all right,' Dreyfus said. 'I've got another witness I need to speak to.'

Just when he thought they were done, that she had said everything she wanted to say to him, Clepsydra spoke again.

'Dreyfus.'

'Yes?'

'I do not forgive your kind for what they did to us on Mars, or for the years of persecution that followed. It would be a betrayal of Galiana's memory were I to do that.' Then she looked him in the eyes, daring him not to reciprocate. 'But you are not like those men. You have been kind to me.'

Dreyfus called by the Turbine hall and sought out Trajanova, the woman he'd spoken to after the earlier accident. He was gladdened to see that two of the four machines were now spinning again, even if they were obviously not operating at normal capacity. The machine nearest the destroyed unit was still stationary, with at least a dozen technicians visible inside the transparent casing. As for the destroyed machine itself, there was now little evidence that it had ever existed. The remains of the casing had been removed, leaving circular apertures in the floor and ceiling. Technicians crowded around both sites, directing heavy servitors to assist them in the slow process of installing a new unit.

'You've obviously been busy,' Dreyfus told Trajanova.

'Field prefects aren't the only ones who work hard in this organisation.'

'I know. And my remark wasn't intended as a slight. We've all been under pressure and I appreciate the work that's gone on down here. I'll make sure the supreme prefect hears about it.'

'And which supreme prefect would that be?'

'Jane Aumonier, of course. No disrespect to Lillian Baudry, but Jane's the only one who matters in the long run.'

Trajanova looked sideways, not quite able to meet Dreyfus's eyes. 'For what it's worth ... I don't agree with what happened. Down here we have a lot of respect for Jane.'

'She's earned it from all of us.'

There was an awkward silence. Across the room someone hammered at something.

'What will happen now?' Trajanova asked at length.

'We work for Lillian, just as we worked for Jane. I don't know what else you've heard, but we have a new crisis on our hands.' Dreyfus chose to volunteer information, hoping it might calm some of the troubled water between them. 'I need to resume interviews with my beta-level subjects: I'm hoping that they can shed some light on what's going on and how we can stop it.'

Trajanova looked at the two spinning Search Turbines. 'Those units are running at half-capacity. I can't risk spinning them any faster. But I could prioritise your search queries, if that would help. You wouldn't notice much difference.'

'I can still run my recoverables?'

'Yes, there's more than enough capacity for that.'

'Good work, Trajanova.' After a moment, he said, 'I know things didn't work out between us when you were my deputy, but I've never had the slightest doubt concerning your professional competence down here.'

She considered his remark before answering. 'Prefect ...' she began.

'What is it?'

'What you said before – the last time we spoke. About how you'd had the feeling your own query had triggered the accident?'

Dreyfus waved a dismissive hand. 'It was foolish of me. These things happen.'

'Not down here they don't. I checked the search log and you were right. Of all the queries handled by the Turbines in the final second before the accident, yours was the last one to come in. You searched for priors on the Nerval-Lermontov family, correct?'

'Yes,' Dreyfus said cautiously.

'Just after your query was shuffled into the process stack, the Turbine began to exceed its own maximum authorised spin rate. It spun itself apart in less than one quarter of a second.'

'It must still have been a coincidence.'

'Prefect, now I'm the one trying to convince you. Something went wrong, but I don't believe it was coincidence. The operating logic of one of these things is complex, and much of the instruction core was lost when the Turbine failed. But if I could ever piece it back together, I think I know what I'd find. Your search query was a trigger. Someone had implanted a trap in the operating logic, waiting to be primed by your question.'

Dreyfus mulled over her hypothesis. It dovetailed with his suspicions, but it was another thing entirely to hear it from Trajanova's lips.

'You honestly think someone could have done that?'

'I could have done it, if I'd had the mind to. For anyone else, it would have been a lot more difficult. Frankly, I don't see how they could have done it without triggering high-level security flags. But somehow they managed.'

'Thank you,' Dreyfus said softly. 'I appreciate your candour.

Given what's happened, are you satisfied that I won't cause any more damage just by querying the system?'

'I can't promise anything, but I've installed manual overspeed limits on both operating Turbs. No matter what traps may still be lurking in the logic, I don't think the Turbs will be able to self-destruct. Go ahead and ask whatever you need to ask.'

'I will,' Dreyfus said. 'But I'll tread ever so softly.'

Delphine Ruskin-Sartorious appraised him with her sea-green eyes, cool as ice. 'You look very tired. More so than last time, and you already looked tired back then. Is something the matter?'

Dreyfus pressed a fat finger against the side of his brow, where a vein was throbbing. 'Things have been busy.'

'Have you made progress on the case?'

'Sort of. I've an idea who may have been behind the murders but I'm still not seeing a motive. I was hoping you'd be able to join a few dots for me.'

Delphine pushed strands of dirty black hair under the cloth scarf she wore as a hairband. 'You'll have to join some for me first. Who is this suspect you're thinking of?'

Dreyfus sipped from the bulb of coffee he'd conjured just before stepping into the room. 'My deputy and I followed an evidence chain, trying to find out who called your habitat to put you off making the deal with Dravidian. The lead we followed brought us to the name of another family in the Glitter Band.'

Delphine's eyes narrowed.

Genuine interest, Dreyfus thought.

'Who?' she asked.

Feeling as if he was treading across a minefield, he said, 'The Nerval-Lermontovs. Do you know of them?'

Beneath the workstained white smock, her slight shoulders moved in an easy shrug. 'I know *of* them. Who doesn't? They were one of the big families, fifty or sixty years ago.'

'What about a specific connection with your family?'

'If there is one, I can't think of it. We didn't move in the same social orbits.'

'Then there's no specific reason you can think of why the Nerval-Lermontovs would want to hurt your family?'

'None whatsoever. If you have a theory, I'd love to hear it.'

'I don't,' Dreyfus said. 'But I was hoping you might.'

'It can't be the answer,' she said. 'The trail you followed must have led you up a blind alley. The Nerval-Lermontovs would never have done something to my family. They've had their share of tragedy, but that doesn't make them murderers.'

'You mean Aurora?'

'She was just a girl when it happened to her, Prefect. Calvin Sylveste's machines ate her mind and spat out a clockwork zombie.'

'So I heard.'

'What are you not telling me?'

'Suppose a member of the Nerval-Lermontov family was planning something.'

'Such as?'

'Like, say, a forced takeover of part of the Glitter Band.'

She nodded shrewdly. 'Hypothetically, of course. If something like that was actually happening, you'd have told me, wouldn't you?'

Dreyfus smiled tightly. 'If it was, can you think of a reason why your family might have posed an obstacle to those plans?'

'What kind of obstacle?'

'All the evidence at my disposal says that someone connected with the Nerval-Lermontov family arranged for the torching of your habitat. Dravidian had nothing to do with it: he was set up, his ship and crew infiltrated by people who knew how to trigger a Conjoiner drive.'

'Why?'

'Wish I knew, Delphine. But here's a guess: someone or something connected with the Ruskin-Sartorious Bubble was considered a threat to those plans.'

'I can't imagine who or what,' she said defiantly. 'We were just minding our own business. Anthony Theobald was trying to marry me into a rich industrial combine. He had his friends, people who came to visit him, but they weren't acquaintances of mine. Vernon just wanted to be with me, even if that meant being spurned by *his* family. I had my art . . .'

The second time he had invoked her, she had mentioned visitors to Anthony Theobald. When he'd pressed her for more information, she'd become reticent. A family secret, something she'd sworn not to talk about? Perhaps. He'd gone easy on her since then, earning her trust, but he knew that the matter could not be put off indefinitely.

He would have to come at it sideways.

'Let's talk about the art. Maybe there's a clue there that we're missing.'

'But we've already been over that: the art was just a pretext, an excuse to disguise the true reason we were murdered.'

'I wish I could convince myself of that, but there's a connection that won't stop surfacing. The family that did this to you had close ties with House Sylveste because of what happened to their daughter. And your breakthrough art – the pieces that started getting you attention – were inspired by Philip Lascaille's journey into the Shroud. Lascaille was a "guest" of House Sylveste when he drowned in that fish pond.'

'Is there an aspect of life in this system that those bloody people *haven't* dug their claws into?'

'Maybe not. But I'm still convinced there's a link.'

She took so long to answer that for a while he thought she was ignoring the question, treating it with contempt. As if a policeman could have the slightest insight into the artistic process ...

'I told you how it happened. How one day I stepped back from a work in progress and felt that something had been guiding my hand, shaping the face to look like Lascaille.'

'And?'

'Well, there was a bit more to it than that. When I made that mental connection, it was as if a bolt of lightning had hit my brain. It wasn't just a question of tackling Lascaille because I felt it was potentially interesting. It was about having no choice in the matter. The subject was *demanding* that I treat it, pulling me in like a magnetic field. From that moment on I could not ignore Philip Lascaille. I had to do his death justice, or die creatively.'

'Almost as if Philip Lascaille was speaking through you, using you as a medium to communicate what he endured?'

She looked at him scornfully. 'I don't believe in the afterlife, Prefect.'

'But figuratively, that's how it felt to you. Right?'

'I felt a compulsion,' she said, as if this admission was the hardest thing she had ever had to do. 'A need to see this through.'

'As if you were speaking for Philip?'

'No one had done that before,' she said. 'Not properly. If you want to call it speaking for the dead, so be it.'

'I'll call it whatever you call it. You were the artist.'

'I *am* the artist, Prefect. No matter what you might think of me, I still feel the same creative impulse.'

'Then if I gave you the means, a big piece of rock and a cutting torch, you'd still want to make art?'

'Isn't that what I just said?'

'I'm sorry, Delphine. I'm not trying to pick a fight with you. It's just that you're the most assertive beta-level I've ever encountered.'

'Almost as if there's a person behind these eyes?'

'Sometimes,' Dreyfus admitted.

'If your wife hadn't died the way she did, you'd feel differently about me, wouldn't you? You'd have no reason to disavow the right of a beta-level to call itself alive.'

'Valery's death changed nothing.'

'You think that, but I'm not so sure. Look at yourself in a mirror one of these days. You're a man with a wound. Whatever happened back then, there was more to it than what you told me.'

'Why would I keep anything from you?'

'Perhaps because there's something you don't want to face up to?'

'I've faced up to everything. I loved Valery but now she's gone. That was eleven years ago.'

'The man who gave the order to kill those people, so that the Clockmaker would be stopped,' Delphine prompted.

'Supreme Prefect Dusollier.'

'What was so abhorrent about that decision that he felt compelled to kill himself afterwards? Didn't he do a brave and necessary thing? Didn't he at least give those citizens a quick and painless death, as opposed to what would have happened if the Clockmaker had reached them?'

Dreyfus had lied to her before. Now he felt compelled to speak the truth, as if that was the only decent thing to do. He spoke slowly, his throat dry, as if he was the one under interrogation.

'Dusollier left a suicide note. He said: "We made a mistake. We shouldn't have done it. I'm sorry for what we did to those people. God help them all."'

'I still don't understand. What was there to be sorry about? He had no other choice.'

'That's what I've been telling myself for eleven years.'

'You think something else happened.'

'There's an anomaly. The official record says that the nukes were used almost immediately after Jane Aumonier was extracted. By then, Dusollier and his prefects knew there was no hope of rescuing the trapped citizens, and that it would only be a matter of time before the Clockmaker escaped to another habitat.'

'And the nature of this anomaly?'

'Six hours,' Dreyfus said. 'That was how long they actually waited before using the nukes. They tried to cover it up, but in an environment like the Glitter Band, wired to the teeth with monitors, you can't hide a thing like that.'

'But shouldn't a prefect, of all people, be able to find out what happened during those missing hours?'

'Pangolin privilege will only get you so far.'

'Have you thought to ask anyone? Like Jane Aumonier, for instance?'

Dreyfus smiled at his own weakness. 'Have you ever put your hand into a box when you don't know what's inside it? That's how I feel about asking that question.'

'Because you fear the answer.'

'Yes.'

'What is it that you fear? That something might have killed Valery before SIAM was destroyed?'

'Partly, I suppose. There's another thing, though. There was a ship called the *Atalanta*. It had been floating in the Glitter Band for decades, mothballed. Then Panoply moved it, at the same time as the crisis, to a holding position very close to SIAM.'

'Why had the ship been mothballed?'

'It was a white elephant, financed by a consortium of Demarchist states with a view to freeing themselves from any dependence on the Conjoiners. Problem was, its drive system didn't work as well as it was meant to. It only ever made one interstellar flight, and then they abandoned any plans to make more of them.'

'But you think it would have made an excellent lifeboat.'

'It's crossed my mind.'

'You think Panoply tried to get those people off during those missing six hours. They brought in this abandoned ship, docked it with SIAM and evacuated the trapped citizens.'

'Or they tried to,' Dreyfus said.

'But something must have gone wrong. Or else why would Dusollier have shown such remorse?'

'All I know is that the *Atalanta* is part of the key. But that's as much as I've been able to find out. Part of me doesn't want to find out anything else.'

'I can see why this is so hard for you,' Delphine said. 'To lose your wife is one thing. But to have this mystery hanging over her death ... I'm truly sorry for you.'

'I have another part of the key. I have this vivid picture of Valery in my head. She's turning towards me, kneeling on soil, with flowers in her hand. She's smiling at me. I think she recognises me. But there's something wrong with the smile. It's the mindless smile of a baby seeing the sun.'

'Where does that memory come from?'

'I don't know,' Dreyfus answered honestly. 'It's not as if Valery even liked gardening.'

'Sometimes the mind plays tricks on us. It might be the memory of another woman.'

'It's Valery. I can see her so clearly.'

After an uncomfortably long pause, Delphine said, 'I believe you. But I don't think I can help you.'

'It's enough to talk about it.'

'You haven't discussed these things with your colleagues?'

'They think I got over her death years ago. It would undermine their confidence in me to know otherwise. I can't have that.'

There was a longer pause before she answered, 'You *think* it might.'

Then her image seemed to twitch back a couple of seconds and she answered his question again with exactly the same words and inflection: 'You *think* it might.'

'Is something the matter?' Dreyfus asked.

'I don't know.'

'Delphine. Look at me. Are you all right?'

Her image twitched back again. Rather than answering the question, she fixed Dreyfus with fearful eyes. 'I feel strange.'

'Something's wrong with you.'

Her voice came through too quickly, speeded up as if on helium. 'I feel strange. Something's wrong with me.'

'I think you're corrupted,' Dreyfus said. 'It could be related to the problems we've had with the Search Turbines. I'm going to freeze your invocation and run a consistency check.'

'I feel strange. I feel strange.' Her voice accelerated, the words piling up on top of each other. 'I feel strange I feel strange *Ifeelstrange Ifeelstrange* ...' Then she found a moment of lucidity, her voice and the speed of her speech returning to normal. 'Help me. I don't think this is ... normal.'

Dreyfus raised his sleeve, tugging down his cuff. His lips shaped the beginning of the word 'freeze'.

'No,' Delphine said. 'Don't freeze me. I'm frightened.'

'I'll retrieve you as soon as I've run a consistency check.'

'I think I'm dying. I think something's eating me. Help me, Prefect!'

'Delphine, what's happening?'

Her image simplified, losing detail. Her voice came through slow, sexless and bass-heavy. 'Diagnostic traceback indicates that this beta-level is self-erasing. Progressive block overwipe is now in progress in partitions one through fifty.'

'Delphine!' he shouted.

Her voice was treacle-slow, almost subsonically deep. 'Help me, Tom Dreyfus.'

'Delphine, listen to me. The only way I can help you is by bringing your murderer to justice. But for that to happen you have to answer one last question.'

'Help me, Tom.'

'You mentioned people who came to visit Anthony Theobald. Who were these people?'

'Help me, Tom.'

'Who were the people? Why did they come to visit?'

'Anthony Theobald said ...'

She stalled.

'Talk to me, Delphine.'

'Anthony Theobald said ... we had a guest. A guest that lived downstairs. And that I wasn't to ask questions.'

He spoke into his bracelet. 'Freeze invocation.'

'Help, Tom.'

What was left of her became motionless and silent.

Dreyfus called Trajanova. She was flustered, not happy to be distracted from the work at hand. She appeared to be squeezed into the shaft of one of her Turbines, suspended in a weightless sling with her back against the curved glass tube that encased the machinery.

'It's important,' Dreyfus said. 'I just invoked one of my beta-levels. She crashed on me halfway through the interview.'

Trajanova transferred a tool from one hand to the other, via her mouth. 'Did you re-invoke?'

'I tried, but nothing happened. The system said the beta-level image was irrevocably corrupted.'

Trajanova grunted and eased sideways to find a more comfortable position. 'That isn't possible. You got a stable invocation until halfway through your interview?'

'Yes.'

'Then the base image can't have been damaged.'

'My subject appeared to be aware that something was corrupting her. She said she felt as if she was being eaten. It was as if she could feel her core personality being erased segment by segment.'

'That isn't possible either.' Then a troubling thought made her frown. 'Unless, of course—'

'Unless what?'

'Could someone have introduced some kind of data weapon into your beta-level?'

'Hypothetically, I suppose so. But when we pulled those recoverables out of Ruskin-Sartorious, they were subjected to all the usual tests and filters we normally run before invocation. They were badly damaged as well. I had Thalia working overtime just to stitch the pieces back together. If there'd been a data weapon – or any kind of self-destruct function – Thalia would've seen it.'

'And she reported nothing unusual to you?'

'She told me she'd only been able to get three clean recoveries. That was all.'

'And we can trust Thalia not to have missed anything?'

'I'd swear on it.'

'Then there's only one answer: someone must have got to the beta-level after it entered Panoply. From a technical standpoint, it wouldn't have been all that difficult. All they'd have needed to do was find some data weapon in the archives and embed it in the beta-level. It could have been programmed to start eating the recoverable as soon as you invoked, or maybe it was keyed to a phrase or gesture.'

'My God,' Dreyfus said. 'Then the others ... I want to talk to them as well.'

'It could be too dangerous if the same code has been embedded. You'll lose your other two witnesses.'

'What do you mean, lose? Don't I get a back-up?'

'There is no back-up, Tom. We lost all duplicate images when the Turb blew.'

'This was all engineered.'

'Listen,' Trajanova said, with sudden intensity, 'I'm going to be stuck in here for a few more hours. I have to get this Turb back up to speed before I do anything else. But as soon as I'm done I'll look at the recoverables. I'll see if I can salvage anything from the one that crashed, and look for a data weapon embedded in the other two. Until then, whatever you do, don't invoke them.'

'I won't,' Dreyfus said.

'I'll call you when I'm done.'

It was only when he had finished speaking with Trajanova that Dreyfus paused to examine his state of mind. What he found was both unexpected and shocking. Only a few days ago, he would have regarded the loss of a beta-level witness as akin to the destruction of some potentially incriminating forensic evidence. He would have been irritated, even angered, but his feelings would have arisen solely because an investigation had been hampered. He would have felt no emotional sentimentality concerning the loss of the artefact itself, because an artefact was all that it was.

That wasn't how he felt now. He kept seeing Delphine's face in those final moments, when she had still retained enough sentience to recognise the inevitability of her own death.

But if beta-levels were never alive, how could they ever die?

Gaffney's first thought was that Clepsydra was dead, or at least comatose. He experienced a moment of relief, thinking that he would be spared the burden of another death, before the truth revealed itself. The Conjoiner woman was still breathing; her deathlike composure was merely her natural state of repose when no one was in attendance. Her sharp-boned face was already turning towards him, moving with the smoothness of a missile launcher locking on to a target, her eyes widening from drowsy slits.

'I was not expecting you to come back so quickly,' she said, 'but perhaps the timing is fortuitous. I've been thinking about our previous conversation—'

'Good,' Gaffney said.

There was a measurable pause before she spoke again. 'I was expecting Dreyfus.'

'Dreyfus couldn't make it. Otherwise detained.' Gaffney came to rest in the bubble, having judged his momentum with expert precision. 'That's not a problem, is it?'

He felt Clepsydra's attention pierce the skin of his face, mapping the bones under the skin. His skull itched. He had never felt so intensely *looked at* in all his life.

'I can guess why you are here,' she said. 'Before you kill me, though, you should be aware that I know who you are.'

The statement unnerved him. Perhaps it was bluff, perhaps not. If she had truly looked into Panoply's archives, then she might have seen employee records. It didn't matter. She could scream out his name and the world wouldn't hear her.

'Who said anything about killing?' he asked mildly.

'Dreyfus came unarmed.'

'More fool him. I wouldn't enter a room with a Conjoiner inside unless I was carrying a weapon. Or would you have me believe that you couldn't kill me in an eyeblink?'

'I had no intention of killing you, Prefect. Until now.'

Gaffney spread his arms. 'Go ahead, then. Or rather, tell me what you were going to tell Dreyfus. Then kill me.'

'Why do I need to tell you? You know everything.'

'Well, maybe not everything.' Gaffney unclipped his whiphound and thumbed it to readiness. 'Nothing would give me greater pleasure than to let you leave this place alive and be reunited with your people. Voi knows you deserve it. Voi knows you've earned the right to some reward for the service you've provided. But it just can't happen. Because if I let you out of here, you'd endanger the state of affairs that must now come into being. And if you did that, you'd be indirectly responsible for the terrible things your people dreamed were coming, the terrible things I'm striving to avert.' He thumbed another stud, causing the whiphound to spool out its filament and move to full attack posture. In the weightless sphere of the bubble, the filament swayed back and forth like a tendril stirred by languid sea currents.

'You have no idea what we saw in Exordium,' Clepsydra said.

'I don't need to. That's Aurora's business.'

'Do you know *what* Aurora is, Gaffney?'

He hoped that she did not catch the subliminal hesitation in his response. More than likely she did. Very little was subliminal to Conjoiners. 'I know everything I need to know.'

'Aurora is not a human being.'

'She looked pretty human to me when we met.'

'In person?'

'Not exactly,' he admitted.

'Aurora was a person once upon a time. But that was a long time ago. Now Aurora is something else. She is a life form that has never truly existed before, except fleetingly. Being human is something she remembers the same way you remember sucking your thumb. It's a part of her, a necessary phase in her development, but one now so remote that she can barely comprehend that she was ever that small, that vulnerable, that ineffective. She is the closest thing to a goddess that has ever existed, and she will only get stronger.' Clepsydra flashed him a smile that did not quite belong on her face. 'And you feel comfortable entrusting the future fate of the Glitter Band to this creature?'

'Aurora's plan is about the continued existence of the human species around Yellowstone,' Gaffney said dogmatically. 'Taking the long view, she sees that our little cultural hub is critical to the wider human diaspora. If the hub fails, the wheel will splinter itself apart. Take out Yellowstone and the Ultras lose their most lucrative stopover. Interstellar trade will wither. The other Demarchist colonies will fall like dominoes. It might take decades, centuries, even, but it will happen. That's why we need to think about survival now.'

Clepsydra formed a convincing sneer. 'Her plan is about *her* survival, not yours. At the moment she is letting you tag along for the ride. When you are no longer useful – and that *will* come to pass – I would make sure you have a very good escape plan.'

'Thank you for the advice.' His hand tightened on the whiphound. 'I'm puzzled, Clepsydra. You know that I can kill you with this thing. I also know that you can influence it, to a degree.'

'You're wondering why I haven't turned it against you.'

'Crossed my mind.'

'Because I know that the gesture would be futile.' She nodded at his wrist. 'Your hand is gloved, for instance. It could be that you wish to avoid forensic contamination of the weapon, but I think there must be more to it than that. The glove extends into your sleeve. I presume it merges with some kind of lightweight armour under your uniform.'

'Good guess. It's training armour, the kind recruits wear when they're learning to use whiphounds. Hyperdiamond cross-weave, edged on the microscopic scale to blunt and clog the cutting mechanisms on the sharp side of the filament. Even if you could bend the tail around towards me, it wouldn't be able to slice through my arm. Still, I'm surprised you didn't try it anyway.'

'I was resigned to death the moment I saw that you were not Prefect Dreyfus.'

'Here's the deal,' he said. 'I know that Conjoiners can shut off pain when they need to. But I'm willing to bet you'd still choose a quick death over a slow one. Especially here. Especially when you're all alone, far from your friends.'

'Death is death. And I can die precisely as quickly as *I* choose, not you.'

'All the same, I'll make you a proposition. I know you looked deep into our files. Minor confession: I was prepared to let that happen because I knew I was going to have to kill you anyway. I thought you might turn something up that I could use.'

'I did.'

'I'm not talking about Aurora. I mean the Clockmaker.'

'I have no idea what you mean.'

He guessed that she was lying. Even if she'd had no knowledge of the Clockmaker prior to her arrival in Panoply – and the Exordium dreamers hadn't been totally isolated from information concerning events in the outside world – she would surely have found out about it during her uninvited rummage through Panoply's records.

He rolled the whiphound handle in his palm. 'I'll let you in on a little secret. Officially, it was nuked out of existence when Panoply destroyed the Sylveste Institute for Artificial Mentation.' He lowered his voice, even though he knew there could be no eavesdroppers. 'But that's not what really happened. SIAM was only nuked after Panoply had already gone inside to extract intelligence and hardware. They believed that they'd destroyed the Clockmaker, true enough. They found what appeared to be its remains. But they kept the relics, the clocks and musical boxes and all the nasty little booby traps. And one of those relics turned out to be ... well, just as bad as the thing itself. Worse, in some respects. It *was* the Clockmaker.'

'No one would have been that stupid,' Clepsydra said.

'Less a question of stupidity, I think, than of overweening intellectual vanity. Which isn't to say they haven't been clever. Just to have pulled this off, just to have kept it hidden for eleven years ... that took some doing, some guile.'

'Why are you interested in the Clockmaker? Are you so foolish as to think you can use it as well? Or is Aurora the foolish one?'

Gaffney shook his head knowingly. 'No, Aurora wouldn't make that kind of mistake. But now the Clockmaker is a very real concern to her. Her intelligence networks have determined that it wasn't destroyed. She knows that a cell working inside Panoply kept it under study in the same place for most of the last eleven years. Aurora fears that the Clockmaker could undo all her good work, at the eleventh hour. Therefore it must be located and destroyed, before the cell has a chance to activate it.'

'Have you already made an attempt to destroy it? Perhaps in the last few days?'

He looked at her wonderingly. 'Oh, you're good. You're very, very good.'

'Ruskin-Sartorious,' Clepsydra said, enunciating the syllables with particular care. 'I saw it in your files. That's where you expected to find the Clockmaker. That's why that habitat had to be destroyed. Except you were too late, weren't you?'

'I can only guess that Aurora had probed around that secret a little too incautiously, and somebody had got nervous. The question is: where did they move it to?'

'Why don't you torture someone useful and find out?'

Gaffney smiled at that. 'Don't think I didn't try. Trouble was the old boy turned out not to know very much after all. I kept my word to him, though: left him with enough of a brain to do some gardening. I'm not a monster, you see.'

'I cannot help you either.'

'Oh, but I think you can. Don't be coy, Clepsydra: I know how transparent our archives must have been to you, how childishly ineffective our security measures, how laughable our attempts at obfuscation and misdirection. You only had access to those files for the brief time you were in Mercier's clinic, and you still worked out what happened to Ruskin-Sartorious.'

'I saw nothing concerning the current location of the Clockmaker.'

'Tell me you didn't see a hint of the cell. Feints and mirrors in the architecture. Faultlines and schisms in the flow of data. Something that would have been nigh-on impossible for a baseline human to spot, even a high-grade Panoply operative. But not necessarily beyond the discernment of a Conjoiner.'

'I saw nothing.'

'Do you want to give that a bit more thought?' He injected a tone of conciliatory reasonableness into his voice. 'We can come to an arrangement, if you like. I can leave you alive, with a modicum of neural functionality. If you help me.'

'You had better not leave me alive, Gaffney. Not if you want to sleep at night.'

'I'll take that as a "no", I suppose.' He smiled nicely. 'No point asking again, is there?'

'None at all.'

'Then I guess we're done here.'

The whiphound felt heavy and solid in his hands, like a blunt instrument. He spooled the filament back into the handle and then clipped it to his belt, for now.

'I thought—' Clepsydra began.

'I was never going to kill you with the whiphound. Too damned risky if you managed to sink your mental claws into it.' Gaffney reached into his pocket and retrieved the gun he had intended to use all along. It was an ancient thing, devoid of any components that could be influenced by Conjoiner mind-trickery. It relied on oiled steel mechanisms and simple pyrotechnic chemistry. Like a crossbow, or a bayonet, it was an outdated weapon for which there were still certain niche applications.

It only took one shot. He drilled Clepsydra through the forehead, just under the start of her cranial crest, leaving an exit wound in the back of her skull large enough to put three fingers through. Brain and bone splattered the rear wall of the interrogation bubble. He paddled closer to examine the residue. In addition to the expected smell of cordite, there was a vile stench of burnt electrical componentry. The pink and grey mess had the texture of porridge, intermingled with bits of broken earthenware and torn fabric. There was something else in there, too: tiny glinting things, silver-grey and bronze, some of them linked together by fine gold wires, some with little lights still blinking. He watched, fascinated, as the lights slowly stopped flashing, as if he was observing a neon-lit city fading into blackout. Some part of her, smeared against that wall, had still been thinking.

Clepsydra was dead now, no doubt about that. Conjoiners were superhuman but they weren't invulnerable. She was floating quite limply, her eyes still open, elevated and turned slightly together as if – as ludicrous as it might appear – she had been tracking the path of the bullet just before it entered her forehead. The look on her face was strangely serene, with the merest hint of a coquettish smile. Gaffney wasn't bothered by that. He'd had enough experience with corpses to know how deceptive their expressions could be. Freezeframe the onset of a scream and it could easily resemble laughter, or delight, or joyous anticipation.

He was nearly done. He returned the gun to his pocket and spoke aloud, very clearly and slowly. 'Gallium, paper, basalt. Gallium, paper, basalt. Reveal. Reveal. Reveal.'

It took a moment, just long enough to stretch his nerves. But he needn't have worried. The nonvelope flickered into existence off to his right, revealing itself as a chromed sphere reflecting back the patterning of wall tiles in convex curves. Gaffney paddled over and cracked the nonvelope open along its hemispherical divide. He removed the forensic clean-up kit he had placed in the nonvelope earlier and for a couple of minutes busied himself removing the immediate evidence of Clepsydra's death from the walls. Had they been made of quickmatter, they would have absorbed the evidence themselves, but the interrogation bubble's cladding was resolutely dumb. Fortunately the clean-up did not need to be a thorough job, and the fact that there would still be microscopic traces of blood and tissue located away from the splatter point – let alone dispersed through the air – was of no concern to him.

He used the clean-up kit to remove forensic traces from both the weapon and his training glove, then packed the gun and the kit back into the nonvelope. He then turned his attention to Clepsydra. The weightless environment made it no simple matter to persuade her inert form into the restrictive volume of the nonvelope, but Gaffney accomplished the task without having to resort to the cutting capabilities of the whiphound. He resealed the nonvelope and ordered it to return to invisibility. In the moment after it had flicked into concealment mode, he fancied that he could just discern its outline, as a pencil-thin circle looming before him. But when he glanced away and then returned his gaze to the spot where the nonvelope had been, he could not see it at all.

He slipped on his glasses, keying in sonar mode. The nonvelope did its best to absorb the sound pulses he was sending it, but it had been optimised for invisibility in vacuum, not atmosphere. The glasses picked it out easily. He reached out a hand and touched the cold, smooth curve of the sphere, which drifted to one side under his finger pressure. He pushed it towards the wall. It was a squeeze getting it through the twin passwalls, but it had made the journey once so it could make it again. Gaffney's only concern was meeting someone coming the other way: Dreyfus, for instance. Two people could easily pass each other, but the nonvelope presented an obstruction too wide to wriggle around.

His luck – or what Gaffney preferred to think of as his calculated access window – continued to hold. He reached the much wider trunk corridor that accessed the interrogation chamber's outer airlock without incident, where there was sufficient room for the nonvelope to hide itself, moving out of the way of passers-by when necessary. He abandoned the sphere to its own detection-avoidance programming. Gaffney was snatching off his glasses when a nameless operative came around the bend in the corridor, pulling himself along by handholds. He was hauling a bundle of shrink-wrapped uniforms from one part of Panoply to another.

'Senior Prefect,' the operative said, touching a deferential hand to the side of his head.

Gaffney nodded back, fumbling the glasses into his pocket. 'Keep up the good work, son,' he said, sounding just a touch more flustered than he would have liked.

CHAPTER 18

Dreyfus pinched the skin at the corners of his eyes until the gemmed lights of the Solid Orrery moved into sluggish focus. For a long while he had been fighting exhaustion, slipping into instants of treacherous microsleep where his thoughts spun off into day-dreams and wish-fulfilment fantasy. Seniors, field prefects and supernumerary operatives were coming and going from the tactical room, murmuring intelligence and rumour, pausing to consult compads or run enlargements and simulations on the Solid Orrery itself. Occasionally Dreyfus was allowed to be party to what was discussed, even to add his thoughts, but the other seniors made it abundantly clear that he was there on their terms, not his. Exasperatedly, he'd listened while the next response was formulated. After much debate, the seniors had decided to send four cutters, one to each silent habitat, each of which would be carrying three Panoply operatives equipped at the same level as a lockdown party.

'That's not enough,' Dreyfus said. 'All you'll have to show for it is four wrecked ships and twelve dead prefects. We can't afford to lose the ships and we damned well can't afford to lose the prefects.'

'It's the logical next step in an escalating response,' Crissel pointed out.

Dreyfus shook his head in dismay. 'This isn't about logical next steps. They've already shown us that any approaching ships will be treated as hostile.'

'So what do you propose?'

'We need four deep-system cruisers, more if we can spare them. They can carry hundreds of prefects. They'll also stand a chance of fighting all the way into the four habitats and making a forced hard dock.'

'To me,' Crissel said, looking pleased with himself, 'that sounds very much like putting all our eggs in one basket.'

'Whereas you'd prefer to keep throwing the eggs one a time, until we run out?'

'That isn't it at all. I'm talking about an appropriate reaction, rather than a sledgehammer strike with all our resources—'

Dreyfus cut him off. 'If you want to recover those habitats, the time to act is now. Whoever's inside them is probably struggling to control the citizenry, enough that they may still be vulnerable to an assault by a small but coordinated squad of prefects. We have a window here, one that's closing on us fast.'

Gaffney had returned to the room – he'd been off on some errand elsewhere. Dreyfus noticed an uncharacteristic sheen of sweat on his forehead, and the fact that he was wearing the heavy black glove and sleeve of whiphound training armour.

'At the risk of endorsing melodrama,' Gaffney said, looking only at the other seniors, 'Dreyfus may have a point. We can't commit four cruisers, or even two. But we do have one on launch standby. We can put fifty field prefects inside it within ten minutes, more if we move some shifts around.'

'They'll need tactical armour and extreme-contingency weapons,' Crissel said.

'The armour isn't a problem. But the weapons are still under wraps.' Gaffney looked apologetic. 'This crisis has caught up with us so quickly that we haven't polled for permission to use them.'

'Jane would have polled already,' Dreyfus said. 'I'm sure she was planning it when I left.'

'It's not too late,' Baudry said. 'I'll force through an emergency poll using the statutory process. We can get a return on it inside twenty minutes. That'll still give us time to equip the cruiser.'

'If they don't turn us down,' Dreyfus said.

'They won't. I'll make it abundantly clear that we need those weapons.'

'And spark off even more unrest into the bargain?' Gaffney asked, head tilted at a sceptical angle. 'Be very careful how you play this one. If the citizenry get even a whiff that we're dealing with something worse than a squabble with the Ultras, we'll have our hands tied just containing the panic.'

'I'll be sure to exercise due discretion,' Baudry said, speaking with fierce self-control.

'I hope the vote goes our way,' Dreyfus said. 'But even if it does, one cruiser won't be anywhere near enough.'

'It's all we can spare at the moment,' Gaffney said. 'You'll just have to take it or leave it.'

'I'll take it,' Dreyfus said. 'Provided I'm allowed to lead the assault team.'

For a moment no one said anything. Dreyfus sensed the conflicted impulses of the other prefects. None of them would have wanted to be on that ship when it got close to House Aubusson.

'It'll be dangerous,' Gaffney said.

'I know.'

Baudry studied Dreyfus with knowing concentration. 'And I presume House Aubusson will be your first port of call?'

He didn't even blink. 'It's the softest target. The one we have the best chance of taking.'

'And if Thalia Ng were elsewhere?'

'She isn't,' Dreyfus said.

Across the Glitter Band, a singular event was taking place, one that had not happened for eleven years, and for more than thirty before that. With the exception of the four that had already been lost, it was happening in all ten thousand habitats, irrespective of their status or social organisation. Where citizens were wired into a high degree of abstraction, whether it was inside the Bezile Solipsist State, Dreamhaven, Carousel New Jakarta or one of a hundred similar habitats, they simply found their local reality – however baroque, however impenetrably bizarre – being rudely interrupted to make way for an unscheduled announcement from the mundane depths of baseline reality. In the many mainstream Demarchist states, citizens felt the intrusion of a new presence into their minds, one that momentarily suppressed the usual nervous chatter of endless polling. In more moderate states, where abstraction was not adopted to the same degree, citizens received warning chimes from bracelets, or found windows appearing in the visual fields provided by optic implants, lenses, monocles or glasses. They paused to pay heed. In states where extreme biomodifications were in vogue, citizens were alerted by changes in their own physiology, or the physiologies of those around them. Skin patterns shifted to accommodate two-dimensional video displays. Entire bodily structures morphed to form living sculptures capable of delivering a message. In the Voluntary Tyrannies, citizens paused to look up at murals on the sides of the buildings that had suddenly flicked over to show the face of an unfamiliar woman rather than the locally designated tyrant.

'This,' said the woman, 'is Senior Prefect Baudry, speaking for Panoply. I am invoking statutory process to table an emergency poll. Please be assured that normal polling will resume after this interruption.' Baudry paused, cleared her throat and proceeded to speak with the slow and solemn gravity of the practised orator. 'As is well known, it is the democratic wish of the peoples of the Glitter Band that Panoply operatives be denied the day-to-day right to carry weapons, beyond those specified in the operational mandate. Panoply has always respected this decision, even when it has meant placing its own prefects at risk. During the last year alone, eleven field prefects have died in the line of duty because they carried no weapon more effective than a simple autonomous whip. And yet each and every one of them walked into danger knowing only that they had a duty to perform.' Having made her point, Baudry paused again before continuing. 'But it is part of the mandate that, when circumstances dictate, Panoply has the means to return to the citizenry and request the temporary right – a period specified as exactly one hundred and thirty hours, not a minute longer – to arm its agents with those weapons that remain in our arsenal, designated for use under extreme circumstances. I need hardly add that such a request is not issued lightly, nor in any expectation of automatic affirmation. It is, nonetheless, my unfortunate duty to issue such a request now. For matters of operational security, I regret that I cannot specify the exact nature of the crisis, other than to say that it is of a severity we have very rarely encountered, and that the future safety of the entire Glitter Band may depend on our actions. As you are doubtless aware, tensions between the Glitter Band and the Ultras have reached an unacceptable level in the last few days. Because of this situation, Panoply operatives are already facing heightened risks to their personal safety. In addition, Panoply's usual resources – people and machines both – are overworked and overstretched. I would therefore respectfully issue two requests at this point. The first is to urge calm, for – despite what some of you may have heard – all the information presently in Panoply's possession indicates that there has been no act of hostile intention from the Ultras. The second request is to grant my agents the right to carry those weapons that they now need to perform their duties. Polling on this issue will commence immediately. Please give this matter your utmost attention. This is Senior Prefect Baudry, speaking for Panoply, asking for your help.'

The deep-system cruiser *Universal Suffrage* sat in its berthing cradle, ready to be pushed out of the hangar into space. Final preparations were under way, with just the latter phases of fuelling and armament still to be completed. The midnight-black wedge of the ninety-metre-long vehicle was offset by the luminous markings delineating general instructions and warnings, power and fuel umbilical sockets, sensor panels, airlocks and weapons and thruster vents. Only when the cruiser was under way would these lines and inscriptions fade back into the absolute blackness of the rest of the hull. Conferring with the pilot, Dreyfus had already worked out an approach strategy. They would come in fast, tail-first, and execute a last-minute high-burn deceleration. It would be bone-crushingly hard, but the cruiser was built to tolerate it and the prefects would be protected by quickmatter cocoons. A slower approach would give Aubusson's anti-collision weapons too great a chance of achieving a target lock.

Satisfied with the status of the ship, Dreyfus pushed his way out of the observation gallery into the armoury, where the other prefects were being issued with Model B whiphounds. He checked the time. Any minute now, the polling results should be in. He'd listened to Baudry's speech and didn't think anyone could have made a better case without galvanising the entire Glitter Band into mass panic. She'd walked a delicate line with commendable skill.

But sometimes the best case wasn't good enough.

Set into one wall was a wide glass panel, oval in shape, with burnished silver pads on either side of it. Behind the panel, set into padded recesses and arranged like museum pieces, was a small selection of the weapons Panoply agents were no longer permitted to carry. There were vastly more weapons hidden from view, waiting to be rolled into place. All were matt-black and angular, devoid of ornamentation or aesthetic fripperies. Some of them were handguns scarcely more lethal than whiphounds. The heaviest weapons, Dreyfus knew, were fully capable of cutting through the skin of a typical habitat.

Baudry and Crissel had just arrived, stationing themselves at either side of the oval window. They each carried one of a pair of heavy keys that needed to be inserted into the pads on either side of the window and then turned simultaneously. Only seniors carried the keys, and it took two seniors to unlock the extreme-contingencies weapons.

'The vote's in?' Dreyfus asked.

'Just a few seconds,' Baudry told him. Most of the field prefects had filed out of the room now, to take their positions aboard the *Universal Suffrage*. Only a handful were still dealing with their armour, or waiting to receive weapons. 'Here it comes,' she said, the set of her jaw tensing in anticipation.

Dreyfus glanced down at the summary data spilling across his bracelet read-out, but it wasn't necessary to see the result for himself. Baudry's expression told him all he needed to know.

'Voi,' Crissel said, shaking his head in dismay. 'I can't believe this!'

'There's got to be a mistake,' Baudry said, mumbling the words as if in a trance.

'There isn't. Forty-one per cent against, forty per cent for, nineteen per cent abstentions. We lost by one per cent!'

Dreyfus checked the numbers on his bracelet. There had been no error. Panoply had been refused the right to bear arms. 'There was always a chance,' he said. 'If House Aubusson hadn't dropped off the network, they might even have swung it for us.'

'I'll go back to the people,' Baudry said. 'The statutes say I can table another poll.'

'It won't make any difference. You made your point excellently the first time. No one could have argued our case more effectively without inciting system-wide panic.'

'I say we just dispense them,' Crissel said. 'There's no technical reason why we need a majority vote. The keys will still work.'

Dreyfus saw the tendons on the back of Crissel's hand standing proud as he readied himself to twist the key.

'Maybe you're right,' Baudry said. There was a kind of awestruck horror in her voice, as if she was contemplating the execution of a glamorous crime. 'These are exceptional circumstances, after all. We've lost four habitats. We can't rule out wider polling anomalies, either. We'd be within our rights to disregard that poll.'

'Then why did you bother tabling it?' Dreyfus asked.

'Because I had to,' Baudry said.

'Then you have to do what the people say, too. And the people say no guns.'

Crissel was almost pleading now. 'But these are exceptional times. Rules can be waived.'

Dreyfus shook his head at the senior. 'No, they can't. The reason this organisation exists in the first place is to make sure the democratic apparatus functions smoothly, without error, bias or fraud. Those are the rules we hold everyone else accountable to. We'd better make damn sure we hold ourselves to the same standards.'

Baudry tilted her head in the direction of the *Universal Suffrage*. 'Even if it means going out there with nothing but whiphounds?'

Dreyfus nodded solemnly. 'Even that.'

'Now I understand why Jane never promoted you above field,' Baudry said, before shooting a conspiratorial glance at Crissel. 'But you're outranked here, Tom. Michael and I have the keys, not you. On three.'

'On three,' Crissel said. 'One . . . two . . . and turn.'

Their hands twisted in unison. A mechanism clunked behind the wall and the oval window slid ponderously aside. The visible weapons emerged from their recessed partitions, pushed out on chromed metal rods. Crissel retrieved a medium-size rifle, sighted along its slab-sided, vent-perforated flanks and then propelled it through the air to Dreyfus.

Dreyfus caught it easily. The weapon felt both reassuring and totally wrong. 'I can't do this,' he said.

'It isn't your call. Senior prefects have just issued you with appropriate ordnance.'

'But the vote—'

'The vote went our way,' Crissel said. 'That's what I'm telling you now. I'm expressly instructing you to disregard any information you might have received to the contrary.'

'This is wrong.'

'And you've said your piece,' Baudry said, 'stated your fine and noble principles. Now take the damned weapons. Even if you won't carry one, Tom, you can at least equip those other prefects. We'll take the fall for this when the dust settles. Not you.'

The weapon felt snug in his hands, solid and trustworthy. *Take it*, a small voice implored. *For the sake of the other prefects, and the hostages in House Aubusson. How likely is it that the eight hundred thousand people in House Aubusson give a damn about democratic principles now?*

'I'll—' Dreyfus began.

But he was cut off by the arrival of a new voice. 'Let go of the weapon, please. Let it float away from you.'

It was Gaffney, accompanied by a phalanx of Internal Security prefects, all of whom were wearing an unusual amount of body armour, with whiphounds unclipped and partially deployed.

'What's this about?'

'Easy, Tom. Just let the weapon go. Then we can talk.'

'Talk about what?'

'The weapon, Tom. Nice and easy.'

Dreyfus had no use for the rifle. Even if there had been an ammo-cell clipped into it, he was hardly going to open fire so close to the docking bay. But it still took a measure of self-control to let it drift out of his fingers.

'What's going on?' Baudry asked.

Gaffney clicked his gloved fingers at the pair of field prefects still waiting to clear the armoury. 'Get aboard the ship,' he said.

'She asked a civil question,' Dreyfus said.

'Field Prefect Tom Dreyfus,' Gaffney said, before the stragglers had cleared the room, 'you are under arrest. Please surrender your whiphound.'

Dreyfus didn't move. 'State the terms of my arrest,' he said.

'Your whiphound, Tom. Then we can talk.'

'My name's Dreyfus, you sonofabitch.' But he still unclipped the whiphound and let it drift after the rifle.

'I think you'd better explain,' Crissel said.

Gaffney appeared to have trouble clearing his throat. His eyes were wide, pugnacious, brimming with an almost religious rage. 'He's let the prisoner escape.'

Baudry's look sharpened. 'You mean Clepsydra, the Conjoiner woman?'

'Prefect Bancal visited her cell about ten minutes ago and found the cell empty. Mercier was called immediately: Bancal assumed that the doctor had moved her back to the clinic for medical reasons. Mercier hadn't, though. She's gone.'

'I want her found, and fast,' Crissel said. 'But I don't see why Dreyfus is automatically assumed—'

'I checked the access logs,' Gaffney said. 'Dreyfus was the last one to see her before she vanished.'

'I didn't release her,' Dreyfus said, directing his answer at the other two seniors, not Gaffney. 'And how could I have got her out of that room even if I'd wanted to?'

'We'll figure that out in due course,' Gaffney said. 'What matters is that you weren't happy about her being locked up in there, were you?'

'She's a witness, not a prisoner.'

'A witness who can see through walls. That makes a difference, don't you think?'

'Where could she be?' Baudry asked.

'She has to be still inside Panoply. No ships have come or gone since Dreyfus's return. Needless to say, I've initiated a level-one search. We'll find her soon enough.' Gaffney touched a hand to his sweat-tangled hair. 'She may be a Conjoiner, but she sure as hell isn't invisible.'

'You're wrong about this,' Dreyfus said. 'Clepsydra was there when I left her. I sent Sparver to check on her. Why would I do that if I'd set her free?'

'We can worry about the how and why of it later,' Gaffney answered. 'The access logs leave no doubt that Dreyfus was the last one in her cell before she disappeared.'

'I want a forensic search of that room.'

'I insist on it,' Gaffney said. 'Now, are you going to make a scene, or can we do this like responsible adults?'

'It's you,' Dreyfus said, with the feeling that he'd just got the punchline to a long, drawn-out joke, hours after everyone else.

'Me?' Gaffney asked, looking perplexed.

'The mole. The traitor. The man Clepsydra spoke about. You're working for Aurora, aren't you? You sabotaged the Search Turbines. You corrupted my beta-level witness.'

'Don't be ridiculous.'

'Talk to Trajanova. See what she says.'

'Oh dear,' Gaffney said, biting his lower lip. 'Haven't you heard?'

'Haven't I heard what?'

'Trajanova's dead,' Baudry said. 'I'm sorry, Tom. I thought you knew.'

Dreyfus stared at her in numb disbelief. 'What do you mean, she's dead?'

'It was a dreadful accident,' Baudry said. 'Trajanova was working inside the casing of one of the Search Turbines when it began to spin up. It appears that some safety interlock had been disabled ... we can only imagine that Trajanova herself must have done it, because she was in a hurry to get the Turbs back up—'

'It wasn't an accident.' Dreyfus was looking at Gaffney now. 'You made this happen, didn't you?'

'Wait,' Gaffney said, unfazed. 'Isn't this the same Trajanova you used to have issues with? The deputy you fired, the one you could barely speak to without the two of you shooting daggers at each other?'

'We got over that.'

'Well, isn't *that* convenient.' Gaffney looked quickly to the others. 'Does this make any sense to anyone? Quite apart from these slanderous accusations of murder, I don't recall Dreyfus mentioning a mole until now. Maybe if he had it would lend this outburst a bit more credibility.' He gave Dreyfus a pitying look. 'I can't begin to tell you how undignified this all sounds. I expected better of you, frankly.'

'He mentioned the mole to me.' They turned as one to see Sparver hovering at the threshold of the chamber.

'This is no business of yours, Deputy Field,' said Gaffney.

'The moment you shot off your mouth about Dreyfus it became my business. Let him go.'

'Escort the deputy out of here,' Gaffney instructed two of his internals. 'Pacify him if he makes trouble.'

'You're making a mistake,' Sparver said.

'Tell you what,' Gaffney said. 'Why don't you dump him in an interrogation bubble until he cools off? Got to keep a lid on that temper, son. I know it's hard, not having a fully developed frontal cortex, but you could make an effort.'

'There's a line,' Sparver said quietly. 'You just crossed it.'

'Not before you did.' Gaffney's hand hovered over his whiphound, a tacit warning. 'Now get out of here before one of us does something he might have cause to regret.'

'Go,' Dreyfus mouthed to Sparver. Then, louder: 'Find Clepsydra. Before Gaffney's people do. She's in danger.'

Sparver touched his hand to the side of his head, enough of a salute to let Dreyfus know he still had an ally.

'Well,' Gaffney said, 'looks like you got an exemption from the rescue mission, at least. Or were you counting on that?'

Dreyfus just looked at him, not even dignifying the statement with a response.

'I'll take his place,' Crissel said.

It fell to Baudry to break the silence that fell after his words. 'No, Michael,' she said. 'You don't have to do this. You're a senior, not a field. This is where we need you.'

Crissel plucked the rifle from the air where it had come to rest. His hands closed around it with probing unfamiliarity, as if he wasn't quite sure which end was which. 'I'll get suited-up and have the rest of the weapons issued,' he said, with a confidence that sounded ice-thin. 'We can launch inside five minutes.'

'You're not ready for this,' Baudry said.

'Dreyfus was prepared to put his neck on the line. Regardless of what's just happened, we can't simply abandon those kids aboard the *Universal Suffrage*.'

'When was the last time you left Panoply on field duty, as opposed to pleasure?' Dreyfus asked.

'Only a few months ago,' Crissel said quickly. 'Six at the most. Definitely within the last year.'

'Did you carry a whiphound?'

Crissel blinked as he retrieved the memories of the trip. Dreyfus wondered how far back he was digging. 'We didn't need them. The risk assessment was low.'

'So hardly comparable to what we're facing now.'

'No one's ever faced anything like this, Tom. It's new to all of us.'

'I'll give you that,' Dreyfus said. 'And I'll give you the fact that you were once an outstanding field. But that was a long time ago, Michael. You've been staring into the Solid Orrery too long.'

'I'm still field-certified.'

'I can still go,' Dreyfus said. 'Overrule Gaffney. You have my word that I'll submit to his arrest order as soon as I return from House Aubusson.'

'That would suit you just fine, wouldn't it?' Gaffney said. 'Dying in the line of duty. Going out in a blaze of glory, never having to face an internal tribunal. Not gonna happen, I'm afraid.'

'He's right,' Baudry said. 'Until this is resolved, you can't leave Panoply. That's the way we do things. I'm sorry, Tom.'

'Take him down,' Gaffney said.

It was the middle of the night in House Aubusson. Thalia already felt as if she had spent half a lifetime in the place, when in fact it was still less than fifteen hours since she had docked her cutter at the hub. But she had not rested in all that time, and now she was pacing back and forth determinedly, fiercely intent on staying both awake and alert, knowing that it would be fatal to sit down with the other citizens and succumb to her tiredness.

'No sign of that rescue of yours, I take it,' Paula Thory said, for about the twentieth time.

'We've only been cut off for half a day,' Thalia replied, pausing to lean against the transparent casing covering the architectural model of the Museum of Cybernetics. 'I didn't promise they'd arrive bang on schedule.'

'You said we might be isolated for a few hours. It's been considerably longer than that.'

'Yes,' Thalia said. 'But thanks to the good citizens of the Glitter Band, a civil emergency was in force when I left. My organisation was doing everything it could to prevent all-out war between the habitats and the Ultras.'

'You think they're still dealing with that, is that it?' asked Caillebot, reasonably enough.

She nodded at the landscape gardener, glad that he had given up some of his earlier outrage. 'That's my best guess. I'm long overdue by now, and they'll be able to see that my ship's still docked with Aubusson. If they could spare the resources to get here, they would.' She swallowed hard, striving to find some of that confidence Parnasse had told her she needed to assert. 'But you can bet we're getting near the top of their list. They'll be here before sunrise.'

'Sunrise is still a long way off,' Thory observed. 'And those machines aren't slowing down.'

'But they're not touching the main stalk,' Thalia replied. 'Whoever's operating them needs to send instructions through this structure, which means they can't risk damaging it just to get rid of us.'

By now it was clear that the construction servitors were engaged in nothing less than the systematic dismantling of the habitat's human buildings and infrastructure. Throughout the night, Thalia had watched – sometimes alone, sometimes with Parnasse, Redon or one of the other citizens – as the robots bulldozed and ripped their way through the outlying structures of the Museum of Cybernetics. They had already torn down the ring of secondary stalks, shovelling the pulverised remains onto the backs of massive debris-carriers. Kilometres away, in illuminated clusters of huddled activity, other groups of machines were engaged in similar demolition work. The machines tackling the museum must already have gathered tens of thousands of tonnes of rubble. Across the entire interior of House Aubusson, they must have gathered dozens or hundreds of times as much. And all that raw material – millions of tonnes of it, in Thalia's estimation – was being conveyed in one direction, toward the great manufactory complex at the habitat's far end. It was feedstock, so that those mighty mills could turn again.

In fact, they were already turning. Though no sound reached Thalia and her cadre of citizens through the airtight windows of the polling core, they had all felt the tremor of distant industrial processes starting up. Near the endcap that rumble must have been thunderous. The manufactories were making something. Whatever it was, they were being cranked up to full capacity.

'Thalia,' called Parnasse, poking his head above the top of the spiral staircase that led to the lower level. 'I need your help with something, when you've got a moment.'

Thalia tensed. That was Parnasse's way of telling her they had a problem without alarming the others unduly. She crossed to the staircase and followed him down to the administrative level, with its unlit offices and storage rooms. Three of the citizens were still working on the barricade detail, collecting equipment and junk from wherever they could find it and then toppling it down the stairs and lift shaft.

'What is it, Cyrus?' she asked quietly, the two of them standing far enough away from the work gang that their conversation would not be overhead.

'They're getting tired, and they've only been on this shift for forty-five minutes. They may be able to last until the end of it, but I'm not sure if they're going to be much use to us by the time they're up for duty again. We're getting worn out down here.'

'Maybe it's time Thory weighed in.'

'She'd be more hindrance than help, with all her moaning. The team getting tired isn't the main problem, though. We're going to start running out of barricade material pretty soon. If not before the end of this shift, then definitely before the end of the next one. Things ain't looking too good. Just thought you should know.'

'Maybe the existing barricade will hold.'

'Maybe.'

'You don't think so.'

'When it's quiet up here, I can hear activity below. The machines are working at the far end of it, clearing it as fast as we can pour new stuff down from our end. That's why the barricade keeps settling down. They're removing the debris at the base.'

'And if we don't keep topping it up—'

'They'll be breaking through before you know it.'

'We need options,' Thalia said. 'I've told the other citizens that we're working on a contingency plan. It's about time we had one, before someone calls me on it.'

'I wish I had an idea.'

'Let's focus on the barricade, since that's all we have right now. If we're running out of material, we'll need to find another supply.'

'We've already cleaned out all the rooms along this corridor. Anything that we can move, and that isn't too large to fit down the holes, we've already thrown.'

'But we've still got the building itself,' Thalia said. 'The walls, the partitions between the rooms ... it's all ours, if we want it.'

'Unfortunately, none of us thought to bring demolition tools to the civic reception,' Parnasse said.

Thalia unclipped the buzzing handle of her whiphound. 'Then it's a good job I did. This thing might be damaged, but it can still just about function in sword mode. If I can start cutting away material—'

Parnasse looked at the whiphound dubiously. 'What will that thing cut through?'

It was almost too hot to hold now. 'Just about any material that isn't actively reinforced, like hyperdiamond.'

'There's nothing like that in this building. I know, I saw the blueprints before she went up. But you'd better not cut the first thing you see. There are structural spars running right through this thing.'

'Then we'll start with something that clearly isn't structural,' Thalia said, remembering the item she had been resting against before Parnasse summoned her below.

'Like what?'

'Right above me, on the next level. That architectural model.'

'We'll need more than that for barricade material, girl. That model's about as substantial as a soap bubble.'

'I was thinking of the plinth – it looked like granite to me. If we could cut *that* into manageable chunks ... there's got to be three or four tonnes of rock there. That would make a difference, surely?'

'Maybe not enough to save us,' he said, scratching his chin, 'but beggars can't be choosers, can they? Let's see if that little toy of yours will hold up for us.'

Thalia clipped the whiphound back to her belt, then rubbed her sore palm against her trousers. Leaving the work gang to their duty, she ascended the staircase to the main level, Parnasse following immediately behind her.

'People,' she called, 'I need some help here. It'll only take a couple of minutes, then you can go back and rest.'

'What do you want?' asked the young man in the electric-blue suit, rubbing a stiff forearm.

Thalia strode to the side of the architectural model and patted the transparent casing. 'We need to remove this thing so I can get at the plinth. I could use my whiphound to cut it up, but I'd rather save it for stuff we can't break apart with our hands.'

The transparent casing was a boxlike shell resting in place by virtue of its weight alone. Thalia squeezed her fingers under one end of it, wincing as she caught a broken nail. The young man worked his fingers under the far end, and between them they heaved the casing into the air, exposing the delicate model underneath. They shuffled sideways until they'd reached a clear spot of floor and were able to lower the casing. They would work out what to do with it later.

'Now this part,' Thalia said, getting a grip under the heavy, flat sheet on which the model had been constructed. This time it took three of them before the model even budged, with Caillebot taking one of the corners. The delicately formed representation of the museum might have been insubstantial, but that could not be said for its foundations. 'Harder,' Thalia grunted, as Parnasse added to the effort.

The sheet budged again, tilting upwards from the underlying plinth. 'Steady,' Thalia said, gritting her teeth with the effort. 'Let's put it down over there, on top of the casing.'

She had already participated in the destruction of several tonnes of museum property, including items that might well have been priceless relics from the history of computing. But there was something about the model that made her unwilling to see it damaged. Perhaps it was because of her suspicion that it had been made by hand, laboriously, over many hundreds of hours. 'Easy,' she said as they reached the casing.

They'd almost made it when the young man yelped and let go as some nerve or muscle in his already strained forearm gave way. The remaining three of them might have been able to take the weight, but they were in the wrong positions. The model crashed to one side, one corner smashing its way through the casing. The impact was enough to dislodge the sphere of the polling core, sending it toppling from the tip of the stalk. The silver-white ball bounced off the tilted landscape and went trundling across the room, until it was lost in the darkness.

Thalia fell to the floor, landing hard on her knees.

'Sorry,' the young man said.

She bit back tears of pain. 'It's just a model. The plinth is what matters.'

'Let's see how that granite holds up,' Parnasse said, helping Thalia to her feet.

Hobbling back towards the plinth, Thalia touched her whip-hound and almost flinched from the contact. It felt white-hot now, as if it had just been spat out of a furnace.

'If anyone has one,' she said, 'I could use a glove.'

Sparver knew he had been lucky not to find himself in a detention cell, but that did not mean he was going to avoid confrontation with Gaffney just to stay out of trouble. The last thing Dreyfus had told him to do was to find Clepsydra, and like Dreyfus he believed that she must still be somewhere inside Panoply. He reasoned that the place to begin his search was the interrogation bubble where Dreyfus had last spoken to the Conjoiner. No matter how cunning or stealthy she might have been, he did not think it likely that she could have travelled a very great distance from the bubble; certainly not as far as one of the centrifuge rings. It might have been in Clepsydra's gift to blind and confuse surveillance systems, but classes were in session now and Sparver doubted that she would find it easy to pass through a bottleneck of prefects and cadets waiting to transition between the weightless and standard-gee sections. In his mind's eye he could see several possible places she might have hidden; his intention was to search them before Internal Security and attempt to reassure Clepsydra so that he could protect her from any rogue elements within the organisation.

But when he reached the passwall into the now empty interrogation bubble, his way was blocked by a couple of Gaffney's goons. Sparver tried to reason with them, without effect. He was certain that the Internal Security operatives were acting sincerely, in the genuine belief that Gaffney was to be trusted, but that did not make them any easier to persuade. He was still trying when Gaffney himself showed up.

'I thought we came to an agreement, Prefect Bancal. You keep your snout out of my business, I'll keep my nose out of yours, and we'll get along famously.'

'When your business becomes mine, I stick my snout wherever I like. It's a nice snout, too, don't you think?'

Gaffney lowered his voice to a dangerous purr. 'Don't push your luck, Bancal. You're only here on sufferance. Dreyfus may like to keep a pet pig around for show, but Dreyfus isn't going to be part of this organisation for much longer. If you want to find a role for yourself, I'd start making new friends.'

'Friends like you, you mean?'

'Just saying, times are changing. We've all got to adapt. Even those of us not exactly equipped for mental agility. How's that frontal cortex working out for you, anyway?'

'Dreyfus didn't have anything to do with Clepsydra disappearing,' Sparver said levelly. 'Either you made her disappear, or she's hiding because she knows you'd rather she was dead.'

'Beginning to flail around a bit there, son. Are you accusing me of something or not?'

'If you did something to her, you'll pay for it.'

'I'm *looking* for her. Do you think I'd go to all this trouble if I had anything to hide? Come on. It's not that much of a conundrum, even for the likes of you.'

'We're not done, Gaffney, you and me. Not by a long stretch.'

'Go and count your fingers,' Gaffney said. 'Call me when you reach double figures.'

CHAPTER 19

Michael Crissel scrutinised himself in the mirrored surface of the cubicle, anxious that no trace of his true state of mind should be apparent when he emerged. His skin was as pale as a reptile's belly, his bloodshot eyes verging on the albinotic. He told himself that his pallor was just as likely to be a function of the cruiser's dehumidified atmospheric mix as his bout of retching, but that was scant consolation. The sickness had come on him hard and fast, with barely enough warning to let him scuttle to the cubicle.

'Get a grip,' he told himself.

He exited the cubicle and moved up through the ship, past the weapons bays and crew quarters, into the main assembly area where the other prefects were waiting, suited and armoured, buckled into deceleration webbing, jammed together like gloss-black toy soldiers, weapons secured between their knees. Not just whiphounds, but the big guns that, technically speaking, the democratic vote had forbidden them. When all this was over, when the people had full access to the information, they'd see that Panoply had done the right thing in disregarding that vote. They'd even applaud when they knew what was really at stake.

The fields watched him as he propelled himself along the gangway, hand over hand in the weightless fall of the *Universal Suffrage*'s cruise phase. None of them had yet snapped down their visors. He could see their faces, feel their eyes tracking him as he passed. He didn't recognise any of them. Even their names, stencilled onto the inert-matter armour of their suits, triggered only glimmers of recognition.

The pressure of their attention demanded a response from him, some rousing, rallying speech. His mouth was raw, filled with the aftertaste of his retching session. Dreyfus would surely have said something, Crissel thought. It didn't need to be much. Just a word or two of encouragement. He brought himself to a halt and turned around slowly, nodding at the young men and women filling those black lobster-like suits.

'None of us are under the illusion that this is going to be easy,' Crissel said, instantly dismayed at how quavery and ineffectual his own voice sounded. 'They'll have the hub airlocks well guarded and we'll more than likely be meeting opposition as soon as we reach the interior. It's quite probable that we'll be outnumbered. But we do have the advantage of training and equipment. Remember, you are Panoply operatives. You have right on your side.'

The reaction was not what he had been expecting, or hoping for. The prefects just looked bewildered and fearful, as if his words had robbed them of the exact measure of morale he had hoped to bolster. 'When I say it won't be easy,' he continued, 'I don't mean we won't succeed. Of course not. I just mean—'

A girl with almond-coloured eyes and a heart-shaped face asked, 'How will we distinguish hostiles from locals, sir?'

He tapped the crown of his own helmet. 'Tactical drop-down will overlay all citizens known to the polling apparatus. Anyone you see who isn't recognised by the overlay must be assumed a non-indigent hostile.' He flashed her an overconfident smile. 'Naturally, you have authorisation to euthanise.'

'Pardon me, sir,' said a young man with a day's growth of chin stubble, 'but we were informed that we'd probably be operating in an environment without local abstraction.'

'That's correct,' Crissel said, nodding. If Aubusson had dropped off the external abstraction, there was every reason to believe its internal systems had gone into blackout as well.

'Then how will the tactical overlays know who is who?' the girl asked, with the tone of someone who genuinely expected a reasonable answer.

Crissel opened his mouth to respond, then felt ominous mental trap doors opening. He'd made a mistake. There could be no guarantee that the overlays would work at all.

'The hostiles will be the ones ... being hostile,' he said.

The prefects just stared at him. If they'd mocked him, or even fired back another question, it would have been preferable to that dumb, expectant staring, as if what he had told them made perfect operational sense.

Something stirred in the dry embers of his gut again. 'Excuse me,' he said, preparing to turn and make his way back to the cubicle. But just as he spoke, the pilot emerged from the flight deck into the assembly area, holding headphones against his skull. 'Visual on Aubusson, sir. Thought you'd like to see it.'

'Thank you,' Crissel said.

He entered the cruiser's spacious flight deck with a shaming sense of relief. House Aubusson looked frighteningly close on the allocated display panes, but that was deceptive; they were still thousands of kilometres away, and the habitat's anti-collision systems would not yet have picked out the approaching cruiser from the confusion of general Glitter Band traffic moving on similar vectors.

'Looks normal enough,' Crissel commented as the end-on view zoomed to reveal the small-scale details of the docking hub, where a handful of spacecraft were still attached. 'I take it there hasn't been any significant change since we left Panoply?'

'Nothing that will affect our approach,' the pilot said. 'But there's something you should know about.' He opened windows over the main view, illustrating side-on views of the habitat captured by some other distant vehicle or camera platform. 'Visible light,' he said. 'Six hours apart. The view on the right is the most recent.'

'They look the same.'

The pilot nodded, confirming Crissel's judgement. 'Now look at the same snapshots in infrared. Anything jump out at you?'

One end of the habitat was a smear of thermal emissions, where it had been cool before. The overlay shaded structures in a gradation of colours, ranging from brick red to fiery orange.

'Judging by those cooling foils, she's putting out a lot of heat all of a sudden.'

The pilot made an affirmative noise. 'Started up in the last four hours, as far as we can tell.'

Crissel risked a silly question. 'Which end is that?'

'Not the one we're intending to dock at. The docking hub's still as cool as it ever was, apart from some small hotspots around the weapons, dumping the waste heat after they fired.'

Weapons, Crissel thought. How easy it was to switch from thinking of the anti-collision systems as instruments for the preservation of life to machines designed to terminate it.

'So what's happening? Why is she getting hotter at that end?'

'Guesswork so far, but one explanation could be that the manufactories have started up.'

'I didn't know Aubusson had manufacturing capability.'

'Years back she was a bigger player, apparently,' the pilot said, tapping a finger against a text summary on his fold-up armrest pane. 'Never as large as any of the heavy manufactories, but still putting out a few hundred thousand tonnes a year. High-value, low-bulk products. Construction servitors, mainly, for use in setting up the new industrial centres on the Eye. Good business for a while, but once the lunar manufacturies were up to speed, places like Aubusson lost their business.'

Old history, Crissel thought. Marco's Eye had been the main industrial supplier in the system for more than a century. 'So what happened to the manufactory?'

'They kept the infrastructure. Must have been betting against a time when they'd be able to compete against the Eye, for one reason or another. Judging by that thermal output, they've got the factory wheels spinning again.'

'But they've only had control of Aubusson for half a day. They can't have started up the manufactory so quickly. It isn't humanly possible.'

'Like I said,' the pilot said defensively, 'just guesswork.'

'This doesn't affect our mission,' Crissel said shakily. 'If anything it makes it more urgent that we get in there and secure the place for Panoply.'

'Just thought you ought to know, sir.'

'You were right to bring it to my attention.' After an uncomfortable pause, during which he was uncertain as to whether his presence on the flight deck was appropriate or not, Crissel said: 'How soon now?'

'We'll be entering the habitat's collision-avoidance volume in six minutes. The cargo drones were intercepted when they were two hundred kilometres into that volume, or about one hundred kilometres from the hub.' The pilot drew his attention to another read-out, crammed with tactical summary data. 'But we'll be ready to target the anti-collision weapons with our guns long before then. We already have positive firing solutions for half of them.'

The back of Crissel's neck bristled. 'Then why don't we fire? If it isn't a stupid question.'

'They'd see us then. We're presenting a highly stealthed cross section now, but as soon as we launch missiles, the enemy aiming systems'll be able to backtrack from our missiles' exhaust vectors.'

'We're talking about anti-collision systems, Pilot, not military hardware. They're programmed to recognise incoming foreign objects, not to extrapolate back from missile exhausts.'

There was a reticence in the pilot's voice. 'Prefect Dreyfus said we have to assume they've been uploaded with new software.'

Crissel coughed. 'Rightly so, of course. Although the likelihood of that being the case ... But are you sure we can't just fire and take out all the weapons in one hit?'

'Can't guarantee it, sir. Best strategy is to hold fire until we have clear solutions on all the weapons, which'll mean suspending our attack until just before we initiate the braking phase.'

'Right. I just needed to be clear on that. And how far outside the avoidance volume will we be at that point?'

'Thirty kilometres inside it,' the pilot said.

Crissel nodded as if the matter were fully settled and need not be raised again. 'Keep on this vector, Pilot. I'm going back to speak to the prefects.'

'You'll need to secure yourself in five minutes, sir. Things will get bumpy, especially if we have to dodge return fire.'

Crissel clambered out of the cool, clinical sanctuary of the flight deck back into the assembly area. The majority of the prefects had now donned their helmets, and of that number more than half had lowered and sealed their visors.

'Pilot informs me that we shall commence braking phase in just over five minutes,' Crissel said, holding himself in position by a padded handrail as he surveyed the massed black ranks. 'Make no mistake, this isn't just a lockdown or disciplinary action. There are more than eight hundred thousand people inside House Aubusson, and each and every one of them is counting on our help. There may be times when the agents of Panoply are feared and hated. There isn't a field in the organisation who doesn't know how *that* feels. I've been there, too. I know what it's like to be despised. But today those people will be praying for the sight of someone in Panoply black. And they'll be expecting us to get the job done. We can do it, too. In all likelihood, we'll be encountering an armed and efficient takeover force. But remember this: no matter how numerous the enemy, no matter how agile or aggressive, we'll have eight hundred thousand grateful citizens on our side. Panoply will prevail today. I have never been more certain of anything in my life.' He raised his fist, clenched in the manner of Panoply's symbol, and drew a cautious roar of approval.

Satisfied with their response, conscious that to push them further might be to risk chastening humiliation, Crissel returned to the flight deck.

'Status, please, Pilot.'

'Braking in four minutes, Prefect. One hundred and twenty-two kilometres to outer edge of avoidance volume. You'd better secure yourself.'

'About those anti-collision systems – you have a clearer view of them now, I take it?'

'Refining all the time.'

'And there's been no change in the tactical situation? We still can't guarantee a clean take-out at this range?'

'Can't promise it, sir.'

But he picked up a nuance in the pilot's voice. 'But the odds have improved in our favour?'

'Slightly, sir.'

'Do you have firing solutions locked in already?'

'Ready to go, sir, as soon as we hit thirty kilometres inside the volume. Which will be in three minutes, thirty-three seconds.'

'I'm securing for braking phase. Do likewise, Pilot.' He turned to the rest of the flight-deck crew. 'Listen, all of you. We're moving the battle plan forward. I want to hit those weapons sooner, while we still have some distance to play with. You have my permission to commence missile strikes in sixty seconds.'

The pilot opened his mouth, as if he was about to frame an objection.

Crissel asked, pleasantly enough: 'Is there a problem with that?'

'It's a change of plan, sir.'

'Nothing's set in stone. We're simply adapting to improved intelligence.'

'We may not take out all the weapons.'

'And we may not take them all out even when we're closer. This is war, Pilot. It involves an element of risk. Kindly execute my revised order at the appropriate time.'

He caught a moment of hesitation as the flight crew glanced at each other. A moment that teetered on the edge of mutiny, before pulling itself back.

'Solutions holding,' the pilot murmured. 'Missiles away in thirty-five seconds.'

Crissel returned to the assembly area and slotted himself into his allocated position. He locked his helmet into place at the last moment, feeling the pressure-tight latch engage at exactly the same moment as a series of sequenced thumps announced the cruiser's missiles darting away from their rapid-deployment launching racks. Until that instant there wouldn't have been a single external clue that the *Universal Suffrage* was about to show her claws.

Crissel had already instructed his helmet to layer a representation of the external situation, compiled from the cruiser's own cams, sensors and battle-management systems, over his normal view of the waiting prefects. He saw the intensely detailed grey disc of Aubusson, the end-on view of the cylinder. The missiles were invisible save for the blue-white hyphens of their fusion exhausts, turned at various angles as they followed different target selections. Green status boxes tracked each missile, filled with tumbling numbers that meant nothing to Crissel. Red crosses marked the intended impact points on the grey disc. Cross hairs, bull's-eyes and vectors slid across the view in a dance of hypnotic complexity, accompanied by their own cryptic digits and symbols.

'Status, please,' Crissel said.

'Missiles are ten seconds from impact,' the pilot's voice buzzed back. 'Commencing braking phase.'

Quickmatter cocoons expanded to wrap the prefects, including Crissel, and then the deceleration burn kicked in with savage force. Now that the *Universal Suffrage* had released its missiles and was directing its exhaust towards House Aubusson, it had become a conspicuous target. The tactical display showed return fire springing up from the anti-collision slug-launchers. The cruiser plotted the trajectories of the slugs, computing and executing high-burn evasive swerves that would allow the slugs to pass by harmlessly. Crissel found himself biting down hard as the gee-force intensified. The angle of his seat was constantly adjusting itself to optimise blood flow to his brain, but he still felt his mental processes growing choppy and interrupted. The hyphenated streaks of the missile exhausts had now diminished to tiny blue-white sparks, almost lost against the looming face of Aubusson. The ten seconds since the pilot had last spoken felt like unendurable hours.

They began to hit home. Crissel didn't need the tactical data to see that the missiles were reaching Aubusson. They damped their fusion fires at the last instant, so as not to trigger a thermonuclear explosion upon impact. Kinetic energy was still enough to do visible harm. Grey-white spheres of expanding debris swelled with dreamlike slowness, cored with hot orange fire. When the spheres had dissipated, each had left a perfect hemispherical crater, cutting tens of metres into Aubusson's crust. They'd have felt that inside,

Crissel thought. Not just the thunder of the impacts, loud as those would have been, but the earthquake-like concussion wave as the energy was dissipated along the sixty-kilometre length of the habitat. No matter what was going on inside Aubusson, the beleaguered citizens would know that someone was knocking on the door.

As the braking phase continued, the habitat's rate of approach diminished. The bulging disc of the endcap now covered half the sky. Most of the impact debris had cleared, revealing the full extent of the damage. The return fire had abated, suggesting that the missiles had indeed neutralised the anti-collision systems in one clean strike. Crissel was also gratified to see that the docking assembly had been spared any visible harm, with the attached vessels still intact.

The gee-force slackened. The cruiser had completed the intense phase of deceleration and was no longer obliged to dodge incoming fire. The cocoon did not relinquish its hold, but Crissel at last found the clarity of mind to manage a sentence.

'Excellent work, Pilot,' he said. 'Complete forced hard docking at your leisure.'

When the incoming fire resumed, it arrived from three points on the outer rim of the endcap, three points which should never have held anti-collision systems of any kind. No missiles had been directed against those sites because the blueprints had shown nothing there that required neutralising.

The *Universal Suffrage* was still at maximum defensive status. It tracked the emerging slugs and evaluated an optimum course of action. Guns sprang out of its hull and began to lay down intercepting fire. Three more missiles were locked on and launched. At the same time, the engines struggled to shove the cruiser out of harm's way, striving to find an open path between the scissoring lines of incoming slugs. With ruthless efficiency, it computed which collision would be the least likely to inflict fatal damage on either itself or its passengers. Crissel felt the swerve, and then the barrage of hammer blows as the slugs chewed into the *Universal Suffrage*'s armour.

Aubusson wheeled to one side as the cruiser lost lateral control and entered a slow tumble. Crissel felt the shove as the steering jets tried to recover stability. The border of his facepatch started flashing red. An emergency siren sounded in his ears, loud enough to be audible but not so loud as to drown out other voices.

'We're going down,' he heard the pilot say.

The three missiles sneaked through the streams of rushing slugs and found their targets. The incoming fire ceased as abruptly as it had begun. Aubusson floated back into the centre of Crissel's facepatch, the docking hub reaching towards them like an eager groping hand, ships nibbling at its fingers. Debris from the latest assault had dislodged a couple of transatmospheric shuttles, which were now drifting away from their berths. One instant they were safely distant, fragile-looking things, harmless as moths. The next they were huge, dangerous-looking obstacles tumbling through space towards the cruiser. The *Universal Suffrage* swerved again and clipped the starboard wing of one of the transatmospherics. Crissel felt the impact rattle down his spine. Everything went dark, the cam view dying in scribbles of ebbing light.

'Pilot?' Crissel said into the silence.

The quickmatter cocoon flowed away and left him unprotected save for his suit. The assembly area was dark, the other prefects all but invisible. Crissel activated his helmet lamp just as three or four of the other suited figures did likewise. He appraised the scene and concluded that no one appeared to have suffered any injury.

Then came a hard thump, too solid and final to be caused by debris knocking against the cruiser. It felt as if they'd hit a landmass, something that didn't yield in the slightest. The hard docking, Crissel thought, amazed. The pilot had brought them in, despite all the odds. He switched to the general suit-to-suit channel.

'I'm going up front to see what our situation is,' he said, releasing his restraints. 'Remain here but be ready to board as soon as I return. The mission is still go. We took more fire coming in than we expected, but the cruiser did its job. Remember, we don't need it to get back. If we go in there and secure Aubusson, we'll have all the time in the world to wait for Panoply to send another ship.'

But as he prepared to enter the flight deck, he was barred from stepping through the connecting passwall. It had detected a pressure loss on the other side. Hard vacuum, if the indicators were to be believed. He tried raising the pilot and flight crew, but this time all he got was the flat warble of a carrier signal.

He looked back at the suited prefects. 'Everyone airtight? Then hold on, because I'm blowing our air.' Crissel moved to the side lock, braced himself, slid up an armoured glass panel and then tugged down on the bright yellow and black bee-striped handle that controlled the atmospheric dump vents. The slats opened almost immediately, allowing the air to gust out in six different directions. No safety interlocks, no cautious queries. Crissel stabilised himself as the air roared and then whistled out. His helmet indicators flicked over to register that he was now in a hard-vacuum environment.

This time, nothing prevented him from accessing the flight deck. But as he stepped through the now-yielding passwall, Crissel found himself looking out through a gaping wound where the front of the *Universal Suffrage* had been. He could see space, the too-bright stars of other habitats, the waxy yellow curve of Yellowstone's nearest horizon. The hull ended in strips of ragged laminate, still twitching from aborted repair processes, oozing with the tarlike slime of quickmatter. Jutting into the space formerly occupied by the flight deck was a metre-thick spar that presumably belonged to the docking hub. All but one of the flight crews' positions had been ripped clean away. The pilot was still there, but impaled on a forking appendage of the docking spar.

The *Universal Suffrage* hadn't achieved the hard docking he had hoped for. But it had come in tantalisingly close. The habitat's own airlock was visible only a few metres beyond the ragged end of the hull. They could reach it easily enough by clambering along the spar. Blanking the predicament of the impaled pilot, confident that it would return to haunt him in due course, Crissel scrambled back into the assembly bay.

'We've lost the flight crew,' he said. 'It's messy ahead, but there's a way into the habitat. We still have a mission to complete, people. Follow me and be prepared to meet resistance as soon as we clear the lock.'

The prefects followed him like a massed black tide, moving with the ease of those well practised in weightless conditions. They divided into two quickly moving formations, traversing the spar like two lines of black ants until they reached the lock ahead of them.

While they worked to open the lock, Crissel at last found the mental breathing space to review what had just happened. The blueprints in Panoply's possession should have included every change made to the habitat since its construction. It was possible that House Aubusson had installed the rim-mounted slug launchers secretively, in covert violation of the legal limit on defensive systems for a habitat of that size. Yet of all the places Crissel could think of, Aubusson was one of the least likely to indulge in that kind of furtive upgrading.

Which left a much less palatable explanation. If the manufactories were truly up and running, and if the fabricators had access to sufficient blueprints and raw matter, then the habitat had the means to create almost anything it needed. Forging and installing additional anti-collision systems would not have taxed even a modest facility – it would only require dealing with a few hundred tonnes of new matter. Installing the guns would have been the difficult part, but even that wouldn't have been insurmountable if one could hijack at least part of the general servitor workforce. The manufactories had been running hot since the cruiser departed Panoply, but they could have been operating for some time before it became necessary to dump that waste heat so visibly. In fact, if all the manufactories had to do was create the new guns, they'd hardly have broken a sweat.

So something else was being made in there.

It did not take long for the prefects to persuade the door to open. It slid into its heavy buttressed frame to reveal the wide mouth of a high-capacity docking connection. It was illuminated, belching pressure into space. A passenger liner could disembark a hundred people down that tube inside a minute, without anyone grazing elbows.

The prefects poured into the empty docking tunnel. Conveyor bands ran the length of the tunnel, moving in both directions. The prefects touched the adhesive bands with one hand and allowed themselves to be hauled toward the far end, as if they had done it a million times before. Crissel followed their lead, but had to press his palm against the band twice before the adhesive bond took hold with enough strength to overcome the momentum of his body and suit. Then he was moving, speeding past a succession of bright, animated advertisements designed to entice the newcomer with deep pockets.

Slowly he became aware of something coming through on the suit-to-suit. It was a small, distant voice, saying something over and over again. The voice, Crissel realised, of a woman.

'Quiet,' he said, silencing what little communication there was. 'I can hear something on our channel.'

'Got it too, sir,' said one of the fields, possibly the girl who had spoken to Crissel earlier. 'It's someone using Panoply protocols, sir.'

Crissel strained to pick out the voice. Somewhere around the third or fourth repetition, the sense of the words suddenly clicked into place.

'... is Thalia Ng, for Panoply. I am recording these words five hours after the end of abstraction. I will keep them on repeat transmission until my bracelet runs out of power. I have secured the polling core, where I'm holding out at the top of the stalk with a small number of survivors. Outside ... we've seen the machines rounding up people. They've started killing them. We don't know who's behind this, but they've managed to take complete control of the local servitors. Please send immediate assistance. I don't know how long we can last up here before the machines find a way through to us.' There was a pause, then the message resumed. 'This is Thalia Ng, for Panoply. I am recording these words five hours after the end of abstraction ...'

'Thalia,' he said. 'Can you hear me? This is Senior Prefect Michael Crissel. Repeat, this is Michael Crissel. Please respond.'

There was nothing, only her endlessly looped message. Crissel repeated his statement, listened again, then shook his head in defeat. 'No good,' he said. 'She obviously isn't—'

'Sir,' came a faint but rushed voice. 'This is Thalia. I'm hearing you. Did you get my message?'

'We got your message, Thalia. Your signal's weak, but audible. We're in the docking complex. Are you still in the polling core?'

'Still holding out, sir.' Her relief was obvious. 'I'm so glad you've arrived. I don't know how much longer we can stand. The machines are getting cleverer, more adaptable—'

Crissel recalled the map of the interior he had committed to memory before leaving Panoply. 'Thalia, listen carefully. We're still a long way from you: many kilometres, even after we make it through the locks.'

'But you're here, sir! I think we can hold out until you get to the stalk, now that we know help's on its way. How many ships have you brought?'

'Just the one, I'm afraid.'

'One?' Disbelief and anger vied in her voice.

'And the ship isn't in too good a state, unfortunately. We have a small force of fields, the best we could muster at short notice. We have weapons and we're ready for a fight.' He made an effort to rally his own spirits. 'We came to take back House Aubusson, and that's what we're going to do. You just hold in there, Thalia, and you'll be right as rain.'

'Sir,' Thalia said, 'I have to sign off now, sir. Not much juice left on my bracelet, and I'd like to conserve what I have.'

'Before you go – something you said back there?'

'Sir?'

'About the machines, Thalia. About the servitors. I presume we're talking about some kind of limited malfunction here? A few machines under the control of an invading party? Not, as you made it sound, a full-scale machine uprising?'

He might have mistaken the hesitation for a failure in the bracelet's transmission if he hadn't known her better.

'No, sir. That's exactly what I mean. The machines have taken over. There is no invading party, as far as we can tell. No one new has arrived in House Aubusson. It's just the machines, sir. They've gone berserk.'

'But abstraction is down. How can machines function without abstraction?'

'There's enough of it left to control or coordinate them. But we still don't know who's doing it. Sir, I'm scared.'

'No need, Thalia. You've done excellently to protect any survivors until now.'

'That's not what I mean, sir. I'm scared that I brought this about. That I played a part in it. I think someone used me, and I was too stupid or naive or vain to notice it. And now it's too late and we're all paying for it, all of us here in Aubusson.'

'Then you don't know,' Crissel said carefully.

'Don't know what, sir?'

'It isn't just Aubusson. We've lost contact with all four habitats you visited. They all dropped off the network at the same time.'

'Oh, God.'

'We can't get near any of them. They shoot down any ship that comes close. That's why we had such a devil of a time getting the *Universal Suffrage* as close in as we managed.'

'What's happening, sir?'

'We don't know. All we do know is that Aubusson's manufactories are running at maximum capacity. And now you've told us something else we didn't know, which is that the machines are part of it.'

Thalia's voice faded and returned. 'I really have to go now, sir. The machines keep trying to get up the stalk. We've barricaded as best we can, but we have to keep fighting them back.'

'We're on our way. Good luck, Thalia. You have nothing to fear, and nothing to be ashamed of.'

'Sir – I'm about to sign off. But I forgot to ask – when help came, I was expecting Prefect Dreyfus to be a part of it.' The tone of her voice became anxious and childlike. 'He's okay, isn't he? Please tell me nothing's happened to him.'

'He's fine,' Crissel said. 'And I'll make sure he hears that you're in one piece. Something came up in Panoply and he had to stay.'

'What kind of something, sir?'

'I'm afraid that's all I can tell you right now.'

The transmission ceased. Thalia must have terminated the endlessly cycling message now that it had reached someone. While he was speaking to her, Crissel and his party of prefects had travelled almost the entire length of the docking tunnel. The conveyor strip ended, losing its adhesive retention at the last moment. In the tunnel's perfect vacuum, Crissel sped on hopelessly until he was grabbed by one of the prefects who had arrived before him, just in time to stop him crashing into the bulkhead at the tunnel's limit. Normally the passengers would have glided to a gentle halt, arrested by the resistance of normal atmospheric pressure.

They were facing a heavy armoured door, stencilled with nymphs and faeries.

'There's air on the other side,' one of the prefects reported. 'Safeties on this door are pretty heavy, and it knows we're in vacuum here.'

'Can you shoot through?'

'Possible, sir. But if there are hostages on the other side, and they aren't wearing suits—'

'Point taken, Prefect. What are our other options?'

'None, sir, except pressurising this part of the tunnel. If we close the door at the other end, the safeties should allow this one to open.'

'Can you do that from here?' Crissel asked.

'Not a problem, sir. We wired a remote trigger on it as we came through. Just wanted to check with you first. It'll mean blocking our exit route.'

'But you can reopen the other door if you have to?'

'Absolutely, sir. It'll only take a few seconds.'

'Go ahead, then,' Crissel told him.

Crissel was braced and ready when the door opened and air

slammed into the vacuum of the tunnel. Beyond lay a much larger space, a free-fall customs volume at the point of convergence of dozens of docking corridors. Advertisements were still running. The spherical space was hung with wire-stiffened free-fall banners in bright silks, some of which had torn free in the draught. Huge iron sculptures of seahorses and seadragons supported a bewildering tangle of colour-coded conveyor bands looping through the open space. Crissel tried to imagine thousands of passengers riding those bands, unselfconsciously gaudy even without their entoptic plumage, an endless flow of twinkling human jewels. He'd seldom visited such a place, seldom felt himself part of the true arterial flow of Glitter Band society. For a moment he regretted the austere trajectory Panoply had forced upon his life.

'The red conveyor will take us straight through,' he said, crushing the thought. 'Let's get moving.'

That was when the machines revealed themselves. They'd been in the volume all along, but hidden amongst the black complexity of the ironwork sculptures. When they emerged, Crissel almost laughed. Amusement, a wry sense of having been bettered, was the only human response to a fatal and inescapable ambush.

'Hostiles,' he said. 'Servitors. Target them. Maximum force. Fire at will.'

But even as he spoke the words, he knew there were too many machines, too few field prefects. The squad had already opened fire; had already destroyed a handful of the approaching servitors. But the machines just kept coming. They were everywhere, oozing out of shadow and darkness, flying through the air or picking their way along the curving lines of the conveyors. Even more were scuttling out of some of the other tunnels that connected with the customs space.

Crissel was used to servitors, so accustomed to their presence that he scarcely noticed them under normal circumstances. Yet these machines did not move like ordinary servitors. Their motions were quick, with something of the speeded-up, slapstick quality of insect activity. As a whole, their efforts were coordinated and deliberate. Individually it was chaotic, with some machines getting trampled under the relentless march of the others or even flung aside when they proved too slow or clumsy. They had no weapons in the usual sense, but every limb, manipulator or probe now served an aggressive function. Some of the attachments even appeared to have been modified to make them more effective: claws sharpened to glinting edges, arms terminating in vicious curved scythes or impaling spikes. It was a killing army. And yet the machines still carried the cheerful colours and logos of their former duties: a domestic machine here, a gardener or kindly medical servitor there. A beetle-backed multi-legged nursery supervisor even had the red and black shell of a ladybird, with a happy face painted on the front.

The prefects unleashed the full force of their guns, but it was only enough to slow the advance, not repel it. Most of the machines were so lightly armoured that they blew apart under a direct hit. But those that followed quickly grabbed the pieces of their shattered comrades and employed the broken body parts as shields or clubs. Then it became more difficult to kill any of them.

Crissel almost failed to notice the first human casualties. As the servitors fell upon the armour-suited prefects, it became difficult to tell the difference between people and machines. There was just a thrash and flail of limbs, a squeal of metal and ceramic on armour. It was only when he saw two headless bodies tumble into the open space between the ironwork sculptures, jetting banners of blood from the open circles of their neck rings, that he knew the servitors had begun to murder.

'Fall back,' Crissel called above the din of battle, the clash of armour and servitor, the panicked shouts of his team. 'Return to the ship! We're outnumbered!'

But even as he spoke the words, Crissel felt himself being pulled to one side by strong metal limbs. He resisted, but it did no good. Then the servitors were upon him, picking apart the puzzle of his armour with the frantic excitement of children trying to get into a parcel.

They were fast about it. He had to give them that.

CHAPTER 20

The holding cell where Dreyfus was detained was not a weightless sphere like the one in which Clepsydra had been imprisoned, but it had the same feeling of deadening impregnability. They had taken away his shoes and bracelet. His only concession had been to loosen his collar so that it didn't chafe so much against his unshaven jowls. In the room's silence he had no way of telling what was happening outside, or of confidently judging the passage of time. He was too alert, too fearful, to begin to feel bored. His mind spun with wild mental permutations, trying to guess what had happened to Clepsydra, and what was now happening to the mission to House Aubusson. What was happening to Thalia. More than likely it was his imagination that had supplied the distant thump as the *Universal Suffrage* detached from its docking cradle.

Dreyfus had put people into cells enough times to have indulged in idle speculation as to what it would feel like to be on the other side of the door when it closed. He realised now that he had never come close to imagining the utter draining hopelessness, or the shame. He had done nothing wrong, he told himself; nothing that merited the slightest degree of self-reproach. But the shame would not listen. The mere fact of confinement was enough.

After what Dreyfus judged to be the passage of two or three hours, the passwall formed the outline of a door. Baudry entered, alone, and had the wall revert to obstruct. She carried no visible weaponry.

'I wasn't expecting another visit. What's the news? Have you heard anything from Thalia?'

She ignored his question. 'If you did this, Tom, now is the time to tell me.' She stood by his bunk, hands folded, the hem of her skirt spilling around her heels like the wax from a thin, black candle.

'You know I didn't do it.'

'Gaffney says you were the last person to see Clepsydra. Did she say or hint at anything that might have indicated she was planning to escape?'

Dreyfus rubbed his eyes. 'No. She didn't have any reason to, because I told her we'd take care of her and make sure she got back to her people.'

'But she left.'

'Or was taken. You've considered that alternative, surely?'

'Gaffney says no one entered that room after you until Sparver went in and found her gone.'

'Did Gaffney catch me leaving with Clepsydra?'

'He speculates that you may have tampered with the passwall settings so that she could make her own way out after you'd gone.'

'I wouldn't know where to start. And even if she did leave, why didn't anyone see her? Why didn't she show up on our internal surveillance?'

'We still don't know the full extent of Conjoiner skills,' Baudry said.

Dreyfus buried his face in his hands. 'They're smarter than us, but they can't do magic. If she left her cell, someone would have seen her.'

'She may have chosen her moment of escape well. You could have advised her as to when there would be the least chance of detection.'

Dreyfus laughed hollowly. 'And the cameras?'

'Perhaps she was able to influence them, to erase her own image from the recordings.'

'She'd still have needed somewhere to hide. Sooner or later she'd have run into people, otherwise.'

'Gaffney speculates that you provided her with sanctuary. That you may still be providing her with sanctuary.'

'You know, I'm hearing the name "Gaffney" a lot here. Don't you think there might be something in that?'

Baudry set her mouth disapprovingly. 'Gaffney's position naturally brings him to the fore in any matter of internal security. And you have no evidence that he has committed any wrongdoing.'

'Would you give a damn if I did?'

'I know we've had our differences, Tom, and I know you didn't like what we had to do to Jane. I respect that, truly I do. But I assure you that our actions were taken in the best interests of Panoply. And I'll be the first in line to swear allegiance to Jane when she's reinstated to full operational authority, as I believe she will be.' She studied him with quizzical eyes. 'You don't believe me. You believe Jane's removal was motivated by self-interest. Or something else.'

'I think Crissel was just too cowardly to stand up to the two of you.'

'And me?'

'You can't tell me self-interest didn't come into it.'

For the first time he saw the hard gold glint of real anger flash in her eyes. 'See it from my position, Tom. I respect Jane. Always have. I was behind her every inch of the way when the Clockmaker made life difficult for us. But she should never have been allowed to stay in power all this time. There's no way that thing hasn't damaged her, mentally or physically.'

'Some might say it's made her the best supreme prefect we could ever have asked for.'

'But the point is, Tom, we've never had any way of knowing for sure. Crissel and I ... and Gaffney, yes, I'll admit it – we've given this organisation our best years, and all we've got to show for it is white hairs and wrinkles, while we wait in Jane's shadow. None of us is going to live for ever!'

'Nor will Jane. You could always wait your damned turn.'

Baudry exhaled. Something in her had relented. 'So I wanted her out of the way. But that doesn't mean it was right for her to stay in command. It doesn't mean we still didn't do the right thing by Panoply.'

'Do you believe that, in your heart of hearts? Look at me when you answer.'

'Yes,' she said, looking him straight in the eye after a long moment.

He nodded, giving nothing away. Let her stew, let her wonder whether he believed her or not. 'You still have to stop Gaffney. He's out of control.'

'Do you want to tell me about the name you mentioned earlier? Aurora, wasn't it?'

'I think we're dealing with Aurora Nerval-Lermontov, who was one of the Eighty.'

'She died, Tom. They all died.'

'I don't think she did. She's out there somewhere, and she's been biding her time for fifty-five years.'

'Just hiding?'

'Until something forced her hand. She learned something from Clepsydra, something that scared her badly. Everything that's happened is Aurora's response to a perceived threat. I think she's taking control because she doesn't trust us to do the job.'

'Clepsydra was her accomplice?'

'Not exactly. Aurora was using the Conjoiners, squeezing them for intelligence.'

'And now the only one of them left's gone missing.'

'I didn't let her out of that room,' Dreyfus said. 'I've made some questionable decisions in my career, but that wasn't one of them.'

'Then who did?'

'You know who.'

'He wouldn't betray us, Tom. He's a good man, Panoply to the core. He's given his soul to this organisation. There's nothing he cares about more than the security of the Glitter Band.'

'Maybe he believes that. But whatever he thinks, he's working for Aurora. Trajanova knew that whoever sabotaged the Turbines and corrupted my beta-level had to have high-level security access. She was only one step away from fingering Gaffney herself. That's why she had to go.'

Baudry shook her head once, as if she was trying to clear out a bad thought buzzing around between her ears. 'I don't believe Gaffney would act against us. More pertinently, why would he ever want Clepsydra outside of that room?'

'Because she knows things he doesn't want us to find out.' Dreyfus craned forward on the bunk. 'Baudry, listen to me. I think Gaffney wants her dead. I think he's going to find her and kill her, if he hasn't done so already. You have to get to her first.'

'We don't know where she is.'

'So start looking. Gaffney controls internal security, but *you* control Panoply. There are still hundreds of prefects he doesn't have an armlock on.'

'Sandra Voi, Tom. Are you seriously proposing all-out war inside Panoply?'

'It doesn't have to be war. Move now and you can stamp down on Gaffney, erase his authority. Security owe him loyalty, but they're loyal to you as well.'

For a moment he had the impression that she was at least considering the idea, giving it house room. Then her face froze, and she offered him only blank denial.

'I can't do that.'

'At the very least, get to Clepsydra before he does.'

'That may not be easy, especially if she doesn't want to be found.' Baudry's bracelet chose that moment to chime, emitting a shrill tone that had no place in the cloistered greyness of the cell. She glanced down, irritated, then lifted the display closer to her face. Dreyfus saw her eyelids grow heavy.

'What is it?'

'The *Universal Suffrage*.' Her voice sounded ghostly, distant. 'We've lost contact with them, during their final approach phase to House Aubusson. Just when the habitat's defences would have fallen within range of their own weapons.'

Dreyfus nodded. He knew that the plan had been to pick off the anti-collision systems with the cruiser's long-range ordnance. 'All comms, or just tactical telemetry?'

'Everything. There's no signal.' She paused, as if she dared not state what was so obviously the case. 'I think we've lost them. I think they're all dead. Crissel, all those young prefects.' Then she looked at Dreyfus with a kind of slow-burning dread. 'What should we do next?'

'Confirm that the ship's really lost,' Dreyfus said. 'Then start pulling in every asset we have elsewhere in the system, no matter what duty it's on. Every cutter, every corvette, every deep-system cruiser.'

'We can't ignore the state of crisis between the Ultras and the Glitter Band.'

'You can,' Dreyfus said, 'because it doesn't matter any more. That wasn't ever a crisis. A distraction, maybe, to take our eyes off the real business. Worked, too, didn't it? What fools we were.'

'We were only ever doing our best,' Baudry said sadly.

'It wasn't good enough. Now we have to up our game. The real crisis starts here.'

'I'm frightened, Tom. They took out a fully armed deep-system cruiser. *That isn't supposed to happen.*'

'I'm frightened, too,' Dreyfus said, 'but we're not finished yet. Find Clepsydra. And make sure you go back to the polls. You can lay it on the line this time. We need those guns. And right now I don't care who gets upset about it.'

Gaffney stared at the surreal spectacle with what he trusted was the appropriate combination of shock and disgust. He stood with his booted feet slightly apart, his back straight, his hands behind his back. His own reaction might be synthetic, but there was no doubting the authenticity of the expressions on the faces of the other internal prefects assembled in Dreyfus's private quarters. Nor was there any doubt concerning the feelings of Senior Prefect Lillian Baudry.

'This can't be right,' she said, shaking her head as if that might clear her vision and reveal the scene to be a psychological mirage. 'I know Dreyfus. We've crossed swords in the past, but he would never have done this. Not to one of his own witnesses.'

'There's never any telling what people will do when they go off the rails,' Gaffney said, with a kind of lofty regret, as if this was a truth he had privately acknowledged many years ago. 'Dreyfus always appeared stable to me as well. But recent events have obviously conspired to push him over the edge.'

'But killing her ... Sandra Voi. It makes no sense, Sheridan.'

'Perhaps the witness knew more than she was letting on,' Gaffney mused. 'None of us really knows exactly what went on inside that rock. It could be that she knew things that would be damaging to Dreyfus's reputation.'

'Why in Voi's name did he bring her back, in that case?'

'Formality, I assume. Perhaps Sparver's presence made it difficult for him not to?'

'And all the while he planned to kill her?'

'Look at the evidence,' Gaffney said, with a humble shrug. 'Speaks for itself, doesn't it?'

Clepsydra had died by a shot to the head. That much at least was obvious to any observer, as was the probable point of entry of the ballistic device that had ended her life.

'Some kind of slug-gun, not a beam weapon,' Gaffney said. 'There's no scorching or cauterisation around the entry wound.'

'Where do you think she was killed?'

Gaffney looked equivocal. 'If he shot her in here, the quickmatter architecture will more than likely have soaked up and processed any traces of blood or larger remains splattered on the walls. There'll be nothing left of it now. If she died a few hours ago, the pieces of her that the room has already absorbed will also have been broken down into their component elements and recycled throughout Panoply by now.' He touched a finger to his lips. 'Have you eaten lately?'

'No,' Baudry said, with a puzzled expression. 'What does that have to do with anything?'

'You might want to avoid the dispensers for a little while. If the idea of eating recycled Conjoiner upsets you, that is. If it doesn't, tuck right in.'

Baudry paled. 'You're not serious.'

'That's the way the recycling system works. It's not programmed to distinguish between human residue and normal domestic waste. There aren't supposed to be murders *inside* Panoply.'

Baudry glanced down at what was left of the body. 'Why wasn't she absorbed completely?'

'Indigestion, I suppose. Quickmatter has a throughput capacity; it can't absorb too much in one go without blocking up.' He forced a pained expression. 'This definitely counts as too much.'

Clepsydra's dead body had been half-absorbed into the floor before the quickmatter had choked and curtailed its efforts to process her. The effect was of a sculpture abandoned: a woman's body half-embedded in smooth black marble. Her crested head and upper torso, her shoulders and upper arms were exposed. Her lower arms, belly and hips gave the impression of being submerged beneath the floorline. The four fingers of her right hand pushed up through the surface like stone sentinels, stiff in death. Her left leg emerged from the floor, rose to the arch of her knee, then plunged back into the absorbing surface.

'Is this . . . all that's left?' Baudry asked.

'I'm afraid so. Your mind insists that there must be an intact body under the floor, like a corpse smothered in quicksand. But really there's nothing there. The protruding parts are disconnected.' Gaffney pushed the toe of his boot against the arch formed by Clepsydra's visible leg, toppling it over. Baudry glanced sharply away, then allowed her gaze to return to the spectacle. Where the leg had been in contact with the floor, it had left two circular depressions. Stringy fibres of partially processed organic matter trailed from the leg to the floor.

'She deserved better than this,' Baudry said. 'There'll be hell to pay when the other Conjoiners find out that she died in custody.'

'We didn't kill her,' Gaffney said gently. 'This is on Dreyfus's shoulders, not ours.'

'I still don't see why he would have done this, let alone how. To get a body from one part of the station to another, without any of us seeing a thing – how did Dreyfus manage that?'

'It isn't any old body, Lillian. It's the body of Dreyfus's prisoner, held in Dreyfus's room. He's the last person known to have seen her alive. That's reason enough to close the vice, in my view.'

'And what kind of vice would that be?'

Gaffney fingered the black shaft of his whiphound, still clipped to his belt. 'We need answers, and we need them fast. Dreyfus may not be inclined to give much away without a little encouragement.'

'I'll talk to him, see what he has to say.'

'No disrespect, but Dreyfus isn't going to just roll over and confess, even if you present him with a body. You saw how eager he was to implicate me.'

Baudry looked down at the atrocity on the floor. 'I still can't see Dreyfus having any part in this. Everything I know about him says he isn't a murderer, or a traitor.'

'It's always the quiet ones.' Gaffney sensed some agonised decision-making churning behind the smooth surface of her brow.

'I don't like the way this is going. But this *is* a state of emergency. I'll consider issuing a trawl order, if you think it necessary. A minimally invasive scan only. I don't want him hurt or distressed in any way.'

'Too many unknowns here, Lillian. Trawling wouldn't be the tool of choice in this instance.'

'Then what do you recommend?'

'There are other methods in our toolkit. Do you want me to be more specific?'

'Please tell me you're not talking about torture.'

Gaffney winced. 'Old term, not really applicable in a modern context. Torture is needles under the fingernails, electrodes to the genitals. Messy and imprecise. The new intelligence-extraction methods are a lot more refined. Really, it's like comparing trepanning to modern brain surgery. Of course, if you'd rather I went in with a deep-cortex trawl—'

Baudry turned away. 'I don't want to hear any of this.'

'You don't have to,' Gaffney said, offering her a reassuring smile. 'You can just sit back and wait for the results.'

'He's one of us,' she said.

Gaffney tapped the whiphound. 'And I'll see that he's treated with the appropriate respect.'

Though she had been scrupulous in concealing her suspicions from the others, Thalia had come to the private conclusion that there would be no rescue, at least not at the hands of Senior Prefect Crissel. Five hours had now passed since they had spoken, and there had been no sign of his promised boarding party. Crissel had warned her that it would take time to reach her, but she knew that she should have seen some evidence of his arrival by now. She had been looking through the windows of the polling core, down the darkened tube of House Aubusson towards the equally dark endcap where she had arrived a lifetime ago. She had detected no trace of human activity, not even the moving lights of the endcap elevators. Nor had there been any further communication from Crissel or any of his deputies. For a little while she had allowed herself to believe that they had met with unexpected resistance, and had pulled back to wait for reinforcements from Panoply. But over the course of those five hours her hopes had steadily eroded. She did not think it likely that Crissel or any of his prefects had survived long after their conversation. More than likely the rogue machines had taken them as soon as they entered Aubusson.

Throughout those five hours, she had watched the external activity continue apace, with no evidence that Crissel's arrival had affected the schedule to any meaningful degree. Construction servitors had worked tirelessly, tearing down the buildings, roads and bridges that had once served the habitat's human population. As Aubusson's night began to give way to a cool, grey dawn, Thalia surveyed a landscape of utter desolation. The stalk of the polling core was the only large structure still standing for kilometres in any direction. The surrounding buildings had been reduced to powdered rubble, sifted of anything that might prove useful for the manufactories. Grey dust had settled on the grass and trees and water. It was difficult to reconcile the scoured, lifeless wasteland with her memories of Aubusson as it had appeared less than a day earlier. A landscape this desolate should only be the product of years of warfare, not hours of mechanised industry.

Crissel's absence was not the only thing sharpening her anxieties. After she had finished cutting up the granite plinth to provide more barricade material, she had resumed her watch by the window. Not long after Crissel's call, she had seen one of the construction servitors pass close to the base of the stalk. It had been one of the open-topped carriers, but instead of rubble it had been carrying a different, infinitely more disturbing cargo. The machine had been full to the brim with human bodies, piled ten or twenty deep. There must have been thousands of them in just that one load, tossed into the container like so much recovered scrap. And that was just what they were, Thalia realised. The machine carrying the bodies was heading in the same direction as all the others, carrying raw material to the manufactories. The dead people would be processed, stripped down, reutilised. Even if their meat bodies yielded nothing of value, there were useful metals, semiconductors, superconductors and organic compounds inside their skulls, courtesy of their Demarchist implants.

Until that moment she had believed that the machines were only imposing totalitarian rule. She had seen bodies being dumped into the ornamental fountain, but had convinced herself that these had been people who'd disobeyed in some fashion. Now she knew that the servitors were engaged in systematic mass murder. The people she had seen outside, being rounded up and lectured to, were not being herded together to make them easier to police, easier to subdue. They were being rounded up so that they could be euthanised and fed to the manufactories.

Thalia had no way of knowing how many of the eight hundred thousand citizens inside House Aubusson had met a similar fate. But she did not think it likely that there were many exceptions. The servitors had assumed control with startling speed, and the constables had unwittingly abetted them by advising the people to remain calm and follow the directives of Lucas Thesiger. But Thesiger could quite easily have been one of those carelessly stacked bodies.

Thalia knew then that she did not have much time left. The only reason the machines had not torn the stalk down already was that the servitors could not risk damaging the polling core. But they would find a way eventually. Whatever intelligence was guiding them, it was cleverer than any individual servitor. And that intelligence, Thalia was certain, knew all about her and her little party of survivors. Even now, it would be working out a way to kill them. If the machines didn't get through the barricade (and she wasn't optimistic about it keeping them out for much longer) then they would explore alternative approaches. Thalia had one deterrent, which was that she could destroy or at least incapacitate the core. But if she played that hand and the machines somehow kept coming, she had nothing else to offer.

'They're getting louder,' Parnasse said quietly, joining her by the little round window.

'What are, Cyrus?'

'The machines on the other side of the barricade. They're working their way through it piece by piece, getting closer and closer to the top. I doubt there's more than ten or fifteen metres of obstruction between us and them. I've tried to play it down, but the others are starting to notice.'

Thalia was mindful to keep her expression fixed, betraying nothing that would upset the nervous disposition of the other citizens. 'How long?'

'It's coming up close to dawn now. We've still got some junk we can throw down the stairs, but most of the heavy stuff's already gone. The barricade may hold until noon, but I'd say we'll be doing extraordinarily well if it's still up by sundown.'

'Cyrus, I need to tell you something. I've seen something very bad out there.' When he said nothing, she continued softly, 'I didn't mention it earlier because you had enough to be thinking about. But now you need to know.'

'The bodies? Being carried away?'

She looked at him sharply. 'You knew already?'

'I saw several loads move through while you were cutting up the plinth. I didn't think *you* needed anything else to worry about. But you're right. It isn't good news.'

'When the machines break through, they'll kill us all.'

He put a hand on her shoulder. 'I reckon you're right. But we're doing everything we can to buy enough time until rescue arrives.'

'I don't think we can count on Panoply to help us,' Thalia said hesitantly. 'I've been putting a brave face on it, but ever since Crissel failed to show ... I don't know what's going on, Cyrus. Crissel said we weren't the only habitat to go silent. But even so, I can't see why it should have taken Panoply so long to reinstate control. I think we have to assume we're on our own in here.'

'Then it's up to us to find a way to survive. I agree, girl. But short of holding out up here, I don't really see what our options are.'

'We have to find a way out,' she said.

'There isn't one. Even if there was another way out of the stalk, do you think any of us would last long out there, with all those machines crawling around? That whiphound of yours might have one more fight in it, if we're lucky. It'll take more than that to get us to the endcap, even if there's a ship to take us away when we get there.'

'But we have to do something. I don't know about you, but I don't particularly want to die in here.'

He looked at her sadly. 'Wish I could wave a magic wand and

get us all somewhere safe. But all we've got is that barricade, and we're running out of stuff to reinforce it.'

Thalia looked across the floor, to the place where the plinth had been. The architectural model rested to one side of it, minus the sphere that had broken off the top of the stalk. Unaccountably, she flashed back to the way it had rolled across the floor when they'd dropped the model. She had paid it no heed at the time, intent only on exposing the granite plinth so that she could hack it into pieces.

'Cyrus,' she said, 'if there was a way to get us out of here, even if it was dangerous, even if it was borderline suicidal, would you risk it, if the only alternative was waiting for those machines to get us?'

'Is that a hypothetical question, girl?'

'I don't know,' she answered. 'It depends. But answer my question first.'

'I'd risk it. Wouldn't you?'

'In a flash,' Thalia said.

Dreyfus looked up as Senior Prefect Gaffney stepped through the passwall. He sat upright on the bed, unable to judge how much time had passed since his last visitor. Through a fog of tiredness and apprehension, a sour taste in his mouth, he nonetheless produced a laconic smile. 'Nice of you to drop by. I was wondering when you'd favour me with a visit.'

Behind Gaffney the passwall sealed itself into impermeability.

'You're very talkative all of a sudden. Let's see how long you can keep it up.'

Dreyfus rubbed a finger along the furred line of his unbrushed teeth. 'I guess the cat's come to torment the mouse while everyone else is looking the other way?'

'On the contrary. I've come to interview you, with full Panoply sanction. Baudry gave me her personal blessing.'

Dreyfus looked down to see if Gaffney was carrying anything. 'No field trawl,' he observed. 'What's wrong: worried that it might reveal some truths you'd rather remained hidden?'

'On the contrary. Worried that it wouldn't give us the hard data we need fast enough. There's a crisis going on out there, Dreyfus. The question is: are you a part of whatever's happening, or did you just kill the prisoner because she looked at you the wrong way?'

'I hear we lost the *Universal Suffrage.*'

'Too bad. There were some good rookies on that ship.'

'Not to mention Senior Prefect Crissel.'

'Worse ways to go than fighting for a cause.'

'This is all about a cause, isn't it? For you, anyway. I've followed your career, Sheridan. I know what makes you tick. You're the most selflessly driven prefect I've ever known. You eat, sleep and breathe security. Nothing matters more to you than guaranteeing the safety of the Glitter Band.'

Gaffney appeared surprised by this outburst of praise. 'If the cap fits.'

'Oh, it does. It fits too well. You're a machine, Sheridan. You're like a wind-up toy, an automaton consumed by a single idea. You've let that cause swallow you whole. It's all you know, all you're capable of thinking about.'

'You think security doesn't matter?'

'Oh, it matters all right. The problem is, in your personal universe it trumps all other concerns. You'll consider any action, contemplate crossing any line, if you feel your precious security is in danger of being compromised. Let's tick the boxes, shall we? Murder of a witness. Betrayal of fellow Panoply operatives. You're about to add torture to the list. And you haven't even really got going yet. What's next on the menu, Sheridan: full-scale genocide?'

'What I do – what we all do – is about the preservation of life, not the destruction of it.'

'That may be the way it looks in your warped worldview.'

'There's nothing warped about it, Tom.' Gaffney tapped a finger against the side of his head. 'I'm sorry – are we on first-name terms now? It's just that you took offence the last time I used yours. "Sonofabitch" was the phrase, I think.'

'Whatever makes you happy, Sheridan.'

'You've got me all wrong. You're the loose cannon in this organisation, Tom. I didn't bring the Spider bitch inside Panoply and let her riffle through our operational secrets. I didn't kill her when I realised my mistake.'

'They'll find out I didn't kill her.'

'There's half a body in your quarters, Tom. It didn't teleport there.'

'Maybe she walked there, with you telling her everything was going to be fine.'

'No, she didn't walk. Forensics found tissue traces in the bubble. That's where she was shot. Whoever killed her didn't hang around to clean up too well. But you'd know that, wouldn't you?'

'How would I have got her from the interrogation bubble to my room without you knowing about it?'

'That's a damned good question. One I'm hoping you can answer.'

'If I wanted to move a body, if I wanted to tamper with access records to hide my own entry into the bubble, being head of Internal Security would certainly make life easier. But even then, I'm not sure how you did it.'

'Why would I have killed a key witness?'

'Because she knew you were working for Aurora. Because there was a chance she could have discovered Aurora's vulnerabilities, given us a clue as to how to take her down.'

Gaffney pointed his finger at Dreyfus. 'Right. That name again.'

'What's she got on you, Sheridan?'

Gaffney looked bored. 'I think we've pretty much covered the preliminaries.'

'And now you're going to kill me,' Dreyfus surmised.

'I'm going to use intelligence-extraction methods on you, Tom, that's all. Nothing you won't get over given time and rest.'

'You know that there isn't a truth to extract. I'm not going to start confessing to crimes I never committed.'

'We'll just have to see what pops out, shan't we?'

'I understand now,' Dreyfus said. 'This is the only way out for you, isn't it? I must die under interrogation. You'll have some explaining to do, but I'm sure you've thought that through already. How's it going to happen? Whiphound malfunction? I hear there've been some quality-assurance issues with those Model Cs.'

'Don't be ridiculous,' Gaffney said as he unclipped his whiphound and thumbed it on. 'I've come to interview you, not kill you. How would *that* go down? I'm not a butcher.'

He ran out the filament and allowed it to find traction against the floor, then relinquished his hold on the handle. For an instant the whiphound stayed where it was, just turning its shaft to shine the red laser of its eye on Dreyfus's face. Then it began to advance, its filament making a slow hissing sound as it scraped its coils against the floor. The handle was tipped down slightly, like the head of a cobra.

Dreyfus knew that there was nowhere to run, nowhere to hide. But he could not help shrinking back against the wall, dragging his legs up onto the bunk as if the corner might provide some sanctuary from the questing machine.

Gaffney stood back, his arms folded across his chest. 'Guess you know the drill, Tom. No point pretending this is going to be pleasant. But tell me what I need to know and it'll all be over with very quickly. Why did you kill Clepsydra, and how did you get the body to your room?'

'You killed her, not me. She was still alive when I left her.'

The whiphound slinked onto the bunk, the elevation of its handle never altering. The red glare of its laser made Dreyfus squint and hold a hand up to his face. It came nearer, until he could hear a shrill electronic buzzing. He edged deeper into the corner, drawing his knees high against his chest. The whiphound continued its advance, bringing the blunt end of the handle to within a hand's-width of Dreyfus's face. The brightness of the laser and the electronic humming combined with hypnotic effect. Around the trembling shield of his hand he saw the filament's tip rise up and quest the air. It began to curl, ready to wrap itself around Dreyfus. Part of him wanted to reach out and grab it, to try to stop it finding a way behind his back. A more sensible part of him knew how futile that would be, and what the attempt would do to his fingers.

'They'll find out what you did,' he said. 'They're better than you, Gaffney. You won't be able to hide from Panoply for ever.'

Then he felt the filament whip around him. It wrapped itself around him twice, constricting him with its blunt edge. His arms were pinned to his sides, his knees jammed hard against his ribcage. The handle remained pointed at his face, its laser eye washing the world into scarlet.

'The whiphound's going to insert the tip of its tail into your mouth,' Gaffney said, 'but we can go with any orifice you like. Your call, Tom.'

Dreyfus closed his mouth, biting down so hard that he tasted salty wetness gush from his tongue. The filament tapped against the portcullis of his teeth, as if asking permission to enter. Dreyfus produced a senseless groan of defiance. The whiphound tapped again. He felt the filament tighten its coils.

'Open wide,' Gaffney said, cheerily encouraging. 'Easy does it.'

The whiphound tapped twice more against his teeth, then withdrew the tip of the filament. Dreyfus wondered if it was going to try to force its way in through a different orifice now that he had barred it from slithering in through his mouth.

He felt the coils loosen. Breathing was no longer difficult. The handle held its gaze on him for a second, and then rotated slowly around until it was directing the horizontal glare of its scanning laser eye onto Gaffney's face rather than Dreyfus's. The coil released Dreyfus completely. He took a grateful breath and slumped against the wall, feeling a stripe of cold sweat ooze down the valley of his spine. The whiphound moved stealthily off the bunk, never releasing its visual lock on Gaffney.

'Stand down,' Gaffney said, keeping the panic from his voice for the moment. 'Stand down. Revert to defence posture one.'

The whiphound showed no sign of having heard or recognised his order and kept on slithering. The filament pushed the handle higher, so that it was level with the standing man's face. Gaffney took a hesitant step backwards, then another, until his back bumped into the wall.

'Stand down,' he repeated, louder this time. 'This is Senior Prefect Gaffney ordering you to stand down and switch to standby mode. You have developed a fault. Repeat, you have developed a fault.'

'It doesn't appear to be listening,' Dreyfus said.

Gaffney raised a shaky hand. 'Stand down!'

'I wouldn't touch it if I were you. It'll have your fingers off.'

The whiphound pressed Gaffney hard against the wall, the filament spooled out to its maximum extension. The handle made an emphatic nodding motion.

'I think it wants you to kneel,' Dreyfus said.

CHAPTER 21

The assembled seniors, internals and supernumerary analysts looked away from the Solid Orrery as the heavy doors of the tactical room swung open. For a second their expressions were as one, conveying a shared sense of indignation that their secret session had been interrupted, and without even the courtesy of a knock. Then they saw that the man stepping through the door was Senior Prefect Sheridan Gaffney and their collective mood changed from one of annoyance to mild puzzlement. Gaffney was perfectly entitled to enter the tactical room, his presence at least as welcome as that of anyone else there. But even Gaffney would normally have had the good manners to announce his arrival before barging in. The head of Internal Security was nothing if not a stickler for observation of the niceties.

'Is there a problem, Senior?' Baudry asked, speaking for the assembled party.

But it was not Gaffney who answered the query. Gaffney himself appeared strangely dumbstruck, incapable of formulating a response. Ten centimetres of black cylinder jutted from his mouth, as if he had been trying to swallow a thick candle. His eyes bulged as if he was seeking to squeeze all meaning through them.

The honour of replying fell instead to Dreyfus, who was following only a couple of paces behind the other man. There was an understandable measure of consternation at this development. Everyone in the room was aware that Dreyfus was under detention, unavoidably implicated in the murder of the Conjoiner woman. A smaller number of those present knew that Gaffney had been tasked to interview Dreyfus, and an even smaller number knew which methods that interview was likely to employ. The thought must have occurred to at least some of the party that Dreyfus had overpowered Gaffney and must now be holding him at knife- or gunpoint. Further inspection, however, revealed the presence of no recognisable weapon about the person of the field prefect. He was not even wearing shoes.

'Actually,' Dreyfus said, 'there is a bit of a problem.'

'Why are you not in your cell?' Baudry asked, her attention flicking from Dreyfus to Gaffney and back again. 'What's happened? What's wrong with Sheridan? What's that thing in his mouth?'

Gaffney's posture was almost rigidly upright, as if he was hanging from an invisible coat rack. When he had walked into the room, he had moved with tiny shuffling footsteps, like a man with his laces tied together. He kept his arms glued to his sides. The thing lodged in his mouth forced him to keep his head at an unusual angle – it was as if he had developed a crick in his neck while looking up at the ceiling. There was a bulge in the skin of his throat, distending the collar of his tunic, that was more than Adam's apple. He appeared unwilling to make the slightest unnecessary bodily movement.

'The thing in his mouth is a whiphound,' Dreyfus said. 'He came to interrogate me with a Model C. We were getting on famously when it just turned on him.'

'That's not possible. A whiphound isn't meant to do that.' Baudry looked at Dreyfus with an appalled expression. 'You didn't do this, did you, Tom? You didn't push that thing into him?'

'If I'd have touched it, I wouldn't have any fingers left. No, it did it all by itself. Actually, Gaffney helped a bit with the final insertion.'

'I don't understand. Why on Earth would he help?'

'He didn't have a lot of choice. It all happened very slowly, very precisely. Have you ever seen a snake swallowing an egg? It pushed the filament into his mouth, then reached down into his stomach. You know how the interrogation mode works on those things: it locates major organs then threatens to slice them in two from inside.'

'What do you mean: interrogation mode? There's no such thing.'

'There is now. It's one of the new features Gaffney had built into the Model Cs. Of course, it has some innocuous-sounding name: enhanced compliance facilitation, or something similar.'

'He could have called for help.'

Dreyfus shook his head. 'Not a hope. It would have sliced him into six or seven pieces before he could say his name into his bracelet.'

'But why did he help it finish what it was doing to him?'

'It was hurting him, letting him know that if he didn't help by pushing the handle into his mouth, it was going to do something really unpleasant.'

Baudry stared at Gaffney with renewed comprehension. The handle of a model A or B whiphound would have been too thick to enter the human throat. But a Model C was thinner, sleeker, altogether nastier. A whiphound handle jammed partway down Gaffney's gullet would certainly explain his stiff-necked posture, his unwillingness to compromise what must have already been a very congested windpipe.

'We have to get it out of him,' she said.

'I don't think it wants you to do that,' Dreyfus said.

'It doesn't *want* anything. It's malfunctioning, obviously.'

'I wouldn't be so sure of that,' Dreyfus said, looking around the party, at the documents and compads on the table. 'But perhaps Gaffney has an opinion on the matter. He can't speak right now, obviously, but he can still use his hands. Can't you?'

Gaffney shuffled around. His eyes were two bulging eggs, ready to pop out of their sockets. His cheeks were the colour of beetroot. He didn't so much nod as make a microscopic twitching suggestion of one.

'I think he needs something to write with,' Dreyfus said. 'Can anyone spare a compad and a stylus?'

'Take mine,' Baudry said, skidding the item across the table. One of the analysts took the compad, unclipped the stylus and passed them both to Gaffney. His arms unlocked from the sides of his body, articulating with painful slowness as if the bones themselves had fused. His hands were shaking. He took the compad in his left hand and fumbled for the stylus with his right. It fell to the floor. The analyst knelt down and gently placed it in his palm.

'I don't see—' Baudry began.

'Tell them what happened to Clepsydra,' Dreyfus said.

Gaffney scratched the stylus across the writing surface of the compad. His movements were pained and childlike, as if he had seldom held a stylus before, let alone written with one. But laboriously he formed recognisable letters, scratching them out in agonised strokes.

He shuffled forward to the edge of the table and dropped the compad.

Baudry picked it up. She studied the scrawl upon it. '"I killed her",' she mouthed. 'That's what it says: "I killed her." She looked up at Gaffney. 'Is this true, Sheridan? Did you really kill the prisoner?'

Again that twitch of a nod, a movement so subtle that the assembled seniors would never have seen it had they not been watching for it.

She handed him back the compad. 'Why?'

He scratched out another answer.

'"Knew too much",' Baudry read. 'Knew too much about *what*, Sheridan? What secret did she have to die to protect?'

Gaffney scribbled again. His trembling was growing worse, and it took longer to spell out one word than it had taken him to spell out three the last time.

'"Aurora",' Baudry read. 'That name again. Is it true, Sheridan? Is she really one of the Eighty?'

But when she handed him the compad, all he wrote on it this time was: 'Help me.'

'I think it might be best to save further questioning for later,' Dreyfus said.

'Why is it doing this to him?' Baudry asked. 'I've heard about the difficulties with the Model Cs, but nothing like *this* has ever happened.'

'He must have switched on the whiphound in Clepsydra's presence,' Dreyfus said. 'Very silly thing to do around a Conjoiner, but I guess he couldn't resist tormenting her. She couldn't stop him killing her – he used a gun for that – but she was still able to tamper with the whiphound.'

'She wouldn't have had time.'

'I doubt it took her more than a second. For a Conjoiner, it would have been about as difficult as blinking.'

'But the programming is hard-coded.'

'Nothing's hard-coded to a Conjoiner. There's always a way in, always a back door. She'd have found it if she knew she was about to die and this was her only way of getting a message through. Right, Sheridan?'

Gaffney twitched another affirmative. Some kind of whitish foam or drool was beginning to erupt around the black plug filling his mouth. The quickening tempo of his breathing was now audible to everyone in the room.

'We still have to get it out of him,' Baudry said. 'Sheridan: I want you to stay very, very calm. No matter what you've done, no matter what's happened, we're going to help you.' She lifted her arm and spoke into her bracelet with a voice on the trembling edge of panic. 'Doctor Demikhov? Oh good, you're awake. Yes, very well, thank you. I know this is unorthodox and that you're mandated to focus only on the Aumonier case but ... something's come up. Something that requires your expertise very, very urgently.'

Dr Demikhov conjured a quickmatter partition, closing off one end of the tactical room to allow him and the other medical technicians to work on Gaffney in privacy. The last clear view Dreyfus had of the senior prefect was of him being gently lowered onto a couch tipped at forty-five degrees to the floor, handled as if he was a bomb that might detonate at any instant. Through the partition's smoky opacity, the team became vaguely outlined pale ghosts, huddled around an indistinct black form. Then the indistinct black form started thrashing, blurred limbs flailing the air.

'Do you think they'll get it out of him?' Baudry asked, breaking the uncanny silence.

'I don't think Clepsydra was interested in killing him,' Dreyfus said. 'She could have achieved that already by embedding a different set of instructions into the whiphound. I think she wanted him to talk instead.'

'He was in no state to tell us anything reliable.'

'He told us enough,' Dreyfus said. 'We can get more out of him when Demikhov's finished.' He eased himself into one of the seats around the table, opposite Baudry. 'I'm taking something of a liberty here, but is it safe to assume that I'm no longer the prime suspect in Clepsydra's murder?'

Baudry swallowed hard. 'I was prepared to believe that you'd been framed, Tom, but I couldn't accept your accusations about Gaffney. He was one of us, for Voi's sake. I had to believe that you were wrong: that you were either striking out against him for personal reasons, or someone was framing Gaffney as well.'

'And now?'

'Following that little spectacle, I think we can safely assume that we know who murdered Clepsydra, and that he was probably acting alone.' Baudry cast a wary glance at the smoky partition, but the huddle of shapes beyond the quickmatter was now too concentrated to separate into individuals. 'Which means you were right, and I was wrong, and I ignored you when I should have trusted you. I'm sorry about that.'

'Don't apologise,' Dreyfus said. 'You had a crisis to contain and you took the best decision you could given the evidence available to you.'

'There's more,' Baudry said. She played with her fingers nervously, as if she was trying to dismantle her hands. 'I see now that Gaffney wanted Jane removed from command. Not because he was concerned for her, or even for Panoply, but because he feared she'd put two and two together before very long.'

'So she had to go,' Dreyfus said.

Baudry's attention flicked to the partition. 'When Demikhov's finished ... I need to talk to him about Jane. Do you think she's strong enough to resume command?'

'Whether she is or not, we need her.'

'Like a circuit needs a fuse, even though it might blow at any time.' Baudry shuddered at the thought. 'Can we do this? Can we subject Jane to something that might kill her?'

'Let Jane decide.'

'Crissel and I didn't want her removed for the same reasons as Gaffney,' she said, apparently oblivious to the other people in the tactical room. 'But that doesn't make what we did any more excusable.'

'Whatever Crissel did wrong, he made it right when he got on that deep-system cruiser.'

'And me?'

'Reinstate Jane, clear me of any suspicion of wrongdoing and I think you'll have made a decent start.'

It was as if she hadn't heard him. 'Perhaps I should resign. I've let down the supreme prefect, allowed myself to be hoodwinked and manipulated by another senior ... failed to trust the one man I should have placed my faith in. In most organisations, what I've done would be punished by instant dismissal.'

'Sorry, Lillian, but you don't get out of it that easily,' Dreyfus said. 'It takes more than a few bad judgement calls to erase a lifetime's loyal service to Panoply. You were an outstanding senior a week ago. From where I'm sitting, not much has changed.'

'That's ... generous of you,' she allowed.

'I'm only thinking of the organisation. We lost a good man in Crissel. That's why we need Jane Aumonier. That's why we need Lillian Baudry.'

'And Tom Dreyfus,' she added. 'And yes, you can consider yourself free of suspicion.'

'I hope that goes for Sparver as well.'

'Of course. He did nothing wrong except support a fellow prefect, and he deserves my personal apology.'

'I want him to start digging into the archives, to find everything he can on Aurora Nerval-Lermontov and the other alpha-levels.'

'I'll make sure he has all the resources, all the clearance he needs. You honestly think this is the same woman?'

Dreyfus nodded at the partition. 'We heard it from the horse's mouth. In a manner of speaking, at least. We're dealing with a ghost in the machine. Now all we need is a ghost-killer.'

The world came back to Jane Aumonier without warning, without ceremony. She had decided, after much deliberation, that she preferred darkness and silence to the limited range of entertainments Gaffney and the others had left her with when they removed her executive authority. That left her alone with only the scarab for company, but in the eleven years since it had attached itself to her neck she had found that she could, when circumstances required it, retreat to a private corner of her own mind, a fortified place where even the scarab could not intrude. She had never been able to stay within that mental bastion for very long, but it had always been there when she needed it. In her place of sanctuary she played glacially cold, achingly melancholy piano pieces. She had often played the piano before the scarab came. Now it would not even allow the small bulk of a holoclavier in her presence, let alone a full-bodied keyboard. Yet she still remembered how to play, and when she was in full retreat her fingers moved in silent echo of the composition she was reciting in her head, ten million parsecs from the chamber in which she floated. The hidden music was the one thing the scarab had never been able to steal from her.

She had her eyes closed when the chamber began to light up of its own volition. It was hazardous to close her eyes for too long, for that invited the spectre of sleep to take a step nearer. But there was a more profound, calmer darkness when her eyes were closed, even in the absolute blackness of the unlit chamber.

'I didn't—' Aumonier began, squinting against the sudden intrusion of brightness, colour and movement. The music shattered into irrecoverable pieces.

'It's all right,' said a voice, coming from somewhere to her right. 'You're getting back everything they took away, Jane.'

She twisted her head towards the voice. The figure was dark on dark, standing in the black aperture of the passwall. 'Tom?'

'In the flesh. Minus shoes, unfortunately.'

The feeds were popping on all around her, gradually filling the interior surface of the sphere. The configuration, the preference given to views of certain habitats over others, was recognisable as one of her usual settings. The Glitter Band, she realised, was still out there. She felt an odd flicker of resentment that her empire had continued running itself while she had been ousted from her throne.

'Where have you been?' she asked as the dark figure fastened on a safe-distance tether and crossed the airspace towards her.

'How much did anyone tell you?' Dreyfus asked as the mounting illumination cast shifting blue highlights on his face. He looked puffy and somehow dishevelled.

'They told me nothing.'

'You're back in command,' Dreyfus said. 'If you want it, of course.'

In the absence of visitors, she'd had little recent practice speaking. The words came out with mushy edges, as if she had just woken. 'What about Crissel, Gaffney, Clearmountain? What about Baudry? They can't have agreed to this.'

'Let's just say the command landscape has changed. The chances are very good that Michael Crissel is dead. Gaffney – who turned out to be a traitor – is being operated on as we speak. I've just had to talk Baudry out of handing in her resignation. I think she's realised the serious mistake she made in ousting you.'

'Wait,' Aumonier said. 'What happened to Crissel?'

'We lost contact with him as he was attempting to enter House Aubusson along with a squad of field prefects. We've also lost contact with that entire habitat, along with three others.'

'No one told me,' she said.

'We're talking about the same four habitats that Thalia was visiting to upgrade their polling cores. Looks as if we were set up, Jane. Thalia's installation may have closed one security hole, but it blew open a much wider one. Wide enough to let a militant faction seize control of those habitats.'

'Do you think Thalia was part of this conspiracy?'

'No, she was set up like the rest of us. I wanted to be on the ship that Crissel took to Aubusson but Gaffney had other ideas.' Dreyfus's expression was one of gloomy resignation. 'Not that it would have made much difference.'

'What about Gaffney?'

'He was working for the enemy faction, from within Panoply. Chances are it was Gaffney who manipulated Thalia's upgrade to make it work the way it did.'

Aumonier shook her head in amazement. 'I never had Sheridan down as a traitor.'

'My guess is he feels he was doing the right and necessary thing, even if that meant going against his own organisation. From his point of view we're the traitors, letting down the Glitter Band by not taking our duties as seriously as he deems necessary.'

'If you're right then we're at least partially culpable.'

'How so?'

'The organisation moulds men like Gaffney. An effective prefect is only one degree from being a monster in the first place. Most of us stay the right side of the line. But we can hardly blame one of us when he strays across it.'

'He's still got some explaining to do,' Dreyfus said.

'I'm sure you're right.' Aumonier breathed in, composing herself. 'Now tell me who we're up against. Do you have a name?'

'The figure behind the takeovers is Aurora Nerval-Lermontov. She was one of the Eighty, Jane. That means she's dead; that she doesn't exist any more except as a set of disembodied patterns stored in the memory of a machine. Patterns that are supposedly frozen, as if they were written down in ink.'

Aumonier digested that, sifting her memories to verify that the Nerval-Lermontovs had indeed been one of the families sponsoring Calvin Sylveste's experiments in mind-uploading. *Fifty-five years ago*, she thought. But the horror of the Eighty still burnt as brightly in the public imagination as at any time in the last half-century.

'Even if I accept this . . . how do we know Aurora's behind it all?'

'A witness told me. She was being held hostage inside a rock owned by Aurora's family. My witness reported coming into contact with an entity called Aurora.'

'This witness—'

'Was a Conjoiner woman named Clepsydra. This is where it gets complicated.'

'Go for it.'

'Clepsydra was one of the survivors aboard an entire ship that was being held captive inside that rock, deep enough underground that there was no chance of them contacting other Conjoiners.'

'With you so far.'

Dreyfus smiled. 'There was advanced technology aboard that ship – a Conjoiner device called Exordium that lets them see into the future.'

'If I was hearing this from anyone other than Tom Dreyfus, I'd get Mercier up here with a full psychiatric renormalisation kit.'

'The Conjoiners have to be in a kind of dream-state just to interpret what it shows them. It's imprecise, but a hell of an improvement on not being able to see into the future at all.'

'I'd buy one like a shot.'

'Not for sale, apparently. Which is why Aurora needed to kidnap the Conjoiners and get them to run Exordium for her. That's what they've been doing in that rock all the while: looking into the future on Aurora's behalf. Seeing things she can't see.'

'And what did they see, Tom?'

'The end of the world. A time of plagues, Clepsydra said. Beyond that, the dreamers couldn't see anything. Aurora kept trying to persuade them to interpret the dreams differently. When they didn't show her what she wanted, she turned the screws on them.'

'I need to speak to this Clepsydra,' Aumonier said. 'The scarab may not like her being in this room, but she doesn't have to be physically present – I only need a voice and a face.'

'I wish you could speak to her,' Dreyfus answered heavily. 'Gaffney killed her, then tried to pin it on me. Given the knowledge she'd already sucked out of our records, there was a very real threat of her being able to pin down Aurora's location, maybe even isolate some weakness we could use against her. That's why she had to go. But it turns out Clepsydra had the last laugh after all.'

'Then what about Gaffney? If he's working for Aurora, we must be able to get something useful out of him?'

'I sincerely hope so. I'm going to find out everything he knows. Then we can start formulating a response. I want those habitats back. I particularly want my deputy field back.'

'You realise Thalia may already be dead, Tom? I'm sorry, but someone has to say it. Better that you start dealing with the possibility now rather than later.'

'She's dead when we recover her body,' Dreyfus said. 'Until then she's behind enemy lines.'

'I fully approve of that sentiment, but don't raise your hopes, that's all I'm saying.' Aumonier closed her eyes and took a deep, cleansing breath before reopening them. 'Now let's talk about me, shall we? You said I am being reinstated to full status.'

'If you want it.'

'Of course I damned well want it. This is what keeps me alive.'

'It could be what kills you. Things aren't going to get any less tense around here any time soon. Are you sure you're ready for that? There isn't anyone I'd sooner see running the organisation in a time of crisis, but you've given Panoply more than enough in the last eleven years. No one would hold it against you if you decided to sit this one out.'

'I'm in command.'

'Good,' called another voice from the still-open passwall. Aumonier recognised the hovering form of Baudry.

'Hello, Lillian,' Aumonier said guardedly.

Baudry attached her own safe-distance tether and drifted out until she flanked Dreyfus, stabilising herself to the same local vertical. 'There's something I need to say, Supreme Prefect. I let you down. I can't speak for Michael Crissel, but I should never have been party to what happened in this room.'

'Prefect Dreyfus tells me you've considered resignation.'

'That's correct. And I will resign, too, if you wish it.'

Aumonier let the other woman wait, until the silence had become as electrically potent as the air before a thunderstorm. 'I don't approve of what you did, Lillian. Gaffney may have played a part in the decision to remove me from power, but you should still have resisted him. It's to your discredit that you failed to do so.'

'I'm sorry,' Baudry mouthed.

'You should be. Crissel as well, were he still with us.'

'We thought we were doing the right thing.'

'And the fact that I expressly requested to be allowed to stay in power – that didn't mean anything to you?'

'Gaffney said we should ignore your pleas, that secretly you would be craving permission to step down.' A little defiance returned to Baudry now. 'We were doing our best. I've told you already that I'm ashamed of what happened. But at the time I did not have the luxury of hindsight, of knowing what we now do about Sheridan.'

'Enough,' Aumonier said, raising a calming hand. She thought about all the testing years that Lillian Baudry, a good, loyal senior prefect, had spent in her shadow. Never once being able to demonstrate true effectiveness, true leadership, never once having the temerity to question or undermine a single one of Aumonier's decisions. 'What's done is done. At least now we both know where we stand. Don't we?'

'I have apologised. I am ready and waiting for either a resignation order or new commands.'

'Both of you might want to take a look at that feed,' Dreyfus said. 'Before you make any rash decisions, that is.'

'What feed?' Baudry asked.

'He means the long-range surveillance of House Aubusson, I think,' Aumonier said. 'Something's happening there, isn't it?'

Dreyfus nodded. 'It started while we were speaking.'

'We've been monitoring the thermal output from the four habitats for a number of hours,' Baudry said, shifting effortlessly back into the detached tones of neutral professionalism. 'Two of them, Aubusson and Szlumper Oneill, show evidence of activity in their manufactories. It's as if the assembler plants have been cranked back up to full operating strength since Aurora's takeover. So far, we've only been able to speculate as to what that means. What we do know is that Crissel's ship was hit by more weapons than we can account for based on the Aubusson blueprints filed with Panoply. One theory, therefore, is that the factories are producing new defence systems, to further consolidate Aurora's hold on the habitats.'

'How long would it take to create and install new weapons if those manufactories were running at standard capacity?' Aumonier asked.

'Allowing for ready provision of raw materials and blueprints, no more than six to eight hours,' Baudry answered. 'It's entirely feasible, given the timescales we're looking at.'

'But now it looks as if they're not just making weapons,' Dreyfus said.

The image of House Aubusson was a three-quarters view captured at long-range by a surveillance cam well outside the attack volume of the habitat's anti-collision weapons. It showed the factory end of the cylinder, not the docking hub where Crissel had presumably met his demise. Vast petal-like structures, curved doors many kilometres long, were opening in the domed endcap, revealing through a star-shaped aperture the blue-gold luminance of intense, frenzied industry.

'Those doors ... are they part of the habitat's original design?' Aumonier asked.

Baudry nodded. 'Back when the habitat had the capacity and

the client base to grow entire ships, they needed those doors to launch them into space. But our records say they haven't opened in over a century.'

'Then why are they opening now?'

'That's why,' Dreyfus said.

Something was spilling through the gaps between the fingerlike doors, billowing out in a gauzy black mass, like an eruption of wasps. It was a cloud composed of thousands of individual elements.

Simultaneously, Dreyfus and Baudry's bracelets started chiming.

'Someone else has noticed,' Baudry said.

'What are we looking at?' asked Aumonier, a queasy feeling in her stomach. Up to this point, her crisis parameters had consisted of a hostage scenario in which Panoply might lose control of four habitats. Four was inexcusable, the worst disaster in eleven years, but it was still negligible compared to the mind-numbing immensity of the ten thousand. Containable, she thought. And yet that emerging black cloud said otherwise. She did not yet know what it was, but she knew with piercing certainty that it was not good news, and that the crisis she had imagined Panoply to be facing was as nothing compared to the one that was now blossoming.

'We need to know what that ... froth is,' she said, fighting to keep her voice from faltering. 'We need numbers and tech assessments. We need to know what it's for and where it's headed.'

'Doors are opening in Szlumper Oneill,' Baudry said, reading a text summary on her bracelet. As she spoke, a window enlarged itself, squeezing others aside as it filled with a long-range view of the other habitat. A black cloud was boiling out of elongated slots near one of the polar docking complexes, smothering detail as it expanded.

'I think it's the same stuff,' Aumonier said.

'Has to be,' Dreyfus said. 'Question is, what about the other two habitats?'

'No excess thermal activity in either Carousel New Seattle-Tacoma or the Chevelure-Sambuke Hourglass,' Baudry said. 'But according to our data, neither of those habitats has any kind of manufacturing capacity.'

Dreyfus scratched at the back of his collar. 'Thalia's upgrade may have been contaminated, but I'm pretty sure she chose those four habitats herself, based on her own selection criteria.'

'Meaning what?' Aumonier asked.

'Meaning Aurora may not have had any influence over which habitats she got control of. Given four, the chances were good that at least one of them was going to have some kind of manufacturing capability. But it wasn't guaranteed. Looks like two of the four were duds, in any case. She's captured them, but right now she can't make them work for her.'

'I'm not taking my eye off any of these habitats.'

'I agree. But it shows us that Aurora isn't pulling all the strings here. She had to work with the hand Thalia dealt her.' Dreyfus flashed a bleak smile. 'I won't say it gladdens my heart, but—'

'Problem is we may already have done the work she needs.'

'I'm hoping that isn't the case.' But Dreyfus still nodded, letting Aumonier know that he shared her fears. 'You're right, though. We need a closer look at whatever those factories are spewing out. How fast would you say that stuff is emerging?'

'I don't know. Judging by the scale ... hundreds of metres a second, maybe faster.'

'I concur,' Baudry said.

'That's what I was thinking,' Dreyfus said. 'Pretty damned fast, anyway. I'll need to look at the Solid Orrery, but given the mean spacing between habitats, it isn't going to take very long before the swarm reaches another one. Let's assume the closest neighbour to Aubusson is sixty or seventy kilometres away, in the same orbit. Even if that stuff is only moving at ten metres a second, we're not looking at much more than two hours. Of course, I hope I'm wrong.'

'You're hardly ever wrong,' Aumonier said. 'That's what worries me.'

Dreyfus glanced at Baudry. 'We need to task ships for a close fly-by of one of those clouds. Automated, if possible, but manned if that's all we can manage in the time available.'

'I'll get on it. We have a deep-system cruiser – the *Democratic Circus* – inbound from the Parking Swarm. I've already asked Captain Pell to swing by Aubusson, to see if he can image the remains of the *Universal Suffrage*, sweep for survivors and get a better look at those weapons emplacements.'

'Tell them to take care,' Dreyfus said.

Baudry said, 'I already did. Now I'll tell them to take even more.'

'The scope of this crisis is now greater than the four lost habitats,' Dreyfus said, directing his words back at Aumonier. 'I'll run the Orrery immediately, but in the meantime I think we should consider an appropriate statement. We've buffered the citizenry so far, but now it may be time to start alerting the wider Glitter Band to the real nature of the crisis.'

Aumonier swallowed hard. 'I don't want mass panic. What should we tell them?'

Dreyfus looked pragmatic. 'Frankly, mass panic may be the least of our worries.'

'Even so . . . we still don't know what we're dealing with, what Aurora wants, what she's doing with those habitats when she gains control of them.'

'Tell them something's trying to take over,' Dreyfus said. 'Tell them that it has nothing to do with the Ultras, and that we'll phase in mass euthanisation if we even suspect that someone's trying to settle an old score with the Swarm. Tell them that Panoply is declaring a Bandwide state of emergency, and that this time we really need a vote in favour of utilizing heavy weapons.'

'We don't have it already?' Aumonier asked.

'I dropped the ball,' Baudry said. 'I went to the polls, stressed that we had a crisis on our hands, but didn't spell out the true severity of the situation. I didn't lie, but I let them think I was just talking about the crisis with the Ultras.'

'Because you didn't want panic?'

'Exactly so,' she said.

'Then you probably did exactly what I'd have done.' Aumonier held Lillian Baudry's gaze for a long moment, signalling to her that, whatever the other woman had done, her professional conduct in Aumonier's absence was not in doubt. She needed allies around her now, people who knew they had her confidence and trust. 'But Tom's right,' she added. 'We need that vote. As a matter of fact, I'll table a request for every emergency privilege in the book. Up to and including mass lockdowns and the curtailing of Bandwide abstraction and polling services.'

'We haven't had to do that in—' Baudry began.

Aumonier nodded. 'I know. Eleven years. And doesn't it feel like yesterday?'

CHAPTER 22

Dreyfus had asked to be alerted the instant Sheridan Gaffney regained consciousness. Mercier – who was now handling the patient following the fraught operation that had been mainly supervised by Demikhov – was predictably reluctant to let Dreyfus anywhere near the recuperating senior prefect.

'If you had any idea of the severity of the procedure he's just gone through, the extent of the internal damage caused by the whiphound,' Mercier said, waving his hands graphically, his treasured fountain pen clutched like a dagger as he guarded the entrance to the medical centre.

Dreyfus looked at the doctor obligingly. He'd always had a good relationship with Mercier and was reluctant to jeopardise it now. 'I understand your concerns. They're admirable. All I need to know is, can he talk?'

'He's suffered severe laceration of the trachea. He has a damaged larynx. About all he can manage right now is a croak, and even that causes him great pain. Please, Tom. No matter what this man did, but he's still a patient.'

'If we could wait, we would,' Dreyfus said, 'but right now we're in a situation where even an hour is too long. Gaffney has information vital to the security of the Glitter Band. I need to speak to him immediately.'

Mercier wilted, clearly aware that this was not a battle he could hope to win. 'You can force this through, can't you?'

'I have Jane's authority. Baudry's, too, as if Jane's isn't enough. Please, Doctor. Minutes are ticking by while you and I debate the health of a man who was quite happy to murder another of your patients.'

Mercier looked disappointed. 'You think I didn't put two and two together, Tom? I'm not that stupid. I guessed exactly what

Gaffney did. But he's still a sick man, no matter what he did to Clepsydra.'

Dreyfus placed a hand on Mercier's green-sleeved forearm. 'I need to do this. Please don't make it any harder.'

Mercier stepped aside. 'Do whatever you have to do. Then get out of my clinic, Tom. The next time you come here, you'd better be the one seeking medical help.'

Dreyfus stepped through into the recovery room. It was a spartan cube lit only by thin blue strips set into the upper walls. Gaffney was in a bed at one end of the cube, attended by a single medical servitor with a swooping white swan's neck. The transparent passwall sealed itself behind Dreyfus, subtly changing the acoustics of the room. He walked to the bedside, then conjured his usual chair out of the floor. Gaffney's face was an impassive mask, almost deathlike, but his eyes betrayed alertness. They tracked Dreyfus with reptilian intensity.

'No flowers?' Gaffney said, scratching the words out. 'That's a surprise.'

'You're more talkative than Mercier led me to expect.'

'What's the use in not being talkative? You're going to make me speak one way or another.' The words emerged dry as charcoal, each one forced out separately. Something horrible rattled down in his lungs.

Dreyfus tucked his hands together in his lap. 'We have a situation, Sheridan. I thought you might be able to shed some more light on it.'

'I told you everything I know.'

'We have a handle on Aurora now, but there's still a lot more we'd like to know.' He checked his bracelet. 'Thirty minutes ago, House Aubusson and Szlumper Oneill began releasing clouds of manufactured entities into Glitter Band space. We're still not sure what those entities are yet, but at least now we have some idea of where they're headed. They're not expanding in all directions. They're moving in two directed flows, like wasps following a scent trail. In less than two hours, those flows will come into contact with two other habitats with combined populations exceeding six hundred and fifty thousand citizens. Do you want to speculate about what might happen when those flows touch the habitats?'

Gaffney's expression hadn't changed since Dreyfus had entered the room. His mask of a face was still fixated on the ceiling. 'If you're so worried, why don't you move the habitats?'

'You know we can't change the orbit of a fifty-million-tonne structure just by clicking our fingers. We can't stop the arrival of the flow of entities either: the individual elements might be vulnerable, but there are just too many of them. The best we can do is alert those habitats, get them to prepare their defences and initiate whatever kind of evacuation programme they have in place. We've already done that, of course, but given the time available, we'll be lucky to offload more than ten thousand citizens by the time the flows hit.' Dreyfus leaned closer to the bedside. 'That's why I'd really like to know what's going to happen, Sheridan.'

'Then you're shit out of luck, Tommy-boy.'

'I'm disappointed, Sheridan. You know better than any of us that there's no sense in withholding information. We'll get it out of you eventually, by hook or by crook. I have the authorisation to run a deep-cortex trawl, for one. Or I could go with one of those Model Cs so dear to your heart. See how *you* like a dose of enhanced subject compliance.'

'In my condition, how long do you think I'd last?'

'That's a fair point,' Dreyfus conceded. 'So perhaps the trawl would be a safer bet. What would you go for, just out of interest?'

'I'm old-fashioned. Never could get on with trawls.'

Dreyfus nodded. 'You'd like that, wouldn't you? I run a whip-hound on you, you die before you spill your guts, end of story.'

'I could think of worse outcomes.'

Dreyfus unlaced his hands and tapped a finger against the side of his brow. 'Here's what I don't get, Sheridan. You're a solid Panoply man, as good a prefect as any of us. What exactly did Aurora have on you that made you turn traitor?'

At last the mask fashioned a grimace-like smile. 'You're the traitor, Tom, not me. You and all the other cowards who turn a blind eye to what's really going on in the Glitter Band. It's been clear to me since we walked away from Hell-Five. The people voted us the power to protect them. Problem is we abdicated that responsibility years ago. We let the people down.'

'That's not quite the way it looks from where I'm sitting,' Dreyfus said.

'If only you saw the bigger picture, you'd understand.'

'Enlighten me, Sheridan. Tell me what I'm not seeing. Would Aurora's glimpse into the future have anything to do with it?'

After a while Gaffney said, 'You know about Exordium, then.'

'Enough to know where to start trawling if you don't tell me about it now.'

'Aurora saw the end of everything we hold precious, Tom. We've created something wonderful around Yellowstone, something glorious, something unheralded in all the human history that's come before us. Something fit to last a thousand years, or ten thousand. And yet it ends. Less than a hundred years from now, all this is over. Humanity opened a window into paradise, and in eighty or ninety years it closes. The Garden of Eden isn't some ancient Biblical story about the fall of paradise thousands of years ago. It's a premonition.'

'How does it end?'

'Everything goes, in a matter of hours and days. Aurora walked amongst their dreams. She saw habitats burning, she saw people screaming in agony, she saw Chasm City turning against its own inhabitants, becoming something monstrous.'

'A time of plague,' Dreyfus said.

'No one sees it coming. There's no time to prepare. It hits us when we feel at our least vulnerable, in our highest, brightest hour.' Gaffney halted and caught his breath, the air rasping in and out of his lungs. 'Aurora couldn't let that happen, Tom. She believes the Glitter Band deserves better than to crash and burn.'

'But we're still talking about something eighty or ninety years in the future. Why is she taking action now?'

'Prudence,' Gaffney said. 'Aurora believes the content of the Exordium prognostications, but not necessarily the detail. She's worried that the Conjoiners were wrong about the timeline, that perhaps it might happen sooner than they predicted. There's no time to wait for warning signals. If action is to be taken to ensure the future survival of the Glitter Band, we must move now, not in twenty years, or fifty years. Only then can she be certain of success.'

'And this action?' Dreyfus ventured, wondering how much Gaffney was going to give up without coercion.

But Gaffney looked disappointed. 'Isn't it obvious? A benign takeover. The installation of a new authority that will ensure the Glitter Band's security for time immemorial.'

'She could have just come to us, if she had reasonable concerns.'

'And how do you think Panoply would have reacted?' Gaffney asked. 'Not by taking the necessary measures, that's for certain. We've already let the people take our guns away. Do you think that kind of ready submission implies an organisation with the necessary spine to take difficult, unpopular action, just because it happens to be in the public good?'

'I think you answered that question for yourself.'

'I love this organisation,' Gaffney said. 'I've given it my life. But little by little I've watched it allow the citizenry to erode its power. We were complicit in that, no question about it. We rolled over and handed the people back the very tools they'd given us to do our work. We've reached the point now where we have to beg for the right to arm our agents. And what happens when we finally issue that request? The people spit it back in our faces. They love the idea of a police force, Tom. Just not one with the teeth to actually do anything.'

'Maybe taking guns off us wasn't such a bad idea.'

'It's not just the guns. When we perform a lockdown, we spend the next year defending our actions. They'll take lockdown authority from us next. Before you know it, we won't even be allowed near our own polling cores. Aurora saw this coming. She knew that Panoply's usefulness was always going to be limited, and that if the people were really to be protected, someone else was going to have to do it for them.'

'This someone else being Aurora, and whoever's with her,' Dreyfus said quietly.

'She's no tyrant, if that's what you're thinking.'

'A takeover sounds more than a little tyrannical, frankly.'

'It won't be like that. Aurora merely envisages a state of affairs in which the people are protected from the consequences of their own worst actions. Under Aurora's regime, life in the habitats will continue exactly as it does now. The citizenry will still have access to the same technologies they've grown to depend upon. No one will be denied longevity treatments, or any other medicines they need. The people will continue to enjoy the same luxuries as they do now, and on a day-to-day level their societies will look much the same. The artists will still work.'

Dreyfus cocked his head. 'Then I'm missing something. What will have changed?'

'Only those things strictly essential for our future security. Needless to say, the Glitter Band will have to be isolated from the rest of human society. That'll mean an end to commerce with the Ultras, and Chasm City. We can't run the risk that some outside agent introduced to the Glitter Band causes its ultimate downfall.'

'You think it will be something internal, something we do to ourselves?'

'We can't know that for certain, so we have to take reasonable precautions against other possibilities. That's only right and proper, isn't it?'

'I suppose so.'

'Likewise, travel between habitats will have to be curtailed. If the destabilising factor arises within the Glitter Band, we can at least stop it spreading.'

'So no one ever gets to leave home.'

Gaffney appeared genuinely perplexed by Dreyfus's point. 'But why would they ever *want* to, Tom? They'll have everything handed to them on a plate: every amenity, every luxury.'

'Except personal freedom.'

'It's overrated. How often do people exercise it, anyway? It's only ever the minority that test the real limits of a society. Reasonable men don't make history, Dreyfus. Most people are content with their lot, content to do today what they did yesterday. They'll still have almost every old freedom within a given habitat.'

'But they won't be able to leave. They won't be able to visit loved ones or friends in other habitats.'

'It won't come to that. Once Aurora has control of the ten thousand, she'll allow a grace period before the strictures come into force. People will be permitted to move around as they wish until they've settled on their permanent place of residence. Only then will the gates be closed.'

'There'll always be some people who regret the choice they made,' Dreyfus said. 'But I suppose you're about to tell me they can always use abstraction to simulate physical travel.'

Gaffney looked almost apologetic. 'Well, actually ... abstraction will need to be policed as well.'

'By which you mean ...'

'A downgrading of the current provisions. For the sake of security, of course. It could be that the destabilising agent gains a foothold as a consequence of the data networks, you see. Aurora can't take that risk. The habitats will need to be isolated from each other.'

'The cure's beginning to sound worse than the disease,' Dreyfus said.

'Oh, don't make it sound worse than it really is. The habitats will still be running internal abstraction services. For many citizens, that's already enough. And the data infrastructure will remain in place, so that Aurora can continue to supervise and assist the ten thousand.'

'So let's get this straight,' Dreyfus said. 'We're talking about a state of curfew, in which no one can move, no one can communicate and in which no one has a democratic say in their own destiny?'

Gaffney winced: Dreyfus couldn't tell if it was because of his injuries, or because of what Dreyfus had just said. 'But they'll be *safe*, Tom. Not just today, not just tomorrow, but for the next ninety years and beyond. Under Aurora's regime, the destabilising event will not be allowed to happen. The Glitter Band will persist.'

'In chains.'

'We're talking about an interim security measure, not something that will have to remain in place in perpetuity. As the years roll on, Aurora will strive to identify the likely focus of the agent. Once the risk is quantified, the people can be handed back their own destiny.' Gaffney peered intently into the depths of the ceiling, as if searching for inspiration. 'Look at it this way, Tom,' he said reasonably, as if the two of them were only a hair's breadth from agreement. 'A man is carrying a sharp instrument in a crowded space. He's about to suffer an epileptic seizure. He could hurt himself, or those around him, if he is not unburdened of that instrument and perhaps restrained. What do you do? Do you sit back and respect his rights? Or do you take the action that will guarantee not only his safety, but that of everyone nearby?'

'I ask him nicely to drop the sharp instrument.'

'And you scare him in the process. He grips the instrument more tightly than ever. Now what?'

'I disarm him.'

'It's too late. He cuts you anyway. Then the seizure kicks in and he starts hacking away at everyone else. Democracy is that sharp instrument, Tom. It's the final weapon of the people, and sometimes they just can't be trusted with it.'

'And you can.'

'Not me, not you. But Aurora?' Gaffney shook his head: not in denial, but in an awed inability to express whatever was running through his mind. 'She's bigger than us. Faster and cleverer. I'd have my doubts, too, if I hadn't been in her presence. But from the moment I first encountered Aurora, I've never had the slightest doubt that she's the one to lead us forward, the one to guide us into the light.'

Dreyfus stood up and conjured the chair back into the floor. 'Thanks, Sheridan.'

'We're done?'

'I think I've learned everything that you're willing to tell me without coercion. You genuinely think this can't be stopped, don't you? That's why you're so content to tell me what Aurora has in mind.'

'It was touch and go for a while back there,' Gaffney said, confidingly. 'And I'll admit that matters were pre-empted by your discovery of Clepsydra. Aurora had been hoping not to have to move until she had complete control of the entire Glitter Band.'

'You mean when Thalia made the upgrade to the entire ten thousand?'

'That was the idea. One second the ten thousand would have been in the hands of the citizenry, the next they would have been Aurora's. It would have been the ultimate bloodless revolution, Tom. No one would have been hurt or inconvenienced. Human distress would have been kept to an absolute minimum.'

'Then I'm sorry I threw a wrench into her plans by doing my job.'

'It wasn't much of a wrench, all told. Aurora had always been mindful that it might be necessary to begin the takeover in a piecemeal fashion, habitat by habitat. It really won't make much difference in the long run, though. Those clouds of manufactured entities you mentioned earlier? You're still in the dark about them, aren't you?'

Dreyfus remained impassive, but something in his expression must have given the game away.

'The machines are mass-produced weevil-class war robots,' Gaffney said. 'Very simple, very rugged, with just enough autonomy to cross space between habitats. By itself, a single weevil can't do much damage. But the manufactories are spewing them out by the hundreds of thousands. That's a lot of weevils, Tom. Weight of numbers'll get you in the end. Always does.'

'What will the weevils do when they reach the other habitats? Cut their way inside and kill everyone?'

'Given that the objective here is to preserve human life, that would be rather counterproductive, don't you think?'

'So what, then?'

'The weevils are carrying copies of the same upgrade Thalia already installed in the first four habitats. Once they reach the target habitats, they'll work their way inside and infect their cores with the same security hole. Aurora will then have complete control of six habitats, not four.'

'Your weevils will have to reach the polling cores first. The local citizenry are already standing by to protect them.'

'They'll slow the weevils, but not stop them. There'll always be more weevils. The manufactories won't stop making them. And once Aurora gains control of another manufactory-equipped habitat, she'll start producing weevils there as well.'

'So we shut down the polling cores. Destroy them, even. Same with the manufactories.'

Again Gaffney looked apologetic, like someone who kept winning against a weaker opponent and was beginning to feel sorry for them. 'Won't work, either. Weevils are more than warriors. They're general-purpose construction servitors. Can't replicate, but there isn't much else they *can't* do. Build and integrate a new polling core? Matter of hours. I gave them the necessary blueprints. Repair a scuttled manufactory? Six hours. Maybe twelve. Ditto on the blueprints. Aurora's covered all the bases, Tom. Why do you think I'd be telling you all this otherwise?'

'I guess you may have a point there,' Dreyfus said. Then he lifted up the cuff of his sleeve to reveal his bracelet. 'Jane?' he asked.

'Aumonier,' she replied, her voice reduced to a doll-like buzz.

'The machines are weevil-class war robots. Someone needs to see what we have on them in the archive. Instruct the *Democratic Circus* to proceed with maximum caution. If they can bring one in intact, they should do so, but I don't want to lose another deep-system cruiser without good reason.'

'Copy, Tom,' Jane Aumonier said.

He cuffed down his sleeve and surveyed the man on the bed. 'Of course, if I find you were lying about any of that—'

'I wasn't lying. And that was spoken like a true leader, by the way. You should have heard yourself. Anyone would have thought you were the supreme prefect the way you dished out instructions to Jane.'

'We have a good understanding. It's called mutual respect.'

'Sounded more like the natural assumption of authority to me. Perhaps you covet her job the same way Baudry and Crissel did?'

'We weren't talking about Jane.' Dreyfus reached behind his back and unclipped the whiphound he had been keeping there, out of

Gaffney's line of sight. He brought it around in front of him and let the other man see what he was holding.

'Oh, now that's *low*. Did Doctor Mercier see you come in with that thing?'

Dreyfus whipped out the filament, letting it hiss against the floor. It sliced the quickmatter like a rapier through water, the floor material healing behind it almost instantly. 'Don't worry. It isn't a Model C. Doesn't have any of those fancy new features you were so keen to see installed.'

'Are you going to kill me now?'

'No. I'll leave killing prisoners to the experts. I want you alive, Sheridan, so I can run a deep-cortex trawl while you still have some brain cells.'

'Trawl me now. See how far it gets you.'

'Sword mode,' Dreyfus said, almost under his breath. The filament flicked to immediate rigidity. He swept it over Gaffney's recumbent form, hard and fast enough to raise a whoosh of parted air. 'I'll spare you the sales pitch. You know what one of these can do in the wrong hands.'

'I've told you everything.'

'No, you haven't. There's an elephant in this room that you're trying very hard to ignore, Sheridan. It's called Ruskin-Sartorious. You set up the execution of that habitat, didn't you?'

'You know the Ultras were behind that.'

'No,' Dreyfus said patiently. 'That's what you wanted us to think. It had to look like an act of spite so we wouldn't go nosing around trying to find the real reason. Dravidian and his crew were used, weren't they? You got someone aboard their ship who knew how to manipulate the engines.'

'Ridiculous.'

'They would have needed expert insider knowledge of Conjoiner systems, but given that you already *had* a shipload of Conjoiners to torture, that wouldn't have been insurmountable. The question is, why? What was it about Ruskin-Sartorious that mattered to you so much? Why did it have to burn?' Dreyfus lowered the blade of the whiphound until it was almost touching the bruised skin of Gaffney's throat. 'Talk to me, Sheridan. Tell me why that had to happen.'

Gaffney said nothing. Dreyfus let the whiphound touch his skin until it drew a beetle-sized drop of blood.

'Feel that, Sheridan?' he asked. 'It would only take a twitch of my hand to sever your windpipe.'

'Fuck you, Dreyfus.' But as he spoke, he appeared to submerge himself even further into the embrace of the bed, trying to lower his throat as far as possible from the whiphound's blade.

'You had those people executed for a reason. Here's my shot at why. There was something about Ruskin-Sartorious, something about that family, or even about that habitat, that was threatening to Aurora. Something that she considered worth mass murder to get rid of. It must have been a major threat or she wouldn't have risked drawing attention to herself when her plans were nearly in place.' He let the whiphound bite deeper, drawing multiple droplets of blood. 'How am I doing? Hot, cold, in the middle?'

'Bring the fucking trawl,' Gaffney said, his voice strangulated as he squeezed his neck even further into the bed. 'See how far it gets you.'

Dreyfus let the filament skim back into the handle, cleansing itself of tiny droplets of blood as it did so. 'You know what?' he said as the fine pink fog settled back towards Gaffney. 'That's an excellent idea. I never did have the stomach for torture.'

Silver-grey daylight penetrated the dust-covered window bands of House Aubusson. Standing at one of the viewing portholes, Thalia contemplated an ashen landscape, utterly ravaged by machines. In contrast to the activity that had been evident through much of the night, all was still now. It had been many hours since she had last seen any kind of robot or construction servitor. The machines must have completed their work, picking the habitat clean of anything that might conceivably be useful for the churning manufactories in the endcap. Structures, vehicles, people: nothing of any utility had been left untouched, save for the polling core itself. Perhaps the servitors were even dismantling themselves now that the hardest work was over.

She picked grit out of the corner of her eye. How long did they have left now? She might not have seen any machines outside, but that didn't mean they'd gone away. The barricade was still holding, but the servitors in the stalk were slowly dismantling it from the other side, working methodically and with a calmness that was somehow more frightening than if they'd come ripping through it at speed. No one could be certain how much of the barricade now remained, but Parnasse thought it unlikely that there was more than ten metres of obstruction left, and perhaps a lot less than that. *They'll be through in a matter of hours*, Thalia thought. She was beginning to think it had been tempting fate to hope they could make it until the end of another day.

'Well?' she asked, as Parnasse joined her. 'Have you looked into what we discussed?'

He pulled a disagreeable face. 'I looked into it, like I said I would. And the more I looked, the less I liked it. I said I'd consider anything, even if it was near-suicidal. But this isn't *near*-suicidal, girl. It's the real deal.'

She spoke through clenched teeth, hardly moving her lips. She didn't want anyone else to guess what they were talking about, even if they saw her expression reflected in the glass. 'The machines are going to kill us, Cyrus. That's guaranteed. At least this way we'd have a fighting chance.'

'We haven't even taken down the polling core,' he said. 'Shouldn't we attempt that first, and see what happens? Maybe the machines will stop being a problem.'

'And maybe they've acquired enough autonomy now that they can keep coming without receiving instructions. Face it: we don't really know what their capabilities are.'

'Can you take down the core?'

'I think I can damage it,' she said, nodding at her whiphound, which was waiting on a nearby chair. 'But that may not be enough to stop all abstraction packets getting through. There's a lot of self-repairing quickmatter in a core. It isn't like cutting dumb matter.'

'And to be sure?'

'I'd have to blow it up. Problem is we only have one shot at that.'

His expression conveyed a mixture of exasperation and admiration. 'And you want to keep the grenade mode for later, don't you?'

'Ignore the likelihood of our survival for the moment,' she answered. 'Just give me the facts concerning the technical side of the problem. Can we weaken the structural members sufficiently if all we have is the whiphound?'

'You said it'll cut just about anything, short of hyperdiamond?'

Thalia nodded. 'Of course, it isn't working as well as it should. But provided the filament stays rigid, it ought to be okay. It coped with granite, after all.'

'Then you can probably do it, provided you follow through with a big bang, in exactly the right place.'

'I don't think the big bang's going to be a problem.'

Parnasse scratched under his collar, looking conflicted. 'Then if we get down into the base of the sphere we can reach what we need to cut. If we weaken the right members, and position the whiphound in *exactly* the right place, we can probably force the sphere to topple in the right direction. Emphasis on "probably", girl.'

'I'll take what I'm given. And then? Will she hold, from a structural standpoint?'

'Your guess is as good as mine.'

'Everyone in here will need to be braced, lashed down. We need to plan for that now or there are going to be a lot of broken bones.'

'Girl, I think broken bones will be the least of our worries.'

'We need to start bringing some of the others in on the plan,' Thalia said. When Parnasse said nothing, she added, 'So that they can start making preparations.'

'Girl, we haven't agreed to this. We haven't discussed it, or put it to the vote.'

'We're not putting it to the vote. We're just doing it.'

'Whatever happened to democracy?'

'Democracy took a hike.' She stared at him with fierce intent, brooking no dissent. 'You know we have to do this, Cyrus. You know there's no other choice.'

'I know it, but that doesn't mean I have to like it.'

'Even so.'

He closed his eyes, reaching some troubled conclusion. 'Redon. She's pretty reasonable. If we can bring her in, she can smooth it with the others, get them to see sense. Then maybe she can start explaining it to *me*.'

'Talk to her,' Thalia said, nodding at the sleeping, exhausted-looking woman. Meriel Redon was resting after having worked on the barricade shift and would probably not welcome being woken prematurely.

'How much do you want me to tell her?'

'The lot. But tell her to keep it to herself until we've made the preparations.'

'Let's hope she's in an optimistic frame of mind.'

'Just a second,' Thalia said distractedly.

Parnasse narrowed his eyes. 'What are you looking at?'

For the first time since the coming of day, movement in the landscape had caught her eye. She squinted for a moment, wondering if she'd imagined it, but just when she was ready to conclude that her mind was playing tricks on her she caught it again. She'd seen something dark move along what had once been the perimeter of the Museum of the Cybernetics, the motion furtive and scurrying. She thought of Crissel and his boarding party, of the black tactical armour of field prefects, and for a cruel instant she let herself imagine they were being rescued. Then she snapped the glasses to her face and zoomed in on the movement, and saw that it had nothing to do with prefects. She was looking at an advancing column of low, beetle-like machines, many dozens of them. They moved faster than any civilian servitor she had ever seen, tearing through or gliding over obstacles like a line of black ink running down a page.

'What is it?'

'Something bad,' Thalia answered.

They were not civilian servitors, she realised. They were some kind of war machine, and they were working their way inexorably towards the polling core.

Terror nestled tighter in her stomach, as if it was making itself even more at home.

'Tell me, girl.'

'Military-grade servitors,' she said. 'I'm pretty sure, anyway.'

'Must be some mistake. There was nothing like that here before.'

'I know. It would have been a lockdown offence even to own the construction files.'

'So where have they come from?'

'I think we already know,' she said. 'They've been made overnight. There are probably bits of people in them.'

'The manufactories?'

'I think so. I can't believe these are the only thing they're spewing out – there'd have been enough material to make millions of them, which is obviously absurd. But at least we know what part of the production flow was meant for.'

'And the rest?'

'I'm too scared to think about it.'

Thalia turned back to the polling core. Perhaps Parnasse was right, that the time had now come to destroy it. The option had been at the back of her mind all along, after all. She believed that the core was playing a vital part in coordinating the activities of the machines via the low-level signals she had already detected. That was why the servitors had not already demolished the stalk, something that she knew would have been well within their capabilities. But she would not risk putting that theory to the test until she took the core out of action. If the machines were somehow able to keep running afterwards, it would all have been for nothing. She had not been prepared to take that risk until now, but the spectacle of the advancing war machines had changed everything.

She walked to the nearest chair and picked up her whiphound. It had become too hot to wear clipped to her belt and she could only tolerate holding it if she had a scarf wrapped around her palm. She let the filament extend and stiffen itself in sword mode, ignoring the buzzing protestation from the handle.

'Are you going to do it?' Parnasse asked.

'I don't know. Maybe you're right. Maybe it's time.'

He steadied her trembling hand. 'And maybe it isn't. Like you said, girl – if chopping at this thing doesn't do the job, we'd better have a pretty good back-up plan in place. Put the sword away for now. I'm going to test the water with Redon.'

CHAPTER 23

A portion of the Solid Orrery had been reassigned to emulate the three-dimensional form of a weevil-class war robot. The one-tenth-scale representation rotated slowly, the light of the room appearing to gleam off its angled black surfaces. In its space-travel/atmospheric-entry configuration, the machine's multiple legs and manipulators were tucked hard against its shell, as if it had died and shrivelled up. Its binocular sensor packages were contained in two grilled domes that bore an uncanny resemblance to the compound eyes of an insect.

'They're as nasty as they look,' Baudry commented to the assembled prefects. 'Banned under seven or eight conventions of war, last seen in action more than a hundred and twenty years ago. Most war robots are designed to kill other war robots. Weevils were engineered to do that *and* kill humans. They carry detailed files on human anatomy. They know our weak points, what makes us hurt, what makes us break.' As she spoke, reams of dense technical data scrolled down the walls. 'In and of themselves, weevils are containable. We have techniques and weapons that would be effective against them in both vacuum stand-off situations and in close-quarters combat in and around habitats. The problem is the number, not the machines themselves. According to the *Democratic Circus*, House Aubusson has already manufactured and launched two hundred and sixty thousand units, and the flow isn't showing any signs of stopping. A weevil only weighs five hundred kilograms, and most of the materials required to make one would be commonplace inside a habitat like Aubusson. If the servitors inside the habitat work efficiently, they can easily supply all the feed materials necessary to build more just by dismantling and recycling existing structures inside the cylinder. We could be looking at an output of millions of weevils before the manufactories need to start eating into the structural fabric of the habitat. Then the numbers become unthinkable.'

'Do we know for a fact that we're dealing with weevils?' Dreyfus asked.

Baudry nodded. 'The *Circus* hasn't secured a sample yet, but the scans are all on the nose. These are weevils, just as Gaffney told us. There's no reason to doubt that they're carrying the Thalia code.'

'What about the rest of what Gaffney revealed?' asked the projected head of Jane Aumonier, imaged on a curving pane of glass supported above an empty chair. 'Do we believe that weevils are capable of hijacking a second habitat?'

Baudry faced her superior. 'If Aurora has embarked on this strategy, chances are she has a high expectation of success. She already has intimate knowledge of security holes in the polling apparatus. There's every reason to think she has the ability to seize another habitat if she can get weevils into it.' All of a sudden Baudry looked shattered, as if the crisis had notched past some personal threshold of endurance. 'I think we must assume the worst.'

The wall displays froze abruptly. Bracelets chorused in unison. The Solid Orrery consumed the weevil and sprang up an enlarged representation of one of the two threatened habitats, a hubless wheel. 'That's Carousel New Brazilia,' Baudry said. 'Anti-collision systems have begun to engage the incoming flow of weevils. We can expect House Flammarion to begin similar engagements within the next fifteen minutes.'

'How are our assets coping?' Aumonier asked.

'We only had time to place three corvette-class vehicles close enough to Brazilia to make a difference,' Baudry said. 'Frankly, their pinpoint weapons are next to useless against the scale of the flow. Even if we dropped a nuke into the middle of it, it would only take out a few thousand units. It's like trying to stop a tsunami with a spoon.'

Aumonier answered calmly: 'Then we need an alternative strategy.'

'Our corvettes are standing by to concentrate their fire on the weevils once they make groundfall on the habitat. The war robots will need time to cut through or force their way in via docking apertures.'

'Let's assume we don't stop them all. What happens if we lose Brazilia and Flammarion?'

'Both habitats have manufacturies of their own,' Dreyfus said, looking up from his compad. 'If Aurora takes them, she'll have two new sites of weevil production. From there she can start leapfrogging to new habitats.'

'I've prepared a simulation on the Orrery,' Baudry said. 'There's a lot of guesswork fed into it, obviously, but I can show you how things might progress under some reasonable assumptions.'

'Go ahead,' Aumonier said.

Baudry shrank the image of Carousel New Brazilia back down to its former size, so that it became simply one gemlike point moving in the stately swirl of the Glitter Band. With another gesture she turned all the points of light to the same emerald green, save for four scattered points of ruby.

'These are the habitats Aurora now controls,' Baudry said, before two more red points lit up, each located close to one of the other four points. 'These are Brazilia and Flammarion, under the assumption that Aurora attains control. I now assume that both these new habitats become weevil-production centres with an output flow similar to what we've already seen. I assume also that each habitat concentrates its weevil output on one other habitat not yet in Aurora's control, in accordance with what we've seen so far. I further assume that in twenty-six hours, a habitat can be attacked by weevils, brought under Aurora's control and direct its own weevil flow against a designated target, crossing space until they make contact.'

'Continue,' Aumonier said.

'In one day, we'll have already gone from two compromised habitats to four. Those four habitats will each infect another neighbouring state, giving us eight infection sites by the end of the second day.' As she spoke, the number of red lights increased in geometric fashion. 'At the end of the third day, sixteen habitats. Thirty-two by the end of the fourth day. Sixty-four by the fifth. One hundred and twenty-eight by the end of the sixth: that's more than one per cent of the entire Glitter Band.'

There were now too many red lights to count. They were still overwhelmed by the green lights, but the inevitability of the process was now painfully apparent.

'How long . . .?' Aumonier asked, voicing the question none of them wanted answering.

'Fewer than half the states in the Glitter Band retain any kind of manufacturing capacity,' Baudry said, 'but that's still over four thousand habitats. Aurora will have taken them all a few hours into the twelfth day. Even if we still hold the remainder by then, we'll lose them very quickly. Aurora will have over four thousand weevil-production sites to turn against us. I doubt that we'd retain a single habitat by the end of the thirteenth day.' She swallowed heavily. 'That includes Panoply.'

'And that assumption of twenty-six hours—' Dreyfus began.

'It's guesswork, a number I pulled out of the air. Perhaps it'll take longer than that. But even if it takes four days to leapfrog from one habitat to the next, she'll still have beaten us within two months. It's anyone's guess how long Chasm City will be able to hold out, but I wouldn't put odds on it lasting much longer than the Glitter Band.'

'We can do something, though, surely,' Aumonier said.

Baudry's expression was that of someone burdened with terrible news. She reminded Dreyfus of a doctor about to deliver the most devastating of verdicts. 'We can do something, yes. Now, while Aurora is still gaining a foothold, and before her efforts touch us. Let's rewind the simulation back to day zero, today.'

Now there were just four habitats highlighted in red. 'The weevil flows have reached Brazilia, and will make contact with Flammarion any minute now.' Baudry glanced uneasily at her bracelet. 'But for the next few hours – maybe even as long as a day – we're only looking at four points of potential spread, if we assume the new habitats can be geared up to weevil production.' Baudry tightened her fingers against each other. 'Aurora is at her most vulnerable now. She has revealed herself, and therefore already played the element of surprise. But she has not yet consolidated enough territory to truly overwhelm us.'

'I thought you said we were already overwhelmed by the weevils,' said Senior Prefect Clearmountain.

'I'm not talking about dealing with the weevils,' Baudry answered. 'I'm talking about taking out the production centres.'

Clearmountain looked unimpressed. 'This isn't surgery,' he said, looking around the table at the others. 'You can't just take out a manufactory and somehow leave the rest of the habitat intact.'

'I'm aware of that,' Baudry said, with icy control.

He blinked. 'Then you're talking about—'

'Mass euthanisation, yes. We nuke the infected habitats. If this was the easy option, do you honestly think I'd have waited until now before raising it?'

'It's murder.'

'We'd be sacrificing a certain number of lives to ensure the survival of vastly more. You saw that simulation I just ran, Senior. Within two months we'll have lost everything. She could be all over us in as little as thirteen days if my earlier assessment was correct. Maybe we don't even have that long. That's one hundred million lives. If we target both Brazilia and Flammarion now, we'll only be losing six hundred and fifty thousand people. Include Szlumper Oneill and House Aubusson and we're still talking about less than two per cent of the total number of citizens in our care.'

'You're talking as if two per cent is a blip,' said Clearmountain incredulously.

'With all due respect,' Baudry answered, 'this is war. There isn't a general in history who wouldn't snatch at the possibility of victory if it could be guaranteed with less than one casualty for every fifty combatants.'

'But they're not combatants,' Dreyfus said testily. 'They're citizens, and they didn't sign up to be part of anyone's war.'

'The balance of numbers still holds,' Baudry said. 'Strike now and we'll be saving many tens of millions of lives. We have to consider this, ladies and gentlemen. We're in dereliction of duty if we don't.'

'It's monstrous,' Clearmountain said.

'So is the prospect of losing the ten thousand,' Baudry replied.

'But would we necessarily be losing one hundred million lives?' asked Aumonier. 'Gaffney told Dreyfus that Aurora was interested in a benign takeover. The life-support systems in Aubusson and the three other habitats are still running: we'd have seen the evidence otherwise. That suggests to me that Aurora has at least the intention of keeping her subjects alive and healthy.'

'Human shields aren't much use unless they're alive,' Baudry said.

'But we still have to consider the possibility that she intends to keep her subjects alive for ever. If her stated goal is to ensure the long-term survival of the Glitter Band, she's not going to start murdering people.' Aumonier's eyes became glazed, as if she was looking at something far beyond the room. 'Oh, wait,' said her floating head. 'Something's coming in from Flammarion. They've made contact.'

Bracelets started chiming. The prefects silenced them and studied the Solid Orrery as it enlarged a thimble-shaped representation of House Flammarion.

'Status on Brazilia?' Dreyfus asked.

Aumonier glanced away, then back at him. 'The anti-collision guns have been picking off one weevil in ten. The rest are getting through more or less undamaged. They've established six bridgeheads on the outer skin of the wheel. Our assets have been concentrating fire, but some weevils appear to be making it through into the underlying structure.'

'Pressure containment?'

'Still holding. It looks as if the machines are at least programmed to break inside without compromising biosphere integrity.'

It would go the same way with Flammarion, Dreyfus knew. The concentration of weevils might not be exactly the same, the anti-collision systems might prove more or less successful at intercepting the arriving forces, but it would make no practical difference in the long run. It would only take a handful of those war robots to storm their way through the citizenry, scything a bloody path to the polling core. And then they would open a door and Aurora, or some facet of Aurora, could pass through.

'How many did we get off Brazilia?'

'Eleven thousand on the commercial shuttles that were already docked. Three from Flammarion.'

'Aurora's reliant on data networks to hop into those habitats,' Dreyfus said. 'Before we start nuking our own citizens, can we block her progress by taking down part of the network?'

Baudry grimaced. 'It's all or nothing, Tom.'

'Then we take the whole damned thing down.'

'We don't know for sure that that would stop Aurora, but it would definitely hurt us. We need the apparatus to track Aurora's spread, to coordinate evacuation operations and the deployment of our own assets.'

'Nonetheless,' Aumonier said, 'Tom is right. Taking down Bandwide abstraction is something we have to consider. In fact, I've been considering it ever since I became aware of the crisis. We shouldn't underestimate the risks, though. We may slow Aurora, but we'll more than likely blind ourselves in the process.'

'Use the nukes and we end this now,' Baudry said. 'Aurora may not be intending to kill people, but she definitely intends to take their freedom from them.'

Dreyfus clutched his stylus so tightly that the nib pushed into his palm and drew blood. 'There's another option, while we still have the apparatus. A given habitat may not be able to fight off the weevils, but at the moment we still have the resources of the entire Glitter Band to call upon.'

'I'm not with you, Tom,' Baudry said.

'I say we table an emergency poll with the people. We request permission to draft and mobilise a temporary militia from across the entire Glitter Band.'

'Define "militia".'

'I mean millions of citizens, armed and equipped with whatever weapons their manufactories can produce in the next thirteen hours. They already have the ships, so moving them around won't be a problem. If we can supply them with weapons blueprints, then place enough of them into the compromised habitats, and into the habitats we think Aurora will go for next, together with military-grade servitors under our control, we may be able to break her back without using nukes.'

Baudry looked regretful. 'You're talking about citizens, Tom, not soldiers.'

'You were the one calling them combatants, not me.'

'They have no training, no equipment—'

'The manufactories'll give them equipment. Eidetics will give them training. Prefects can lead small units of drafted citizens.'

'There are a hundred million citizens out there, Tom, ninety-eight per cent of whom face no immediate threat from Aurora. Do you honestly think many of them are going to race to throw themselves against those weevils?'

'I think we should at least give them the choice. We won't be proposing to draft the entire citizenry. Ten million would give us an overwhelming advantage, especially if they're backed up by servitors. That's only one citizen in ten, Lillian. The majority can agree to our draft safe in the knowledge that they're not likely to be called up.'

'Do you want to put some numbers on casualty estimates?' Baudry asked. 'One in ten, two in ten? Worse than that?'

Dreyfus tapped his stylus against the table. 'I don't know.'

'Lose two million and you'll have killed more people than if we go in now with nukes.'

'But it would be two million people who chose to put themselves on the line, for the greater good of the Glitter Band, rather than two million we press the button on just because some simulation says so.'

'Maybe we can come to some kind of compromise,' Aumonier

said, her crystal-clear voice cutting through the tension between Dreyfus and Baudry. 'We all find the idea of nuking habitats abhorrent, even if we differ on the necessity of doing so.'

'Agreed,' Baudry said cautiously.

'Which criteria did you use to identify Aurora's next targets?' Aumonier asked.

'Proximity and usefulness, with allowance for varying distances due to differential orbital velocities. I reasoned that Aurora would concentrate her efforts on the nearest habitats with manufacturing capability.'

'Sounds reasonable to me,' Aumonier said. 'The question is, can we get the people out of those habitats before the weevils arrive from those that are now under assault?'

'You mean evacuate and then nuke?' Dreyfus asked.

'If we can do it, we'll be clearing a line in a forest. Aurora's weevils may well be able to cross that line and leapfrog to even further habitats, but at least it'll have bought us time, with no expenditure of human lives.'

'If we get them out in time,' Clearmountain said.

'We can't be certain which habitats she'll go for,' Baudry said, pointing at the Solid Orrery. 'I selected likely candidates, but I couldn't be precise.'

'Then we'll have to cover more bases.' Aumonier said. 'I'm going to initiate an emergency evacuation order for ten probable targets.'

Dreyfus said, 'I suggest we concentrate any enforcement activities on one habitat, just to show we mean business. The others will hopefully assume we're capable of dishing out the same treatment to them.'

'I agree,' Aumonier replied. 'The one thing the people mustn't suspect is that we're overstretched. As for assistance in the evacuation effort, I'll go through CTC. They can requisition and re-route all spaceborne traffic without the need for a poll. We'll be limited by ship capacity and docking hub throughput, but we'll just have to do the best we can.' She looked directly at Baudry. 'I want the names of ten habitats, Lillian. Immediately.'

'I'd like to re-run the simulation, varying the parameters a little,' Baudry said.

'There isn't time. Just give me those names.'

Baudry's mouth fell open, as if she was about to say something but the words had suddenly escaped her. She reached for her stylus and compad and started compiling the list, her hand shaking with the momentous enormity of what she was doing.

'How long are you going to give them?' Dreyfus asked. 'Before you go in with the nukes, I mean.'

'We can't wait a day,' Aumonier said. 'That would be too long, too risky. I think thirteen hours is a reasonable compromise, don't you?'

She knew that it could not be done, Dreyfus thought. Save for the tiniest family-run microstates, there was no habitat in the Glitter Band that could be emptied of people that quickly. Even if evacuation vehicles were docked and ready, even if the citizens were briefed and prepared, ready to leave their world in an orderly and calm fashion, a world that many of them would have spent their entire lives in.

It just couldn't be done. But at least those people would have a chance of getting out, rather than none at all. That was all Jane was counting on.

'I have those names,' Baudry said.

Aumonier floated rock-still, anchored in space at the epicentre of her own sensory universe. Most of her feeds were blanked out, leaving a bright equatorial strip focusing only on those twenty-five or thirty habitats at immediate or peripheral risk from Aurora's takeover. The views kept shuffling, playing havoc with Dreyfus's sense of his own orientation.

'We're going to lose Brazilia and Flammarion,' she said, by way of acknowledging his presence. 'Weevils are deep inside both habitats and the local citizenry can't hold them back. They've already taken appalling losses, and all they've done is slow their approach to the polling cores.'

Dreyfus said nothing, sensing that Aumonier was not finished. Eventually she asked: 'Did they get anything out of Gaffney?'

'Not much. I've just read the initial summary from the trawl squad.'

'And?'

'They've cleared up at least one mystery. We know how he moved Clepsydra from the bubble to my quarters. He used a nonvelope.'

'I'm not familiar with the term,' Aumonier said.

'It's an invisibility device. A shell of quickmatter with a degree of autonomy and the ability to conceal itself from superficial observation. You put something in it you don't want people to find.'

'Sounds like exactly the sort of thing that should be banned by any right-thinking society. How did he get hold of it?'

'From Anthony Theobald Ruskin-Sartorious, apparently. Anthony Theobald must have procured it through his black-market arms contacts. He used the nonvelope to escape from his habitat just before it was torched by Dravidian's ship.'

Aumonier frowned slightly. 'But Anthony Theobald didn't escape. All you had to interview was his beta-level copy.'

'Gaffney knew differently, apparently. He intercepted the nonvelope before it fell into the hands of Anthony Theobald's allies.'

'And then what?'

'He cracked it open. Then he ran a trawl on Anthony Theobald to see if he could find out where the thing Ruskin-Sartorious was sheltering had got to.'

'Voi. Gaffney *trawled* him?' Reading her expression, Dreyfus could imagine what was going through her mind. It was one thing to be trawled inside Panoply, where strict rules were in force. It was another to receive the same treatment elsewhere, inflicted by a man acting outside the bounds of the law who cared nothing for the consequences of his actions.

'He didn't get as much information as he was hoping for, unfortunately.'

'I presume he kept digging until he'd burnt away Anthony Theobald's brain?'

'That's the odd thing,' Dreyfus said. 'He appears to have held back at the last. He got something out of the man, enough for him to stop before he burnt him out completely.'

'Why didn't he go all the way if he thought there was something more to gain?'

'Because Gaffney doesn't see himself as a monster. He's a prefect, still doing his job, still sticking to his principles while the rest of us betray the cause. He killed Clepsydra because he had no other option. He killed the people in Ruskin-Sartorious for the same reason. But he's not an indiscriminate murderer. He's still thinking about the tens of millions he's going to save.'

'What else did he get?'

'That was where the trawl team hit resistance. Gaffney really didn't want to give up whatever he had learned from Anthony Theobald. But they got a word.'

'Tell me.'

'Firebrand.'

Aumonier nodded very slowly. She said the word herself, as if testing how it sounded coming from her own lips. 'Did the summary team have anything to say about this word?'

'To them it was meaningless noise. Firebrand could be a weapon, a ship, an agent, anything. Or it could be the name of the puppy he owned when he was five.'

'Do you have any theories?'

'I'm inclined to think it's just noise: either noise that came out of Anthony Theobald, which Gaffney assumed was significant, or noise that came out of Gaffney. I ran a search on the word. Lots of priors, but nothing that raised any flags.'

'There wouldn't have been any,' Aumonier said.

Dreyfus heard something in her tone of voice that he hadn't been expecting. 'Because it's meaningless?'

'No. It's anything but. Firebrand has a very specific meaning, especially in a Panoply context.'

Dreyfus shook his head emphatically. 'Nothing came up, Jane.'

'That's because we're talking about an operational secret so highly classified that even Gaffney wouldn't have known about it. It's superblack, screened from all possible scrutiny even within the organisation.'

'Are you going to enlighten me?'

'Firebrand was a cell within Panoply,' Aumonier said. 'It was created eleven years ago to study and exploit any remaining artefacts connected with the Clockmaker affair.'

'You mean the clocks, the musical boxes?'

She answered with superhuman calm, taking no pleasure in contradicting him. 'More than that. The Clockmaker created other things during its spree. The public record holds that none of these artefacts survived, but in reality a handful of them were recovered. They were small things, of unknown purpose, but because they had been made by the Clockmaker, they were considered too unique to destroy. At least not until we'd studied them, worked out what they were and how we could apply that data to the future security of the Glitter Band.' Before he could get a word in, she said: 'Don't hate us for doing that, Tom. We had a duty to learn everything we could. We didn't know where the Clockmaker had come from. Because we didn't understand it, we couldn't rule out the possibility of another one arising. If that ever happened, we owed it to the citizenry to be prepared.'

'And?' he asked. 'Are we?'

'I instigated Firebrand. The cell was answerable only to me, and for a couple of years I permitted it to operate in absolute secrecy within Panoply.'

'How come Gaffney didn't know about it?'

'Gaffney's predecessor knew – we couldn't have set it up without *some* cooperation from Security – but when he handed over the reins there was no need to inform Gaffney. By then the cell was self-sufficient, operating within Panoply but completely isolated from the usual mechanisms of oversight and surveillance. And that was how things continued for a couple of years.'

'What happened then?'

'There was an accident: one of the seemingly dead artefacts reactivated itself. It killed half the cell before the rest brought it under control. When the news reached me, I took the decision to shut down Firebrand. I realised then that no benefits could outweigh the risks of allowing those artefacts to remain in existence. I ordered all the remains to be destroyed, all the records to be deleted and the cell itself to be disbanded. Those involved were dispersed back to normal duties, resuming the jobs they'd never officially left.'

'And?' Dreyfus asked.

'Shortly after, I received confirmation that my orders had been implemented. The cell was no more. The artefacts had been destroyed.'

'But that was nine years ago. Why would Firebrand come up again now?'

'I don't know.'

'Someone's stirring up old ghosts, Jane. If Firebrand is really connected with Panoply, how did Anthony Theobald know about it?'

'We don't know for sure that he did. That could be a rogue inference from the trawl.'

'Or it could explain why Gaffney was so interested in the Ruskin-Sartorious family,' Dreyfus said. 'You shut down that cell, Jane. But what if the cell had other ideas?'

Her eyes flashed nervously. 'I'm not with you.'

'Try this on for size. The people running that cell decided their work was too important to be closed down, no matter what you thought. They told you it was all over for Firebrand. But what if they just relocated their efforts?'

'I'd have known.'

'You already told me this cell was damn near untraceable,' Dreyfus said. 'Can you really be sure they couldn't have kept it running without your knowledge?'

'They'd never have done such a thing.'

'But what if they believed they were acting in the right? You clearly thought there was a justification for Firebrand when you started it. What if the people inside thought those reasons were still valid, even after you tried to kill it?'

'They were loyal to me,' Aumonier said.

'I don't doubt it. But you'd already set a bad example, Jane. You'd shown them that deception was acceptable, in the interests of the common good. What if they decided that they had to deceive *you*, to keep the cell operational?'

For a long moment Aumonier said nothing, as if Dreyfus's words had not just stunned her, but undermined her every certainty. 'I told them to put a stop to it,' she said, so quietly that Dreyfus would not have caught the words had he not already attuned himself to her voice. 'I ordered them to end Firebrand.'

'It appears they thought differently.'

'But why would all this surface now, Tom? What does any of this have to do with Anthony Theobald, or Gaffney, or Aurora?'

'There was something in the Ruskin-Sartorious Bubble that had to be destroyed,' Dreyfus said. 'Something that even we didn't realise was there, but which Aurora considered an impediment to her plans, something that had to be removed before she could begin the takeover.'

'You think Firebrand relocated to the Ruskin-Sartorious Bubble nine years ago.'

'If you'd pulled the plug on the cell, it would have been too difficult for them to remain operational inside Panoply, especially if something went wrong again. Too risky to relocate elsewhere in the system, either, since that would have involved travel they couldn't easily explain away as routine Panoply business. So why not another habitat? Somewhere close enough to be easily reachable, but still discreet enough to contain something so secret even we didn't know about it?'

'What would Anthony Theobald's involvement have been?'

'I don't know,' Dreyfus said, still getting things straight in his head. 'Did he have any prior connection with Firebrand?'

'Not to my knowledge.'

'Then he was probably just told to keep his mouth shut in return for certain favours. Whatever those favours were, it looks as if he was prepared to screw his own family to safeguard them. He was the only one who bailed out, just before the Bubble was destroyed. I'm assuming your cell had ready access to funds, without going through the usual channels?'

'Like I said, it was superblack. If they needed something – resources, equipment, expertise – they got it, no questions asked.'

'Then I imagine they could have made someone like Anthony Theobald very comfortable indeed.'

'He must have had advance warning that the Bubble was going to be hit,' Aumonier said.

'Or he was good at putting two and two together. According to Gaffney's trawl, Firebrand moved out of the Bubble at the last minute. They must have received intelligence that someone was closing in on them, trying to hunt down the Clockmaker artefacts.'

'Aurora,' Aumonier said.

'Almost certainly. Whatever it was was enough to scare them out of hiding. Maybe they tipped off Anthony Theobald: get your family out of here now, while you can, that kind of thing. Then change your identities and lie low for a couple of centuries, until the trail goes cold. But Anthony Theobald obviously decided to prioritise the saving of his own neck instead.'

'Except Gaffney was cleverer.'

'We need to find out who's still running Firebrand, Jane. Something they were holding in that Bubble scared Aurora really badly. For obvious reasons I'm interested in finding out what it was.'

'If it still exists.'

'They didn't destroy it nine years ago. Chances are they didn't destroy it this time, either. They moved it somewhere. Find someone with ties to Firebrand and we'll have a shot at getting hold of the artefacts.'

'That might not be easy.'

'It's all we have. I need names, Jane. Everyone who was part of the original Firebrand cell, when you closed it down. You remember, don't you?'

'Of course,' she said, apparently dismayed that he even had to ask. 'I committed them to memory. What are you going to do with them?'

'Ask hard questions,' Dreyfus said.

Thalia and Parnasse were alone beneath the lowest public level of the polling core sphere. They'd been down to these corridors and rooms once before, scouting for barricade material, but the expedition had been largely fruitless. Thalia had not expected to be making a return trip into the unwelcoming space, and certainly not with the destructive intention that was now occupying her thoughts. She was grateful that Parnasse knew his way around. Although it was now full daylight outside, very little of that light reached these gloomily lit sub-levels.

'Now we go deeper,' he said, pausing to lever up a floor hatch that Thalia would never have noticed. 'Gonna be a bit dusty and dark down here, but you'll cope. Just try not to make too much noise. The elevator, polling core conduit and stairwell rise right through this part of the sphere, and there's only a few centimetres of material between us and them. I don't think the machines have got this high yet, but we don't want to take chances, do we, girl?'

'If they get this high,' Thalia said, 'what's to stop them breaking through the walls and bypassing our barricade completely?'

'Nothing, if they get the idea into their thick metal heads. That's why it might be an idea for us not to make too much noise.' He lowered himself into the underfloor space, then extended a hand to help Thalia down.

'How did Meriel Redon take it, by the way?' she asked as she pushed her legs into the darkness.

'She thought I was taking the piss.'

Thalia's feet touched metal flooring. 'And afterwards, when you explained it was my idea?'

'She changed her mind. She thought *you* were taking the piss. But I think I brought her round in the end. Like you say, it's not as if we really want to take our chances with those servitors.'

'No,' Thalia said, grimly resigned. 'That we don't. Did you see any sign that anyone else has noticed the military-grade machines?'

He kept his voice low. 'I don't think so. Cuthbertson started nosing around the windows, but I managed to steer him away before he saw anything.'

'That's good. The citizens are spooked enough as it is, without having to deal with the thought of war robots. I don't expect I have to tell you what those machines would be capable of doing to unarmed civilians.'

'No, got enough of an imagination on me for that,' Parnasse said, taking a kind of grim pleasure in the remark. 'What do you think they're going to do – try coming up the inside, like the others?'

'No need. These machines are designed for assault and infiltration. They wouldn't need to climb the stairs to reach the polling core. They can come up the outside, even if they have to form a siege tower with their own bodies.'

'They don't seem to have started climbing yet.'

'Must be evaluating the situation, working out how to take us down as quickly as possible. But we can't count on them dithering for ever. You'd better show me where to cut.'

'This way,' Parnasse whispered, pushing Thalia's head down so that she did not knock it against a ceiling strut. 'You might want to put those glasses of yours on,' he added.

'What about you?'

'I know my way. You just take care of yourself.'

Thalia slipped the glasses on. The image amplifier threw grainy shapes against her eyes. She clicked in the infrared overlay and locked on to Parnasse's blob-like form, following his every move as if they were passing through a minefield. As silently as they could, they negotiated a forest of crisscrossing struts and utility ducts, descending slowly until they reached the trunk-like intrusion of the three service shafts Parnasse had already described. Thalia had a clear sense that they'd reached the base of the sphere, for she could see where the curve of the outer skin met the top of the stalk. Surrounding the cluster of service shafts was a series of heavy-looking buttresses, arcing back over Thalia's head into the depths of the chamber. Wordlessly, Parnasse touched a finger against one of the spoke-like buttresses. It was as thick as her thigh.

'That's what I have to cut?' she asked.

'Not just this one,' he whispered back. 'There are eighteen of these, and you're going to have to take care of at least nine if we're to have a hope of toppling.'

'Nine!' she hissed back.

He raised a shushing finger to his lips. 'I didn't say you had to cut through 'em all. You cut through four or five, say two on either side of this fellow, and you cut partway through another two on either side, and that should be enough. We want to make damned sure the sphere topples in the right direction.'

'I know,' Thalia said, resenting the fact that he felt she needed reminding.

'You want that magic sword of yours?'

'No time like the present.'

Parnasse passed her the thick bundle he'd made of the

whiphound. Between them, they unwrapped the insulating layers, then re-wrapped the cool outer part around the scorching-hot shaft of the handle. Her hands trembling as they had done before, Thalia took the damaged weapon and prayed that the filament would extend for her one more time.

Then she started cutting.

Not for the first time, Jane Aumonier found herself both awed and frightened by the submarine processes of her own mind. She had scarcely given the names of the Firebrand operatives more than a second's thought in nine years, but the process of recall was as automatic and swift as some well-engineered dispensing machine. She dictated the names to Dreyfus while he scratched them into a compad, floating at the end of the safe-distance tether. He always looked awkward when writing, as if it was a skill his hands had not quite evolved for.

When he was done he left her alone, the past amok in her head, while the weevil-class war robots rampaged through the gilded plazas of Carousel New Brazilia.

Many public data feeds had been severed, but the habitat would not be completely isolated until the weevils reached the polling core. The cams would maintain their dispassionate vigilance until that final moment of transmission, even as the streets turned slippery with citizens' blood, congealing too thickly to be absorbed by the municipal quickmatter. The war robots moved very fast once they were inside the airtight environment of the wheel-shaped structure. They tumbled out of doorways and ramps in a slurry of dark armour, their traction legs a furious grey-black blur. They whisked through plazas and atria in a rampaging column of thrashing metal, as if lumpy black tar was being poured along the alleys and boulevards of the habitat's great public spaces, a tar that ate and dissolved people as it swept over them. It looked disorganised, almost random, until Aumonier slowed down the time rate and studied the invasion in the accelerated frame of machine perception. Then she saw how fiercely systematic the invaders were, how efficient and regimented. They cut down the citizens with brutal precision, but only when they were directly opposed. Bystanders, or those running in panic, were left quite alone provided they offered no immediate obstruction to the weevils. Local constables, recognisable by their armbands and activated from amongst the citizenry under the usual emergency measures, were taking the brunt of the casualties. The constables' non-lethal weapons were hopelessly ineffective against the war machines, but still they tried to slow down the invading force, spraying the weevils with immobilising foam or sticky netting. Using their special constabulory authority, they tried to conjure barricades out of the ambient quickmatter, but their efforts were panicked and ineffective. The weevils barged through the obstacles as if they were no more substantial than cobwebs. Most of the constables ran for cover as soon as they'd used their weapons or conjured obstacles, but a few stood their ground and paid a predictable price. Death, when it came, was always mercifully quick – Aumonier remembered what Baudry had told them about the weevils carrying anatomical knowledge – but while there appeared to be no specific cruelty in the machines' actions, that did not make the process of invasion any less horrific.

The polling core in Carousel New Brazilia lay at the heart of a dizzying multi-tiered atrium crisscrossed by railingless pedestrian bridges. Here the constables had converged from all over the wheel, ready for a courageous last stand. They'd taken up defensive positions around the core, covering the endpoints of all the bridges. In addition to their usual non-lethal weapons, some of them now carried heavier armaments dispensed under the emergency provisions. Aumonier watched as a trio of constables tried to assemble some kind of tripod-mounted cannon, two of them arguing over the right way to attach the angled blast screen. By the time they had the cannon operational, the weevils were already crossing the bridges from the surrounding galleries. The constables opened fire, their gun chugging silently as it spewed out low-velocity munitions, trailing banners of pink smoke. It made no practical difference. Weevils were constructed for the rigours of vacuum warfare, hardened to withstand direct hits from high-energy pulses or penetrating slugs. The constables managed to dislodge a couple of the robots, sending them plummeting from the bridges, but it was as nothing compared to the numbers still crossing. Belatedly, some of the constables realised that they had the authority to conjure gaps in the bridges, and a couple of them ran bravely out into the middle to issue the necessary close-proximity commands. The bridges puckered apart, like strands of toffee being pulled too hard.

But by then it was much too late. The weevils bridged the openings with their own bodies, locking together while other machines flowed over them. They flung the retreating constables aside, into the open space of the atrium. The constables fell with silent screams.

Then the weevils were at the polling core. Aumonier watched until the last bitter instant, until the cam feeds greyed out, filling with static and cascading error messages.

Panoply had just lost Carousel New Brazilia. Aurora now held five habitats.

Aumonier switched her attention to House Flammarion, where the weevils were only just beginning to reach the interior. Something compelled her to watch, as if the futile but dignified resistance of the constables demanded a witness, even though she could do nothing to affect the outcome.

Before very long Aurora held her sixth prize.

CHAPTER 24

It was the first time Dreyfus had returned to his quarters since his release from detention. He knew that the forensics team had worked the place over with their customary thoroughness, removing every atom of Clepsydra that had not already been digested by the quickmatter. And yet he could not shake the sense that this temporarily allocated space – it was now functioning as his living room – remained unclean, materially despoiled by the act of her murder. Death had visited in his absence, stroked his furniture, made himself at home and left a sour mortuary smell that mostly lingered just below conscious detection.

Dreyfus conjured thick, hot coffee and enveloped himself in a cloud of bitter aroma. He sat back in his usual chair and brought the compad to life. He had not looked at the names until this moment since Jane had dictated them to him, and even now he angled the compad steeply to his chest, as if someone might be looking over his shoulder. It was a pointless gesture – it made no more sense than the smell – but he was equally incapable of suppressing it. Even though he was engaged on Panoply business, even though the names had been divulged by the supreme prefect herself, he felt a furtive sense of wrongness.

He sipped the coffee. It rushed down his throat, acrid and black, and for a moment he forgot Clepsydra.

There were eight names. He had no doubt that these were the eight original members of Firebrand, assuming that Aumonier herself was not to be counted amongst them. He recognised all of the names, too, and could even put faces to some of them. Panoply's compartmentalised structure, with each field prefect being assigned a tightly knit team of deputies, ensured that there was only limited communication between field units. Units with very different field assignments might go years before their members met.

And yet he knew these eight names and could put faces – blurred, admittedly – to five of them.

He read them again, just to make sure he wasn't missing something obvious:

Lansing Chen (FPIII)
Xavier Valloton (DFPIII)
Eloise Dassault (DFPIII)
Riyoko Chadwick (FPI)
Murray Vos (FPII)
Simon Veitch (FPII)
Paula Saavedra (FPIII)
Gilbert Knerr (DFPII)

But there'd been no mistake, and the more he thought about the names the more he convinced himself he could put at least sketchy faces to all of them, not just the five he'd thought of first. Veitch in particular – that name loomed larger in his memory than the others for some reason. But he couldn't think of a case or training exercise where he'd worked with any of them. The faces, such as they were, hung in contextless limbo, like portraits where the background had only been roughed-in.

What now? he wondered. Save the flicker of recognition he'd felt upon seeing Veitch's name, there was no single prefect who jumped out at him as an obvious starting point. But it would definitely help his cause if at least some of them were actually inside Panoply at the moment.

Using Pangolin clearance, Dreyfus pinged the locations of all eight names. Bracelets tracked prefects inside Panoply, and duty schedules and flight plans dictated what they were up to when they were outside. It wasn't foolproof – Gaffney had proved that – but it was the only tool available, and Dreyfus had to trust that Gaffney's replacement was working for the organisation, not against it.

The pings came back almost instantly, together with recent images and bio snapshots.

Six of the eight, including Veitch, were indeed outside Panoply, on what appeared to be plausible errands. Nothing too fishy about that: they *were* field prefects, after all. The other two – Lansing Chen and Paula Saavedra – were supposedly somewhere inside the rock, on normal downtime between duties. Dreyfus used additional

Pangolin clearance to dig through Chen and Saavedra's duty schedules for the last few days. No surprises there: like most prefects who weren't already tied to high-priority assignments, they'd been outside fighting fires between the Glitter Band and the Parking Swarm. Pulling triple shifts, too. Dreyfus couldn't speak for these two in particular, but most of the prefects who'd returned to Panoply were in need of that downtime.

Pangolin clearance gave him sleep schedules. Chen and Saavedra were both meant to be awake by now. Again using Pangolin, but this time running an appreciably greater risk of detection, Dreyfus had the system locate the two prefects. He'd been hoping to catch them alone, but that wasn't to be. The two were apparently sitting together in the main refectory. It was as good a place to start as any.

Dreyfus finished his coffee and slugged the cup back into the floor.

Dreyfus paused at the entrance to the refectory, casting his gaze over the assembled prefects gathered there to eat, drink, exchange professional gossip and simply pass the time of day between shifts. The tables, mostly unoccupied, bent upwards in long, low lines, following the gentle curvature of the floor. As was the case in the refectory during certain shift cycles, the lights had been dimmed to a drowsy, candlelit level of illumination. Prefects, all of whom were wearing their uniforms, were gathered in clots of blackness, most of them sitting in groups at the tables. Some were returning from the serving hatches with trays and cups. Others were standing in ones and twos at the display panes that smothered the refectory's walls. At any other time they'd have been reading case summaries and ongoing investigation reports, getting a feel for the work their colleagues were engaged in, but now the panes had been given over to a running analysis of the Aurora crisis. They were filled with multiple images of the six habitats she had now taken, all external views since there were no longer any active internal feeds. Other panes showed images and diagrams of weevils, coupled with views of the spaceborne containment effort. Few of the prefects in this room knew more than the basic details of the crisis – Aurora's identity was still a Pangolin-only operational secret – but all of them were aware of the severity of the situation.

Including Chen and Saavedra. He found them sitting together in the far corner of the room, at the very end of a row of tables, a long way from any other prefects. They were facing each other, leaning together in a worried, conspiratorial manner that left Dreyfus in no doubt that he was looking at two elements of Firebrand. The other prefects were concerned, no doubt about it, but they were also animated and enthused by the exigencies of the crisis. It was giving them a chance to prove themselves, to compete for promotional favours. But Chen and Saavedra just looked scared, like a pair of illicit lovers convinced they were about to be found out.

Dreyfus moved through the room to the nearest vacant serving slot. The aproned human orderly behind the slot was a deliberate touch. People came to the refectory because they had some profound psychological need not to eat alone or be served by a machine. The food might have been created using the same quickmatter processes utilised elsewhere, but at least it was handed over on a warm china plate, by a living person.

But Dreyfus just asked for an apple and a glass of water. As he strolled away from the slot, he polished the apple against the fabric of his trousers. He ambled between the tables, acknowledging those prefects who looked up or spoke to him, but offering nothing more than a distracted nod in return.

Chen and Saavedra still hadn't noticed his approach. What had looked like a lovers' tiff from a distance revealed itself to be a full-blown, heated argument as he neared. They were conducting the argument in whispers, but their expressions and the tension in their gestures gave them away. At first he wondered why they'd chosen to meet in the refectory rather than in the seclusion of their rooms. But if they'd been called upon to explain their meeting, at least the refectory allowed the possibility of an accidental encounter.

He rounded the end of one of the tables. Now he was closer to the two than anyone else in the room. He raised his apple and took a crunching bite through the emerald-green skin of the perfectly spherical fruit. Chen looked up, registering less surprise than mild affront that Dreyfus should dare to invade their privacy. Lansing Chen was still a youthful man with a broad, high-cheekboned face and thick black hair that he wore carefully parted.

'Prefect,' he said, friendly enough, but not in such a way as to sound as if he was inviting Dreyfus to sit down with them.

'Lansing,' Dreyfus said, taking another bite from the apple. 'Mind if I join you?'

The woman, Paula Saavedra, flashed unmasked animosity in Dreyfus's direction. She was thin and bony, like the articulated wooden dolls artists used instead of human models. Everything about her was pale, washed out, as if she'd spent too long under very bright lights. Even her eyes were colourless, as if the ink in them had faded from whatever colour it had once been.

'Actually, Prefect—' she began.

That was when Dreyfus heard footsteps behind him and felt a hand land on his shoulder. 'Tom,' he heard a voice say. 'I'm glad I found you. Had to invoke Pangolin. I almost didn't believe it when it said you were in the refectory. This was about the last place I expected you to be.'

Dreyfus snapped around, prepared to be angered until he saw that the man who had spoken was the lantern-jawed Demikhov. 'Doctor,' he said quietly. 'Actually, would you mind ... I'm in the middle of something right now.'

Demikhov nodded understandingly. 'So are we all, Tom. But you and I need to talk right now. Trust me on this, okay?'

Dreyfus studied the doctor's fatigue-mapped face. He'd never once known Demikhov overstate the seriousness of an issue. Whatever the man wanted to discuss, it was clearly urgent.

'What's it about?' Dreyfus asked, still keeping his voice low.

'Have a guess, Tom.'

'Jane?'

'There's been a development. Not a good one. We have to make a very difficult decision and I need your input. Immediately, Tom. Can you come down to the Sleep Lab?'

'It's okay, Prefect,' Lansing Chen said, standing up from the table with a scrape of chair against floor. 'Paula and I were just leaving anyway.'

'I'd like to see you back here in an hour,' Dreyfus said, tapping his bracelet.

'Is something the matter, *Field Prefect* Dreyfus?' Chen asked innocently, but obviously reminding Dreyfus that they shared exactly the same rank.

'Yeah. Something's the matter. And in sixty minutes we're going to have a chat about it.' He turned his attention to the woman. 'You too, Field Prefect Saavedra.' He watched them flounce out of the refectory, leaving their trays and food on the table.

'I'm sorry to have interrupted you,' Demikhov said, while Dreyfus swigged down the water and threw the remains of the apple onto Chen's dinner tray. 'But please believe me – I wouldn't have disturbed you were it not regarding an issue of the utmost concern.'

In the Sleep Lab Demikhov said, 'How was Jane the last time you spoke to her?'

Dreyfus rubbed at the back of his neck. 'Compared to what?'

'The time before. Or how she was last week.'

'She wasn't too happy. Understandably, since she'd been removed from power.' He raised a reassuring hand. 'Don't worry, Doctor. I don't hold you responsible for that. You were just doing your job, looking after Jane's ultimate health. I can guess how manipulative Gaffney must have been.'

'It wasn't just Gaffney. It was Crissel and Baudry, too.'

'Well, Crissel got to make amends. And while I might not approve of the decisions Baudry says we have to make, I can see that she's just trying to discharge her obligations.'

'Back to Jane – did you notice anything else? Did she appear to be under a higher degree of stress than usual?'

'Well, let's review the situation. We've now lost control of six habitats, four of which have weevil-manufacturing capacity. The agency that now has control of them is poised to grab another four habitats inside the next twenty-six hours, maybe sooner. We'll soon be in double figures, and then it won't be long before we hit triple figures. We're running a mass-evacuation programme to clear a fire break around the infected habitats so that we can nuke the very structures we're supposed to protect. There are probably still going to be people inside those structures when we push the button. Meanwhile, we're losing agents and machines faster than we can think. So – all told – yeah, I'd say Jane's under a bit more stress than usual.'

Demikhov batted aside Dreyfus's sarcasm like a man shooing a fly. 'I think the time has come to intervene.'

'Not now. Not until we're done with Aurora.'

'There's been another change in the scarab. Did Jane tell you?'

'No,' Dreyfus said warily.

'It's pushed one of its prongs deeper into her neck. It's applying pressure to her spinal cord. She can feel it.'

Dreyfus thought back to his last conversation with Aumonier. 'She didn't appear to be in pain.'

'Then she was doing a good job of hiding it from you. It's not agony – yet. But the scarab's been changing faster and faster lately. It's sending us a warning, Tom. We don't have much time.'

'But it's only been a few days since the last time we talked. You didn't have a strategy then; nothing that would get it off her in under four-tenths of a second. Are you telling me you've come up with something new since then?'

Demikhov could not quite meet his eyes. 'I've not been entirely truthful with you, Tom. There's always been a strategy, one that we're confident can remove the scarab before it has time to retaliate. It's just that we wanted to make sure all other options were exhausted first.'

Dreyfus shook his head. 'Tango was your best option. Yet it still wasn't down to four-tenths or less.'

'There's always been something faster than Tango. We've held it in reserve, barely discussed it since the groundwork was put in place. We always hoped we'd come up with something better in the meantime. But we haven't. And now there isn't any more time. Which leaves us three choices, Tom.'

'Which are?'

'Option one is we do nothing and hope that the scarab never triggers. Option two is we go with Tango. All the sims – incorporating the work we've put in during the last week – say that Tango will achieve scarab extraction in point four nine six seconds. The sims also estimate that that isn't quite enough time for the scarab to do anything.'

'But there's not much of a margin of error.' They'd agreed long ago that no action would be taken until the extraction could be achieved in under point four seconds. Warily, Dreyfus asked, 'What's the third option?'

'We call it Zulu. It's the last resort.'

'Which is?'

'Decapitation,' Demikhov said.

'You're not serious.'

'It's been analysed into the ground. We have a plan, and we think it will work.'

'You *think*?'

'Nothing's guaranteed here, Tom. We're talking about operating on a patient we haven't been able to get within seven and half metres of for eleven years.'

Dreyfus realised that he was taking out his exasperation on the hapless Demikhov, a man who had selflessly dedicated the last eleven years of his life to finding a way to help Jane Aumonier. 'All right. Tell me what's involved. How does cutting her head off score over just shooting the scarab right now? And how are you going to get a surgical team in there to decapitate her, anyway?'

Demikhov steered Dreyfus towards one of the partitions that divided the central area of the Sleep Lab, bright with diagrams and images of both the patient and the thing clamped to her neck. 'Let's deal with one thing at a time. We've considered forced removal of the scarab – shooting it off, if you like – since day one. But we've always been concerned that there might be something in it that can still hurt Jane even if it isn't physically connected to her.'

They'd been over this before, but Dreyfus still needed his memory jogging. 'Like what?'

'An explosive device, for instance. We're confident the Clockmaker couldn't have got antimatter inside it, but there might be conventional explosives or spring-loaded cutting mechanisms concealed in the structures we haven't been able to map.'

'Enough to hurt Jane?'

'Easily. You've seen what it managed to build into some of those clocks. If we can get the scarab on the other side of some kind of blast screen, no harm will befall the patient. That's how we'll kill two birds, Tom.'

'Two birds? I'm not sure what you mean.'

Demikhov tapped a finger against one of the diagrams. Dreyfus had the vague impression that he'd seen this picture a hundred times without ever paying it due attention. It was a cross section of the chamber in which Jane floated.

'You'll have noted this ring-shaped duct running around the bubble,' Demikhov said.

'I assumed ...' But Dreyfus trailed off. He hadn't assumed anything, beyond the fact that the ring-shaped structure was nothing to do with the bubble itself.

'We installed that duct, Tom. We opened up that space because one day we feared we might need to proceed with Zulu.'

'What's in it now?'

'Nothing: it's just an empty ring encircling the bubble. But everything we need to install in it is stored elsewhere in Panoply, ready to go.'

'Show me.'

Demikhov tapped a finger and the diagram tilted around so that they were looking down on the bubble and the ring instead of seeing them in cross section. A series of modular structures were shown being inserted into the ring through a single opening, then pushed around until they joined up to form a kind of thick, barbed necklace.

'What is it?'

'A guillotine,' Demikhov said, matter-of-factly. 'When the structures are in place, they'll project those bladed segments through the wall of the sphere. We've weakened the outer wall where they need to cut through, so there's no need to do anything on the inside of the bubble. It'll happen very quickly. The segments will close in and bisect the chamber in two-tenths of a second: well inside our margin of error.'

The diagram flipped back around to cross-sectional form. A figure appeared, floating in the middle of the chamber. A red line bisected the figure's neck. The blades sprang through the wall, severing the figure's head from its body. The head floated up into one half of the bisected space. The decapitated body floated down into the other half.

'We cut high enough to remove the scarab,' Demikhov said. 'We bisect between the submaxillary triangle and the hyoid bone. If we're lucky, we get a clean separation of the third and fourth cervical vertebra. The scarab goes into the lower half. Even if it blows up, the blades will have interlocked to form a blastproof shield.'

'What about Jane's body?' Dreyfus said.

'We don't care about the body. We'll grow her a new one, or fix any damage the old one sustains. Then we reattach the head. But the head's the most important thing. Provided we get a clean decapitation, she'll live.'

Dreyfus knew he was missing something. 'But you still need to get a surgical team in there somehow. She needs to be prepped for the procedure.'

'No, she doesn't.'

'I'm not following.'

'We don't prep Jane, Tom, because we can't. We can't anaesthetize her because that's exactly what the scarab's waiting for. And if she knows what's coming her stress levels are going to shoot through the roof. The only way this will work is if we go in fast, without warning.' Demikhov nodded at Dreyfus's reaction. 'You see it now, I think. You understand why this has only ever been an option of last resort.'

'This is a nightmare. This can't be happening.'

'Listen to me,' Demikhov said urgently. 'Jane's had eleven years of living hell inside that chamber. Nothing we can do to her to get rid of the scarab even begins to stack up against that. She'll have no warning, and therefore she'll have no time to get scared. When the blades close, the upper half of the chamber is ours. Then we send in a crash surgical team, ready to stabilise Jane and put her under.'

'How long?'

'Before the team goes in? Seconds. That's all. We'll just need confirmation that the hemisphere's really clear, that the scarab hasn't left any surprises, and in we go.'

'Jane will still be conscious at that point, won't she?'

The question troubled Demikhov visibly. 'There's anecdotal evidence . . . but I really wouldn't put too much store by it. The shock of blood loss is just as likely to plunge her into deep unconsciousness within five to seven seconds. Clinical death, if you like.'

'But you can't guarantee that. You can't promise me that she won't have awareness after those blades have closed.'

'No,' Demikhov said. 'I can't.'

'She has to be told, Doctor.'

'She's always made it clear that we don't need her consent to attempt an extraction.'

'But this isn't the same as sending in a servitor to disarm the scarab,' Dreyfus protested. 'This is a completely different form of intervention, one that'll probably involve pain and distress above and beyond anything Jane's ever expected to endure.'

'I agree wholeheartedly. I also think that's exactly why we can't breathe a word of this to her.'

Dreyfus looked at the diagram again. He recalled the red line cutting through Jane's neck, just above the point where the scarab was attached. 'The position of those blades is fixed, right? You can't steer them if she's not floating at the right height?'

'That's correct.'

'So how will you be able to cut in the right place?'

'We mount a laser on the door. It's small enough that she won't notice it. The laser draws a line across Jane, indicating where the blades will pass.'

'Cut. That's the word you're looking for.'

'Thank you, but I'm fully aware of what we're contemplating here. I'm not taking any of this lightly.'

'And what happens if the line doesn't hit her in the right spot?'

'We wait,' Demikhov said. 'She bobs up and down. Sometimes she does it herself, paddling the air. Sometimes it's just currents in the chamber, pushing her around. But sooner or later that line's going to touch the right spot.' He looked hard at Dreyfus. 'My hand will be on a trigger. It'll be my call as to when the blades go in, not some machine's. I have to feel it's the right moment.'

'What about the crash team?'

'I've arranged for three shifts. There'll always be one team on stand-by.'

Dreyfus felt numb. He could see the logic. He didn't have to like it.

'Have you spoken to the other seniors?'

'They've been informed. I have their consent to proceed.'

'Then you don't need mine.'

'I don't *need* it, but I want it. You're closer to Jane than anyone else in the organisation, Tom. Even me. From the word go it's always been clear to me that I'd need your permission before I go ahead with this. She trusts you like an only son. How many other field prefects have Pangolin?'

'To my knowledge, none,' Dreyfus said candidly.

'You're the one she'd want to have the final say-so, Tom.' Demikhov shrugged resignedly, as if he'd done all he could. 'I've stated the medical case. If you give me the nod, we can install the blades in thirteen hours. She could be out of that room and stable in thirteen hours, ten minutes.'

'And if I say no?'

'We'll run with Tango. I can't risk doing nothing. That would be true negligence.'

'I need time to deal with this,' Dreyfus said. 'You should have told me about this years ago, so I'd have had time to think it over.'

'Do you think it would have helped? You'd have listened to me, agreed how unpleasant it was and then shoved the whole matter to the back of your mind because you didn't need to deal with it there and then.'

Dreyfus wanted to argue but he knew that Demikhov was right. There were some horrors it was pointless spying on the horizon. You had to deal with them at close range.

'I still need time. Give me an hour. Then you can start installing the equipment.'

'I lied to you,' Demikhov said softly. 'We've already started. But you still have your hour, Tom.' He turned away and picked up one of the dismantled plastic scarab models, distracted by some waxy grey internal component, a snail-shaped thing he'd apparently only just noticed. 'You know where to find me. I'll be awake, just like Jane.'

CHAPTER 25

Dreyfus was leaving the Sleep Lab when his bracelet chimed. It was Sparver.

'Think you need to drop by the nose, Boss. Caught a couple of fish trying to swim away.'

'Thank you,' Dreyfus said, glad that he'd taken the initiative to have Sparver shadow Chen and Saavedra. 'I'll be there immediately.'

Sparver had detained them in the docking bay that formed the nose of Panoply's pumpkin-face, the bay that handled cutters and corvettes as opposed to civilian vehicles or deep-system cruisers. As field prefects, the Firebrand operatives were regular users of both light- and medium-enforcement vehicles and would have been familiar faces to the technical staff manning the bay. Although they did not have clearance to take a ship, they had managed to talk their way aboard a cutter that had just come in for refuelling and re-armament and had been well advanced in pre-flight checks when Sparver blocked their escape by closing the main bay doors. Dreyfus would have to reprimand the staff who had allowed the prefects aboard the ship without the right clearance, but for now his only concern was extracting information from the two unsuccessful fugitives. They were still aboard the cutter, the ship still poised on its launching rack, with the doors blocking its egress.

'I had a hard time tailing them,' Sparver said, floating next to the cutter's suitwall, inside the air-filled connecting tube. Two internal prefects flanked him, whiphounds drawn. 'For run-of-the-mill fields, these two knew a few tricks.'

'They're not exactly field prefects,' Dreyfus said. 'That's just an operational cover for what they really do. They're specialists, assigned to a superblack cell called Firebrand. Jane pulled the plug on the cell, but the cell had other ideas. They've been carrying on without her authority for nine years.'

'Now that's just naughty.'

'Naughtier than you think. Firebrand has to take some of the responsibility for what happened to Ruskin-Sartorious.' Dreyfus unclipped his whiphound and motioned for Sparver to do likewise. 'Let's get them off the vehicle. We can't keep these bay doors closed for ever.'

They set the passwall to yield and entered, Dreyfus leading with Sparver just to his rear. Dreyfus sealed the passwall behind them, with the internals keeping guard on the other side so that there was no possibility of the Firebrand agents escaping back into Panoply.

Like all cutters, it was a small vehicle with a limited number of hiding places. It was powered, but the cabin illumination was dimmed almost to darkness. Dreyfus fumbled in his pocket for his glasses, but he'd left them in his room before he went to the refectory.

He called into the cutter's depths. 'This is Tom Dreyfus. You both know me by reputation. You're not going anywhere, so let's talk civilly.'

There was no answer.

Dreyfus tried again. 'You don't have anything to fear from me. I know about Firebrand. I know about your operational mandate. I understand that you did what you did because you thought you were doing the right thing by Panoply.'

Again there was no reply. Dreyfus glanced back at Sparver, then pushed further into the ship, in the direction of the flight deck. He made out the watery blue glow of instrumentation seeping around the corner of the bulkhead that separated the flight deck from the adjoining compartment.

'I haven't come to punish you for the consequences of any actions you may have taken that you believed to be in the best interests of the Band.' Dreyfus paused heavily. 'But I do need to know the facts. I know that Firebrand was using Ruskin-Sartorious until just before the Bubble was destroyed. At some point, you're all going to have to answer for the mistake of hiding your activities inside that habitat. It was a mistake, a bad one, but no one's accusing you of premeditated murder. All I'm interested in is *why* that habitat had to die. Panoply needs whatever Aurora was scared of, and it needs it *now*.'

At last a voice emerged from the direction of that blueish glow. 'You have no idea, Dreyfus. No idea at all.' It was a woman's voice – so Saavedra, not Chen.

'Then it's up to you to put me right. Go ahead. I'm ready and waiting.'

'We weren't just working with relics,' Paula Saavedra said. 'We were working with the Clockmaker itself.'

Dreyfus recalled everything that Jane Aumonier had told him. 'The Clockmaker doesn't exist any more.'

'Everyone believes that the Clockmaker was destroyed,' Saavedra said. 'But it left relics of itself. Souvenirs, like the clocks in the Sleep Lab and the thing clamped to Jane. And other things, too. We got to study them. We thought they were toys, puzzles, vicious little trinkets. Mostly, they were. But not the one we opened nine years ago.'

'What was it?'

'The Clockmaker had encapsulated itself, squeezed its essence down into one of the relics. It knew Panoply was closing in on it eleven years ago, so it survived by tricking us. It compressed itself into a seed and waited for us to find it.' Before Dreyfus could frame an objection, she continued: 'It had to discard much of itself, accept a weakening of both its intellectual and physical capabilities. It did so willingly because it knew it had no other option. And also because it knew it could rebuild all that it lost at some point in the future.'

Dreyfus pushed himself closer to the flight deck. 'And you – we – helped it?'

'It was a mistake. But when we reactivated the Clockmaker, it was still weak, still ineffectual compared to its former embodiment. Even so, it still nearly won.'

'How much of this did Jane know?' Dreyfus asked, beginning to wonder why Lansing Chen wasn't contributing to the conversation.

'She was informed that one of the relics had run amok. She was never told that it was the Clockmaker itself that had come back from the grave. It was felt that the news would have been too upsetting.'

'But she still closed you down.'

'Perhaps she was right. Needless to say, we didn't agree. Although Firebrand had taken grave losses, we felt that we had come closer than ever before to learning something of the Clockmaker's true nature. We who survived were convinced that the future security of the Glitter Band depended on the discovery of that nature. We had to know what it was, where it had come from, so that we could ensure nothing like it ever emerged again. That was our moral imperative, Prefect Dreyfus. So we decided to remain operational. We were already superblack; it took very little effort to submerge ourselves to an even deeper level of secrecy, beyond even Jane's oversight.'

'And what did you learn, Paula?'

'Don't come any closer, Prefect Dreyfus.'

But Dreyfus was already within view of the flight deck by the time she finished her sentence. The connecting door was open. Blood droplets formed a cloud of little scarlet balloons, pulled into perfect spheres by surface tension. Lansing Chen was dead. He was buckled into the right-hand command seat, his head lolling at an unnatural angle, swaying slowly from side to side as the air shifted. His neck had been gashed open with the whiphound Paula Saavedra was still holding. She was buckled into the left-hand chair, rotated around to face Dreyfus and Sparver. She had one leg hooked higher than the other. She held the whiphound in her right hand, while her left hovered above one of the luminous blue controls on the console.

'You didn't have to kill Chen,' Dreyfus said, tightening his grip on his own whiphound.

Behind, he heard Sparver speak into his bracelet. 'Get me Mercier. We need a crash team at the nose. This is a medical emergency.'

'I didn't want to kill him,' Saavedra said, with real menace. 'Chen was a good man, Prefect. He served Firebrand well, until the end. It's not his fault that he's been having doubts.'

'What kind of doubts?'

'None of us liked what happened to Ruskin-Sartorious, but most of us saw it as an unfortunate but unavoidable occurrence. A casualty of war, Prefect. Not Chen, though. He felt we'd gone too far; that nine hundred and sixty lives were too high a price to pay for security. He felt it was time to blow our cover.'

'He'd have been right.'

The tip of her whiphound gleamed dark red. 'No, he wouldn't. Nothing matters more now than keeping the Clockmaker's new location hidden.'

'I agree wholeheartedly. Aurora mustn't learn of the Clockmaker's whereabouts. But Panoply needs that information more than ever.'

'Ordinarily, I might have agreed you. But Panoply is compromised. Someone's been sniffing around Firebrand for days.

Probably the same someone who helped arrange the attack on Ruskin-Sartorious.'

'That was Senior Prefect Gaffney. He's out of the picture now. I took care of that myself, so you can start trusting me.'

'Can I, really? You've done very well to track us down, Prefect. How do I know you aren't just following up on Gaffney's unfinished business?'

'I am, in a way – I had to find you. Why'd you have to kill Chen, Paula?'

'I told you – he got cold feet at the last moment. Decided he'd rather stay here and face the music. I couldn't let that happen, Prefect. Just as I can't let you keep me here now.'

'Nothing bad will happen to you,' Dreyfus said. But if he'd meant it earlier, it was an empty promise now. Nothing could excuse the murder of a fellow prefect.

'Even if killed myself, you'd trawl my corpse to get the location of the Clockmaker. Therefore I must leave. Can you see my left hand, Prefect?'

Dreyfus nodded. 'I guess you're holding it there for a reason.'

'When I boarded this ship, I brought four whiphounds with me. They're set to grenade mode, maximum yield, keyed to this console. Don't go looking for them – they're well hidden.'

'Whiphounds won't detonate inside Panoply. There's a positional safeguard.'

'Which I overrode, without difficulty.' She shook her head disappointedly. 'I'm Firebrand, Prefect. Can you imagine the lengths we've had to go to to maintain our effectiveness and secrecy over the last nine years? There isn't a trick in the book we don't know.'

'Don't do it, Paula. We need this bay in one piece.'

'I won't do it unless you prevent me from leaving. But if you try to prevent me, I won't hesitate. The blast won't do significant damage to Panoply – it might put this bay out of action, true – but it definitely won't leave enough of me for you to trawl.'

'I need to know where the Clockmaker is,' Dreyfus insisted.

'I can't take the risk of telling you. As far as I'm concerned, Panoply is already compromised. Firebrand is the only remaining part of the organisation capable of handling things from now on.'

'If you think I can't be trusted, why did you tell me that the Clockmaker's still alive?'

'I told you nothing Aurora won't already know. Now leave the cutter, Prefects.'

'We'll track you. Wherever you go. You're just prolonging the inevitable.'

'There isn't a ship in Panoply that can be prepped and launched in time to follow me.' She allowed a glint of self-satisfaction to shine through. 'I know: I checked. And you won't be able to track me. This cutter is CTC-dark. Maybe if there wasn't a Bandwide crisis going down, stretching all our resources, you might have a chance. But you don't, so you may as well not even bother. I'm dropping off the map. You won't hear from me again.'

'You might hear from me,' Dreyfus said.

'Get off this ship. Then make sure those bay doors are opened. You've got two minutes.'

'Give us Chen's body.'

'So you can run a post-mortem trawl to find out what he knew about the Clockmaker? Nice try.'

No, Dreyfus thought: not for that reason at all. He'd never counted on extracting anything useful from the dead. But he was sure Demikhov's crash team would welcome some practice at stabilising a severed head before they had to do it for real.

'Have it your way, Paula.' Dreyfus looked back at Sparver. 'We're leaving. She may be bluffing about those whiphounds, but we can't take the chance.'

'Boss,' Sparver said quietly, 'I already have her marked. I can put my own whiphound on her in under a second.'

'Try it,' Saavedra said. 'If you're feeling lucky. You have about ninety seconds now, by the way.'

'You're making a terrible mistake, Paula,' Dreyfus said.

'So are you. Get off the ship.'

Dreyfus nodded at Sparver and the two of them retreated back into the docking connector. The airlock closed, isolating the ship. Dreyfus cuffed his bracelet and called through to Thyssen, the officer in charge of bay operations. 'This is Dreyfus. Open the doors. Let her go.'

'Prefect, we can't afford to lose that cutter,' Thyssen said.

'We lose the bay if we don't lose the cutter. Open the doors.'

Thyssen didn't need to be told twice. A moment later the vast jaws of the armoured doors began to ease wide, interlocking teeth pulling away from each other to reveal a sea of false stars and the darkside curve of Yellowstone, cusped by a line of indigo. The launching rack pushed out on pistons, shoving Saavedra's cutter into open space. Engines kicked in, spiking out needle-thin thrust lines. The cutter surged away at maximum burn.

'Can we get another ship out there?' Dreyfus asked.

'Not fast enough to intercept,' Thyssen said. 'We'll track her as best we can, but I can't promise anything.'

Through the window of the docking connector, Dreyfus watched Saavedra's ship fall into the sea of stars, following it by eye until he could no longer distinguish it from the lights of distant habitats.

'It's very, very bad,' Jane Aumonier's hovering face told Dreyfus and the assembled seniors, while the Solid Orrery displayed six red lights amidst a sea of twinkling emerald. 'Weevils penetrated and occupied Carousel New Brazilia nine hours, thirty minutes ago. We detected manufactory warm-up two hours ago. Eighteen minutes ago, the doors opened and newly minted weevils began to emerge. Squadron density and flow throughput is consistent with what we've already seen in Aubusson and Szlumper Oneill.' She paused, allowing that to sink in before delivering the grim remainder of her summary. 'We lost Flammarion not long after Brazilia. The manufactories are on-line there as well. Based on what we've observed in the other habitats, we can expect weevil output to commence in ten to fifteen minutes. We've failed to contain the outflow from Aubusson and Szlumper Oneill, but we were at least able to reduce the number of weevils, which must have had some measurable effect on Aurora's rate of spread. Now we'll have no chance, short of nuclear intervention at the production sites. Of course, that won't stop any weevils that have already departed.'

'Which habitats are the new weevils targeting?' asked Clearmountain.

'If there's one crumb of comfort to extract from any of this,' Aumonier said, 'it's that Lillian's simulation appears to accurately predict Aurora's intentions. That may change in the future if Aurora realises that we're guessing her movements, but for the moment it does at least allow us to concentrate our evacuation efforts where they're most useful. The weevil flow from Brazilia is aimed at the Toriyuma-Murchison Spindle, one of the ten habitats we've already prioritised.'

'How are we doing, evacuation-wise?' asked Dreyfus, rubbing at his eyes.

'If I might ...' Baudry began, clutching a compad as if it was the only thing in the universe she could depend on. 'The

Toriyuma-Murchison Spindle contains ... contained ... five hundred and eleven thousand citizens. According to docking staff, we've now processed four hundred and sixty thousand, leaving a surplus of—'

'Fifty-one thousand,' Dreyfus said, before Baudry could finish. 'How long until we get them out?'

'Local constables report a non-compliance level of one per cent. I'm afraid we'll just have to abandon them – we don't have time to argue with people if they really don't want saving. As for those still awaiting transport, our current estimate predicts complete evacuation within four hours, twenty minutes, assuming we can get the liners in and out without incident.'

'There's a liner docked now?' Dreyfus asked.

'Not a high-capacity vehicle. The biggest ship we have on-station is the medium-capacity liner *High Catherine*. She can carry six thousand at a time, but she takes a long time to load. The larger ship we've been using, the *Bellatrix*, can take ten thousand, but we're also using her to offload people from the Persistent Vegetative State.'

'Why are we risking the lives of living citizens to save a bunch of self-induced coma-cases?' Clearmountain asked.

'Because they're citizens as well,' Aumonier snapped. 'No one gets priority treatment here. Not on my watch.'

'It's a moot point in any case,' Baudry said, for Clearmountain's benefit. 'Even if we reassigned the *Bellatrix* to deal solely with the evacuees from the Toriyuma-Murchison Spindle, we still wouldn't get them all out in time.'

'Correct,' Aumonier said. 'Weevil contact is anticipated in ... fifty-five minutes, eleven seconds. With local constables tasked to assist in the evacuation at the docking hubs, the weevils will have a clear run to the polling core. If events follow the pattern we've already seen, the Toriyuma-Murchison manufactory is scheduled to start weevil production in under ten hours.'

'Then the evacuees still have all that time,' Dreyfus said. 'We can get them out.'

'I'm sorry,' Aumonier said, her image looking at him as if no one else was in the room, 'but what we're dealing with here is akin to a state of plague. So far as we know, Aurora can seize control of habitats by reaching their polling cores. What we don't know is what other capabilities she might have up her sleeve if we give her the chance to try them out. I cannot run the risk of letting her hop from habitat to habitat by another means. And that includes evacuation vehicles.'

'But Jane—'

'We keep moving them out until the absolute last moment,' she said. 'But the instant weevils make groundfall on Toriyuma-Murchison, I'm pulling out the liners.' Just to be absolutely clear to all concerned, she added: 'Even if there are still people in the docking tubes.'

'And then what?' Dreyfus asked, even though he knew what she was going to say.

'We nuke. We remove one of Aurora's stepping stones.'

'There'll still be tens of thousands of people inside the Spindle.'

'About thirty-five thousand, if the *Bellatrix* can get in and out one more time. But there's no other way, Tom. We'll target the manufactory first, of course, but we'll have to hit it so hard to take it out completely that we might as well be attacking the entire habitat. We'll have ships standing by in case, but I'm not expecting survivors.'

'There must be another way.'

'There is. We could nuke the six habitats Aurora already holds, and the two she's about to take. That would stop her. But then we'd be talking about killing several million people, not just tens of thousands.'

'Taking out that one habitat won't necessarily stop her.'

'It'll inconvenience her. I'll settle for that for now.'

'This is bigger than Panoply,' Dreyfus said desperately. 'We need to call in assistance. Anyone who has a ship and can help.'

'I've issued requests for help through the usual channels. Maybe something will arrive, but I'm not counting on it.' She hesitated, her attention still fixed only on him. Dreyfus had the feeling that he was participating in a private conversation, to the exclusion of everyone else in the room. 'Tom, there's something else.'

'What?' he asked.

'I'm going to have to take down polling and abstraction services, Bandwide. There's just too much danger of Aurora utilising the network for her own purposes.'

'She spreads by weevil.'

'The weevils are her main agents, but we don't know for sure that she isn't using other channels to assist in her spread. I've already received a mandate to use all emergency powers at our disposal. That means authorisation to commit mass euthanisation if it means saving other lives. It also means I can take down the networks.'

'We'll need those networks to coordinate our own efforts.'

'And we'll retain skeletal data links for just that purpose. But everything else has to go. It's the only way to be sure.'

Dreyfus examined his thoughts. It startled him to realise that he was less shocked by Aumonier's planned use of nuclear weapons than he was by the idea of blacking out the entire Glitter Band. But the fact of the matter was that for most of the ten thousand habitats, life was continuing more or less as normally. Some of the citizens would be aware of the crisis, but many would be completely insulated from it, snug in the hermetic cocoons of their private fantasy universes. That wouldn't necessarily change when Panoply started nuking. But no one – save the citizens of the Bezile Solipsist State, or the Persistent Vegetative State, or the harsher Voluntary Tyrannies – could fail to notice the withdrawal of Bandwide data services. Reality was about to give them a cold, hard slap in the face, whether they liked it or not.

The lights were about to go out across the Glitter Band. There was no choice: it had to be done.

'Just do one thing for me,' Dreyfus said, 'before you pull the plug. Tell them Panoply isn't giving up on them. Tell them that we're going to be outside, fighting, and that we won't let them down. Tell them not to forget that.'

'I will,' she said.

CHAPTER 26

Thalia's trembling hands nearly dropped the whiphound as she finished weakening the final support spar in the sphere of the polling core. It had been agonisingly slow, and not just because the whiphound had grown too hot to hold for more than a minute at a time, even with a scarf wrapped around her palm. The weapon's sword function had begun to falter, the filament occasionally losing its piezoelectrically maintained stiffness, the molecular cutting mechanisms losing some of their efficacy. The whiphound had ghosted through granite as if she was cutting air with a laser, but now towards the end she had to strain every muscle to persuade the filament to keep working its way through the structural members. The ninth had been the worst; it had taken nearly half an hour just to cut partially through, so that the strut would give way when she detonated the whiphound in grenade mode.

'Is that enough?' she whispered, even though the sound of the buzzing, crackling whiphound seemed loud enough to render whispering pointless.

'It'd better be,' Parnasse said. 'I don't think that thing of yours is good for much more cutting.'

Thalia retracted the filament. 'No, I don't think it is.'

'I guess we'd best just thank Sandra Voi that that thing held out as long as it did. Only has to do one more thing for us now.'

'Two things,' Thalia said, remembering that she still intended to sabotage the polling core. 'Show me where we have to place it, anyway.'

'Anywhere around here should do the trick. A centimetre's not going to make the difference between life and death.'

Thalia placed the bundled whiphound under one of the weakened spars. 'Like here?'

'That'll do, girl.'

'Good. I should be able to find this spot when I come down again.'

'How does grenade mode work on that thing?'

Thalia eased aside the wrapping surrounding the shaft until she had revealed the whiphound's twist-controls. 'You twist that dial to set the yield. I'll turn it to maximum, obviously. It'll give us about point one to point two kilotonnes, depending on how much dust's left in the power bubble.'

'And time delay?'

'Those two dials there, in combination.'

'How long a delay will it give you?'

'Long enough,' Thalia said.

Parnasse nodded wordlessly. They had done what they could down there, and while it might have been possible to weaken one or two more struts, Thalia doubted that they had the time. The barricade teams were already reporting that the noise of the servitors was louder than it had ever been, suggesting that the machines were only metres from breaking through. Thalia had heard them while she had been cutting. They had begun to climb past the top of the stalk, into the sphere itself. *We've probably get less than an hour*, she thought. *Even thirty minutes might be pushing it now.* And that was without considering the war machines that she believed were planning to ascend the outside of the stalk, or even the inside of the elevator shaft.

Thalia and Parnasse climbed back through the forest of structural supports until they reached the ceiling door that led into the lowest inhabitable section of the sphere. A minute later they reached the floor of the polling core, where most of the party were now awake and nervous, aware that something was afoot but as yet ignorant of Thalia's plan.

They had questions for her, but before she spoke to them, Thalia moved to the nearest window and looked down towards the very base of the stalk. She noted, with a knife-twist of apprehension in her stomach, that the concentration of military-grade servitors was now much less than it had been before. It could only mean that most of the machines were now ascending the stalk, working with methodical inevitability towards the level of the polling core.

'Call off the work squad,' she told Caillebot. 'Tell them to drop what they're doing and get back up here.'

'Why?' he asked. 'What about the barricade? Someone needs to keep watch on it.'

'Not now they don't. It's served us well but we won't be needing it any more.'

'But the machines are getting close.'

'I know. That's why it's time we got out of here. Get the squad, Jules. We don't have time to debate this.'

He stared at her, frozen as if on the verge of framing an objection, then turned and descended the short staircase down to the next level, where the current barricade team was still doing what they could to reinforce the obstruction.

'What's going to happen?' asked Paula Thory, standing up from the sprawl of clothes that she had made into a makeshift bed.

'We're getting out of here,' Thalia said.

'How? You're not expecting us to climb down those stairs, are you? We can't very well fight our way past those machines.'

'We won't be fighting our way past anything. If all goes well, we won't have to deal with a single servitor. Before you know it, we'll be outside House Aubusson, in clear space, waiting to be rescued.'

'What do you mean, *in space*? None of us have suits! We don't have a ship. We don't even have an escape pod!'

'We don't need an escape pod,' Thalia said carefully. 'We're in one.'

Dreyfus noticed that Aumonier was clenching and unclenching her hands, her chest rising and falling with deep breaths. 'I thought you'd appreciate some company,' he said. 'In person, I mean.'

'Thank you, Tom. And yes, you're right. I do appreciate it.' She paused. 'I just issued that statement, by the way – including your remarks.'

'They needed reassurance.'

'They did. You were right.'

'Have we gone dark yet?'

'No – I'm holding off on removing network services until we've finished with the Spindle. I want the citizens to know that we're dealing with something bad, but that we're doing all in our power to keep as many of them safe as we can.'

'Won't seeing the Spindle nuked to kingdom come scare them half to death?'

'More than likely. But if it means they start listening to local constabulary, it's a price worth paying.'

Dreyfus looked at the largest screen. 'How long now?'

'Three minutes.'

Three minutes until the weevil flow hit the Toriyuma-Murchison Spindle, he thought. Panoply ships had done what they could to thin or deflect the flow, but their efforts had proved almost entirely ineffectual. They were only holding station now in case there were survivors after the *Democratic Circus* had done her work.

The deep-system cruiser hovered aft of the Spindle, two missiles locked on target and armed, dialled to a yield high enough to take out the as-yet-dormant machinery of the habitat's manufactory. Panoply had always had a contingency procedure in place for the act of destroying a habitat, and the crew would have run through such a scenario many times during training. The sequence, from the issuing of the command to the firing of the weapons, was supposedly immune to error. It required not just the authorisation of the supreme prefect, but also a majority of seniors. Mechanisms even existed to deal with the possibility of sudden changes in rank due to death or injury, so that the order could still be given even if there'd been a direct attack on Panoply.

And yet, Dreyfus thought, the crew wouldn't have been human if they didn't at least consider the possibility that the order was erroneous, or had originated through malicious action. They were being asked to do the one thing that cut against everything Panoply stood for. Like a surgeon putting out his hand to receive a scalpel, and being handed a gun instead.

But they'd do it, he thought. They'd allow themselves that one flicker of doubt, and then they'd get over it. The protocol was watertight. No mistake was possible: if the order had come in, then it was logically guaranteed that it had been issued by the supreme prefect herself, with the approval of her seniors.

The crew had no choice but to act upon it.

'One minute thirty,' Aumonier said. Then her tone shifted. 'Tom: I've been meaning to ask you something.'

'Go on.'

'It may be a difficult question. You may be uncomfortable about answering it truthfully.'

'Go on anyway.'

'Is something happening? Something I don't know about?'

'What kind of something?'

'I've been hearing sounds. I've been in this room for eleven years, Tom, so I've become quite astonishingly attuned to my surroundings. I've almost never heard any noises from elsewhere in Panoply, except for today.'

'What kinds of noises?'

'The kinds of noises people make when they're trying very hard to do something without making any sound. Something that involves heavy machinery and tools.' She faced him directly. 'Is something going on?'

He'd never lied to her, in all the years they'd known each other. Never lied, or bent the truth, even when that would have been the kinder thing to do.

Today he chose to lie.

'It's the mouth bay,' he said. 'The launching rack was damaged when one of the cruisers came in too hard. They've been working around the clock to get it back into shape.'

'The mouth bay is hundreds of metres away, Tom.'

'They're using heavy equipment.'

'Look at me and say that.'

He met her gaze steadily. 'It's the bay. Why? What else do you think it might be?'

'You know exactly what I think.' She glanced away. He couldn't tell whether he'd passed or failed the test of her scrutiny. 'I've been trying to get Demikhov to talk to me. He's using every excuse in the book not to return my calls.'

'Demikhov's been busy. That business with Gaffney—'

'All right, so he's been busy. But if you knew something was happening ... if you knew they were planning something ... you'd tell me, wouldn't you?'

'Absolutely,' Dreyfus said.

Except now.

'It's time,' she said, returning her attention to the display. 'Weevil contact in three ... two ... one. Impact is confirmed. They've made groundfall.' She raised her arm and spoke into her bracelet. 'This is Aumonier. Detach the *Bellatrix* and instruct her to proceed at full-burn. Repeat, detach the *Bellatrix*.'

They still had cam feeds from the docking hub of the Toriyuma-Murchison Spindle. Hundreds of people were still crammed into the boarding tubes, being ushered aboard the waiting liner. Dozens of constables, marked by their armbands, were assisting in the boarding process. Dreyfus already knew that many constables had elected to remain inside the Spindle rather than leave on earlier evacuation flights. A few hours earlier they'd just been ordinary citizens, going about their daily lives.

'*Bellatrix* is secured for space,' Aumonier said, reading a text summary on her bracelet. 'She's moving, Tom. She's undocking.'

The feed had locked on to a single boarding corridor. The viewpoint was from inside a transparent-walled tube filled with civilians, constables and servitors, floating in an unruly multicoloured jumble. The vast, white, porthole-sprinkled side of the *Bellatrix* loomed beyond the glass, huge and steep as a cliff. And the cliff was starting to move: pushing away from the tube with a dreamlike slowness. At the far end of the tube, hundreds of metres from the cam, Dreyfus made out a sudden puff of silvery white vapour escaping to vacuum. He presumed that the airlock doors had closed, but a small amount of air had been sacrificed into space.

The *Bellatrix* kept receding. He focused on the golden glow of her airlock. Formless debris spilled out. Something was wrong there, he realised. The liner's outer doors should have closed by now.

'Jane . . .' he began.

'They can't close the doors,' she said numbly. 'The locks on the *Bellatrix* are jammed. Too many people are trying to squeeze through.'

'It's not just the liner,' Dreyfus said.

Air was still rocketing into space from the end of the docking tube. But now it was carrying people with it, sucked out by the force of decompression. It started at the far end and then raced up the tube, towards the cam. Dreyfus watched in horror as the people nearest the cam realised what was coming. He saw them scream and reach for something to hold on to. Then it hit them and they were just *gone*, as if they'd been rammed down a syringe by an invisible plunger.

He watched them spill into space by the hundreds: civilians, constables, machines, clothes, possessions and toys. He watched the people-shaped things thrash and die.

The cam greyed out.

Another feed showed the *Bellatrix* turning, giving a view along its white flanks. The outrush from the open airlock had ceased. Interior doors must have closed.

'She's on drive,' Dreyfus said. The liner's quadruple engines cranked wide, spitting tongues of pink fire. The enormous vessel hardly appeared to move at first. Gradually, though, the slow but sure acceleration became apparent. The *Bellatrix* began to put distance between itself and the habitat. Departing from the Spindle's forward docking hub, the liner would have the entire bulk of the habitat between it and the fusion explosion when the missiles hit home.

Aumonier lifted her bracelet again. 'Connect me to the *Democratic Circus*,' she said, barely breathing before speaking again. 'Captain Pell: allow the *Bellatrix* to achieve ten kilometres. Then you may open fire on the habitat's aft assembly.'

Since the *Bellatrix* was maintaining a steady half-gee of thrust, it took only sixty seconds for the liner to reach the designated safe distance. By then, all surrounding habitats – those that hadn't already been taken by Aurora – were on a state of high defensive alertness, anticipating not just the electromagnetic pulse of each nuclear strike, but also the likely risk of impact debris. For Dreyfus the seconds slowed and then appeared to stall altogether. He knew that Aumonier would have preferred to give the liner more space, but she was mindful of the weevils escaping and doing more harm if they waited. The evacuees aboard the *Bellatrix* would just have to hope that the shielding between them and the engines would serve to protect them from the worst effects of the blast.

A voice, rendered small and reedy in transmission, spoke through her bracelet. 'Pell, Supreme Prefect. *Bellatrix* has cleared safe-distance margin.'

'You already have my authorisation to fire, Captain.'

'I just wanted to be certain that nothing'd changed, Ma'am.'

'Nothing's changed. Do your job, Captain Pell.'

'Missiles launched and running, Ma'am.'

The cam feed switched to a long-range view of the Toriyuma-Murchison Spindle. With distance foreshortened by the cam angle, the *Bellatrix* almost appeared to be still docked.

The missiles surged in, etching two bright streaks of exhaust fire, as if they'd gashed open space to reveal something luminous and clean behind it.

They detonated.

The nuclear explosion – the double bursts occurred too close in time to separate – whited out the cam view. There'd been no sense of the fireball expanding; it was just *there*, consuming everything in a single annihilating flash.

It happened in deathly silence.

All the displays in Jane's room flickered momentarily as the electromagnetic pulse raced across the Glitter Band.

Then the whited-out view dulled through darkening reds until the background blackness was again visible, and something mangled and molten was drifting there, something that had once been a habitat, but which now resembled more the blackened, tattered remains of a spent firework. The nukes had destroyed the manufactory, but in doing so they'd blasted away at least a third of the habitat's length, leaving the rest of the structure cracked open along structural fault lines. The air inside wouldn't have had time to escape through those cracks before it became searingly hot. No one would have had time to suffocate, either. But they'd have had time to see the fire surging towards them, even as that fire burnt the eyes out of their sockets.

If only for an instant, they'd have known what had been done to them.

'Status, Captain Pell,' Aumonier said.

'Initial indications suggest complete destruction of the manufactory. *Bellatrix* reporting minor damage, but no additional casualties. Likelihood of further survivors is ... low.'

'That's what I expected,' Aumonier said, with almost infinite resignation. 'Destroy the rest of the habitat, Captain. I don't want those weevils using it as a bridgehead even if they can't make new copies of themselves.'

Dreyfus felt the weight of what they had just done squeeze in on him like a vice. In the time since he had last blinked, thirty-five thousand people had ceased to exist. He couldn't focus on that kind of number, any more than he could focus on the nine hundred and sixty who had died in Ruskin-Sartorious. But he had seen the faces of the people in the Spindle's docking tube; he'd seen their inexpressible terror when they knew that the air was going to suck them out into space and they were going to die, unpleasantly, with their lungs freezing into hard, cold husks before their hearts stopped beating. The face of one middle-aged woman came back to him now, even though she'd just been one of many people squeezed into the boarding tube. She'd been looking directly into the cam, looking – so it seemed to him now – directly at him, her expression one of quiet, dignified pleading, placing her utmost faith in him to do something about her predicament. He knew nothing of that woman, not even her name, but now she came to stand in his imagination for all the good and honest citizens who had just been erased from existence. He didn't need to imagine her death multiplied by thirty-five thousand. The loss of one decent citizen was shame enough. That it had happened by Panoply's hand made it all the more repellent.

But that didn't mean Jane had been wrong to do it.

'I never thought I'd have to do this,' she said. 'Now I'm wondering if I've just committed the worst crime in our history.'

'You haven't. You did the right thing.'

'I killed those people.'

'You did what you were meant to do: think of the majority.'

'I haven't saved them, Tom. I've just given them time.'

'Then we'd better make it count, hadn't we? If nothing else, we owe it to the citizens of the Spindle.'

'I keep thinking: what if I'm wrong? What if they really will be better off under Aurora's government?'

'The people gave us the authority to protect them, Jane. That's what we just did.'

Jane Aumonier said nothing. Together they watched as Captain Pell finished off the rest of the habitat. Now that there was no possibility of sparing survivors, the yields were dialled as high as they could go. The blasts snipped the remains of the Spindle out of existence.

Perhaps it was Dreyfus's imagination, but he detected an easing in Aumonier's mood when the evidence of her actions had finally been erased.

'You know the hard part?' she asked.

Dreyfus shook his head. 'No.'

'The hard part is we have to do exactly the same thing to the Persistent Vegetative State. By the end of the day I'll be lucky if I have less than a hundred thousand dead on my hands.'

'They're not on your hands,' Dreyfus said. 'They're on Aurora's. Don't ever forget that.'

She came to them shortly afterwards. Her transmission rode a secure Panoply-restricted data channel, one that remained active when the public networks were silenced and the citizens roused from the great dream of abstraction. The incoming data signal was subjected to ruthless scrutiny, but it was free of any hint of concealed subliminal influence or embedded weaponry. After consultation with the supreme prefect, it was concluded that nothing would be lost by displaying the image to the seniors gathered in the tactical room.

They found themselves looking at a girl: a child-woman on a throne wearing elaborate brocaded clothes. Her parted hair was reddish-brown, her expression watchful but not hostile.

'It's high time we spoke,' Aurora said, in a strong, clear voice with excellent elocution.

'State your demands,' Jane Aumonier said, her projection addressing the image from her usual position at the table. 'What do you want?'

'I don't want anything, Supreme Prefect, except your absolute capitulation.'

'Keep her talking,' Dreyfus mouthed. Panoply's best network hounds were trying to backtrack the transmission all the way to Aurora herself, wherever she was hiding.

'You must have demands,' Aumonier persisted.

'None,' the child-woman said firmly, as if it was the answer to a parlour game. 'Demands would imply that I need something from you. That is not the case.'

'Then why have you contacted us?' asked Lillian Baudry.

'To make recommendations,' Aurora replied. 'To suggest a way in which this whole matter can be settled with the minimum of inconvenience to all parties, as swiftly and painlessly as possible. But make no mistake: I will succeed, with or without your cooperation. I am merely concerned that the citizenry should be subject to the least amount of disruption.'

'You sound very confident of success,' said Aumonier.

'It is a strategic certainty. You have seen how easily I can take your habitats. Each is a stepping stone to another. You cannot stop the weevils, and you will not fire on your own citizens except as an absolute last resort. Ergo, my success is logically assured.'

'Don't be so sure of yourself,' Aumonier replied. 'You are still in a position of weakness, and I have no proof that you haven't murdered all your hostages. Why shouldn't I assume they're all dead, and just destroy the habitats you now control?'

'Be my guest, Supreme Prefect. Go ahead. Fire on those habitats.'

'Give me proof that the citizens are still alive.'

'What would be the point? You would rightly distrust anything I showed you. Conversely, even if I showed you a smoking ruin, the corpses of a million dead, you would suspect an ulterior motive, that I was encouraging you to attack for nefarious reasons of my own. You would still not fire.'

'You're wrong,' Dreyfus said. 'You can convince us that the people are alive in one very easy way. Let us speak to Thalia Ng. We'll trust her testimony, even if we don't trust yours.'

Something crossed her face – a moue of irritation, quickly suppressed.

'You can't,' Aumonier said, 'because you've either killed her, or she's out of your control.'

One of the network analysts pushed a compad in Dreyfus's direction. He glanced at the summary. They had narrowed down Aurora's location to a locus of thirteen hundred possible habitats.

'My concern is for the absolute welfare of the citizens,' the child-woman said. 'Under my care, no harm will come to any of them. Their future security will be guaranteed, for centuries to come. The transition to this new state of affairs can be as bloodless you wish. By the same token, all casualties incurred during the transition will be upon your conscience, not mine.'

'Why do you care about people at all?' Dreyfus enquired. 'You're a machine. An alpha-level intelligence.'

Her fingers tightened on the edges of her armrests. 'I used to be alive. Do you think I've forgotten what it feels like?'

'But you've been a disembodied intelligence for a lot longer than you were a little girl. Call me judgemental, but my instincts tell me your sympathies are far more likely to lie with machines than with flesh-and-blood mortals.'

'Would you stop caring for the citizens if they were slower and weaker, stupider and frailer than yourself?'

'We'd all still be people,' Dreyfus countered. 'Tell me something else, Aurora, now that you've confirmed your origin. Are there more of you? Were you the only one of the Eighty who survived?'

'I have allies,' she said cryptically. 'You would be as unwise to underestimate their power as you would mine.'

'But for all that power, there's still something that scares you, isn't there?'

'Nothing frightens me, Prefect Dreyfus.' She said his name with particular emphasis, making it clear that she knew of him.

'I don't believe you. We know about the Clockmaker, Aurora. We know how it keeps you from sleeping at night. It's a machine intelligence stronger and quicker than you, even with your allies to back you up. If it got out, it would rip you to shreds, wouldn't it?'

'You overestimate its significance to me.'

'It can't be that insignificant. If you hadn't destroyed Ruskin-Sartorious, none of us would have been any the wiser that you were planning this takeover. You'd have achieved your goal in one fell swoop, taking the entire ten thousand at a stroke. But you were prepared to risk everything to remove the Clockmaker. That doesn't sound insignificant to me.'

The analyst drew his attention to the compad again. The locus of habitats had now shrunk to eight hundred candidates.

'If you had control of the Clockmaker, you would have turned it against me already.' She leaned forward slightly, her voice hardening. 'In truth, you neither control nor understand it. Even if it was in your possession, you would fear to use it.'

'That would depend on how much you provoked us,' Aumonier said.

'There has been no provocation. I have merely begun the process of relieving you of the burden of care of one hundred million citizens. I care about them more than you do.'

'You murdered nearly a thousand people in Ruskin-Sartorious,' Dreyfus answered. 'You killed the prefects sent in to regain control of House Aubusson. That doesn't sound like a very caring attitude to me.'

'Their deaths were necessary, to safeguard the rest.'

'And if it takes a million, or ten million? Would they be necessary deaths as well?'

'All that matters is that no one else need suffer. We have already discussed the inevitability of my success. If you resist me, people will die. People will die anyway, because people panic and do irrational things and I cannot be held accountable for that. But there is a way to bring this to an immediate conclusion, with the absolute minimum of fatalities. You have my takeover code: it's the instruction set your agent so helpfully installed in the first four habitats. Make it universal. Broadcast it to the rest of the ten thousand. I will have them all eventually; this way it will be with the least pain and bloodshed.'

'You're out of your mind,' Aumonier said.

'Then I shall give you an incentive. I am convinced that many millions of lives will be saved by speedy transition to my rule. So convinced, in fact, that I am prepared to sacrifice a certain number of citizens to underline my point. You have six hours, Supreme Prefect. Then I shall begin humane euthanisation of one in ten of the citizens already under my care.' The child-woman eased back into her throne. 'You may stop the deaths at any time by broadcasting the code to the ten thousand. If you choose not to, the deaths will continue. But my weevils will still give me the ten thousand, whatever you do.'

'One hundred and thirty habitats,' the analyst whispered in Dreyfus's ear. 'We're zeroing in.'

'Before I sign off,' Aurora said, 'let me assist you in one matter. Doubtless you are trying to localise the origin of this transmission. If you are employing your usual search methods, you will have narrowed the field down to between one hundred and one hundred and fifty habitats by the time I utter these words. Were I to stay on the line, you would locate my point of origin inside two minutes. I'll spare you the trouble, shall I? You will localise me to Panoply. I'm sure it's one of your candidates.'

Dreyfus looked at the analyst. The analyst nodded briefly, his face losing colour.

'I'm not really in Panoply. It's a mirror bounce; very difficult to crack in the time I'm giving you.' Aurora smiled slightly. 'Just in case you were thinking of turning those missiles on yourselves.'

It had never exactly been day in House Aubusson – the dust-smeared window panels hadn't let in enough light for that – but now even that half-daylight was sliding back into twilight, and another machine-stalked night would soon be upon them. Thalia supposed they had done well to last this long, but she could extract no comfort from the realisation. They had pushed their luck, that was all. They would not see another dawn unless they left Aubusson, and there was only one way that was going to happen.

She refrained from more detailed elaboration until Jules Caillebot had returned with the barricade squad. Paula Thory was almost incandescent with rage and incomprehension, and her mood was beginning to rub off on some of the others. But Thalia held her ground, standing with her arms folded in front of her. Nothing would be gained by showing even the slightest trace of doubt now. She had to appear in absolute command, utterly certain of success.

'We're leaving,' she said as soon as Parnasse and Redon managed to quieten the party. 'Cyrus and I have already made the preparations. We either do this or wait for the servitors to arrive. No one's going to rescue us in the meantime.'

'We can't leave,' Thory said. 'We're in a *building*, Prefect. Buildings don't move.'

Without answering her, Thalia walked to the architectural model. It was now resting on the flat, damaged surface of the transparent casing that had once covered it. Between them, Meriel Redon and Thalia had removed most of the structures surrounding the stalk, corresponding to the actual demolition work that had taken place overnight.

Thalia reached into her pocket and removed the white ball that represented the sphere of the polling core, dusted it against her thigh and placed it gently atop the stalk. 'For the benefit of anyone who hasn't been paying attention, this is us. Machines are trying to get at us through the stalk, and more than likely they're climbing up the outside as well. So we have to leave. Here's how it's going to happen.'

She touched a finger against the side of the ball and toppled it from the stalk. It dropped to the side and rolled away across the denuded grounds of the Museum of Cybernetics until it ran off the edge of the model and fell to the floor.

'Oh. My. God,' Thory said. 'You're insane. This isn't going to happen.'

'That ... doesn't look survivable,' said Jules Caillebot.

'It's not as bad as it looks,' Thalia said. 'For a start, we're not going to just drop half a kilometre. We're going to topple and roll. The sphere will travel down the side of the stalk, but it won't ever hit the ground. The stalk widens near the base and then flares out until it's almost horizontal. We'll be moving fast, but there's nothing to stop us rolling around the bend and continuing along a horizontal trajectory. It's going to be bumpy, sure, but with the momentum we'll have gained during the drop we should roll a long way, particularly as there isn't much left out there to slow us down. We can thank the robots for that. If they'd left the surrounding stalks in place, we wouldn't have a hope.'

'Girl's right,' Parnasse said, standing next to Thalia with his arms folded and a look on his face that dared anyone to contradict him. 'Structurally, the sphere'll hold. We can expect to roll two, three kilometres before we run out of momentum.'

'But surely we won't be able to just roll off the stalk like that,' said the young man in the electric-blue suit. 'What do you want us to do? Run back and forth until we topple over?'

'We've taken care of the rolling part,' Thalia said. 'Cyrus and I have weakened the connections between the stalk and the sphere. It'll hold for another hundred years as it is, but I'm going to give it a little nudge in the right direction with my whiphound. I'll set it to grenade mode, on maximum yield. It'll give us a pretty big bang. It should sever the remaining connections and push us in the right direction. We'll topple.'

'We'll be smashed around like eggs in a box,' Caillebot said.

'Not if we secure ourselves first.' Thalia indicated the metal railings encircling the polling core. 'You're going to strap yourselves to these guards, as tight as you can. Meriel's going to make sure everyone has enough clothing to do a good job. You'll need to be secure during the roll. I don't want anyone breaking loose when we end up upside down.'

'Maybe I'm missing something,' Caillebot said. 'You talk of us rolling two or three kilometres.'

'Correct,' Parnasse said.

'That isn't going to help us much, is it? By the time we've unlashed ourselves, the robots will have caught up with us again.'

Parnasse glanced at Thalia. 'I think you'd better tell them the rest, girl.'

'The robots won't be catching up with us,' she said.

Caillebot frowned. 'Why not?'

'Because we're not stopping. We said we could roll two or three kilometres. That should be enough to take us across the nearest window band.'

'Oh no,' Thory said, shaking her head. 'Don't even *think*—'

Thalia grimaced. She walked over to the woman and faced her down. 'Here's the deal, Citizen. I don't have a fully functional whiphound any more. If I did, I'd run you through some of the more interesting things I can do with it. But I do have a pair of hands. If you make one more remark, if you open your mouth to speak, even if you so much as give me a funny look, I'm going to wrap those hands around that fat neck of yours and keep squeezing until your eyeballs pop into your lap.'

'I think you'd better listen to the girl,' Parnasse said.

Thalia stepped back and resumed her earlier position. 'Thank you, Cyrus. Yes, we're going to roll across the window band. The band's pretty tough, I admit – it's already holding back air at atmospheric pressure, and it's designed to tolerate occasional stresses above and beyond its normal loading. It could withstand collision by a small ship, a volantor or a train coming off one of the bridges. But it isn't designed to cope with something as substantial as the sphere. Parnasse and I both agree that the band will collapse under our weight, allowing us to drop into open space.'

'Where we'll suffocate and die,' Caillebot said. 'Followed quickly by everyone else still inside House Aubusson as the air rushes out through the hundred-metre-wide hole we'll have just dropped through.'

'There's no one else to worry about,' Thalia said. 'We've kept it from you until now, but all the evidence at our disposal says that the machines have embarked on the systematic murder of all the other citizens. They've been rounded up, euthanised and shipped off to the manufactory to be stripped down and scavenged for useful elements.'

'You can't be certain that there are no other survivors,' said the woman in the red dress, her face pale.

Thalia nodded. 'No, we can't. Some other groups may have held out for a while. But we're the only party able to protect ourselves by virtue of being near the polling core. No one else will have had that security. There'll have been nothing to stop the machines storming everyone else en masse.'

'But what about us?' asked Cuthbertson, his mechanical owl still perched on his shoulder. 'We'll still need air, even if everyone else is already dead!'

'We've got it,' Thalia said. 'There's enough air inside here to keep us alive until we're rescued. It won't be going anywhere because the sphere's already airtight. Provided the portholes hold, we'll be fine. Internal doors will stop the air leaking out of the bottom of the sphere, where it used to meet the stalk. If there's a slow leak, we can live with it. Rescue should be on us within a few minutes of break-out, if my guess is right.'

'You're confident of that?' Caillebot asked.

'I'm even more confident that we won't have a chance against those machines when they break through.' Thalia planted a hand on her hip. 'That good enough for you, or do you want it in writing?'

Meriel Redon coughed. 'I know it sounds like madness, at first. That's what I thought initially when they told me about this plan. But now that I've had time to think things through, I see that this is the only way we're going to survive. It's roll or die, people.'

'How soon?' Cuthbertson asked.

'Very,' Thalia said.

'We need to think about it. We need time to talk it over, see if we can't come up with another plan.'

'You've got five seconds,' Thalia said, looking at him belligerently. 'Thought of anything? No, didn't think so. Sorry, but this *is* the plan, and there's no opt-out clause. I want you all to start securing yourselves. Anything you can't do, I'll help you with. But we haven't got time for a debate on the matter.'

'It's going to work,' Redon said, raising her arms to silence the party. 'But we have to do it fast, or those machines are going to be through to us before we know it. Thalia's given us a way out when we had nothing. Don't think for one second that I'm thrilled about what we're going to attempt, but I see that we have no choice.'

'What about the polling core?' Caillebot asked. 'Have you forgotten about sabotaging it?'

Thalia produced the whiphound, gripping it in a glove-wrapped hand. 'I'm going to take it down now. Then I'll head downstairs to see if I can hear any activity behind the barricade. If I don't, and there's no sign of the machines trying to break in elsewhere, then I may reconsider our escape plan. But if I decide to go ahead, I won't have time to come back up and tell you until we're almost ready to roll. You'd better assume that's what's going to happen.'

She stepped through the gap in the railinged enclosure, extending and stiffening the whiphound's filament. Without ceremony, she swung it into the polling core's pillar at chest height, straining to push it deeper until the resistance was too much. The core flickered in protest at the damage she was inflicting, fingers of sharp-edged black radiating away from the wound. She withdrew the filament and came in again, slicing at a different angle. The whiphound buzzed fiercely, the handle throbbing in her hand. Thalia sweated. If she failed to disable the core and somehow incapacitated the whiphound's grenade mode, it would all have been for nothing.

She removed the whiphound. Now most of the pillar was consumed by geometric black shapes. At some level it was still functioning – her glasses confirmed that there was still some low-level abstraction traffic – but she had certainly impaired it, perhaps to a degree where it would not be able to send coherent packets to the servitors. That would have to suffice. The marrow of quickmatter at the heart of the core would prove resilient against the whiphound, healing as the filament passed through it, and she could not risk overtaxing the weapon.

Thalia let the filament go limp and spool back into the handle. She had done all that she could.

'Let's see if we did any damage,' she said to Parnasse.

She left the polling core level, glancing back to make sure the citizens were all engaged in securing themselves to the railings. She was pleased to see that they were, despite the ramshackle nature of some of their bindings. There was some grumbling going on, some indignation, but Meriel Redon was doing her best to make them understand that there was no other way.

Maybe it wouldn't be necessary, she thought. Maybe taking down the polling core would be the end of it.

But when Thalia and Parnasse reached the top of the barricade, she knew that the machines were still alive. If anything they sounded louder and closer than ever. Thalia had the palpable impression that they were about to break through the obstruction at any second. The machines sounded enraged, their dim mechanical fury only doubled by what she had just attempted.

'Roll it is,' Parnasse said.

'Looks like it.'

They started jogging away from the barricade, towards the next set of stairs.

'Any idea why those things are still moving if we just took down the core?'

'Your guess is as good as mine, Cyrus. Could be they were uploaded with enough autonomy to keep functioning even without direct supervision. Could be I didn't damage the core enough. Could be they made another one, somewhere else. It isn't that difficult if you know the protocols.'

They reached the next level down and arrived at the trap door in the floor, still open as they had left it. Parnasse rolled up his sleeves, moving to lower himself into the gap ahead of Thalia.

'It's all right,' she said. 'I memorised the way pretty well the last time we came down here. You showed me where to place the whiphound. I'm sure I can find my way without you.'

'All the same, girl, I'm coming with you.'

'I'd rather you were back up with the others, Cyrus, making sure they do what they're told.'

'Redon's got them under control. I think you convinced them there was no other choice.'

Thalia had been striving to maintain a façade of certainty, but all of a sudden doubts magnified inside her. 'There isn't, is there?'

'Of course there isn't.'

'But what if I'm wrong?'

'Nothing could be worse than waiting for those bastards to break through. Even if this doesn't work, it'll be a hell of an improvement on being ripped apart by killer robots. At least we'll go out with style.'

'Even though there'll be no one to applaud our efforts?'

'We'll know, girl. That's all that matters.' He gave her an encouraging pinch on the arm. 'Now let's get that whiphound in place.'

They clambered through the tangle of intervening supports until they reached the area where the struts had already been weakened or cut through entirely.

'Thank our lucky stars this isn't quickmatter,' Parnasse said, 'or those cuts would have healed over by now. But the rules say you can't have quickmatter anywhere near a polling core.'

'I like rules,' Thalia said. 'Rules are good.'

'Let's unwrap the baby.'

Thalia removed the whiphound from its protective bundle. It was trembling, with parts of the casing beginning to melt from the heat. The smell of burning components hit her nose. 'Okay,' she said, twisting the first of the dials. 'Setting yield to maximum. Looks as if it's accepted the input. So far so good.' She paused to let her fingers cool down.

'Now the timer,' Parnasse said.

She nodded. She twisted the first of the two dials necessary to input the setting. It was stiff, but eventually the dial moved under her fingers until it reached the limit of its rotation. The double-dial fail-safe existed to stop the whiphound being set to grenade mode accidentally. 'Five minutes,' she said.

'It'll start counting as soon as you twist the other dial?'

Thalia nodded. 'It should give us enough time to get back upstairs and lashed down. If you want to go ahead now, to make sure—'

'I'm not going anywhere without you. Set the timer.'

Thalia took hold of the end of the whiphound and began to twist the other dial. It moved easily compared to the other one, clicking around through its settings. Then it stopped, long before it had reached the correct limit. Thalia tried again, but the dial would not pass beyond the point where it had jammed.

'Something's the matter,' she said. 'I can't get the second setting locked in. Both dials have to be reading three hundred seconds or it won't start the countdown.'

'Can I try?'

She passed him the whiphound. 'Maybe you can force that dial past the blockage.'

He tried. He couldn't.

'It's jammed pretty good, girl.' Parnasse squinted at the tiny white digits marked next to the dial. 'Looks like we're stuck at one hundred seconds, or less.'

'It isn't enough,' Thalia said. 'We'd never get back up and lashed down in one hundred seconds.'

'There's no other way of setting that counter?'

'None.'

Then something came over her, a kind of awesome calm, like the placidity of the sea after a great storm. She had never felt more serene, more purposeful, in her life. This was it, she knew. It was the point she had waited for, with guarded expectation, knowing it would arrive at some time in her career, but that she might not notice it unless she was both alert and open-minded. This was her opportunity to redeem whatever it was her father had done wrong.

'Girl?' Parnasse asked, for Thalia had fallen into a momentary trance.

'It's okay,' she said. 'We can still do this. I want you to leave now, Cyrus. Get back to the others and strap yourself down. Make sure you close all airtight doors on the way.'

'And you?'

'I'm going to wait a whole three hundred seconds. Then I'm going to complete what I came here to do.'

'Which is?'

Her voice trembled. 'Uphold the public good.'

'Is that right?' Parnasse said.

'Yes,' she answered.

'I don't think so, girl.'

She started to protest, started to raise her arm in defence, but Parnasse was faster and stronger. Whatever it was he did to her, she never saw it coming.

CHAPTER 27

Thyssen's face was slit-eyed and puffy when it appeared on Dreyfus's compad.

'I know you're meant to be sleeping now, and I apologise for disturbing your rest. But something's been nagging at me and I need to talk to you about it.' He neglected to tell Thyssen that the thing that had been bothering him had only revealed itself fully when he woke from his snooze.

'Is this urgent, Prefect?'

'Very.'

'Then I'll see you in the bay in five minutes.'

Thyssen looked surprisingly alert when Dreyfus arrived, feeling less than clearheaded himself. Thyssen was talking with his shift replacement Tezuka, the two of them peering through a window at the ongoing ship operations. Technicians were performing vacuum welds on the damaged hull of a cutter. Both men were sipping something from drinking bulbs.

'Prefect Dreyfus,' Thyssen said, breaking away from his conversation. 'You look like you could use some of this.' He offered Dreyfus the drinking bulb. Dreyfus declined.

'The ship Saavedra took,' Dreyfus said.

'You mean Saavedra and Chen.'

Dreyfus nodded: he'd forgotten that Thyssen hadn't been informed of Chen's murder. 'I'm just wondering why they took that one, out of all the choices they had. Am I correct in thinking that cutter was a Type B?'

'Correct,' Thyssen said. 'Most of the new vehicles are Type C or D. They don't have the—'

'Transatmospheric capability,' Dreyfus finished for him. 'That's what I reckoned.'

'Since the segregation of security responsibilities between Chasm City and the Glitter Band—'

'Prefects hardly ever need to take a ship into Yellowstone's atmosphere. And all that aerodynamic bodywork makes for fuel-draining mass that we don't need in normal duties. I know. But we still keep a small number of transat vehicles on readiness, in case we do need them.'

Something clicked behind Thyssen's eyes. 'You think they've gone to Yellowstone.'

'It's a possibility. I need you to look into your logs. I'm going to give you the names of some prefects and I want you to correlate those names against the vehicles they've signed out for routine duties. Can you do that for me?'

'Yes. Immediately.'

'Here are the names.' Dreyfus handed Thyssen his compad, allowing him access to the area where he had input the identities of the eight Firebrand operatives. Thyssen retired to an office space, Dreyfus shadowing him, and transferred the names into his own compad with a finger stroke.

Thyssen chucked his bulb into the wall and conjured a console. 'I'm checking the logs right now. How far back do you want me to go?'

Dreyfus thought of the likely activity that would have preceded the destruction of the Ruskin-Sartorious Bubble. Moving the Clockmaker and its associated relics – including any equipment required to study them – would have certainly required more than one trip.

'Two months should do it.'

'Conjure yourself a coffee, Prefect. This is going to take a couple of minutes.'

Thalia woke with the worst headache she could remember, one that felt as if someone had driven an iron piton into the side of her skull. She was just beginning to speculate on the precise origin of that pain when she became aware of less intense discomfort afflicting almost her entire body. It was difficult to breathe, and her arms were tugged so far behind her back that she felt as if her shoulders had been dislocated. Something squeezed her chest. Something hard dug into her spine. She opened her eyes and looked around, wondering where she was and what had happened to her.

'Easy,' said Meriel Redon, who appeared to be bound in a similar position next to Thalia: sitting on the ground with her back against the railings that encircled the polling core, her arms crossed and bound behind one of the uprights. 'You're okay now, Prefect Ng. You took a bad bump on the head, but there's no bleeding. We'll get you checked as soon as we're out of this.'

Through a curtain of pain, Thalia said, 'I don't remember. What happened?'

'You were down in the basement, getting ready to set the timer on your whiphound.'

'I was,' Thalia said foggily. She had a groggy recollection that there had been some kind of problem with the whiphound, but the details refused to sharpen.

'You banged your head on one of the struts, knocking yourself out.'

'I banged my head?'

'You were out cold. Citizen Parnasse carried you back up here on his own.'

The events began to come back to her. She remembered the second timing dial jamming, how she had come to the decision that she would have to detonate the whiphound manually. She remembered that awesome calm she had experienced, as if every trifling detail in her life had just been swept aside, leaving a breathtaking clarity of mind, as empty and full of possibility as the clear dawn sky. And then she remembered nothing at all, except waking up here.

'Where is Parnasse?'

'He went back down to set the timer,' Redon said. 'He said you'd shown him what to do.'

'No—' Thalia began.

'We're expecting him back any minute. He said he'd be able to tie himself down when he arrived.'

'He isn't coming back. There was a problem with the whiphound, with setting the five-minute fuse. I didn't bang my head. Parnasse must have knocked me out.'

Redon looked puzzled. 'Why would he have done that?'

'Because I was going to set it off myself, while I was still down there. It was the only way. But he wouldn't let me. He's decided to do it himself.'

Comprehension came to Redon in horrified degrees. 'You mean he's going to die down there?'

'He isn't coming back up. I showed him how to set the whiphound. He knows exactly what to do.'

'Someone has to go down there, tell him not to do it,' Redon said. 'He can't kill himself to save us. He's just a citizen, just one of us.'

'When did he go?'

'Quite a long time ago.'

'He can't set the fuse for longer than a hundred seconds. There's no reason why he needs to wait that long, if he's in place.'

'You mean we could go any second?'

'If the whiphound works. If the machines haven't already broken through and stopped him.' She knew she ought to feel gratitude, but instead she felt betrayed. 'Damn him! He shouldn't have brought me back up here. It wasted too much time!'

'Maybe it wouldn't be a bad idea if one of us—'

Redon never got to finish her sentence. Judging by the force of the blast, felt through Thalia's spine as it transmitted itself through the fabric of the polling core sphere, the whiphound must have detonated at nearly its maximum theoretical yield. It had been a new unit, she remembered belatedly: she'd checked it out of the armoury only a couple of weeks ago. There would still have been a lot of energy left inside it, anxiously seeking release.

The sphere rocked appreciably: Thalia saw the landscape tilt and then settle again at its former angle. The blast had been very brief: a spike of intense sound followed by a few seconds of echoing repercussions. Now all was silent again. The sphere was still. The landscape outside was still.

'It didn't work,' she said. 'We're not moving. It didn't fucking work.'

'Wait,' Caillebot said quietly.

'It didn't work, Citizen. We're not going anywhere. The blast wasn't sufficient. I've failed you, used up our one chance.'

'Wait,' he said.

'Something's happening,' Cuthbertson said. 'I can hear it. It sounds like metal straining. Can't you?'

'We're tilting,' Redon said. 'Look.'

Thalia craned her neck in time to see the white ball of the model polling core sphere roll across the floor, towards the window facing them.

From somewhere below there came a kind of twanging sound, as if the energy stored in a stretched spar had just been catastrophically released. The twanging sound was followed in quick succession by another, then a third, and then a volley of them too close together to count.

The tilt of the floor increased. Thalia felt her weight beginning to tug on the upright to which she was bound. The sphere must have been at ten or fifteen degrees to the horizontal already. She heard another series of metallic sounds: shearing and buckling noises, less like the failure of structural components than the cries of animals in distress.

The angle of the tilt reached twenty degrees and continued increasing.

'We're going over,' she said. 'It's happening.'

Loose clothes and debris skittered across the floor, coming to rest along the curve of the outer wall. The architectural model slid noisily, then shattered itself to pieces. Thirty degrees, easy. Thalia felt an unpleasant tingling in her stomach. The landscape was tilting alarmingly. Through the windows, she could see aspects of the surrounding campus that had been obscured before. Suddenly it looked much further down than she had been imagining. Five hundred metres was a long way to fall. She remembered Caillebot's reaction when she'd outlined the plan: *That doesn't look survivable.*

Maybe he'd been right all along.

Now the tilt was increasing faster. Forty degrees, then forty-five. Thalia's arms felt as if they were being wrenched out of their sockets, but it was only the effect of her bodyweight so far. When the sphere started rolling, it was going to get much worse. Fifty degrees. The lower extremity of the stalk was beginning to come into view through the windows. In one brief glimpse she knew she'd been right about the war machines. They covered it like a black mould, reaching as high up the shaft as it was possible to see. They must have been very close to the sphere itself.

Something gave way. Thalia felt the sphere drop several metres, as if the upper part of the stalk had crumbled or subsided under the changing load. And then suddenly they were rolling, pitching down the side of the stalk, the angle of tilt exceeding ninety degrees and then continuing to climb. The sphere shook and roared. There was no time to analyse the situation, or even judge how far down the stalk they had rolled. There was only room in Thalia's head for a single, simple thought: *It's working . . . so far.*

She felt a momentary increase in the forces tugging at her body and judged that the sphere had reached the base of the stalk and changed its direction of roll from the vertical to the horizontal. She tried to time the duration of each roll, hoping to judge the distance they had travelled and detect some evidence that the sphere was slowing. But it was hopeless trying to concentrate on such matters.

'I think,' she heard Caillebot call out, between grunts of discomfort, 'that we've cleared the perimeter.'

'Really?' Thalia called back, raising her voice above the juggernaut rumble of their progress.

'We're still rolling pretty fast. I hope we don't just bounce right over the window band.'

It was a possibility neither Thalia nor Parnasse had considered. They'd guessed that the sphere would have enough momentum to reach the edge of the band, but they had never thought about it moving so fast that it would skim right across, moving too quickly to stress the window enough to break. Now Thalia realised that they were open to the awful possibility that the sphere might traverse the entire window band and come to a rolling halt on the next stretch of solid ground.

'Can you see the band yet?' she asked.

'Yes,' called out Meriel Redon. 'I think I can. But something's wrong.'

'We're coming in too fast?'

'Not that. Shouldn't we be rolling in a straight line?'

'Yes,' Thalia said. 'Aren't we?'

'We seem to be curving. I can see the window band, but we're approaching it obliquely.'

Thalia was confused and worried. They'd always assumed that the sphere would follow a straight course once it reached the base of the stalk, with only minor deviations caused by obstacles and friction. But now that she concentrated on the tumbling landscape and tried to make out the grey line that marked the edge of the window band, she knew that Redon was right. They were clearly off-course, at far too sharp an angle to be explained by the sphere crashing through the remains of the campus grounds.

'I don't understand,' she said. 'We went over this. It should be a straight roll all the way to the window band.'

'We're still going to hit the window band,' Cuthbertson said, his voice reduced to a strangled approximation of itself. 'You've just forgotten about Coriolis force.'

'We should be moving in a straight line,' Thalia said.

'We are. But the habitat's rotating, and it's trying to get us to follow a helical trajectory instead. It's all about reference frames, Prefect.'

'Coriolis force,' Thalia said. 'Shit. After everything they taught me in Panoply, I forgot about Coriolis force. We're not on a planet. We're inside a fucking spinning tube.'

She'd become aware that the rate of roll was diminishing, the landscape cartwheeling around at half the speed from when they had begun the journey. She could begin to pick out details, landmarks that the Aubusson citizens had already noted.

'We'll be okay,' Cuthbertson said. 'We're just going to hit a different part of the window band than we were expecting.'

'Will that make any difference?' she asked.

'Don't think so. We should break through as easily there as anywhere else.'

'Any second now,' Meriel Redon said. 'We're coming up on the band. Get ready, everyone. There's going to be a jolt when we hit the edge of the land strip.'

Thalia braced herself, in so far as bracing was possible when she was already bound like a sacrificial offering. She felt a moment of giddy vertigo as the sphere rolled over the edge of the landscape strip and crashed down onto the vast glassy plain of the window band. The ride became eerily smooth as they trundled over the geometrically perfect surface. With little friction save air resistance, the rate of roll was holding more or less steady.

'Break,' Thalia whispered. 'Please break. And please let us be airtight when it happens.'

Dreyfus knocked on the door to the tactical room before stepping through. A certain deference was advisable. Dreyfus knew that his Pangolin clearance put him on a level footing with the seniors in some respects, but he saw no point in rubbing salt into that particular wound.

'Dreyfus,' Baudry said, breaking off from whatever discussion she'd been having with the other seniors. 'I'm afraid you're too late. You've just missed the demise of the Persistent Vegetative State.'

Without sitting down, Dreyfus moved to a position close to the Solid Orrery. The number of red lights hadn't changed since last time he'd seen it, but he could draw no consolation from that, knowing what it had cost just to slow Aurora's advance. 'How many'd we get out?'

'One hundred and seventeen thousand, out of a total population of one hundred and thirty. Not bad, all things considered, especially as we were basically dealing with corpses.'

'We've now concentrated our evacuation efforts on the targets we think Aurora will go for next,' Clearmountain said. 'Our monitors show that the weevil flows are already changing direction, now they know the Spindle and the PVS are out of the picture.'

'You mean "nuked",' Dreyfus said.

'Whatever. So far, though, we can't say where the flows are most likely to hit next. There are a number of possible candidates. Unfortunately, none of them are habitats where we've already started evacuating. We're starting from scratch.'

'Where are the evacuees going?'

He could tell from their reactions that his question wasn't a popular one. 'In an ideal world, we'd ship them far across the Glitter Band, well beyond Aurora's expansion front,' Clearmountain said. 'But even with the high-burn liners, that would involve an unacceptable round-trip delay. Our only practical strategy has been to move the citizens to relatively close habitats, so that the turnaround time can be minimised.'

'Go on.'

Clearmountain cast a glance at the other seniors. 'Unfortunately, Aurora's projected front is now beginning to impinge on some of the habs where we've been moving people.'

'I see.'

'Which means that when we start evacuating those habs, we're also going to have to shift the recent refugees. With our current resources the situation is borderline containable, but as the front expands, and the number of endangered habitats grows geometrically, the refugee burden will soon become the predominant limiting factor.' Clearmountain offered his palms in a gesture of well-intentioned surrender. 'Some tough calls may have to be made when that happens, Prefect Dreyfus.'

'Today we nuked two occupied habitats. We've already made tough calls.'

'What I mean,' Clearmountain said, with a strained smile, 'is that we may have to focus our activities where they can do the most good.'

'Isn't that exactly what we're already doing?'

'Not to the degree that may shortly become necessary. In the interests of maximising the number of citizens we can evacuate away from Aurora's takeover front, we may have to prioritise assistance to those citizens least likely to hinder our efforts.'

'I see where you're going. You think we should leave the coma cases to die.'

'It's not as if they'll know what hit them.'

'All those citizens went into voluntary coma on the understanding that the PVS would be looking after them, and that Panoply would be standing by if the PVS failed in its care. That was a promise we made to those people.'

Clearmountain looked exasperated. 'You're worried about breaking a promise to a citizen with the brain functions of a cabbage?'

'I'm just wondering where this ends. So the coma cases are inconvenient to us. Fine, we lose them. Who's next? Citizens who can't move as fast as the rest? Citizens we just don't like the look of? Citizens who maybe didn't vote the right way the last time there was a poll on Panoply's right to arms?'

'I think you're being needlessly melodramatic,' Clearmountain said. 'There *was* a reason for this visit, wasn't there, other than to cast doubts on an already complicated evacuation programme?'

'Clearmountain's right,' Jane Aumonier said, her image speaking from her usual position at the table. 'The coma cases are a blessed nuisance, and we'd have a much easier time of it if we just pulled life-support on the lot of them. They're going to retard our evacuation programme and therefore increase the danger to the rest of the citizenry. But Tom's even more right. If we cross this line just once – if we say these citizens matter less than those citizens – we may as well hand Aurora the keys to the kingdom. But we're not going to do that. This is Panoply. Everything we stand for says we're better than that.'

'Thank you,' Dreyfus said, his voice a hushed whisper.

'But we can't let the coma cases impose too heavy a drag on the evacuation programme,' Aumonier continued. 'That's why I want them dealt with *now*, so we won't have to worry about them in the future. I want them leapfrogged well ahead of the front – out of the Glitter Band, even, if we can identify a suitable holding point.'

'That'll tie up ships and manpower,' Baudry said.

'I know. But it has to be done. Do you have any suggestions, Lillian?'

'We might consider an approach to Hospice Idlewild. They're used to dealing with sudden influxes of incapacitated sleepers, so they should be able to handle the coma cases.'

'Excellent proposal. Can you sort that out?'

'I'll get right on it.' After a lengthy pause she said, 'Supreme Prefect Aumonier . . .'

'Yes?'

'It's been nearly six hours now. Since Aurora's transmission.'

'I'm well aware of that, thank you very much.'

'I'm just saying . . . given what we now know of her capabilities . . . and the difficulties we're having with the evacuation effort, and the finite number of nuclear devices in our arsenal—'

'Yes, Lillian?'

'I think it would be prudent at least to consider Aurora's proposal.' Her words came out awkwardly, the strain written in her face. 'If her success is guaranteed, then we have an onus to do everything we can to protect the citizenry during the transition phase. Aurora has threatened to start euthanising citizens in the habitats she already holds. I believe she will follow through on that threat unless we broadcast the takeover code to the rest of the ten thousand. If we wish to save as many lives as possible, we may have no choice but to comply with her demand.'

'I don't think we're quite ready to hand her the keys to the castle,' Dreyfus said, before anyone else had time to respond to Baudry's words.

'With all due respect, Field Prefect Dreyfus—' she began exasperatedly.

'With all due respect, Senior Prefect Baudry, shut up.' Dreyfus looked pointedly away from Baudry, to Clearmountain. 'I dropped by for a reason, and it wasn't to rubber-stamp our surrender. You have any objections if I commandeer the Orrery for a moment?'

'If you need to run the Orrery, you have authorisation to conjure a duplicate in your quarters,' Clearmountain said.

'Let him run it,' Aumonier said warningly. 'What have you got for us, Tom?'

'It may be nothing. On the other hand, it may be a clue to the present location of the Clockmaker.'

Aumonier lifted an eyebrow. He hadn't briefed her in advance, so she was as much in the dark as everyone else in the room. 'Then I think you should continue, with all haste.'

'I'll need to wind back a few hours. Everyone happy with that?'

'Do what you need to do,' Aumonier said.

Dreyfus began to spin back the Solid Orrery to the point when he had begun tracking Saavedra's cutter. 'Let's remind ourselves what we're looking at here,' he said, as the timetag digits reversed themselves. 'The Orrery's more than just a real-time record of the disposition of the Glitter Band and its habitats. It also shows Yellowstone. That isn't just some static representation of what the planet looks like from space. It's a constantly changing three-dimensional image, pieced together from countless orbital viewpoints.'

'We're well aware of this,' Clearmountain said.

'Hear him out,' purred Aumonier.

'Everything that happens on Yellowstone, the Orrery keeps a record of it. Changes in the weather, the cloud colouration ... it all goes into the memory. Even those rare occasions when the clouds clear to reveal the surface. But there's more to it than that.' The digits froze: the Orrery had wound back to the time of Saavedra's flight. Dreyfus dabbed a finger into the jewelled disc of the Band. 'Here's Panoply.' He moved his finger a few centimetres to the right. 'Here's the last known position of Saavedra's vehicle before she dropped beyond our sensor horizon. In clear space we'd have been able to track her at a range of several light-seconds, even with her hull stealthing. But it's hopeless in the thick of the Band, even more so with the present crisis, and Saavedra knew it.'

'You said we lost her,' Aumonier said. 'Has something changed?'

'Saavedra told me I had no hope of chasing her since there were no other ships ready to go. She was bluffing – maybe there were no other ships fast enough to catch her, but there were certainly other vehicles that had more fuel and heavier weapons loads.' Dreyfus looked up from the Orrery. 'So I did some nosing around. Turns out the Firebrand operatives – I presume you've all been briefed concerning Firebrand? – have been using a lot of transat vehicles lately, even signing them out for duties that wouldn't require that capability. Now, why would they do that?'

'You think they've moved the Clockmaker to Yellowstone,' Aumonier said.

Dreyfus nodded. 'That's the way it's looking. Of course, that's not particularly useful data in and of itself. It's a big planet with a lot of hiding places.'

'So why didn't they take the Clockmaker there first, instead of using the Ruskin-Sartorious Bubble?' Baudry asked.

'Because it would have been much more risky,' Dreyfus said. 'Visiting the Clockmaker in the Bubble was so easy that they kept it up for nine years without any of us suspecting. But it's a lot more difficult to conceal flights in and out of Yellowstone. They must have looked on it as a temporary holding point until they could prepare somewhere else in the Band. But then Aurora made her move.'

'This is good work, Tom,' Aumonier said. 'But the point still holds. Neither Panoply nor the local enforcement agencies have the resources to comb the whole planet looking for a secret hide-away, especially not now.'

'We don't have to comb. I think I know exactly where they are.' Dreyfus indicated the night-time face of Yellowstone in the Solid Orrery. It was almost entirely black, except for a cold blue flicker of frozen lightning at the southern pole. 'Saavedra's ship was stealthed, but nothing's truly invisible, not even a nonvelope. To avoid being pinned down, Saavedra had to move quickly and exploit gaps in CTC's tracking, just like any prefect on sensitive business.'

'How does that help us?'

'It means her options were limited when she hit atmosphere. I'm sure she'd have preferred to come in slowly, but that would have meant spending too much time in near-Yellowstone space. So she came in hard and fast, using the atmosphere itself as a brake.'

'And we got a hit,' Aumonier said.

Dreyfus smiled. Jane was one step ahead of him, but he liked it that way. He felt as if the two of them were a double act, feeding each other lines so that they both looked better before the other prefects. The others must have thought that the whole performance had been rehearsed.

'The cams detected this flash,' Dreyfus said, letting the Orrery scroll forward to the point he had tagged. A tiny pink spot of light waxed and waned near Yellowstone's equator. 'It matches the expected entry signature for a cutter-sized vehicle moving at about the same speed Saavedra had just before she dropped out of range. It's her, Seniors.'

'Ships are coming and going from Yellowstone all the time,' Clearmountain said.

'But not that fast. Most ships come in slow, settling down into the atmosphere on controlled thrust. And there's hardly been any routine traffic since the supreme prefect polled for the use of emergency powers. People are keeping their heads down, hoping this will all blow over.'

'But an entry point is just an entry point,' Baudry said.

'Agreed. I can't rule out the possibility that Saavedra travelled a lot further within the atmosphere. But if she did, planetary traffic control didn't pick her up. I think she came in hard and fast close to her destination.'

'But there's nothing there,' Baudry said. She craned her head slightly. 'I can see the weather pattern over Chasm City, on the sunward face. Unless my knowledge of Stoner geography's seriously flawed, Saavedra came in thousands of kilometres from any other settlements.'

Dreyfus sent another command to the Orrery. 'You're right, Lillian. The nearest surface community would have been Loreanville, eight thousand kilometres to the west. But Firebrand wouldn't have been interested in Loreanville, or any of the domed settlements: there'd have been too much local security for them to continue their activities.'

'So where was she headed?'

'Clear to surface,' Dreyfus told the Orrery. The quickmatter envelope of the planet's atmosphere dissipated in a puff, revealing the wrinkled terrain of Yellowstone's crust. It was an icy landscape riven with fissures and ridges, spotted here and there with simmering cold lakes, lifeless save for the hardiest of organisms capable of enduring the toxic chemistry of the methane-ammonia atmosphere.

'There's still nothing there,' Baudry said.

'Not now. But there used to be.' Dreyfus gave another command and the surface became dotted with a dozen or so vermilion symbols, each accompanied by a small textual annotation.

'What are we looking at, Tom?' Aumonier asked.

'The sites of former Amerikano colonies or bases, predating the Demarchist era. Most of these structures and digs go back three hundred years. They've been ruins for more than two hundred.' There was no need for him to labour the point: Saavedra's entry trajectory had positioned her directly above one of the abandoned colonies. 'Now, this could be coincidence, but I'm inclined to think otherwise.'

'What is that place?' Aumonier asked.

'The Amerikanos called it Surface Operations Facility Nine, or Ops Nine. If they had another name for it, we have no record of it.' Dreyfus shrugged. 'It's been a long time.'

'But not so long that there isn't still something there.'

'Firebrand wouldn't have needed a fully operational base, just somewhere to hide the Clockmaker and keep an eye on it. An abandoned facility would have served them adequately.'

'But is there anything there at all, after all this time?'

'Not much on the surface according to the terrain maps, but the old records say Ops Nine went down several levels. This is quite a stable area, geologically speaking. The subsurface areas may still be relatively intact: even to the extent that they'll still be airtight.'

Clearmountain blew out slowly. 'Then we'd better get a task force down there immediately. There may be nothing in this, but we can't take that risk. Our top priority is to secure the Clockmaker.'

'All due respect, Senior,' Dreyfus said, 'but I wouldn't recommend any kind of visible response to this intelligence. Since nothing's happened so far, we can be reasonably sure that Aurora hasn't made the same deductions we have. But if we start retasking assets – sending deep-system vehicles into the atmosphere – Aurora's going to see that and wonder what's got us so interested in an abandoned Amerikano base.'

'And I wouldn't expect her to take long to put two and two together,' Aumonier said. 'No: Tom's correct. We need to respond, but it has to be a covert approach. We need to secure and protect the Clockmaker before Aurora even has a *hint* as to what we're up to. That rules out any mass concentration of assets or personnel.' She paused heavily. 'But someone will still have to go in. I'd volunteer to do it – I've already survived direct contact with the Clockmaker – but for obvious reasons my participation isn't an option.'

'We wouldn't risk you anyway,' Dreyfus said. 'You were a field when you encountered the Clockmaker back then. It's still a field's job to go in now.'

'But it doesn't have to be you.'

'This has been my case from the moment I spoke to that Ultra captain. I propose talking with it.'

'It doesn't talk. It kills.'

'Then I'll just have to find some common ground. A negotiating position.'

Clearmountain looked appalled. 'Even if that means giving it something in return?'

'Even if.'

'I won't permit it.'

'Then I suggest you start looking into alternative career options.

I don't think Aurora's going to have a lot of use for senior prefects when she takes over.'

Someone knocked at the door. Dreyfus recognised the girl – she was the operative who'd informed the tactical room of the hostile action taken by the first four habitats claimed by Aurora.

'Bad news for us again?' he asked.

'Sirs, I'm not sure,' she said, looking nervously at the strained faces of the seniors. 'I was asked to bring this to your immediate attention. There's been a development in the House Aubusson situation.'

'What kind of development?' Dreyfus asked, secretly dreading her answer.

'Sirs, I have imagery obtained by the deep-system cruiser we have on monitoring standby near Aubusson.' With shaking hands, she placed a compad on the table. 'There's been a pressure breach, a major one. Air's blasting out through a hundred-metre-wide hole in one of the window bands.'

Dreyfus snatched the compad across the table, flipping it around to face him. He made out the sausage-shaped habitat, a jet of cold, grey air geysering out from its side.

'The cause of this breach?'

She was facing Dreyfus now, answering him to the exclusion of everyone else present, even the supreme prefect herself. 'Sir, it appears something crashed through the window band. The cruiser's tracking a metal object, a sphere, moving on a slow free-fall trajectory away from the habitat.'

Dreyfus's throat was very dry. 'The nature of this object?'

'Unknown, sir, but it doesn't resemble any orthodox space vehicle or weapons system. The cruiser's asking permission, sir.'

'Permission for what?'

She blinked. 'To fire, sir. To destroy the unknown object.'

'Over my dead fucking body,' Dreyfus said.

'We can't be too careful,' Clearmountain replied. 'This could be another part of Aurora's takeover strategy.'

'It's Thalia.'

'How can you be so sure? We don't know what Aurora might have planned.'

'She's been using weevils to spread her influence from habitat to habitat,' Dreyfus answered. 'Why would she change, put all her eggs in one basket, when her existing strategy's working just fine?'

'We can't guess what she has in mind.'

'I can. She's going to keep using force of numbers, the way she already has. Whatever this is, it isn't part of her plan.'

'Which doesn't automatically mean it's anything to do with Thalia Ng,' Baudry said. 'I'm sorry to remind you of this, but we have no evidence that she survived the initial takeover phase.'

'If we think they're all dead, why haven't we nuked Aubusson already?'

'Because there's a chance, however small, that the citizenry may still be alive. But that doesn't necessarily imply that Thalia is amongst the survivors.' Baudry offered Dreyfus a sympathetic look. 'I know this is tough on you, but we need to take the rational view. How likely is it that Thalia Ng is behind this development, whatever it represents? We don't even know what the object is, let alone how it came to smash through the habitat. Thalia was just a single deputy field, Tom. She knew a lot about polling cores, and I don't doubt that she'd have done her best to protect the citizens, but we have to be realistic about the chances of her succeeding. She had next to no experience in high-risk field situations. Correct me if I'm wrong, but isn't it true that she'd only participated in a single lockdown before all this happened?'

'I know Thalia,' Dreyfus said. 'She'd have done whatever it took.'

'Tom, I know you mean well, but we can't afford to let this foreign object—'

'Put me through to the deep-system cruiser,' Aumonier said, cutting over Baudry.

The operative touched settings on her bracelet. 'Connection should be open, Supreme Prefect.'

'This is Jane Aumonier,' said the projected figure. 'To whom am I speaking?'

A woman's voice crackled across the room. 'Captain Sarasota, Supreme Prefect. How may I be of assistance?'

'I believe you're tracking something, Captain, something that emerged from House Aubusson?'

'We have a weapons lock on it, Supreme Prefect. We can fire at your command.'

'I'd rather you didn't do that, Captain. Maintain your maximum defensive posture, but approach the unidentified object close enough to sweep for infrared hotspots. I want to know if there are survivors aboard that thing.'

'And if there are?'

'Bring them in. As fast as you can.'

CHAPTER 28

Dreyfus fastened the safe-distance tether with an unshakeable conviction that this would be the last time he performed the action. Either he would not be coming back from Yellowstone, or Jane Aumonier would not be waiting for him here, in this weightless room, upon his return. The significance of either outcome caused his hands to shake as he locked the catch into place.

'How long before you leave?' Aumonier said as Dreyfus came to a halt.

'Thyssen says there'll be a ship fuelled and prepped within thirty minutes.'

'A deep-system cruiser, I take it?'

'No, I opted for a cutter. The amount of armament's immaterial. All that matters is that we sneak in unobserved.'

'We, Tom?'

'Pell will fly me to the drop-off point. I'll walk the rest of the way.'

'Walk?' she asked, frowning. 'No one said anything about walking.'

'There's no other way. Firebrand will have Ops Nine guarded against the approach of any unauthorised vehicle. But if Pell drops me over their sensor horizon, I should be able to walk in without triggering the perimeter defences.'

'How will you know where their sensor horizon ends?'

'They want to stay hidden, so their coverage will be necessarily limited. They won't be floating drones up in the air to spy on someone approaching overland.'

'You hope.'

'I'll take my chances. If you could clear the paperwork for a Breitenbach rifle, that would help.'

'Take whatever you want from the armoury,' Aumonier said

dismissively. 'If I could spare a nuke, I'd give you one of those as well.'

'Not on my kit list, but would you really give me one if I asked?'

'Probably, but with misgivings. The problem is we don't have an inexhaustible supply, and we need to make sure we curtail all weevil production when we take out a habitat.'

'How many nukes do you have left?'

Aumonier glanced away: he could tell that she'd rather he hadn't asked that particular question. 'We're down to our last fifty warheads. For some of the larger habitats on the evacuation front we'll have to use three or four to guarantee total destruction of all manufactory centres. It's bad enough that we're driven to this, Tom. But no one ever imagined Panoply would need more than a few dozen nukes, even in the worst crisis scenarios we ever imagined.'

Dreyfus smiled thinly. 'Can we make more nukes?'

'Not on a useful timescale. We've put in so many safeguards to stop people making these horrors that it's going to take days of frantic red-tape cutting before we can even begin to utilise civilian manufactories. They won't come through in time to help us, I'm afraid.'

'If we had another weapon to use against the evacuated habitats, would we consider it?'

'You mean something with the destructive potential of nukes?' Aumonier shook her head sadly. 'There just isn't anything in our arsenal, I'm afraid. If we deployed every foam-phase warhead we have, we might be able to destroy a single habitat. But it would take hours, and we'd always run the risk of missing a chunk of functioning manufactory, something with the capacity to keep churning out weevils.'

'I wasn't thinking about our armoury,' Dreyfus said. 'I was thinking about the people we blamed for starting this whole thing in the first place.'

'I'm not following you, Tom.'

'The Ultras,' Dreyfus said. 'We've already had a comprehensive demonstration that one of their ships can destroy one of our habitats, no problem. Granted, Ruskin-Sartorious was one of the smaller states, but I think the principle still applies. They can help us, Jane.'

'Will they go for it?'

'We won't know unless we ask,' Dreyfus said.

She looked down, surveying her weightless form, the tips of her dangling feet. Dreyfus wondered if she had noticed the thin, red scratch of the laser that was now cutting across her body just below her neckline. If she had cause to raise a hand, she would notice it shining across her wrist. Demikhov's guillotine was in place, the laser's sub-millimetre accuracy good enough for surgical purposes, so Dreyfus had been informed. If the laser happened to transect her throat above the upper extremity of the scarab, and if all other physiological parameters were satisfactory, Demikhov would initiate the decapitation process. Demikhov had even argued against Dreyfus visiting Aumonier in person, for he would not trigger the blades while another prefect was in the same room. Dreyfus understood that, and that his presence was therefore not in Aumonier's best interests. But he'd had an overwhelming need to see her before he left.

'I don't want to keep you, Tom,' she said hesitantly. 'But before you go—'

He cut her off, more out of nerves than intention. 'There's been no news from Captain Sarasota?' he asked.

'I'm still waiting. Her last report said that there appeared to be thermal signatures consistent with survivors, but they won't know until they've docked with it and cut a boarding aperture. I've no idea what the hell that thing is, but I suppose we'll find out soon enough.'

'It's not done anything hostile, has it?'

'No. On that score your intuitions were correct.'

There was a silence. Dreyfus was conscious of the ship waiting for him down in the bay, almost ready for departure. As little desire as he had to be aboard it, he knew that he could not delay. It might take many hours to reach Ops Nine, but every minute was critical.

'You were about to say something,' he said. 'Then I interrupted you.'

Aumonier could not meet his eyes. 'This is difficult for me.'

'Then save it for later. I'm not planning on staying down there.'

'It can't wait until later, unfortunately. This whole business with the Clockmaker has precipitated something I had hoped to avoid for a very long while. Perhaps for ever. I've had to make a very difficult decision, Tom. Even now, I don't know if what I'm about to do, what I'm about to say to you, is the right thing.'

'Perhaps you should just say it and see how things go.'

'Before you board the ship, I'm going to make a document

available to you. I'll have it transferred onto your compad.'

'You want me to read a document?'

'It isn't that simple. You have Pangolin clearance now, but this is a matter above Pangolin. You'll need Manticore.'

'I don't have Manticore.'

'But I can grant it to you. The choice will be yours as to whether you use it or not.'

'Why should I hesitate?'

'Because of what's in that document, Tom. It probably won't come as a great surprise if I tell you that it concerns the last Clockmaker crisis, and what happened to the Sylveste Institute for Artificial Mentation. By implication, it concerns Valery.'

'I understand.'

She answered very gently. 'No, you don't. Not yet. Not until you've read the contents. Something happened back then, Tom, that was personally very difficult for you.'

'I lost my wife. It doesn't get any more difficult than that.'

Aumonier closed her eyes. He could sense the distress this was causing her. 'What happened in SIAM was . . . not what was entered in the public record. There were good reasons for this. But you chose not to live with the facts as they were.'

'I don't understand.'

'You were more closely involved in the Clockmaker affair than you have led yourself to believe these last eleven years. After the crisis, you were . . . troubled. You could no longer function as an effective prefect. You recognised this yourself and requested the appropriate remedial action.'

Though he was floating weightless, Dreyfus had the impression that he was falling down a deep, dark shaft, into invisible depths.

'What do you mean?'

'Selective amnesia was applied, Tom, at your request. Your memories of the Clockmaker crisis were forcibly suppressed.'

'But the records say I was nowhere near SIAM,' Dreyfus protested.

'The records were incorrect. Since so much of what happened that day was destined to remain secret anyway, it was an easy matter to place you elsewhere. It was done with my full authorisation.'

Dreyfus knew she wasn't lying. She had no reason to, not now. The stress of speaking the truth was almost ripping her in two.

'And the missing six hours? What happened with the *Atalanta*?'

'It's all in the document. Take Manticore and you'll understand why we had to lie. But understand that it was the truth that nearly broke you. I've spent eleven years protecting you from the memories you wanted suppressed. In return, I've got back the best field prefect I could ever have asked for. But now I have to give you the key, so you can unlock them again.'

'Will digging up the past really help?' Dreyfus asked, his own voice sounding small and childlike.

'I don't know. But I can't let you go down there without knowing everything there is to know about the Clockmaker. Ultimately, though, the choice has to be yours.'

'I understand.'

'I'm sorry I have to do this to you, Tom. If there was any other way in the world ...'

He looked at the thin red line etched across her throat like a premonitory scar. 'You don't have anything to apologise for.'

Captain Pell was talking to Thyssen when Dreyfus arrived in the pressurised observation platform overlooking the nose bay. Pell had already been briefed on the general nature of the mission, though not its precise objective.

'We'll make our approach into the atmosphere just like any other ship on its way to Chasm City,' Dreyfus said. 'But once we're under cover of the clouds, you fly me to the other hemisphere. Can you do that without Aurora picking up our movement?'

'Nothing's guaranteed,' Pell said. 'If we go supersonic, and she happens to have sensors pointed down at the right part of the sky, she may see the disturbance in the atmosphere caused by our Mach cone.'

Dreyfus didn't welcome the news, but he'd been expecting it. 'Then we'll have to hold subsonic. How long will that take?'

'Eight, nine hours, depending on the trajectory. Too long for you?'

'It's still faster than using surface transportation, even if I could get closer than Loreanville.'

Pell tapped a stylus at the compad he held in the crook of his arm. 'There are some deep canyon systems we can use for cover. I may be able to take us supersonic for brief periods, using the canyon walls to soak up most of our shockwave.'

'Just give me the fastest approach you can consistent with our staying hidden from orbital surveillance.'

'You want me to drop you right on the doorstep of that place?'

Dreyfus shook his head. 'I'm not expecting a warm welcome

when I get there. You'll have to assess the terrain and put me down as close as you can without risking detection by anti-ship systems. If that means I have to walk twenty or thirty klicks overland, so be it.'

'It's your call, Prefect. I'll try to pick a spot where you'll have an easy approach.'

'I know you'll do your best, Captain, but I'm not expecting miracles.' Dreyfus glanced through the nearest window at the waiting form of the cutter, a flint-like wedge of black poised on the end of its launch rack. 'Are we good to go?'

Pell nodded. 'We can move out as soon as we're aboard and lashed down.'

'There's a surface suit aboard?'

'Everything you asked for on the checklist, and as many weapons as Thyssen's people could cram into the remaining space.'

'I'm hoping it won't come to a gunfight,' Dreyfus said, 'but I'll take what I can get.'

He was about to board the ship when an internal prefect came rushing into the observation area, braking himself to a halt against a restraining strap.

'Prefect Dreyfus!' the man called. 'I'm glad I caught you, sir. We were told you're shipping out and that you'll be out of comms range. But you need to hear this before you go.'

'Is it about Thalia?'

The man smiled. 'She's alive, sir. She's alive and well and she's managed to get a whole party of Aubusson citizens out of that place.'

'Thank God.' Despite his nerves, Dreyfus couldn't help smiling as well. 'I want to speak to her. Is she back yet?'

'Sorry, sir. We need that deep-system cruiser out there for the time being.'

'But she's okay?'

'We have reports of minor injuries, sir, nothing worse than that. But Thalia had some bad news for us. It looks like there are no other survivors from Aubusson.'

'None?'

'It wasn't the decompression, sir. According to Thalia the servitors inside the habitat have been rounding people up and killing them for hours. She doesn't think anyone else made it through the night.'

'Thank you,' Dreyfus said. 'You'll make sure the supreme prefect is informed, won't you? If Aubusson is depopulated, she needs to know. It could make all the difference.'

'She already has the intelligence, sir. Is there anything else?'

'Just this: I want you to pass on a message to Thalia Ng when she gets back to Panoply. Tell her I was very pleased to hear that she made it out in one piece. Tell her that I'm very proud of her actions. Tell her that she's a credit to the organisation, and that I look forward to telling her that in person.'

'I'll see the message gets through, sir.'

Dreyfus nodded. 'You do that for me.'

Pell boarded the cutter first, sealing the flight-deck passwall while Dreyfus attended to the organisation of his suit, weapons and equipment, satisfying himself that everything he had requested was present. It was a more complicated ensemble than could be created by a standard suitwall. There had been no oversights, he was glad to see. If anything, the technicians had stocked more armour and weapons than he could ever have hoped to carry. It was all lashed down or fixed into place via conjured restraints. He resisted the urge to suit-up now; there would be time enough for that during the long subsonic flight to the drop-off point, once they were safely inside Yellowstone's atmosphere.

Dreyfus felt a tightness in his stomach. It was fear, moving back in like an old lodger.

He felt the cutter move on the rack. He buckled in for launch, wishing he had remembered to shave. His neck hairs rasped against his collar and he could smell his own sweat seeping out of his pores.

His bracelet chimed. It was Jane Aumonier, as he had anticipated.

'They say we should remain out of contact once you've cleared Panoply,' she said, 'just in case Aurora can eavesdrop on our long-range comms.'

'It's a sensible precaution.'

'Concerning the matter we discussed, Tom – the document is now available on your compad. There's also a package under your seat. I had it loaded aboard before you arrived. You'll know exactly what it is when you open it.'

'I've made my decision,' Dreyfus said. He was on the verge of adding something, feeling that he ought to wish Aumonier well, but he did not want to risk her guessing Demikhov's intentions. 'I'll see you back in Panoply,' he said.

The cutter surged forward. He waited until the vehicle had ramped up to full thrust and then carefully loosened his webbing. He reached under the seat and found the package Aumonier had mentioned. It came loose with a gentle tug. He settled the black box onto his lap, allowing the cutter's thrust to hold it in place. The box was unfamiliar, but his fingers located a catch and the lid sprang open easily.

Dreyfus examined the contents.

The box contained six boosters of the same basic type that maintained his Pangolin clearance. He took one of them out. The label on the side read: *Manticore clearance. To be self-administered by Senior Prefect Tom Dreyfus only. Unauthorised use may result in neurological injury or permanent irreversible death.*

He felt as if he was holding a bomb in his hands, and the bomb had just stopped ticking.

'Senior Prefect Dreyfus,' he said, mouthing the words as if there must have been some mistake.

But he knew there hadn't been.

The thrust sequence ended. The cutter was now in free fall and would remain so until it commenced its braking phase prior to atmospheric insertion. Through the window he'd sketched in the wall upon his arrival, Dreyfus saw that they had already cleared the main orbits of the Glitter Band. Habitats of all shapes and sizes crowded upon each other, sliding silently through space as if they were the ornamented, treasure-bedecked barques and argosies of some marvellous flotilla. The clear space between them, which he knew was at least fifty or sixty kilometres, looked too narrow to allow the passage of a single cutter. He could see now, with a forcefulness that had never really struck him when staring into the Solid Orrery, that it would be the simplest matter in the world for Aurora to spread her infection from state to state. Her weevils had almost no distance to cross. The habitats were stepping stones towards total dominion.

And yet nowhere in his line of sight was there the slightest evidence of the crisis itself. Even if it now encompassed thirty or fifty habitats, including those on the fringe of the evacuation effort, that was still much less than a hundredth of the total number of states under Panoply's protection. The serene panorama before him looked startlingly normal, like a snapshot of the Glitter Band during the most routine of days. And yet he recalled the swiftness with which Lillian Baudry's simulation had demonstrated the takeover could spread. No comfort could be extracted from this apparent normality.

Satisfied that the cutter would not be making any high-acceleration swerves for now, Dreyfus replaced the Manticore box beneath his seat and propelled himself through the cabin. He knocked quietly on the passwall before letting himself through into the flight deck.

'Thanks for getting us away in good time, Captain Pell,' he said, before his eyes took in the fact that Pell was not alone on the flight deck. Sitting behind and to his left, in one of the other flight positions, was Sparver.

'Hi, Boss.'

Dreyfus was too stunned to feel anger, or even annoyance that his orders had been disobeyed. 'What are you doing here?' he asked.

Sparver looked at Pell. 'Now, I ask you – is that any way to talk to your deputy?'

Aumonier floated alone, striving to keep her thoughts on the matter at hand rather than Dreyfus's mission to Yellowstone. She had cleared all but four display facets in her sphere, and had enlarged those until they filled almost the entire facing hemisphere. They showed the four habitats where Thalia Ng had performed the initial upgrade to the polling core software: Carousel New Seattle-Tacoma, the Chevelure-Sambuke Hourglass, Szlumper Oneill and House Aubusson. No contact had been made with any of these states since the installation of the core patch, more than twenty-six hours earlier. All along, Aumonier had assumed that the citizenry were alive and well, albeit under some new and possibly repressive system of government. She had always assumed that if Aurora wished to kill those people, she would achieve it the easy way, by depressurising the habitat or tampering with the life-support in some equally decisive fashion. It was only now that Aumonier realised the fatal flaw in her thinking. Aurora had indeed wanted those people dead: not because she hated them, not because they were capable of derailing her plans, but because they were of no conceivable use to her. And yet, as Thalia's debriefing testimony made clear, Aurora had been at pains to conceal her murder of the citizenry from the outside world. It had to be done the old-fashioned way, the historical way: not with a single catastrophic release of air or heat, something that would have been detectable from afar, but with the apparatus of state: armed force, applied via her new army of servitors. The citizens had been rounded up, pacified with lies and then executed by machine. And then their remains had been shovelled into bigger machines and conveyed to the matter-consuming furnaces of the manufactories, where they were smelted down and made into parts for other machines.

Aumonier cursed the way Aurora had manipulated her unwillingness to strike against habitats that she still believed contained living citizens. But without Thalia's escape with her tiny party of survivors, she would still not have known. There was probably no one left alive in any of those four habitats. Even if some survivors had managed to hide or hold out against the machines, Panoply could do nothing for them now.

Well, there was one thing, Aumonier reflected. It could end their torment now, before the machines reached them. It was not much of a kindness, but it was the only one she had left to give.

'Captains Sarasota, Yokosuka, Ribeauville and Gilden. This is Jane Aumonier. You have my permission to open fire on your designated targets.'

This time there was no questioning of her order, no doubt that she meant what she had said.

'Nukes deployed and running,' Gilden said.

'Deployed and running,' Yokosuka reported.

'Deployed and running,' Sarasota and Ribeauville said, in near-unison.

Aumonier closed her eyes before the first flash reached her. Even though she was only seeing a monitor feed, the brilliance of the nuclear explosions – twelve in all, three per habitat – still pushed through her eyelids. She counted twelve pink flashes.

When she opened her eyes, nothing remained of the targets except four slowly expanding nebulae: the atomised, ionised remains of what had once been homes to more than two million of her citizens. There'd been beauty and misery in those habitats, wonder and sadness, every facet of human experience, history reaching back two hundred years. Between one breath and the next all that had been wiped out of existence, like a delirious dream that never happened.

'Forgive us,' she said to herself.

*

A little later, she received confirmation that the weevil flows from Aubusson and Szlumper Oneill had both been curtailed. The weevils that had been manufactured just before the attack were still crossing space, but their predicted destinations were already subjects of the evacuation effort. Aumonier knew that they would not clear all the citizens out in time, that they would be doing well to remove seventy per cent of them before the weevil contamination infected another habitat. Nothing more could be done, given the limiting bottlenecks of airlocks and ships and round-trip travel times. Her best people had been on the problem around the clock, and she had no doubt that they had already squeezed the last fraction of a percentile out of that figure. Attempts were now under way to mobilise enough ships to change the orbits of habitats lying beyond Aurora's current expansion front, but the technical challenge of moving a billion-tonne city state was awesome, and Aumonier knew that this was not a solution she could count on in the long term. At best, it would just take the weevils a little longer to reach their targets.

Her bracelet chimed. She glanced down and saw that it was the call she had been hoping for.

'This is Baudry, Supreme Prefect.'

'Go ahead, Lillian.'

'We're receiving reports from CTC.' Aumonier heard a catch in Baudry's voice. 'They're tracking massive ship movements from the Parking Swarm. Dozens of Ultra vessels, Supreme Prefect. Lighthuggers leaving their assigned orbits in the Swarm.'

'Are they leaving the system, Lillian?'

'No.' Baudry sounded flustered. 'Some of them, yes. Most of them ... no. Most of them appear to be on vectors that will bring them into the Glitter Band.'

'How long until they arrive?'

'Six to seven hours, Supreme Prefect, before the lead vehicles enter Glitter Band airspace. If we are to consider a tactical response, we need to start making arrangements now. Deep-system vehicles will need to be retasked, fuelled and weaponed in readiness—'

'You consider this a hostile gesture?'

'What else could it be? They've had designs on control of the Glitter Band for decades. Now that we're facing a crisis, they've seen their moment. They're going to use the Aurora emergency to stage a takeover of their own.'

'I don't believe so, Lillian. I actually requested assistance from the Ultras. I sent my plea to Harbourmaster Seraphim. I'd heard nothing from him since Dreyfus's departure, so I assumed ... but I assumed wrongly, I think.' Aumonier paused, conscious that it had been a mistake not to inform the other seniors of her contact with Seraphim. 'Have any attempts been made to speak to the incoming ships?'

'Standard approach queries were transmitted, Supreme Prefect. No valid response has been received.'

'That doesn't mean anything. We're dealing with Ultras here. They have their own way of doing things.'

'But Supreme Prefect ... we have to assume the worst.'

'I'll assume the worst when I have evidence of hostile intent. Until then, no one so much as fires a ranging laser on one of those ships. Is that clear?'

'Clear,' Baudry said sullenly.

'Lillian, we have less than forty nuclear devices left in our arsenal. Do you honestly think we'd get very far if it came to open war against the Ultras?'

'I'm just saying ... we can't trust them. We've never been able to trust them. That's always been a cornerstone of our operational policy.'

'Then maybe it's time we got a new cornerstone. They're people, Lillian. They might be people who make us uncomfortable, people with very different values from ours, but when we're facing local extinction at the hands of a genocidal machine intelligence, I don't think the differences between us look massively significant, do you?'

'I'll keep you informed,' Baudry said.

'You do that. I'm not having the best of days here, Lillian, and the one thing I'm sure of is that we really, really don't want to add any new enemies to our list.'

She closed the connection with Baudry and allowed her hand to drift down from her mouth. As it did so, she saw the red scratch of the laser cut across her cuff. She had been aware of that thin line for some hours now, without allowing herself to be distracted by pondering its purpose. Now, however, there was a window in her schedule. The Ultra ships would not arrive for six or seven hours. Dreyfus would take even longer to reach Ops Nine.

She had time to ponder.

She raised the bracelet again and spoke softly. 'Put me through to Doctor Demikhov.'

He answered almost immediately, almost as if he'd been watching her place the call. 'Supreme Prefect. This is a surprise.' Aumonier smiled: for all his talents, Demikhov was a poor liar. 'I wasn't expecting to hear from you.'

'Doctor,' she said, 'perhaps I'm mistaken, but I can't help feeling that you have something planned for me.' She waited a handful of seconds, listening to his breathing. 'I'm right, aren't I? This laser, which wasn't here yesterday. The noises Dreyfus did his best to explain away. What's going to happen, Doctor?'

After a silence that made her wonder whether the link had been broken, Demikhov said, 'It's best if you don't know.'

'You're probably right. It's not as if I've ever had cause to doubt your clinical wisdom, after all. But I just wanted to say something.'

'Go ahead,' Demikhov answered.

'I've done all I can for the next few hours. If you're intending to remove the scarab, now might be the best time to try it.'

'There'll be risks.'

'Just as there are risks in allowing it to remain clamped on my neck. I know the score, Doctor.'

'After the procedure we have in mind,' Demikhov said hesitantly, 'there's a possibility that you may be incapacitated.'

'In which case Senior Prefect Clearmountain will assume temporary authority. But only until I'm fit to resume command. Don't keep me out of it for too long, Doctor. All I need is a pair of eyes and a mouth to give orders. Understood?'

'Understood,' he answered.

'Then I urge you to execute whatever plan you've been putting in place. You are good to go, aren't you?'

'We're good to go.'

'Then do your best, Doctor. I'm submitting myself to your care.'

'If I fail—' he began.

'You'll still have my undying gratitude. Now get this fucking thing off my neck.'

'You're in position,' Demikhov said. 'Please don't move a muscle, Supreme Prefect. Not even to answer me.'

Jane Aumonier held her breath. She heard something go *click*.

CHAPTER 29

Doctor Demikhov watched events unfold with a curious sense of retardation, as if he was replaying one of his simulations at half normal speed. The blades pushed through the weakened part of the wall and raced together, their cutting edges forming a tightening circle with the supreme prefect at the precise centre. Aumonier floated motionlessly, her expression unchanging: she did not have time to react to the blades' intrusion into her private space. They closed on her, reaching her throat and passing cleanly through, interlocking with micron precision as they met. Demikhov was now forced to take in two distinct views, captured from cams in the two isolated halves of the former sphere. In the upper hemisphere, the supreme prefect's severed head began to drift away from the blades with almost imperceptible slowness. In the lower hemisphere, her body and the scarab drifted in the opposite direction. In the same decelerated timeframe, Demikhov saw the scarab react to the violent intrusion of a large foreign object into its volume of denial. The lower part of Aumonier's neck, below the cut, puffed apart in a cloud of pink and grey. Blood continued to spurt from the neck in inky profusion. The heart was still pumping. The drifting remains of both the decapitated body and its damaged parasite were quickly obscured.

Demikhov's attention flicked to the upper sphere. Time accelerated. The head's slow drift became an ungainly tumble. The head was also leaking blood, albeit with much less ferocity than the body.

Servitors rushed into both chambers, moving too quickly for the eye to follow. The machines reached the scarab, detached it from the neck and encased it in a cocoon of blast-smothering quickmatter. In the upper chamber, machines reached the head and arrested its motion away from the shining floor formed by the blades.

'Scarab is neutralised,' reported one of Demikhov's analysts. 'Repeat, scarab is neutralised. Upper chamber is now secure for crash team.'

'Go,' Demikhov said, with all the urgency he could muster.

And then he too was moving as if his own life depended upon it.

He was only slightly behind the crash team when he arrived at the head. The servitors had braced it, pinning it gently in place between telescopic manipulators. There'd been a temptation to simply immerse the head in a vat of curative quickmatter, but Demikhov had resisted. The quickmatter would undoubtedly stabilise the head, flooding the brain to preserve neural structure, and would make a start on the necessary tissue-repair. The drawback was that the quickmatter would most likely wipe short-term memories and delay the return to full consciousness by many days. Demikhov had considered every angle and knew that this was a time when hard-won clinical judgement, the cumulated knowledge of his own eyes and experience, outweighed the easy option.

He meant only to look at the neck, to judge the accuracy of the cut and assess the damage to the major structures. He saw instantly that the blades had transected the cervical vertebrae between C3 and C4, as he had always hoped. The cut had been so accurate that only the cartilaginous disc between the bones had been destroyed. The carotid artery, internal and external jugular veins and vagus nerve had all been severed within a millimetre of his optimum cut points. Had he been looking at a simulation, Demikhov would have rejected it as unrealistically optimistic. But this was reality. Zulu – this stage, at least – had worked as well as he could have dreamed.

Then he looked at the face. He didn't mean to. It was clinically irrelevant, and he'd told himself to pay no heed to any signs of apparent consciousness he saw behind Jane Aumonier's eyes. But he couldn't help it. And there was something there: a sharpness in her gaze, a sense that she was focusing on no one in the room but him, that she was utterly, shockingly aware of her condition.

Less than ten seconds had passed since the blades had gone in.

'Begin stabilisation,' Demikhov said. 'Plan three-delta. We have a job to do here, people.'

He risked another look at the eyes. This time there was a fogged absence where a mind had been.

*

It took three hours to fall towards Yellowstone. The cutter could have made the journey in a third of the time, but then it would have appeared to be moving anomalously fast, running the risk of attracting Aurora's attention. Dreyfus could not be certain of the extent of her surveillance, but it was likely that she would be alert to any traffic that appeared to be out of the ordinary, be it civilian or law-enforcement. As much as it pained him to watch the clock ticking, he knew that the slow and unobtrusive approach was necessary.

'Captain says to buckle up,' Sparver said, prompting Dreyfus to put aside the compad he'd been studying. 'We'll be slowing for atmosphere in about five minutes.'

Dreyfus nodded curtly. 'You can tell him you passed on the message.'

Sparver had braced himself with an arm and a foot. 'You still sore at me for sneaking aboard?'

'What do you think?'

'I had Jane's blessing. Who else do you think put that stuff under your seat?'

'I expressly requested that I go in alone,' Dreyfus said.

Sparver shrugged, as if none of this was his fault, merely the outcome of a series of circumstances beyond his control. 'Look, it's done. I'm aboard. So make the most of me.'

'I will. You can keep Pell company when he flies this cutter back to Panoply.'

'Actually, I intend to keep you company during that little stroll you've got planned.'

'Then it's a pity we didn't load two surface suits, isn't it? I only requested one, I'm afraid. And it wouldn't fit you anyway.'

'Which is why I had a word with Thyssen and asked him to stow a spare,' Sparver said. 'The extra weapons were my idea as well. You didn't think you were going to carry them all on your own, did you?'

Dreyfus sighed. He knew Sparver meant well, and that there was no other prefect he'd sooner have at his side than his own deputy. But he had resigned himself to going in alone. Now that he had crossed that mental Rubicon, he could not easily accept the idea of placing another's life at risk.

'Sparv, I appreciate the gesture. But like I said to you before, you're one of the few people who have been following this investigation since the outset. I cannot in conscience accept that you should be placed at risk. Especially not—'

'Save it for later, Boss,' Sparver said. 'There's no secret now. Jane and the other senior prefects know everything we do. We've just become expendable again. And isn't that a wonderful, liberating feeling?'

'You're right,' Dreyfus answered forcefully. 'We are expendable. And you know what? We probably won't come back from this mission. If the Clockmaker doesn't get us, Firebrand or Aurora will.'

Sparver lowered his voice. For once he was serious. 'So why are you doing this, if it's guaranteed to fail?'

'Because there's a chance it will succeed. Not much of one, but it's better than any other option on the table.'

Sparver nodded at the compad. 'Does that have anything to do with all this?'

'I don't know.' Dreyfus turned the compad around so that Sparver could see the display, with its dyslexia-encrypted read-out. 'This still makes as much sense to me as it does to you, and you don't even have Pangolin, let alone Manticore.'

'Did Jane give you Manticore?'

Dreyfus nodded humbly. 'Not that it's made any difference to me yet.'

But that was a lie, albeit a small one. Dreyfus had to stare hard at the scrambled text, but every now and then he'd feel a premonitory sense of something about to reveal itself, like a kind of mental hiccup that never quite arrived. The text was still illegible, but he recognised the feeling from his Pangolin exposure. The neural architecture necessary for the decoding stage was beginning to assemble. It might take another six or nine hours until it was fully functional, but the process was already beginning to affect his comprehension.

'But it'll come, eventually?' Sparver asked.

'That's the idea.'

'What does she want you to know, Boss?'

'How should I know if I can't read this yet?' Dreyfus snapped.

'She must have given you an idea.'

'She did.'

'It's about the Clockmaker, I assume.'

'Yes,' Dreyfus said tersely. 'It's about the Clockmaker. Now would you mind leaving me alone with it so I at least have a chance of making some sense of this before we land?'

'It's all right,' Sparver said, with more sympathy than Dreyfus felt he deserved. 'I understand, Boss. If it's about the Clockmaker, then it's also about Valery, isn't it?'

'Valery died,' Dreyfus said. 'I'm over her death. Nothing in this is going to change that.'

Sparver had the good sense to leave him alone after that.

The braking phase commenced shortly, entailing several minutes at high burn. When it had subsided, Dreyfus was experiencing nearly full gravity and the cutter had already begun to ease its way into the upper atmosphere of Yellowstone. This was no fiery insertion, nothing like Paula Saavedra's high-speed re-entry, but rather a progressive submergence into thicker and thicker air, with the cutter using its engines to avoid excessive aerodynamic friction. To a casual observer, they would look like one more passenger ship returning to Chasm City from the glitz and glamour of the orbital communities.

Dreyfus found himself dozing. It was something to do with Manticore making him sleepy while it worked on his mind. He did not feel markedly different when he woke, but when he resumed his perusal of the compad, he knew that he had taken another step closer to comprehension. Now whole phrases kept slipping in and out of clarity, like animals prowling behind tall grass. He saw:

Sylveste Institute for Artificial Mentation . . .
Emergency measures instituted during Clockmaker crisis . . .
Prototype ramscoop vehicle, mothballed but otherwise intact . . .
Heavy Technical Squad boarded and assumed command . . .
Ramliner Atalanta *deemed functional . . .*
Containment effect of magnetic field . . .
Risk of civilian casualties reduced, but not eliminated . . .
Unavoidable losses . . .
Assignment of emergency powers to Field Prefect Tom Dreyfus, authorised by Supreme Prefect Albert Dusollier . . .

And then he felt something open in his mind, like a heavy trap door, one that had been shut and forgotten for eleven years. He saw Valery's face, lit up with childlike delight, kneeling in soil, turning to him from the bed where she had been arranging flowers.

And he knew that he had done a very bad thing to his wife.

*

Mercier watched the proceedings from the elevated observation room overlooking Demikhov's dedicated operating theatre. Though the theatre had been fully equipped since its inception, it had seen few occupants in all that time. Demikhov's team had occasionally employed it to rehearse a surgical procedure, but they had usually done so under the assumption that the scarab would be removed by more conventional means, leaving Aumonier with only superficial injuries. It was only lately that the theatre had been staffed around the clock, with the crash team preparing for the increasingly likely eventuality that Zulu would have to be implemented.

When he wasn't busy with his own patients, Mercier had sometimes watched the crash team working on eerily accurate medical dummies, using microsurgical techniques to reknit head and body. Sometimes the body had been intact below the neck, but they'd also worked under the assumption of varying severities of injury occasioned by the removal of the scarab. Now they were dealing with a real case that fell somewhere in the middle of their simulated outcomes. The head had been severed with superhuman precision, but the scarab had inflicted major damage to the three cervical vertebrae below the bisection point. Nothing that couldn't be fixed – it wasn't going to be necessary to grow the supreme prefect a new body – but there was a lot of restorative work to be done.

Little of the surgical activity was visible to Mercier. Pale-green medical servitors crowded over and around the body and head, which were currently situated on separate tables a metre apart. The hulking machines appeared clumsy until one focused on the speed with which their manipulators were knitting tissue back together. Secrets of the flesh lay obscured behind a flickering blur of antiseptic metal. Now and then one of the swan-necked servitors would whip around to swap one manipulator extremity for another, lending the whole scene the faintly comedic look of a recording on fast-forward. Demikhov's human staff were situated several metres away from the whipping machines, gowned and masked but having no direct contact with their patient. They stood before pedestals, studying panes filled with anatomical images, not so much controlling the machines as offering advice and guidance when it was merited. They did not need to be in the same room, but they were all ready to intervene in the unlikely event of some catastrophic machine failure.

Mercier had a shrewd idea of what was happening. The machines were identifying severed nerve fibres, cross-matching them between the two detached body parts. Reverse-field trawls were being used to stimulate areas of Jane Aumonier's brain, with particular focus on the sensorimotor cortex. When the machines identified the function of a particular nerve, they capped it with a microscopic cylinder primed with regenerative quickmatter. Myoelectric stimulation was being used to map the nerve bundles emerging from Aumonier's body. When head and neck were rejoined, the two cylinders corresponding to a single nerve would identify each other and promote flawless tissue reconnection. Much would remain to be done – Aumonier could expect partial or complete paralysis for some time after the procedure – but Demikhov had been confident that basic life-support processes could be restored during the first phase of surgery.

Mercier watched until he was satisfied that everything was under control. Demikhov's team were working urgently, but there was nothing about their movements that suggested anything untoward. They had prepared for this and did not appear to be encountering anything they had not anticipated.

Reluctantly Mercier turned from the spectacle. He wanted to see the moment of reunion, but he had his own matters to attend to. He'd learned about Thalia Ng's escape from House Aubusson, accompanied by a party of local citizenry. There were no reports of serious injuries amongst that group, but they would all benefit from medical attention when the deep-system vehicle redocked at Panoply, even if the worst Mercier had to deal with was a few cuts and bruises.

He returned to his section of the infirmary. Through the windowed partition he made out the recumbent form of his only current patient, asleep on a bed. Mercier opened the partition. He stepped through and moved to the side of Gaffney's bed, cradling a compad in the crook of his arm. He tapped a stylus and brought up a summary of Gaffney's progress since the removal of the whiphound and his subsequent interrogation by trawl.

Mercier did not approve of the way Dreyfus had insisted upon his patient being scanned so soon after the fraught process of removing the object lodged in his throat. Gaffney had been medically fit, traumatised yet otherwise free of serious injury, but the principle of it still galled Mercier. Now, however, he was forced to admit that Gaffney had no need of further medical supervision.

He could be transferred to a normal holding facility somewhere else in Panoply, freeing up space that could be used when Thalia's party arrived.

'Sheridan,' he said softly. 'Can you hear me? It's time to wake up now.'

At first Gaffney didn't stir. Mercier repeated his instruction. Gaffney mumbled something and opened his eyes with resentful slowness.

'I was sound asleep, Doctor Mercier,' he said, his voice still a painful croak.

'I apologise. You still need rest.' Mercier tapped the stylus again, bringing up a different set of diagnostic summaries. 'Unfortunately, I've got a ship coming in with an unspecified number of injured citizens aboard. I can't afford to tie up this bed for much longer.'

'Are you discharging me?' Gaffney croaked.

'Not exactly. I'm still ordered to keep you under lock and key, but there's no reason why you can't be transferred to a normal detention cell.'

'I'm surprised Dreyfus isn't here to give you a helping hand.'

'Dreyfus is outside,' Mercier said.

'That's a shame. Can't say I really miss his bedside manner, though. You didn't hear where he was headed, by any chance?'

'No,' Mercier said, after a trace of hesitation.

'Well, let's hope he doesn't come to grief, wherever it is. I think we still need to clear the air between us. Are you sure he didn't put you up to this, Doctor?'

'This has nothing to do with Dreyfus. I don't approve of what you did, Sheridan, but that doesn't mean I approve of the way you were treated, either.'

'Aumonier, then? Did she issue the order?'

'Jane's in no fit state to issue any kind of order,' Mercier said, and then regretted it instantly, for Gaffney had no need to know of the operation in progress.

'What do you mean by that?'

'I mean ... I've said enough.'

'Where is she?' Gaffney cocked his head. 'Has something happened, Doctor? Are they *doing* something to her? Come to think of it, this place has been a little quiet lately.'

'Never mind Jane. I assure you that you won't be any less comfortable in a holding cell than you are here, and you'll be under constant machine observation. If you do experience any complications, someone can attend to you almost immediately.'

'You put it like that,' Gaffney said sarcastically, 'how can I possibly refuse?'

'I wish there was another way, Sheridan.'

'Yeah. So do I, son.' Gaffney set his face in a look of resigned determination. 'But needs must when the devil calls. Can you help me out of this bed? I seem to have become a little stiff in my spine.'

Mercier put down the compad and stylus and leaned over to assist Gaffney to his feet. In a flash Gaffney was standing by his side, twisting Mercier's right arm behind his back, pushing the stylus hard against the side of his throat. The stylus was blunt, but Gaffney was applying so much pressure that the pain was unpleasantly sharp.

'Got to admit, I was feeling a bit stronger than I looked,' Gaffney said. 'Sorry about that, Doctor, but there's no way you're moving me to a holding cell.'

The pressure on his throat made it difficult for Mercier to answer. 'You can't get out of here.'

'Let's take a stroll to your office.'

With Gaffney still pressing the stylus into his neck, Mercier shuffle-walked sideways, his heart hammering and his breathing beginning to rocket. 'My arm,' Mercier protested.

'Fuck your arm. Open the door.'

Mercier admitted the two of them into his administrative annexe. He held out a forlorn hope that there'd be someone in there who could pacify Gaffney or raise the alarm. But with all the other medical staff either participating in Demikhov's operation or up in the bay awaiting the arrival of the deep-system cruiser, the medical centre was deserted.

'Don't even think about calling out,' Gaffney warned. 'Now move to your desk. Pull out the chair and sit down.'

Mercier's office was all inert matter. The furniture was studiedly old-fashioned, the way he liked it. But even if he'd had the means to conjure one, he wouldn't have had the necessary control or presence of mind to fashion a weapon or restraining device.

'What do you want with me?' he asked as he sat down in the chair, with Gaffney still jamming the stylus into his neck. 'You're going to dislocate my arm!'

'That's what happens to arms. Now open the desk drawer on your right.'

'My drawer?'

Gaffney intensified the pressure on both the stylus and the arm. 'I'm not really in the mood to say things twice, son.'

With his left arm, Mercier opened the drawer. 'There's nothing in here except papers,' he said, tugging it open enough to demonstrate that this was the case.

'You do like your paperwork,' Gaffney commented. 'Now reach all the way to the back of the drawer.'

'There's nothing at the back.'

'Do it.'

Mercier started as his fingers brushed against something unfamiliar, lodged at the back of the drawer where it would not interfere with his beloved paperwork.

'Pull it out,' Gaffney said.

Mercier tugged and the item snapped loose. It felt heavy in his hand, like a bar of cold iron. Something about its shape was familiar, though he had never handled anything remotely like it. 'This isn't possible,' he said. 'There shouldn't be—'

'How many times have you had this office swept by Internal Security?' Gaffney asked.

Mercier's hand emerged from the drawer. He was clutching the black shaft of a whiphound. 'How did—'

'I put it there. I put them in a lot of places, wherever I felt I might need one. The possibility of my being exposed and arrested was not something I could ignore. Matter of fact, there's one in that holding cell you were probably intending to take me to. Impossible, you say. Security would never have allowed it! Getting the picture now?' Gaffney croaked out a guttural laugh. 'Put the whiphound down on the table.'

Mercier dropped the whiphound. It clunked heavily on the table, denting the polished wood surface beneath his writing lamp. In a single fluid movement, Gaffney released Mercier's arm, alleviated the pressure from the stylus and snatched up the whiphound.

He spooled out the filament.

'You know what one of these can do in the wrong hands,' he said. 'So let's not dick around, shall we?'

Pell brought the cutter to a halt on a ledge just under the rim of the canyon they had been following for the last twenty kilometres. He powered down the in-atmosphere engines, allowing the weight of the vehicle to settle onto its tripedal landing gear.

'This is as close as I can get you.'

Dreyfus felt an unsettling crunching movement as the gear forced its way though the ice crusting the shelf.

'Are you sure?'

Pell flipped up his goggles and nodded. 'I'd caution against flying any closer, unless you have a burning desire to find out what kind of perimeter defences Firebrand have managed to get their hands on.'

'Fair enough.' Dreyfus knew better than to debate the point with Pell, who he knew would have done the best possible job. 'How long a stroll are we looking at?'

Pell indicated a contour map conjured onto his flight-deck console. 'You're here,' he said, stabbing his finger at the head of the canyon. 'Ops Nine is *here*.' He moved his finger a few centimetres to the right. 'Ten or eleven kilometres as the crow flies. Good news is that the terrain's pretty level between here and there, with only one crevasse you'll want to avoid, so your route should be less than fifteen kilometres. Those surface suits have amplification, don't they? I hope so, given the size of those rifles. With power-assist, I'm guessing you can keep to three or four klicks per hour. Say, four or five hours to the nearest entry point.'

'If that's the good news,' Sparver said, 'what's the bad?'

'You'll have limited cover, which is the reason we can't fly any closer. You'll have to stay low and avoid exposed ground. If something paints you, hunker down and don't move for at least thirty minutes. The perimeter system may just assume it picked up a scavenger drone, wandering the surface looking for Amerikano trinkets.'

'What about our way in?' Dreyfus asked.

'Imagery points to several possible entry points. I don't recommend going in through the front door.' Pell moved his finger slightly. 'If you approach the way I'm suggesting, you should hit some kind of secondary access ramp about here. It's all locked into your suits, so don't worry about that.'

'We won't,' Dreyfus said.

'That's about all I have to say. You can get off the ledge easily enough: there's a dried-up river bed that climbs up onto the plateau. Keep low once you're up there, and exploit whatever natural features you can find for cover. You've got a good shot at getting to Ops Nine by sundown. I suggest you aim to achieve that objective.'

'If we don't?' Sparver asked.

'It cools down pretty fast here. In infrared, those suits of yours are going to light up the landscape like a pair of beacons.'

'Then we should move out right now,' Dreyfus said, readying his suit for exposure to Yellowstone's atmosphere. He picked up the heavy bulk of the Breitenbach rifle and slung it over his shoulder. 'Thank you for the ride, Captain. I appreciate the risk you took in bringing us this close.'

'I'm not the one taking the risk here.' Pell touched a control on this console then studied a read-out for a moment. 'We're stable. You're free to cycle through.'

Dreyfus nodded at Sparver and the two of them moved towards the cutter's suitwall.

'One thing I forgot to mention,' Pell said. 'When you were suiting up, word came through from Panoply.'

'They weren't supposed to contact us.'

'They didn't, not specifically. It was a general broadcast, to all assets. It sounded like a code. It meant nothing to me, but I thought you might know better.'

'Tell me,' Dreyfus said, swallowing hard against the tightness in his throat.

'The message was, "Zulu has occurred. Repeat, Zulu has occurred."' Pell shrugged. 'That was all.'

Dreyfus moved to snap down his faceplate. 'You're right. It does mean something.'

'Good or bad?'

'Too soon to tell,' he answered.

CHAPTER 30

Gaffney held the stiffened filament of the whiphound against Mercier's throat in much the same way that Dreyfus had held the whiphound against his own. They were standing outside the operating theatre where the Zulu team were still at work.

'I can't let you in there, Sheridan.'

Gaffney let the sharp edge of the filament draw a dab of blood. 'It's not a question of "can't", I'm afraid. You're going to do it, or they're going to have another head to reattach when they're done with Jane.'

'I can't allow you to hurt the Supreme Prefect.'

Gaffney's thumb caressed the handle of the whiphound. 'Open the door. I won't ask again.'

Mercier palmed the door, ignoring the signs warning him against entry. The door slid open, revealing the gowned backs of Demikhov's crash team standing at their pedestals with the medical servitors beyond them. For a moment all was deceptively normal. Mercier heard the urgent but calm voices of the surgeons discussing the progress so far; he saw gloved fingers reach out towards data panes, switching between display options. Then one of the gowned figures became aware that the door had opened. She glanced over her shoulder, her eyes widening as she took in the spectacle of Gaffney holding Mercier hostage.

'Is there a problem?' Demikhov asked.

'What does it look like, shit-for-brains?'

'We're in the middle of a delicate procedure here,' Demikhov said, still keeping admirably cool. 'If you've got a problem, if there's something you want, I suggest you take it up with Senior Prefect Clearmountain.'

'Tell your staff to suspend the machines and step away from their pedestals.'

'I'm afraid that's not possible.'

'I'll kill Mercier if you don't.'

'We're trying to save the life of the supreme prefect. In case you haven't been informed, her head and body were separated when we removed the scarab.'

'I don't like repeating myself. Tell your staff to do what I just said.'

'Whatever you want, whatever demands you might have, we can't give it to you.'

'I'll be the judge of that.' Gaffney let the whiphound bite deeper, until blood began to trickle down Mercier's throat in a continuous flow. 'I won't ask again. Do what I say and I promise that neither Mercier nor the supreme prefect will come to harm. *Fuck* with me and you're going to be mopping up into the middle of next week.'

'Please,' Mercier said.

Demikhov breathed in deeply and nodded to his staff. Gloved fingers touched panes. The surgical robots halted.

'Now step away from the pedestals,' Gaffney said. 'As far as you can go.'

The staff shuffled back until they had all taken at least ten paces. Gaffney pushed Mercier forward, keeping the whiphound in place. They walked between the pedestals, then eased past the poised medical servitors to stand by the patient. Since Mercier had last viewed the scene, the two tables had been brought closer so that the gap between head and neck was only ten centimetres. The complexity of the operation was even more humbling in close-up. Aumonier's head rested in a padded cradle, with constantly swivelling trawl probes arranged around her shaven scalp in a barbed halo. Oxygenation of the head was being maintained by a tangle of arterial shunts inserted into the skin of the neck or up through the stump itself. A handful of nerves had already been rejoined across the divide, using jumper cables to bridge the gap between the quickmatter cylinders that tipped the end of each nerve.

'You're a doctor,' Gaffney told Mercier. 'How long do you think she can last without those lines running into her head?'

'Without blood? Not very long.'

'Put some numbers on that for me. How many minutes are we talking about? Three? Five? Six?'

'Four at the most. Why?'

'Four it is, then. Snap off your bracelet and hold it up to my mouth.'

Mercier did as he was told, fumbling as he released his bracelet.

'Put me through to Clearmountain,' Gaffney said.

The acting supreme prefect answered almost immediately. 'This is Clearmountain. Is something the matter, Doctor—'

'This isn't Mercier. It's Gaffney.'

Clearmountain comprehended the implications quickly enough. 'This is unexpected, Sheridan.'

'Don't worry, I'm not staying around.'

'Where are you?'

'I'm down with Demikhov, in the theatre. I'm standing right next to Jane. Nice work he's done so far.'

'Don't lay a finger on Aumonier,' Clearmountain said.

'Jane's going to be just dandy. That is, provided you don't do anything to annoy me.'

'I'm sure we can work something out.'

'Actually, I'm sure we can't. I'm finished here. I've burnt my bridges. It might surprise you, but I'm a rational man. I did everything I did because I believed it was the right thing for the citizenry. I still believe that. I love this goddamn organisation, or at least what it used to stand for. But I know I have no future unless Aurora wins against Panoply.'

'She's a machine, Sheridan. You've been working for an alpha-level intelligence, the ghost of a girl who should have died fifty-five years ago.'

'Aurora's nature is irrelevant. It's her intentions that count.'

'She's a mass murderer. We've received direct confirmation that all the citizens inside House Aubusson were murdered shortly after the takeover.'

'Nice try,' Gaffney said.

'It's the truth.'

Mercier thought he caught a twitch of hesitation before Gaffney answered. 'She wants to protect people. She'd hardly start murdering them if that was her objective.'

'Listen to me, I'm begging you. Aurora is not what you think she is. Her only goal is her own survival.'

'You know,' Gaffney said, 'I really think you could have tried a bit harder than that. I mean, *honestly*. Do you think I'm going to drop everything and roll over like a puppy just because you tell me some people have been murdered?'

'I'll show you,' Clearmountain said. 'I'll let you interview Prefect Ng as soon as she returns to Panoply.'

'Sorry, but I'm not planning on staying that long.' Without warning, he released his hold on Mercier, pushing him away with such force that the doctor tripped over his own feet and fell backwards against one of the servitors, toppling it noisily. 'Join the others,' he said.

'Sheridan?' Clearmountain said.

'Still here.' Gaffney had snatched Mercier's bracelet as he pushed him away. He snapped it around his own wrist and continued speaking. 'I'm leaving, but not before you've done a couple of things for me. You can begin by telling me where Dreyfus is.'

'I can't do that.'

'I'm standing less than a metre from the supreme prefect, with a whiphound. Do you want to rethink your response?'

Clearmountain answered after a pause. 'Dreyfus is somewhere else in the Glitter Band. I can give you the coordinates in a moment—'

Mercier pulled himself to his feet, bruised but otherwise unhurt. He touched a hand to the drying scab on his throat, judging that the wound was superficial.

'Oh, nice try,' Gaffney said. 'Let's have a little look here, shall we?' He reached down and tugged at one of the lines running into Aumonier's neck until it popped out. 'I've just pulled something free. I don't know if it was important or not.'

'Sheridan—'

'I'll ask again. Where is Dreyfus? Don't lie to me, Clearmountain. I've spent my entire professional life spotting liars.'

'A secure holding facility on Marco's Eye—'

'Oh, *please*. I wonder what this one does? A bit of blood squirting out there. Okay, you get one more try. I'd give this one a *lot* of thought, if I were you.'

'He's gone to Yellowstone.'

Gaffney cocked his head and nodded. 'Like it so far, Prefect. Where on Yellowstone? Don't tell me they moved it to Chasm City?'

'It's in Ops Nine.'

'Mm. Going to have to jog my memory on that one.'

Clearmountain's voice was flat with defeat. 'A disused Amerikano research station.'

'Good, now we're getting somewhere. That sounds plausible. Do you think you can spare a ship, Gaston? I'm thinking something like a corvette, one with transat capability. I'll want a full fuel and weps load, and the coordinates of Ops Nine programmed into the autopilot.'

'I can't give you that,' Clearmountain said.

'Oh dear, there goes another tube. The liquid's kind of watery this time. What does cerebrospinal fluid look like, anyone?'

'We don't have a corvette on the rack. They're all out.'

'I'll settle for a cutter, then, but I'm not budging on the fuel and weps. Throw in a surface suit while you're at it.'

'I'll . . . talk to Thyssen.'

'Better make it quick. I'm on my way up to the cutter bay. And I'm bringing some insurance with me.' Gaffney started tugging out the rest of the wires and nerve shunts. 'I'd say you've got about four minutes.'

He tugged Jane Aumonier's severed head free of its support cradle.

Dreyfus and Sparver walked across an undulating landscape of frozen methane-ammonia ice. Their shadows lengthened ahead of them as the orange smear of Epsilon Eridani lowered towards the horizon to their rear, burning through ochre-brown clouds that had been tugged into weird anatomical shapes by high-altitude winds. The sky ahead of them was an ominous purple, palpitating with distant electrical storms. Above, it was coloured and knotted like old wood, curdled like bad milk.

'Do you want to talk about what was in that document now?' Sparver asked.

'Not really.'

Dreyfus altered his course to exploit the shadowing effect of a natural boulder formation. They had covered seven kilometres from the touchdown point; approximately the same distance remained to be traversed. With the power-assisted suits, the physical effort was minimal. But the continuous chore of choosing a safe route, one that would avoid unstable ground and keep them low enough to avoid being detected by Firebrand, was itself taxing.

'Boss, you've hardly said a word since we left Pell. Aren't you happy that Thalia got out okay?'

'Of course I'm happy. I'm just not really in the mood for banter. I didn't ask for company, remember.'

'But now you've got it. Was that document something to do with the Clockmaker?'

'Have a guess.'

'Okay, so what was so earth-shattering about it? What did you read that you find so personally difficult to deal with?'

'That's between me and the document.'

'And I'm your deputy. We share things.'

'Do you have Manticore clearance?'

'No. But I've never had Pangolin, either, and that hasn't stopped you from feeding me the occasional crumb of restricted information.'

'This is different.'

'Because it concerns the Clockmaker? Or because it concerns Tom Dreyfus?'

'We should talk less.'

'They're not going to hear our conversation.'

'I mean we should concentrate on walking. If you fall though ice, I'm not stopping to haul you out.'

'Nice to know you care.'

They trudged on, zigzagging around a labyrinth of crevasses and deadfalls. After at least a kilometre, Dreyfus said, 'I found out something about myself I didn't know. I've always believed that I played no part in that day's events, but now I know I was there. I was in SIAM, directly involved in the unfolding of the Clockmaker crisis. I must have been nearby when it broke loose. I was probably visiting Valery, or on my way from visiting her.'

'You don't remember?'

'I had the memories blocked. They're becoming clearer now that I've seen the document, but I still feel as if I'm looking at them through thick glass.'

'Why would you have had the memories blocked? Was that a security thing?'

'Not exactly. I wouldn't have been allowed to function as a field with the knowledge I gained that day, but that wouldn't have been an issue if they'd promoted me to senior, which is what they wanted to do. That's not why I had the memories blocked, though. I made a decision that day, Sparver. It fell to me. But I couldn't live with what I'd done afterwards.'

'What kind of decision?'

'I worked out a way to save the people in SIAM, the ones that the Clockmaker hadn't got to already. That's why there was a delay. I've always wondered about the six hours between Jane's release and us going in with the nukes. Now I know what happened.'

'Did you succeed?' Sparver asked.

Dreyfus walked on. After a dozen paces he turned and said, 'Yes, I succeeded. I saved them all. Including Valery.'

There was a coldness beyond cold, and then a light. Aumonier felt weightless and the thought formed itself in her mind that after everything they had failed, that she was back in the room with the scarab. For an instant the prospect was intolerable and she sought to crawl back into the unconsciousness from which she had just emerged. But then she became aware that she could no longer feel the scarab. Its absence was so profound that it almost felt like a negative image of the thing itself.

'Open your eyes,' Doctor Demikhov said softly. 'Everything's all right. You're going to be fine.'

'I was sleeping, wasn't I?'

'Yes. You were asleep, after all these years. I'm sorry it was necessary to wake you.'

Demikhov was leaning over her, green gown and mask against a tiled backdrop of sterile green walling. She tried speaking, but the words wouldn't form. Instead she heard a harsh-sounding imitation of her own voice, as if someone standing next to her had anticipated exactly what she wished to say. 'Where am I?'

'In post-operative. Do you remember anything?'

'I remember calling you. I remember that we were discussing your plans for me.'

'And afterwards?'

'Nothing. What's wrong with my voice?'

'We're reading your intentions with a trawl. Don't be alarmed; it's only a temporary measure.'

By degrees, Aumonier became aware that she had scant sensation below the neck. She could move her eyes, but little else. Her head was fixed in place, unable to tilt from side to side.

'Show me what you've done, Doctor.'

'I've done something quite drastic, but there's no cause for alarm. You're going to be up on your feet in no time at all.'

'Show me,' she said, the simulated voice picking up her insistence.

Demikhov motioned to one side. A gloved hand passed him a mirror. He held it before Aumonier so that she could see her face, pinched tight in a padded restraint.

'I haven't seen my face in eleven years. No one could get a mirror close to me, but that wasn't the point. I didn't want to see the scarab, even accidentally. Now I look so old and thin.'

'It's nothing time won't put right.'

'Tilt the mirror.'

Her neck came into view. It appeared to have been stapled to her body, the wound still raw. Cables and wires plunged into her skin, or into the gap between the two edges of skin.

'You understand what we had to do?' Demikhov said.

'How did you . . .?' she began.

'It took a lot of planning but the process itself was very quick. You had a few seconds of consciousness before the crash team reached you, but I doubt you remember much of that.'

She realised, in an instant of comprehension, that it was very important to her that she not remember. But she did. She remembered bright lights and a concerned, lantern-jawed face looking at her with clinical intensity, and the face had belonged to Demikhov. She remembered a cold beyond cold, as if the interstellar vacuum itself was groping its way up her neck, reaching freezing fingers into the empty cavity of her skull.

Demikhov didn't need nightmares for the rest of his life.

'You're right,' she said. 'I don't.'

'The damage to your body was severe but treatable. We neutralised the remains of the scarab and my intention was to keep you under until your head and body were fully reunited. There was a minor complication, however.'

'With me?'

'Not exactly. I'll explain things later, but all you need to know right now is that Gaffney managed to escape from Panoply. He took a cutter and went after Dreyfus.'

She had a thousand questions, but most of them would have to wait. 'How did he know where to go? Surely nobody told him about Ops Nine.'

'Gaffney was . . . persuasive,' Demikhov said. 'Clearmountain had no option but to reveal the suspected location of the Clockmaker. In his shoes, I'd have done exactly the same thing.'

'Is there any word from Dreyfus?'

'Nothing. But given the anticipated timing, we can assume he's making his way by foot from the drop-off point.' Demikhov returned the mirror to his aide. 'That's not why I had you brought to consciousness, though. As you can see, the process of reuniting your head and body is only partially complete, but we were making good progress. Once you've dealt with the matter at hand, I have every confidence of being able to reinstate full control.'

'The matter at hand, Doctor?'

'Perhaps it would be better if Acting Supreme Prefect Clearmountain explained.' Demikhov gestured at the wall, turning part of it into a display pane. From her inclined position, Aumonier could see it without difficulty. Clearmountain was looking at her from the tactical room, the edge of the Solid Orrery peeping into view behind him.

'Can I talk to her?' he asked.

'She's perfectly lucid,' Demikhov replied.

'Supreme Prefect Aumonier,' Clearmountain said, trepidation in his voice, 'I am sorry that this was necessary. I assured them that you had delegated authority to me, but they wouldn't listen.'

'Who wouldn't listen?' Aumonier asked.

'They're still waiting to talk to you. They won't take orders from anyone else.'

'Who are you talking about?'

'I can put them through, if you wish.'

'If this is why you woke me up, that would be a very good idea.'

Clearmountain vanished. He was replaced by the visage of a monster, a man who had once been human but who now faced the world through a mask of leathery, radiation-hardened skin and articulated metal plating embossed with florid bronze patterning. His eyes were two telescopic cameras, emerging from skull sockets like a pair of cannon. Glue-stiffened dreadlocks spiked back from his scalp.

'This is Captain Tengiz, of the lighthugger *Wrath Ascending*. We stand ready to assist you.'

'Thank you,' Aumonier said.

The image switched. Now she was looking at the vastly magnified head of a praying mantis, or something very like one, emerging from the ring-shaped neck of an ancient spacesuit. The mantis's mouthparts opened, revealing teeth and tongue of human semblance.

'This is Captain Rethimnon, of the lighthugger *Frost Wind*. We stand ready to assist you.'

'Thank you.'

The image changed again. Another face, more recognisably human this time, despite the absence of a nose. 'This is Captain Grong, of the lighthugger *Stasis in Darkness*. We stand ready to assist you.'

She started to answer, but the image had already changed.

'This is Captain Katsuura of the lighthugger *Pharaoh's Daughter*. We stand ready to assist you.'

'This is Captain Nkhata, of the lighthugger *Black Narcissus*. We stand ready to assist you.'

'This is Captain Vanderlin, of the lighthugger *Dawnrazor*. We stand ready to assist you.'

'This is Captain Teague . . .'

'Captain Voightlander . . .'

The roll-call continued; a dozen ships, then a dozen more, until she had lost count.

'Thank you, Captains,' she said, when the last Ultra had spoken. 'I am grateful that you have responded to my request for help. You can, I think, provide a decisive contribution. I must warn you – though I am sure you already appreciate as much – that you will be placing your ships and crew in grave danger.'

The face of Tengiz, the first Ultra to speak, reappeared on the pane. 'I have been tasked to speak for the other ships, Supreme Prefect Aumonier. Rest assured that we are fully aware of the risks. It is still our intention to help.'

'I'm grateful.'

'Tell us what you want us to do.'

'You can be of benefit to me in two ways,' Aumonier said. 'Your ships have a capacity exceeding anything in the Glitter Band, even the largest in-system liners. If you can start taking aboard evacuees, that will be incalculably helpful to us.'

'We will do what we can. How else may we help?'

'Doubtless you've witnessed our efforts to contain Aurora's expansion by destroying those habitats contaminated by her war machines. Unfortunately, we're running out of nuclear weapons. If there was any other way—'

'You wish us to intervene.'

'Yes.'

'In a military sense.'

'I don't doubt that you have the means, Captain. At the risk of opening an old wound, we all saw what Captain Dravidian's ship was capable of doing. And his vessel wasn't even armed.'

'Tell us where and when,' Tengiz said.

'I'd dearly like to. Unfortunately – as you're probably aware – I'm somewhat indisposed right now and need further surgery. I appreciate your insistence on speaking only to me, but it would simplify matters enormously if you would allow me to designate Prefect Clearmountain to speak for me.'

Tengiz looked at her with his blank telescopic eyes. She couldn't read a single human emotion in the mongrel collision of machine and flesh that was his face.

'Do you have confidence in Clearmountain?'

'Yes,' she said. 'Absolute confidence. You have my word, Captain. Allow Clearmountain to speak for me.'

Tengiz paused, then nodded. 'So be it.'

'I'm going to sleep again now, if that's all right with you. Good luck, Captain. To you and all the others.'

'We'll do what we can. As for you . . .' Tengiz halted. For the first time she sensed indecision. 'We have long been aware of your predicament, Supreme Prefect Aumonier.'

'I never imagined I was of the slightest interest to Ultras.'

'You were wrong. We knew of you. We knew of you and . . . you've long had our respect. You would have made an excellent captain.'

Dreyfus and Sparver surmounted the last rise and found themselves looking out across a shallow depression in the terrain, like an old crater that had been gradually eroded and filled in by slow and mindless processes of weather and geochemistry. Yet there was something out of place at the base of the depression, even though Dreyfus nearly missed it on his first glancing survey. It was a ramp, sloping down into the ground, its walls and sides fashioned from some kind of fused construction material with the ebony lustre of burnt sugar. It had cracked and distorted in places, evidence of shifts in the underlying landscape, but it was still remarkably intact for something that had been out there for more than two hundred years. The ramp angled down into the ground and vanished into a flat-roofed tunnel, the lip of which had formed a portcullis of dagger-like ammonia-ice stalactites or icicles. Dreyfus pointed to the middle part of the opening, where a number of the spikes had been broken off at head height.

'Someone's been here recently,' he said. But without knowing how long it had taken for the stalactites to form, he knew he could have been talking about a visitation that had happened days, years or even decades ago.

'Let's take a look-see inside,' Sparver said. 'There's nothing I like better than unwelcoming tunnels leading underground.'

If a surveillance system had detected their arrival, there was no sign of it. They crunched across the last few metres of surface ice until they were standing at the top of the ramp, and then began a cautious descent towards the portcullis. The ground was slippery under their feet. Dreyfus stooped to avoid dislodging any more stalactites; Sparver only needed to nod his head slightly. Beyond the opening, the ramp continued to slope down into unseen depths. The suit's acoustic pick-up conveyed the sounds of trickling, dripping liquids to Dreyfus's ears. As the gloom deepened, he angled his helmet lamp down, mindful of treacherous cracks in the flooring. He supposed that this must once have been an entry point for vehicles, though it was clear that nothing large had come down here in a long time.

After fifty or sixty metres, the ramp terminated in a black wall set with a single wide door. The door consisted of a set of hinged panels that would have rolled down from a mechanism in the ceiling. It had stopped half a metre short of the floor, above an airtight slot into which the lowest part of the door must have been intended to lock.

'Someone was careless,' Sparver said.

'Or in a hurry. You think we can squeeze under that?'

Sparver was already on his knees. He undid some of his equipment and weaponry and slid it through ahead of him. Then he lowered onto all fours and scraped through the gap. 'It's clear,' he told Dreyfus, grunting as he stood up. 'Send me through what you can.'

Dreyfus unclipped the bulkier pieces of his kit and passed them to his deputy. Then he lowered himself to the cracked black floor and squeezed under the door, scraping his backpack in the process. Something jammed, and for a horrible instant he thought he was trapped, pinned in place with vicelike pressure. Then whatever it was worked loose and he was through, standing up next to Sparver. His suit reported no damage, but had the door been a couple more centimetres lower, he wouldn't have been able to get through wearing it.

Dreyfus reattached his equipment and hoped silently that he wouldn't be sliding under any more doors. They had arrived in what was clearly a cargo airlock, designed to allow vehicles and heavy equipment to pass between Ops Nine and the outside world. A similar door to the one they'd just crawled under faced them on the opposite wall, but this one was sealed down tight.

'We can cut through,' Sparver said, tapping a glove against the torch on his belt. 'Or we can try opening it. Either way, if there's a single soul alive in this place they'll know about it. Your call, Boss.'

'See if you can get it to open. I'll try to close the other one. I'd rather not flood the place with Yellowstone air if we can avoid it.'

'Because you're feeling charitable towards Saavedra and her friends?' Sparver asked sceptically.

'They committed crimes against Panoply. I'd like them alive to answer for that.'

Dreyfus brushed icy yellow caulk off a raised panel next to the door they had just crawled under. The panel contained a simple arrangement of manual controls labelled with Amerikano script. He pushed the stud with a downward-pointing arrow and heard a laboured whine of buried machinery. The door began to inch its way towards the floor, spitting chunks of yellow ice out of its tracks as it descended.

'Looks like someone's been paying their power bills,' Sparver said.

Dreyfus nodded. If he'd harboured lingering doubts that Ops Nine was truly where Firebrand had gone to ground, they had just been thoroughly dispelled. The facility was powered and functional, at least on a spartan basis. Amerikano technology was robust, but not robust enough to open doors after two hundred years.

Dreyfus flinched as slats rattled open in the walls without warning. Red lights stammered on behind ceiling grilles and he heard the roar of powerful fans. The environment sensor on his suit began to record the change of gas mixture and pressure as the air in the room was swapped for breathable atmosphere. The process took less than three minutes. The fans died down and the slats clattered shut again.

'I think I can open the door now,' Sparver said.

Nothing would be gained by waiting, Dreyfus knew. 'Do it,' he said, mentally preparing himself for whatever was on the other side. Sparver hit the control, then moved to stand next to Dreyfus, his Breitenbach rifle held doubled-handed. But as the door rose, it became clear that there was no one waiting for them on the other side. Dreyfus allowed the muzzle of his own weapon to dip slightly, but remained alert. The two prefects stepped over the threshold.

A curving corridor, triangular in cross section, walled and floored with metallic grille, stretched away to either side. An illuminated red strip ran the length of the corridor at the apex of the two angled walls. Behind the grilles snaked corroded and mould-caked piping and machinery, much of it eaten away, probably by rats. Steam jetted from ruptured lines, hot enough to scald if they hadn't been wearing suits. But Dreyfus noticed that some of the plumbing was shiny and new. Firebrand must have done just enough to make this facility habitable again. They hadn't been intending to make it comfortable, or homely.

'You want me to toss a coin?' Sparver asked.

'Clockwise,' Dreyfus said, leading the way.

The grilled flooring clattered heavily under their boots, the din echoing around the curve of the corridor. Dreyfus had no good idea of the dimensions of the facility, but it wasn't difficult to imagine that noise reaching far enough to alert someone of their arrival, if that hypothetical person hadn't already been notified by the airlock activity. Since his suit assured him that the ambient air was now breathable, Dreyfus reached up and risked removing his helmet. He attached it to his belt, just as he'd had cause to regret doing in the Nerval-Lermontov rock when Clepsydra touched her knife against his throat. But he didn't think knives were going to be the problem now.

'Yeah, getting kind of stuffy in here,' Sparver said, undoing his own helmet. He took a deep breath, sucking in the same cold, metallic air Dreyfus had just tasted. 'Feels better already.'

'Watch out for those steam jets,' Dreyfus said. 'And be ready to jam your lid on again.'

They continued walking, following the slow curve of the corridor until they arrived at a junction. They paused to decide which way to go, while pink-tinged steam snorted in dragon-like exhalations from a severed pipeline. Dreyfus shone his light on a burnished metal panel stencilled with Amerikano text. 'Central operations is this way,' he said, raising his voice above the angry snort of the steam jet. 'Sounds like the right place to start, doesn't it?'

'Or the right place to stay a long way away from.'

'Nothing I'd like better. But we came here to do a job, Field.'

After a moment Sparver said, 'Don't you mean "deputy", Boss?'

'I mean field. Jane just promoted me to senior, so I don't see why I shouldn't elevate my deputy to full field status. How does it feel, Field Prefect Bancal?'

'It feels great. Though I imagined it might happen under different circumstances.'

Dreyfus smiled to himself. 'You mean slightly less suicidal ones?'

'Now that you mention it . . .'

'That's exactly the same way I felt when I got my promotion, so that makes two of us.'

'But it's still a promotion. I mean, that's what it'll say in my obituary, right?'

'It would,' Dreyfus affirmed. 'Only problem is, I'm the only one who knows about it. Apart from you, obviously.'

'So it would really help if one of us survives, is what you're saying.'

'Yes. Me, preferably.'

'Why you, Boss, and not me?'

'Because if you survived, you wouldn't be needing an obituary, would you?'

'That makes sense,' Sparver said, sounding only the tiniest bit puzzled.

Dreyfus tightened his grip on the Breitenbach rifle. 'There's something ahead,' he said, lowering his voice.

Pale-blue light was leaking around the curve of the corridor, highlighting the hexagonal meshwork of the grilles. Dreyfus judged that they were approaching the central operations section. Conscious that there was little they could do to quieten their approach, he nonetheless slowed his walk and edged closer to the angled wall on the inside of the curve, hoping to use it for cover until the last moment. As he crept forward, he saw that the corridor terminated in a hollowed-out cavern that extended several storeys below their present level. The blue illumination originated from a grid of lights suspended from the bare rock ceiling that arched ten or twelve metres above them. The corridor brought them out onto a railinged balcony that encircled the entire cavern. Doors were set into the smooth-panelled wall at regular intervals, marked with spray-painted numbers and cryptic symbols that must have once referred to different administrative and functional departments of the facility. Dreyfus looked over the railing, down to the floor of the chamber. It was a kind of atrium, he realised. Tiled walkways encircled what might once have been flower beds or small ponds. The flower beds now contained only grey-black ash, the ponds nothing but dust. There were even a couple of benches, cut from solid rock. Rising from the ground in the middle of the atrium was a complicated-looking metal sculpture whose design he couldn't easily fathom from this angle, but which almost resembled an iron cactus.

Dreyfus realised that he'd had preconceptions about the people who'd lived here originally. The Amerikano culture might have felt distant from his own, its values foreign, but the inhabitants of this place had still needed a place to relax and mingle, away from the pressures of their duties. In its way, this place would not have felt very different from his own place of work. He wondered what kinds of ghosts would haunt Panoply, two hundred years after he was gone.

He pulled back from the railing with a tingle of disquiet. Sparver was already a quarter of the way around the balcony, testing each door as he passed. So far they had all been locked, but as Dreyfus watched, Sparver reached a door that was ajar. He nudged it with the muzzle of his rifle, then beckoned Dreyfus forward. Glancing occasionally down at the atrium, Dreyfus approached the newly promoted field and examined what Sparver had discovered.

'I guess you were right about Firebrand, Boss.'

The room would once have been the personal quarters of one of the Amerikano staff. Now it had been converted into makeshift accommodation for one of Saavedra's people. A sleeping hammock had been strung between two walls. On an equipment crate, Dreyfus saw part of a Panoply uniform, a belt and whiphound clip, minus the whiphound itself. He found a coffee bulb that still had coffee in it, albeit cold. There was no dust on any of the items.

They continued their inspection of the upper level, pausing to investigate those rooms that were not locked. They found more personal effects and equipment, even a pair of compads. The compads were still operational, but when Dreyfus activated one he could not decipher the contents, even with Manticore. The Firebrand unit must have had its own security protocol.

Sparver and Dreyfus descended to the next level via a staircase, negotiating it slowly in their suits and armour. They found another ring of rooms, but most of these were larger and appeared to have served an administrative or laboratory function. There was even a medical complex, a series of glass-partitioned rooms still illuminated by pale-green secondary lighting. Old-fashioned equipment formed abstract, vaguely threatening shapes under a drapery of plastic dust sheets. The sheets had brittled and yellowed with age, but the machines under them showed little sign of decay.

'What happened to the people who used to live here?' Sparver asked, in little more than a whisper.

'Didn't they teach you anything in school?'

'Cut me some slack. Even fifty years is ancient history from a pig's point of view.'

'They went insane,' Dreyfus said. 'They were brought here in the bellies of robots, as fertilised eggs. The robots gave birth to them, and raised them to be happy, well-adjusted human beings. What they got was happy, well-adjusted psychopaths.'

'Really?'

'I'm simplifying. But children don't grow up right without other normal people around, so that they can imprint on reasonable social behaviour. By the time the second generation was being raised, some nasty pathologies were bubbling to the surface. It got messy.'

'How messy?'

'Axes through doors messy.'

'But they couldn't all have been insane.'

'They weren't. But there weren't nearly enough stable cases to hold the society together.'

Another staircase brought them to the lowest level of the atrium, where the pathway ambled between dried pools and ashen flower beds. Dreyfus speculated that it might once have been an agreeable place to pass time, at least in comparison with the claustrophobic confinement of the rest of the facility. But now he felt like an intruder breaking the stillness of a crypt. He told himself that the Firebrand agents had violated the sanctity of the place before Sparver and he had arrived, but the sense of being unwelcome did not abate.

Rooms, all of them larger than any they had seen on the upper levels, ringed the atrium space, cut back into the rock for many tens of metres. Corridors plunged even deeper, curving away to other parts of Ops Nine. At the far end of one, Dreyfus saw the daylit glow of what he presumed was another atrium space, perhaps at least as large as the one they were in. Several corridors ramped down into the ground, suggesting that there were further levels of habitation beneath. Dreyfus paused, unsure which route to take. He had expected to encounter *someone* in the central operations area, or at least find a clue as to where everyone had gone. But apart from the Panoply items they had already seen, there was no evidence of immediate human presence.

He was about to debate their next move when Sparver made an odd clicking noise, as if he'd got something lodged in his throat. Dreyfus snapped around to look at his deputy.

'Sparv?'

'Check out the sculpture, Boss.'

Dreyfus had paid little attention to the metal object since arriving on the lowest level. He'd appraised it just enough to see that it was indeed what it had appeared to be from above: a spiky black structure fashioned from something like wrought iron, suggestive of a cactus, anemone or angular palm tree, but equally likely to be a purely abstract form. It towered three or four metres over his head, throwing jagged shadows across the flooring. It consisted of dozens of sharp bladelike leaves radiating out from a central core, most of which were angled towards the ceiling. What he hadn't noticed – but which had not escaped Sparver's attention – was that there was a human skeleton at the base of the sculpture.

Despite all his years as a prefect, Dreyfus still flinched at the sight. He had seen corpses, but not many of those. He had seen even fewer skeletons. But the shock subsided as he realised that the skeleton could not have belonged to someone who had died recently. Most of the flesh had been consumed, leaving only a few grey-black scraps attached here and there. The bones, those that had not crumbled, were mottled and dark. Of clothes, and whatever else the corpse had been wearing, no visible trace remained.

The hapless victim must have been tossed from the high balcony, or perhaps dropped from some makeshift bridge stretched across the atrium, to fall on one of the larger spikes. The skeleton lay at its very base, the spike having rammed apart its ribcage. The skull lolled to one side, empty eye sockets regarding Dreyfus, the lopsided tilt of the jaw conveying incongruous amusement, as if it was taking a ghastly posthumous delight in the horror it caused.

But the real horror, Dreyfus decided, was not that someone had been murdered here. Dreyfus hardly approved of summary justice, but at this remove there was no telling what the victim might have done to deserve this brutal end. The horror was that the agents of Firebrand had not seen fit to do something with the bones. They had gone about their business, equipping this base for rehabitation, as if the skeleton was merely an unavoidable part of the decor.

Dreyfus knew then that he was dealing with more than one kind of monster.

'Put down your weapons,' a voice said.

Dreyfus and Sparver spun around, but it was already too late. The muzzle of another Breitenbach rifle was aimed down at them from the intermediate-level balcony. With the weapon on maximum beam dispersal, Dreyfus knew, it could take out both of them with a single pulse.

'Hello, Paula,' Dreyfus said.

'Put down the weapons,' Saavedra repeated. 'Do it immediately, or I will kill you.'

Dreyfus worked the sling of the rifle over his shoulder and set the weapon down on the ground. With obvious reluctance, Sparver followed his lead.

'Step away from the guns,' Saavedra said. She began to walk around the balcony, keeping the muzzle of her rifle trained on them all the while. Reaching the staircase, she began to descend. She wore Panoply trousers, but her upper body was clothed only in a sleeveless black tunic. It made her look thinner, more doll-like, than when Dreyfus had confronted her in the refectory. Yet she cradled the rifle as if it weighed nothing. The muscles that moved under her skin looked as hard and sleek as tempered steel.

'I haven't come to kill you,' Dreyfus said, as her booted feet clattered down the stairs. 'You'll have to answer for what you did to Chen, and Firebrand will have to explain its part in the death of the Ruskin-Sartorious Bubble. But I have no difficulty believing you acted out of a sense of duty; that you thought you were doing the right thing in sheltering the Clockmaker. A tribunal will see both sides, Paula. You have nothing to fear from justice.'

She reached the floor and started walking towards them. 'You finished?'

'I've said my piece. Let me walk out of here with the Clockmaker and I'll do all I can to make things easier for you.'

Saavedra kicked the rifles aside. 'Why are you so interested in the Clockmaker, Dreyfus? What does it mean to you?'

'I won't know until I've got it.'

'But you're interested in it.'

'I'm not the only one, am I?'

'You mentioned Ruskin-Sartorious. Do you know why we had to move the Clockmaker?'

'I presume someone was sniffing around.'

'And who would that someone have been, I wonder? Who was so concerned to locate it, after all the years it had been hidden? Who is still concerned?'

'Gaffney was working for Aurora. She's the one who wanted to locate and destroy the Clockmaker, because she perceived it as a threat.'

'And you think it's safe?'

'Aurora was afraid of it. That's good enough for me.'

'Thing is, Dreyfus, I don't have any proof that you're not lying to me.'

'How about this? If I wanted to destroy the Clockmaker, I could have dropped a missile on this whole facility thirteen hours ago. Instead, my partner and I have walked in with the intention of negotiating.'

'It's true,' Sparver said. 'We just want access to the Clockmaker. You've kept it all this time because you thought it might be useful one day. Well, guess what? This is the day.'

'I really don't know much about Aurora,' Saavedra answered. 'Yes, I'm aware of the crisis in orbit, the loss of the habitats, the evacuation effort. But I still don't have a clear picture of who's behind it. Can you enlighten me?'

'Is anything we say going to make you point that gun elsewhere?' Dreyfus asked.

'Let's see how you get on.'

Dreyfus took a deep breath, as much to calm his nerves as to prepare to speak. 'We think we know what Aurora is. She's a rogue alpha-level; one of the original Eighty. Unlike the others, she didn't fade or loop. She just made it look that way. In reality, she'd moved on, become stronger and faster.'

Saavedra's lip twitched derisively. 'So where's she been for the last fifty years, or however long it's been?'

'Fifty-five. And we don't know where she's been all that time, except that she's been planning something for much of it. The takeover is just the start. She wants complete control of the Glitter Band. Humans won't be allowed to live in it any more. It'll just be one vast support infrastructure for an immortal mind.'

'Why the sudden megalomaniacal intentions if she's lived happily enough under our noses all this time?'

'Because she thinks we're going to do something bad to the Glitter Band, something that will make it impossible for even an evolved alpha-level intelligence to remain safe.'

Again that lip-twitch. 'Something *bad*?'

'The point is, she's convinced herself that we can't be trusted with the safekeeping of the infrastructure she needs to stay alive, so we have to be removed from the equation. It isn't a takeover, since there isn't going to be anyone left alive under her regime – unless you count the handful of human slaves she'll need to fix the servitors when they break down. It's mass genocide, Paula.'

'And why does she fear the Clockmaker?'

'I think it's because the Clockmaker's the only thing in the system with an intelligence even approaching her own. It may even be cleverer. That means it's a threat to her sovereignty. That means she has to remove it.'

'That's what she was trying to do when she took out Ruskin-Sartorious,' Sparver put in. 'Gaffney set that up, but it was Aurora pulling the strings all the time. Only problem was, she was too late. You'd sensed her interest and moved the Clockmaker here.'

'Which is a pity, given that nine hundred and sixty people died because of false data,' Dreyfus said.

'Those people – the inhabitants of the Ruskin-Sartorious Bubble – were not meant to die,' Saavedra said.

'Then you regret their deaths?' Dreyfus asked.

'Of course.' She snarled her answer back at him. 'Don't you think we'd rather it hadn't happened? We assumed that whoever had shown interest had backed away. The relocation was a precaution. We didn't think there'd be *consequences*.'

'I'm prepared to believe that,' Dreyfus said.

'Believe what you like.'

'I also believe that a portion of the blame must be placed on Anthony Theobald's doorstep. He must have known he was endangering the lives of his family, even if he didn't know exactly what he was giving houseroom to.'

'He didn't need to know. None of them needed to know. None of them did know, right until the end.'

'One of them came close, though.'

She looked at him with sharp eyes. 'What do you mean?'

'Delphine Ruskin-Sartorious. The daughter. The artist of the family. Or didn't you realise?'

'Realise what?'

'She was in contact with the Clockmaker. It was something of a one-way dialogue, but it was contact all the same.'

She looked at him for a moment, then shook her head in flat dismissal. 'No, that wouldn't have been possible. Delphine was never allowed anywhere near it. Nor were any of the family members, including Anthony Theobald. It was kept inside an armoured cell, locked away unless *we* wanted to communicate with it. Not only could it not escape from the cell, it couldn't send a signal beyond it, either.'

'It still found a way to reach her.'

'Impossible.'

'Like it or not, it happened. My guess is that the cell wasn't as data-secure as you thought it was. Or maybe the Clockmaker slipped a signal through when you were talking to it, or whatever it was you did during your visits.'

'A signal needs a receiver,' Saavedra pointed out.

'Delphine had one. It was in her head. Like any good Demarchist citizen, she had a skull full of implants. She used them to direct the machines that helped her with her art. The Clockmaker found out how to manipulate one or more of those implants to place imagery in Delphine's mind and shape her artwork.'

Now Saavedra tilted her head sceptically. Dreyfus knew that he had some way to go before she was convinced, but he had certainly succeeded in intriguing her. 'Imagery?'

'The Clockmaker used her as medium, expressing itself through her work. She thought she'd tapped a seam of miraculous self-inspiration, but in truth she'd just become a conduit for the Clockmaker.'

'Ridiculous,' she said, but not with quite enough conviction.

'Maybe that's what attracted Aurora in the first place,' Dreyfus said, the idea occurring to him more or less at that moment. 'Of course, for the threat of the Clockmaker to have impinged on her consciousness, she must have a good idea of what the Clockmaker actually *is*.'

'And what is it? Seeing as you appear to have all the answers.'

Dreyfus couldn't help smiling. 'You mean you really don't know? After all this time?'

'And you, presumably, do?'

'I've got an inkling.'

'Nice try, Dreyfus, but if you think you're going to bluff your way out of this one—'

'A crime was committed,' he said. 'It all goes back to a single, simple deed: the murder of an innocent man. The Clockmaker is a direct consequence of that.'

'Who was murdered?'

'Point that gun elsewhere and I might tell you. Better yet, why don't you show me the Clockmaker?'

'Remove your suits,' she said. 'I want to check that you're not carrying any other weapons. If I even think you're about to trick me, I'll kill you.'

Dreyfus glanced at Sparver. 'Better do as she says.'

They removed their armour and suits, laying them out in neat piles before them. Under the suits, they both wore standard-issue Panoply uniforms.

'Turn around,' Saavedra instructed.

They turned their backs to her.

'Now turn to face me. Remove your whiphounds. Do not activate them.'

Dreyfus and Sparver unclipped their whiphounds and tossed the handles to the ground.

'Kick them to me.'

They did as they were told. Still training the rifle on them, Saavedra knelt down and clipped the whiphounds to her own belt. Then she single-handedly unclipped her own unit, a Model C, and deployed the filament. It hissed against the floor, its sharp edge a coiling scratch of bright silver. Deftly flipping the haft in her hand to turn the laser eye towards Dreyfus and Sparver, she marked them both then released the handle.

'Confirm target acquisition,' she said; the whiphound nodded its handle in reply. 'Maintain target surveillance. If targets approach within five metres of me, or move more than ten metres from me, intercept and detain both subjects with maximum lethal force. Indicate compliance.'

The whiphound nodded.

'I think we're clear on the ground rules,' Dreyfus said.

Saavedra moved to the rifles she had told them to discard, put down her own weapon and removed the ammo cells from the other two guns. She clipped the cells to her belt, next to the two captured whiphounds. Then she collected her own rifle and shrugged it back over her shoulder, the muzzle aimed at the ceiling.

'This is called a gesture of trust. Don't abuse it.'

'We're cool with not abusing it,' Sparver said.

'Follow me, and remember what I just told the whiphound. I'll show you the Clockmaker, if you really want to see it.'

CHAPTER 31

Saavedra led them deeper into Ops Nine, down one of the sloping ramps that Dreyfus had already noticed leading away from the atrium. Her whiphound slinked along behind the party, constantly triangulating the distance between Saavedra and her guests, waiting for one of them to transgress the parameters she had laid down. Dreyfus was relieved not to have a gun aimed at him, but the whiphound was only a marginal improvement. If he had been concerned about dying because of a twitch from Saavedra's finger, now he had to worry about the inflexible thought processes of a machine that really wasn't much brighter than a guard dog. Not that he had any intention of deliberately violating the rules, but what if he tripped, or accidentally crossed the five-metre line?

'I will show it to you,' she said, 'but you can forget any idea of negotiating with it. It is not a rational intellect.'

'It doesn't have to be rational to understand that Aurora wants it dead,' Dreyfus replied.

'You think that will give you leverage?'

'It's all I've got. Better make the most of it.'

'How did you manage to install a containment facility down here at such short notice?' Sparver asked.

'We didn't. There was only just time to clear out of Ruskin-Sartorious before it was destroyed. Fortunately, there was a kind of cage already here. It needed some alterations, but nothing beyond our resources.'

'You're talking about the tokamak,' Dreyfus said, wonderingly.

'The what?' Sparver asked.

'He means the fusion reactor that would have powered this facility during the Amerikano era,' Saavedra said loftily. 'And he's right. That's exactly what we used. It's one large magnetic containment bottle. Hideously inefficient compared to the portable generators we brought with us, but it has its uses. It needed to be checked, and the field geometry adjusted, but none of that was particularly taxing. It was much easier than installing our own containment equipment: we'd have needed to hollow out another cavern for that.'

'I hope you trust Amerikano engineering,' Dreyfus said. 'Keeping a psychopathic machine prisoner wasn't exactly in the design specs.'

'I trust it not to fail. Do you think I'd have come here if I didn't?'

'Where's everyone else?' Dreyfus asked.

'The rest of Firebrand? Apart from Simon Veitch, I'm the only one down here.'

Dreyfus remembered that name from the list of Firebrand members Jane had given him. It had impressed itself on his memory for a reason.

'Where are the others?'

'Wherever their duties require them to be. Since Jane pulled the plug on us, we've all had to live dual lives. How do you imagine we managed to maintain Firebrand while we also had our regular duties to attend to?'

'I did wonder.'

'The same therapeutic regime designed to keep Aumonier awake proved equally useful to the agents of Firebrand. Most of us have been getting by on only a few hours of sleep a week.' Saavedra lifted her arm and spoke into the bracelet clamped around the pale stick of her wrist. 'Simon? I've found the intruders.' She paused, listening to Veitch's reply. 'Yes, just the two. I'm bringing them down to the reactor.' She paused again. 'Yes, I have them under control. Why else would I have allowed them to live?'

The tunnel levelled out. They passed along a corridor lined with equipment storage rooms, then emerged onto a balcony overlooking a chamber only slightly smaller than the atrium they'd left behind. There was enough room for all three of them on the balcony without triggering the whiphound into action. The reactor filled most of the chamber, squatting on shockproof supports like an enormous magic cauldron. It was painted a pale green, with faint lines of rust along panel joints. A handful of panels and parts shone like chrome. Other than that it appeared superficially intact. Dreyfus guessed that little repair had been necessary before its magnetic generators were coaxed back to strength.

A catwalk girdled the reactor at its fattest point. A figure, dressed in black, was attending a monitor panel next to a dark observation window. The figure looked around and up, a grimace on his face. Veitch was as thin and cadaverous-looking as Saavedra, but conveyed the same impression of wiry strength.

'You should have killed them,' he said, raising his voice above the low hum of the reactor.

'They have information about the Clockmaker,' she said. 'Dreyfus says he knows where it came from. I'd like to hear what he has to tell us.'

Veitch looked irritated. 'We know where it came from. They made it in SIAM. That's where it ran amok.'

'But it didn't begin there,' Dreyfus said. 'It came of age in SIAM, reached its true potential there, but it originated somewhere else entirely.'

'Descend the stairs,' Saavedra snapped.

'You can call the whiphound off now,' Dreyfus said. 'I'm not going to hurt you.'

'Just descend the stairs. I'll worry about the whiphound.'

Dreyfus and Sparver edged past Saavedra, taking care not to come closer to her than five metres. They clattered down the stairs and crossed the chamber's equipment-cluttered floor until the reactor was looming over them.

'Climb to the observation deck,' Saavedra said, 'and tell Veitch why you want the Clockmaker.'

Looking up at Veitch, Dreyfus reiterated the argument he had already presented to Saavedra – that the Clockmaker was now the only effective weapon against Aurora.

'So what are you proposing? That we just let it loose and hope it crawls back to us when it's done?'

Dreyfus placed a hand on the railing and began to climb the stairs to the observation deck, Sparver immediately behind him.

'I'm hoping we won't have to let it loose at all. It's a matter of self-preservation. If I can impress upon it how much Aurora wants to destroy it, I can make it see the sense in defeating her. It will help us by helping itself.'

'From inside the cage?'

'It's a form of machine intelligence,' Dreyfus said. 'So is Aurora, no matter what she started out as.'

'How does that help us?'

'Aurora isn't a disembodied intelligence. She's a collection of software routines emulating the structure of an individual human brain. But she's nothing unless she has a physical architecture to run on.'

Above him, Veitch nodded impatiently. 'And your point is?'

'Somewhere out there, a machine has to be simulating her. More than likely she's controlling her takeover from within a single habitat. It probably isn't one of those she's already taken over, since she wouldn't want to risk being wiped out by one of our nukes. Unfortunately, that leaves almost ten thousand other candidates to consider. If we had all the time in the world, we could comb through network traffic records and pin her down. But we don't have all the time in the world. We have a few days.'

'You think she has free roam of the networks?'

'Almost certainly. She's stayed under our radar for fifty-five years, which means she can move herself from point to point without difficulty. But she can't duplicate herself. That's a limitation embedded in the deep structure of alpha-level simulations by Cal Sylveste himself. They cannot be copied, or even backed-up.'

'Perhaps she's got around that one by now.'

'I don't think so. If she could copy herself, she wouldn't be so concerned about safeguarding her own survival. She's scared precisely because there's only one of her.'

'But the notion of "machine" is nebulous, Prefect. Aurora might not be able to copy herself, but there's surely nothing to prevent her from spreading herself thinly, using thousands of habitats instead of one.'

'There is,' Dreyfus said, puffing as he reached the observation deck. 'It's called execution speed. The more distributed she is, the more she has to contend with light-speed timelag between processor centres. If part of her was running on one side of the Glitter Band, and another part on the far side of the Band, she could be afflicted by unacceptable latencies, whole fractions of a second. She'd still be just as clever as she is now, but the clock rate of her consciousness would have slowed by an intolerable factor. And that's her problem. Being clever isn't good enough on its own, especially when she's trying to win a war on ten thousand fronts. She has to be fast as well.'

'There's a lot of supposition there,' Veitch said as Dreyfus approached him cautiously, Sparver, Saavedra and her whiphound close behind.

'I agree, but I think it's watertight. Aurora can't afford to be spread out, therefore she has to be running on a single machine, inside a single habitat. And that means she's vulnerable to a counterstrike if that habitat can be identified.'

'And you're hoping the Clockmaker can pin her down?'

'Something along those lines.'

Veitch looked puzzled, as if he knew he was missing something obvious. 'It would need access to the networks.'

'I know.'

'You're insane. What if it escapes, loses itself in the networks the same way Aurora did?'

'There'd be a risk of that, but it's one I'm prepared to take given the alternative. I'd rather have a monster on the loose if it's a choice between that or dying under Aurora.'

'Do you have any idea what the Clockmaker did to its victims?'

Dreyfus thought of everything he had learned since gaining Manticore. Examining those new, fresh memories was like opening a wound that had just begun to scab over. 'I know it did bad things. But it wasn't indiscriminate. It spared more than it killed. Aurora won't spare a soul.'

'Show him what it is,' Saavedra said. 'He may as well know what he's talking about letting loose.'

'You've searched him for weapons?'

'He's clean. Show him the window.'

Veitch stood back from the monitor panel. 'Take a look for yourself, Prefect.'

'It's on the other side of this glass?'

'Nearly. We usually keep it away from the window. I'll rotate the magnets to bring it into view for a few moments.'

Dreyfus glanced back at Saavedra, waiting for her permission to move. She nodded. He joined Veitch and stepped onto the small pedestal beneath the viewing window. Two upright handrails provided support on either side of the armoured porthole. Dreyfus touched the pale-green skin of the reactor and felt it tremble under his hands. The tremor was irregular, with powerful surges.

'How did you get it in here?'

'There's a door on the other side, for swapping out the magnets. We kept the Clockmaker in a portable confinement rig while we moved it from Ruskin-Sartorious. We had to move fast, since the rig's only good for about six hours. The Clockmaker was testing it all the time, flexing its muscles, trying to break out, even though we did our best to stun it before the relocation.'

'Stun it how?' Dreyfus asked.

'With a heavy electromagnetic pulse. It doesn't put it under completely, but it does subdue it. But by the time we arrived here, it was back up to full strength. We got it inside and locked down with the big magnets just in time. You know how a tokamak works?'

'More or less.'

'Normally the magnets trap a ring-shaped plasma, steering it away from the walls. You heat and squeeze the plasma to a few hundred million degrees, until you get fusion. There's no fusion going on inside there now. Just hard vacuum, and the Clockmaker. We had to adjust the magnets to create a localised bottle, but it wasn't too difficult.'

'It's still trying to get out, isn't it?' He touched a hand to the reactor's throbbing skin again. He was feeling the Clockmaker's exertions as it tested the resilience of those magnetic shackles.

'It never stops trying.'

Dreyfus looked through the window. At first he saw nothing save a deep-blue darkness. Then he became aware of a faint pink glow encroaching on the darkness from his right. The glow flickered and intensified. To his left, Veitch made delicate adjustments to the configuration of the trapping magnets. The pink became a halo of flickering silver. The silver brightened to incandescent white.

'Why does it glow?'

'The field's stripping ions off its outer layer, a kind of plasma cocoon. When we collapse the field, the Clockmaker appears to suck the plasma back into itself. It doesn't suffer any net mass loss as far as we can tell.'

'I can see it now,' Dreyfus said, very quietly.

'It's beautiful, isn't it?'

Dreyfus said nothing. He wasn't exactly sure how he felt. He had thought of the Clockmaker many times since losing Valery, but the appearance of the thing had never been something he dwelled upon. He had been concerned only with its effects, not its nature. He knew from the victims' testimonies that the Clockmaker was amorphous, capable of shifting its shape with fluid ease, or at least of conveying that impression. He knew also that some of the survivors had spoken of a humanoid form underpinning its quicksilver transformations, like a stable attractor at the heart of a chaotic process. But those accounts had barely registered. It was only now that he truly appreciated that this was no ordinary machine, but something more like an angel, rendered in glowing white metal.

It hung in the tokamak, pinned in place by magnetic fields fierce enough to boil the electrons off hydrogen. Any normal machine, anything forged from orthodox matter – be it inert or quick – would have been simultaneously shredded and vaporised by those wrenching stresses. And yet the Clockmaker endured, with only that silver-pink halo conveying the extreme physical conditions in which it floated. It had the vague shape of a man: a torso, arms and legs, the suggestion of a head – but the humanoid form was elongated and spectral. The details shimmered and blurred, layers phasing in and out of clarity. For a moment the Clockmaker was a thing of jointed armour, recognisable mechanisms. Then it became a smooth-surfaced, mercurial form.

'He's seen enough,' Saavedra said. 'Move it away from the window before it breaks confinement.'

Veitch worked the controls. Dreyfus watched the Clockmaker recede from view. He was glad when it had gone. Though its face was featureless, he'd had the overwhelming impression that it was looking straight at him, marking him as a subject for future attention.

'That's my side of the arrangement,' Saavedra said. 'Now tell me what you know about it.'

'If I do, will you let me talk to it?'

'Just tell us what you know. We'll worry about the other stuff later.'

'I only came down here for one reason. The longer we delay, the harder it's going to be to stop Aurora. People are dying up there while we hesitate.'

'Tell us where it came from, like you promised. Then we'll talk.'

'It didn't come from SIAM,' Dreyfus said. 'It was created somewhere else, more than ten years earlier.'

'Could you try to be less cryptic?' Veitch said.

'Does the name Philip Lascaille mean anything to you?' Dreyfus asked rhetorically. 'Of course it does. You're educated prefects. You know your history.'

'What does Lascaille have to do with anything?' Saavedra asked.

'Everything. He became the Clockmaker.'

'Don't be absurd,' Veitch said, looking away with a dismissive smile on his lips. 'Lascaille went mad after he got back from the Shroud. He died years ago.'

Dreyfus nodded patiently. 'As you'll doubtless recall, he was found drowned in the Sylveste Institute for Shrouder Studies. It was always assumed that he'd committed suicide, that the madness he came back with had finally caught up with him. But that wasn't the only explanation for his death. He'd been silent for years, but just before his death he'd opened up to Dan, the scion of the family. He'd imparted clues that allowed Dan to go off on his own expedition to the Shrouders, confident of success where others had failed. People concluded that Lascaille, having relieved himself of this enormous burden of knowledge, had viewed his life's work as being complete. Either way, it was still suicide.'

'You don't think it was,' Saavedra said, curiosity vying with suspicion in her voice.

'Like I said, a man was murdered. I think that's where this all began.'

'But why?' she said. 'He was already mad. If people were worried about what he might say to Dan, the time to kill him would have been before they spoke, not after.'

'That's not the reason he died,' Dreyfus said. 'He wasn't killed because certain people were worried about the knowledge inside his head. He was killed because certain people wanted to get at that knowledge more than anything else in the universe. And killing him was the only way they knew to reach it.'

'You're not making much sense,' Veitch said.

'He's talking about alpha-level scanning,' Saavedra said, with dawning comprehension. 'Lascaille had to die because the process was fatal. Right, Dreyfus?'

'They wanted the patterns in his head, the structures left behind when he returned from the Shroud. They thought that if they could understand those structures, they'd have another shot at understanding the Shrouders. But to scan at the necessary resolution meant cooking his mind alive.'

'But things have improved since the Eighty,' Veitch said.

'Not by the time Lascaille died. All this took place thirty years after the Eighty, but for most of that time there'd been a moratorium concerning that kind of technology. They took him and did it anyway. They burnt his brains out, but they got their alpha-level scan. Then they took his body and dumped it in the fish pond. He was known to be insane, so no questions were asked when it looked as if he'd drowned himself.'

'Who would have done this?'

Dreyfus shrugged at Saavedra's question. He hadn't got that far yet, and his mind was freewheeling with the possibilities. 'I don't know. It would have needed to be someone high up in the Sylveste organisation. I doubt that it was Dan himself – it would have been against his own interests since he already had an insight into how to contact the Shrouders. But who's to say he didn't have a rival, a spy in the clan, interested in beating him to the prize?'

'But you'll go looking, won't you?' she said.

'I can't let a murder go uninvestigated. Of course, there are a couple of matters we need to deal with first. Surviving the next fifty-two hours would be a good start.' Dreyfus turned his attention to Veitch. 'Which is why we need the Clockmaker. I've stated my case as best I can. Now I want you to show me how to communicate with it.'

'It's an interesting theory you have, concerning its origin,' Veitch said. 'It may even be true. But that doesn't mean it makes any sense to let it loose now.'

'I'm not talking about letting it loose,' Dreyfus replied patiently. 'I'm talking about—'

'You think it makes a scrap of difference to the Clockmaker whether you open that cage or give it a hotline to the networks?'

Dreyfus felt a powerful wave of exhaustion crash over him. He had done his best. He had explained things to Saavedra and Veitch as clearly as he could, trusting that they would see his sincerity and understand that the Clockmaker really was the only effective weapon against Aurora, as unpalatable a prospect as that undoubtedly was. And it hadn't worked. Perhaps Saavedra had begun to come around, or at least believe that he had not come to destroy it. With time she could have been turned. But Veitch was showing no inclination to see things Dreyfus's way.

'I came here to negotiate,' he said, offering his hands in surrender. 'I could have had you killed, you and the Clockmaker. A single nuke would have done it. Do you think I'd have come here if I felt there was another option?'

'Prefect, listen to me,' Veitch said. 'No matter how bad things are up there, no matter how desperate they look, nothing can possibly be bad enough to justify giving the Clockmaker an angstrom of freedom. This is pure fucking evil incarnate, understand? It's the devil in chrome.'

'I know.'

'You *can't* know. No one really knows unless they've had direct experience with it, day after day, year after year, the way we have.'

'I was there,' Dreyfus said calmly.

'What do you mean, you were there?'

'When we went into SIAM. I was one of the prefects who went inside, before it was nuked out of existence.'

Veitch shot a nervous glance at Saavedra. Dreyfus recognised the look. They thought he was losing it. He looked at Sparver and saw the same expression on the face of his former deputy, though only Dreyfus would have recognised it.

'Prefect, we have clearance that exceeds Pangolin, clearance that exceeds even Manticore,' Veitch answered, in tones of slow reasonableness. 'We know everything that happened that day, to the last minute. We know who was involved, where they were, what they were doing.'

'Except the facts were changed,' Dreyfus said. 'My involvement was expunged from the record, from all documents except those intended for the eyes of Jane Aumonier alone. But I was there. I just didn't remember much about it until now.'

'He's losing it,' Veitch said.

'Dusollier committed suicide shortly after the Clockmaker crisis,' Dreyfus continued, 'but it wasn't because of decisions he took for himself. He killed himself rather than deal with the consequences of the actions I initiated, acting with Dusollier's blessing.'

'What do you mean, actions you initiated?'

'There was no prefect of higher rank in the vicinity of the crisis. The Clockmaker had already reached Jane. She was out of the equation. Dusollier authorised me to go in and use whatever measures were necessary to save the people still inside SIAM.'

'Then you failed,' Veitch said.

'No, I succeeded. I saved most of them.' Dreyfus paused. He found the words difficult to say out loud. It had been one thing to read the account of what he had done that day. But it was only now that he was speaking of his deeds that he felt he was really internalising what had happened. 'They survived. They're still alive.'

'No one survived,' Saavedra said. 'We nuked SIAM.'

'Yes, but not until six hours after Jane was pulled out, with the scarab on her neck. What happened in that gap? Why was it expunged from the public record? I've always wondered.' Dreyfus smiled weakly. 'Now I know.'

'Just come back to you, has it?' Saavedra asked snidely.

'Jane felt it might be tactically useful for me to recover the memories of my previous encounter with the Clockmaker. She knew it would be painful for me, given everything else that came with that baggage. But she was right to do it.'

'I agree with Veitch – you're losing it,' Saavedra replied.

'There was a ship orbiting nearby,' Dreyfus said quietly, 'a type of starship built by the Demarchists in an effort to lessen their dependence on the Conjoiners. It was a prototype, built around Fand. It used a different drive system, one that owed nothing to Conjoiner science. It had made one flight to our system and then been mothballed because it was too expensive, too slow, too clumsy. It was being stored against the day when even a ship like that became economical.'

'What was the name of this ship?' Saavedra asked.

'*Atalanta*,' Dreyfus replied.

'There was a ship with that name,' Veitch said, frowning. 'I remember that they wanted to rip it apart for scrap.'

'They did. It doesn't exist any more.'

'Tell us what happened,' Saavedra said.

'Yeah, you do that,' Sparver said.

Dreyfus was about to speak when two bracelets began to chime in unison. Saavedra and Veitch stared down in what was at first irritation and then alarm.

'Are the surface guns online?' Saavedra asked Veitch.

He nodded. 'They've acquired, but they won't open fire until it's closer.'

'Until what's closer?' Dreyfus asked.

Saavedra's eyes snapped to him. 'There's a ship coming in from space. It's making a direct insertion from orbit, at high-burn. It's not even attempting to conceal itself. Do you know anything about this, Dreyfus?'

'I went out of my way not to draw attention to your location. I didn't want Aurora following me to you.'

'But only Panoply knows we're here.'

'Then something must have happened,' Dreyfus said. 'It's a fair bet that whoever's flying that ship wants to put the Clockmaker out of action.'

'Let's get to operations,' Saavedra said. She fixed Dreyfus with a warning look. 'I'm calling off the whiphound now, but you know how quick these things are. I can put it back on you before you can blink.' She turned to Veitch. 'Is the containment stable?'

'Steady as a rock.' He flipped an armoured cover across the viewing window, secured it with a heavy latch, then followed the other three along the catwalk and down to the reactor floor. Saavedra's whiphound was now clipped to her belt again, but Dreyfus was under no illusions that he had gained her unequivocal trust. She was accepting his story provisionally, until he slipped up or circumstances changed.

'It could be Gaffney,' he said as they ascended the sloping tunnel back to the main habitation and operations level. 'The last time I saw him he was lying on his back recovering from surgery. But he wasn't dead. Maybe that was my big mistake.'

'Presumably he was under guard, though?' Saavedra said, looking back over her shoulder as they jogged up the slope.

'He was, but perhaps that wasn't enough. Gaffney was already able to sabotage the Search Turbines and murder both Clepsydra and Trajanova. He was clever, and he had the entire security apparatus at his fingertips, but he's not superhuman. I think Aurora may have been helping him, even inside Panoply.'

'And now she's helped him escape?'

'Possibly, but regardless, this feels like Gaffney. Did I hear you mention guns?'

'Portable self-burrowing anti-ship emplacements,' Veitch said. 'We installed them in case anyone came snooping without an invitation. You'd have found out if you hadn't come overland.'

'I'm glad we did. The walk did me good.'

Firebrand's operations centre had been set up in what must once have been a conference room when the facility was under Amerikano control. The walls were covered in monochrome photographs of scenic panoramas with only shallow three-dimensionality. One wall showed a deep canyon, possibly taken on Mars. Another showed a horseshoe-shaped waterfall. A third showed a rock face carved with enormous stone likenesses: eight vast heads, the fifth and seventh of which were women.

A cluster of display panes rested on the table, arranged hexagonally so that they formed a makeshift holographic tank. Veitch sent a gestural command to the apparatus, causing it to fill with luminous green wireframe graphics. Dreyfus recognised the contoured landscape of Ops Nine and its surrounding terrain. Markers signified the placement of weapons and tracking devices. An arrowhead symbol high above the landscape indicated the incoming craft.

'Signature matches a light-enforcement vehicle,' Veitch said, peering at the numbers accompanying the symbol. 'Would Gaffney be able to fly one of those?'

'He'd have the necessary experience,' Dreyfus said.

'It's not good news. It may be a cutter, but it could easily be carrying nukes.'

'Only if Jane had any left,' Dreyfus said. 'And if she did, they were probably already outside Panoply aboard deep-system cruisers, ready to be deployed as and when they were required. I don't think Gaffney would have been able to get his hands on one. More than likely it was all he could do to escape from Panoply.'

'I hope you're right,' Veitch said.

'I hope your guns are good. When will they open fire?'

'Not until he's below about thirty klicks,' Saavedra replied. 'The guns know the kinds of evasive routines and countermeasures a cutter has up its sleeve. Unless the cutter shoots first, they won't waste a shot until they have a chance of making a difference.'

Dreyfus saw that the cutter was still more than one hundred and twenty kilometres above them, but falling fast enough that it would pass below the weapon ceiling in only a couple of minutes. 'Gaffney wouldn't come unless he thought he could do damage,' he said. 'He'll be expecting to meet anti-ship fire.'

'I could take our cutter,' Saavedra said doubtfully. 'It still has enough fuel to get me airborne.'

'You wouldn't last five seconds against Gaffney,' Dreyfus said. 'Even if you could get up in time.'

She stared at the display, mesmerised by the falling arrow. 'He can damage the complex if he has foam-phase weapons, but he won't be able to touch the Clockmaker, inside the tokamak. He must know that.' A thought drained colour from her face. 'Voi, maybe he does have a nuke after all.'

'If he does, it'll be clean and fast for all of us,' Dreyfus told her. 'But I don't think he's intending to take out the Clockmaker in one hit. He must be planning to flush it out, then pick it off on the surface. It can't *fly*, can it?'

'If you gave it enough time,' Veitch said, 'I don't think there's much it couldn't do.' Then he studied the tank again. 'At present rate of descent, weapons will engage in ... forty-five seconds.' He looked anxiously at the others. 'There isn't much more we can do here. Maybe we should get below again?'

'Missile inbound,' Saavedra said, with dreamlike calm.

The display showed the missile streaking down from the cutter, leaping though the intervening atmosphere with ferocious acceleration. Any faster and friction would have incinerated the warhead before it reached its target.

'Guns retargeting,' Saavedra reported. 'Engaging.'

The room tremored. Dreyfus heard a low, rolling report, like distant thunder. He shuddered to think of the energy that had just been dissipated only a few hundred metres over his head. The weapons would have blasted their way out of concealed bunkers, just like the guns buried in the Nerval-Lermontov rock. But that had taken place in vacuum, not under a smothering methane-ammonia atmosphere. On the planet's surface, it would have looked like a series of choreographed volcanic eruptions, as if fists of molten fire had punched through the very crust of the world.

'Missile intercepted,' Saavedra said, though they could all see the result for themselves. 'Second incoming. Third incoming. Guns responding.'

The room tremored again, the earthquake-like rumble longer than before. There was a moment of silence as the guns retargeted to intercept the third missile, then the noise recommenced. 'Second missile destroyed. Partial intercept on third,' Saavedra announced. The room shook again, but Dreyfus knew that the guns would struggle to shoot down the third missile on the second attempt. It had been damaged, but it was still arcing down towards the facility.

'Brace,' Veitch said.

The missile's impact came a fraction of a second later. Dreyfus felt the shockwave slam through his bones. There was a roar louder than the guns, loud enough that it felt as if he was out there, standing under Yellowstone's poison sky with his eardrums naked to the air. He felt a violent shove, as if the room and all its contents had just lurched several centimetres to one side.

'One emplacement out,' Saavedra said as the appropriate icon pulsed red and faded to black. 'Fourth missile inbound. Guns acquiring.'

The roar of the anti-ship weapons sounded more distant now: Dreyfus guessed that the disabled emplacement had been the nearest one, taken out in a direct hit by the damaged missile.

'Tell me you have an intercept,' Dreyfus said.

'Partial,' Saavedra said. 'Attempting recontact.'

The guns droned. The room shook. The sense of helplessness

Dreyfus felt was suffocating. Machines were running his life now: machines and software. The system running the anti-ship emplacements was locking antlers with the system controlling the cutter's onboard weapons. Like familiar adversaries, the systems had a thorough understanding of their mutual capabilities. In all likelihood, his survival could already be ascribed a fixed mathematical probability. One participant knew it would eventually lose, but was still going through the motions for the sake of formality.

The fourth missile had lost much of its effectiveness when it struck home, but still retained enough potency to do real damage. The noise was a continuous deafening avalanche of sound. The room shuddered, chunks of ceiling material crashing down. A deep crack jagged its way down one wall, dividing the eight carved heads. The room's illumination failed, leaving only the pale-green glow from the holographic display, which was itself faltering.

'Generator complex is down,' Veitch said, with grim resignation. 'We should have buried it deeper. I *said* we should have buried it deeper.' He began to tap instructions into his bracelet. 'Back-up generator should have kicked in automatically. Why isn't it working?'

'Fifth missile inbound,' Saavedra said as the holographic display flickered. 'Guns attempting to acquire. Two emplacements down. What about that back-up generator, Veitch?'

'I'm doing the best I can,' he said through gritted teeth.

The roar of anti-ship guns was like a distant avalanche.

'Intercept?' Veitch queried.

'Partial,' Saavedra said.

Dreyfus was about to ask something when the fifth missile came slamming in. There was no sound this time; it was too loud to register as noise. It *felt* like a cosh to the skull. Deafened, but with scarcely a moment to register the fact, Dreyfus observed events compress themselves into a single frantic instant. The room darkened, filling with choking black dust, scouring eyes and skin, burning throat and lungs. His last glimpse gave the impression of the ceiling bowing down, riven with cracks. He saw a similar crack rip through the already damaged wall. And then there was neither light, nor sound, nor consciousness.

CHAPTER 32

Dreyfus came round to a world coloured in degrees of pain. He was cognisant of the pain map of his body, traced in his mind's eye by a flickering green mesh. There was a knot somewhere around his lower right leg, the contours bunching together until they formed an angry little eye. There was another knot in his chest, to the left of his sternum. A third on his upper right arm. The rest of him was merely aflame with discomfort. His throat felt as if it had been etched with acid. When he breathed, it was as if the lining of his lungs had been replaced by powdered glass.

And yet he was breathing. That was more than he'd expected to be doing.

He remembered the attack, but had no sense of how much time had passed since the arrival of the final missile. Everything was very still now. Not exactly silent, for his ears were ringing, but when he moved slightly he could hear his own groans of discomfort, so he had not been entirely deafened. He must have screamed at the end, he thought. He lay still, breathing heavily, ignoring the stab of pain that accompanied each breath, until he had regained some clarity of thought.

He forced his eyes open. At first he could see nothing, but then he became conscious of a faint glow. One of the holographic panes was still flickering, casting insipid green light around the wreckage-strewn room. Most of the dust and debris appeared to have settled, suggesting that more than a few minutes had passed since the assault. His eyes were stinging, watering, but slowly Dreyfus became accustomed to the gloom and began to pick out details of his surroundings. He was lying on his back on the floor, with his legs and hips pinned under the table, which had collapsed when the ceiling thrust down upon it. As the table gave way, the cluster of display panes had toppled to the floor to Dreyfus's right, including the one unit that was still aglow. He was trapped, and he could only speculate as to the true extent of his injuries, but he knew that he was very lucky to be alive at all. Had the table not shielded him, he would have been killed by the rubble that had crashed in through the ceiling. He tried moving his right arm again. The knot of pain had died down slightly, and as the arm moved he drew some comfort from the fact that it was probably not broken. He flexed his fingers, watching them move like pale wormlike things, seemingly disconnected from his own body. His left arm felt intact, but he could not reach the edge of the table from where he was pinned. Groaning again, pain flaring in his chest, he tried to move his right arm enough to begin to lever the table, hoping to lift it away from his trapped lower half. But as soon as he applied pressure, he knew it was hopeless. The pain in his arm intensified, and the table did not move at all. Dreyfus realised that he would not be able to escape unassisted.

He looked to his side, trying to distinguish between rubble and bodies. He began to fear that the others had been killed in the attack. But slowly he realised that the only other body in the room belonged to Simon Veitch. Of Sparver and Saavedra there was no sign.

'Veitch?' Dreyfus called, barely hearing his own voice over the ringing in his head.

Veitch answered almost immediately. 'Prefect,' he said, sounding as if there was a thick layer of insulating glass between the two men. 'You're alive, then.'

Dreyfus paused to recover strength before speaking again. Each word cost him more energy than he felt he could spare. 'I'm trapped under this table. I think I've broken a rib, maybe a leg. What about you?'

'Worse than that. Can't you see?'

Dreyfus could see, now that his eyes were finally adjusting to the minimal light. A silvery pipe, probably one of those installed by Firebrand when they were reactivating the facility, had buckled down from the ceiling to plunge through Veitch's thigh.

'Are you losing blood?'

'I hope so.'

Dreyfus coughed and tasted his own blood. 'What does that mean?'

'It means I think I have a chance of dying before it finds us.'

'Then it's loose?'

'The back-up generator should have activated immediately to

ensure a smooth handover. It didn't. Containment failed.'

'But we don't know for sure that it's loose. Not until someone goes down there ...'

Veitch laughed. It was the vilest, most inhuman sound Dreyfus had ever heard coming from another person. 'It's out, Prefect. Don't worry about that. It's just a question of how long it takes to find us. Because you can bet your life it's looking.'

'Or maybe it's already run away, trying to hide itself.'

'You don't know the Clockmaker. I do.'

'And you hope you're going to die before it gets here.'

Veitch touched a hand to his thigh. In the green glow his fingers came up tipped with something wet and dark, like melted chocolate. 'I think I've got a shot. How about you? You could always try holding your breath, see how far that gets you.'

'Tell me something, Veitch,' Dreyfus said, in the tone of a man changing the subject of a conversation that had begun to weary him.

'What?'

'When Jane gave me the list of Firebrand operatives, your name was familiar to me for some reason.'

'I get around.'

'It was more than that. It struck an old chord. It just took me a little while to remember the rest.'

'Meaning what?'

'You were involved in the case against Jason Ng, weren't you?'

The silence that followed was enough of an answer for Dreyfus. 'Simon?' he asked.

'Still here.'

'You're going to die soon. More than likely so am I. But let's clear this one up, shall we? Thalia's father was innocent. His only mistake was to get too close to your operation. He was investigating Firebrand, long after Firebrand had supposedly been shut down, and you had to do something about it.'

'Looks like you've already made your case.'

'I'm just putting pieces together. You concocted a case against Jason Ng to protect the operational integrity of Firebrand, didn't you? You fabricated evidence and watched a good man go down. And then you had him murdered, making it look like suicide, because you couldn't risk his testimony coming out in a Panoply tribunal. Which makes you no better than the people who murdered Philip Lascaille, does it? In fact, I'd put you on about the same moral pedestal.'

'Fuck you, Dreyfus. Fuck you and fuck Panoply.'

'I'll take your views into consideration. Before you die on me, answer one last question. Where are the others?'

Veitch's answer came more slowly this time, his words slurred. He sounded like a man on the edge of unconsciousness. 'I woke up once and your pig was still here. Saavedra was already gone. When I came around the second time, the pig was gone as well. Before I passed out the first time, he said something about taking care of Gaffney.'

Dreyfus absorbed that. As gladdened as he was to hear that Sparver was alive, he was troubled by the other prefect's intentions. 'Where did Saavedra go?'

'I don't know. Why don't you go and ask her?'

'Veitch?' Dreyfus asked, a little later.

But this time there was no answer.

'Good for you,' Dreyfus said, under his breath.

It was dark when Sparver finally found his way to the surface again, his suit donned hastily, sacrificing the armour he would have needed assistance to lock into place. Much of Ops Nine had collapsed during the attack, but the sloping tunnel by which he and Dreyfus had entered was still intact, and with care he had been able to ascend through the facility and squeeze past the obstructions on his way, using his suit's power to force open the surface doors. For once being a hyperpig had been to his advantage; he doubted very much that a fully armoured and suited baseline human would have been able to navigate some of the crawlspaces he'd had to pass through, especially not while dragging a Breitenbach rifle.

When he'd first regained consciousness, Saavedra had been about to leave the collapsed room, intending to find a way to restore the Clockmaker's containment. Sparver knew then that he had to get out of that room, even if it meant abandoning Dreyfus for the time being. He'd talked Saavedra into handing over the ammo cells she had confiscated earlier and clipped to her belt, telling her that he would attempt to take down Gaffney – or whoever it was – on his own. Saavedra obviously hadn't liked the idea of giving him access to weapons, but she presumably liked the idea of the attacker going unpunished even less. Eventually she'd relented and Sparver had taken the cells, watched Saavedra go and then lain very still while the room suddenly resettled, filling with pale dust and pinning him temporarily again before he worked loose and made his exit. He'd found the suit and weapon near the sculpture on the atrium level, right where he and Dreyfus had been ambushed what felt like a lifetime ago.

He emerged from the sloping ramp, crouching low as he passed through the toothlike formation of icicles. Overhead, the sky surged with the unbridled energy of a storm, clouds billowing and flickering with electrical discharges and strange, seething shifts in local atmospheric chemistry. Yet above the roar of the wind and thunder, his suit was conveying another sound to his ears. It was high-pitched and steady: the shrill whine of engines. Still using the upper slope of the ramp for cover, he knelt with the rifle between his knees and scanned the howling dark sky. It was not very long before he made out the hovering form of the cutter, poised nose-down like a stabbing dagger, with its hull-mounted weapons deployed and ready. Sparver guessed that Gaffney was loitering over the remains of Ops Nine with the intention of catching the Clockmaker making its escape. Whatever firepower had yet to be discharged would be directed in a single berserk frenzy of concentrated destruction. Perhaps Gaffney had no real expectation of killing the Clockmaker, but he would certainly be hoping to maim it.

Sparver flipped open the Breitenbach's weather cover, exposing the muzzle with its delicate battery of plasma emitters and laser-confinement optics. He powered-up the weapon, mindful that the cutter might be sniffing the local electromagnetic environment. The weapon ran through its start-up cycle, then signalled readiness. Sparver settled the long barrel of the rifle onto his shoulder, bazooka-style. A portion of his faceplate filled with a sighting reticle, superimposed over a view of the rifle's current target. Sparver eased back on his haunches until the hovering cutter bobbed into the middle of the reticle. He squeezed a stud on the side of the primary grip, telling the weapon to lock on to this target. A red bracket pulsed around the cutter, signifying target acquisition. Instantly Sparver felt the suit stiffen and adjust his posture for him. The rifle had assumed command of the power-assisted suit; it was using it as an aiming platform, with Sparver just going along for the ride.

The cutter's engine note shifted. Sparver watched the ship rotate and then start to drift in his direction. Its weapons slewed slowly towards him, like a nest of snakes moving in unison. The cutter must have detected him. Gaffney was scouting closer, not wanting to discharge his weapons against a false target. The rifle, tracking the moving ship, made Sparver's suit adjust his position. A stutter of light erupted from the side of the hull. A rain of slugs tore into the upper lip of the ramp entrance, dislodging the icicles just before the lip crumbled away entirely. Sparver took a hit above one knee, a glancing shot that must have ricocheted off the ground. The impact nearly floored him, but his suit wasn't holed.

He fired the rifle, squeezing off three closely spaced pulses before regaining control of his suit and falling back into cover. *Confirmed hit*, the weapon informed him.

He peered back over the rim. The cutter was still airborne, but it wasn't doing any more shooting. The engine note had become erratic. The weapons were jerking around haphazardly, locking on to dozens of false targets. Sparver resettled the rifle on his shoulder and fired another three shots, this time relying on his own aiming ability. Crimson light poured from the hole he'd blown in the side of Gaffney's ship. The engine note quietened to silence.

The cutter dropped.

A second or so later, Sparver felt the impact slam through the ground. He braced, but there was no explosion. He waited a decent interval, then hauled himself from the cover of the shattered ramp and made his way across the pulverised ground, keeping the rifle aimed nervously ahead of him. The cutter had come down a kilometre away, close to the main entrance point to Ops Nine, where Saavedra would have docked and hidden her own ship. When Sparver reached it he found that the cutter had buried the front three metres of its nose in the frost, urine-coloured rivulets of melted methane-ammonia snow dribbling away from the impact point. The airlock was open, the outer door blasted off and lying to one side some metres away. The inner door was also open, revealing the faintly glowing interior of the crashed vehicle. Sparver's suit started warning him that radiation levels were above tolerable norms. He ignored its protestations and used a handy boulder to climb into the shell. He pointed the rifle into the interior, using its sighting facility to see around the corner. But it only took a glance to confirm that the cutter was empty.

Gaffney was missing.

'Even for a cockroach, you take a lot of killing,' Sparver said.

*

Dreyfus snapped to consciousness again. He had no recollection of sliding back under, although he did remember that he had been about to make another attempt to free himself of the table. Perhaps the pain, or simply the exertion, had been enough to loosen his hold on the waking world. Either way, once more he had no clear idea of how much time had elapsed; whether it was seconds or minutes or hours.

'Stay still,' a woman's voice told him. 'You're safe now.'

He realised that he wasn't pinned under the table any more, and that the overall blanket of pain had dampened to a vague numbness. His ears were still ringing, his eyes still watering, but he did not feel any worse off than when he had been speaking with Veitch.

'Paula?' he asked, recognising the voice as Saavedra's, and that she was standing to one side of the bed or couch upon which he was resting. 'What happened? Where am I?'

'I rescued you from the collapsed room. You're in a different part of the facility, deep enough that it escaped the damage.'

Saavedra was almost lost in the shadows, with only dull red highlights tracing her form. She stood demurely, her hands linked before her, against the ruddy glow from a wall panel.

'Did you check Veitch?'

She nodded stiffly. 'He was already dead when I got back.'

Dreyfus moved his head enough to survey his body. It was difficult, since there was hardly any light in the room. The lower part of his right leg was covered with dried blood, but there was no sign of any bones sticking through the fabric. The pain had eased now: his uniform would have begun secreting topical antiseptic and painkillers as soon as it detected his injury, and by now they'd had time to take effect. His right arm was still sore – the uniform was allowing him to feel just enough pain to remind him not to hurt himself further – but again the injury could have been much worse.

'I don't know what's happened to Gaffney, but we should probably think about getting out of here,' Dreyfus said. 'Before he lost consciousness, Veitch told me that there'd been a containment breakdown. He was convinced that the Clockmaker would have escaped.'

'Do you think there'd be any point in running from it?'

'I'd rather run than sit here waiting for an audience.'

'Well, you don't need to worry just yet. Containment failed, but not long enough for the Clockmaker to escape. It's still inside the tokamak. The back-up generators won't keep it there for ever, but we're safe for an hour or so.'

'I'm glad. But you should still be thinking about getting out of here now.'

She cocked her head, puzzled by his response. 'Me, Dreyfus? After all that's happened?'

'You came here by ship, Paula. Find Sparver, then collect your cutter. If you have fuel to reach orbit, do so. Otherwise get back to Chasm City and contact the authorities. If there's anything left of Panoply, they can probably put you in touch.'

'And then what?'

'Tell them what I told you concerning the Clockmaker. Make sure someone finds out about it. If Jane Aumonier is still alive, tell Jane.'

'How will that knowledge help matters?'

'Maybe it'll come in useful when they have to put the Clockmaker back in the bottle.'

'You are not seriously injured, Dreyfus. You don't have to die down here.'

'Someone has to go down to the tokamak. Someone still has to talk to the thing and persuade it to do what it can to turn back Aurora.'

'You think you can persuade the Clockmaker?'

'I'll give it a shot.'

'How? You don't even know how to communicate with it.'

'I'll find a way. Even if I have to open the tokamak and let it out.'

'It would almost certainly kill you.'

'But it might want to talk first. I'll have to count on that. If I can make it see what a threat Aurora presents ... if it hasn't already worked that out for itself, of course.'

Saavedra unclasped her hands. She touched one index finger to her lips, studiedly conveying thoughtfulness. 'I made a mistake in not trusting you when you arrived, didn't I? I should have listened to you properly; learned everything I could about Aurora.'

'You can make amends by getting through to Panoply.'

'I'll do what needs to be done. But first I need to know more about Aurora, not just the Clockmaker. You said she was one of the original Eighty, didn't you?'

Dreyfus nodded wearily. It seemed unnecessary to rake over this again, given what he had already told Saavedra. 'My colleague knows about as much as I do.'

'But I'm asking you, not your deputy. What was her full name?'

'Aurora Nerval-Lermontov. She was just a girl when they scanned her. I don't think she was a monster then. Maybe it was society's hatred and fear that drove her to become what she is, when they knew what Calvin Sylveste had brought into existence. Or maybe she always had it in her, like a seed waiting to flourish. Maybe she was a sick little girl from the moment she was born. Either way, she has to be stopped, wiped out of existence, before she takes over the entire Glitter Band. She won't stop there, either.'

'Where is she located?'

'We've been over this, Paula. We don't know. There's about ten thousand habitats up there, any one of which could be hosting her unawares.'

'Could she distribute herself, like a program executing on a massively parallel architecture? A piece of herself running on thousands of habitats, so that the loss of any one processing centre would not be catastrophic?'

'Like I said, she won't do that because the timelag would slow her thought processes down to a crawl.'

'All the same. If she is to coordinate a takeover, she must make use of the network infrastructure to send commands and receive intelligence.'

'Yes, but she's obviously become expert at concealing herself. We just don't have the overview to pick out the signal from the noise.'

'Whereas you think the Clockmaker may be able to.'

'That's the idea.' He was growing increasingly irritated at having to repeat the argument he'd already presented to Saavedra and Veitch. 'Paula, why are we going over this again? We don't have time. Either you agree or you don't.'

'I do agree,' she said, so quietly that he almost didn't catch the reply. 'It's your only hope of survival. Put one alpha-level mind against another. What could be more logical?'

That was when Dreyfus had the first tingling suspicion that something was very wrong.

'Paula?' he asked.

She turned away from him so that he was looking at her face in profile. Silhouetted against the illuminated wall, her body held the erect pose of a dancer about to begin some demanding routine. Dreyfus saw that there was something attached to the back of her head, neck and spine. It was like a thick metal caterpillar, a segmented thing with many legs. Her sleeveless black vest had been gashed open from neck to coccyx. As she turned even more, he saw that this was also true of her skin. He could see her backbone, grinning white through meat and muscle. The caterpillar had dug its needle-tipped feet through to her spinal nerve column.

Quite without warning, she dropped to the floor.

Dreyfus lay perfectly still, paralysed by the horror of what he had just witnessed. It must have found her, tortured or tricked her just enough to extract the basic details of Dreyfus's mission. Then it had slashed her open and made her into a meat puppet.

Now it was done with the puppet. On the floor, Saavedra twitched and spasmed like a fish out of water.

'You're here,' he said, finding the strength to speak. 'You're with me, aren't you? In this room. You did escape after all.'

There'd been a humming sound all along, but it was only now that his ringing ears became fully attuned to it. Moving his neck by the tiniest of degrees, he looked around to face the other side of the bed, opposite where Saavedra had been standing. That side of the room was dark, but he was still aware of the form waiting there. It was larger than a man, towering towards the ceiling, stooping over to fit into the confined space. The red light gleamed off a dripping chrome ribcage, off the sickle-shaped fingers of a huge metallic hand, off the hammerhead width of a huge eyeless skull. The humming intensified. To Dreyfus, it became the most malevolent sound in the universe.

'What do you want with me?' he asked, expecting no answer.

But the Clockmaker spoke. Its voice was surprisingly soft, surprisingly avuncular. 'It was very brave of you to come here, to find me. Did you expect that it would end like this?'

'I didn't know what to expect. I had no other choice.'

'You expected to persuade me to help you?'

Dreyfus licked his lips. They felt as dry as clay. His heart was trying to tunnel its way out of his chest. 'I only wanted to show you the way things are.'

'With Aurora?'

'Yes. She won't stop. You're the only thing that can touch her. Therefore she has to destroy you. And she will, sooner or later. Unless you destroy her first.'

'Aurora will murder all of you.'

'I know.'

'What makes you think I'm any better?'

'Because you didn't kill everyone in SIAM.'

The Clockmaker sounded amused. 'And that gives you hope? That makes you think I'm the lesser of two evils?'

'I don't think you're evil. Not really. I think you're furious and driven, like an avenging angel. You've been hurt and you want to give back some of that hurt. I think that makes you bad. But I don't think it makes you evil.'

The Clockmaker contorted itself even more, bending at the middle to lower its upper chest and head to only a metre above Dreyfus. Still he could see only highlights, where the red light caught a sleek metal edge. The head, which had appeared hammer-like only a moment ago, now had the form of an anvil.

'You presume to know what I am?'

'I know *who* you are,' Dreyfus said, each word feeling as if it might be his last. 'I know what they did to you, Philip.'

The Clockmaker did not answer. But something sliced through the air, one of its arms moving so quickly that the motion became a scything blur of darkness and shadow. The whipping arm touched Dreyfus's forehead. His skin felt suddenly cold. Something trickled into his eye, warm and stinging.

'I know what they did to you,' he repeated. 'They took you and burnt out your mind, trying to extract an alpha-level simulation. Then they dumped your body in a fish pond and made it look like suicide. They only wanted those alpha-level patterns for one thing, Philip. Not to give you immortality, but to help them program a machine that could travel into the Shroud without being ripped apart. You'd survived, where others hadn't. They made a robot and loaded your alpha-level simulation into it, in the hope that something in those brain patterns would make a difference.'

The Clockmaker was listening. It hadn't killed him yet. Perhaps it was planning something worse than death, some ingenious new cruelty that would make even Jane Aumonier's eleven years of sleeplessness seem like a kindness.

'They must have sent you into a Shroud,' Dreyfus continued. 'One within a few light-years of Yellowstone, so that you had time to go there and back before you showed up in SIAM. That's what happened, isn't it? You were sent into the Shroud as a machine running Philip Lascaille's alpha-level simulation, and you came back ... *changed*, just the way Philip had all those years before. Something inside the Shroud had remade you. You were still a machine, but now you were a machine with alien components. And you were angry. You were worse than angry. You were a machine that knew its soul had been stolen from an innocent man, a man who'd already been driven half-mad by the things he'd seen inside the Shroud.'

Still the Clockmaker loomed over him, the mantra-like rhythm of its humming beginning to fill his brain, squeezing out rational thought. Dreyfus swore he could feel its breath, a cold, metallic exhalation like a steel breeze. But machines didn't breathe, he told himself.

'I don't know how you ended up in SIAM,' Dreyfus went on, 'but I'd guess you were in a state of dormancy when you returned from the Shroud. The people who'd sent you there didn't really know what to make of you. They knew they'd got back something strange, but they couldn't begin to comprehend your true origin, your capabilities, what was driving you. So they transferred you to the people in the Sylveste organisation best suited to probe the nature of an artificial intelligence. More than likely, the scientists in SIAM had no inkling of where you'd come from. They were fed a story, led to think that you were the product of another research department in the institute itself. And at first you were very obliging, weren't you? You were like a newborn baby. You made them happy with the clever things you made. But all along you were recovering memories of your true nature. The fury was welling up inside you, looking for a release valve. You'd been birthed in pain and terror. You naturally assumed that pain and terror were what you were meant to give back to the world. So you did. You began your spree.'

After a silence that stretched on for centuries, the Clockmaker spoke again. 'Philip Lascaille is dead.'

'But you remember, don't you? You remember how it felt to be him. You remember what you saw in the Shroud, the first time.'

'How would you know?'

'Because I recognised your face in Delphine's sculpture. You were communicating through her art, finding a channel to the outside world even when you were a prisoner.'

'Did you know Delphine?'

'I knew her after she was murdered, via her beta-level simulation.'

'Why was she murdered?'

'Aurora did it. She was trying to destroy you. Delphine and her family got in the way.'

The humming became slower, ruminative. 'And the beta-level simulation?'

'Aurora found a way to get to that as well.'

'Then she has murdered Delphine twice.'

'Yes,' Dreyfus said, surprised that the truth of that had never really occurred to him before.

'Then another crime has been committed. Is that why you came here, to solve a crime?'

Dreyfus thought about everything that happened to him since he first learned of the destruction of the Ruskin-Sartorious Bubble. With each step the case had opened wider, until he was embroiled in a full-blown emergency, a crisis upon which the future existence of the Glitter Band rested. It was difficult now to remember how parochial he'd expected the outcome of the inquiry to be. A simple case of revenge or spite. How laughably wrong he'd been.

But the Clockmaker was right. The path that had brought him here had begun with a simple murder investigation, albeit one that encompassed nine hundred and sixty victims.

'In a manner of speaking.'

'Aurora would have needed an accomplice. Who did her bidding?'

'A man called Gaffney. A prefect, like me. He's the one attacking this facility, trying to get to you.'

'A bad man?'

'A man who believes bad things.'

'I should very much like to meet this Gaffney.' The Clockmaker's tone was momentarily pensive, as if it was daydreaming. 'What will happen to you now, Prefect?'

Dreyfus almost laughed. 'I don't think that's really in my hands, is it?'

'You're right, it isn't. I could kill you now, or do something to you that you would find infinitely worse than death. But I could also let you leave.'

Dreyfus thought of the way cats toyed with birds before finishing them off. 'Why would you do that?'

'Murders have been committed, Prefect. Isn't it your duty to investigate those murders, to bring those responsible to justice?'

'That's part of it.'

'How far would you go to see justice served?'

'As far as it takes.'

'Do you believe that, in your heart of hearts? Be careful how you answer me. Your skull is a stained-glass window, an open book revealing the processes of your mind. I can tell a lie from the truth.'

'I believe it,' Dreyfus said. 'I'll do whatever it takes.'

He saw the great fist rise high and then descend, dropping towards his skull like a chrome-plated pile driver.

Gaffney halted at the sight of the figure ahead of him. Her thin form stood silhouetted against the glowing wall to her rear. She had one hand on her hip, her head at an angle. There was something almost coquettish about that stance, as if she'd been waiting for him, like a lover keeping an assignation.

'As you can see,' he said, his voice booming out beyond the suit, amplified to monstrous proportions, 'I'm unarmed.'

'As you can see,' the woman said, 'so am I. You can put down that weapon now, Prefect Gaffney. You have nothing to fear from me.'

'It's more a case of what you have to fear from me. Saavedra, isn't it?'

'Got it in one. Should I be flattered that you know of me?'

'You can if you want to be.' Gaffney stepped closer. He was limping. He had been injured in the crash and the power-assist of his suit was beginning to malfunction. 'I only want one thing from you. You've got the Clockmaker down here.'

'It's already escaped,' Saavedra said. 'You're too late. Go home.'

'What if I said I didn't believe you?'

'Then I'd have to prove it to you, wouldn't I?'

'How would you do that?'

Still holding that coquettish pose, still mostly in shadow, the woman said, 'I could show you the reactor, the tokamak we were using to contain it. You know about magnetic fields and the Clockmaker, don't you?'

'Of course.'

'We had it pinned down until you showed up. If you hadn't attacked us, you could have infiltrated our facility and then worked out a way to destroy it.'

'Like you wish I'd done that. Where's Dreyfus?'

'You killed Dreyfus in your attack.'

'So the day hasn't been a complete waste of time.'

'Did you hate him that much, Prefect Gaffney? Did you hate him enough to want him dead?' Only now did she adjust the tilt of her head, moving it with the stiffness of a puppet that needed oiling. Something about the movement triggered a profound unease on Gaffney's part, but he suppressed his qualms. 'Did you hate him the way you hated Delphine?'

'Delphine was a detail that got in the way. She had to go.' He waved the muzzle of his rifle. 'Do you want to become a detail as well?'

'Not really.'

'Then show me the tokamak. I want concrete evidence that the thing's escaped. Then you're going to help me locate it, before it gets off-planet.'

'Are you going to kill it as well?'

'That's the idea.'

'You're a very determined man,' she said, with a note of admiration he hadn't been expecting.

'I get things done.'

'You know, so do I. Maybe the two of us have more in common than we might have imagined.' Her hand moved on her hip. Her arms were stick-thin, less like limbs than jointed sword sheaths. She pivoted on her heels, turning with the eerie smoothness of a battleship turret. Gaffney blinked, thinking he'd seen something on her back, tracing the course of her spine.

'I'd like to see where you had it hidden.'

'I'll show you that and more. I can prove to you that it escaped.' She beckoned him forward. 'Would you like that?'

'Very much so,' he said.

CHAPTER 33

Dreyfus came around for the third time that day. He was still lying where the Clockmaker had left him, his head still ringing with that last fateful moment when the machine's fist had come crashing down. He'd been expecting to die then, more certain of it than anything in the universe. Yet here he was, looking up at Sparver.

'I . . . ' he began.

'Easy, Boss. Save the questions for later. We've got to get you suited and out of here. Whole place is starting to cave in.' Sparver had his helmet cradled in his arm but was otherwise suited, a Breitenbach rifle slung over his shoulder.

'My leg's hurt,' Dreyfus said, his throat still raw. 'I'm going to have trouble walking.'

'You made it here. How did you get out of that collapsed room?'

'I didn't. I was brought out while I was unconscious.'

'By whom? When I left, Saavedra was gone and Veitch was out cold. I tried shifting that table but I couldn't manage it on my own. Veitch was in a bad way. I don't think he was in any shape to help you.'

'It wasn't Veitch.' Dreyfus paused, sucking in his pain while Sparver helped him off the couch. 'I came around in here, and I was talking to Paula Saavedra. But it wasn't her. It was the Clockmaker, Sparv. I was in the same room as it. It was talking to me, speaking through her body.'

'You sure you weren't hallucinating?'

'Later I saw it for what it was. It revealed itself to me when I guessed what was going on. I thought it was going to kill me. But it didn't. I woke up and I'm looking at you instead.' As the pain ebbed, Dreyfus was struck by an unpleasant possibility. 'It had time to do something to me, Sparv. Is there anything on me? Anything missing?'

Sparver inspected him. 'You look the same way you did when I left you, Boss. The only difference is that thing on your leg.'

Dreyfus looked down with apprehension. 'What thing?'

'It's just a splint, Boss. Nothing to be alarmed by.'

There was a thin metal cage wrapped around his lower right leg made up of a series of thin chrome shafts, bracing his leg at several contact points. The metal shafts had a still-molten quality about them, as if they were formed from elongated beads of mercury that might quiver back to liquid form at any instant. The longer Dreyfus studied it, the more clearly it looked like the work of the Clockmaker, rather than any human artificer.

'I thought it was going to kill me, or do something worse,' he said, in a kind of awed shock. 'Instead it did this.'

'That doesn't mean we misjudged it,' Sparver said, 'just that it has nice days.'

'I don't think that's why it did this. It just wants me kept alive so I can serve a purpose.'

Sparver helped him to begin hobbling towards the door. 'Which purpose would that be?'

'The usual one,' Dreyfus said. Then another troubling thought crystallised in his head. 'Gaffney,' he said. 'Veitch said—'

'I took care of Gaffney. He isn't a problem any more.'

'You killed him?'

'I shot down his ship. He survived the crash and escaped into Ops Nine before I had a chance to finish him off. But he isn't an issue any more.'

'How do you know?'

'Because I passed him on the way down to fetch you,' Sparver said, taking the bulk of Dreyfus's weight as they started ascending stairs. 'Most of him, anyway.'

With Dreyfus suited, an outcome that was somehow achieved despite the cumbersome bulk of his splint, they made their way to the surface, taking a different route than the one Sparver had used earlier. Although there were some tight squeezes along the way, neither of them was wearing tactical armour and Sparver discarded the rifle after a while on the assumption that it would prove inadequate against the only foe they stood a chance of encountering.

'It's gone,' Dreyfus said, attempting to reassure his deputy. 'You won't be seeing it again.'

'I didn't see it the first time.'

'Figure of speech.'

'Anyway, what do you mean *I* won't be seeing it?'

'Wherever it's gone, wherever it ends up, I think it'll be keeping its eye on me,' Dreyfus said. 'That's why it left me alive. It wants me to see that justice is served.'

'Justice for what?'

'The murder of Philip Lascaille. It was a long time ago, but some of the people involved may still be in the system, maybe even still working for House Sylveste.'

'You're talking about avenging the Clockmaker?'

'It still has a right to justice. I don't deny that it's a perversion of whatever Philip Lascaille once was. They took the mind of a man who'd been driven insane by the Shrouders and then fed the mind of that man – terrified even more because he knew he was going to die – into a machine for making contact. What they got back was an angel of vengeance, forged in a strange and alien place. I'm not saying the thing has my sympathies. But the earlier crime still stands.'

'And you'd be the man to look into it?'

'I don't care *who* wants justice, Sparv. It's a thing unto itself, irrespective of the moral worth of the wronged party. The Clockmaker may have committed atrocities, but it was still wronged. I'll do what I can to put that right.'

'And then what?'

Dreyfus grimaced as a spike of pain shot up his leg. 'Then I'll go after the Clockmaker, of course. Just because it was wronged doesn't mean it gets an exemption.'

'Presupposing, of course, that this minor business with Aurora blows over. Or had that slipped your mind?'

'I'm not too worried about Aurora any more.'

'Maybe you should be. The last time I checked, we were getting a whipping up there.'

'The Clockmaker interrogated me,' Dreyfus said. 'It grilled me on her capabilities, her nature. It wanted to know exactly what she was. Then it escaped. Doesn't that tell you something?'

'It's going after her.'

'It's at least as smart as she is, Sparv. Maybe smarter. And it has a very good reason to take her out of the picture.'

'At which point we'll be left with the Clockmaker to deal with, instead of Aurora. Is that really an improvement?'

'It wants vengeance, not genocide. I'm not saying any of us are going to sleep easy with that thing out there, but at least we'll be sleeping. That wouldn't have been an option under Aurora.'

Dreyfus and Sparver completed the last stage of their ascent. They passed through the collapsed remains of a subterranean landing area where Saavedra's cutter was still parked and waiting. A ceiling spar from the sliding weather cover that concealed the landing deck had pinned the ship to the ground. Sparver went aboard and tried to communicate with Panoply, but the cutter was dead.

'Don't worry,' Dreyfus said. 'They'll come for us.'

By the time they arrived on the surface, the storm had abated. The starless sky was a moving vault of poisonous black, but according to Sparver it had nothing of the howling ferocity of earlier. Unafraid now to stand on high ground, Dreyfus activated his helmet lamp and surveyed the fractured dark landscape, picking out suggestive details that made him flinch until he saw that they were merely conjunctions of ice and rock, light and shade, rather than the furtive presence of the Clockmaker. He sensed that it had left this place, putting as much distance as it could between itself and the magnetic prison of the tokamak.

'It must still be out there somewhere,' Sparver commented.

'I don't know about that.'

'It can't have left the planet. It's a machine, not a ship.'

'It can take whatever form it wants to,' Dreyfus replied. 'What's to say it can't change itself into anything it needs to be? I watched it manipulate its form right in front of me. Now that it's free of the cage, I wonder if there's anything it can't do.'

'It's still a thing. It can be tracked, located, recaptured.'

'Maybe.'

'What are you thinking?' Sparver asked.

'Maybe it will have taken a leaf out of Aurora's book. An alpha-level intelligence is easy to contain if it confines itself to a single machine, a single platform. But it doesn't have to be like that. Aurora worked out how to move herself around, to embody herself wherever it suited her needs. What's to say the Clockmaker won't do likewise?'

'To meet her on her own terms, you mean?'

'If I was it, and I thought she wanted to kill me, that's what I'd do.'

'That would also make it more difficult for us to kill it, wouldn't it?'

'There'd be that as well,' Dreyfus admitted.

They stood in silence, waiting for something to come out of the sky and rescue them. Occasionally a strobing flash pushed through the darkness: evidence of lightning or – perhaps – something taking orbit around Yellowstone, something that had nothing to do with weather.

After a long while, Dreyfus started speaking again. 'I had a simple choice, Sparv. The nukes were available and ready to go. They'd have destroyed SIAM and taken out the Clockmaker. We'd already got Jane out, so we knew what it was capable of. We knew the things it could do to people even if it didn't kill them. And we knew there were still survivors inside that structure, people it hadn't got to yet. Including Valery.'

'You don't have to talk about this now, Boss. It can wait.'

'It's waited eleven years,' Dreyfus said. 'I think that's long enough, don't you?'

'I'm just saying ... I pushed you earlier. But I had no idea what I was doing.'

'There was something else, of course. We still needed to know what we'd been dealing with. If we nuked SIAM without gaining any further intelligence on the Clockmaker, we'd never know what to do to stop something like it happening again. That was vital, Sparv. As a prefect, I couldn't ignore my responsibility to the future security of the Glitter Band.'

'So what happened?'

'From the technical data we'd already recovered, and Jane's testimony, we knew that the Clockmaker was susceptible to intense magnetic fields. Nothing else – no physical barrier or conventional weapon – seemed able to stop or slow it. I realised that if we could pin the Clockmaker down, if we could freeze it, we could get the surviving citizens out alive. That's when I knew we had to power up the *Atalanta*.'

'The *Atalanta*,' Sparver echoed.

'It was a ship designed to undercut the Conjoiners in the starship-building business. Thing is, although it worked, it never worked well enough to make it economical. So they mothballed it, left it in orbit around Yellowstone while they worked out what to do with it. It'd been there for decades but was still perfectly intact, exactly the way it had been when it was last powered down.'

'What was so special about this ship?'

'It was a ramscoop,' Dreyfus said. 'A starship built around a single massive engine designed to suck in interstellar hydrogen and use it for reaction mass. Because it didn't have to carry its own fuel around, it could go almost as fast as it liked, right up to the edge of light-speed. That was the idea, anyway. But the drive system was cumbersome, and the intake field generated so much friction that the ship was never as fast as its designers had hoped. But that didn't matter to me. I didn't want the ship to move. I just wanted its intake. The scoop generator was fifteen kilometres across, Sparv: a swallowing mouth wide enough to encompass SIAM in its entirety.'

'A magnetic field,' Sparver said.

'I sent a Heavy Technical Squad aboard the *Atalanta*. We attached high-burn tugs to shift its orbit, to bring it close to SIAM. We couldn't get its reactors back on line fast enough, so we jump-started the ramscoop using the engines on our corvettes. In an hour the field was building strength. In two we had it positioned around SIAM.' Dreyfus paused, the words suddenly drying up in his mouth. 'We knew there was a risk. The human survivors in SIAM were going to be exposed to that same magnetic field. There was no telling what it would do to their nervous systems, let alone the implants most of them were carrying. The best we could do was to try to focus the field on the area where we'd last pinpointed the Clockmaker, and try to hold the field strength as low as possible elsewhere.'

'It was better than just nuking. At least you gave them a chance.'

'Yes,' Dreyfus said.

'You said they survived. When you told me about it earlier.'

'They did. But the effects of the field had been ... worse than we feared. We froze the Clockmaker, recovered its relics, studied it as best we could and then retreated with the survivors. That took the rest of the six hours. Then we nuked. We thought we'd destroyed the Clockmaker, of course. In truth, it'd had packed itself down into one of the relics, waiting to be reopened like a jack-in-the-box.'

'And the survivors?' Sparver asked eventually.

It took Dreyfus an equally long time to answer. 'They were all taken care of. Including Valery.'

'They're still alive?'

'All of them. In Hospice Idlewild. The Mendicants were asked to look after a consignment of brain-damaged sleepers. They were never told where those people really came from.'

'Valery's with them, isn't she?'

Dreyfus's eyes were beginning to sting. 'I visited her once, Sparv. Just after the crisis, when it had all blown over. I thought I could live with what she'd become. But when I saw her, when I saw how little of my wife was left, I knew I couldn't. She was tending the gardens, kneeling in soil. She had flowers in her hand. When she looked at me, she smiled. But she didn't really know who I was.'

'I'm sorry.'

'That was when I went back to Jane. I told her I couldn't live with what I'd done to them. So she authorised the memory block.'

'And Valery?'

'I never went back to see her. Not in eleven years.'

Presently Dreyfus became aware of a rising sound, louder than the wind. He looked up in time to see a large ship come slamming through the clouds, its hull still glowing from a high-speed re-entry. He recognised it immediately as a deep-system cruiser, although he could not identify the ship itself. It circled overhead, landing gear clawing down from its reptile-smooth belly, weapons erupting through the hull as if they were the retractile spines of some poisonous fish. The pilot selected a patch of level ground large enough to accommodate the ninety-metre-long vehicle and descended slowly, using brief coughs of steering thrust to manage the descent.

Dreyfus and Sparver raised their hands in salute and started walking towards the parked ship, Dreyfus's stiff right leg dragging in the ice. A ramp lowered from the belly. Almost immediately, a suited figure began walking down it, picking its way cautiously down the cleated surface. The figure's small stature, the way she walked, told Dreyfus exactly who she was.

'Thalia,' he called out, delighted. 'It is you, isn't it?'

She answered on the suit-to-suit channel. 'Are you okay, sir?'

'I'll mend, thanks to Sparver. What are you doing here?'

'As soon as Prefect Gaffney got to you, we knew there was no point in concealing this location from Aurora. We would have come sooner, but we've been tied up with evacuees.'

'I understand completely. You came quickly enough as it is.'

Thalia walked across the rough ground until they were only a few metres from each other. 'I'm sorry about what happened, sir.'

'Sorry about what?'

'I screwed up, sir. The upgrades . . . I was unprepared.'

'It wasn't your fault.'

'But maybe if I hadn't gone in alone, if I'd had a back-up squad with me ... things might have been different.'

'I very much doubt it. Aurora had already considered every possible eventuality. She'd have found a way through no matter what precautions you took. It might have taken longer, but it would still have happened. Don't cut yourself up about it, Deputy.' Dreyfus extended a hand, inviting her closer. She crossed the remaining ground and let her suit touch his. Dreyfus held one of her arms, Sparver the other. 'I'm glad I got you back in one piece,' he said.

'I wish I could have done something for all the other people.'

'You saved some. And you got word back to us that Aurora had no intention of keeping anyone alive once she was in control. You did good, Thalia. I'm not displeased.'

'That's praise,' Sparver said. 'I'd take it if I were you.'

'What about Gaffney, sir?'

'Gaffney's gone,' Dreyfus answered.

'And the rest of Firebrand? The Clockmaker?'

'You've been well briefed, I see. I thought you'd have wanted to rest.'

'Well, sir?'

'Veitch and Saavedra are dead. The Clockmaker escaped.'

Behind her faceplate, Thalia nodded. 'We did wonder, sir.'

'Why?'

'Something's happening. We could only assume it had some connection with the Clockmaker, that you'd managed to persuade it to act against Aurora.'

'I wouldn't exactly say I persuaded it.' But Dreyfus was encouraged by this information. 'What's been happening, Thalia?'

'We're not really sure. The good news is that the Ultras have been contributing to the evacuation effort and helping with the destruction of contaminated habitats. Overnight we've cleared and evacuated another six along Aurora's expansion front.'

'Total evacuations?' Dreyfus probed.

'No, sir,' she said, hesitantly. 'Some people were still left aboard at the end. But a lot less than before.'

'I guess we can't expect miracles.'

'Sir, there's something else. A couple of hours ago, weevil flows reached two habitats before we were in place with nukes or lighthuggers. We'd got most of the citizenry out, but local constables were still assisting with the evacuation when the weevils broke through.'

'Go on,' he pushed.

'The constables started encountering the expected weevil resistance. They were doing their best to slow the weevils as they worked their way to the polling core, but they were taking heavy casualties. Then the weevils started behaving strangely. They became uncoordinated, erratic. They stopped their advance. The surviving constables managed to deploy heavy guns and started inflicting losses on the weevils.'

'But there'd still have been millions more in the flow, even if there was a local malfunction at the head of the assault.'

Thalia shook her head urgently. 'It wasn't a local malfunction, sir. It's started happening everywhere, wherever there are weevils. They have a degree of autonomous programming, like any servitor, but whatever controlling influence was guiding them appears to be absent, or at least distracted.'

'As if Aurora's mind's on other things.'

'That's what it looks like. Which is why we assumed you must have had some success with the Clockmaker.'

'It's already engaged her,' Dreyfus said marvellingly, as if he'd just witnessed some staggering phenomenon of nature. 'It knew it couldn't afford to wait very long. Even though Gaffney hadn't succeeded, Aurora would have found another way to destroy this facility. It *had* to leave.'

'We should probably be leaving as well,' Thalia said. 'Unless you still want to admire the scenery, that is.'

'I've had enough scenery,' Dreyfus replied. 'I'm not really a planet person.'

'Me neither, sir.'

'Thalia,' he said gently. 'There's something else you need to know. It's about your father.'

'Sir?' she asked, cautiously.

'It's good news,' Dreyfus said.

When Dreyfus returned to Panoply, even before Mercier had attended to his injuries, his first port of call was the tactical room. There he found Clearmountain and Baudry engrossed in study of the Solid Orrery, running it back and forth through time under different assumptions. As the outcomes of their simulations varied, so did the number and distribution of the red points of light in the emerald swirl of the Glitter Band. Sometimes there were dozens of red glints, but never the hundreds or thousands that had figured in the earlier forecasts, when Aurora's expansion had appeared unstoppable.

'Dreyfus,' Clearmountain purred. 'Welcome back to Panoply. I understand you now have senior status?'

'That's what it said on the Manticore booster. You'll have to talk to Jane to see whether it's a permanent status change.'

'You received the message, I take it?' Baudry asked him sharply. 'Demikhov went ahead with Zulu.'

'I heard.'

'There were ... complications, but when I last spoke to him, Demikhov was optimistic that Jane will make a complete recovery.' She shot an awkward glance at Clearmountain. 'There'll be no reason for her not to resume her duties.'

'After she's had a long rest,' Dreyfus said forcefully. 'She deserves that, no matter what *she* says.'

'Yes. No one would begrudge her that,' Baudry replied.

'I lost the Clockmaker.'

Clearmountain nodded at Dreyfus. 'From what we heard, it was tactically unavoidable. We could have nuked Ops Nine, but then we'd still be fighting Aurora on our own. You did well, Senior Dreyfus.'

'Thank you.' Dreyfus rubbed at the sore spot on his arm. 'Concerning Aurora ... I heard from Thalia that there've been some changes. Is this correct?'

Baudry answered him. 'The picture still isn't completely clear. All we know is that weevil activity has now become much less organised, much less systematic. We're still not able to seriously affect the flows before they reach target habitats, even with the assistance of the Ultras. But constables and field prefects are making real strides in preventing the weevils from reaching the cores once they achieve habitat penetration.'

'Enough to mean you don't need to nuke any more?'

'That's a possibility. For now, it should at least give us time to complete the evacuations before we sterilise. In the longer term, once the current flows are exhausted, we should see a total cessation of all weevil activity. We'll have halted Aurora.'

'She may just have stalled, not gone away for good.'

'We're mindful of that,' Baudry said. 'We'll continue evacuating well beyond her current expansion front, even if it means emptying fifty or a hundred habitats. We'll have nukes and lighthuggers in place to incinerate those habitats if we see renewed weevil activity.' She laced her fingers together. 'It should be enough, Senior. The emergency could be over in two to three days.'

'How many habitats will we have sacrificed by then?'

'Forty-five, most likely,' Baudry answered automatically. 'Twenty-five in the best-case scenario, more than a hundred and twenty in the worst.'

'Civilian losses?'

'Assuming that we can move to complete evacuation for the remaining occupied habitats within twenty-six hours, we'd be looking at total casualties in the range of two to three million citizens.'

'Just over a thirtieth of the entire citizenry,' Clearmountain said. 'It's a catastrophe, no doubt about it. But we have to thank our stars we're talking about millions, not tens of millions. And if we get out of this and we've lost forty-five habitats ... it's nothing against the ten thousand, Dreyfus.'

'I wouldn't say it's nothing, but I take your point.'

'The citizenry will get over it,' Baudry said. 'They'll move on with their lives, choosing to forget how close we came to disaster. For some of them, the forgetting will be quite literal. At the moment we're in the middle of an emergency. In a few days, if all goes well, it'll have been reduced to the status of a crisis. This time next year, we'll look back on it as an incident. Ten years from now, it'll be something no one outside of Panoply remembers, something our new recruits learn about with bored indifference.'

'Not if I get my way,' said Dreyfus. 'What about Aurora's prognostication? The time of plagues?'

'We'll keep a weather eye open,' Clearmountain said.

Baudry looked at Dreyfus with interest. 'Do you have plans, Senior?'

'We haven't won,' he told her. 'We've just postponed the day of reckoning. If it isn't Aurora, we'll be facing the Clockmaker.'

'There is such a thing as the lesser of two evils,' Clearmountain observed.

'I'll remind you of that when it crawls out of the woodwork again.'

'Where do you think they are?' asked Baudry.

'Dispersed,' Dreyfus said. 'Spread out over the network, two alpha-level intelligences smeared as thin as they can go before they stop being conscious entities at all.'

'How can you be so certain?'

'Because it's the only way for them to survive. If Aurora concentrates herself in one habitat, the Clockmaker will find a way to engage and destroy her in a single attack. The same applies to the Clockmaker. But distributed, spread out across the entire Glitter Band, they're almost invulnerable.'

'Why didn't Aurora adopt such a strategy already?'

'Because there's a cost. The speed of her thought processes depends on the distance between processing nodes. The Clockmaker's forced her to spread out just to survive. The downside for her is that she can't think quickly enough to defeat *us*.'

'But we can't kill her either,' Clearmountain said.

'No. Finding her would be almost impossible now. Maybe if we listen to network traffic long enough, we'll see the tiny slow-down caused by Aurora's presence. But that still wouldn't help us destroy her. We'd have to take out thousands of nodes, thousands of habitats, before we began to hurt her.'

'And by then we'd have hurt ourselves even more,' Baudry said, nodding as she understood what Dreyfus was driving at. 'So what you're saying, if I get you rightly, is that there's nothing we can do. We just have to sit back while these two monsters slug it out in slow motion, parasiting our network infrastructure.'

'That's right,' Dreyfus said. 'But I wouldn't worry unduly. If they've been slowed down as much as I think they have, it's going to be a long time before one of them emerges as victor. You're talking about a chess match between two opponents of almost limitless intelligence and guile. The only problem is they only get to make one move a year.'

'I hope you're right,' Clearmountain said.

Dreyfus smiled. 'So do I. In the meantime, we still have jobs to do. We can't dwell on the gods fighting over our heads.'

'Gods will be gods,' Baudry said.

'But that doesn't mean I'm finished with this case,' Dreyfus continued. 'With the permission of the acting supreme prefect, I'd like authorisation to dig into the murder of Philip Lascaille. If there's still a body, I want it exhumed for analysis. I want to see if there's any evidence that his brain was subjected to alpha-level scanning.'

'You have my permission, of course,' Clearmountain said. 'I don't doubt that Jane would give it to you. But you should realise what you're getting yourself into, digging into ancient history like that. You'll be going up against the legal apparatus of House Sylveste. That's an organisation that protects its secrets even more zealously than we do. It isn't to be trifled with.'

'With respect,' Dreyfus said, standing up, 'neither is Panoply.'

A little while later he called upon Demikhov. The man resembled a spectral shadow of his former self, spent beyond exhaustion.

'I heard that there were complications,' Dreyfus said.

'Nothing medical, you'll be glad to hear. The cut was as clean as a guillotine. Nerve reconnection could not have been less problematic. The only difficulty was occasioned by the intervention of your former colleague.' Demikhov shrugged philosophically, bony shoulders moving under the green fabric of his surgical gown. 'It was undignified, what he did to her. But at least she was unconscious throughout the whole sorry escapade.'

Dreyfus had no idea what he was talking about. He assumed he would learn all about it later.

'And now?'

'I completed partial reattachment, then brought her round to talk to the Ultras. She was lucid and comfortable. I then put her under again to complete the procedure.'

'How did it go?'

'She's whole again. It would take a better doctor than me to tell that Zulu ever happened.'

'Then she'll be fine?'

'Yes, but it's not going to happen overnight. At the moment she can breathe for herself and make some limited body movements, but it'll be a while before she can walk. Having the wiring back in place doesn't mean her brain's ready to use it again.'

'I'd like to see her,' Dreyfus said.

'She's sleeping. I'd like to keep her that way until there's another emergency.'

'I'd still like to see her.'

'Then you'd better follow me,' Demikhov answered with a heavy sigh, standing up to lead the way.

He brought Dreyfus to the quiet green room where the supreme prefect was recuperating. Jane Aumonier lay under bedsheets, sleeping normally. Aside from her thinness, the baldness of her skull and the grey pallor of her skin, there was nothing to hint at what she had endured, either in the last day or the last eleven years. She looked peaceful, serenely restful.

Dreyfus moved to her bedside. 'I won't wake her,' he whispered.

'You wouldn't be able to. I've put her under for her own good. It's quite safe to talk normally.'

Dreyfus touched the back of his hand against the side of Jane Aumonier's face. Despite all the time they had known each other, this was the first moment of physical contact between them.

'I'm going now,' Dreyfus said. 'There's something I need to attend to, before I put it off any longer. I have to go to Hospice Idlewild. There's someone there I need to see, someone I haven't seen in a very long while. I probably won't be in Panoply when you come around, but I want you to know that I'm going to be with you every step you take. If you need a hand to hold, you can count on mine.'

'I'll tell her what you said,' Demikhov said.

'I mean it. I don't break my promises.'

Demikhov was about to usher Dreyfus from the room when he paused. 'Prefect ... there's something I should show you. I think it's rather wonderful.'

Dreyfus nodded at the sleeping figure. 'This is enough for me, Doctor.'

'I'll show it to you anyway. Look at the wall.'

Demikhov conjured a pane into existence, filled with trembling neon-blue lines whose meaning Dreyfus couldn't fathom.

'What am I looking at?' he asked.

'Dreams,' Demikhov said. 'Beautiful human dreams.'